INTO THE
LIGHT

INTO THE
LIGHT

DAVID WEBER
AND
CHRIS KENNEDY

TOR

A TOM DOHERTY ASSOCIATES BOOK

INTO THE LIGHT

Map by Jennifer Hanover

A Tor Book
Published by Tom Doherty Associates
120 Broadway
New York, NY 10271

www.tor-forge.com

Tor® is a registered trademark of Macmillan Publishing Group, LLC.

Library of Congress Cataloging-in-Publication Data

Names: Weber, David, 1952- author. | Kennedy, Chris, 1965- author.
Title: Into the light / David Weber, Chris Kennedy.
Description: First edition. | New York : Tor, 2021.
Identifiers: LCCN 2020042334 (print) | LCCN 2020042335 (ebook) |
ISBN 9780765331458 (hardcover) | ISBN 9781250766953 (ebook)
Subjects: GSAFD: Science fiction. | Fantasy fiction.
Classification: LCC PS3573.E217 I58 2021 (print) | LCC PS3573.E217 (ebook) |
DDC 813/.54—dc23
LC record available at https://lccn.loc.gov/2020042334
LC ebook record available at https://lccn.loc.gov/2020042335

Our books may be purchased in bulk for promotional, educational, or business use.
Please contact your local bookseller or the Macmillan Corporate and Premium Sales
Department at 1-800-221-7945, extension 5442, or by email at
MacmillanSpecialMarkets@macmillan.com.

First Edition: January 2021

Printed in the United States of America

0 9 8 7 6 5 4 3 2 1

This one is for Sheellah and Sharon, the ladies we love
and who put up with both of us while we were working on this.
We hope the margaritas helped!

AUTHORS' NOTE
The authors wish to thank Commander Wieslaw Gozdziewicz,
Polish Navy, and Lieutenant Colonel Cezary Reginis, Polish Army,
for checking our Polish. They were incredibly helpful, although we
ended up "regularizing" the grammatical shifts so as not to confuse
our English readers even though they told us better than that!

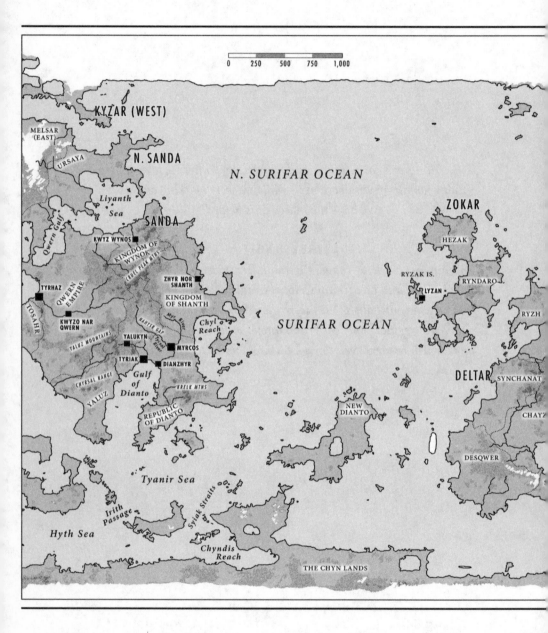

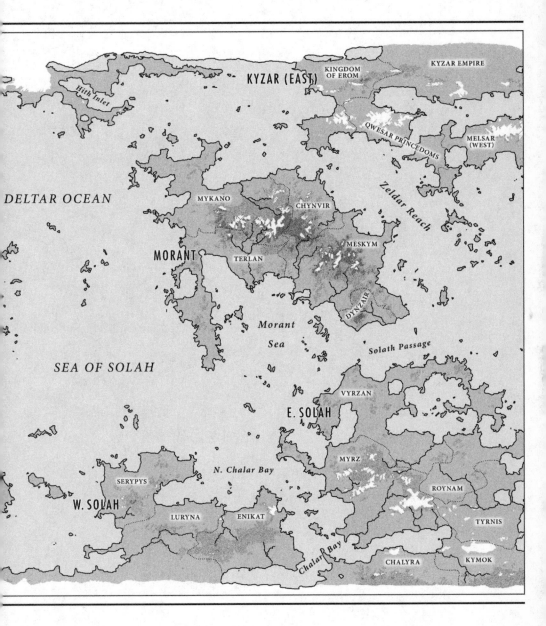

KYZAR (EAST)

KINGDOM
OF EROM

KYZAR EMPIRE

Hith Inlet

QWESAR PRINCEDOMS

MELSAR
(WEST)

DELTAR OCEAN

MYKANO

CHYNVIR

Zeldar Reach

MORANT

TERLAN

MESKYM

DYNZAIR

Morant
Sea

Solath Passage

SEA OF SOLAH

E. SOLAH

VYRZAN

N. Chalar Bay

MYRZ

ROYNAM

SERYPYS

W. SOLAH

LURYNA

ENIKAT

TYRNIS

Chalar Bay

CHALYRA

KYMOK

YEAR 1 OF THE TERRAN EMPIRE

AURORA, MINNESOTA,
UNITED STATES

The wet, soft sound of an ending world burned in Lewis Freymark's ears as he crouched to drop more wood into the fire. Spits of sleet hissed as they filtered into the flames, and the tarp he'd rigged to break the worst of the wind flapped in the drenched, blowing darkness.

It was almost enough—*almost*—to drown out the sound of his daughter's cough.

He hunched his shoulders, bending over, using the end of a limb to rearrange the burning branches. They didn't really need it. But it gave him a few more minutes before he had to look up, face Janice and the kids again, and he couldn't do that. Not yet. His heart cried out to take them all in his arms, shelter them against the cold, promise them that he was there and that somehow they'd get through this as they'd gotten through everything else. But he couldn't do that, either. He couldn't because this time he couldn't be their strength. Because this time his own despair would only have broken whatever scraps of hope might still sustain them.

There'd been no weather reports in months—not since the "Shongairi" had brought nightmare and destruction to Earth—but there was snow somewhere beyond the sleet. Freymark could smell it. He could feel it in the icy little teeth biting into the back of his neck as he crouched, using his body to give Janice and Stevie and Francesca and Jackie—oh, especially Jackie!—any extra fragment of windbreak he could.

And in his heart, he knew it didn't matter. He'd grown up in Duluth, fifty-odd miles from this unquiet, hopeless refugee camp. He knew northern winters. He knew how cruel they could be, even without murderous aliens from beyond the stars. And because he did, he knew exactly what would happen.

For a while, he'd thought they'd make it. The farmhouse outside the town of Babbitt had belonged to his cousin, but Jake and Suzanne had been in St. Paul when the initial Shongair kinetic strike turned the entire Minneapolis–St. Paul metropolitan area into fire, ash, smoke, and death.

Freymark and Janice were supposed to have joined them for the river cruise . . . until Francesca's impacted wisdom teeth required immediate surgery, instead. They'd just gotten home from the oral surgeon's when the initial strikes went in.

Minneapolis–St. Paul hadn't died alone. Washington, Los Angeles, San Francisco, Denver, Spokane, London, Paris, Berlin, Moscow, Ottawa . . . the dirge of murdered cities had rolled like the fanfare of Apocalypse. And the unending list had only grown and grown in the months since. There'd been fresh reports almost daily, at least until the Internet, the communications satellites— even the emergency band radios—had gone down. Duluth had been destroyed two months after Minneapolis–St. Paul in one of the Shongairi's "reprisal" strikes. Freymark didn't have a clue what the "reprisal" had been for, but it didn't matter. Not really. Not beside the death toll which had swept across his country and his world like some black, bottomless tide.

Yet he and Janice and the kids had been safe. They'd loaded up the SUV, headed north for sleepy little Babbitt, where there was nothing for the invaders to waste their "kinetic bombardments" upon. Where they'd known Jake and Suzanne's farmhouse would stand empty. Indeed, his greatest fear had been that they'd find someone else already squatting on the family farm, but civilization hadn't gone into the crapper that quickly. Not then.

Jacqueline coughed wetly behind him again, and he clenched his jaw tighter, feeling the cold closing in, staring into the flames as they crackled against the hateful dark.

Jake and Suzanne's family garden had helped a lot over the summer, and he and Janice had preserved what they could. Neither of them had known a thing about canning, but they'd dragged out Suzanne's canning supplies, chased down instructions on the Internet, and printed them out while they still had electricity (and before the Puppies took out the Net), and they'd managed to put up a lot of food. Or it had seemed like a lot, just looking at it in the pantry. Until he'd thought about feeding a family of seven through a Minnesota winter.

Yet they could've made it. He *knew* they could have. Babbitt was still a functional town, its mayor and city council had managed—somehow—to hold their community together, and if they hadn't been delighted to see strangers, neither had they tried to turn them away. Besides, he hadn't *been* a stranger. Not really. And Douglas and Carla Jackson had spoken for them—Carla had been Suzanne's sister, and Freymark had known her since he was nine, visiting his aunt and uncle in Babbitt—and helped the Freymarks settle in at the farm. And there were still deer to eke out their food supplies, and there were always fish in Birch Lake. And so he'd been able to tell himself that whatever happened to the rest of the world, *his* family would make it.

Until three weeks ago, anyway.

There were a lot of things Lewis Freymark would never know, and one of them was why the Puppies had decided to strike Babbitt. The town had never had more than fourteen or fifteen hundred citizens, although it had probably crept higher than that over the summer and early autumn as other refugees filtered in. How it could have posed any kind of threat to star-traveling aliens was more than he could imagine. Maybe it had been a reprisal for something someone had done, or maybe it had been no more than pure viciousness on the Shongairi's part. He didn't know, and it didn't matter anyway.

What *did* matter was that Babbitt had disappeared into the same horrific fireball which had claimed a seventeen-year-old boy—a boy turning into a man any parent could have been proud of—named Dennis Freymark.

Dennis had taken the SUV to town to trade some of their precious canned food for medicine. The Babbitt Medical Center had continued to serve the town and its froth of refugees, but Mayor Oswald and the city council had collected the stock of Babbitt's half-dozen pharmacies under lock and key—and armed guard. They probably would have let Dennis have at least some of what he needed, anyway, but it never hurt to contribute a little something to the town's food stocks in exchange.

Only there'd never been an exchange. And the blast front and fire had swept outward from the devastated town, burning through the tinder-dry leaves of autumn with no one left to fight it. He'd had just enough warning to get Janice and the kids, grab Jake's sportorized Lee-Enfield deer rifle, a couple of boxes of ammunition, and all the food they could carry, and get as far as the lake before the flames swept through, devouring everything in their path. He'd sheltered in the lake water—icy cold, even at the height of summer, much less in the fall— neck-deep, holding Jacqueline in his arms and feeling her shiver—as the fire roared and bellowed around them. And when the flames were done, the farm was gone.

So they'd come here. Almost twenty miles west of Babbitt, to what had been the almost equally small town of Aurora. All of Babbitt's handful of survivors had ended up here, in the refugee camp that sprawled across the high school's athletic field on the west side of the town, near the lake. There was another on the football and baseball fields between Forestry Road and Third Avenue, on the other side of town, but there were precious few amenities for either. The high school had long since filled every classroom with refugees; there was no space inside it for late arrivals, however desperate their need, and so they crouched in whatever shelter they could while the exhausted city government tried hopelessly to find better asylum for them.

He could smell the overstrained portable toilets—and the communal latrine pits—from here. Water had to be hauled in from the lake, using some of the town's old water trucks, drawn by the priceless handful of horses who'd survived and been pressed into service as supplies of gasoline and diesel vanished. Food was already scarce and getting scarcer every day, despite mandatory rationing that restricted adults to no more than fourteen hundred calories a day, and medical supplies were nonexistent. The surviving doctors and nurses worked eighteen-hour shifts at the local hospital, a mile southeast from where he crouched feeding the fire, but they were swamped by far too many patients with far too little nourishment, shelter, and warmth, and that was only going to get worse. Winter was coming on fast, there'd be no new shipments of fuel, there was no electricity, none of the refugees had anything remotely like the clothing needed to survive it, and housing was desperately short. There would have been far too few supplies, far too few roofs, under the best of circumstances, far less the ones they actually faced.

The authorities were trying hard to find someplace for the fresh influx to go, but the town was already packed—by Freymark's lowest estimate, the city's population had to have at least tripled—and most of them were at least as malnourished, and cold, and wet as his own family. And so he crouched here, burning scavenged branches, praying someone could find them a roof, wondering where the next armload of fuel was coming from, while Jackie coughed behind him in her mother's arms, and there was nothing—nothing at all—he could do.

He looked up as someone dumped another scant pile of branches beside him.

"City police just dragged in a flatbed of downed trees," Alex Jackson said, squatting on his heels and laying the ax he'd salvaged from the burned farm's barn beside him. He looked at least a decade older than his fifteen years. "I was over there with the ax." He twitched a parody of a smile. "Gave me first dibs for helping cut it." He shrugged. "Supposed to be a wheelbarrow load headed this way in another half hour or so."

"Good, Alex." He reached out, squeezed the boy's shoulder. "*Good.*"

He put all the approval left in him into those three words, and God knew Alex deserved it. His parents and his sister had caught a ride into Babbitt with Dennis on that terrible day. The Freymarks were all he had left, and Lewis Freymark put an arm around him and hugged hard, eyes burning as he thought about Dennis. Thought about his broad shoulders, his curly hair, his mother's eyes. About the way his son—*his son*—had always had a smile for his mom, a joke for his kid brother, his sisters. And Freymark had been even prouder of his boy when he paused quietly outside the closed bedroom door one rainy autumn night and heard Dennis—Dennis, the perpetually smiling, the always optimistic—weeping with quiet desperation when he thought no one else could hear.

Dennis, who the Puppies had taken from him and from Janice. His death had torn his father's heart in half and shattered his mother's. Only one more death among *billions*, but the one death which had reached right up inside them and ripped out their souls. So yes, Freymark understood Alex. Understood his pain, the strength that somehow kept him going, and he hugged the son of his dead friends, the son who needed a father as he'd never needed one before, because he would never hug his own again.

And now they were losing Jacqueline. Jackie, the baby, the laughing sprite who'd turned into a solemn-eyed ghost as the grim reality ground its way through every shield her parents—and Dennis—had tried to erect against it for her sake. She was only *seven,* for God's sake! Only seven. She would've been eight in another three months, but she didn't have three months. Maybe none of them did, if the rumors of the Puppies' bioweapon were true, but it didn't matter for Jackie.

He wasn't a doctor, but he didn't need to be one. It was pneumonia. He could hear it in the wet cough, the labored breathing—feel it in the raging tempera- ture, see it in the chills. In the way she was just . . . fading away. And without the medicine Dennis had died trying to get and Aurora simply didn't have, there was nothing they could do about it. Nothing but keep her as warm as they could, try to get fluids into her somehow . . . and hug her. Hold her. Be there for her as that last, precious ember flickered its way forever into the dark. Man- age somehow to *smile* for her when she roused and called out for "Mommy" or, most heart-wrenching of all, for "Poppa." To tell her it would be all right and urge her to rest, torn between the terror that she might slip away without ever awakening again . . . and the prayer that she would, because the father who loved her more than life itself knew it was the only peace she would ever find again.

And there was nothing—*nothing*—he could do for her, or for Stevie, or Camila, or Francesca. Not in the end. He was their father. It was his *job* to save them, and he couldn't do it, and dying himself would have been easy compared to that.

His daughter coughed again, and he looked over his shoulder.

Janice sat on an overturned plastic crate, hunched forward, trying to shelter the tiny, blanket-wrapped body in her arms. Janice—his strength and his rock, who was always there for him and the kids, whose face had grown thin and gaunt, and whose eyes could no longer share the hope she promised her children. Janice, whose cheek rested on the crown of that small head while she whispered lullaby words so softly he couldn't hear them through the rattle of sleet, the sigh of the ice-fanged wind, and the weeping of his own heart.

He made himself stand, straighten his spine, square his shoulders, and somehow produce a smile. It was his turn to be Dennis, he thought, steeling himself before he bent to kiss his wife, take his own turn holding their daughter while she trickled away from them. It was—

He froze, his head jerking up as a sound he hadn't heard since before The Day came thumping out of the windy, frigid dark.

"*Lewis!*" Janice cried, struggling to her feet with Jackie in her arms while the other kids jerked upright in the pitiful nest of blankets where they'd huddled together, sharing body warmth.

"I hear it!" he said tautly, and picked up the rifle he'd clung to through fire and water and cold. He could remember Jake teasing him the summer when he'd loaded the magazine by hand, without stripper clips, and gotten the overlap on the rimmed .303 cartridges wrong and locked up the magazine. This time, he was sure he had them in the right sequence, even if it wasn't going to matter in the end.

"Stay here," he said flatly. "Alex, stay with Aunt Janice. Keep her and the babies safe. Frankie," he took time to throw one arm around his fourteen-year-old daughter, hugging her hard. "Take care of Mom."

"*Dad,*" she whispered into his chest, "don't go!" She looked up, eyes gleaming with upwelling tears in a face that was far too thin. "*Stay* with us!"

"I can't, Punkin," he told her gently and released her to reach down and ruffle Stevie's hair as he and Camila clung weepingly to their mother.

He looked up, met Janice's eyes, and saw the knowledge in them. The knowledge that she would never see him again. And that it probably wouldn't matter in the end, but that he had to *try* anyway.

"If—when—the shooting starts, head farther into town. Find a place to hide with the babies," he told her, cupping her cheek in his hand. "I'll find you . . . after."

"I know you will," she lied, pressing her cheek harder against his palm. "We'll be waiting for you. We love you."

Her voice wavered on the last three words, and he closed his eyes for a moment. Then opened them again.

"I know," he said, and leaned close, kissed her forehead. Then he drew a deep breath and headed off into the wind and the cold through the suddenly panicked refugee camp as the running lights of not one helicopter, but at least three, came out of the lowering cloud and circled.

They were the first aircraft he'd seen since "Fleet Commander Thikair" had made what would happen to any human aircraft which dared take to the air perfectly clear. Freymark had seen the video Admiral Robinson had posted on the Internet, watched three dozen Shongair shuttles being torn apart by just four F-22s, so he'd understood exactly why Thikair had been so emphatic.

A part of him was surprised Puppy helicopters sounded exactly like human helicopters, but he shook that thought aside. Rotary wing aircraft were rotary wing aircraft, he supposed. No doubt they *had* to sound alike. But these were clearly headed for the parking apron between the high school and the sports fields. It was probably the only open area big enough for them to set down—the city cops kept it clear as the area where any available supplies could be distributed to the camp—and he made himself move faster, joined by other armed men and women in ones and twos and threes. There were at least two dozen of them by the time they reached the parking lot, armed with a motley assortment of weapons—everything from modern AR-15s to his own ancient Lee-Enfield and God knew what sort of handguns. But two things they all had in common: desperate determination . . . and no hope at all.

Freymark found a position on the edge of the parking area, kneeling behind a bare-leaved tree in a concrete planter box, and chambered a round. At least two or three helicopters continued to circle, but another one came in slowly, sliding down the darkness behind the blinding glare of its landing lights, and his heart hammered. He had no way of knowing what the Puppies intended, but every man and woman around that parking lot knew the Shongair policy. They knew what would happen to every human soul in Aurora if they opened fire. Yet their families—everything in the world they had left to love—were in the camp behind them, and if the rumors were true, if the Shongairi *were* seeking human test subjects for bioweapon research and they'd come to collect them, then every human soul in Aurora might as well die cleanly right here, right now, in the sizzling inferno of yet another kinetic strike, instead.

It would be the final, and the greatest, gift he could give his wife and children, and he knew it.

The single helicopter—it was even larger than he'd thought—was impossible to make out through the dazzling light pouring from it, and spicules of sleet glittered against the brilliance as the icy downblast from the rotors pounded over him. He felt himself hunching together in his thin, sodden jacket as it touched down at last and the thunder of its rotors eased. They didn't stop turning completely, but they rotated much more slowly now, and he settled behind his rifle, waiting. He'd never seen a Shongair himself, but he'd seen plenty of them on video and heard them speaking through their mechanical translators before the Internet died, and now he waited for the inevitable loudspeaker to issue its demands.

But it didn't. And then he froze as the first silhouetted shape appeared against the flood of light.

It wasn't a Shongair. It was a *human!*

It stood there, by itself, motionless for a good thirty seconds, and then Lewis Freymark watched in disbelief as three more figures joined it. Then the landing lights switched off, although the running lights remained lit, and for the first time he could actually see them.

Three men and a woman stood there, waiting with obvious patience, and Freymark swallowed hard as he recognized the U.S. Army's camouflage-pattern uniform. But the Army was *dead*. Everyone knew that! And how could human-operated aircraft survive in Shongair-controlled airspace?! It was impossible. It *couldn't* happen.

But then he realized he was on his own feet, moving forward, the rifle heavy in his hand, muzzle pointed at the ground, and the compact, dark-haired man—the one who'd disembarked first—looked up at him. Green eyes glittered with an odd intensity as they reflected the running lights, and he held out his hand.

Freymark took it.

"Torino," the man said. "Daniel Torino, Major, U.S. Air Force."

The words made perfect sense. They just couldn't mean what it sounded like they meant.

"Lewis Freymark," he heard himself say. "What—? I mean, how—?"

The question stammered into fragmented silence, and Torino smiled crookedly. He looked—they all looked—impossibly clean, impossibly neat and professional.

"That's going to take some explaining," he said. "Short version, the Puppies got their asses kicked."

"*What?!*"

Freymark felt his eyes bulging in disbelief, and Torino shook his head with an odd compassion.

"I said it's going to take explaining, and it is. Important thing right now? I've got five Chinooks loaded with around sixty tons of supplies and a complete medical team. I need someplace to unload and set up."

His hand tightened on Freymark's as desperation, disbelief, and despair turned into sudden, searing hope in the eyes of a father.

"Think you could help me out with that?"

II

WIDAWA,
POLAND

*S*tarszy Chorąży Szymański looked up from his paperwork with an incipient snarl as someone knocked once on his office door, then opened it.

It was late, they were running low on ballpoint pens (among altogether too many other things), the wind outside the unfortunately ramshackle "headquarters block" was cold, his fingers were clumsy because of the chill, and the old-fashioned kerosene lamp on his desk was remarkably frugal with its illumination.

None of which was designed to put him in what anyone would have called a happy mood.

"What?" he growled.

"Sorry, *Panie Chorąży,*" *Starszy Sierżant* Jacob Makinowski replied. "I know you don't want anyone disturbing you, but I think you'd better talk to this guy."

"And what 'guy' would that be?" Szymański's tone wasn't a lot more pleasant.

"Says he's Ukrainian." Makinowski shrugged. "His Polish is pretty damned good, if he is. Big guy, blond hair, blue eyes. But he also says he's a captain in the Ukrainian Army, only he's not wearing Ukrainian uniform."

"And this is a surprise because—?" Szymański asked sarcastically, twitching his head at Makinowski's own lack of sartorial splendor.

The *starszy chorąży* had a point, Makinowski conceded, looking down at his own sturdy but worn civilian boots, the two layers of knitted sweater under his summer-weight army tunic with its homemade epaulets. One of the two five-pointed stars of a *starszy sierżant* was homemade (and undeniably more lopsided than the other), since the shoulder boards had belonged to a *plutonowy*—a corporal—before the invasion, and the supply chain had been pretty thoroughly disrupted when ninety percent of the Polish military went up in the fireballs of the Shongairi's initial bombardment.

More than ninety percent, really. That was how a civilian had become a staff sergeant and inherited the epaulets of a corporal named Krystian Szymański when the corporal in question became a sergeant major. *The* Sergeant Major, actually.

"Sorry," Makinowski said again. "What I meant is, he's in uniform, but it's not Ukrainian. Not Russian, either. I think it's American."

Szymański laid down his ballpoint and shoved back in his chair, both eyebrows rising.

"Let me get this straight. This *wieśniak* says he's Ukrainian, but he's in *Jankeskim mundurze*—an American uniform? And he just turned up in the middle of the night? And you think he's important enough to interrupt me at a chore you know I love so much?"

"*Panie Chorąży*," Makinowski said frankly, "I think you need to talk to him, and then you're probably going to get into a shitpot of trouble when you wake up the *Pułkownik*. And *he's* probably going to have to wake up the *Generał Brygady*."

"You're serious, aren't you?" Szymański said slowly.

"Damn straight I am."

"Then I guess you'd better show him in."

· · · · ·

PUŁKOWNIK MAREK PEPLIŃSKI, who'd been a *starszy chorąży* until five or six months ago, blinked bleary eyes and took another sip of the ersatz tea. The cup didn't match the saucer, but at least they were both intact. Not that the liquid the cup contained was anything to celebrate. Except that it was at least warm.

They did have some tea and coffee left, but very little, and what they had was dwindling rapidly. *Generał Brygady* Lutosławski had decreed that the remaining supplies would be conserved and doled out as rewards for service above and beyond the call of duty. Pepliński supported the decision. In fact, he thought it was a very good idea. But he did miss the caffeine.

He missed a *lot* of things, actually. He especially missed the ability to know what was happening beyond their brutally truncated horizon here in Widawa. It probably wouldn't matter much in the end, but it would be nice to know why they hadn't heard a single word from the Shongair invaders over their remaining radios in almost two weeks. He'd never thought he would miss those broadcasts or the combination of threats and promises that came with them. (Some of the oldest citizens of Widawa had compared them—unfavorably—to the worst of the old Stalinist "news broadcasts" from their "fraternal Soviet comrades." Personally, Pepliński had always been grateful he was too young to remember those.)

But he'd discovered he *did* miss the Shongairi's version. The silence was unnerving, like some vast, quivering void. He had enough other problems and uncertainties. He damned well didn't need the fucking Puppies deciding to go silent on him on top of everything else!

He held the cup under his nose, inhaling the steam's warmth, then set it back on the saucer. His office was cold, but at least it was free of drafts. That was quite a lot, with winter already upon them. Whether it would be enough in the end was yet to be seen.

And aren't you a cheerful fellow when they wake you up at two in the morning? he asked himself. *Gotten too used to being an officer, have you?*

The thought restored at least a little badly needed humor and he set the cup carefully on its saucer and inhaled deeply.

"All right, Krystian. I suppose I'm as awake as I'm getting."

"Yes, Sir."

Szymański came briefly to attention, then turned sharply and marched out of the office, and Pepliński smiled tiredly as he watched the sergeant major go.

Szymański had been one of Pepliński's motor pool corporals before the attack. The two of them had been off-base, returning from a NATO training exercise. If Pepliński hadn't been delayed by a last-minute piece of paperwork idiocy and caught a ride back in Szymański's Jelcz truck, neither of them would have been alive today. Despite which—or, possibly because of which—Szymański was always careful to maintain proper military formality between them. Which was undoubtedly wise of him. Private habits could spill over into public behavior, and the one thing none of Lutosławski's officers and noncoms could afford was to let the illusion that the Polish military still existed slip.

Not that it was likely to hold up a lot longer, no matter what they did.

Ludwik Lutosławski had been a *porucznik*—a first lieutenant—in the Polish Army when the Shongairi attacked. His current rank wasn't quite completely self-awarded; theoretically, he'd been promoted by Fryderyk Sikorcz, the sole surviving member of the *zarząd województwa,* the executive board of Województwa Łódzkiego. That made him the closest thing to a governor available, and he'd named Lutosławski *military* governor of *gmina* Widawa, commanding all regular and reserve military personnel in it. There hadn't been a lot of those.

The *gmina*—an administrative district of perhaps seven thousand, before the invasion—was centered on the village of Widawa, fifty-odd kilometers southwest of what had once been the regional capital of Łódź. None of Łódź's 700,000 people had survived the initial bombardment, and casualties in the immediately surrounding urban areas had been close to total, as well. For that matter, the town of Łask, the seat of *gmina* Widawa, had been destroyed at the same time, probably because of the Air Force base located there, which had killed over a quarter of the *gmina's* total population. The bombardment's survivors—not just from Łódź but from *every* major city and most of the larger towns—had fled to the farming country which had escaped attack, and the predictable result had been chaos as what remained of local government collapsed and starving refugees fought to keep themselves and their children fed.

Initially, many of the farmers had shared generously, but that had changed as the locusts flowed over them and they'd realized how completely and totally their country had been devastated. As they'd realized they would need that food to keep their *own* families alive in the face of such an utter collapse of transportation and all the other infrastructure people had taken so much for granted. As that understanding swept through them, they'd begun refusing to feed refugees. They'd started hiding food to protect it from looters, and they'd organized to defend what they had by force.

Until Ludwik Lutosławski . . . changed their minds.

No one had denied the farmers owned their own food. It simply hadn't mattered who owned what. Not in the face of such disruption and starvation. And so "hoarding" had become a capital offense and squads of Lutosławski's troopers—the majority of whom had been civilians only weeks earlier—had swept over every farmhouse pantry and barn to make that perfectly clear. Perhaps some of them, even the majority of them, had sympathized with the farmers, but that hadn't mattered anymore, either. What had mattered was feeding as many people as possible while simultaneously building at least some cushion for the looming winter, and the *generał brygady*'s men had taken their cue from him.

Marek Pepliński didn't actually like Lutosławski very much. The one-time lieutenant had a streak of brutality he wasn't shy about showing. Pepliński couldn't decide whether that brutality had always been there or whether it was a response to the nightmare situation in which Lutosławski had found himself. For that matter, he wasn't certain how much of it was genuine and how much of it was theater, designed to make sure no one defied him or his authority. It wasn't the brutality itself that worried the promoted sergeant major. Hanging on to some semblance of order, dealing with the flood of refugees, and somehow keeping people fed—so far, at least—*required* a certain degree of brutality. No, what worried him was that he wasn't at all confident *Lutosławski* still knew how much of it was born of necessity and how much was his . . . default setting. So far he'd at least given accused hoarders, or thieves, or rapists a drumhead court-martial before he had them shot, but over the last couple of months, he'd seemed less and less firmly anchored. And that frightened Pepliński. Winter would have them by the throat within weeks, and for better or worse, Lutosławski was the core of *gmina* Widawa and its survival. If he truly was beginning to crumble. . . .

Someone rapped crisply on the opened door's frame and then Szymański waved a tall, broad-shouldered, blond-haired man through it. The newcomer certainly looked Slavic, but he was improbably neat, obviously well fed, and impeccably attired in what really did look like the uniform of the United States military. Although, Pepliński realized, its epaulets carried the four Maltese crosses of a Ukrainian army captain rather than the silver bars an American officer should have worn.

"*Kapitan* Ushakov, *Panie Pułkowniku*," the *starszy chorąży* said crisply.

"*Kapitan*," Pepliński said a bit warily, then nodded to Szymański. "That will be all for now, *Starszy Chorąży*."

"Yes, Sir."

The noncom came briefly to attention once more and withdrew, not without a wary sidelong glance of his own as he left his colonel alone with the stranger.

"So, *Kapitan*," Pepliński said as the door closed behind him. "I understand you want to see the *Generał Brygady*?"

"Yes, Sir. I would indeed appreciate a few moments of conversation with *Generał Brygady* Lutosławski," the stranger—Ushakov—replied. "I realize it's rather late, however there are certain . . . logistic constraints in play." He smiled slightly. "I fear it will be some time before I could arrange to be here during his normal working hours."

His Polish was flawless, Pepliński realized. Indeed, he suspected it was better than his own, grammatically. Which didn't explain why a Ukrainian in American uniform was standing in his dreary, chill little office in the middle of the night.

"Might I inquire as to precisely why you want to see him?" he asked.

"I have a message for him from my own superiors." Ushakov shrugged. "Given the state of the world communications net, a personal emissary was the only practical way to deliver it."

"I see." Pepliński looked the stranger up and down, then cocked his head.

"I'm sure you can understand why I'd have some questions, *Kapitan*," he said. "For example, how does a *Ukrainian* officer find himself in *American* uniform? And who might those 'superiors' of yours be?"

"Reasonable questions," Ushakov acknowledged with a nod. "Answering them may take a while, however."

"We're both already awake, *Kapitan*," Pepliński pointed out with a thin smile, and pointed at the wooden chair—it had been salvaged from someone's dining room—in front of his desk. "Have a seat."

· · · · ·

"THIS HAD BETTER be good, Marek," Ludwik Lutosławski growled as he stalked into the parlor of the farmhouse which had been requisitioned for his HQ. A fresh fire had been lit in the parlor's open hearth, but it hadn't even begun taking the chill off the room yet, and his hands were buried deep in the pockets of a thick dressing gown. "You do realize what frigging time it is?"

"Yes, Sir," *Pułkownik* Pepliński replied. There was something just a bit odd about his voice, although Lutosławski was too irritated—and groggy from being awakened at three o'clock in the morning—to notice.

"Then what the fuck is this about?" the one-time lieutenant demanded.

"Sir, there's someone here you need to talk to."

"At three in the goddamned morning?! I don't think so!" Lutosławski snapped.

"Sir, I wouldn't have roused you at this hour if it wasn't really important," Pepliński said. "You know that."

"What I *know* is that I didn't get to sleep until after midnight," Lutosławski snarled. "And that I'm going to be back up in less than three hours for that sweep towards Marzeńska to deal with those goddamned hoarders."

"Sir, I—"

"Excuse me for interrupting, *Generał Brygady*," the third man in the parlor said, "but I'm afraid I'm the one who insisted the *Pułkownik* disturb you."

"And who the fuck are *you*?" Lutosławski demanded, turning his head to glare at the stranger. It was a glare whose anger transmuted—slightly, at least—into something else as he truly saw the other man's uniform for the first time.

"*Kapitan* Pieter Ushakov." The stranger bowed slightly as he introduced himself.

"And you're here because—?"

"I bear a message for you from my superior," Ushakov replied.

"And who might that be and why might I want to hear whatever he has to say?" Lutosławski asked unpleasantly.

"There are several reasons you should want to hear what he has to say," Ushakov said calmly. "The best reason is that he wants to offer you assistance, under certain conditions."

"What sort of 'assistance'?" Suspicion edged Lutosławski's tone. "Everyone else who's offered to 'assist' me had no intention of doing anything of the sort. Which is why most of them are *dead* now," he added warningly.

"I'm here on behalf of Governor Judson Howell," Ushakov said, apparently oblivious to the not-so-veiled threat. "He's in a position to offer medical assistance and at least limited assistance with food and other logistic issues. Assuming you're able and willing to meet those conditions I mentioned."

"Howell?" Lutosławski repeated the name. His expression was puzzled for a moment, but then his eyes narrowed. "Howell! The asshole who was collaborating with the Puppies?!"

"That's how the Puppies described it," Ushakov acknowledged. Howell's "cooperation" with the Shongairi had figured prominently in some of the aliens' broadcasts. "Actually, he was outsmarting them 'three ways to Sunday,' as an American friend of mine would put it." The big Ukrainian smiled thinly.

"They didn't like what happened when he was *finished* outsmarting them very much, either."

"Sure they didn't, and I can believe however much of that I want," Lutosławski growled suspiciously. He glowered at his uninvited visitor. "Even assuming there's a word of truth in that, are you seriously suggesting an *American,* on the other side of the world, could help us here even if he wanted to?"

"In fact, North Carolina, Governor Howell's state, is less than seventy-five hundred kilometers from Widawa, which isn't even a quarter of the way around the world," Ushakov observed. "The actual distance doesn't matter, however." He shrugged. "I assure you, the Governor has the capability to reach you here at any time he chooses."

"Oh, of *course* he does!"

"You might want to reflect upon the fact that *I'm* here," Ushakov pointed out.

Lutosławski started a quick reply, then paused, and Ushakov smiled ever so slightly.

"And what would those 'conditions' of his be?" the Pole asked instead, after a moment.

"The most immediate would be that you will refrain from seizing any supplies or assistance directed to you," Ushakov said levelly. "The ruthlessness you've shown in forcibly confiscating food and other supplies is . . . understandable, under the circumstances you've confronted. And the Governor knows as well as you do how unlikely you are to survive the winter without losing all too many of your people to malnutrition or sickness. But if he agrees to help you, he'll expect his assistance to be passed on through you to the communities around you. Even to *Wojewoda* Konarski."

Lutosławski's nostrils flared and he darted a glance at Pepliński. The *pułkownik*'s expression was as bleak as his own, and both of them looked back at Ushakov.

Tadeusz Konarski had declared himself governor of a territory somewhat smaller than *gmina* Widawa's current size, centered on the tiny village of Zabrzezie, just over thirty-five kilometers from Widawa itself. His and Lutosławski's foragers had clashed more than once. Indeed, they'd fought a pitched battle over a newly discovered hoard of rye only three days ago.

Lutosławski's people had won that one, but they'd taken losses. And they hadn't won all of the other clashes, either.

"That bastard's willing to starve all of my people!" he snarled. "Why should I give him the sweat off my balls?!"

"Because if the two of you—and the other people around you who have managed to hold on to at least a little of what passes for civilization—don't cooperate with one another, the Governor will be unable to help *any* of you. More than that, he won't even try. Believe me, he has any number of at least equally pressing emergencies much closer to home, and that means he has to prioritize ruthlessly. If he can count on local cooperation, he can make a significant difference to your chance of surviving the winter, because that cooperation will be what you might call a 'force multiplier' for his own resources and people. If that cooperation isn't forthcoming here, he'll concentrate his efforts on other places where it is."

"And you're seriously suggesting someone only a *quarter* of the way around the world could offer assistance remotely great enough to convince that murderous bastard to 'cooperate' with me?"

"You are aware *Wojewoda* Konarski thinks of you in much the same terms?" Ushakov asked with a crooked smile. "To be fair, I think the label applies rather better to him than to you, but you've both had to be fairly 'murderous' to survive this far, *Generał Brygady*. My Governor understands that. But if you wish his assistance in *continuing* to survive, the two of you will have to learn to work together."

"Assuming for the moment this American governor really could reach Poland with some sort of assistance, what's to keep Konarski—or me—from agreeing to cooperate and then seizing all of that assistance for himself?"

"I can think of several moral arguments which should dissuade you. However, I'm a practical man, so I'll move straight to the most pressing reason neither of you should do anything so foolish. If you do, you'll die."

Lutosławski's eyes widened.

"Are you *threatening* me?!"

"Not unless I must," Ushakov said in that same calm tone. "And I would prefer not to, to be honest. While I might quibble with some of your methods, you've done a remarkable job of maintaining order in the area under your control. We would very much prefer to work with you rather than replace you."

"I see."

Lutosławski looked at the other man for a moment. Then his right hand came out of the house coat pocket with a WIST-94 pistol. It was the 94L variant, and he showed his teeth in a humorless smile as the crimson dot of the integral laser settled on the center of Ushakov's chest.

"I don't think you're in a very strong position to be throwing around threats, *Kapitan* Ushakov," he said very softly.

"Actually, I'm in a far stronger position than *you* are." Ushakov seemed remarkably unfazed. "I anticipated this situation might arise after I'd studied your methods a bit, so why don't we go ahead and get it over with? Feel free to squeeze the trigger."

Lutosławski's eyes narrowed as the lunatic smiled at him and made a small welcoming gesture with his right hand. The *generał brygady*'s index finger tightened on the double action trigger, a half kilogram or so from firing, but he stopped himself.

"Don't think I won't," he warned.

"Oh, I'm quite certain you would," Ushakov replied. "If I permitted it, that is."

"If you—?"

Lutosławski stared at him in disbelief, and then the other man . . . *blurred*. That was the only description for it. The lighting was poor, but not poor enough to explain the way in which Ushakov seemed to *flow* suddenly through the air. The Ukrainian—if that was what he truly was—vanished, transmuted into a coil of smoke that snaked across the parlor towards him. The impossibility of it froze him for half a pulse beat . . . and that was long enough for the smoke to suddenly re-consolidate three feet from him and a sinewy hand to twist the pistol out of his hand with humiliating ease.

"A fine weapon," Ushakov observed, stepping back in a more normal fashion to stand before the parlor's small hearth with the pistol in his own hand. "I believe I would probably prefer it to the Makarov or the FORT." He smiled. "I like its ergonomics, and I always felt the Luger round was superior. Unfortunately, neither round is adequate for what you intended to do, *Generał Brygady*."

Lutosławski gawked at him, trying to understand how he could have moved that quickly. It wasn't possible! He darted a quick look at Pepliński, but his executive officer seemed as frozen as he was.

"*Pułkownik* Pepliński," Ushakov said, never looking away from Lutosławski, "would you be kind enough to ask the sentries to step into the parlor? I wouldn't want there to be any . . . misunderstandings."

Pepliński looked at Lutosławski, and the *generał brygady* glared for a moment. Then he inhaled.

"Do it, Marek," he said.

Pepliński nodded. He disappeared, and Lutosławski stood glowering at Ushakov until the *pułkownik* returned with the two men from his headquarters guard force who had the night's sentry duty. They looked more than a little apprehensive, and their apprehension clicked up another notch as they saw the stranger standing there with their CO's pistol in his hand.

"Thank you, *Pułkowniku*," the stranger in question said politely, and nodded to the newcomers. "I didn't want you to feel alarmed," he explained, then pressed the muzzle of the pistol to his temple and squeezed the trigger.

The sudden, explosive "CRAAACK!" of the shot hit their ears like a sledgehammer in the small parlor's confines, a plate displayed on the mantel above the hearth shattered into dozens of pieces, and every man in the room flinched, their eyes wide with horror as they realized Ushakov had just shot himself in the head in front of them! What kind of maniac—?

But then they realized Ushakov hadn't collapsed to the floor. In fact, he was *smiling* at them, the pistol still against the side of his head. For an instant, Lutosławski wondered if the deafening shot still reverberating in his bones had been some sort of illusionist's trick. But then a large fragment of broken plate slid off the mantel and splintered on the hearth.

And Ushakov was totally unmarked. His temple had seemed to . . . ripple under the force of the shot, but there wasn't even a powder burn in its wake!

"As you can see, *General Brygady*," he said, lowering the pistol with a faint smile, "shooting me would accomplish very little beyond leaving holes in my uniform." His voice sounded far away, distant beyond the ringing in Lutosławski's ears. "It certainly couldn't prevent me from reaching you, wherever you might be, whenever I chose." His smile disappeared. "And before you ask, I've already demonstrated that fact to *Wojewoda* Konarski, as well."

"What—" Lutosławski swallowed hard. "What *are* you?" he asked hoarsely.

"That really doesn't matter at the moment," Ushakov replied. "What matters is that I'm here, that I can do what I've said I can do, and that Governor Howell can—and wants to—help you and all the people under your control survive. So, what reply would you like me to take home to him?"

III

COLD MOUNTAIN,
TRANSYLVANIA COUNTY, NORTH CAROLINA,
UNITED STATES

A remarkably beady pair of blue eyes considered Dave Dvorak across the cheerful kitchen table, dark with distrust as he folded the phone and shoved it into his pocket.

It wasn't actually a "phone," of course, although it was already obvious that was what people were going to go on calling it, just as they'd called the portable computers companies like Apple and Samsung had been selling their customers for years "phones," despite how little they resembled the device he remembered hanging on his parents' kitchen wall. Of course, this one went a bit farther than iPhones or Galaxies had . . . although, now that he thought about it, "Galaxy" might not be all that bad a name for it. While it resembled the flip phones that smart phones had long since made obsolete, the folding unit was actually only the interface for the slim two-inch-by-two-inch, wafer-thin sliver of molecular circuitry unshakably attached to his belt via a nanotech-based "sticky surface" whose physics would probably have been enough to induce massive migraines even in someone who actually *understood* the laws of physics.

Or someone who understood what humanity had *thought* were the laws of physics six months earlier, anyway.

The communications satellites the Shongairi had parked in geosynchronous orbits to replace the human satellites they'd exterminated once they realized the Internet was more trouble than it was worth, were still there and operating under new management. The "phone" attached to his belt could reach any other "phone" anywhere on the planet—or within several light seconds of Earth, for that matter—courtesy of that satellite net. According to Chester Gannon, a Lawrence Livermore physicist who'd happened to be visiting relatives in Kernersville when the Shongairi arrived, it could also perform somewhere around two "petaflops" worth of calculations in a second. Dvorak was a historian by inclination, and a pretty fair gunsmith, but he'd always been a bit fuzzy about the magic that went on inside even merely human computers. So he understood that a "petaflop" meant "a whole big bunch" of calculations and that packing that kind of power into a small, portable unit that ran on self-contained power was going to change the world more than iPhones and Galaxies ever had. Beyond that, it was just better magic than he'd had before . . . and he hoped to hell that autocorrect worked better on it than it had on his iPhone!

And the reason you're thinking about that is because you don't *want to think about the fact that the love of your life just heard your end of the conversation, Dave,* he reflected.

"'Sam and Longbow and Howell are out of their damn minds if they think I'm going to agree to run for the Senate,' I believe you said," Sharon Dvorak quoted from memory with devastating accuracy. "'Oh, no, you're not getting *me* into Washington—or Raleigh, or wherever the hell else we put the capital once we get around to rebuilding it! I've got me a cabin up in the hills with a bunker, by God, and I'm a-staying in it!'" She leaned back and folded her arms. "Did I get that approximately right?"

"Nobody said anything about the Senate," he said in a hopeful sort of tone, and she raised one eloquent eyebrow with a magnificent snort of disdain. "Well, they *didn't*!" he protested. "Not one single word!"

"Of course they didn't," she retorted. "After all, you might lose an election, 'Mister *Special Advisor*,' so of course they decided to do a workaround!"

"But, Honey," he said reasonably, "I can't just sit around up here in the mountains while they're trying to put an entire world back together. You know that."

"No. I *don't* know that." She glowered at him. "There are a lot of *other* things you could be doing, including getting your sorry butt well again before you go charging off after the next windmill on your list."

"Hosea says I'll be fine, and it feels a lot better already, honest!"

He shifted his left shoulder cautiously, and it really did hurt a lot less than it had a couple of weeks ago. Which wasn't to say it didn't still hurt like a son-of-a-bitch if he moved it without thinking about it. On the other hand, for a joint which had been thoroughly shattered—as in "reduced to the consistency of fine gravel"—by a Shongair bullet, it was doing remarkably well. And once the rebuilding process was complete, it should be good as new. Really! Not that Sharon (and he himself, if he was going to be honest about it) hadn't experienced the odd qualm about volunteering as the first test subject for the medical nanotech Doctor James Hosea MacMurdo and a dozen or so docs from the Duke University School of Medicine had reprogrammed to work on humans instead of Shongairi, Kreptu, Barthoni, or any of a dozen other alien species.

The neural educators Mircea Basarab—otherwise known as Vlad Drakulya—had left in Governor Judson Howell's care were capable of "teaching" almost anyone with incredible speed. It turned out they couldn't teach *quite* everyone—about eleven percent of human brains didn't seem to take to it—but that was still pretty damned good, and the computers aboard the fabrication ships Vlad had left behind contained pretty much the entire technical and scientific database of the Galactic Hegemony. So—theoretically—any human could learn anything in that database overnight. And MacMurdo, who'd happened to be one of the best physicians Howell had available, had been tapped to dig into the medical portion of that database and drag out anything that could possibly help in the face of the appalling wreckage the Shongair invasion had left in its wake.

As it turned out, there were quite a few things in that medical portion that could help quite a lot . . . assuming the human physicians involved got their sums right when they reprogrammed it. The Galactic Hegemony's practice of medicine was just a *bit* more advanced than Earth's had been, including a body of knowledge literally tens of thousands of years deep which had been distilled down into techniques and custom-tailored nanotech that could be programmed to work with scores of different physiologies, as long as the people responsible for the programming knew what they were doing.

That was where the "theoretical" bit about the neural educator learning process came into play. There was a difference between simply acquiring *data* and learning to use it as *knowledge,* and it wasn't too surprising Sharon had nursed a few reservations about using her one and only husband (not to mention the father of her three children) as a test subject. So far, though, it seemed to be working as advertised, and he hadn't turned green or started growing antennae at all.

Yet, at least.

"It may—and I stress, *may*—be 'fine' *eventually,*" she said now. "It isn't *yet,* though, and the kids need you right here being part of the stability in their lives."

He sighed and sat back in his own chair, looking across the table at her in the cheerful, sunny kitchen of the cabin where they and their family had ridden out Apocalypse and, beyond all expectation, survived it. And he knew she had a point. On the other hand, so did Howell.

"Honey, you're right," he said quietly and watched her eyes widen at his admission. "But there are millions—probably *billions*—of other kids out there in the holy, howling *hell* of a mess the frigging Puppies left in their wake, and they need somebody to pull *them* out of it. I can't be out with the contact teams like Longbow or Pieter or even Rob and Sam. Not with this." He tapped the sling supporting his left arm with his functional hand. "And nobody's asking me to be out there, either. But we've got to build something better on the ruins, and we've got to build it fast. And Howell needs all the help he can get doing that."

"You don't have to kill yourself." Sharon's tone was almost pleading. "It's not like you're the only person he could ask! Hell, Dave—most of the North Carolina University system survived! You're telling me that with all of that available, *you're* the one guy he needs? I mean, I love you, and I think you're pretty darned smart, but *really*? And he needs you right now—can't even wait the couple of months Hosea says it'll take to finish fixing your shoulder?"

Her fury was obvious to him . . . and so were the real reasons for it.

"There are a lot of other 'guys' available to him," he said. "And, frankly, I think a lot of them are a lot smarter than me. But he trusts me. Maybe just as importantly, Pieter and Longbow—and *Vlad*—trust me. It's likely to take a while for them to start trusting anyone else as much as they already trust me."

"So what?" She glared at him. "The one thing we've *got* is time, Dave! Given how long it takes to get from star to star, it'll be centuries before anybody else from the Hegemony—" her lips twisted with disgust as she used the term "—gets here to see what the Shongairi did to us. Or to do anything *else* to us, for that matter."

"It'll *probably* be centuries," he corrected gently. "I'll even give you that we almost *certainly* have centuries, but we can't guarantee that. Besides, the Hegemony's not who I'm worried about. Not right now, anyway."

Her blue eyes narrowed, and she cocked her head with a questioning expression he'd learned to recognize over the years.

"Right this minute, Howell has a monopoly on the tech base Vlad left behind, and I trust him," he said. "Matter of fact, he's one of the very few people I *would* trust with that kind of lever. And with Longbow and Pieter and the other vampires looking over his shoulder, I doubt he's likely to succumb to any latent delusions of Godhead. But there's an entire planet out there, and most of it—especially the developed 'most of it'—has been shot to hell. Best estimate right now, we're down to maybe—*maybe*—a quarter of the planetary population we had this time last year. Think about that. I know you understand—we all understand—what that means in human terms, in terms of dead parents and children and learning to live with all the holes it's torn in our lives. But it also means virtually every government in the world's been destroyed or at least mortally wounded and left for dead. Now that the teams are starting to spread out, I'm beginning to realize—*really* realize, I mean—what an unbelievable job Howell did of maintaining order and stability here in North Carolina, even if he did have to pretend to collaborate with the Puppies to pull it off."

"Most of the rest of the world wasn't that lucky, Honey."

He shook his head, his eyes haunted as his memory replayed the recon images Judson Howell had relayed directly to his contact lenses courtesy of that "phone" attached to his belt. He hadn't shared those with Sharon, and he didn't intend to unless she insisted. Better that only one of them should have those particular nightmares.

"There *are* spots that had their own Howells," he continued, "but they're few and far between, and as nearly as we can tell, none of them managed it on the scale he did. North Carolina, southern Virginia, what's left of South

Carolina, and eastern Kentucky and Tennessee represent the biggest single organized unit of governance in the entire world. Think about that. In the *entire world,* Honey. Everything else is patchworks, bits and pieces—warlords here, county or state governments over there, self-organized communes somewhere else. The only places where central authority held up over big geographic distances were like rural Canada or Australia, where there weren't any people. I mean, theoretically Canada's still there, but its total population is no more than fifteen million or so, and that's less than Howell has right here. And Brazil's still *technically* intact, but the Federal government doesn't really control anything outside the acting capital.

"The world's broken, Babe. Even before the Puppies, there were countries that were . . . dysfunctional, let's say. Now?" He shook his head again. "Now there's nothing *but* 'dysfunction,' once you get past the purely local level. Hell, as far as we can tell, aside from Representative Jeffers, none of our own senators or congressmen are even still alive! And I'm talking about 'our' in terms of the entire damned *country.* I'm sure there have to be at least *some* of them left, but we don't know where they are, and even if we did know, Jeffers is right: Vlad left Howell in charge for a reason, and until we can start fixing all the broken places, nobody in his right mind wants to start screwing around with that."

"I know all that," she said when he paused. "Oh, I haven't been watching the data feeds he's been sending you, and I don't want to." Her face was suddenly twenty years older. "I can't hug all those babies, Dave. I can't pick them up, feed them, find their moms and dads for them. And if they have faces, then I *have* to, and the fact that I can't would just—"

"I know." He reached across the table, held out his hand, and she took it. "I *know,* Babe, believe me. And that's part of the problem. I did look, and they do have faces, and there are thousands of almost-Howells out there who aren't going to trust anybody outside their own little enclaves. People who forted up, dug in to defend themselves and theirs against all comers. Some of them would love to work with us, assuming they could really trust us. Others enjoy being in charge or are sure to figure their claim to the Puppies' tech stash is just as good, just as legitimate, as Howell's. They sure as hell won't see any reason to leave *him* in charge of it instead of themselves, but somebody—some *one* body, for at least the foreseeable future—has to be in charge. Right now that's Judson Howell, God help him, and somehow he has to convince all these people not just to let us help them survive but to come together and build a genuine world government."

"And how did that work out with the UN?" Sharon asked cynically. "You're the historian—you and Malachi. So tell me again just how well that worked!"

"It never worked because it was never intended to be a *government,*" he replied. "Howell's not talking about a debating society, or a place to posture on the international stage for domestic consumption. He's talking about a genuine government, one with the ability to make—and enforce—not just pious policy hopes but actual *law* anywhere on the face of the planet. A government that would supersede all other governments . . . including *ours*."

"You're serious," she said slowly, after a moment.

"Dead serious." Dvorak nodded. "I don't know if even Howell can pull that one off, but I do know that if he can't, *nobody* can, and we've got to do it. We're one planet with maybe—*maybe*—a couple of billion people left on it, and from everything I can see from the limited amount of galactic history I've been able to look at so far, the Hegemony's going to want all of us dead once it gets to know us better."

"What?" She stiffened in her chair, eyes wide, and he shrugged.

"I've been looking for trends. Seventy-five thousand of their years—next best thing to *a hundred and fifty* thousand Earth years—of recorded history isn't something you can just whip right through, even with a neural educator, but some things are pretty damned glaringly obvious, and one of them is that the Hegemony prizes 'stability' above almost anything else. That's one reason they were willing to point the Shongairi in our direction. The Puppies were already destabilizing things, so the Hegemony figured it might as well use them to keep *us* from becoming a problem in the fullness of time. I have to wonder just what sort of contingency plans some of the older races might have been putting together to deal with the Shongairi in the long run, but in the meantime, they made a convenient hammer to deal with another pugnacious bunch of violent primitives. That would be us. But, I gotta tell you, Honey, I don't think the Hegemony researched the problem carefully enough before they handed this over to Thikair and his people, because the Puppies were *nothing* compared to us."

"What do you mean?"

"It's obvious from Thikair and Shairez' notes and memos that nobody in the Hegemony expected us to be as technologically advanced as we were when they got here. Got *back* here, I should say; they paid us their first visit back in the fifteenth century. Honey, they expected us to just be getting around to inventing flintlocks and crude steam engines. The Shongairi are quite a bit more innovative than the Hegemony as a whole, and compared to us they're the Mikado closing his borders to keep out dangerous foreign innovation. Once the rest of the Hegemony realizes humans aren't big fans of stagnation, it's going to decide we're the Puppies on steroids, and I just can't rid my mind of the possibility that they might be willing to burn down the house to get rid of the damned cockroaches."

"You mean they might come back to finish what the Puppies started," she said.

"No. I mean worse than that." He met those beloved blue eyes levelly. "The

Shongairi *started out* to enslave us, to channel our taste for innovation to support their own designs against the Hegemony. Thikair's own memos make that clear enough. They only decided to wipe us out once they realized they'd never be able to conquer the planet and *keep* it conquered as long as there were still humans living on it. When they figured that out, they were perfectly willing to exterminate us . . . and figured the rest of the Hegemony would give them a pass on it. I'm not sure they were right about that, but I sort of suspect that if any of the other races had objected it would have been because they saw what happened to us as a club to use against the Shongairi, not because they really cared about a bunch of primitive, hairy monkey boys and girls on a planet in the back of beyond.

"More to the point, I'm pretty damn sure that if the *Hegemony* catches up with Thikair's evaluation of us and realizes how fundamentally . . . at odds with their basic matrix humanity and human nature really are, none of *them*'re going to be interested in just conquering us. From what I can see, the 'older races'—who are almost all herbivores, as nearly as I can tell—have spent a lot of time looking down on the 'murderous' carnivorous Shongairi, but I doubt they'll hesitate for a moment to swat us like mosquitoes once they realize how much worse we're likely to destabilize things for them.

"And that means that somehow we have to get big enough and nasty enough to make that impossible—or at least as difficult as hell, hopefully difficult enough they decide not to try it. And for that, we need a world government that *works*. One that can take the knowledge Vlad left behind for us, build on it, and present a *united front* to the Hegemony when we meet up with them again."

"And that's why Howell wants *you*," she said flatly. "Because you understand that. And because you're so damned stubborn, so damned *bullheaded,* that you've just *got* to do something about it, don't you?" She glared at him, those blue eyes gleaming with sudden tears. "Can't just sit here and figure you've done enough, that you can take a few months—hell, maybe even a couple of *years*!—to spend with the people who love you and who thought they'd *lost* you when Rob brought you home more dead than alive. Damn you, Dave Dvorak! We love you. We *need* you and we—*I*—almost lost you!"

"I know," he said softly. "I know. And I love you, and I need you. But I can't walk away from this. I just can't! There are too few of us left, Honey. And way too many of the better paid thinkers and philosophers and diplomats are gone. Howell's trying to put together a team that can hit the ground running, get this thing launched before somebody else starts trying to pull the wheel out of his hands. I'm not the best man in the world for the job—God knows *I* know that if anyone does! But he's decided I'm the man he's got, and I can't just walk away. I can't because I love you. Because I love the kids. Because somebody's got to help him do it, and, God help me, it looks like one of those somebodies is me."

"But why *you*?"

"Because he knows me—now, at least. And because he trusts me and knows Pieter and Longbow and the others trust me, too. And because he thinks I'm the best he's got. But the real reason?" He squeezed her hand fiercely. "The real reason I'm taking this job is that I don't trust anyone else to do what I know has to be done to keep you safe, and I will do anything—*anything*—to keep you and our kids safe. And they're all 'our kids' now, Sharon. Every single one of them out there being hungry and afraid in the dark are *our kids*, and when the rest of the frigging Hegemony gets around to us again, our kids, and their kids, and their *grandkids*, are going to be ready to put a bullet right between its frigging eyes if that's what it takes."

· IV ·

ST. JOHNSBURY, VERMONT,
UNITED STATES

The snowplow chugged along slowly, clearing a lane of two feet of the purest, whitest snow Abu Bakr bin Muhammed el-Hiri (Abu Bakr, son of Muhammed, the Wildcat) had ever seen. A native of New York City, his experience with snow was that it was white on its journey through the sky, but upon making contact with the ground, it immediately turned a shade of black darker than his own skin.

He'd never seen this much unbroken white before in his life, and it almost made him forget the devastation of the war. Almost.

Abu Bakr's truck was at the front of the aid column which followed the snowplow north along Interstate 91 through Vermont. Although he'd spent plenty of time in New England during the war—and killed a number of the Shongairi while operating in Concord, New Hampshire, not too far away—that had been during warmer months. After an hour of nothing to see but the eternal blankness of snowfall, though, the desolation lost its thrill, and Abu Bakr's mind began to wander as road hypnosis set in.

"Well, here's something you don't see every day," his driver remarked as he slowed the truck. "At least, not anymore."

Abu Bakr snapped out of the semiconscious haze he'd fallen into and scanned the area around them with the practiced eyes of an insurgent. "What?" he asked, after not finding any immediate threats.

The driver chuckled at Abu Bakr's reaction, but then indicated the off ramp to St. Johnsbury with a twitch of his chin. "The road's plowed once you get past the off ramp," the driver said. "First indication of civilization I've seen since we left I-89, what? About forty miles and two hours ago?"

"Huh. Is that all it's been?"

"What do you want me to do?" the driver asked.

"Call the plow and tell him to come back," Abu Bakr replied. "Looks like someone put out the welcome mat; let's go say hi."

The driver nodded, then waited as the plow came back and cleared the ramp. As the bladed vehicle reached Highway 5, Abu Bakr's driver sped up, passed the plow, and headed into town.

"Easy," Abu Bakr cautioned. "Just because the welcome mat's out, doesn't mean it's out for *us*. Let's not race into something we'll have to fight to get back out of again."

The driver throttled back to a more stately fifteen miles per hour, giving Abu Bakr a chance to survey his surroundings. Highway 5 ran alongside a set of train tracks that followed the western bank of the Passumpsic River. After about half a mile, he began to see the normal signs of pre-invasion civilization—light industry and a gas station. Although there were lights on in some of the buildings, it was impossible to tell if all of them were still functional, and no one came out to greet them. In fact, there was no one to be seen. If not for the plowed road and electric lights, Abu Bakr would have thought the area abandoned.

"Want me to stop and check out some of the buildings?" the driver asked, his tone indicating he didn't particularly want to go out into the cold Vermont late afternoon weather.

"No, keep going," Abu Bakr replied, motioning forward with his hand. He shuddered as a cold shiver ran down his spine. "This place is giving me the creeps. It feels like we're being watched—closely—but I don't see anyone doing it."

"Me, either," the driver replied, his eyes jumping back and forth as if trying to take in everything at once.

"Just take it nice and slow. I don't think we're in any danger, yet, but be ready to stand on the gas if I say so."

They drove another tenth of a mile past several restaurants and the Chamber of Commerce, and were just entering St. Johnsbury proper when the driver slammed on the brakes and pointed to a man standing in the intersection of Highway 5 and Eastern Avenue. The man was dressed for the weather, with a long winter coat covering most of his figure and a winter stocking cap on his head. He also had both hands in his pockets, which looked big enough to hold a number of things Abu Bakr hoped the man wasn't hiding.

The driver turned to Abu Bakr, and the former insurgent noticed he didn't volunteer to go out this time. Abu Bakr gave him a half smile. "Guess this one's mine, huh?"

The driver nodded as Abu Bakr buttoned up his coat and pulled on his gloves. "Be right back," he added as he got out, shivering as a blast of freezing air immediately went down his neck and back.

The man in the road simply waited, unmoving, as if unaffected by the cold, as Abu Bakr trudged over. The intersection was surrounded by four-story buildings on three sides, with what looked like small businesses on the ground floor and apartments on the upper floors, but there were no lights on in any of them.

"Now, what's this all about?" the man asked, nodding to the convoy, as Abu Bakr approached.

"The aliens left, and we're putting the country back together," he replied.

"So?"

"So what?" Abu Bakr asked, shivering as another blast of the frigid wind found its way past his jacket.

"So, what's in it for us?" the man asked. "In case you haven't noticed, we're doing okay on our own. We've got water, power, and food, and we don't rightly need a whole lot more than that. What are you offering to get us to join back up?"

Abu Bakr sighed. Although the contact team leaders had discussed the possibility that some of the survivors might not want to reunite without a good bit of convincing, he hadn't expected it *here*—where it looked like civilization *hadn't* broken down—and he cocked his head in exasperation, his mouth slightly open, while he tried to decide if it might not just be easier to kill the man and try to work with his second in command.

"You're not the first group that wanted to integrate us, you know," the man said, when he didn't get an answer to his question.

"We're not?" Abu Bakr asked.

"Newp. A group from New York showed up about a month ago. Told us we were being 'repatriated.'"

"What happened?"

"We sent most of them back home." The man smiled, but it had no humor in it. "About twenty of them chose to stay."

"That so?"

"Ayup. They thought they could force us to do something against our will. They're all buried up at Mount Pleasant Cemetery." He pulled a hand out of a pocket to jerk a thumb over his shoulder. As he did so, Abu Bakr caught movement from above him, as windows on all of the nearby buildings opened, and the barrels of at least thirty rifles poked out. More men with rifles appeared on the rooftops overlooking the intersection, aiming their weapons at the convoy from over the parapets.

"So," the man asked, "what's it going to be? You going to turn around and go back to your 'union' peacefully, or would some of you folks like to stay with us, too?"

"No, I don't imagine any of us want to stay here," Abu Bakr replied. "We'll just take our supplies on down the road and find someone a little more appreciative to give them to."

One of the man's eyebrows went up. "Supplies? What kind of supplies do you have, and what are they going to cost?"

"I don't think you understand," Abu Bakr explained. "They're free. We're here to help you folks out."

The man chuckled. "Nothing's free in this world, son. That said, you may have heard the folks next door have a saying, 'Live free or die.' Happens we believe in that saying, too, and we definitely aren't paying anymore to support the decisions of people in Washington or from the Left Coast, or to do anything else that isn't of benefit to us."

"And we aren't asking you to."

The man started. "You're not?" he asked, disbelief evident on his face and the way he held his body.

"Nope." Abu Bakr blew into his hands to warm them. "Look. Hopefully you've decided by now that we're the legitimate representatives of the former government, not some group of thugs or bullies. Can you at least agree to that much?"

"Ayup. That sounds fair enough."

"So, is there someplace we might go inside and talk about this like men, over a nice hot cup of coffee?"

The man looked down at the pavement a second, then back up to Abu Bakr. "I've got someplace warm we can talk, but coffee's been scarce in these parts for a number of months. Best I can offer's a homebrew tea that tastes like shit. 'Bout all you can really say for it is that it's warm."

"Tell you what," Abu Bakr replied. "You let us pull into town and unpack a bit, and you can have all the coffee we brought."

The man's eyebrows went up to touch the bottom of his cap. "You have *coffee*?"

Abu Bakr nodded. "And it's all yours. Free."

The man smiled. "What did you say your name was?"

"I didn't, but it's Abu Bakr bin Muhammed el-Hiri. My friends call me the Wildcat."

"Well, Mr. Wildcat," the man said, holding out a hand to shake, "welcome to St. Johnsbury, Vermont. I think we're going to be great friends."

GREENSBORO, NORTH CAROLINA, UNITED STATES

"Come in, Dave!"

Dave Dvorak paused, despite the invitation and who'd issued it, because this was the first time he'd actually seen the conference room. He was more than a little surprised by the quality of the accommodations, and his lips twitched as he remembered Sharon's incredulous response when *she* heard about his destination.

"A mall?" she'd demanded. "You're telling me the new birthplace of the United States of America is a *shopping mall*?"

"But it's a really *nice* mall," he'd said a bit defensively. "I mean, I've never actually seen it, but now that the Net's back up, I checked it out. The Four Seasons Mall is right in the middle of Greensboro, with scads of room—I understand they're going to remodel the JCPenney store for the new House chamber and Dillard's for the Senate. And the Sheraton Greensboro's *huge*! There's plenty of room for everybody—for now, at least—and there's a major convention center attached to the Sheraton, with all *kinds* of facilities. It's got a heck of a lot more space than Independence Hall ever had, anyway!"

"But a *mall*?!"

"Well, Governor Foster's going to need every square foot of space in Raleigh just managing the state and dealing with all the refugees right here at home," he'd pointed out. "It makes more sense to let the people doing that stay where they've already settled in while the new kids on the block have to fit in somewhere else. And unless Howell wanted to take over one of the university campuses, this probably really is his best bet."

"A mall." She'd shaken her head.

"Don't worry, Honey. I'm sure history will come up with a much fancier name to hang on it. One that neatly camouflages its sordid origins."

In fact, there was nothing sordid about *this* conference room. Greensboro was still on the power grid, and it still had running water. Food was in somewhat shorter supply than either of those, but at least no one was dying of exposure . . . unlike other places in the world. Until the Shongairi, Americans especially had taken a limitless supply of electricity for granted, just as they had oxygen. The catastrophic consequences when an energy intensive society was suddenly denied that electricity had been far more than simply sobering.

But here, in this room, there was indirect lighting, the circulating whisper of warm air, and deep carpet underfoot.

He wondered how long it would take for this kind of setting to blunt someone's awareness of how terrible things were outside its comfortable walls.

The moderately tall, brown-haired man at the head of the conference table interrupted his thoughts, waving a greeting that repeated his invitation. Dvorak stepped just a bit hesitantly into the room, and the brown-haired man pointed at a chair about halfway down one side of the long table.

"Sit," the man who'd been *Governor* Judson Howell until very recently commanded with a smile, then turned back to the sandy-haired, uniformed officer standing at the large screen TV with a pointer in hand. "General Landers is just bringing us up to speed on search and rescue operations." The smile faded for a moment, but then it was recovered with something suspiciously like an actual chuckle. "Too bad you missed the part about Major Torino's current expedition. It sounds like it's going to be downright memorable."

"The Major does have a way about him," the very dark-skinned young woman sitting at the foot of the table agreed. She nodded to Dvorak. "It's good to see you again, Mister Dvorak. How are the kids?"

"They're fine, Jasmine," he replied. "I think Pieter's going to have more trouble than he expects getting Renfield away from them, though. After all, we've more or less adopted Zinaida and Boris while he's off gallivanting around Europe. The kids don't see any reason we shouldn't keep them and their mom and brother. *And* Renfield, of course."

Jasmine Sherman chuckled and shook her head. Unlike Pieter Ushakov, she'd known exactly why Vlad Drakulya had suggested that name for Ushakov's German Shepherd puppy. It had amused her no end, and she shared more than a sense of humor with Vlad and Ushakov. A pre-invasion petty officer of the U.S. Navy, she was one of only four survivors from Stephen Buchevsky's mixed force of Americans and Romanians who'd fought to the last against the Shongairi, fighting and dying to protect the villagers who'd taken them in. Like Buchevsky himself, she'd been mortally wounded and left for dead by the invaders, only to be pulled back from the brink—or perhaps pulled *across* the brink—when Vlad returned.

She didn't breathe anymore . . . unless her vocal cords needed the air.

"I'm sorry I interrupted, Sir," Sherman said now, turning back to the three-star general by the TV. "I haven't seen Mister Dvorak in several weeks now."

"Not a problem, Ms. Sherman," Truman Landers replied. Technically, Sherman was still a U.S. Navy noncom, and third-class petty officers did not, as a general rule, interrupt lieutenant generals. But Sherman had been transferred to a rather different armed force in which precise military ranks meant very little, and Landers not only knew that, but accepted it, which was quite a different thing. He obviously understood that what mattered was that she was effectively the third-ranking vampire on Earth, serving as Pieter Ushakov's chief of staff and also his representative to the steadily evolving Howell Administration.

"Continue, please, General," Howell said now, tipping back in his chair and clasping his hands behind his head.

"Of course, Mister President," Landers said, and Dvorak watched Howell's expression very carefully as the general gave him his brand-new title.

That expression gave away very little as Landers resumed his briefing, using the satellite feeds and the big TV to give real-time reports on their rescue expeditions. Howell was only about five-feet-ten, a good five inches shorter than Dvorak himself, with pleasantly plain, rather blunt features. There were a lot of fresh lines in that face, and he'd started to gray at the temples. Dvorak had never known him before the Shongair invasion, but people who had known him longer all agreed the gray was a new development.

Howell wore his trademark blue dress shirt, red bow tie, and black suspenders. The political cartoonists had loved those before the invasion, and Dvorak doubted they were going to stop using them now that Howell had risen to a rather more prominent role. But if Howell cherished any concerns about the burdens—or, for that matter, the *legality*—of his new role, those blunt features did a remarkably good job of hiding it.

Dvorak looked around at the conference room's other occupants while Landers finished his briefing. Only four members of Howell's new cabinet were present.

Doctor Nancy Kaufman, the Assistant Secretary of Health and Human Services, was a petite, silver-haired oncologist with twinkling green eyes. The former head of the University of North Carolina Department of Pathology and Laboratory Medicine, she and Hosea MacMurdo were Secretary Leonard Gillespie's chief lieutenants in the evaluation of Hegemony medical tech.

Secretary of Homeland Security Patrick O'Sullivan was an inch or so taller than Howell, with red hair, blue eyes, and freckles. In fact, he looked exactly like what he preferred to call himself: an old-fashioned Irish cop . . . with a southern accent. A career policeman until his late thirties, he was in his early fifties now, and he'd become the North Carolina State Secretary of Public Safety about a year and a half before the invasion. He'd never expected to inherit national office, although, admittedly, the "nation" in question consisted of only parts of four or five states at the moment, but he seemed to be bearing up well.

Kacey Zukowski had been Howell's Secretary of Military and Veteran Affairs before the invasion. Now she'd handed that title off to her pre-invasion chief of staff to become Howell's Secretary of Defense, although Dvorak knew she and Howell both favored returning to the original title of the Secretary of *War*, instead. He also knew why they both favored that change, and he agreed with their reasoning wholeheartedly. Zukowski was fifty-one, five and a half feet tall, with dark hair and eyes, and she'd risen to the rank of major in the U.S. Air Force before a catastrophic helicopter landing invalided her out with a shattered right knee and seriously impaired vision in her right eye. A skilled surgeon by the name of Hosea MacMurdo had put the knee back together, however, and she was almost dauntingly fit: a long-distance runner and an avid tennis player, although Dvorak suspected she was finding it hard to steal court time given her new and crushing responsibilities.

And, finally, there was Doctor Fabienne Lewis, Howell's Secretary of Information Technology. At thirty-one, she was the youngest person in the room, with black hair and dark eyes. Her son, Raymond, was the same age as Dvorak's own Malachi, and the two of them were far too much alike for his peace of mind. They'd taken to one another on sight, and Dvorak knew from personal experience that the amount of mischief a boy child could get into increased exponentially with each additional boy child plugged into the equation.

He turned his attention back to Landers as the general completed his report. Truman Landers had been a colonel before the invasion, the commanding officer of the 1st Attack and Reconnaissance Battalion of the 130th Aviation Regiment, a component of the 449th Theatre Aviation Brigade, one of the three major units of the North Carolina National Guard. He'd been on leave when President Palmer called the snap nationwide antiterrorism exercise that had inadvertently concentrated so much of the U.S. military and state-level first responders on convenient bull's-eyes for the Shongair KEWs. He'd been on his way to Fort Bragg—indeed, his chopper had been only fifty miles out—when the enormous base was reduced to flaming rubble by half a dozen kiloton-range KEW strikes. The blast front had nearly swatted him right out of the air.

It had been agonizingly obvious there was nothing he could do at Bragg, so he'd returned to Raleigh to do what he could to assist the governor in the new nightmare world which had come for all of them. He'd never expected to end up a three-star general, nor to almost certainly become the senior uniformed officer of the United States . . . assuming Howell really could put that particular Humpty Dumpty back together again. He wasn't the smartest man Dvorak had ever met—the general was obviously somewhat in awe of Secretary Zukowski's razor-sharp intelligence, actually—but he was methodical, organized, unflappable, and approached problems with an analytical dispassion far more effective than mere brilliance. Dvorak thought of him as Ulysses S. Grant, not Robert E. Lee, and he'd always thought Grant was actually the better general (although he'd been careful to keep that opinion to himself growing up in the South).

"Thank you, General," Howell said as Landers finished. The newly elevated president puffed his cheeks for a moment, then shook his head. "I hate how many people we're still going to lose," he said more grimly. "All of your people are performing superbly, Kacey," he added quickly, looking at his Secretary of Defense, "and none of that was meant as any criticism, General Landers! It's just that it's such a deep damned hole and we don't have nearly enough shovels. We're going to lose people to starvation and hypothermia right here in North Carolina, despite all we can do. God only knows what it's going to be like someplace like northern *Russia*."

He shook his head again, and the same cold wind whispered through Dvorak's bones. There was snow on the ground here in Greensboro. Not nearly as much as other places, but far more of it than Greensboro usually saw, especially this early in the winter. It would appear that all the dust blown into the atmosphere by the Shongair KEWs had turned the planetary thermostat back down, at least temporarily, and no one needed the vanished National Oceanic and Atmospheric Administration to tell them it was going to get worse before it got better.

And from Judson Howell's expression, it was going to be a long time before this palatial room's comfort blunted *his* awareness of what was happening outside it.

"All we can do is the best we can do, Mister President." Landers' quiet response sounded almost compassionate, Dvorak thought. "And our capabilities are increasing rapidly. Secretary Jacobi really is working some miracles on his end."

Howell nodded, but his eyes were hooded, and Dvorak knew why. The industrial modules they'd "appropriated" from the Shongairi had begun turning out landing shuttles, aircraft, prefabricated emergency housing, and a veritable cornucopia of incredibly capable hardware. But Howell and Brian Jacobi, his Secretary of Industry (the previous title of Secretary of *Commerce* had been changed, in light of how little actual "commerce" there was at the moment) had to balance an agonizing equation. How much of their growing capacity could they use to support *immediate* search-and-rescue operations and how much of it did they devote to expanding their overall industrial base? Every shuttle they built now was two shuttles they could have built three months from now if they hadn't diverted the effort to build it *now*. And how badly were they going to need those additional shuttles when winter really hit . . . or when it was the southern hemisphere's turn to be socked in by snow and ice?

And how did they explain to a starving child in Finland why there was no rescue flight to pluck him and his family to safety today?

Not for the first time, Dave Dvorak was uncomfortably aware that he vastly preferred the role of advisor to being the one forced to actually make those gall-bitter decisions. Perhaps he *could* have made them, if he'd had to, but he'd seen what actually making them cost Judson Howell, and he was prayerfully grateful to have been spared that price.

"It's like we've entered a new Dark Ages," Doctor Kaufman murmured.

"Actually, that's not a bad parallel in a lot of ways," Dvorak said. "I know what you mean, given how grim things look right now, Nancy, but there's another side to it, too, because people tend to forget that the 'Dark Ages' weren't really all that dark."

Kaufman's eyes widened in polite disbelief, and Dvorak shook his head and leaned back in his chair. It was a posture with which his friends and family were only too familiar, and Jasmine Sherman hid a smile as she sat back on her own side of the table to listen.

"When most people use the term 'Dark Ages,' they're using it in a . . . pejorative sense," he began. "They're using it to describe a time in European history when life was 'nasty, short, and brutish,' to misappropriate Mr. Hobbes' phrase. A time when the light of Classic civilization had gone out and left everyone living in muddy misery. But that's not really fair. The real reason they're the 'Dark Ages' is that we don't have a lot of written records from them, compared to other eras. We don't know as much about them, so they're 'dark' to us. And a lot of what we *thought* we knew about them for a long time was projected backward from the fourteenth century. The truth is, what we call the Dark Ages was actually a fairly stable culture that served its society's needs pretty well . . . until the Black Death came calling in the 1340s. As we've just found out for ourselves, any society that loses somewhere around half its total population is going to have problems, and the Black Plague killed between seventy-five and two hundred million people in Europe and Asia in just six years, between 1347 and 1353. For that matter, the net *world* population declined from somewhere around four hundred fifty million to maybe three hundred and sixty million during the fourteenth century, almost all of it because of the Plague. In fact, it took two hundred years for the population to get back up just to the pre-Plague numbers!

"So, yeah, folks in the Renaissance, looking back on that kind of an experience, called everything on the other side of the Plague 'dark,' and it's kinda hard to blame them. And we've lost one hell of a lot more people—even in relative terms, as a percentage of the total population, far less in absolute numbers—in a lot less time than the Plague ever killed. So right this minute, we're in the middle of our very own Dark Ages for sure."

It was very quiet in the conference room, and he looked around the watching faces.

"But you know what lay on the other side of the Black Death?" His eyes circled the conference table again. "The Renaissance. The explosion of art and literature—and commerce, for that matter—that led directly to the Scientific Age. From the fall of the Western Roman Empire to the start of the sixteenth century—a thousand years—nothing changed very much in terms of technology, because there was no pressure to change it. But you can only compress a spring so long. Then it breaks loose, and that's what happened in the Renaissance and the Age of Reason. In five hundred years, we went from feudalism to the Moon . . . all on our own."

The silence was deeper than ever, and he shrugged.

"I've just really started digging into Hegemony history, people, but I can already tell you no other species in that history *ever* moved that quickly from plowing with oxen to riding rocket boosters into space. We chained the lightning—chained it on our *own*—and nobody—*nobody*—else ever did it in that teeny, tiny a window. That blink in the eye of eternity. But we did. The monkey boys and the monkey girls—*we did it*. Our ancestors crawled up out of the grave of the Black Death, and they launched a trajectory that would have taken us to the stars on our own faster than anyone else in the history of the *galaxy* if the Shongairi hadn't tried to kill us all.

"They had to do it from scratch, so what kind of Renaissance d'you think *we'll* be able to pull off when our starting point means the stars are already in our grasp?"

He smiled, his eyes on Landers and Zukowski, and that smile was cold and thin.

"The bastards didn't just give us their tech. They gave us one hell of a motivation to use it—and to improve on it—so we can show our teachers just how well we've learned the lesson when we meet up with them again."

. . . . .

"GOOD JOB AT the meeting this afternoon, Dave," Judson Howell said as he handed Dvorak the beer stein.

"I beg your pardon?" Dvorak asked, cocking his head.

"I felt like you were channeling a little Winston Churchill there." Howell flashed a quick grin. "He was a pretty fair historian, too, if I recall correctly."

"And one tough-minded son-of-a-bitch," William Jeffers added. Despite his choice of phrase, Jeffers was a lifelong Baptist who never touched alcohol, although he'd never been prudish about people who did. Instead of a beer, he nursed a can of Cheerwine with the care of the truly addicted who know their supply is limited. Soft drink production wasn't high on the new government's priority list, and despite its popularity in the Carolinas and Georgia, Cheerwine was available in rather smaller quantities than beer.

Which probably said something interesting about the actual drinking habits of the "Bible Belt," Dvorak reflected.

"He was that," Howell agreed. "He was that."

"No brooding," Sarah Howell said, and her husband looked up with another of those quick grins which had been one of his political hallmarks for so long.

"You'll be just as tough-minded as you need to be, Judson," she said in a gentler tone. "Don't go worrying yourself about all the crap piled up around you any more than you have to."

"Good advice," Jeffers said firmly, and Dvorak nodded. It *was* good advice, and having Jeffers endorse it only gave it more point.

William Jeffers was sixty-one, with gray hair and brown eyes, and as far as anyone knew, he was also the sole surviving member of the pre-invasion U.S. Congress. He'd represented Kentucky's Sixth Congressional District for almost eighteen years, and the truth was that, legally, he had an arguably far stronger claim to the Office of the President than any mere state governor. It was probable that there were other Congressional survivors, although none of them had so far surfaced. And it might actually be less probable than Dvorak had assumed, since Congress had been in session when the Shongairi attacked. Jeffers had been outside the District of Columbia, en route from Washington to visit a friend in Petersburg, Virginia, when the KEWs hit. He'd headed home to his family immediately . . . and gotten as far as North Carolina before word reached him that Lexington had been annihilated, as well. His wife, three of their children, and seven of their grandchildren had died in that attack, leaving him only his son, Bryant, and his wife and two children, who'd happened to live in High Point, less than twenty miles from this very sitting room.

Jeffers knew a "tough-minded son-of-a-bitch" when he saw one, Dvorak thought. He saw one every morning in his mirror, because there wasn't an ounce of quit in him. In fact, what he wanted more than anything else was revenge on the Hegemony who'd thrown his home world to the Shongairi.

That determination made it even more astonishing, in some ways, that he hadn't asserted his own claim to the Presidency when the state legislature— acting in the name of the entire United States—named Howell President and he'd handed the state government over to Lieutenant Governor Alvin Foster. Of course, the law would actually have been pretty ambiguous, even in Jeffers' case. The Presidential Succession Act had never been extended beyond the cabinet level, despite concerns following 9/11, but it was certainly arguable that someone elected to national office would have a better claim than someone elected to state office, if he'd chosen to assert it.

Jeffers hadn't, for several reasons—the most important of which was that he was a very, very smart fellow. As he'd pointed out, he'd been elected to Congress by less than eight hundred thousand people, whereas Judson Howell had been elected governor by over ten million voters. Demographically speaking, that was a bit broader mandate than he'd enjoyed. Howell had also been the head of the only functional, intact state government in the country—nothing else above the county level had survived—and Jeffers had refused to joggle his elbow in the face of such an existential crisis. He was also almost twenty years older than Howell, and dealing with the ruin the Shongairi had wrought was a job for a younger man's energy. And perhaps even more importantly— and the reason he'd agreed to serve as Howell's *Vice* President—was that *his* acceptance of Howell's presidency would go a long, long way in legitimizing that succession if some other senator or congressman turned up and chose to challenge it.

Dvorak had to wonder how many people in Jeffers' situation, especially knowing the new president would very probably end up calling the shots for pretty much the entire human race, could have made that decision. The one thing he was certain of was that it hadn't been the result of any moral cowardice, any need to evade responsibility, on Jeffers' part.

"Listen to Bill," Sarah Howell said now, swatting her husband lightly on the shoulder. "He always was one of the smartest people in Washington."

"You only say that because I was always willing to come on your program," Jeffers said with a slow smile, and she laughed.

Before Judson Howell's election to the governorship, Sarah Howell had been one of the more visible cable news anchors and commentators. She was blond, gray-eyed, and extraordinarily attractive, none of which had hurt her prospects at all. More importantly, however, she was also articulate and quite possibly the smartest person in a room which, Dvorak had to admit, with all due modesty, wasn't exactly brimming over with dummies. As the First Lady of North Carolina, she'd been forced to put her journalistic career aside, which had to have been hard for her. Especially since Howell had clearly been headed for na- tional office of one sort or another after the governorship, which meant her career as an independent journalist had almost certainly been over forever. Not that she'd ever anticipated exchanging Burke Square in Raleigh for the White House.

Of course, Dvorak's mood darkened for a moment; there *wasn't* a White House anymore. Or a National Mall, or a Smithsonian Institute or Library of Congress. No Lincoln Memorial or National Gallery.

"I'm only saying it because it's true," she told Jeffers now, affectionately. "And I knew you had to be *brilliant,* not just smart, because you almost always agreed with *me!*"

Jeffers chuckled and sipped Cheerwine, and Dvorak took a pull at his own stein of Pilsner. Personally, and despite his family origins, he'd never been that fond of Pilsner. His father had tried—without much success—to guilt-trip him over that, but he much preferred the darker lagers and porters or a good oat- meal stout. Under the circumstances, however, he was prepared to settle even for Pilsner . . . especially, he admitted, Victory Prima. He had no idea where Howell had found it, although reports suggested Downingtown, Victory Prima's Pennsylvania hometown, had survived.

"Yes, he did," Howell said. "And Bill here really is one of the smart ones, Dave. Which is one of the reasons that I wanted him here this evening."

"Oh?" Dvorak heard the slight wariness in his own tone. He'd come to know Howell fairly well in the immediate aftermath of the Shongairi's defeat. Along the way he'd discovered the new president rarely said enigmatic things by accident. He'd assumed this was simply one more meeting with one of Howell's "kitchen cabinet" advisors, but something about the President's expression. . . .

"I'm about to really, really piss Sharon off," Howell said, and Dvorak felt a sinking sensation as the other man's lopsided smile confirmed his own trepidation. "I know she never wanted you to come to Greensboro in the first place, and I know she thinks—rightly, I'll add—that she and the kids need you right now. The problem is that I need you, too."

"She and I both know that," Dvorak said slowly. "That's why I'm here."

"I know, but right now you're here as an unpaid 'special advisor,' and I need to change that."

"I won't object to being a *paid* advisor!" Dvorak said quickly, and Howell's smile deepened at his obvious effort to deflect the conversation.

"That'll have to wait until we get the currency running again. At the moment, the U.S. dollar has about the same market value as the quatloo. Besides, I have something else in mind for you."

"What?" Dvorak asked bluntly.

"Secretary of State," Howell replied, equally bluntly, and Dvorak's nostrils flared. Secretary of *State*? That was ridiculous! And Sharon would shoot him dead if he came home and told her he'd accepted the offer. Or maybe not. Maybe she'd settle for just shooting him in both kneecaps, since the kids did need a father.

"Sir, I—" he began, but Howell's raised hand stopped him.

"I know you hadn't considered it," he said, "but I've actually been thinking about this for a while. It's the real reason I left the Secretary of State's position unfilled instead of putting Jessica Tallman into it. The thing is, I can't leave it that way any longer. You know I've been in touch with Jeremiah Agamabichie up in Saskatchewan?"

He paused, eyebrows rising slightly, and Dvorak, despite his shock—nodded. Jeremiah Agamabichie, the Premier of Saskatchewan, was one of only two provincial premiers to survive the Shongairi's initial decapitation strike. Regina, the capital of Saskatchewan, had been spared throughout the war, in fact, despite total Canadian casualties which had been at least as grievous, proportionately, as those of the United States. The other premier, Anson McLarty of Alberta, had been in office for a much shorter period of time, was a younger man, and less well-known outside his home province. Ottawa had disappeared in its own fireball, along with Washington, D.C. . . . and London, which had left the lieutenant governors of Saskatchewan and Alberta as the senior officers of the Crown in Canada, and they—along with McLarty—had agreed that Agamabichie was the only person to serve as Acting Prime Minister, despite the fact that Alberta's population was over three times that of Saskatchewan.

Agamabichie was said to be a tough, no-nonsense sort of a fellow with bulldog pugnacity, and he—and McLarty, who'd become Acting Deputy Prime Minister—had done a remarkable job in their home provinces. The rest of the country had fared less well, however, and despite the vast size of the two provinces, both of them together had boasted barely half the pre-invasion population of North Carolina by itself. The Canadian infrastructure had sustained less damage, but Canadian winters were far more severe, even in normal conditions, than those of their neighbors to the south, and it was obvious Agamabichie needed all the help he could get, as well.

"Bill just said Churchill was a tough-minded fellow," Howell went on, "and from what I can see so far, that's just as true of Agamabichie. But after what we have right here, he and McLarty between them have held together the largest region of unified, functional government in North America. They've got less than twenty percent of the warm bodies we do, but geographically, the area under their control—nominally at least—is six times our size. More than that, Agamabichie's got a damned good claim to be the legitimate, legal chief executive of Canada, with a lot less breaks in the chain of succession than just about anywhere else on the planet. That gives him even more legitimacy as the head of an existing national government than I have. That means I need him on my side when we start trying to put things back together, and that means I need someone to be my official spokesman with him. Which is pretty much the definition of a Secretary of State, isn't it?"

"Well, yes," Dvorak said after a moment. "But I'm the kind of guy who runs a *shooting* range, Judson—not a diplomat! I couldn't tell a canapé from a croissant!"

"That's not the kind of diplomat we're going to need for the immediate future, Dave," Jeffers put in. "And the way you and your brother-in-law handled yourselves during the invasion's a pretty clear indication you have the qualities to be the kind of diplomat we *are* going to need."

"Bill's right," Howell said seriously. "And even if you hadn't handled yourselves so well, I'd still need you, because I need somebody who's a historian. Somebody who's at least tried to understand how people outside his own bubble of time and place think. I'm always astonished how few people ever manage to pull that off. I guess we do all still live in our own villages, at least intellectually. But I've listened to you for long enough to know you *do* try. I don't think you always succeed, but your batting average's pretty damned good, all things considered. And I need that. *We* need that."

"I appreciate the compliment," Dvorak said after a moment, "and you're right, I do try to do that. And you're right that I don't always succeed. I think I can even see where you're coming from on this, but I genuinely don't have the stature and the training for it."

"Been a lot of that going around lately," Howell observed, and Dvorak was forced to nod. "Look," the President went on, "there are all kinds of people I could pick from UNC's and Duke's political science faculties. People who probably would have at least the theoretical training you're talking about not having. But I don't know them the way I know you, I don't *trust* them the way I trust you, and most of them—no shame to them—pretty much sheltered in place during the invasion. You and Rob didn't."

"We'd *planned* to," Dvorak half-muttered, and Howell snorted.

"Of course you did—neither of you is an idiot! But when the Resistance came knocking on your door, you didn't hesitate, either of you, and you almost got your fool selves killed. That's a pretty hefty credential, in my eyes. And from what I've seen of Agamabichie, it'll probably carry a lot of weight with him, too. When I can get that in the same package as someone who's studied history the way you have and has such a clear view of what we need to do before those Hegemony bastards come calling again, I don't have any choice. I need you, and I'm an unscrupulous, devious bastard who'll do anything he has to do to get you."

"In his own thankfully inimitable fashion, he's saying he thinks you're the best man for the job and that he'd really, really like you to go be his spokesman to Prime Minister Agamabichie," Sarah Howell put in, with a half-humorous, half-scolding look at her husband. "And he's dead right," she continued, looking back at Dvorak. "You have the qualities he needs, I think you and Agamabichie will like each other, and it's hugely important we get him on board."

"On board?" Dvorak looked back and forth between her and her husband. "From everything I've heard, they need our help a lot more than we need theirs right now!"

"So they do . . . right now," Jeffers said, drawing Dvorak's eyes back to him. "But that's not going to be true forever, especially if Judson here really hopes he can get away with his more grandiose plans."

"Grandiose?" Dvorak repeated.

"Yep." Jeffers shook his head, brown eyes gleaming with something suspiciously like admiration. "Our Judson's not content with just 'usurping' the office of President from such an august personage as myself. He's got bigger plans, starting with unification of what's left of us and Canada into a single country."

Dvorak's eyes narrowed. It wasn't as if he hadn't seen the need for something like that coming, but he hadn't realized Howell was that far along with the process. After all, they still hadn't put the *United States* back together again!

"*Starting* with unification with Canada?" he said.

"Starting," Howell confirmed, and there were no smiles in evidence now. "We can't stop there, and right this minute I've got the stick to make it happen, thanks to the combination of the Puppies' industrial base and Vlad and people like Pieter and Jasmine. I control all access to that industry, which means I decide who gets to use it—and survive—and who doesn't, so I could beat just about anybody into signing on the dotted line if I wanted to. But what we need to build won't work if *all* I use is a stick. It won't have legitimacy, because every other potential political type out there will figure he only agreed to it under duress. And that means it won't have the staying power it needs. I need somebody who understands that, and who can help me build something that *will* have legitimacy. And I've decided the somebody in question is you. So, how do I go about convincing Sharon to not shoot both of us when you finally surrender to the inevitable and accept the office?"

· VI ·

KEY WEST, FLORIDA,
UNITED STATES

End of the line," the driver said, stopping the car.

Major Daniel "Longbow" Torino, U.S. Air Force, glanced through the windshield and sighed as he inspected the empty space the Seven Mile Bridge should have filled to the west of Marathon, Florida. Several spans of both the new bridge and the old one had been dynamited since the last satellite pass. The destruction of infrastructure—by humans—was an all-too-frequent problem in the aftermath of the Shongairi. Don't like your neighbors? Knock down the bridge connecting you. Problem solved. Want to set up your own little fiefdom? Just isolate your community and proclaim yourself the new ruler. In the post-apocalyptic nightmare of the months following the Shongairi retreat, if you had the guns to back you up, you could probably get away with it. Longbow was just glad he wasn't in charge of infrastructure. Whoever got saddled with that chore was going to have their work cut out for them.

Longbow shook his head. Unfortunately, this was more than a case of bad neighbors. The people who'd likely dropped the bridge—and who waited five miles west—*were* the bad neighbors, as evidenced by the crudely drawn signs his eyes could see in the dark at the end of the bridge. The skull and crossbones motifs indicated quite well what you could expect if you continued.

The contact forces had heard stories for a while about missing fishing boats and pleasure craft. After the invasion, the fishing boats had continued to work the waters, at least as long as they had fuel—people had to eat, after all—and, with increasing frequency as time went on, many didn't return. Similarly, there were rumors of civilian pleasure craft that had left ports on the East and Gulf coasts—their owners trying to flee to the islands to get away from the Shongairi—who'd never called back to report arriving at their destinations. To hear the locals tell it, the Bermuda Triangle was operating at peak efficiency. Garbled messages sometimes gave an indication of something being wrong, but the Shongair prohibition of human aircraft precluded any sort of aerial search, and by the time surface rescue craft reached the area, the vessels had simply disappeared. It didn't matter what type of ship—fisherman or pleasure craft—if it went to sea by itself, all too often it vanished without a trace.

Longbow Torino didn't believe in the Bermuda Triangle any more than he believed in the goodness of people's hearts; he'd suspected foul play, even before he'd seen the satellite photos of the missing ships in port. He motioned for the trucks loaded with supplies to begin the slow process of backing down the highway to where they could turn around, then got back in the car with another sigh. Although he'd been able to use the carrot with most of the communities he'd contacted, he suspected Key West was going to need the stick.

· · · · ·

"HELICOPTER APPROACHING KEY West, this is Key West Tower on Guard. You are entering restricted air space. Turn around now or you will be destroyed."

"What the hell is that?" asked the pilot, Captain Jim "Boot" Hill, as he looked over his shoulder into the back of the Florida Army National Guard HH-60M Black Hawk.

"Those are our new friends," Longbow replied, switching the cabin radio to 121.5 Mhz—the international distress frequency, or "Guard."

"Doesn't sound like the way any of my friends talk to me."

Longbow smiled. "Maybe that's because they don't know how charming I am, yet."

"Yeah, that's probably it."

Longbow switched the wafer switch to VHF and transmitted, "Key West Tower, this is Rescue One, flight of four Army Guard helicopters for landing at Key West."

"Rescue One, you do not have authorization to land at Key West. Remain clear of our air space or you will be destroyed."

"And how exactly do you propose to do that, Key West?" Longbow asked.

"Stand by."

Longbow switched back to the intercom. "This is starting to piss—fuck!" he yelled as a gray blur rocketed past the formation in the post-sunset twilight.

"What the hell was that?" Boot asked, scanning the sky for more aircraft.

"An F-18," Longbow replied, also searching for more. "The recon sats said they have at least one hangered here. Problem is, they might have two. We're not sure about that bit."

Boot gave him the very speaking glance of someone who, for some reason, felt he had been insufficiently briefed.

"Rescue One, Key West Tower. I understand you are now aware we could destroy you at will?"

"Tower, we understand your warning," Longbow replied. The fly-by hadn't given him the opportunity to see if the aircraft had been armed—which was probably intentional—and he wasn't ready to concede the point. It did, however, prove they had at least one operational fighter jet, which was more than *he* had at the moment.

"Good," the tower replied. "Turn around and vacate our airspace immediately."

"I can do that," Longbow replied. "But if I do, I'm going to come back with a flight of four F-22s, and we'll see who owns the sky." *Two could play the bluff game.*

"I don't believe you can," the tower replied. There was a pause and then the voice asked, "What is it you want?"

"Rescue One would like to land and talk to whoever is in charge. I am a representative of the legitimate national government," Longbow replied. *Well, mostly legitimate, anyway,* he added to himself.

The pause was even longer this time, and Longbow knew he was making progress if the controller had to go talk to someone higher in the chain of command.

"Rescue One," the voice eventually replied, "you are cleared to bring one helicopter to Conch Republic International Airfield. Do not attempt to land at Boca Chica Field, or you will be destroyed. The other three helicopters in your flight must turn around now, or all four of you will be destroyed."

"What is it with this guy?" Boot asked. "He's got a bad case of 'or you'll be destroyed.' Sounds like somebody with a Dalek complex!"

"No idea," Longbow said, "but at least we have clearance to proceed. Send the other helos back while I talk to him."

He switched back to the radio.

"Copy all, Tower. We are proceeding to the international airfield and sending three back to base."

He saw the other helicopters peeling off and turning around, and he felt a sense of unease pass through him. While he was pretty sure he could survive a helicopter crash—heck, he'd "spacewalked" without any protection through hard vacuum from a stolen shuttle to take the Shongair flagship—still, he wasn't one hundred percent sure. Nor did he particularly want to try it to find out. Then there was the crew to think about. They certainly *wouldn't* survive it, and that made him feel something else he hadn't felt in a while . . . uncomfortable. He'd never liked losing people under his command.

"You sure about this?" Boot asked, probably feeling the same way.

"Yeah, just get me on the ground, and I'll work it all out."

"I'm sure you'll be good when we get there," Boot said. "I've heard . . . stories . . . about you. My co-pilot and I, though . . . We're a little more . . . vulnerable to enemy fire, if you take my meaning."

"We'll be fine," Longbow replied. Although his voice sounded sure, deep down, he was decidedly less so. What exactly was this whole "vampire thing"? Did it have limits? Did it have an expiration or a damage limit? He'd been shot and survived, but what if he got blown out of the sky? Could he survive that? If so, would he still be in one piece?

He didn't have the information on any of that. He'd wanted to spend more time discussing the limits of vampirehood with Vlad before the captured dreadnoughts had headed out on their mission of vengeance, but they'd never quite gotten around to it. Oh, Vlad had made the chain of command abundantly clear to all of them, left them with a stack of admonitions about things they were forbidden to do, and given Longbow and Pieter Ushakov a separate list of things to watch out for, but all that had left little time to explore the physical limits of what a vampire could face and survive, which left him somewhat in limbo. He knew he was more than human . . . but how much more? Would it be enough?

He shrugged and put the questions aside, compartmentalizing his fears as he'd learned to do long ago as a fighter pilot. Worrying about things you couldn't affect was distracting and not conducive to mission completion. He had clearance to the airport, and he was en route. He'd make it work.

"Look out the port side," Boot said, interrupting his reverie.

They were passing the former naval air station on Boca Chica Key, and he could see the flashing lights of an F-18 landing.

"I see it," he said.

"Suppose that's the one that buzzed us?" Boot asked.

"Probably. I can't imagine they have too many of them. If there'd been a squadron deployed here, I doubt they would've escaped the loving attention of the Shongairi."

"Looks like the Hornet has missiles on its wingtips. He might have been able to shoot us, after all."

"Maybe, maybe not," Longbow replied. "They always have Sidewinders on their wingtips. I think it helps their aerodynamics. No idea whether those missiles are live or just training rounds, though."

"Fair enough. I'm just saying, let's try not to do something where we find out, okay, Sir?"

"Sure thing," Longbow replied.

"Huh," the co-pilot, Captain David Packer, said a few seconds later. "You should see the marinas we're about to go past."

"Why's that?" Longbow asked.

"They're full. And not just with a boat in every slip. The entire tidal basins are full of ships at anchor. They're packed in like sardines."

"Might be some of the missing boats," Boot added. "There's certainly a bunch of them."

"Yep, that's them," Longbow replied. "We confirmed their identities with the overhead imagery." He didn't have long to deliberate over it further as they reached the international airfield another minute later. A truck with flashing lights and a "Follow Me" sign was waiting for them, and Boot followed it to the ramp in front of the terminal building and a parking spot surrounded by klieg lights. A ground crewman took it from there, landing them and then having them shut down the helicopter as several trucks arrived carrying men with rifles.

Longbow slid out of the helicopter, keeping his hands where the men—now pointing the rifles at him—could see them. "Let's go," one of the men said, motioning towards the closest truck with his rifle.

"What about them?" Longbow asked, nodding towards the two helo pilots.

"They can stay here," the same man replied. He gave Longbow an evil grin. "Don't worry; nothing will happen to them . . . assuming you're a good boy, of course. *Now get in the truck!*"

Longbow got in the back of the truck, and it roared off down the ramp and onto Highway A1A. After a couple of minutes, they pulled into a set of luxury condos, and he was led to a room on the top floor. The leader of the group knocked, and the door was opened after a few seconds by a woman wearing . . . not much of anything. Longbow guessed it was a bathing suit, but the amount of material she wore could have functioned as a Band-Aid. For a very small cut.

She walked past them with her nose in the air and headed in the direction of the pool, so Longbow decided it actually was a bathing suit. One of the thugs pushed him in the back, and Longbow turned to glare at him.

"Go!" the heavy said. "Stop looking at the governor's girlfriend."

Longbow decided an object lesson would be lost on the Governor if he didn't actually see it, so he ignored the man and walked into the room, where he was greeted by another woman wearing something similar to what the first woman had worn. He shrugged; maybe it was some sort of a uniform. This woman smiled and pointed to the balcony.

"The governor will see you on the veranda."

Longbow snorted—a hotel balcony was hardly a veranda—but walked out to find the governor seated, looking out at the Gulf of Mexico across the street. He took a sip from a fruity drink and waved Longbow to the seat on the other side of a small glass table from him.

"So," he said without any introduction, "you're some sort of representative from the government?"

"I am," Longbow said as he sat. Two of the thugs followed him out onto the balcony and stood behind his chair, making the balcony seem crowded. "I'm Major Daniel Torino, U.S. Air Force, and I'm here to talk with whoever's running this little operation."

"*Little* operation?" the man asked. "You wound me. I've put a lot of effort into it, and we've got a nice thing going on here. It may not be as big as we'd like yet, but it's growing every day. Drugs, piracy . . . we may even dabble a bit in the sex trade. We have big dreams."

"And you are?"

"I'm Paul Beach, governor of the Conch Republic." He cocked his head. "What government are you from, exactly?"

"The government of the United States of America."

"I didn't think that existed anymore, just like your Air Force. The Shongairi got rid of both of 'em."

"That may have been true for a while," Longbow said, "but we got rid of the Shongairi, and we're putting the United States back together. The leadership has bigger dreams this time around—"

"—don't we all," the governor interrupted.

"I'm sure you have visions of taking advantage of the anarchy the Shongairi brought about—"

"—Where there is anarchy, there is profit," the governor quoted, interrupting again.

Longbow frowned. "Do you want to hear what I have to say, or not?"

"Actually, no, I don't," the governor replied. "We're quite happy here with the government we've established. People bring us their toys—" he waved at the lights of ten sailboats anchored offshore "—and we turn them into drugs or cash—whatever we need—and purchase the imports we need. All things considered, we have it pretty good here right now, and we don't need any government up north telling us what we ought to do or how much of our money we ought to be sending them."

The governor turned back to Longbow and smiled. "I do thank you for the gift of your helicopter, though. It'll make our logistics a lot more manageable going back and forth to Cuba."

"I see." Longbow stood, ignoring the thug behind him and the pistol leveled at the back of his head. "I take it this is your final position, and you aren't interested in what I have to offer?"

"Anything you offer will have strings attached. We here in the Conch Republic don't like strings." The governor made a shooing motion with his hand. "Now, run along. I'm sure we can find some transportation for you so that you can take my message back to your government."

"I can't do that," Longbow said. "What I neglected to mention was that my offer is non-negotiable. You can take it . . . or I'll kill you and find someone else who *will* take it. We *will* put a government together, regardless of how many criminals we have to execute to make it happen."

"I don't like the way you're talking to the governor," the thug who'd pushed him earlier said, holding his pistol to Longbow's temple.

Longbow turned so the barrel was between his eyes, and he was looking around it at the thug. "Are you trying to frighten me? Because if you are, you're going to have to try harder."

"Are you kidding me, man?" the thug asked. "*I'll kill you!* I'll kill you right here, right now!"

"Nope. Still not buying it."

"Why's that?" the governor asked. "Because you think someone's going to come save you? Maybe some special forces from that government you mentioned? You're wrong. Maybe you think we're afraid of your pretend president, or whatever he's calling himself? Well, we're not. We're the Conch Republic now, and you're on *our* land."

"No, I'm not afraid because I could kill all of you if I wanted to, and there's no way you could stop me."

"What?" asked the thug. "You think you're some kind of karate master?"

"No," Longbow replied, holding up a hand, "I'm a vampire." Jaws dropped across the balcony as his fingertips lengthened and the nails grew into claws.

"Fuck me!" the tough yelled.

He fired, but Longbow was already in motion. His hand swiped across the hoodlum, and the man's eyes went wide as Longbow tore out his throat in a spray of blood. The other tough started to pull the trigger on his pistol, but Longbow swept it up and away, then chopped across the man's neck, breaking it. Longbow grabbed the fresh corpse—almost half again his size—picked it up easily, and threw it over the balcony. It landed with a thud just after the first tough hit the balcony floor. A scream sounded from the suite's interior.

"No thanks," Longbow said, looking at the corpse on the balcony. "You're not my type."

The governor slid his chair away from Longbow until he was brought up short by the wall. One hand pointed at Longbow over the remains of his spilled drink as it dribbled from the table's edge.

"H-h-how . . ." he stuttered, his eyes wide. "How did you do that?"

"He missed me," Longbow said, looking distastefully at a drop of blood on one of his claws. "Probably drug-tainted," he noted, then wiped it off on the dead thug's pants.

"No, he didn't miss," the governor replied, pointing at a depression on Longbow's head that closed before his eyes. "I saw it! The bullet went through your head!" The man's teeth chattered, and Longbow could see he was quickly losing control of his faculties. "How are you still alive?"

Longbow shrugged. "I told you. Vampire." He smiled as he righted his chair and sat back down. "Now, we were talking about what message I was going to take back to my president. Is it your intention to rejoin the Union, or do you want to see some of the other things I can do?"

"No." The governor gave Longbow a terrified smile and shook his head sharply. "No, I think I've seen enough," he said. "Where do I sign?"

GREENSBORO, NORTH CAROLINA,
UNITED STATES

I'm telling you, you might as well just give up, smile, and go with it," Dave Dvorak told his brother-in-law.

"The hell I will!" Rob Wilson shot back grumpily, prodding at the mashed potatoes on his plate.

The food court around them was filled with the hum of conversations and the clatter of cutlery. Despite the food court's serve-yourself cafeteria style, disposable plastic tableware and plates had not yet been added to the printers' production queues, so the total dinnerware and flatware inventory of the Walmart Supercenter four miles west on I-40 had been purchased by the fledgling national government. The job of dishwasher had made a strong, although probably temporary, comeback, and the entire eating experience had gotten rather noisier.

"You really think you're going to be able to turn him, and Sam, and Landers down?" Dvorak said skeptically.

"Hey! Just because you got sucked into this dog-and-pony show doesn't mean I've gotta do the same thing," Wilson growled. "Besides, it's not my job. It's not even what I did when I was still in the Suck!"

"Oh, is that true?" Dvorak sat back in his own chair. "I guess my own lengthy career in diplomacy and sensitive high-level international negotiations explains how he browbeat *me* into taking *my* new job?"

"Don't even go there!" Wilson waved an index finger under his brother-in-law's nose. "I had a lengthy conversation with my beloved baby sister about this 'Secretary of State' gig of yours. I believe her exact words were 'like a bee to honey.'"

"I put up a substantially stiffer struggle than she gives me credit for," Dvorak said with dignity. "She's still . . . just a little pissed, is all. I'm sure she'll get over it in time. Like, sometime in the next, I dunno—you think maybe ten years? That sound about right?"

"*Hah!* More like twenty—if you're *lucky*!"

"Then that's another reason you should sign on the dotted line. Misery loves company."

"No," Wilson said mulishly.

"Rob, it's going to happen. And you know, as well as I do, whether you want to admit it or not, that if Howell personally hits that 'But we *need* you' while giving you that earnest, eagle-eyed look, he'll get what he wants. He always does. Look at me!"

"I am trying so hard not to do that," Wilson retorted. "Look at you, I mean." He shuddered. "This is the first time I've seen you in a tie since you and Sharon renewed your wedding vows."

"Well, at least it won't be as big a shock to your system. You're used to wearing uniforms."

"I haven't worn one in almost six years!"

"And your point is? I believe that vow renewal you're talking about happened *seven* years ago."

"But—"

"Jesus, Rob." Dvorak shook his head. "Look, I know you have to put up a good fight out of self-respect. But I also know you don't want to be sitting on the sidelines when all this gets built, either. So, what the hell is the problem?"

Wilson half-glared at him for a moment, then grimaced.

"He wants to make me a fucking *officer*," he growled finally. "I was a frigging E-8—a *master sergeant*—Dave. What do I know about being an officer? Hell, I *worked* for a living!"

"Um." Dvorak sat back again, rubbing his beard. He hadn't heard that bit, and he had to admit it made a lot more sense out of Wilson's recalcitrance. But still—

"Rob, there's going to be a lot of people doing a lot of things they don't think they're really qualified for, and that's probably truer on the military side than anywhere else, in a lot of ways," he said in a gentler tone. "The Puppies kicked the shit out of the U.S. military, and you know it. An awful lot of vets got themselves killed fighting back on their own, too. You came close enough a time or two, yourself, and you handled yourself pretty damn well." He rubbed his still recovering shoulder, looking levelly across the table at his brother-in-law. "You might say you've got a pretty good résumé where Howell is concerned. And I know you were never an officer, but you spent twenty damned years—twenty-*three,* if anyone's counting, really—figuring out how to save officers from themselves. You think that's not a point in your favor?"

"I don't have the education for it," Wilson said, looking away. "You know I screwed up, didn't use the education benefits."

"Yeah, I do." Dvorak nodded. He did know it, just as he knew how bitterly Wilson had sometimes regretted that. "But I also know that whether you want to admit it to anyone else—or yourself—you're one of the smartest guys I know. Maybe your 'book learning' is a little thin on the ground, but you've got tons of what my mom used to call 'wisdom,' and all those hard knocks you've picked up along the way have pounded a lot of savvy into that thick Irish skull of yours."

"You always say the sweetest things," Wilson replied. Dvorak's lips twitched, but he refused to be deflected.

"Look, let me point something out to you," he said. "You don't have a college degree. Well, I've got three of 'em, and when the Puppies got here, I was doing what I *wanted* to do, which was running a shooting range and selling firearms. Don't think all those degrees of mine were exactly part of the job description. And, even if your lack of formal education would have been a disqualifier before the Puppies hit us, what the hell makes you think it would be one now? Not just because of how badly Howell and Landers need your experience, you idiot, but because we've got neural educators now. And I happen to know you've been spending a lot of time with them. Making up for some of those education benefits a younger version of you passed up, aren't you? I got a hunch from the few things Landers already said to me that with NET available, the traditional educational requirements for commissioned rank will be substantially *revised*, let's say."

"Maybe," Wilson said after a minute.

He sat looking at something only he could see, and Dvorak waited patiently. Finally, Wilson's eyes refocused.

"You realize that I know exactly what you're up to, right?"

"What makes you think I'm 'up to' anything?"

"Looking for cover—that's what you're doing. Next time Crazy starts in on you over this whole Secretary of State business, you'll throw me right under the bus, won't you?"

"In a skinny New York minute," Dvorak said with a smile.

"Well, you do realize that my . . . reservations about my own qualifications for higher office, let's say, are only part of the problem, right? You know what they want to call this new abortion they're cooking up, don't you?"

"No, not really." Dvorak shrugged. "Frankly, it's not my monkey. I've got plenty of those of my own."

"Well, I can see why they're talking about renaming it. Can't very well call it the U.S. military when the current President of the U.S. is busy cooking up something considerably grander, now can they? So, I guess calling it the 'Continental Union Armed Forces' makes some kind of sense. But they're talking about abolishing the term 'Marine' *entirely*." He shook his head. "That's a step too far, Dave. A step too far!"

"So what are they planning to use instead?"

"Oh, they're still working on that. The latest, according to my sources, is something along the lines of 'Continental Union Armed Forces Expeditionary Forces.'"

"You're kidding—right?"

"Oh, no I'm not. Just think of the acronym—CUAFEF. How the hell do you pronounce that? Sounds like a cat throwing up in the corner, damn it!"

"So, what would *you* call them?"

"Gotta be Marines," Wilson said firmly. "Don't care about anything else, but they gotta be Marines. 'Space Marines,' maybe. That's got a nice ring to it."

"You were just complaining about acronyms," his brother-in-law pointed out. "You do know that if they go with 'Space Marines' instead, it's going to get pronounced S&M, don't you? Are you ready for all those kinds of jokes?"

Wilson folded his arms, set his shoulders, and glowered.

"It's better than sounding like a puking cat," he said mulishly. "And, trust me, they're gonna hear from me about that one!"

"Good luck," Dvorak said, shaking his head with a chuckle. Then he reached across the table with his good hand and smacked Wilson lightly on the shoulder. "You go get 'em, Tiger."

"I will. You see if I don't!" Wilson said. "I am *so* not going down without a fight on this one!"

SÃO SALVADOR DA BAHIA DE TODOS OS SANTOS, BAHIA, BRAZIL

Y ou're sure of this?" Fernando Garção asked, looking out the window of the conference room. The conference room—and the entire suite of offices on the fourth story of the building—had once belonged to the governor of the state of Bahia, Brazil.

They'd belonged to the governor, anyway . . . until the *demônios* came. Now, it was his office—the Office of the Acting President of Brazil. It was a position he'd never wanted or ever expected to have. A career lawyer and judge, he'd never had political aspirations. Even if he had, they would have been out of reach—several months prior to the coming of the Shongairi, he'd assumed the position of President of the Supreme Federal Court and become the chief justice for Brazil's Supreme Court, which had pretty much ruled out any pursuit of elected office.

After being sworn in, he'd returned to his hometown of São Salvador da Bahia de Todos os Santos, or Salvador, as it was more commonly known, to support his youngest daughter during the birth of her first child. Unfortunately, the *demônios* had chosen that time to arrive, and they'd bombed the cities of São Paulo and Rio de Janeiro, as well as the Federal District of Brasília. In the following days, a number of other, smaller cities and towns had been hit, as well as all of Brazil's military facilities. Salvador, for some reason, had been spared, but by that point the damage had already been done.

The strike on Brasília had decapitated the government, killing the President, the President of the Chamber of Deputies, and the President of the Federal Senate. The only other government authority above Garção in the presidential line of succession, Vice President Victor Lopez, had been killed when an orbital bombardment round hit Rio de Janeiro just north of the Christ the Redeemer statue atop Mount Corcovado where Lopez had been conducting a photo opportunity.

Fourth in the line of succession, President of the Supreme Federal Court Fernando Garção had become Acting President Garção, responsible for discharging the duties of the presidency, pending elections to choose a new president and vice president who would be expected to complete the current presidential term.

He laughed ironically to himself. As if it were that easy. Hold new elections for a country suddenly reduced from almost 200 million people to just under half that, which had just lost the majority of its federal legislative, executive, and judicial branches, as well as much of its infrastructure and communications facilities. Belo Horizonte, Manaus, Guarulhos . . . the list of murdered cities had been both long and terrible, but he'd done what he'd been able to. He'd held the country together as best he could.

He wasn't all that satisfied with his "best," though.

Bahia, like the rest of the Brazilian states, was semiautonomous and had its own constitution, justice system, and legislative assembly. That had helped keep the country stable, mostly, as the surviving governors—over a third of them had died with their capital cities—stepped in to control their states under the iron rule of the *demônios*. Although some of the more rural states in the west hadn't been heard from in some time—they appeared to have set themselves up as new mini-nations—most of the urban states along the Atlantic coast had survived the winter and the Shongairi rule, and they had avoided the complete collapse of civilization.

But then Garção had discovered there was something even worse than having aliens ruling their society: having those aliens vanish suddenly, with nothing in place to fill the power void they left behind.

Before the aliens' arrival, eighty-two percent of the country's population had lived in its cities. While some people had left the remaining cities after the bombardment to shelter in the rural areas—those with the means to do so had, anyway—the vast majority still lived in Brazil's coastal enclaves. When civilization fell, it had fallen quickly as desperate—or unscrupulous—human beings took their own turn at inflicting misery, mayhem, and murder on their fellows. The already-wounded authority of what remained of local government had collapsed under an onslaught of violence and terror as crimelords who saw the opportunity to become *war*lords fought over the ruins the Shongairi had left behind. Recife and Natal along the coast had disintegrated into chaos, and much of the urban areas which had survived the Shongair bombardments had been burned. Thousands, and some reports said hundreds of thousands, of people were dead at the hands of their fellow humans in those two towns alone, and God alone knew how many more had died in the smaller cities which had also fallen to general uprisings and criminal activity.

Although the local police had held things together—so far—in Salvador and most of Bahia, the Comando Vermelho, a criminal organization engaged primarily in arms and drug trafficking, had taken over Aracaju, approximately three hundred kilometers to the north, and it was expanding its influence in Bahia. The gang was attractive to young, poverty-stricken males—with which the slums of Salvador had overflowed even before the invasion—and recruited them by sponsoring sporting events and karaoke funk-music parties where the Comando Vermelho exposed them to a variety of narcotics.

The Comando Vermelho had enjoyed a following even in pre-Shongair Bahia, which had suffered from one of the highest poverty rates in Brazil prior to the invasion and also held the title of the nation's murder capital. In post-Shongair Brazil, the organization was a siren's call for men with nothing better to do and no other options. It hadn't taken much to embolden the criminal element to attempt a takeover of Bahia, and he knew much of Bahia's poverty-stricken populace—facing the upcoming winter—was primed to rise with them if they promised something the government hadn't been able to provide much of recently—food.

"You're sure of this, Raul?" Fernando Garção asked again. "The Comando Vermelho is organizing a food riot for next week?"

"I am." Raul Beltrame, his Minister of Justice, was responsible for the Federal Police and enforcement of Brazil's federal laws. "We've heard about it from too many of our informants to be mistaken."

"What do they hope to gain from a food riot? More dead? Haven't we had enough death in Brazil already?"

"They hope to take over the country," Beltrame replied. "And they don't care how many people outside their organization die to support that cause." He shrugged. "They barely care how many of their own low-level operatives perish in the operation. Life is cheap to the leaders of the Comando Vermelho."

"So they get the people to riot. Then what?"

"They swoop in and give them food," Edson Padilha, the Minister for Agriculture, Livestock, and Supply replied. "If they do that, they're suddenly heroes in the people's eyes, and they've positioned themselves to do exactly that." His lips twisted. "They've been buying up all the stocks they can find, which is part of why we're having so hard a time supplying the cities. They either force the farmers to sell it to them, or they kill the farmers and take it from them. In either case, they dry up the stream of food heading into Salvador."

"So, what are our options? What can we do about it?"

Padilha shrugged. "Kill the killers?"

"Is that possible, Raul?" Garção asked. "Can you find them and stop them? And maybe take back the food they've stolen along the way?"

"We're trying, but every time we get someone into their operation, they're exposed and murdered by the Comando Vermelho." Beltrame sighed. "It appears we have a mole in the Federal Police, and that's making it hard to find volunteers to try to penetrate their organization."

"Maybe we should just invite the demônios back," Edson Soares, the Minister of Foreign Affairs muttered. "Sure, they killed half our people, but at least they knew how to enforce their will."

"That isn't funny," Natalia Perez, the Minister of Human Rights, said. "Half our population is dead, and you think it's a joke?"

"No, I'm just saying things were better when they were here," Soares replied with a shrug. "I also know they'll be back. A race that powerful? There's no way they just 'ran away' when they were winning. Something must have caused them to focus their attention elsewhere—maybe they were losing a war on another planet and needed the forces—but there isn't anything *we* did to cause them to leave. We didn't make them leave, and we can't prevent them from coming back. Why not have them come back now so they can drop some rocks on the heads of the Comando Vermelho?"

"While I do *not* want them back, that *is*, however, a subject I would like more information on," Garção noted. His eyes moved to his Minister of Defense. "Do we have any idea where the *demônios* went? Do we know whether they're gone not only from Brazil, but from the entire world?"

Diego Sanchez shook his head. "We can't confirm it, but the aliens appear to have left all of Earth. We have no idea why, though."

"I can confirm it," Mateus Romero, Minister of Science, Technology, Innovation, and Communications, replied. "My people have been on the HF radio to stations across the planet. Not only have the aliens left Brazil, they've vanished entirely from Earth."

"Do these *stations* say why that is?" Sanchez asked, obviously annoyed to be just hearing this for the first time. Garção turned back to the window to hide his own displeasure at not having been given the news earlier.

Romero chuckled. "I wish we knew. They're saying creatures from our dreams and cinemas—*vampires*, believe it or not—appeared and drove them away. The Shongairi appear to have left Europe or Asia first, and now they're gone from the Americas as well. What caused them to do so, though, hasn't been revealed yet. Not to my satisfaction, anyway. That is why I haven't said anything before now."

A sound . . . or a feeling—or something—set Garção's teeth on edge, and he looked up into the sky outside the window.

"Hold on, everybody," he said, pointing up beyond where they could see from their seats at the table. "I think we have bigger problems, Diego."

"What do you mean?"

"I think Edson was right," Garção replied as a massive shape floated down softly to fill the entire window. "It looks like the *demônios* are back."

The enormous aircraft set down in the street in front of the building—at least Garção thought it was an aircraft; it had wings and was generally aircraft-shaped, although it was over two hundred meters in length, or at least three times the size of the American C-5 Galaxy aircraft he'd ridden in once. Its multiple wheels found good purchase on the pavement on one side and the parched earth—thanks to water rationing—on the other.

"How does . . . How does it land like that?" Natalia Perez asked in a voice full of wonder. "The wings look like a regular airplane's, but it's coming down like a helicopter."

Romero shrugged. "My science and technology folks looked at that. It must have some sort of counter-gravity technology that allows it to lift off and land, and then jet engines that propel it through the sky like an airplane. They would greatly like to take a closer look at it, but we haven't been given the opportunity, for obvious reasons."

Garção turned to Sanchez. "We're going to need some of your forces here, as soon as possible."

"You don't intend for us to attack it, do you?"

"No, but I want to make sure we keep our people well back from it. I don't want a member of the Comando Vermelho—or even one of your troopers—to do something stupid like shoot one of them and have them drop a bombardment round on Salvador. Our country's suffered enough devastation already, I think."

"That's a good point," Sanchez said. He turned and raced from the room, shouting orders to someone as soon as he was in the hallway outside.

"Well, I guess I should go welcome our overlords back to Brazil," Garção said in the voice of a man going to his own funeral. He turned to look back a second, swore, and then hurried to the door.

"What is it?" Romero asked.

"It's not the Shongairi!"

· · · · ·

GARÇÃO HIT THE doors to the main entrance at a run, but then drew up short. He hadn't been wrong—there was a human supervising several other humans. The supervisor—a woman—wore a flight suit with two silver bars on the shoulders. A tall blonde, she was speaking English to the two, no four, men who were positioning things at the top of the craft's ramp. She stood at the top of the ramp pointing to something. Garção's English wasn't very good, but it sounded like—*could it be true?*—they were getting ready to start unloading things from the craft.

He approached the woman at a more dignified pace.

"*Boa tarde, Capitão,*" he said in a loud voice.

"Good afternoon," the woman replied in perfect Portuguese, although she appeared to hesitate slightly, as if having to think about the words. "Although I'm a lieutenant, not a captain. I'm in the U.S. Navy; it's the same insignia but different rank."

"I see, thank you," Garção said with automatic courtesy. "I apologize for my error. But—" his voice sharpened "—how is it that you have this . . . this . . ." He pointed to the craft but ran out of words to describe it.

"The *Starlander*?" The woman smiled. "I know this is going to sound hard to believe, but we made it. It was faster to redesign and build them new than to rework the controls for humans on the ones we'd captured." She held up a hand when Garção started stammering again. "Trust me, I'll tell you all about it after we get it unloaded."

"You are the pilot of this . . . this *Starlander*?" Garção asked, unable to help himself as the rest of his cabinet gathered around him, staring up at the woman in awe. Seeing them gawk at her made him realize he was doing the same, and gave him the ability to shut his mouth.

"Actually, I'm the mission commander on this run," the woman replied. "I have two nugget pilots up in the cockpit holding it up on its counter-grav system so I don't put holes in your parking lot. Like I said, though, they're nuggets, so I don't want to have them do it too long. Besides, we have two more ships orbiting overhead with food and supplies, and I need to get them down here, too." She paused, looking at their faces. "What?" she asked after a moment.

"A nugget is flying this craft? What kind of a nugget?" Romero asked, and the woman chuckled.

"Sorry, that's slang for a new pilot. Like a diamond, my two pilots need a little more polish—and perhaps some additional pressure—to become fully-qualified." She waved them away from the ramp. "Now, if you'll move, I've got an awful lot of aid onboard to unload." A stream of people began issuing forth from the craft's cavernous interior. "Oh!" the woman added, "I also have some other folks onboard to help you."

"Who are they?" Garção asked, unable to keep the wonder out of his voice.

"A variety of professionals," she replied. "Health professionals, mostly, but some logistics folks to help distribute what we've brought you. There are also a few military and security people to help you work on your defensive posture. And there are a few other . . . specialists . . . too. That's about it."

"That's it?" Garção asked, incredulously. "That is more than we deserve, and far more than we could ever have hoped for! Who do we owe for all of this . . . this . . . largesse?"

"All of this is from President Howell in the United States," she said, waving to the supplies and people moving down the ramp. "He's hoping you'll meet with him soon to discuss some ideas he has for the way forward."

"I would very much love to," Garção replied. He looked down at his shoes. "I'm afraid that I don't have transportation to get me to the United States, however, nor does the security situation here permit me to travel at the moment."

"The security situation?" the woman asked as two men and two women in flight suits came to stand behind her in the shade of the cargo bay. "Do you mean the Comando Vermelho and the other gangs that are running roughshod over your country?" Garção nodded, and the woman gave him a smile that chilled his blood, despite the hot summer day. "You won't need to worry about them much longer. My friends—" she indicated the people standing behind her "—are here to take care of them."

IX

AURORA, MINNESOTA,
UNITED STATES

Lewis Freymark smiled as he heard/felt the Shongair *Starlander*-class shuttle go past overhead, and he threw his jacket and outerwear on quickly. Even though he'd been overflown by the shuttles on several occasions now, he still couldn't determine whether he *heard* the vibration of the counter-grav, just *felt* it, or some combination of the two. Actually, he was pretty sure it had to be a combination, since the counter-grav put off some kind of waves that were a cross between a vibration and a sound. It was really hard to describe, but the feeling wasn't; it set his teeth on edge whenever they flew past.

Freymark wasn't a military person, but even he could see some of the disadvantages of using such a system in combat. Although the massive craft was quiet—far quieter than any six-hundred-foot-long airplane had any right to be—the fact that you could hear/feel it coming undermined its stealthiness badly. Of course, it had been built by the Puppies for use against cultures armed with bows and arrows, so that characteristic had never been a problem for them. Until they came to Earth, anyway. That brought a smile, something he found himself doing more of recently.

He was still pulling on his second glove as he rushed out of the pre-fab hut that had become his home. He closed the door quickly behind him. Although the material the hut was constructed of insulated as efficiently as a double-walled, vacuum-filled thermos, holding the door open let the Arctic air sweep through the little structure like an icy hurricane. Aside from that one drawback, the hut was miraculous. Even a small heater was enough to keep them warm despite the minus-six-degree temperature outside.

It was too small for a family of seven—his six plus Alex Jackson—in pre-Shongairi terms, but it was a blessing he and Janice thanked God for every day. They'd made do, learning to sleep together like cordwood. It had probably brought them closer together as a family, or at least he liked to think it had. As long as Stevie and Frankie didn't have to sleep next to each other, anyway. Elbows tended to jab when that happened.

He'd heard the hut could keep you just as cool in a Sahara summer with its micro air conditioner—part of the standard equipment delivered with it—installed. Amazing.

He shivered as a chill wind found its way down his neck while he raced over to where the ramp was coming down from the back of the craft. Several people bundled up in layers of clothing started down the ramp, but paused when the cold air hit them. Freymark chuckled. While you could protect yourself from the worst of the cold, mostly, you never really got used to it.

The group was just starting to edge back up into the cavernous belly of the lander—and impeding the people trying to unload the supplies within—when Freymark reached them.

"Hi!" he called, and the group turned back to him. "Can I help you?"

One of the group pulled down a scarf that wound around a balaclava that protected the owner's head. If the lipstick was any indication, the owner was female, a fact that was confirmed when she spoke.

"I hope so," she said. "I'm Doctor Sarah Rollins with the UNC Children's Hospital System. We're supposed to be here to check out your kids and any young adults who might need medical assistance."

"That's great!" Freymark replied. "Thanks for coming; we're really glad to have you. I'm Lewis Freymark, the leader of this community. If you'll come with me, I'll take you somewhere warmer."

"That would be . . . brrrr . . . lovely," she said, shivering as another gust came up.

"Follow me then," Freymark replied, "and try to stay close." He wasn't expecting more snow today, but that didn't mean nature wouldn't throw it at him, anyway. The way the weather worked in northern Minnesota, you could go from sunny to a white-out in what seemed like seconds.

He led the group through the foot-deep snow to the former high school school building on the southeastern side of town that now served as the area's combination relief headquarters and medical facility. Once they were indoors and everyone had removed enough clothing to be able to talk, he smiled and said, "Hi everyone, and welcome to sunny—if not warm—Aurora, Minnesota. I'm Lewis Freymark."

"You're the mayor of this town?"

"Yes, ma'am, I am." Freymark's cheeks reddened slightly. "As of about a month ago, anyway. I happened to be the first person the relief effort met when they arrived here, and their leader, a Major Torino, told me to take charge of where things needed to go. After they left, the residents here decided to make me mayor so I could continue organizing the relief efforts. I think it was just so I'd be the one outside in the cold all the time. It wasn't something I wanted, but as a refugee here, myself, it wasn't like I had anything better to do."

"Is this the Aurora High School?" one of the other people, a tall, serious-looking man asked.

"No, it's not," Freymark replied. "Or not anymore, anyway. We moved our headquarters down here because this was the only place with a big enough cleared area to land your *Starlanders*. This building was empty, since they built the new high school up by the lake, and we're using one wing to administer the relief efforts and the other as our clinic."

Freymark turned back to Dr. Rollins. "I take it your group is all doctors?"

"We do have one oral surgeon with us, in case he's needed," she replied, "but you're right; most of our team are doctors from the UNC Children's Hospital. We brought a variety of specialists with us—as well as enough equipment to set up a small operating room, if required—and enough medicine to start a small pharmacy." She chuckled. "We thought we had more equipment than we'd be able to transport, until we saw the size of the beast that brought us here. There were teams from UNC, Duke, and Wake Forest, and we didn't even fill up half that thing."

"There are other teams coming here?" Freymark asked. He looked around, wondering where he would station the other groups. "They only told me to expect your group."

Dr. Rollins chuckled. "Unfortunately, no matter how badly you have it here, I'm sorry to say you haven't cornered the market on misery; those other groups were for other areas. We dropped them off on our way here."

"Well, I'm certainly thankful to have you here in Aurora," Freymark replied, his cheeks darkening further. "My daughter is one of the people Major Torino's first supply run saved; there's no telling how many people are alive today because of that."

"Great," Rollins replied. "Well, if you'll show us where we are supposed to set up, we'll see how many more people we can save this time 'round."

X

GREENSBORO, NORTH CAROLINA,
UNITED STATES

M ind if we sit down?"
The pleasant contralto pulled Dave Dvorak out of his reverie, and
he looked up, his mouth full of food.

"Hmpf?" he asked indistinctly, then felt his face heat as he saw Doctor
Fabienne Lewis and Brian Jacobi. They held trays of food, and the sable-haired
IT secretary shook her head with a smile as his eyes refocused on the world
around him. He swallowed and tried again.

"Sorry. What?" he asked more clearly.

"I asked if you minded if we joined you." Lewis held her tray with one hand
and waved the freed hand at the other tables in the food court, all of which were
full. "The more government comes online, the harder it gets to find somewhere
to eat."

"Sure. I mean, yes—have a seat, please." Dvorak stood and pulled out one of
the small table's other chairs for her with his good arm while Jacobi set his tray
on the small round table and pulled out his own chair. Lewis smiled in obvious
amusement, but Dvorak didn't care. He was a Southern boy, and his mama had
taught him about holding chairs for ladies.

"Sorry," he said. "I was kind of lost in thought."

"I'm sure the new Secretary of State has lots of things on his mind."

"Not any more than everybody else, I expect," Dvorak replied, resuming his
own chair as she and Jacobi unwrapped their silverware from the paper napkins.
Portion sizes were much smaller, even here in Greensboro, than they'd been
before the invasion, but Lewis dug into her chicken and dumplings with obvious
gusto.

"Everyone has a lot on his or her mind just now," he continued, nibbling
on one of his own French fries. "I'm no different! It's just that my own biggest
worry—and frustration, really—is more internal than external. I'm not what
you might call convinced that I'm the best person for the job."

Lewis swallowed a bite of dumpling and nodded sympathetically.

"I totally get that. As a matter of fact, I said the same thing when the President decided to make me his chief scientific advisor, in addition to 'only' his
IT secretary."

"You did?" Dvorak cocked his head. "I can see that's a pretty significant expansion, but at least you were a scientist by trade before the Puppies!" She had, in fact, been pulled out of the private sector, where she'd been one of the better—and more brilliant—R&D types specializing in advanced AI applications. "Sure, there's a lot more to being in charge of all 'science' than just the info tech stuff, but at least you're still in the ballpark!"

Lewis chuckled.

"Spoken like a true historian—as in, not like a scientist, Mister Dvorak," she said, "because what you just said shows that you don't know the depth and breadth of what's involved in being the science advisor. It's a lot more than just extrapolating from the one little corner I know into all the areas I don't. And when you throw in the fact that he wants me to decide on which parts of Hegemony tech to prioritize for adaptation when we start pushing beyond the immediate imperatives of our rescue efforts. . . ." She sighed. "It's exhausting, and I had almost no idea where to start."

"It sounds like you figured it out, though."

"I did." Lewis nodded with a smile. "At least a little."

Dvorak set down his French fry and gave her his full attention.

"So what did you do?"

"Well, the first thing I did was to sit down with Brian here." She waved at Jacobi as she spoke. "He's the guy who's really on the front line with the existing industrial base, after all."

Dvorak nodded. The Secretary of Industry had responsibility for the actual management of the captured Shongair industrial platforms, and he and Jessica Tallman worked closely with General Landers, whose SAR teams were carrying the lion's share of the rebuilding effort. Tallman was the Secretary of Federal Management, a brand-new cabinet level position Howell had created when he pulled FEMA out from the Department of Homeland Security's umbrella and handed it over to the woman who'd been his state's Secretary of Administration. Her years as what amounted to North Carolina's business manager stood her in very good stead in her new duties.

"Bryan gave me a comprehensive picture of where we are right now—how we're allocating resources, what the President's established as our core priorities for the rescue efforts, and how they're prioritizing production. Neither of them have had much time to do any real long-range thinking, though."

"You might put it that way," Jacobi put in dryly, looking up from his own hamburger. "Personally, I like Truman's pithy little phrase, though."

"Which would be—?" Dvorak asked with a slight smile. He'd encountered Truman Landers' pithiness, himself.

"He says we're too busy clubbing alligators to worry about what *else* may crawl out of the swamp to bite us on the ass," Lewis said, and Dvorak chuckled.

"He's absolutely right, though," Jacobi said more seriously. "Truman's people decide what we need worst; my people figure out how to build it for him; and Jessica spends her time as the umpire, managing the balance between our current production and expansion for *future* production. None of us can afford to take our eyes off of our own ball to think about long-term implications or how to prioritize tech *as* tech."

"They're coming at it from the perspective of engineers and emergency managers rationalizing production to meet our immediate needs, which are pretty damned dire," Lewis said. "That doesn't leave much room for long-range, what you might call 'strategic,' thinking."

She paused, looking at Dvorak, and he nodded in comprehension.

"I'm afraid we sucked Fabienne into our own task areas, though," Jacobi observed with a crooked smile.

"Well, one of the things I realized when I really started looking at my new assignment was that there's not much *I* can do about long-term analysis right this minute, either. So I figured I should look at other ways to make myself useful until I get my own people—and myself—up to speed on the basic Hegemony scientific platform. Until we manage that, it's *all* engineering and figuring out the best immediate applications for our problems, really," Lewis pointed out. "And even with neural educators, getting at the underlying principles in a knowledge base as deep as the Hegemony's is going to take what I believe you Southerners call 'a while.'"

Dvorak nodded again. He'd already encountered the same problem himself where galactic *history* was concerned, and he suspected it had to be a lot worse for someone who probably needed to *unlearn* quite a few things she'd always known in the past. Like the fact that faster-than-light travel was impossible, for instance.

"And in the meantime?"

"In the meantime, while I start familiarizing myself with the basic theory, I'm helping Brian and Jessica look at current problems and needs. That's not really something I was trained for, either, and I didn't have a clue about where to start. So, faced with such an overwhelming number of things I didn't know, I fell back on the things I *did* know. I turned the whole problem into a giant, worldwide IT solution."

Dvorak cocked his head, and she smiled at the obvious interest in his eyes.

"Once I could relate it to something I knew, some of the questions started answering themselves. I may not know about worldwide food and fuel distribution, for example, but I do know about networking. When I turned it into a networking issue, I realized it was very similar to what I'd do in the IT world; I just needed to learn the new terminology required. In this case, it's infrastructure, and with Brian here as a tutor, I was able to at least start getting a handle on it."

"Fabienne's being a little too modest," Jacobi said. "The truth is that she's been useful as hell when it comes to clubbing alligators, too."

"I can leave you and Jessica—and General Landers—to do the heavy lifting while I sit back and think about things," Lewis pointed out. Then her smile faded and she reached out to lay a hand on Jacobi's forearm. "All three of you have way too much on your plates for that, and we're luckier than we deserve that you're handling the short term as well as you are, because if you weren't, there might not *be* a long term."

Jacobi shook his head and looked at Dvorak.

"We've been focused on what Truman calls the 'airdrop' approach. We're delivering supplies and medical teams by shuttle—by helicopter where we can, but mostly by shuttle, now—and we can reach any place on the planet that way. The problem is that we can only reach one place with each shuttle at any given moment, and that means we're building up isolated enclaves whose only physical communication with one another—or with us—is *by* shuttle. A *Starlander* has a lot of capacity, but not enough to meet any logistic need beyond that. But because we *have* that capacity, that's what we've been totally focused on using."

He paused until Dvorak nodded in understanding, then shrugged slightly.

"Fabienne is looking beyond that stage, and I think the approach she's taking has implications for everything else we're up to."

"And that approach is?"

"Before the Puppies came calling, we had a functioning infrastructure for food and fuel distribution," Lewis said. "It may not have been perfect, and some of it may have been vastly in need of update—even here in the U.S.—but there was an infrastructure in place.

"But when they dropped their KEWs on us, they blew gaps in that infrastructure—gaps big enough to cause it to collapse completely. Now food no longer goes where it's needed, and the fuel no longer flows. Where I erred though, was in thinking we needed to create an entire new infrastructure to get things where they were needed."

"That wasn't *your* error, Fabienne; it was ours," Jacobi interrupted.

"Well, maybe," Lewis allowed. "But what really matters is that we don't—need to create an entirely new infrastructure, I mean. Like any networking solution where a gap exists, we just have to close the gap. The rest of the infrastructure's already there."

"I guess that makes sense," Dvorak agreed.

"Here's an example of what she's talking about," Jacobi said. "Canada needs some items of food and fuel to get from the east to the west, and other items of food and fuel need to go the other way—from the west to the east. We've been focused on using our existing *Starlanders*—and building more of them—to do the transporting because of how devastated the pre-invasion transportation systems are, and that's been a pretty serious problem, because shuttle production is one of our bottlenecks. A *Starlander*'s built almost completely out of synthetics, and that uses up a lot of critical resources and a lot of our printer capacity.

"But Fabienne took a closer look at that transportation system, and she realized the major rail nets are still pretty much there. The problem is the number of bridges that were taken out, and the number of freight yards that went up when the Puppies hit major cities. Those are all fixable problems . . . it takes a lot less of our capacity to turn asteroidal iron into steel rails—or bridge girders, for that matter—than it does to make *Starlanders*."

Dvorak's eyes narrowed, and Lewis shrugged.

"The Puppies left us complete plans for fully automated, self-directing engineering vehicles and construction units," she said. "In fact, they also left us a complete assembly line that was just about ready to start churning them out for the occupation when they decided we were too much trouble to conquer. It wasn't that difficult to turn the line on and let it churn out some of those units for us, and then program them to build bridges." She frowned. "Actually, it *was* a little more difficult than I'd expected. It's probably a good thing the Puppies didn't have true AI in the sense of fully sentient systems, because something like that might have objected to finding itself under new management. But it looks like what they really have is what we'd call 'brilliant software.' In a lot of ways, it's so capable it might as *well* be sentient, but it isn't, and getting the engineering units to understand exactly what we wanted out of them took longer than I'd have expected."

"But she managed it in the end," Jacobi said. "So instead of trying to haul tons of food and fuel back and forth, my *Starlanders* only have to land a few dozen loads of rails and steel girders and drop off some of those engineering units of hers. Then I can switch them back to the 'airdrop' approach and get the hell out of the way. In about another two weeks, we'll have trains running between Vancouver and what's left of Newfoundland again, and a single freight train can carry one hell of a lot more than a dozen *Starlanders*!"

"That makes sense," Dvorak said. "You're not trying to build from scratch; you're just . . . patching the holes."

"Exactly." Lewis nodded. "It's kind of like this mall. What do you suppose people said when the President decided to set up the government—what will ultimately be the *world* government, if he has his way—in a shopping mall?"

"You probably don't want to know what Sharon said," Dvorak replied with a smile. "Let's just say that if the comments were anything like hers, they weren't very complimentary."

"Exactly," Lewis said again. "And yet here we are, eating in the food court of the world government." She smiled. "It's actually got better facilities—the Koury Convention Center, for example—than a lot of the pre-Shongair governments had, and it's at the junction of a number of major interstate highways *and* it's got its own airport, so getting in and out of here is relatively easy . . . as much as it is anywhere else in the world these days."

"So," Dvorak said, "if it's silly, but it works, then it *isn't* silly."

"Yep." Lewis smiled and took another bite of dumpling. "And until we get through the immediate recovery stage, that's the kind of thing I'm going to focus on. I'll still be *thinking* about where we go in terms of pure science, but I'm pretty sure I'll be more useful helping Brian and Jessica with those alligators for right now. Would it be better in some sort of perfect, ideal world if we could start from scratch and build the kind of planetwide transportation system that's possible with Hegemony-level tech? Of course it would! But we don't live in an ideal world, and everything doesn't have to be perfect. All it has to do is to work for now. After we get through the crisis, we can start worrying about perfection."

"Works for me," Dvorak agreed with a slow smile.

"I figured it would." She smiled back at him. "And it's occurred to me that you should take some of the same approach yourself. I mean, if you're concerned that you're not the man for the Secretary of State's job, you're the only person I know who thinks so."

"I beg your pardon?" His surprise showed, and she shook her head.

"You're a smart man, Dave. And you'll have all of Hegemony history at your fingertips, once you've had a chance to delve into it—just like I'll have all of the Hegemony's tech and science at my fingertips. You don't have time to drill down into it yet, just like I don't, but you *do* have a pretty solid grasp of *human* history, and I'm sure there are plenty of things you can use there as corollaries when it comes to your duties. Humanity never had a world government that was a real parallel for its transportation net. Or, rather, never one that worked as efficiently as its transportation net did. But it had a lot of governments, and they *talked* to each other. There were plenty of . . . interfaces, let's say. You just need to find them, start putting some of them back online. Trust me, only the real idiots won't understand that we need something a lot better than we ever had before. So all you really need is to open those interfaces back up and get them all talking to you—and to President Howell—again. After that, an awful lot of things will start taking care of themselves. So *how* you get them talking doesn't have to be managed perfectly—"

"It just has to work," Dvorak finished for her, and she nodded.

"Exactly," Fabienne Lewis said yet again, and smiled.

PETTY BUILDING, UNC-G,
GREENSBORO, NORTH CAROLINA,
UNITED STATES

Well, *that's* weird," Trish Nesbitt said.

"Did you ever see the movie *The Princess Bride*?" Warren Jackson asked without looking away from his own computer display.

"What about it?" Nesbitt asked suspiciously.

"My favorite character's Inigo Montoya," Jackson said, looking up at her for the first time. He was a very tall, very black, very thin man who looked a good twenty years younger than his calendar age, and he stroked his mustache with an index finger. A mustache, Nesbitt realized for the first time, which looked a great deal like Inigo Montoya's. "I think he gets most of the best lines. Of course, 'You killed my father. Prepare to die,' is sort of the classic, but there was another one. About the meanings of words."

"I know exactly the scene you're talking about, and it doesn't apply. The word means exactly what I think it means—*weird*. Although, now that I think about it, 'inconceivable' *would* run a fairly close second."

"Well, maybe." Jackson rolled his chair back and stood. He stretched mightily, then ambled across to Nesbitt's desk. "It's just that what we call 'weird' is probably only one more manifestation of the fact that the aliens are . . . well, they're *aliens*, Trish. Of course the way they do things is going to strike us as a little odd."

"A *little* odd?" Nesbitt looked at him incredulously. She was blond and the next best thing to two feet shorter than he was, and her blue eyes widened as she shook her head. "Warren, I've come to the conclusion that the only thing that would really be 'odd,' is for anything these bastards do to make *sense*!"

"Might be putting it a bit too strongly." Jackson chuckled. "On the other hand, might not be, either. So, what's 'weird' today?"

Nesbitt smiled back at him. Jackson's easy-going manner had fooled some people into missing the keen-edged brain behind it, but Nesbitt never had. She was used to leaving other people in her intellectual dust, but that never happened with Jackson. More than that, she considered him probably the best boss she'd ever had, especially in academia. He was one of the very few people she'd ever met who seemed genuinely able to check his preconceptions at the door, and that was a very valuable trait indeed as they began picking their way through the cornucopia of the Hegemony's industrial and scientific base.

"All right, look at this," she said, pointing at her monitor.

It was an eighty-two-inch LCD with PIPPBP functionality . . . and as obsolete as a wax tablet, as soon as they got around to replacing it. It was, however, quite good enough for her current purposes, and Jackson bent over her shoulder to look at the pair of schematics on it. One was about a quarter the size of the other, and he frowned.

"I'm looking. What would it happen I'm looking *at*?"

"This," Nesbitt said, pointing at the larger of the two, "is the basic counter-grav generator built into the Puppies' ground vehicles. It's smaller and less capable than the one built into their shuttles, and that one's smaller and less capable than the one built into their work boats, which is then scaled up even further for larger ships, etc. Right?"

"Sure." Jackson nodded. The Hegemony was a great believer in standardization, and apparently once it had a design that worked—especially one that scaled—it saw no reason to produce competing designs.

"Well, this one over here," Nesbitt pointed at the smaller schematic, "is what their workboat counter-grav *should* look like."

"What?" Jackson quirked an eyebrow. "Trish, I'm willing to concede that the Hegemony over-engineers like mad, but this—" it was his turn to indicate the smaller, simpler schematic "—is the *workboat* counter-grav and it's—what? Seventy percent smaller than the ground version?"

"Yep." Nesbitt shook her head, her expression disgusted.

"I know they go for multiply redundant features, but are you saying *seventy percent* of this thing doesn't need to be here?"

"No, it's worse than that." She tapped a key and a portion—a *small* portion—of the larger schematic flashed red. "I'm saying that this is what actually does all the work in the ground vehicle version. So, no, it's not seventy percent of the ground version that doesn't need to be there. It's more like *ninety* percent, and all the rest of this is all what you might call *multiply* multiply redundant features. Not one bit of it needs to be there, Warren. I mean, I kept double backups for every feature, and I was still able to cut the workboat version to less than a third of its original bulk. I know we're talking molecular circuitry. I know we're talking about a degree of miniaturization that was never possible for us before the invasion. But this is one of their more volume intensive components. In fact, if they'd been willing to accept this level of redundancy, they could've put counter-grav into every single one of their vehicles, not just their tanks, and still have saved a good ten or fifteen percent of the volume their engines and transmissions used. Not to mention most of the suspension, the steering gear—all of it."

"Hm. That *is* 'weird,' even for the Hegemony," Jackson acknowledged. "You'd have thought the *Puppies* would've recognized the advantages even if the rest of the Hegemony didn't."

"Well, I ran a simulation and analysis. Basically, the installation the Hegemony and the Puppies are using is designed for a mean time between failures of right around one-point-eight-million hours." Jackson looked at her skeptically, and she nodded. "That's right, this design—which is for their *ground* vehicle, mind you—will fail about once every four hundred and twenty years. This one," she pointed at her revision, "will only go about eighty years between failures. Now, I understand it's really convenient when the troops can't break things in the field, but I find it just a little hard to imagine that they could be on constant operations without general overhaul for eighty fricking years, Warren! And their design margins get even greater as you move up to the larger, more capable units."

"Jesus." Jackson ran his fingers through his close cropped, curly hair.

"Yep." Nesbitt sat back, folding her arms so she could glare at the monitor better. "I couldn't believe it when I started stripping out the redundancies and realized just how damned many of them there really were. This is . . . overcompensating, even for the Hegemony. And, take a look at this."

She tapped the image of the original design, and the touch sensitive screen obediently zoomed in until a single portion of the image filled practically the entire width of the display.

"Know what this is?" she asked brightly.

"Not a clue," he told her obediently. "You may recall that you were put in charge of this particular project?"

"Indeed I was. What this is is an inhibitor whose sole function is to prevent the counter-grav generator coil from reversing polarity."

"Say what?"

"Well, we're still working out the proper terminology, but essentially, it's designed to prevent a counter-gravity generator from turning into a *gravity* generator."

"I can see why they might consider that unfortunate if it happened," Jackson said with a slight smile.

"But so far we haven't found any indication anywhere in their literature that they generate increased gravity, Warren. In fact, *so far* I haven't even found any suggestion that they *could,* which is why their starships have spin sections. It wasn't until I started trying to figure out what the hell this thing—and its four backups—were for that I realized what it had to be. So whoever designed this thing figured there was at least the possibility that someone could try to flip it from counter-grav to gravity generation. I don't even want to think about the power consumption—it's bad enough just *canceling* gravity—and I don't have a clue how you'd actually do it. Not yet. I've got a pretty good idea that taking the inhibitor apart would point us at how to do it, assuming we wanted to. But this is just plain crazy, even by Hegemony standards. I don't see any way that something like that could happen accidentally, which means they're designing to prevent things that could only happen as the result of a conscious operator decision."

"Yeah." Jackson nodded slowly, rubbing his mustache again, then shrugged. "Actually, it's not the first time we've seen a design intended to prevent an 'accident' that could only happen if someone *made* it happen. And, to be fair, looking at some of the tech we're starting to play around with, that might not be a terrible idea. I mean, some of this stuff is planet-killer level hardware, Trish. Given the Hegemony's apparent mindset, if somebody went off the rails and used one of these things as a weapon—the Hegemony equivalent of a terrorist, for example—just once, they'd make *damned* sure no one could ever do it again!"

"I guess so," she acknowledged almost unwillingly, and Jackson patted her on the shoulder.

"I imagine you've just moved the capabilities of whatever new ground vehicles we start designing ahead by—oh, nine or ten thousand percent, Trish. And, you're right. I think a MTBF of eighty years is probably adequate. *Barely,* you understand, but adequate."

She looked up and back to grin at him, and he smiled back. But then his smile faded.

"Actually, what I'm more interested in is this notion that it's possible to generate an artificial gravity field. Mind you, I can't really see a use for it right off the top of my head, but that sure doesn't mean there *isn't* one."

· XII ·

DOCTOR FABIENNE LEWIS' OFFICE,
GREENSBORO, NORTH CAROLINA,
UNITED STATES

What do you think about Nesbitt and Jackson's little discovery?"
Fabienne Lewis asked.

"Which one? You mean how much smaller *we* can make counter-grav generators?" Doctor Marcus Ramos asked.

Ramos' father's family was from the Philippines. Although his mother's family was primarily Scottish, he strongly favored his dad, with curly black hair and a dark complexion that went a bit oddly with the gray eyes he'd inherited from his mother. At the moment, he sat in the comfortable chair on the other side of Lewis' desk, lounging at ease in his preferred cargo pants and the Clemson sweatshirt he wore to—as he put it—remind all of his current colleagues that some people had gone to *practical* universities.

Now he shrugged.

"You know, nuts and bolts and molecular circuitry aren't really my thing, Fabienne. So I don't really have an opinion on how much we can strip down their hardware when we design our own. Except that it's pretty obvious we can take a lot of it out." He shrugged again. "From where I sit, that's probably a good thing."

"Oh, I'm sure it is." Lewis tipped back in her own chair. "The thing is, I'd really like to be able for us to wrap our collective brain around whatever version of logic they use when they're designing this stuff. Rog MacQuarie and his guys and gals figure on ripping a lot of redundancy out in the name of tweaking efficiency, and I think it would be kind of neat to have some sort of roadmap of the reasoning behind the original designs. We know there are good reasons for *some* of their safety features, but when you start looking at something like this counter-grav—"

She shook her head, and Ramos snorted.

"I'm only starting to get a handle on that, and trust me—Freud, Jung, James, Dewey, and Skinner would all need psychoanalysis of their own after dealing with this stuff!"

"So why should they be any different from the rest of us?" Lewis asked sourly, and he chuckled.

"Point," he acknowledged.

"Look, I've got a meeting with the President in a couple of hours, and he's taken a special interest in what Jackson and Nesbitt are up to. I think there's a part of him that worries about whether or not the Hegemony is really as paranoid about this crap as we may think they are or if we're about to convince ourselves that *all* of their safety measures are unnecessary and delete the one that eats us in the end. So, *are* they really as paranoid about it as we think they are?"

"Paranoia isn't really the term you want," Ramos said. "And I'm serious when I say that our understanding of human psychology and how human brains work is still a lot less than perfect. Understanding the same things about not just one alien species but apparently an entire *stack* of alien species is a whole lot steeper order. So anything I can tell you at this point is going to be a generalization that may or may not stand up as we get deeper into it."

He paused, both eyebrows raised, until Lewis nodded, then resumed.

"All right, with that proviso.

"I think there are several things in play here. I'm not totally sold on the Hegemony model that says fundamental psychological approaches are *inevitably* shaped by whether a species is a predator, an herbivore, or an omnivore, but it certainly does offer some useful handles. Since we'd never met another tool-using species with . . . different dietary practices before the Shongairi came our way, there's no way we can test their theories with independent research, and everything I've found so far in their database has taken those classifications so completely for granted for thousands upon thousands of our years that nobody worries about a rigorous examination of the foundation upon which they rest.

"Having said that, it's not unreasonable for a species which was preyed *upon* rather than chasing *down* its prey, to have evolved a civilization focused on threat avoidance. As nearly as we can tell, most of the Hegemony's species built their civilizations and their use of tools as ways to avoid being eaten by other critters rather than as a way to more efficiently hunt the critters *they* wanted to eat. Even most of the omnivorous species I've been able to look at so far skew that way, especially as opposed to someone like the Shongairi, whose total focus was on better ways to hunt down or domesticate and raise meat animals."

"I can see that," Lewis said. "I guess that's sort of inevitable."

"As I said, the concept does offer useful handles. One of them is that risk avoidance and stability go hand-in-hand, at least in the Hegemony's view of the universe. I'm pretty sure that plays into the fact that humans appear to be so much more innovative than the Hegemony is. Maybe the best way to put it is that the Hegemony *likes* stagnation, because while things are stagnant, nothing bad is likely to surprise you. And the fact that they have a genuine post-scarcity economy means they can maintain that status quo—that stagnation—indefinitely. There isn't any pressure on them to be producing new technology to more efficiently utilize resources, because they have an effectively unlimited energy supply and their printer technology can produce anything they need in effectively unlimited quantities. There aren't going to be very many 'lean and hungry' species in the Hegemony. Even the Shongairi, who obviously prided themselves on cutting against the grain, being the 'bad boys and girls' who scorned the safety nets and 'cowardice' of the rest of the Hegemony, were *highly* risk-averse by our standards. How much of that was inherent in their own psychology before they met the Hegemony and how much of it was assimilated, maybe without their even realizing it, is another of those questions I can't even begin to answer at this point."

"Interesting," Lewis murmured. "I hadn't thought about the Puppies being . . . domesticated by the Hegemony."

"And I'm not saying that's what happened. I'm saying it *could* have happened," Ramos pointed out. "And if it is, that may be the reason they didn't see the advantage of stripping down the redundancies in their military equipment the way it jumped right out at Doctor Nesbitt."

"Understood. Go on!"

"Well, another facet that plays into that desire for stasis is that the Hegemony's technology simply doesn't break. Not very often, and not under anything like normal operating conditions, at any rate. Part of that is probably just that they've had millennia to refine their designs. Another part is all of those multiple layers of redundancy that they build into everything, though. Again, they can get away with that because their technology is good enough to produce that post-scarcity economy of theirs anyway, but the degree to which they built in the redundancies because of the risk-avoidance—the 'cowardice,' from our perspective—which is part of their basic nature and the degree to which they built them in simply to increase design lifetimes and be *positive* stuff wouldn't break is another one of those questions we can't answer at the moment. I would think those two desires, coupled with the fact that they aren't planning on producing a 'new, improved' version of any of their tech anytime soon, mutually reinforce one another.

"And, while I'm hypothesizing wildly on the basis of virtually non-existent evidence, I might also suggest that the enormously long lifespans the Hegemony antigerone therapies make possible is probably another factor in avoiding risk. I mean, if you're potentially going to live for another six or seven hundred years, you might get just a little hinky about running avoidable risks."

"Makes sense," Lewis murmured.

"Which is one reason I'm hesitant about investing too much confidence in it," Ramos said. "It's always way too easy to fall in love with your own impeccable logic."

"I'll bear that in mind," Lewis said dryly.

"Good." Ramos grinned, then shrugged. "On the other hand, your question

about all of the safety features in their tech probably points out another difference between our mindset and theirs which I think could grow directly out
of our shorter lifespan and the fact that we haven't had the level of technology
they've got for thousands and thousands of years. I think we're more . . . *impatient,*
perhaps, than they are. Historically, we haven't had time to burn the way they
have. Some of our human cultures, like the Chinese, for example, have thought
in generational terms, but we've always been limited by what we can accomplish, even as part of some generational strategy, by the size of our personal
time windows. We haven't had all the centuries the Hegemony's species do, so
we're more rushed to get things done.

"And another thing we have going for us—right now, at least—that they
don't, is that first, we're used to things that break, and, secondly, our knowledge
curve has been bending sharply upward for a couple of centuries now instead of
having flatlined about the time Cro-Magnon turned up here on Earth."

"I think I can see the knowledge curve part of it, but *breaking* things is an
advantage?"

"In a way. Look, Nesbitt says the counter-grav unit they installed in their
ground vehicles was designed to be good for over four hundred years, I think
she said, between failures. I can't think of anything much more complicated
than a sundial—certainly not anything with moving parts—that any human
being would expect to run at all for over four centuries, much less without a
single failure. That's exactly what the Hegemony does appear to expect, though.
So, if I'm going to buy a spaceship that's undoubtedly going to go even longer between failures than a ground vehicle, I'm going to plan on keeping it for a while,
and I'm going to plan on its not breaking. That means I don't have a 'replacement' mindset. In fact, I have exactly the reverse of a 'replacement' mindset.
And because that's my basic mindset, my attitude towards technology and the
universe in general, I'm going to continue to design things that fit comfortably
into it.

"Then you look at the fact that they haven't needed to change anything in so
long. I'm not joking when I say they're still using essentially the same technology they had in their possession ninety or a hundred thousand of our years ago.
It works, it meets their needs, and there's no reason to improve upon it. And
with no reason to improve upon it, they have even greater incentive to build it
to *last.* But we haven't had a mature, stable technology for that long. Hell, I'm
not the historian that Secretary Dvorak is, but I don't think the *Egyptians* had
a mature, stable technology for anything remotely like that long! So when we
look at technology, we automatically assume that this year's model is going to
be obsolete by *next* year, and our experience has confirmed that assumption.
We're not at the top of a hill, standing on a plateau. We're still climbing the hill,
and it's going to be very interesting to me as a psychologist to see if we fall prey

to the same status quo mentality once we finally catch up with the Hegemony and its member races. How much of our 'better model next year' is dependent upon the fact that our current institutions and belief structures have evolved in an environment where that's literally true, and how much of it is inherent in human nature? I guess it's that old nature-versus-nurture argument all over again."

"Interesting," Lewis said again, pursing her lips thoughtfully. "I'll tell you this, though, Mark—we damned well better not change our mindset until after we've figured out how to kick the Hegemony's ass!"

"No, I can see where that would be a Bad Thing," Ramos agreed.

"It's definitely something to keep in mind, though," she went on, "and not just where increasing the efficiency of their hardware is concerned. For example, this notion of Nesbitt's that it's within the scope of Hegemony-level technology to generate gravity, as well as *counter*-gravity. She still hasn't found anything in their database about doing that, but we're still only sort of scratching the surface there, and she and Jackson have turned up a few interesting possibilities. They've had to hand them off to another team right now—I need them doing exactly what they've been doing, at least until Brian Jacobi has *Invictus* and *Provocatio* up and running at absolute maximum capacity. But I think we need to question every single conclusion in the Hegemony's accepted theory and practice. If we're the 'monkey boys and girls' Dvorak keeps talking about, then we need to look for every single 'oh, shiny' moment we can find. As you say, the Hegemony's had a highly advanced technology for over a hundred and fifty thousand years that we *know* of. There have to be quite a few 'roads not taken' buried in all those years. I think it's time we started straying off the beaten path."

"On the whole, I agree with you," Ramos said, after a moment. "I would, however, remind you what used to be printed around the outer edges of maps."

"Maps?" Lewis raised both eyebrows.

"Maps," Ramos confirmed. "They used to say 'Here There Be Dragons,' and—as we know—they were wrong about that. It's just possible the Hegemony isn't *always* wrong, though, and I really, really don't want to get eaten by any dragons."

REGINA, SASKATCHEWAN,
CANADA

S o, what do *you* think I should tell him?" Prime Minister Jeremiah Agamabichie asked.

He stood with his hands clasped behind him, looking north through
the conference room's windows across Legislative Drive towards the landscaped trees of Queen Elizabeth II Gardens. He could just see the statue of the
Queen riding her horse Burmese, and he felt a familiar spasm of grief and regret for what had happened to her and her family when the KEWs hit London.
At least King Henry and the Queen Consort had been in South Africa at the
time, so there still *was* a Royal family, although the new King had been without
communications while what was left of Canada was trying to decide who ought
to be Prime Minister. Agamabichie still wasn't positive how he'd ended up in
that office. Despite the next best thing to forty years in politics, he'd never anticipated moving into 24 Sussex Drive.

And now you never will, he thought grimly, his eyes bleak as he looked at
the heavy snow covering the Gardens. An icy wind whistled in across Lake
Wascana, lifting the powdery flakes in snow devils along the walkways, and a
leaden sky promised more snow by late afternoon. It was early in the winter for
that . . . and it was going to get a lot worse before it got better.

"I think we should be cautious," Adam LaCree said from behind him after
a moment. Which wasn't exactly a surprise. LaCree was the leader of the
Saskatchewan New Democratic Party, and he'd been quite a bit to the left even
for the NDP. He hadn't been particularly fond of the U.S. before the invasion,
and he was acutely aware that the entire surviving population of Canada was
no greater than—and probably *less* than—the estimated sixteen million survivors
in "President Howell's" current vest pocket slice of the United States.

"I'm forced to agree, in this instance," Jared Timmons said, and Agamabichie allowed the eyebrows none of the others could see to arch slightly. Timmons
was Deputy Premier and Cabinet Secretary, and he and LaCree *never* agreed. It
was almost a matter of pride for both men, although when pressed individually,
each of them would admit it was . . . counterproductive.

"I know Adam's never liked the Yanks much," Timmons went on now, getting in the obligatory dig at the Opposition Leader, "and I know we've all spent
a long time living in their shadow. But let's face it, all of Canada had less citizens

than their California alone! From everything we've heard, California's disintegrated into a bunch of miniature warring states after the way it got hammered,
and a lot of the rest of the states have done the same thing. In the end, though,
they'll still have a hell of a lot more warm bodies than we do, and we're sitting
on a lot of stuff they'd like to get their hands on. Athabasca oil sands, anyone?
If we sign on with them, and we disappear into their electorate, what's to keep
them from exploiting Athabasca—or anything else we own—if they want to?"

Agamabichie snorted quietly. He was far less concerned about the exploita-
tion of known oil reserves than he once might have been. If even a tenth of
the little Howell had already shared about the capabilities of the "Hegemony"
industrial base which had fallen into his hands was true, there was an entire
star system's worth of "natural resources" out there to be exploited. Yes, and effectively infinite clean energy, given what the "Hegemony" could apparently do
with solar power satellites and beamed energy. On the other hand, he suspected
Jared was voicing his own concern—the inevitable loss of Canada's identity in
any "equal" partnership with its southern neighbor—in comfortable, familiar
terms.

"I think Adam and Jared both have valid points," Jansen Moore said. At
forty-five, Moore—Speaker of the Legislative Assembly—was the youngest
man in the room, although he'd been active in politics for over half his life.
The last year or two had put a lot of white into his dark hair, but he was still a
vigorous, determined fellow.

"I think they both have points," he reiterated, "but I'm afraid all of them
may very well be trumped by a greater imperative: survival." He looked around
the room, grimly. "We've kept our heads above water so far, but housing's critical, and despite Athabasca, fuel's in dangerously short supply. Without the
help 'President Howell' says he's prepared to provide, we're going to lose a lot of
lives this winter." He paused for emphasis, and his tone was slow and measured
when he added, "That's simply the way it is, Mr. Prime Minister, and I think
every person in this room knows it."

"I agree we need assistance if we can possibly get it," LaCree said. "I just hate
the thought of selling our collective soul in the process."

"Belinda?" the Prime Minister asked, never turning away from the window.

"In my opinion, you must at least listen to what they have to say." Belinda
Timmerman's British public school accent seemed a bit more pronounced than
usual. Aside from that, her tone was calm, dispassionate. One would hardly
guess her entire family, aside from her husband, one daughter, and a single
grandchild had been wiped out back home in the U.K.

"I'm not saying you have to accept whatever they're offering," the Acting
Governor continued. "I'm saying that given the current realities, I don't believe
you have any option but to at least hear them out."

"And how do you think Whitehall—" the old terminology lingered, even if London was a charred pattern of overlapping KEW impact craters and the city of Bristol had become the new capital of the U.K. "—will react to 'whatever they're offering'?" Agamabichie half-challenged.

"I haven't the foggiest," Timmerman admitted with a tiny shrug. "But despite our . . . erratic communications, I understand His Majesty has assumed rather greater powers than the Crown possessed prior to the invasion." She gave another shrug. This one was bigger. "I haven't the least notion how that will play out, ultimately, but given what happened to Parliament and all of the Ministries, it's difficult to see what other option he had, once he managed to return to the U.K."

"And you mention this because—?" Agamabichie prompted when she paused.

"I mention it because even though I feel confident the King never expected to inherit the crown, I suspect he takes his new responsibilities very seriously and that he has a clear appreciation of the present state of the planet . . . and what needs to be done if we are all to survive. It's obvious that none of us—even, or perhaps especially, you, Mr. Prime Minister—can accept any constitutional modifications without the Crown's consent, but I shouldn't be at all surprised if that consent were forthcoming, so long as the nature of the modifications wasn't especially egregious."

Agamabichie nodded. That was how he read things, as well. And even if King Henry *didn't* approve, there'd been more than enough upheaval to justify— or allow, at least—what was left of Canada to act as seemed best to it.

He turned away from the window at last, facing the inner circle of his political allies and, in LaCree's case, cooperating opponents, and clasped his hands behind him. He spread his feet slightly, his shoulders squaring as the weight of responsibility pressed down upon them, and his brown eyes were hard.

"Well, whatever we ultimately tell them, we have to at least listen to them first," he said. "And, as Belinda points out, we can't officially accept anything without Crown approval, which will buy us a little wiggle room if we need it."

Timmons looked around the conference room, then back at the Prime Minister.

"All I can say, is that I am unspeakably grateful that you have to do the talking to them, and not me," he said.

· · · · ·

DAVE DVORAK FOLLOWED Felicity Knight, Prime Minister Agamabichie's chief of staff, into the office. He had no idea if this was the same office *Premier* Agamabichie had used when he was merely the chief executive officer of a province, but it wasn't huge. Bookshelves filled one wall, another wall of windows looked out into the snowy gloom as the afternoon's flakes swirled ever more densely, and Jeremiah Agamabichie rose behind his desk in greeting.

"Secretary Dvorak," he said, holding out his hand, and Dvorak suppressed a spinal reflex to look over his shoulder and see who the other man was really talking to. He didn't *feel* like a "Secretary Dvorak."

Shut up, he told himself, and gripped the proffered hand firmly.

"Mr. Prime Minister," he replied, bobbing his head above their clasped hands in an abbreviated bow. "Thank you for agreeing to speak to me."

"Oh, I could hardly refuse," Agamabichie said with a tight smile. "Even if your President hadn't contacted me to clear the way, the arrival of an alien shuttle in U.S. Air Force markings would have gotten my attention quite nicely."

Dvorak returned his smile, and the Prime Minister waved at the comfortable armchairs in one corner of the modest office. Dvorak obeyed the silent invitation and studied Agamabichie with frank curiosity as the two of them settled into the facing chairs.

The Prime Minister was sixty-two, with a full beard that was still mostly black, although his head had gone completely white. He was only an inch or two shorter than Dvorak himself, and very broad shouldered, with legs that seemed disproportionately short for someone of his height. He looked weary, with the sort of bone-deep fatigue that only endless months of unremitting responsibility could impart, but those shoulders were square, and the eyes under those bushy white eyebrows were very steady.

Agamabichie took the opportunity to return the other man's regard, and he was cautiously inclined to think he liked what he saw.

His people had altogether too little background information on Judson Howell, and even less on this Dvorak. "Less" as in "virtually none," actually. According to what they did know, he was in his late thirties or early forties, he'd never served in government in his life, and—assuming the more outrageous reports were accurate—he'd run a *shooting range* in his pre-invasion life. That would scarcely have endeared him to the pre-invasion Ottawa crowd, but Agamabichie had been born and raised in a rural province, where agriculture and hunting lived side by side.

Physically, Dvorak was brown-haired and eyed, with a more closely cropped version of Agamabichie's own beard. He was tall, and he carried one arm in a sling. If their reports were accurate, that was because he'd damned nearly gotten himself killed in a successful shootout with the invaders who'd killed so many billions of human beings.

And that, Jeremiah Agamabichie admitted to himself, was probably the real reason he liked what he saw.

"I hope your communications with Greensboro are better than they were, Sir?" Dvorak began.

"Now that we've received the first of the new model communicators, they're at least as good as they were before the invasion," Agamabichie confirmed. "I wish I could say the same for the rest of the planet. Our link to Bristol is . . . less than reliable, I'm afraid."

"We were aware you were experiencing some difficulties communicating with the King, but we hadn't realized they were still severe," Dvorak said. "Would it help if we deployed a new model com center to Bristol to use the Shongair satellites? We would, of course, instruct your own IT people on methods of encryption."

"That would be very kind," Agamabichie said, although Dvorak sensed a tad less than total confidence in the security of any encryption Howell's people might show the Brits.

"Well, assuming President Howell's more ambitious plans have any hope of success, you'll obviously have to discuss them with the Crown," the new-minted secretary of state said reasonably. "We should've thought of that and gotten into direct contact with the King already, especially given how close the U.S. and the U.K. have been for so long. But to be honest, we thought you were still communicating using the transatlantic cable."

"I'm afraid not." Agamabichie shook his head. "As I'm sure you're aware, Newfoundland suffered massive damage, and that cost us our cable connection. Oh, the damage to the rest of the country's communications didn't help, but the cable terminals themselves are just *gone,* and getting anyone in there to restore them is simply beyond our capabilities at this time."

The Prime Minister's expression was grim, and Dvorak understood perfectly.

No one knew exactly what the Province of Newfoundland and Labrador had done to piss off the Puppies, although it was most likely the province had simply been in the wrong place. All three of its genuine cities and an awful lot of its towns had received their own KEWs in the initial bombardment wave, probably because the Puppies had established a major satellite base at Grand Falls–Windsor, in the center of Newfoundland. Which most likely also explained why they'd spent so much time "cleansing" the island and a sizable portion of the rest of Newfoundland and Labrador. There'd never been more than around a half million people in the entire province; there were a hell of a lot less now, and those who remained were in a grim, no-holds-barred struggle to survive as winter closed in. Average temperatures were usually fairly moderate in Newfoundland, ranging between sixty-one degrees in the summer and thirty-two degrees in the winter, but *this* winter was already proving far worse than "usually," and too much of the infrastructure had been ripped to shreds.

"We'd very much like to be able to offer them at least humanitarian assistance," Agamabichie continued, "but we don't have the transport or, frankly, the assistance to spare. And we certainly don't have the capability to establish some sort of enclave and rebuild the cable terminals."

"Understood." Dvorak nodded.

Saskatchewan's pre-invasion population had been just over one million. Despite its own grim death toll, its current population was at least 1.5 million, thanks to the refugees who'd poured in from farther east. Alberta had suffered its own influx as citizens of British Columbia sought safe havens. The Puppies had paid particular attention to the coastal regions in both Canada and the U.S., possibly because so much of the population and so many of the major ports had been concentrated there. That would certainly explain why California had taken so much damage, and it might explain what had happened to British Columbia, as well. Both Victoria and Vancouver had been wiped from the face of the Earth in the initial strike, and the province's decapitated central government had crumbled quickly. Many of B.C.'s survivors had sought the relative security of Alberta and Saskatchewan, and at least there'd been little starvation. Those two provinces had contained over forty percent of all Canadian farms, and the crops and livestock which had been produced for export had been available to carry their people—and their visitors—without the grim starvation which afflicted so much of the rest of the planet. Agamabichie and his government had even managed to put aside a sufficient bumper for the winter. What they didn't have was the capacity to move any sizable percentage of that food to places like the howling wilderness which had once been Newfoundland and Labrador.

Fuel was in extremely short supply, which was bitterly ironic, considering that Canada had been the sixth-largest oil-producing country in the world and the refineries of Western Canada had produced forty percent of all Canadian petroleum products. But the Puppies had clearly grasped that human technology ran on fossil fuels, and precious few of those refineries remained. The situation was similar in the U.S., where the Gulf Coast and the Great Lakes ports had taken a special pounding.

That was bad enough from the viewpoint of transportation; it was far worse from the viewpoint of heating oil and gas. The government had been forced to throw up temporary housing for the enormous influx of refugees, and speed of construction and lack of materials, all hampered by Shongair interference at every step, meant very little of that housing would have met code. It was drafty, it wasn't all that well insulated, and an awful lot of people were going to get awfully cold in the coming weeks.

"We're aware of at least some of the difficulties you face, Mr. Prime Minister," he continued after a moment. "Secretary Tallman and Secretary Jacobi have done their best with the limited data available to them to estimate your most serious needs, but we're certain you have a far better grasp of that than we do.

One of the things President Howell's instructed me to get from you is a list of them so we can see how we can help most effectively.

"Some things we already know we won't be able to do, I'm afraid. For example, our supplies of gasoline, diesel, natural gas—all the petroleum products—are extremely tight right now. We would be able to make some additional stocks available to you, but not in anywhere near the quantities we expect you actually need. That's partly because we don't have them ourselves, and partly because—frankly—you aren't the only place that desperately needs help.

"There are a couple of things we can do to alleviate that, however. We're now producing trucks configured for human operation with Shongair power plants. They use what Doctor Gannon—he's a Lawrence Livermore physicist in North Carolina—tells me is a fully developed version of the low-energy nuclear reaction technology people like NASA were playing with prior to the invasion. Don't ask me to explain what 'low-energy nuclear reaction' is or how it works." He flashed a quirky grin. "I know the acronym is LENR, that it uses a lot of nickel, and that because it uses 'slow neutrons'—whatever the hell those are—it doesn't generate radiation or radioactive waste. Which means," his smile disappeared, "that we can put them into trucks, into houses, into *aircraft,* and have a low-cost, long-endurance, high-output power plant that doesn't need fossil fuels at all. They're also a lot smaller than anything like them that we could have built before Fleet Commander Thikair was kind enough to leave us his orbital industry. We're turning them out as quickly as we can, and some of our more clever techs have figured out how to mount them in existing pre-invasion truck designs by switching out the internal combustion engines for steam turbines, so in addition to new-build vehicles, we're turning out a growing stream of conversions.

"We're also producing small, portable units that can heat—or cool—homes and public buildings. The need's so great that balancing output against expansion is our greatest nightmare right this minute, but President Howell told me to tell you that he will make absolutely as much of the new technology available to you as he possibly can."

"And the price for this will be . . . what? Our acceptance of this plan of his to merge our two nations?"

"There *is* no price for it, Mr. Prime Minister," Dvorak said levelly. Agamabichie's eyebrows arched, and Dvorak shook his head. "We're making this tech available as broadly as we can on the basis of need," he said. "In fact, we're probably sending more of it to northern Europe and Scandinavia than to Canada, despite the logistic issues. Their need, frankly, is far worse than yours, because most of Europe lost cohesion when the Puppies moved in.

"Yours—and President Garção's, down in Bahia—are the two largest geographic areas to maintain unified government. You've faced harsher environmental issues; he's faced a lot more civil unrest—warlordism, to call it by its true name. But nobody in Europe managed to hold society together on the same kind of scale. And that means the two of you will be able to use what we can provide more efficiently, without its being hijacked, or diverted, or simply lost, than anyone else. Which means what we give you will go farther . . . and that we have to give proportionately *more* to the areas where it *won't* be used efficiently, because we'll have to compensate with quantity to overcome the lack of efficiency. Within that limitation, though, you'll get everything we can send you. No price tags, no strings attached."

Agamabichie sat back in his chair, his eyes suddenly intent, and Dvorak leaned back and crossed his legs.

"I . . . find that difficult to believe," the Prime Minister said after a long, thoughtful pause. "And—" visions of Adam LaCree danced in his imagination "—I expect that some of my ministers and advisors will find it even more difficult to believe than I do."

"I won't pretend President Howell doesn't hope his willingness to assist will buy some goodwill, Sir." Dvorak flashed another brief smile. "Probably a proper diplomat would beat around the bush and put that ever so much more delicately, but I don't think President Howell picked me because I'm a 'proper diplomat.' He picked me, I think, because I have a tendency to call a spade a spade, as we put it back home. But you're a smart man, so you have to be as aware as I am that helping your people get through this winter has to earn us at least some good press up here in Canada.

"On the other hand," the smile vanished again, "there is such a thing as common decency, Mr. Prime Minister. Our . . . core constituency in North Carolina's probably in better shape than any other spot on the face of the planet. You would not believe—or want to see—what the satellites are showing us out of China." He shook his head, his face suddenly decades older than it had been. "We don't know who issued the call for a general uprising, but the casualties were beyond catastrophic. We're trying to reach out to China, but so far we're having an awful time finding anyone in all that chaos in a position to cooperate effectively with us.

"But that only underscores the fact that anywhere we *can* help, we *must* help. No matter what we do, we're going to lose too many more people, and at least some of the survivors will blame us for it, after the dust settles. They won't believe we couldn't have done more for the people *they* loved, and it's hard to blame them for that. Whatever they think, though, it won't be because we didn't do everything we damned well could, because all of us need to live with ourselves afterward."

Agamabichie nodded slowly, digesting the sincerity behind that not-a-diplomat's eyes.

"You *do* hope we'll join this scheme of yours to merge Canada and the States, though, don't you?"

"Of course we do. And I hope that after I've had a chance to share our intelligence on why the Shongairi attacked us in the first place—and why it's imperative for us to get ourselves organized as a species before the Hegemony gets around to round two—you'll agree with us."

"Round two?" Agamabichie sat straighter, his expression suddenly intent.

"Yes, Sir," Dvorak said grimly. "Our belief, which we believe you'll share after looking at the records and the data we've captured, is that this was only the first wave. Given the limitations of even the 'Galactic Hegemony's' faster-than-light technology, they won't be back next week, or next year, or even next decade, but they *will* be back, and we have to be outnumbered literally trillions to one. So the one thing we can't afford is to still be squabbling with one another when the next Hegemony starship drops out of phase-drive somewhere around Jupiter."

Agamabichie's blood ran cold, but he couldn't pretend he was really surprised. And he was looking forward to poring over any records Howell's people might have. But in the meantime . . .

"You have to understand how many reservations Canadians are going to have about losing their identity and control of their own destinies if they merge with something like the United States. Assuming President Howell can put your own country back together again, you'll easily outnumber us many times over, and I can't believe anyone in North America would suggest a system of governance in which population doesn't count for a lot when it comes to elections."

"Of course you have reservations!" Dvorak chuckled. "In your place, I'd have a lot more than just 'reservations,' Sir! But the President's given quite a bit of thought to this." *And,* he did not add out loud, *he's discussed it a lot with the poor son-of-a-bitch he drafted as his Secretary of State, too.* "And as a consequence, what he intends to propose is a step back towards the compromise between the larger states and the smaller states at the time our own Constitution was drafted."

"Ah?" Agamabichie leaned forward, elbows on his chair arms, and tented his fingers under his bearded jaw. "I have to admit I don't know as much about your early history as I do about Canada's."

"You probably know a hell of a lot more about U.S. history than I do about Canada's history," Dvorak said. "Most Americans don't read or study Canadian history at all, I'm afraid."

"I'm not surprised, given the . . . disparity in our populations."

"Gracious of you, and probably more gracious than your typical U.S. citizen would be. I mean, after all, we routinely call ourselves 'Americans,' as if all the rest of you live on another continent somewhere. That's one of the things President Howell would like to fix."

"How?" Agamabichie's tone was blunt. "Frankly, that reminds me of the story about Hercules and the stables."

"Basically, he intends to propose a Constitution based on the original U.S. Constitution, minus one or two of its amendments. Specifically, he intends to exclude the Seventeenth Amendment."

"Which would be the one that—?"

"It would be the one that establishes the direct election of Senators," Dvorak said. "Originally, Senators were chosen by their state legislatures and represented the states' interests in a federal system that emphasized a much broader degree of local sovereignty than became the case in the last century."

"And why does he want to change that?"

"Because he's looking at a bicameral legislature, with a Senate and a House of Representatives, and each sovereign nation which ratifies his new constitution and joins his Continental Union will have the same number of Senators, regardless of population. That is, in the upper house, the former Canada and the former United States will have equal representation, and the Senate will retain not simply its legislative role but its right of advice and consent for cabinet officers, members of the judiciary, and everything else it oversees under the current U.S. Constitution. Which means Canada and the U.S. will have *equal voices* on those issues.

"In addition, he wants to incorporate the Electoral College. Before the invasion, a lot of people in the States felt that the Electoral College system was antidemocratic, and they were right. Its function was to ensure that smaller states, all of whom had a minimum of two Senators and at least one or two Representatives, wouldn't simply be steamrollered by a few bigger states which happened to have far more massive populations. Those issues aren't new; they confronted the original thirteen states, and the Electoral College was the compromise adopted to protect the little guys. Which is why President Howell wants to extend that same protection to any smaller sovereign nation that signs on the dotted line. Money bills will originate in the new House of Representatives, and every seat in the House will be up for reelection in every general election, which means the nations with more people will still have far more clout than ones with smaller populations, but the Senate—especially if its members owe their loyalty to their home nations rather than to the Continental Union's federal power structure— will prevent the federal *republic* from becoming a centralized *democracy*. What member states of the Continental Union want to do within their former national borders will be largely up to them, with as much local autonomy as possible, as long as minimal human rights guarantees are met."

Agamabichie frowned thoughtfully. That was a far more generous offer than he'd anticipated, but it made sense. Assuming Howell truly understood the . . . un-wisdom of *forcing* other nations to ratify his new constitution, that was.

"Should I assume you've brought a more detailed version of what you've just described along with you?" he asked finally.

"I have," Dvorak acknowledged. "And, with your permission and agreement, we intend to present a copy of those same plans to King Henry in Bristol. I don't think many of us folks from below the forty-ninth parallel really understand how the Commonwealth works, but it did occur to us ignorant colonials that it would *probably* be a good idea to get the Crown to sign off on this. For that matter, I might as well admit that President Howell sees the Continental Union as only the first step. And I don't think he'd object at all if the entire Commonwealth 'spontaneously' decided to get in on the ground floor, as it were."

"At least I doubt anyone's ever going to accuse President Howell of thinking small," Agamabichie said dryly.

"No." Dvorak shook his head. "No, I don't think that would be the very best way to describe him, somehow."

Agamabichie chuckled, then leaned back again.

"If you could deliver that communication center to Bristol at the same time as you deliver President Howell's proposals, I think that would be a very good thing," he said. "In the meantime, you're absolutely right about the amount of help we're going to need, and those new reactors of yours sound *wonderful*! My people have already drawn up provisional lists to ask for. Once we've had a chance to look at what sort of help you can deliver, we'll fine-tune them. And I'll consult with the Cabinet and the Opposition on President Howell's . . . political initiative. I have to tell you, though, that while I'm far more optimistic about their ultimate willingness to consider it now that you've described the safeguards President Howell has in mind, it's going to take a while to bring them around. And I think all of them will insist on studying the data—the intelligence—you've gathered on the Shongairi and this 'Hegemony.'"

"And they damned well should," Dvorak responded. "*I* would, in their place, at any rate!"

"I'm glad you understand. And I also hope—" Agamabichie's eyes narrowed again "—that you'll shed a little light on just what the hell *really* happened to the Shongairi?! All anyone here in Canada seems to really know is that one minute they were about to kill the entire human race and the next minute President Howell had control of all their assets in the solar system!"

"I thought we'd told everyone how that happened." Dvorak raised his good hand shoulder high and waggled it back and forth in a tipping motion. "Didn't the broadcast come through here in Regina?"

"Oh, the *broadcast* came through," Agamabichie assured him. "It's just that nobody really believes it."

"Well they should," Dvorak replied.

"Really?" Agamabichie's skepticism was abundantly clear, and Dvorak chuckled.

"Really," he said. "It really was Vlad Tepes, or Vlad Drakulya, or whatever you want to call him, and if he isn't a classic 'vampire,' he's certainly the most convincing counterfeit to come around in a long time."

"*Vampires*?" Agamabichie shook his head. "In this day and age?"

"Well, he's been around for five hundred years or so," Dvorak pointed out, "so you might say he *predates* 'this day and age.' I'll concede that quite a few people have problems believing it until they've actually met him . . . or one of the other vampires, anyway."

"So you're seriously suggesting there are more of them around?"

"Oh, yes!" Dvorak chuckled. "In fact, I've brought one of them along. She's Vlad's personal representative to President Howell's cabinet. I think you'll like her. And—" there was a curiously steely twinkle in his eye "—Jasmine is very, very convincing. Trust me."

· XIV ·

T hank you for fitting me in, Mister President."

"Frankly," Judson Howell smiled a bit thinly as he pointed at the chair on the other side of his desk, "it's more a matter of *squeezing* you in, I'm afraid. The delegation from Fort Worth is inbound. I expect they'll be on the ground within the next twenty minutes, and I can't keep them waiting. This 'visit' will probably decide whether or not Texas rejoins the Union voluntarily."

"I understand that," Fabienne Lewis said, settling into the indicated chair, "and I promise I'll be as brief as possible. This is something I need you to put into your 'Things to Consider Down the Road' mental file, though. And, frankly, it'll almost certainly have some bearing on *Invictus.*"

"Ah?" Howell cocked his head. "What sort of bearing?"

"I think it may speed things up appreciably, maybe even as much as the reductions in redundant safety features we've already made," Lewis replied. "I can't promise that, but it's something Director MacQuarie and I have been looking at for the last couple of days. Well, actually, what we've been looking at is a report from Damianos Karahalios. You remember him, Mister President?"

"Vividly." Howell grimaced and rolled his eyes, and Lewis chuckled.

Damianos Karahalios was one of the senior computer and IT professors from North Carolina State University. He was also supposed to be a fairly brilliant researcher, and Howell was prepared to accept that. It didn't make the professor's meticulous, step-by-step, I'm-making-this-as-simple-as-I-can-for-you-idiots explanations that rambled on forever—interspersed with lengthy pauses which would have led anyone unfamiliar with him to assume he was finished, except, of course, that he wasn't—any less irritating, though. He really was very well thought of in his field, however, and he'd been a regular consultant for CERT/CC—the Computer Emergency Response Team Coordinating Center—which had been responsible for researching software bugs and Internet security for the Internet as a whole. Unfortunately, CERT/CC had been part of the federally funded Software Engineering Institute at Carnegie Mellon, which had been wiped out when the Shongairi finally lost patience and destroyed Pittsburgh along with virtually every other remaining urban center in the Northeast.

Leaving Judson Howell with Damianos Karahalios.

"I know he can be a pain," Lewis conceded, "but he really is very good at what he does, and he's completed his preliminary survey of the differences between Hegemony and human computer systems."

"Has he?"

Howell's eyes narrowed with the first true interest he'd felt since the conversation began. One thing they'd already discovered was that there was often a difference between neural education and true understanding. A neural educator could teach anyone to run an existing Hegemony computer system in barely five minutes, for example, but that didn't mean the operator was actually familiar with many of its features. And it certainly didn't mean someone like Judson Howell grasped the fundamental principles of the hardware . . . or the software! For that matter, even someone who had downloaded the entire neural module for cybernetics and information technology had to learn his way through an absolutely enormous knowledge base. Moreover, because he'd acquired it literally "overnight," rather than gradually building on his existing platform of knowledge, it was remarkably difficult to make point-to-point correlations between what he'd known before the neural education and what he'd acquired from it.

From Karahalios' previous presentations to Howell, the professor found that particularly irritating. In fact, he seemed to consider it a personal affront. The problem was that he possessed two separate, very extensive bodies of knowledge. One of them he'd spent a lifetime building, and he could find his way through with impressive speed and precision. The other was brand new, and using it was like running an online search that led to innumerable branching references, *none* of which were part of the searcher's fully digested and internalized database. When that difference—and how incredibly frustrating it must be—had percolated through Howell's understanding, he'd found that he almost sympathized with Karahalios' fussy, finicky, nuanced, and unendingly qualified lectures.

Almost.

"I have his entire report—which runs to something like twenty thousand words, with charts, diagrams, and quite a few footnotes—and I'll be forwarding that to you," Lewis continued. "I assume, however, that you'd prefer me to break it up into . . . more digestible bites, Mister President?"

"I have no doubt his report would be fascinating reading if I understood more than, say, one word in thirty," Howell said dryly. "So, yes, I think you can safely assume I'd prefer the ignorant layman version."

"All right, let me begin by saying that while Shongair computing technology is vastly more technologically advanced than our own, it's an incremental improvement. Well, a little more than just incremental, since, unlike us, they've figured out how to use qubits, and that radically changes what you can do with a programming language or with operations. I'm not going to try to get into quantum tunneling or any of the other concepts involved, but to put it very simply—and a bit inaccurately—our computers operate in binary. Data is expressed in ones and zeros, and any given bit can be in only one state at any given time. Think of it as carrying only one meaning, one value, at a time. The computers we're looking at now use bits—qubits—which can be in superpositions of states. That means a qubit doesn't have a value of one or zero, but rather contains both of those values as a weighted probability. There's no way to tell which of the two possible states actually pertains until—"

She paused as Howell tipped his chair back and looked at her reproachfully.

"Sorry, Mister President. Basically, what I'm saying is that the Shongairi— the Hegemony—have cracked a step in computer capabilities which we've theorized about since the 1980s. We'd actually built a small quantum computer for experiments, but we were still a long way from actually making the concept work. Its advantage over the binary system is that a quantum computer can solve certain problems much more quickly than any 'classical' computer, because everything depends on the algorithms of the systems, and quantum algorithms run faster than any probabilistic classical program.

"All of that's exciting, and suggests lots of possibilities, but what's really interesting is what the Shongair *haven't* done with it."

"I beg your pardon?" Howell arched an eyebrow.

"We don't see *anything* in this system that hadn't already been part of our theoretical models. They've figured out how to do things we hadn't, but they haven't figured out—so far as we can tell—how to do anything we hadn't already worked out pretty fully in theory *as* theory. Doctor Karahalios didn't find any great conceptual leaps. No miracle memory devices, no hyper-space shunts connecting all computers into an artificial brain. In fact, despite the qubits, their computers are simply faster and far, far smaller—built on the molecular scale, not the printed circuits we've used—but not extraordinarily more *capable.*"

"Excuse me, but doesn't 'faster and far smaller' equate to 'more capable'?"

"For certain values of the word 'capable,' yes." Lewis nodded. "But before the invasion, the experts all said that any spacefaring society would need artificial intelligence—AI—to support their civilization. Even we Earthlings, stuck here in a single star system, sent ten or more robotic probes into space for each manned mission. And aside from a handful of deep space probes, we'd only truly explored one other planet in that star system in the process. But there are supposed to be hundreds or even thousands of stars in the Hegemony, and it takes years to travel between them, so logically, the Hegemony should have AIs to support them. Why send a manned—well, crewed—starship on a sixty-year voyage to deliver cargo or a message, when you could send an AI on the same mission while your flesh and blood citizens got on with their lives? But they don't. They don't have an AI they *can* send."

"I don't know," Howell said slowly, pulling his "phone" from his pocket and tossing it onto his blotter. He pointed at it. "I talk to this, and it finds me schedules, information on any topic I tell it to search, or whoever I want to talk to. I may not know which of General Landers' people I need to get hold of to ask a question, but I ask this—" he tapped the "phone" with an index finger "—and it not only figures out who I need to talk to, it gets hold of him—or her—even if I've only given it a very rough description of who I need. Seems pretty intelligent to me."

"That's not really artificial *intelligence,* Mister President." Lewis shook her head. "That's just what Doctor Karahalios is fond of calling 'an overblown expert system.' It's certainly artificial, but it's not truly *intelligent*. It can't think outside the limiting parameters of its basic programming.

"The first wave of AI was all about teaching computers to sort through large lists of information and find the connections. That meant the programmers were constructing hierarchies which allowed the construction and manipulation of information lists. The second wave created voice interfaces and language translation that allowed those systems to take verbal or written commands and *apply* them to the information list. When you tell your phone you need to talk to one of General Landers' officers, it has access to a list of *all* of General Landers' officers. When you provide it with specifics about the officer in question, it eliminates everyone on the list who doesn't match those specifics. It may seem to you that you're giving it only fragmentary descriptions, but until you give it *enough* fragments, it can't find whoever you're looking for. It can't . . . intuit its way to that specific officer. And if you tell your phone to do something—enter a new appointment on your calendar, print out a hard copy of the memo you've been reading electronically—it can do only things it's already programmed to do and only if you *tell* it to.

"So, basically, what you might call 'AI' is just a very sophisticated library of data and—especially—programs that require human direction, human decisions. Some of those decisions—many of those decisions—can be automated, but in that sense they aren't really 'decisions' so much as automatic responses that the programmers built into the system. The computer doesn't *care* what it does. It simply does what it was told to do at every step and in response to recognized outcomes of previous steps, either through its internal programming or as the result of a typed or verbal input from a human operator.

"The *third* wave of AI, though—which DARPA and quite a few other people had started to look at before the invasion—was designed to apply actual reasoning and decision-making to computers. To allow them to function independently of human decision-making. To—to go back to my earlier example—to build AI pilots capable of flying autonomous starships between the stars so that Shongair or Barthon or Kreptu crews don't have to. They do have systems to control ships while the crews are in cryo, but they aren't autonomous; they aren't able to think for themselves if something unexpected by their programming comes up. In that case, they have to wake the ship command crew to seek guidance and direction.

"From our own work, we're convinced we can build on their existing 'brilliant software' to create AI systems which truly *are* autonomous. Whether or not we could build AI systems which were *self-aware* is another matter, of course, but we should certainly be able to build something that gives an awful convincing imitation of self-awareness. Assuming we decide we want to, that is. There's an awful lot of science-fiction about the potential downsides of creating a self-aware intelligence that decides it doesn't like taking orders from its creators." Her lips quirked briefly in amusement, but then her expression sobered again. "From an efficiency perspective, though, autonomous AI would be a huge multiplier. Despite which, the Hegemony doesn't have it when, by all human standards and the self-evident capabilities of its tech base, it should."

"Hmmmm. . . ." Howell rubbed his chin, his expression thoughtful. "So if we were able to use their technology to create this 'third-wave AI' of yours for ourselves, we'd have an advantage? A big one?"

"A *very* big one, Mister President. But Damianos—Doctor Karahalios—raises a few other points in his current report. Our science-fiction writers and quite a few serious scientists have been looking at neural interfacing for a couple of decades now, and we've achieved it, at least to a degree. There's been some very encouraging work being done with the use of neurally accessible computer chips to store memories for Alzheimer's patients, for example. That's not the same thing as a direct brain-*computer* connection, but it's headed in the same direction, and the implications of actually achieving that sort of connection are huge. You've had plenty of experience giving verbal commands to a computer, even before the invasion. It's frustrating—or it *was* frustrating—when the computer misunderstood you, maybe because of background noise, maybe because you weren't speaking clearly. But consider if you'd had to physically enter every command, instead. Even tapping the screen on your iPhone or your Galaxy generally took longer than a verbal command. But now imagine that you could give your computer commands *at the speed of thought* and never have it misunderstand you. Do you think that might . . . enhance your efficiency?"

"Yes, I imagine it would," Howell said slowly.

"Of course it would, yet we don't see any sign of that in the Hegemony's computer tech. This despite the fact that they've mastered the art of neural education, so they clearly have the ability to send immensely complicated dumps of *data* at least one way through a neural interface, and they've had it longer than

Earth has had to put up with *Homo sapiens*! So why, in all that time, haven't they developed the ability to send mental commands *into* the system? We don't even see any speculation about the possibility in the literature we've been able to access so far!"

"Why not?"

"That we would love to know, Mister President. But we have noticed a few other things, most of which appear related to the same sort of . . . caution that seems to be hardwired into the Hegemony's entire industrial base. Their programming language is recursive, which means a function can call itself, and it's also what we might call 'type safe,' which means it's designed to prevent the system from running an operation against the wrong type of variable.

"Most human programming languages are designed to do that, too, but from what we can see, Hegemony coding takes the concepts to a ridiculous extreme. Consistency checking for acceptable values and variables is built directly into the code for an incredible range of variables. For example, the Hegemony has over five hundred languages, which means—as one of Doctor Karahalios' programmers pointed out—that using the Hegemony's programming language to write the equivalent of 'Hello, world!' for a planet you'd never visited before or a species whose language you didn't already speak would involve loading a million-line module. Their protocols would require the module to search the entire Hegemony database to make certain that the world you're talking to exists—even if you're currently in orbit around it—and sort through every one of those languages—every language spoken anywhere in the entire *Hegemony*, not just on the planet in question—and the societal constructs that go with them, to be sure 'hello' is the proper greeting, in the proper language, properly spelled and punctuated, in that particular sociopolitical context."

Howell stared at her in disbelief, and she shrugged.

"It's not that terrible a problem, given their computing speeds and storage ability. The codebase is bloated beyond belief—the executable for 'Hello, world' would be hundreds of gigabytes, just to carry all the baggage—and as far as we can tell, their libraries never get pruned, but—"

"Pruned?" Howell interrupted.

"There's no automatic memory management, what a human programmer would call 'garbage collection' to reclaim memory occupied by objects the program isn't using anymore, Mister President. They just store *all* of them. That's why their modules are so blasted big. But despite that, it doesn't slow down the output appreciably. There's some bottleneck in terms of storage, but not enough to make a significant difficulty, given how much memory their systems have. It's certainly not anything they can't handle. We could probably shave some time off of their operations, but not enough for it to make any perceptible difference to the speed at which their programs execute.

"The problem is that the same 'check everything again and again' attitude carries over to their control systems as well as the programs themselves. Oh, we use redundancy in critical systems—like aircraft flight systems, for example, in which there are three completely separate processors running the same calculations. As long as at least two of them come up with the same answer, that's the one used. If they come up with three *separate* answers, the system reverts to 'manual,' and human supervision is called in. We generally employ systems like that only when failure could have catastrophic consequences, like the loss of human life, though. As nearly as we can tell, the Hegemony applies the same idea to almost *everything*."

"Everything?" Howell repeated.

"An example, Mister President. A minor component—a motor, say—will have a dedicated processor running dedicated code. You could 'ask' it to do something, like turn in one direction at a specified speed for a given length of time, but the central control module tasking the motor doesn't have direct control over it and can't override the dedicated processor. And if the dedicated processor senses a potential fault condition, it will simply refuse to *let* 'its' motor turn, no matter what the central system is telling it to do.

"Now, take that same situation, and apply it to an entire assembly, like one axis of a gantry platform in *Invictus*. You've got dozens or hundreds of motors and similar components, each with its own processor with its own code and multiple redundancy to keep that particular component within safe operating parameters as defined by *its* programming, and *any one of them* can shut down the entire gantry if it detects any potential hazard to the single component *it's* running. And just to be sure all those individual components have enough ability to see those potential hazards, the gantry has an entire multilevel sensor suite watching every aspect of its environment, and every one of those sensors has *its* own processor running its own code."

"Crap," Howell muttered.

"The only thing that makes this workable, and that generates the level of production we've seen out of the original platforms the Shongairi left behind, is the speed of Hegemony-level computer operations. They're so blindingly fast by our standards that they can actually keep this ridiculous balancing act moving forward . . . most of the time. I'm sure you've read some of Director MacQuarie's comments on how often *Invictus* simply shuts down until some trivial fault's been corrected?"

Howell nodded, and Lewis shrugged.

"In some ways, that's probably not a bad thing. We're still learning how to run it all, so having it stop while we figure out what's caused its current temper tantrum is one way to really familiarize ourselves with its gizzards. And, as I say, the system actually works. In relative terms, by its own potential standards, it works really, really poorly, you understand, but in *absolute* terms it's genuinely capable of producing a post-scarcity economy, something our species has never seen. But we're estimating—conservatively—that if we could only identify the redundancy levels that are totally unnecessary for safe operation, we could probably increase output by at least another forty or fifty percent—and probably one hell of a lot more than that—just by eliminating all those unnecessary steps and all the inter-processor negotiating that goes with them. And we could save a lot of refinery time and resources—and especially printing time—if we were able to eliminate some of the multiple layers of sensors they build into their hardware. I mean, one sensor and maybe a couple of backups should be sufficient for almost any situation. We're pretty sure we don't need *twelve* of them, though!"

"Um." Howell pinched the bridge of his nose and grimaced. "I had a friend before the invasion who worked for the Tennessee Valley Authority," he said from behind his hand. "One evening, over a couple of beer steins, he described the redundancy of the safety features built into U.S. nuclear plants. According to him, if they'd been allowed to build and operate to realistic threat levels, nuclear plants would have been cheaper than coal or natural gas. And he pointed out that for all the publicity, the Three Mile Island's reactor design prevented a catastrophic failure despite the fact that the operators did pretty much everything wrong." He lowered his hand and looked at her levelly. "Now, I'm a firm believer in belts-and-suspenders where something like a nuclear reactor just outside a major city is concerned, but it sounds like you're talking about the steroids version of the . . . superabundant redundancy he had to put up with."

"Pretty much, Mister President," Lewis acknowledged, then smiled crookedly. "You know, this whole conversation seems a bit . . . surreal to me. On the one hand, I'm sitting here talking about how much more efficiently the Hegemony could run its computers and its printers and all the rest of its infrastructure. On the other hand, the way it *is* running them is still incredibly productive—'incredibly' in the sense of literally *unbelievable*—by any human standard."

"I can see that," Howell said, then let his chair come upright again as the phone on his desk chirped at him and flashed a digital time display.

"I'm actually sorry to say we're out of time," he said. "I'll try to look over Karahalios' report, although if it's anything like the last one he sent me, I probably actually learned more from you this afternoon than I'll ever get out of it. Right now, though, I really do have to meet with the Texans."

"Of course, Mister President."

Lewis rose and started for the door of his office, but Howell halted her with a raised index finger.

"Mister President?"

"There's one point about your explanation that stuck in my mind. Right at the end, when you said the Hegemony's technology is incredible by any *human* standard."

"Yes, Mister President?" Lewis looked puzzled, and he smiled at her.

"I know it's early days, and we're only really just starting to tear into the possibilities, but I want you and Karahalios and everyone else involved in this project to look for every single way we can improve on what the Hegemony's willing to accept. When we meet them again, I want *them* to be the ones thinking about how incredibly efficient and productive human technology is by *their* standards." His smile turned cold and hard. "I want that 'third wave' of yours, and I want that neural interface, and I want to leave those bastards in our *dust* when the time comes."

"Understood, Mister President." Fabienne Lewis' smile was just as cold and hard as her president's. "Why don't I just go and get started on that?"

XV

DREADNOUGHT *TÂRGOVIȘTE*,
PHASE-SPACE,
1.5 LY FROM EARTH

"What? You're out of your mind! *Dark Passage* is *tons* better than *The Big Heat*."

"How can you say that? Ford is the classic avenger of wrongs, whereas Bogart is out to avenge himself and prove his *own* innocence!"

"But he's *Bogart*! Ford is always so . . . so fueled by nervous tension. And it's not just Bogart; it's *Bacall*, too!"

"And in one of her stronger performances, I admit, my Stephen. But Bogart was 'off his game,' as I believe you Americans put it, in that film. And aside from the way in which his appearance is changed, the character of Vincent Parry is sadly two-dimensional. Oh, the cinematography was very clever, especially the way in which the viewer never saw the hero's face until *after* the 'plastic surgery,' that I grant. Yet despite that, I cannot say that Bogart's ability to support a film was at its best in *Dark Passage*."

"But *Glenn Ford*? I like a lot of his work, but I never thought action movies were really his forte. I like him a lot more in movies like *Fate Is the Hunter*. I mean, Pleshette overacted in that one—she usually did, really—but Ford *nailed* McBane, and Taylor was damned good as Savage. The model work's . . . pretty bad, in a lot of ways. I'll give you that. But it was made in 1964, for God's sake! And I personally think it was one of Ford's best movies."

"In which, once more, he is avenging a wrong done to others! You see? You make my own case for me!"

Stephen Buchevsky sat back in his unreasonably comfortable chair and glowered across the small table. He'd always loved a good movie, but he'd never thought of himself as a student of classic cinema. In fact, most of the movies he'd seen dated from no later than the seventies or eighties. But he'd had more exposure than he'd realized to earlier cinematic fare. He might be out of his league as a cinematic scholar compared to his present company, but how could anyone prefer Glenn Ford to Humphrey Bogart? That was just . . . wrong.

"Oh, cheer up!" The green-eyed, sharp-faced man on the other side of the table waved his beer stein. "Perhaps we should watch *Blacula* again! That always seems to improve your mood."

"No," Buchevsky said very, very firmly. "We are *not* watching *Blacula* again. In fact, if I have my way, we are *never* watching *Blacula* again!"

"So sad." Vlad Drakulya shook his head, his expression sorrowful. "And it shows so little empathy. If I must endure all of the . . . imperfect cinematic presentations of my own life, then surely it is only fair that you should endure Prince Mamuwalde—who, after all, at least *begins* his unbreathing life as a truly heroic figure!"

"Life isn't always fair," Buchevsky replied. His own eyes darkened for a moment, as memory of just how *un*fair it could be ambushed him, but then he shook himself. "Although, I will grant you that as blaxploitation movies go, it's one of the best. I'll even grant you that it's an arguably serious attempt at a horror movie with a Black protagonist and the producers went out and actually found an actor with the chops to pull it off. Yeah, and they managed it without pimps or drugs. I did like that! I just can't handle William Marshall with hair glued all over his face and a mouthful of fangs. My God! Did you ever see the video of his *Othello*? That man could *act*, Vlad!"

"Yes, I have, and yes, he could. Indeed, he was *far* better than Burbage was in the original presentation, not to mention actually being Black. Of course, he had certain technological advantages not available to the Globe in 1605, as well." Vlad's eyes went unfocused for a second or two, then sharpened and focused once more on Buchevsky. "Very well, we will leave that one for another time. Is there another film you would prefer to request?"

Buchevsky pondered that question, because the options were . . . many.

One thing he hadn't suspected during his sojourn in Romania was that "Mircea Basarab" had been an even bigger cinema junkie, and for far longer, than Stephen Buchevsky. In fact, longer than anyone else on the planet had been alive! Nor had he guessed that Vlad Drakulya had amassed one of the world's great digital movie collections on the servers under his villa above the Arges River. He'd built that villa, almost within sight of Poenari Castle—a fortress which had served him well in its time—over four hundred years ago, although it had never appeared on anyone's maps, and it had served him even better— and far longer—than the castle had. It had also been equipped with all the "modern conveniences," including an enviable computer suite. He'd been very careful to power down anything which might have attracted Shongair sensors to his home, but before he'd left Earth behind, he'd uploaded the entire content of those servers to the dreadnought he'd renamed *Târgovişte* and found a way to interface his video files with the starship's holograph projectors. Watching at least one of those films every day had become one of their more enjoyable rituals.

"You're the only one who has any real idea what you have stashed away in the computers," he said finally. "I'll let you choose—as long as it's not a Glenn Ford movie!"

"So sad that you are so small minded." Vlad shook his head mournfully. "In that case, however, why do we not consider a complete change of pace and watch something a bit less dark?"

"What did you have in mind?" Buchevsky arched one eyebrow.

"One of my favorite Cary Grant films." Vlad smiled. "*Father Goose.*"

Buchevsky suppressed a chuckle. Vlad Drakulya had an unmistakable partiality for the film noir genre, which was probably inevitable, but Buchevsky rather doubted the world in general would have been ready to believe the true weakness of the historical reality behind the most enduring, bloodthirsty villain in cinematic history was for comedies. Especially—the temptation to chuckle disappeared—comedies which incorporated a deadly serious thread centered upon a character who rose above his flaws to protect that which he had learned he loved.

"All right, I could do with a little Grant," he allowed. "Assuming that *you'll* sign off on *The African Queen* next."

"Ah! I sense a theme of sorts! Very well. Although—" Vlad's smile turned sly "—I *was* thinking in terms of *Human Desire.*"

"Oh my God!" Buchevsky rolled his eyes. "Thank goodness I managed to avoid repeating *that* one. If you really need to add another Ford movie to the calendar, try to find one with at least one character I can empathize with."

"Fair, fair," Vlad conceded, then pulled the slim human-style keyboard out of the edge of the tabletop and began entering commands.

Buchevsky sat back with his beer, watching him, and the sheer . . . unlikelihood of his life flowed through him yet again.

He looked around the compartment—the equivalent of what a human would have called the captured Shongair dreadnought's wardroom—which the ship's printers and servomechs had reconfigured to meet human notions of comfort and convenience. The overhead remained too close for someone Buchevsky's height, because the Puppies were short even by the standards of normal-sized humans, but the ship systems had done a remarkable job of modifying *Târ-goviṣte*'s interior. Of course, he thought, at the moment only he and Vlad were awake to take advantage of that, and he tried to imagine how far from the world of his birth he'd come. The starship's best speed in hyper was just under six times that of light, and they'd left the Sol System astern three months earlier, which meant they'd covered a light-year and a half as normal space measured things. It would take them another forty years to reach their destination: the Shongairi's home star system. And when they did. . . .

His jaw tightened. A part of him absolutely agreed with Vlad. There was only one way to be certain the Shongairi never again threatened humanity, and as Gunny Meyers had pointed out, the one thing that couldn't be disputed about capital punishment was that it had a very low rate of recidivism. Yet another part of him remembered the tearing anguish of losing his own daughters without even one last chance to hug them, tell them how much he'd loved them. And that part of him shied away from becoming the very creatures he'd most hated in the name of retribution.

Maybe that's a good thing, he reflected. *I told Dave Dvorak I wouldn't let Vlad turn into a monster again, so maybe it'd be just as well if I didn't turn into one, either. Speaking of which—*

"There are still some things about this whole vampire business I'm trying to figure out," he said, and Vlad paused in the commands he'd been entering.

"Only some?" Vlad's eyebrows quirked.

"Well, a lot, really," Buchevsky admitted. "Like why I don't feel any need to be drinking human blood. Or why sunlight makes me itch like hell but doesn't melt me into dust that blows away on the breeze."

"You may, perhaps, have already perceived that the legends of the *nosferatu* are somewhat less than completely accurate," Vlad replied dryly.

"You might say." Buchevsky snorted.

"Well, my Stephen," Vlad sat back in his chair, one hand on the table, "I am reasonably certain you cannot have been more taken aback by those differences than I. It would appear my sturdy Romanian peasants' grasp of our condition was less than perfect. In *so* many ways, actually. It was not until the headlong progress of science in the twentieth century that I began to realize just how imperfect."

"Really?" Buchevsky folded his arms across his chest. "Somehow I hadn't thought of putting 'Count Dracula' and 'scientist' together in the same sentence."

"Scarcely surprising. However, when one lives for several centuries, one acquires at least a smattering of knowledge about a great many things. And, for obvious reasons, I was what I suppose one might call moderately curious about my own origins and state. I have never been able to discuss it openly with breathers, of course, but that has not prevented me from thinking about it a great deal. Especially about the fact that it bears so little resemblance to the legends and folklore about it."

"I can see that. And what have your smatterings of knowledge told you about it?"

"Well, as I am certain you are yourself aware, however cursed we may be in some ultimate sense, at least we are not 'cursed' to be ravening, blood-drinking monsters every night." Vlad spoke lightly, but Buchevsky sensed a weary lifetime behind the words. "As I say, it took quite some time for me to develop a theory as to why that is, and why, I suspect, you 'itch' so badly in direct sunlight. Despite the folklore, it is not the 'purifying and cleansing' effect of sunlight which causes our kind so much distress, particularly when we are newly come to it, my Stephen. The problem is that we are . . . overeating."

"Overeating?" Buchevsky repeated, and Vlad snorted.

"We do not sustain ourselves on the stolen life force of others, Stephen! Rather we absorb energy directly from our environment—both electromagnetic and radiant, it would appear—and our sensitivity to it is strongest when we are youngest. Or perhaps it would be more accurate to say that as we become older as vampires our ability to tolerate the absorption without pain grows. I have theorized for many years that in direct sunlight we are simply overloaded until we learn to deal with it, and our experience when we seized Thikair's ships would seem to confirm that. Would you not say so?"

Buchevsky's shudder wasn't at all feigned as he remembered the exquisite agony of the journey to orbit on the exteriors of the Shongair shuttles. It was fortunate that Vlad had warned them what they were about to experience—and that every one of them had been so . . . motivated to endure it. It had been considerably worse than being killed, as he knew from personal experience, and it had taken several minutes for them to recover even after the shuttles entered their docking bays.

"To be honest, I was not at all certain that we would survive the intensity of radiation in space, especially in the concentrations of the Van Allen belts," Vlad admitted.

"Kind of forgot to mention that to the rest of us?" Buchevsky asked with a wry smile.

"Oh, no, my Stephen! I did not *forget*. I simply chose not to concern you with things which could not be controlled. Would you have declined to attempt the journey if I had shared my thoughts with you?"

"No." Buchevsky shook his head, expression momentarily grim. "No, Vlad, I don't think a single one of us would have turned back, even if you'd told us we *probably* wouldn't make it. Hell!" His expression lightened, and he snorted. "Every one of us had already beaten the odds just to make it that far! Of course we'd have figured we'd make it all the way!"

"No doubt." Vlad smiled, but both of them knew the truth. It wouldn't have been optimism that sent them on a potential death ride; it would have been determination, rage, and fury.

"At any rate, our experiences on the journey appear to me to offer ample confirmation of my original theory. And it is also the reason that our fellows who chose to sleep away the voyage found it so easy to go into 'hibernation.' I have done so myself on occasion, although it requires isolation from the energy all about us. Earth and stone were the only materials available for 'insulation' when I first began to comprehend how the process worked. No doubt that explains the legend that the vampire must return to his 'native earth' during daylight. The only way he could get any true sleep was to bury himself!"

"Yeah," Buchevsky agreed with a laugh. "I can see that—if you're right about 'absorbing' energy."

"I am as certain of it as I am of any other aspect of our existence, my Stephen. And while we can subsist on extraordinarily meager amounts of energy, we lose much of our capabilities if we are left in a state of energy deprivation for an extended time. The shielding on these ships is sufficient to protect breathers from the radiation hazard even here in the hyper-space, which means that it 'protects' us, as well. Fortunately, it would appear even Hegemony electronics leak sufficient energy to sustain us at minimum operating levels. But that's the reason our fellows could retire to the missile magazines, shut down the electronic systems, and hibernate until we choose to wake them once more."

"I was tempted to join them," Buchevsky admitted. "It's gonna be a *long* trip. But if I had, I wouldn't have figured out you were a fellow film nut and gotten my postgrad course in cinematography!"

"Indeed," Vlad said, but his smile acknowledged that the true reason Buchevsky had remained awake was to keep *him* company.

"I have to say that if I've turned into an energy eater, I'm at least grateful that I can still enjoy the occasional beer," Buchevsky said.

"Liquids are relatively easy for our kind to imbibe and . . . process, although we scarcely need them on any regular basis, which may be another part of the notion that we drink blood, since we so seldom consume solid food. I fear you can experience only the taste in your present state, however; I have become 'inebriated' on an excess of sunlight upon occasion, but alcohol no longer affects us. I do believe that eating and drinking also helps to sustain us in some fashion, as we grow older. I would postulate that it provides a form of . . . call it replacement biomass. I was quite surprised the first time that I realized I actually felt *hungry* again, and our appetite for food and drink never becomes more than a shadow of what it was when we were still breathers. Within a few more decades, however, you will once again be able to eat and enjoy a good steak or salad upon occasion. Until then, I would recommend against it, however."

"Yeah, figured that part out for myself. Talk about heartburn!" Buchevsky shook his head. "But, man, wrapping my head around this seems to get harder, not easier, as I go along!"

"I realize that. It has been difficult for me, many times. And I regret that I inflicted this upon you without your permission. That is something I have always tried to avoid, whatever the novels and the films or legends may say."

"Not like you had a lot of choice," Buchevsky pointed out. "If you hadn't, I'd be dead—and so would Jasmine, Calvin, and Francisco. And everyone else on Earth, by now, now that I think about it."

"True." Vlad nodded. "Yet the fact remains that I did not ask, and the fact that you would have died otherwise does not absolve me of that." He looked away for a moment, his expression troubled, then returned his gaze to Buchevsky. "In the early days, immediately after I realized what had happened to me, I acted without thought—and without restraint. Too many of those I brought over in those early days were even darker than I, and some of them . . . reacted poorly to what I had done to them. Indeed, some of them. . . ."

His voice trailed off, and his expression was bleak.

"I was monster enough before the change, my Stephen," he said, after a moment. "To see what I could do *after* the change was sufficient to terrify even me, however, and some of my 'children' were far worse than I, when the change came fully upon them. Take Bratianu is the oldest of us all, after myself. Indeed, he is the only of my original 'children' who remains."

"What happened to the others?" Buchevsky asked softly, and Vlad's mouth tightened. Then he faced the ex-Marine squarely.

"Destroyed, every one of them—by my own hand. I had no choice. Too many of them came through the change only to descend into madness . . . or worse. And others grew impatient of the restraint I imposed upon them. They saw no reason why such as we should not make ourselves princes or even kings."

"I can sort of understand that. But why didn't you? Make yourself a prince or a king, I mean?"

"I *was* a prince. I had no desire to take that upon my shoulders once again. All it had ever brought me was grief and guilt, and when I awakened, it was too late to stop the conquest which was already upon us by the time I ceased breathing."

"Awakened?" Buchevsky leaned forward in his chair slightly. "You mean like I did after you brought me across?"

"No, my Stephen." Vlad shook his head. "For you, the transition was a matter of days, only. For me—? Forty years passed between my last breath as a mortal man and the moment I opened my eyes once more."

"What?" Buchevsky blinked. "Why did it take that long?"

"If I knew the answer to that, I would know many things I do not," Vlad said dryly. His index finger tapped slowly, thoughtfully, on the tabletop, and then he shrugged.

"I have never actually described what happened to me to another, Stephen," he said very seriously. "Perhaps it is time I did."

"I'd sure like to know, anyway," Buchevsky replied, and Vlad snorted again.

"No doubt you would, but there are many aspects of the experience which remain confusing to me, even now. So, where shall I begin?"

He sat silent for several moments, eyes unfocused as he stared at something only he could see. Then he gave his head a little toss and his attention focused on Buchevsky once again.

"First," he said, "so far as I am aware, I am the only vampire who has no 'parent,' and I have never understood how that could be. We may not drink blood as the legends declare, yet so far as I have ever been able to discover, blood transfer is the only way to make a vampire. The blood flows in the opposite direction, perhaps—from sire or dam to . . . offspring—and offers no sustenance to the sire, yet it is necessary, the only way to bring someone through the change. Yet there was no blood exchange in my own case."

Buchevsky frowned, and Vlad waved one hand.

"Tell me, what do you know of my actual history?" he asked.

"Not as much as I wish I did," Buchevsky admitted. "I know you were technically Prince of Wallachia three different times." He shook his head. "From everything I've been able to find, it must've been like living in the middle of a dogfight!"

"One way to put it, indeed. Although the title *voivode* does not actually translate as 'prince.' A closer approximation might be 'duke,' although there was little difference, in practice. And so far as the situation in Wallachia at the time is concerned, to call it a dogfight is to make things far neater and simpler than they actually were. What is today Romania was the bulwark between Christian Europe and the Ottoman Empire, especially after the fall of Constantinople, the year I turned twenty-one. Both the sultans and the kings of Hungary—not to mention the Pope, the Albanians, and the Saxon merchants who did so much business in the Balkans—were all deeply involved in Wallachia. It is important to remember that, just as it is important to remember that most of the official record of my life was written by my enemies. That is not to say that it is all false. Much of it is, however, and much which is not false is presented in . . . rather different terms than the ones in which I would have presented it.

"I have told you of what the boyars did to my father and brother." He paused, one eyebrow raised, and Buchevsky nodded. "At the time, my younger brother Radu and I were hostages in Adrianople. Sultan Murad had not trusted my father—with reason, I must confess—but promised to help him regain his position as *voivode*. Technically, he had been a vassal of Hungary prior to that, but there was bad blood between him and John Hunyadi, who drove him out and replaced him with his cousin, Basarab II. Murad promised his support to restore Father in return for an annual tribute, and Radu and I were the 'insurance' he demanded to ensure Father's loyalty. I was eleven at the time, and while Father returned to Wallachia, Radu and I remained in Adrianople for several years. Indeed, Radu eventually converted to Islam and became a trusted member of the Sultan's court. Suffice it to say that in my time as a breather, no man could trust another, betrayal was the common coin of all involved—myself not least among them—and if sufficient bloodshed could have procured peace, Romania would have been a garden, with no need of walls or swords."

He fell silent for a long moment, brooding over a past long dead. Then he shook himself.

"I will not bore you with the complexities of my own . . . dealings with Hunyadi, Corvinus, the Dans, and the Sultan. Suffice it to say that I knew my position must always be precarious and that anything that smacked of indecision or weakness would be my downfall. I had concluded that the only way to secure my position was to eliminate all within Wallachia who might turn against me and to create a new nobility—new *boyars*—whose loyalty would be solely to me, and I attempted to do so by destroying the old *boyars* mercilessly and without pity. Perhaps I might have succeeded, had I been given more time. But from the perspective I have since been granted, I do not think there was ever much likelihood of that.

"Still, I did do my best to terrorize those who would be my enemies, and at the same time, I sought to protect the commons against the pillaging, rape, and brutality which had become their lot. Partly, of course, that was to bring them to my side against the *boyars* and our 'foreign' enemies in general, yet not all of it was. There came a time at which *someone* had to take their side, and if I could simultaneously buy their support, so much the better. There is a reason the folklore about my reign extols my determination to protect the property and persons of my subjects. And, of course, I did it in my own way—the way of the time in which I was born—with brutal punishment for any who violated my justice.

"I do not seek to excuse myself, my Stephen, or to make myself any less of the monster I was, yet it is fair to say that a punishment intended to deter must be such that no one would lightly risk incurring it. When it is not, one tends to think in terms of 'what have I to lose,' which means that in desperate times, punishment must be severe enough to deter even desperate individuals. And so I handed out death sentences on every hand, and I decreed that the executions must be public and terrible enough that no one would willingly risk a similar fate. I found that impalement worked quite well in that regard."

His voice was calm, almost detached, but his green eyes were dark and shuttered, and his mouth was grim below his bushy mustache.

"Yet, in the end, my position was ultimately hopeless, particularly when fresh warfare against the Turks rolled across Wallachia. It was not because of lack of valor; my men followed me into battle against terrible odds more than once. And it was not because we won no victories—this very ship is named, now, for one of those victories. But the odds were simply too great. We were outnumbered ten- or even twenty-to-one, which is the true reason I dealt with so many Turks—not all of them soldiers, I confess to my shame—as I dealt with those Shongairi in the forest near Lake Vidaru, creating forests of impaled dead in the Turkish armies' path. I suppose I was the classic enemy against whom you fought in Afghanistan, my Stephen. It was 'asymmetrical warfare' in which I, as the weaker side, embraced terrorism as a . . . psychological weapon. And it was effective. That, of course, is the reason it has been employed so often throughout history.

"But be a man's cause however just it may, the cost of setting one's hand to tactics such as those is the loss of one's soul, so perhaps it is fitting that I became what I have become. And, in the end, terror was not enough, especially when I had no monopoly upon it. Your military may have frowned upon 'fighting fire with fire,' but the Turks and my Romanian and Hungarian foes did not. In the end, my Wallachians began to desert to the invaders in ever greater numbers, and who shall blame them? My cause was ultimately doomed, and who did not have family or position to think of? And so, ultimately, my small army was crushed in a battle near Bucharest and I was forced to flee the field accompanied by a handful of my loyal Moldavian bodyguards.

"That is not, of course, the end that history has recorded for me. According to my foes, I was slain, my body was dismembered, my head was taken to Constantinople, and what was left of me was buried in an unmarked grave. I have no idea who was actually dismembered in my place or whose head was displayed by Mehmed the Conqueror, although I am quite certain that *he* knew it was not mine, as we knew one another quite well. On the other hand, his need to 'prove' my death to deal the final blow to any who might have continued to follow me was understandable. And he no doubt believed I had, indeed, been killed and that my actual body had simply never been identified.

"In fact, a handful of my Moldavians and I cut our way out of the battle. There were only eleven of us, several with minor wounds, and we fled north, seeking to reach at least temporary safety. Yet we were forced away from the direct route home and became lost, until we found ourselves in a high, narrow Carpathian valley. It was December, the falling snow and bitter winds made it almost impossible to see, and we knew we were in danger of freezing to death. There was no shelter to be found, but then—miraculously—Yoet, one of my most loyal bodyguards, literally fell into the opening of a cavern. Or, we thought it was cavern, at least initially."

He paused once again, his eyes very distant. Then he inhaled a sharp breath that he no longer needed and exhaled it in a long sigh.

"Tell me, my Stephen. I know you and I have never watched it together, but would it happen that you have seen the movie *Dracula Untold*? It was released in 2014, I believe, so it would fall within your admittedly narrow viewership envelope."

He smiled with the last sentence, but those distant eyes remained dark.

"Well, yeah," Buchevsky admitted. "Have to say it wasn't the best Dracula movie I ever saw. Not the *worst,* you understand, but definitely not the best."

"A fair assessment, although it did represent the more recent trend towards rehabilitating my tattered reputation. And, alas, I was never as handsome as Luke Evans' Dracula! However, although it created its 'origin' story line out of whole cloth, it struck uncomfortably close to the truth."

"You met a monster inside the cavern?" Buchevsky knew he sounded incredulous, and Vlad shook his head.

"No, my Stephen. To this day, I do not know what we *did* meet, but it was not the monster of the film. Nor was the cavern actually a cavern at all, I believe. My memory is less than clear, you understand. All of us were suffering from hypothermia by the time we found what seemed to be shelter. We were more concerned with getting ourselves and our remaining horses under cover than with anything else. Yet as we moved deeper into the 'cavern,' the walls—visible but poorly in the light of our two or three torches—appeared unnaturally smooth to me. And deep in the cavern, I . . . sensed something. A vibration, perhaps, like that given off by the Puppies' counter gravity. It was not that, but I had no other reference for it. And then, I turned a bend, and there was a glow before me. I believed it was natural fluorescence clinging to a stone face, but when I reached out to touch it, my hand seemed to pass straight through it. I had only a moment to register that it had, and then the world exploded."

"Exploded?" Buchevsky repeated, and Vlad nodded.

"It is the only word that seems to apply. There was a tremendous burst of blinding brilliance—of course, our eyes were so acclimated to the dark that *any* light might have seemed blinding, yet this struck my eyes with a physical agony I had never felt before. And I had very little time to feel it before *something*—something my blinded eyes could not see—slammed into my face. It invaded my nostrils, as if I had inhaled a living flame, and then it was my brain's turn to explode and I plummeted into a deep, bottomless darkness."

He pushed up out of his chair to pace back and forth across the compartment.

"Eventually, I crawled back up out of that darkness, but I was . . . disoriented, scarcely able to recall even my own name. It was only later that I realized I could see perfectly in the total darkness of the 'cavern,' but what I saw made very little sense to me in my state. I have scattered, chaotic memories of the way in which I made my way out of the cavern. Among those memories, however, is that I was alone. Utterly alone. I stumbled and almost fell when I tripped over the armor of one of my Moldavians, but there were no bodies. There was only the empty armor, the empty *garments,* lying as my bodyguards must have fallen, yet they were empty. There were no bones, no dust. Simply . . . nothing."

"It was night when I emerged from the cavern, and it was also summer. In my state, that meant little to me, but I staggered down the valley, seeking aid and shelter from pure instinct, for I was incapable of anything so clear as rational thought. I do not know how far from the cavern I had come before the sun arose, but when it did, the pain was terrible. I crawled into the forest, burrowed under the leaves like an animal, hiding myself from its punishing brilliance. And when merciful darkness fell once more and I was again able to think—however poorly—I realized what I must have become and that I must at all costs stay away from other humans. So I became one more beast, living—or subsisting, at least—in the trackless mountains.

"I do not know how long I remained in that state of confusion and animal instinct, but it was long enough for my clothing to become rent and tattered and my beard to grow long and tangled. It was only later that I learned to command hair and beard to grow—or not to grow—as suited me best. I recall the day my mind was finally clear enough to be called my own again, however. I recall looking down into a pool of water from which I had been drinking like an animal and seeing my own reflection in the light of an evening sun which merely made me 'itch,' as you have put it. And I remember thinking that I had never seen a more demented-looking lunatic in my entire life.

"I will not bore you with the long, painful time I spent hiding in those mountains, seeking to understand how I had become what I was. Learning that I had been transformed into whatever had formed the basis for the legends of the *nosferatu*—the *vampyr* in which I had never truly believed, despite the time in which I was born. One thing I knew was that I could never return to who and what I had been, and that was even before I discovered that it was the year 1519, forty-three years since my final battle against the Turks.

"But that is the true story of how I became what I—what *we*—have become, my Stephen."

"Jesus," Buchevsky said. "That's one hell of a lot different from all the legends!"

"Believe me, you are no more aware of that than I." There was far more of his usual tart humor in Vlad's tone. "In truth, I have never really understood why Mister Stoker chose me as the central figure for his novel, and he got virtually every detail about the historic 'Dracula' wrong . . . assuming he ever intended to use more than simply my name. But given how wrong even my peasants' folklore proved about our state, I feel little temptation to criticize him for his artistic license."

Buchevsky snorted in amusement, then tipped back in his chair once more.

"Did you ever go back and explore that 'cavern' of yours?"

"No." Vlad shook his head. "Not for want of trying, you understand. But I had wandered so far from it by the time something which approached rationality returned to me that I could never find my way back to it."

"Damn. I sure would like a peek inside it myself!"

"I sought it because I wanted some fuller explanation for my curse, yet the truth is that the very thought of returning to it filled me with terror," Vlad admitted with stark honesty. "My memories of that night, of what followed from it, were my own Purgatory, in many ways, my Stephen. Not sufficient to cleanse me of my sins, of the blood upon my hands, but the most terrifying punishment ever visited upon me."

"I can see that," Buchevsky said softly.

"Perhaps you understand now why I stayed so close to hand during your own . . . transition," Vlad told him. "It took me the better part of a half century to begin truly coming to grips with all of the ways in which I had been transformed. I had no guidance. Certainly the legends about what I had become offered none! But, in time, I began to accept what I had become and learn to control it."

Buchevsky nodded, and wondered how many other men in Vlad's situation could have accomplished that.

"And, in the centuries since," Vlad continued more briskly, "I have continued to improve my control and in the process I have learned how to . . . assist others in making the same change. The process takes far less time now, and I am able to bring others across as I did you, without the disorientation, the loss of memory. Although even today, not all make the transition successfully. In the early days, perhaps one in twenty of those I attempted to bring across survived. Today, I *lose* only about one in twenty. Even today, however, some of those I bring across succumb to the madness which must, in fact, be the basis for the legends of vampires' murderous nature. In the grip of that madness, they would rend and destroy anyone they encountered, and so, in those cases, I must . . . undo that which I have done, take away the renewed life I have given. And sometimes, as I warned Pieter and Longbow, in the fullness of time that same madness comes upon even some of our kind who appear to have weathered the change intact.

"But, by the time I had achieved sufficient control to once again move among the breathers, I was a man adrift. No one I had known before was still alive, I certainly had no throne—nor any desire for one! And so I became some*one* else just as I had become some*thing* else. I turned away from the man who had created the legend of Vlad the Impaler, and until the Puppies' arrival, I had never reverted to him. Not as fully as I have now. There were times when I . . . intervened, but for the most part, Take and I have lived quiet lives, drawing little attention to ourselves. And I would so very much have preferred for it to stay that way."

"I understand," Buchevsky said. "I really do. But if you had, the Puppies *would* have wiped out our entire species. You know that, too."

"Aside from the minor qualifier that I am not certain *Homo sapiens* remains our 'species,' you are correct," Vlad admitted. "But perhaps you understand now why I seem a trifle . . . detached upon occasion."

Buchevsky snorted again, but behind the humor, he knew he understood something else now, as well. He understood why the man who had been Vlad Tepes was so drawn to flawed cinematic heroes who sought to protect and to avenge *others*.

"But enough of that!" Vlad flopped back into his own chair. "I believe we were about to watch a movie, were we not?"

"Yes, we were," Buchevsky agreed. "Bring it on!"

"I shall," Vlad said, and tapped the PLAY key.

XVI

MOOSE JAW, SASKATCHEWAN,
CANADA

Right here," Constable Jamie Ibson said, pointing to the fast food restaurant's oversize parking lot just off Highway 2 in Moose Jaw, Saskatchewan. He buttoned up his jacket as the driver turned the massive vehicle into the parking lot, leaving enough room for the second truck with the crane to pull in alongside. Since each truck was over thirty meters long, the two of them easily filled two-thirds of the parking lot.

The trip from Regina had gone fairly smoothly. The Trans-Canada was still open and in pretty good shape, and the small portion of the Manitoba Expressway they'd had to traverse had been plowed earlier in the day. Still, he knew the race was on, as the area around Regina was prone to extremes.

It had been plus forty-eight degrees centigrade, or "stupid hot" as his friend, Stephan Blackwolf, had said, on their arrival for training at the Royal Canadian Mounted Police Academy in July. As the country headed into the throes of winter, though, he knew there would be storms where the temperatures would reach "stupid cold," or about minus forty degrees centigrade, as well.

Ibson pulled the toque over his dark brown hair, flipped up the hood of his jacket, and then pulled on his gloves. As prepared as he could be, he climbed down from the giant transporter and walked to the southeastern corner of the lot and shook his head. The railroad overpass had decided that the coming of winter was a good time to fail, and had done so as the train bearing the relief supplies for the refugee camp at Medicine Hat, Alberta, was going over it.

In addition to the failure of the overpass, which cut the key trans-Canadian rail line, the resulting derailment of the train had snarled everything going into the yard at Moose Jaw. It was a mess, and people were going to die, hungry and cold, if he didn't get it fixed. While they had pulled the train clear of the yard and removed the rubble from Highway 2, the rail bridge was completely gone, and the tracks were a mangled, twisted mass on both sides.

He shook his head again. Rebuilding overpasses wasn't something that was normally in the job description of a new graduate of the RCMP academy. Usually, a graduate wasn't even considered a fully trained constable until he'd had another six months under the guidance of a coach. In the aftermath of the Shongairi invasion—with winter coming on full bore, though—the position had been "adjusted" slightly.

When the call had come for able-bodied men and women to help with the relief effort coming in from the "United States"—whatever part still existed, anyway—the RCMP had volunteered all of its graduates. They didn't really have jobs yet, which made them more expendable—or dispensable, at least—than the seasoned RCMP officers they'd have had to pull from the field.

So Ibson had become a relief worker.

He'd overseen two convoys of aid going from the Regina supply depot out to the hinterlands . . . and his presence had been necessary on one of them when they'd come to the "tariff station." A band of locals at one of the small towns along the route, who didn't have enough supplies of their own, had been enterprising enough to set up a roadblock where they said they would "just take a small amount as tax." Judging by the vehicles he could see in the area, the tax was on the order of one hundred percent. While his mandate allowed for distributing some of the supplies along the way, *if necessary,* showing up without anything would not have endeared him to his boss, so he had respectfully declined.

While the hunting rifles the men carried had been effective against the earlier passers-through, the C7 assault rifles Ibson and the two army privates he commanded carried—and the C9 light machine gun mounted on the Iveco VM 90 leading the convoy—had dissuaded the men from any further tax collection. Permanently, when they hadn't taken "no" for an answer.

He'd returned from that trip to find out that he was now a bridge repairman. He'd complained about being the wrong person for the job—he didn't have the knowledge or skills for the job—and he'd been right. Until they'd brought one of the Shongair neural educators along with the bridge repair kit that had come in on the next *Starlander.*

So now he had the knowledge, if not "the skills."

Now all he needed was the manpower, which, as he turned around, was just pulling into the parking lot as well. Two large passenger vans with 15 WING, CFB MOOSE JAW on the sides stopped next to the transporters, and twenty men piled out. They were young airman from the airbase on the south side of town, who knew even less about fixing bridges than he did. A man who looked a little older than the rest came over to him while the rest shared a couple of cigarettes, each taking a drag before passing it to the next person. The man had three stripes on his uniform jacket and piercing blue eyes; everything else was protected by several layers of clothing.

"I'm Sergeant LaCroix," the man said. "You Constable Ibson?"

"I am," Ibson replied. "Thanks for coming, eh?"

"Well, we're here, but I don't know what good we're going to be to you." LaCroix jerked a thumb over his shoulder at the group of airmen. "Simmons over there was on a road crew for a summer after a . . . shall we say, minor indiscretion, but no one else has any experience with roads or railroads, and no one has any heavy construction experience. We're jet mechanics for the Thunderbirds demonstration squadron . . . well, when we have planes again, we are, anyway."

"That's all right. I think I know what I'm doing."

"You think you know, eh?" LaCroix asked. "What are you, some kind of civil engineer?"

"No, I'm a Mountie, but I did stay at a Shongair Inn last night, and they gave me the info I needed to show you what needed to be done."

"How long's this going to take?" LaCroix asked. "It's going to get cold once the sun goes down."

"Yes, it is," Ibson said, nodding. "And I'm sure you're looking forward to getting back to your nice, warm barracks. But it's also going to get cold in Alberta when the sun goes down, and all the people there don't have fuel, because it's stuck in Regina while this bridge is out. Those folks are going to get cold, too, when the wind starts whipping across the plains. *Really* cold."

The man looked down at his boots, realizing he was probably lucky to have them, and Ibson let him reflect for a moment before he added, "We need to get this bridge up, but the aliens at least made it easy on us—a lot easier than it would have been. I know how to do it, but I'll need your guys to manhandle some things."

The sergeant looked up and took a deep breath, squaring his shoulders. "What do you need us to do?"

Ibson chuckled, then motioned towards the restaurant. "Less than you might think, believe it or not." He nodded his head at the two massive transporters, where the crane operator on one of the vehicles was already lifting the giant synthetic crates down to the ground, under the supervision of his driver and with the assistance of Ibson's driver. "It'll take them a little to get all that stuff off the transporters. Why don't we go inside where it's warm and talk about what needs to be done over a couple of pizzas, and then come back and open up the railway again?"

"Sounds good," LaCroix replied.

"Then, when we're done, there's a bar next door, too. The first round's on me."

The sergeant looked over as they walked and nodded. "Now you're talking."

· · · · ·

"HERE'S THE DEAL," Ibson said to the crowd of twenty young men, about a half hour later as they stood looking at the various piles spread across the parking lot. Once the transporters had been unloaded, the drivers had moved them down the street so they wouldn't be in the way. "The Puppies left us the plans for fully automated, self-directing engineering vehicles." He pointed to the oversized synthetic crates. "That's them. I hear that these things run on something called 'brilliant software.' It's like the next, best thing to having a fully sentient artificial intelligence."

He could see several of the men's eyes glaze over, and he tried again. "Put simply, these things are robots—smart robots—that can almost do the entire job by themselves."

"Then what the hell are we doing here out in the cold?" one of the airmen muttered.

"Good question," Ibson replied. "I'm glad you asked. Even though they're really smart, that's not entirely the same as being able to think for themselves, and, as I understand it, they aren't always programmed for everything that needs to be done. We're here to help them and provide a certain level of safety and quality assurance."

"What's that mean?" another airman asked.

"Would you like to go over a bridge built entirely by robots that no one else ever looked at to see if it was done right?" Ibson asked.

"Uh, no," the airman replied.

"Me, neither. So we're going to make sure the bridge is built right."

"But I don't know anything about building bridges," a third said, to the agreement of most.

"I understand that," Ibson replied. "And, to tell you the truth, I don't either. But you guys do know about fixing planes, and joining metal and circuitry together, and you can tell if *that's* been done right, eh?"

"Well, yeah."

"And that's most of what I need you to do. Stay out of their way, watch what they do, and make sure it looks right, as much as you're able. Got it?"

The airmen nodded, and Sergeant LaCroix raised his hand. "So what do we need to do first?"

"Stay there, and I'll get them started." Ibson walked over to the first crate, about two meters to a side and three meters tall, which had a giant number *1* marked on all sides. It was made of something that looked like white plastic but was a lot harder. He'd seen the chemical formula for the synthetic; he had enough of a chemistry background to know it was well beyond his ability to comprehend. He found the touchpad on the side of the crate, turned it on, and entered the activation code he'd been given.

The side of the crate opposite the touchpad folded down, and a giant, quadrupedal robot nearly as large as the crate marched out. The robot turned to Ibson and asked, "Are you the supervisor?"

Ibson nodded, dumbstruck. While he'd been neurally educated on what would happen, it was a lot different to see RoboCop walk out of a box and ask you a question. The robot was a shiny silver and generally humanoid—or maybe the right word was "centauroid" (if that *was* a word)—although its four arms and four legs announced it wasn't "human."

It continued to look at Ibson, and a red light blinked on its chest.

"Yes, I'm the supervisor," Ibson said when he realized a nod wasn't good enough. He pointed to the sergeant and added, "That is my assistant."

"Noted," the robot replied. "What is the task?"

"We need a new train bridge across that opening." Ibson pointed to the former overpass. "The bridge cannot obstruct the vehicular traffic lanes that go below it."

"I understand you need a bridge. What is a train bridge?"

"A train is a vehicle that runs on the tracks—the steel rails—that lead up to where the bridge used to be and then extend on the other side."

"Understood. What weight must the bridge support?"

"Uh." Ibson frowned. Somebody should have given him that information, and no one had. So how—? "Can you analyze the old bridge and see what weight it was designed to bear before it collapsed?"

"That is possible," the robot replied.

"In that case, build the new one to support a weight twenty percent greater." Better to build in a safety margin than rely on a machine's minimum estimate, he figured. "Oh, and be sure to leave the lanes under it clear. Can you do that?"

"Yes."

"Good, and once it's built, you need to lay these tracks—" Ibson gestured at the small mountain (well, hillock) of gleaming new tracks stacked to one side "—across the bridge. Please."

It felt strange to say "please" to a robot, but it would have felt even stranger if he hadn't.

"Understood. Analyze original bridge. Build new bridge to cross gap and support one-point-two times original bridge's weight. Do not obstruct lanes beneath bridge. Lay track and connect it to other side. Are these directions correct?"

"Yes they are."

"Shall I assemble the team and begin?"

"Yes, please."

The foreman robot walked to the next crate, extended one "finger," and plugged it into a data port on its side. When it did, Ibson realized all four of the fingers on that hand were subtly different from one another.

The robot that emerged from the second crate looked nothing like the first robot. This one had long limbs, like on a forklift, that snapped down as it emerged. As it cleared the crate, additional limbs snapped into place on its opposite side, although these ended in claw-shaped appendages with three "fingers" opposed by three "thumbs" on each. After a brief pause, it rolled over to one of the piles of steel girders on its tank-like treads, picked up a load, and began carrying them to where the bridge would be built.

"First thing I need your guys to do," Ibson told LaCroix, "is you better go stop traffic, eh? Looks like that robot's heading to the street and we don't want anyone to run it over . . . or cause a wreck while they're trying to figure out what it is."

By the time the sergeant had four airmen on traffic patrol, the construction foreman robot had opened another three crates, and more robots were on the job. One robot had some sort of torch, or laser, or *something* that cut metal, and it was slicing through the existing bent railroad tracks as if they were made of butter. A second was preparing the site for where the bridge's support structure would go, in between the lanes of vehicular traffic in the underpass, and a third robot—one that was built lower to the ground, with four sets of tracked wheels and a bladed appendage—was leveling the ground on the closer side.

"So . . ." the sergeant started, then his voice trailed off and he pursed his lips in thought.

"Yes?" Ibson asked.

"What exactly are we supposed to be doing now?"

"Staying out of the way of the robots while they work, mostly," Ibson said. "We're supposed to manage the big picture—like stopping traffic—things that the robots might not be familiar with. They know how to build bridges, and the foreman's smart enough to look out for the things that are dangerous in building a bridge, but they don't know anything about humans."

A new robot rolled onto the site and started slamming the ground with an appendage.

"What the hell is that one doing?" the sergeant asked.

"Measuring the density of the ground?" Ibson asked. "How much it's going to flex when a train rolls over it? I don't know. Hell, I really don't know any more about it than you do. I do, however, know that *this* one's on me." He pointed towards where a man was cautiously approaching the site with a deer rifle in his hands. Although Canada's citizenry didn't have as many firearms as their counterparts in the south did, firearms *did* exist, and it looked like the man was trying to decide whether he should shoot the strange, alien things which appeared to be taking over one end of his town.

Ibson glanced over his shoulder as he approached the man, then turned back to smile at the newcomer's obvious confusion. The site was now a hive of activity, with twenty separate robots working on various aspects of the bridge. Most of the support structure on Highway 2 was already built and in place, and the first girders were being positioned by a robot with a mini crane on its back. It was the damnedest thing he'd ever seen.

"Can I help you?" he asked as he approached the man, keeping his hands in plain sight. The man appeared to be in his early sixties, with white hair and a beard. He also was quite heavyset, and he would have almost have looked like Santa Claus . . . if not for the weapon.

"What the . . . what the hell is going on there?" the man asked, motioning at the bridge with his rifle.

"It's a robot construction crew," Ibson replied.

"What the hell's it doing?"

"They're rebuilding the railroad bridge."

"Didn't know robots could do that."

"They're new. We're just trying them out for the first time, eh?"

"Is that safe?"

"We think so, but it'd be safer if I watched them," Ibson said, pulling out his badge. "I'm Constable Ibson. Now why don't you just go back to your house and put away the rifle, and let me take care of this."

"You're a Mountie?" the man asked, apparently noticing Ibson's RCMP parka for the first time. He seemed happy to have something he understood and could count on.

"Yes, sir, I am, and I have this all under control." *Even if I don't understand half of what I'm doing.*

"Well, okay then," the man said. He turned away, shaking his head. "Damnedest thing I've ever seen."

· · · · ·

"LAST ONE," THE robot foreman said.

Ibson nodded, amazed to have the task completed so quickly. He looked at his watch—he hadn't even been on-site for six hours, and they were already finished.

"Clear?" asked one of the three remaining robots.

"Your call," Ibson said to Sergeant LaCroix, who stood on the other side of what Ibson had come to think of as the "pile-driving robot."

The sergeant nodded and gave a quick scan. "Clear!" he called. "Fire!"

The robot fired some sort of coilgun on its arm, and a spike emerged from it to slam into place, holding the final rail to the tie. Not satisfied with the spike's placement, the robot's sledgehammer arm descended once, driving it the rest of the way home.

"Satisfactory," the robot pronounced.

"Satisfactory," LaCroix agreed.

The pile-driver robot turned and began rolling towards its crate at some unspoken signal from the foreman robot, who was networked in with all of them. Except for their interaction with the humans, the robots worked silently, based on the electromagnetic orders given them by the foreman.

"Bridge to cross gap completed," the foreman informed Ibson. "Lanes below bridge remain unobstructed. Track in position and connected to original track on both sides. Job complete. Do you agree?"

"I agree," Ibson said. "It was a job very well done. Thank you."

"We are ready for the next task. Two units will require servicing after that," the robot said, then walked to its crate and backed into it. As it came in contact with a switch inside the box—Ibson had looked earlier—the crate sealed itself, just like all the previous ones had.

"Now what?" the sergeant asked.

"Now I get the drivers to load the crates back onto the transporters, and we head back to Regina."

"I think you're forgetting something, first, though."

Ibson scanned the job site, looking for something he missed. "No, I think we're good."

The sergeant chuckled. "No, there was also the mention of a beer, and the fact you were buying . . ."

XVII

COLD MOUNTAIN,
TRANSYLVANIA COUNTY, NORTH CAROLINA,
UNITED STATES

I t's good to see you guys," Dave Dvorak said as Daniel Torino and Pieter Ushakov walked into the dining room.

"No, it's not," Sharon Dvorak said. "I can't think of two people I'd less prefer to see."

She smiled as she spoke, and crossed the room to wrap her arms first around Ushakov and then around Torino. She kissed each of them on the cheek, then pointed imperiously at chairs while a platoon or so of children laughed.

"This is not the proper example to be setting for dutiful children." Ushakov glowered at the audience—especially at Zinaida Karpovna—although the severity of his tone was sadly undermined by the twinkle in his eye.

"I tell her that," Larissa Karpovna, Zinaida's mother, said mournfully. "But it does no good, Peten'ka." She shook her head and smiled at Sharon; she'd learned to do that again. "She cannot help it. She is American."

"Durn tooting," Sharon said.

"Sit down—sit down!" Dvorak urged. "Can we at least offer you two beers?"

"I would like that," Ushakov agreed, slipping into the indicated chair at the very large table.

"Actually, could I have coffee, instead?" Torino asked. Dvorak raised an eyebrow, and the ex-fighter pilot shrugged. "I was a fighter pilot. We lived on that stuff, so if I'm going to pretend that I'm drinking for effect, I might as well pretend I'm getting buzzed on caffeine instead of alcohol."

"The scary thing is that actually makes sense to me," Dvorak said, and both of the visitors chuckled as they settled in at the table.

Not exactly what comes to mind when you think about "vampires," Dvorak reflected as he watched the children—three of his and Sharon's, his niece Keelan, and Zinaida and her younger brothers Boris and Ermolai—swapping greetings (and jokes) with "Uncle Pieter" and "Uncle Daniel." *Then again,* his mood darkened briefly, *none of the kids have ever seen the two of them in an "offer you can't refuse" mode. Except Zinaida, maybe.*

He pondered that for a moment, then shook the reflection aside as Morgana and Maighread hopped up to go fetch a bottle of beer for Ushakov and another coffee cup for Torino. He'd have to return to it later, but for right now he could just enjoy having two friends stop by for dinner with the family.

"It's Tuesday," he observed aloud, looking down the table at Malachi when the twins had returned and resumed their seats. The ten-year-old looked back gravely, then bowed his head.

"Thank you for the blessings of this day and of every day, and especially this meal. Amen," he said, and Dvorak nodded in approval.

"And now," he said, "somebody pass the mashed potatoes, please!"

. . . . .

CONSIDERABLY LATER THAT evening, Dvorak sat on the cabin's front porch. They'd finally made it past winter, but March nights were cold in the Appalachians and tonight's temperature hovered just below freezing. The porch, however, had acquired a roof and walls of Hegemony crystoplast. The side panels irised obediently open at the touch of a switch if its occupants wanted a breeze, but at the moment they were tightly closed and the porch was a bubble of warmth and light under a high and frigid moon. Despite that, Dvorak sensed the cold hovering outside the warmth, and he shivered as he thought once more about all the people who had neither heat nor light.

"It's not your fault," Ushakov said quietly, and Dvorak looked at him. "I have come to know you rather well, Dave. You are brooding again."

"Takes one to know one," Dvorak replied, and Ushakov snorted. But he also nodded, and Dvorak leaned back, looking up through the crystoplast at that icy moon and the tiny glittering dots of the solar collector satellites beaming power down to the electrical grid steadily regenerating itself across the face of the planet. He rather missed the larger, brighter dots which had been the industrial platforms "acquired" from the Shongairi, but he understood why Howell had decided to relocate them to the Lagrange points, especially given the president's ambitious plans for their eventual expansion. Besides, the science-fiction reader in him was tickled by the notion that the L5 Society and its successor, the National Space Society, had been vindicated at last.

"You're right, though," he went on. "I guess I *am* 'brooding' again. Hard not to, especially with the vantage point I have now from Greensboro. At least things seem to be going pretty well with Agamabichie and Garção, and King Henry's turning out to be a hell of a lot more decisive—and influential—than I would've expected. But France is a mess, Poland's worse, and I don't even want to talk about China or India and Pakistan."

"This is a large planet, in case you hadn't noticed," Torino put in, "and the Puppies fucked it up pretty damned thoroughly." His tone was almost whimsical; his green eyes were not. "We're moving as fast as we can, and you're a big part of that, but there's a limit to how quickly we can un-fuck it."

"I know. I know! And I guess that's why I try to get home to Sharon and the kids every weekend. And I have to admit that having my very own air car available helps a lot." Dvorak twitched his head at the small, sleek VTOL vehicle parked in the clear space which had once been their vegetable garden. It was capable of speeds of up to 120 mph on a good road . . . or just over Mach 1 with its configurable wings deployed in swept mode. "When I'm not seeing it as one more perk to feel guilty over, at least."

"Don't you dare get maudlin over my air car," his wife told him as she stepped out onto the porch. Unlike Dvorak, she loathed coffee, so she'd brought along one of her prized and hoarded Sierra Mist soft drink cans.

"Your air car?" Torino asked mildly. "I seem to remember it being issued for official use only."

"*My* air car," Sharon repeated, seating herself beside her husband on the glider. "They *promised* me an air car way back at the '64 World's Fair, and they never delivered. Until now."

"I don't think this is quite what they had in mind, Honey," Dvorak said, and it was her turn to snort.

"Don't care, and don't want to hear it," she replied firmly. "Besides, it won't be a lot longer before there're enough of them they won't have to be restricted to 'official use.'"

"True, and another illustration of what I was just telling your husband—known around here as the Gloomy One," Torino said. "Right this minute, it still looks pretty dark, but once we reach the tipping point, things are going to start getting better really, really fast. And we're getting closer to that point every day. Trust me, Pieter and I see plenty of evidence of that out on SAR ops."

"I know, but that's one of the things I really wanted to talk to you two about," Dvorak said, setting his coffee cup on the rattan table at the end of the glider.

"Dave, you promised no business," Sharon said.

"I promised no more business than I could help, Babe." He put his good arm around her and hugged. "And I waited until you had the kids showered and off to bed before I brought up word one about it."

She glowered at him for a moment, torn between actual irritation and worry about the bone-deep fatigue she felt inside him. But then she nodded grudgingly.

"I suppose you did. But you'd better keep this brief and to the point, Buster! You're already up past curfew. So none of your no doubt brilliant but . . . excessively loquacious discourse. Got it?"

"Got it," he agreed.

"What part of Search and Rescue did you want to talk about?" Torino sounded a bit puzzled, and Dvorak didn't blame him. Actual field ops weren't part of the Secretary of State's duties, after all, and the truth was they were going very well.

"I don't know if it's actually anything to worry about or not," he replied a bit slowly, "but if anybody knows about that, it'd probably be you two. And I think it's got Jasmine a little worried—or maybe the word I want is 'uneasy.'"

"You begin to sound a bit ominous," Ushakov observed.

"It's just . . . just that we've been getting a few after-action reports, not so much about the SAR missions as the intervention teams, that are generating a few concerns in Greensboro."

"The intervention ops are bound to be messy sometimes, Dave," Torino said. "The kinds of people we go to call on aren't all like Lutosławski in Poland or Mitsotakis in Greece. Mostly we're dealing with people like that bastard Beach down in Key West." He shook his head. "The only things people like that understand are examples, and it's going to get worse when we start getting into the real shitholes. The Cartels down in Mexico, for example, once we finally get around to them."

"I know that, and I saw quite a bit of 'messy' right here in North Carolina," Dvorak reminded him, reaching up to rub gently at the shoulder which continued to improve steadily under the nanites' ministrations. "That's not what's worrying anyone."

"Then what *does* concern them?" Ushakov asked.

"I guess you could say it's an attitudinal thing," Dvorak replied, speaking slowly as he chose his words with care. "Some of the vampires seem to be enjoying their work a bit more than others." Ushakov and Torino frowned, but he continued. "I'm thinking specifically of Cecilia. I hate to say it, but there seems to be an increasing tendency on her part to pull the wings off the flies when she doesn't have to."

"Cecilia is very effective." Ushakov's tone was unnaturally neutral, and Dvorak nodded.

"No question about that," he agreed. "And as Dan just pointed out, the people you've got her dealing with require a pretty big—and graphic—clue stick. Nobody's questioning that. But I'm sure the two of you can understand why people like Pat O'Sullivan and General Landers get a little nervous when someone who seems to be both immortal and indestructible starts . . . looking forward to her work a little too enthusiastically."

He looked very levelly at his guests, both of whom were also apparently immortal and indestructible, and they looked back at him for several of his breaths. Then they glanced at one another, and Torino shrugged very slightly.

"Go ahead." He sounded almost resigned. "You knew we were going to have to tell someone sooner or later. Seems to me Dave might be a good place to start."

"I suppose." Pieter drew a breath and let it out in an audible sigh, then turned back to Dvorak.

"I hope that your concerns about Cecilia prove unnecessary," he said, "but I cannot be as confident of that as I would prefer. Do you, by any chance, remember Vlad saying that he chose more carefully about the vampires he made this time?"

"I don't remember hearing *Vlad* say that, but Stephen said something like it."

"I am not surprised. Serëžen'ka is the closest to him of us all. But the reason he said that was that the first vampires he created are undoubtedly much of the basis for the horrendous stories told of the 'undead.' He himself was not what one might have called excessively rational in those early days, and many of those he brought across in his loneliness were far more unstable than he. In truth, when one considers all that he endured, both before and after his death, it is truly remarkable that he is *not* the bloodthirsty monster of legend. I think perhaps he was very close to that for some time, yet he pulled himself back from the brink and refused to become—or perhaps I mean that he refused to *remain*—the thing of darkness he might have been."

"Not all of his 'children' did that." Ushakov's expression was grim. "No doubt some of them had no desire to refuse, given what life had cost them before they ceased to breathe. Vlad was less careful about that in those early days. But even some who could have—who one would think *should* have—proved most resistant to the dark desire to, as you put it, pull wings off of flies did not. They sank into that darkness, and what one such as we can do in the grip of that madness is truly horrible.

"As I say, he refused to bring across any of the truly broken for his new vampires. Indeed, before Zinaida and her family entered my life, he would probably have refused to bring *me* across because of the darkness which filled my soul. But before he departed, he warned me, as his deputy here on Earth, and Daniel as *my* deputy, that some of our kind may descend into the dark rather than climb into the light."

"Meaning what, exactly, Pieter?" Sharon asked quietly.

"Meaning that for some, the change is a gateway to madness." Ushakov's voice was flat. "It may not come upon us overnight, and it affects only a small percentage of us, but when it does, we become the very creatures of the night of legend. Not because we must feed upon our victims blood, but because we feed upon their *fear*. Because something in us embraces the power we have to terrify and hurt, and, I think, because when that happens to us we believe we have become superior beings—near gods, perhaps—and that the breathers about us exist only as our toys."

"I remember reading that the common characteristic of almost all serial killers is a lack of empathy," Dvorak said. "That they don't see their victims as fellow human beings. They see them as *things*, as toys that they can do anything they want to."

"Thank you," Ushakov said softly, then smiled crookedly as Dvorak's eyebrows arched. "Thank you for reminding me that madness and cruelty are part of humanity, not something that emerges only in vampires."

"That's true, but you seem to be talking about some sort of . . . progressive loss of empathy. And maybe something that goes deeper than that. I'm not about to try to psychoanalyze Cecilia or anyone else, but from what you're saying, Pat and Landers' concerns may just be justified. And if they are, what do we—what *can* we—do about it?"

"For the moment, I think it is probably wisest to leave her where she is," Ushakov said after a moment, and glanced at Torino. "Longbow?"

"I think you're right." Torino looked troubled, but not hesitant. "We both need to keep an eye on her—and having Jasmine as part of that wouldn't be a bad idea. But if this is what Vlad was talking about, the only person who can pull Cecilia back is Cecilia herself. *We* sure as hell can't. So probably better to leave her with the teams where at least she'll be dealing with the sort of scum most of us won't miss very much at the end of the day."

"And what if that accelerates whatever's happening inside her?" Dvorak asked.

"I do not think it will," Ushakov said. "Not if this is, indeed, the gradual collapse Vlad described to us. That seems to work its way through, either to the final darkness or to the triumph over it that Vlad found, regardless of anything else. And one cannot deny that she is very effective in her work."

"That's certainly one way to put it," Dvorak agreed with a shiver that owed nothing to the mountain night outside the porch as he remembered some of the reports he'd viewed. "And if she does reach the tipping point and goes . . . feral, for want of a better word, on us? What then?"

"If that happens, it will be my job, or Daniel's, to ensure that she is no longer a problem," Ushakov said flatly. "I believe you described her as someone who *seems* to be both immortal and indestructible, and that was perhaps an even better choice of verb than you realized. Under the right circumstances, we are neither of those things, and if it is necessary to protect others from one of our kind, we will demonstrate that."

His blue eyes were colder than the distant moon, and the iron in his promise was colder still.

XVIII

SPACE PLATFORM *INVICTUS*,
L5 LAGRANGE POINT

W hat the fu—?!"

Arturo Sanchez looked up from his multifunction displays as Quintin O'Malley cut off the last word of his muttered imprecation. Samantha Twain, their shift supervisor, wasn't what anyone could call prudish. In fact, in most ways, she was a pleasure to work for. But she did object to casual profanity, and the overuse of that particular verb was one of her trigger buttons. O'Malley knew that, and he was usually pretty good about honoring her objections. Which meant something out of the ordinary must have attracted the other controller's attention.

O'Malley stared down at his panel, frowning as his hands darted across the keyboard. Eventually, all of the platform staff would have the new contact lenses, capable of projecting displays and a virtual keyboard without needing the actual hardware, but that hadn't happened yet. For that matter, Sanchez wasn't sure he wanted it to happen. Reconfiguring Hegemony control interfaces for humans was hard enough with physical keyboards and displays. Besides, it was good to have *something* relatively familiar, given the environment into which he and his fellows had been pitched. The overheads were too low, the lighting was wrong, the human-style furniture looked out of place in the alien environment, and all of them were aware that they were one hell of a long way from home.

"What is it?" he asked as O'Malley continued to tap keys and his frown grew steadily more intense.

"I don't know," O'Malley half-muttered. "I'm getting structural integrity warnings on Arm Three."

"What?" It was Sanchez' turn to frown. "That's crazy!" Arm Three had been certified complete by the inspection teams the day before yesterday, and one thing the hyper-cautious, ultraconservative Hegemony-style instrumentation didn't miss was a lack of structural integrity!

"I know!" O'Malley entered another command, and his expression shifted from one of baffled irritation to the beginning of genuine alarm. "I've got three more warnings," he said. "Different subsystems, too."

"That's—" Sanchez began, then broke off, whirling back to his own console as a red light began to flash. He tapped keys and smothered a few colorful comments of his own.

"I'm getting the same warnings on Arm Two!" he said tersely.

"That really *is* crazy," O'Malley said, and keyed his com.

"Twain," a contralto voice responded almost instantly in his headset.

"Sam," O'Malley said into his headset mic; *Invictus'* personnel were comfortable with informality, "we've got a problem down here. Arms Two and Three are both showing structural faults."

"That's crazy," Twain said, and O'Malley and Sanchez shared a nervous grin at her choice of adjective. "Hold one."

A musical tone beeped in both controllers' headsets as the supervisor logged directly into their displays. Even as she did, two fresh warning lights began to blink on Sanchez' display. He muttered and began typing a query into the system when—abruptly, with zero additional forewarning, dozens of other lights flashed brightly.

More telltales turned crimson on displays all around the large compartment, and an audible alarm warbled.

"Warning," a dispassionate computer voice said suddenly. "Warning. Structural failure imminent. Structural failure imminent."

"Can't be!" Twain sounded stunned by the speed of the totally unexpected threat's expansion, but she reacted quickly. The neat columns of data on the status of structural components arriving from the already active printers vanished from the master display on the large compartment's forward bulkhead as she reconfigured it to a visual feed. The camera she'd selected had an excellent view of Refinery Six, her crew's current responsibility, and—

"What the *fuck*?!" Samantha Twain blurted as the brilliant sparkle of shorting circuits flared along a third of Arm Two's length. Sanchez stared at the display in disbelief, then swallowed an incredulous curse as his entire panel went red.

"Warning," the computer voice said. "Structural failure Arm Two. Structural failure Arm Two. Structural failure Arm Two. Struc—"

The warning died in mid-word as the heel of Twain's hand slammed down on the big red button on her console. The one no one had ever expected to need.

"Emergency shutdown procedures initiated," the voice said calmly. "Proceeding. Shutdown confirmed. All drones at standby."

"Well, that's a hell of a mess," Sanchez said quietly, to no one in particular, as a four-hundred-foot length of Arm Two simply . . . detached from the refinery and began drifting slowly away from it.

"Yeah, and somehow I don't think Director MacQuarie's gonna be real pleased about it," O'Malley agreed.

· · · · ·

"DAMN, DAMN, *DAMN!*"

Despite its low volume, Major Sheila McIlhenny could almost physically feel the intensity of Roger MacQuarie's soft-voiced profanity as it came over her headset. Partly, she thought, that was because she knew he practically never swore. Or maybe she only recognized it because both of them could see what had evoked it simply by glancing through her cockpit's crystoplast and she knew exactly how . . . frustrating it must be for him. She was MacQuarie's personal pilot. She'd come to know him well over the last few months, and she'd decided he was one of the best bosses she'd ever had. He was hardworking, conscientious, considerate of his personnel, imaginative, and willing to think outside the box.

And at the moment, he was also very, very frustrated and angry.

"Well, at least we know what happens when we get too enthusiastic. That's useful," Doctor Claude Massengale said over the com channel. His tone was deliberately bright, almost chirpy, and McIlhenny smothered a chuckle as MacQuarie scowled.

"Listen, half pint—you aren't doing yourself any favors where my Christmas list is concerned," MacQuarie replied, glaring at the construction drones drifting inertly between him and the Refinery Six platform, and McIlhenny turned another chuckle into a rather unconvincing cough as Massengale made a rude sound over the com.

It would have been difficult to imagine two men with less in common, physically speaking. MacQuarie was six and a half feet tall, the father of three, with Herculean shoulders, blond hair, hazel eyes, and a thick, closely cropped beard which had been on the wild and bushy side until he found himself forced to deal with space helmets. At fifty-seven, Massengale was fifteen years older, a wiry confirmed bachelor, ten inches shorter, built more for speed than power, clean-shaven, with brown hair, brown eyes, and a café au lait complexion. He was also the veteran of nine orbital missions and two assignments aboard the International Space Station prior to the Shongair invasion, whereas MacQuarie had never been off Earth until he was assigned as Director for *Invictus*. Despite which, they had formed a tightknit working relationship and an equally tight friendship.

It probably helped, McIlhenny thought, that both of them were smart, organized, and absolutely determined to succeed. And Massengale's attempt to divert MacQuarie from his self-anger with humor didn't surprise her one bit.

"I doubt I was very high on your list to begin with," Massengale said now. "And such petty threats don't invalidate my observation."

"No, they don't," MacQuarie sighed. "And you were right. We should have been more conservative."

"Maybe." Massengale's voice was considerably more serious now. "On the other hand, you had a point when you quoted Fisher, too—the best scale for an experiment *is* twelve inches to a foot." MacQuarie visualized his assistant director's shrug. "It's not like we have time to be cautious about these things, and you did restrict the tweak to Refinery Six. And it's not like it was a total disaster, either."

"Not quite," MacQuarie muttered, gazing through the crystoplast at the huge, half-wrecked refinery platform two kilometers from the workboat. When it was completed, it would be capable of ingesting tons of pulverized asteroid, liquid gasses mined from Jupiter's atmosphere, or ice quarried from Ganymede—or anything else, for that matter—and separating it into the finely divided components Hegemony-level printers required.

Of course, it wasn't going to be completed quite as soon as it might've been, he reflected moodily.

"I got too carried away," he said after a moment. "Or too optimistic, maybe, about our grasp of the system mechanics. And Karahalios even warned us about exactly that." He grimaced. "God, he's going to be hard to live with when he finds out about this!"

"I suggest we don't tell him," Massengale said, and MacQuarie snorted in sour amusement. Neither of them considered Damianos Karahalios their favorite person. "Seriously," Massengale went on, "you and I both know the real reason he gave you that warning was to cover his own ass in case something like this happened. Oh, this time he was right—damn it—but that's what he *always* does. And this kind of crap is bound to happen. This isn't just a simple matter of moving back and forth between human-designed applications and operating systems, Rog, and we're all going to be cursed with the 'book learning' aspect of neural education until we've had more field experience."

"Tell me about it!" MacQuarie growled.

"Well, if he does hear about it and he gets snippy, I suggest we—very respectfully, you understand—point out to him that he doesn't have *any* field experience," Massengale suggested, and despite his mood, MacQuarie laughed. Not that the situation was all that amusing. And despite Massengale's encouragement, Roger MacQuarie knew exactly who was responsible for it.

Unlike Massengale, who held a doctorate in astrophysics, MacQuarie had spent the last ten years in various administrative posts. On the other hand, he held a Masters in Robotics System Integration, which was the reason—combined with that Human Resources background—Judson Howell had picked him to run *Invictus*. Well, that and the fact that he and Howell had roomed together in college and remained close personal friends. Judson Howell wasn't the sort who operated on the basis of favoritism, but he did believe in trust, and he trusted both MacQuarie's intelligence and his integrity. Besides, as he'd said at the time, when he already knew the round peg he needed for the hole in question, there wasn't much point interviewing other candidates.

And it's that SI crap that got you in trouble with Refinery Six, he told himself. *It's the reason you knew what you were doing—you thought—and you were so pleased with how you were going to tweak efficiency by stripping out all those redundant steps.*

Once upon a time, *Invictus* had been named *Sword of Empire* in a language no human would ever be able to pronounce and Doctor Tiffany Samuelson's Space Platform *Provocatio,* located at the L4 Lagrange point, had been named *Stellar Dawn* in the same language.

MacQuarie much preferred their new names, but he and his crews had experienced plenty of hiccups in learning to use an alien-designed technology. There were any number of places for humans to stub their toes, and he was pretty sure he and his people would soon run smack into any they'd managed to avoid so far. It wasn't just sizes or shapes or life support requirements, either. It was entirely different units of measure and—far worse, in many ways—entirely different conceptual starting points.

The differences between how the Hegemony and humanity approached cybernetics and systems integration threw the truly alien origin of "their" new technology into stark contrast, and the Hegemony's approach only got more frustrating as they gained more familiarity with it. The incredible profusion of fail-safes, checking processes, safety protocols (especially where what a human would have called AI and the Hegemony called SMS, for Self-Managing Software, was concerned), sensors, sensors that watched the *sensors,* independent processors, and multiply redundant code was enough to drive any self-respecting human insane. For example, any SMS program had a minimum of not one, not two, but *at least* three additional programs doing nothing but making sure it stayed within its designed parameters at every single step. And when those programs had to negotiate with every other program—the literally tens of *thousands* of other programs—in something like Refinery Six, the efficiency degradation had to be seen to be believed. A human programmer, once he was confident an AI app had been properly debugged, preferred to put a human decision maker into the loop at any critical points and otherwise let the computers do what the hell they'd been designed to do without seven billion other programs looking over their shoulder to pounce if the app strayed one photon beyond its proper bounds. The Hegemony, on the other hand, didn't seem to believe its SMS *could* be debugged thoroughly enough for that. It was almost as if their cyberneticists were convinced Skynet really did lurk just across the horizon!

He and his staff had been stripping out the inhibitory aspects on Hegemony AI functions from the beginning, and the same . . . design timidity applied where things like construction and repair drones were concerned. MacQuarie's crews had been able to increase efficiency by over thirty-five percent just by giving the drone software more discretion about how to prioritize and reallocate task elements, and he'd been confident their ongoing efforts would soon double *that* increase, at least. But he'd gone a bit too far in that respect in his enthusiasm where Refinery Six was concerned. Or, more probably, one of his programmers had missed a problem.

Which was still MacQuarie's responsibility, since it had happened on his watch and the platform staff took their cue from him.

One of the most frustrating of the *many* frustrating things about working with Hegemony software was the multi-layered confirmation prompts. MacQuarie appreciated being asked if he really wanted to do something, especially if the "something" in question was critically important. It was the way programmers reminded themselves and other users that computers didn't care what you told them to do, only that you told them to do it, and he'd worked with enough of them over his lifetime to fully understand how necessary that reminder was. And that it didn't always prevent someone from making a serious mistake anyway. But like everything else connected to its IT, the Hegemony took it to ridiculous lengths. It didn't matter what you wanted to change; *any* programming change was queried at least twice. And anything that changed something the original programmer had classified as critical—which seemed to be true of at least two-thirds of the code in their industrial modules—was queried a dozen times. Literally. The Hegemony used base-twelve numbering, and apparently someone, somewhen had decided that a round dozen was a suitable number of confirmation prompts. Which meant that even normally attentive human programmers' brains tended to numb out and they simply automatically punched "yes" whenever they were prompted.

He wasn't positive that was what had happened here, but he suspected they'd discover it had been something along those lines. The consequences were clear enough, however.

The Refinery Six construction drones were divided into multiple arrays, each responsible for a particular facet of its construction, all under the supervision of a master controller (which, in turn, was supervised by twelve additional consulting controllers). Within each array, each drone was driven by its own processor (with consulting controllers), and each of its internal systems was driven by its own processor (with consulting controllers), and each component of each internal system was driven by its own processor (with consulting controllers). What had been supposed to happen was for all but two of the consulting controllers to be deactivated at each stage and to give each drone's master processor authority to override fault warnings so long as they were reported by only one of the three controllers on any of its subcomponents.

What had *actually* happened was that, in addition to the desired changes, they'd somehow shut down the master control link. That ought to have brought everything to a screeching halt, but it hadn't—almost certainly because someone had automatically hit that "yes" button the umptiumpth time it appeared— and the consequences had been . . . spectacular as the construction arrays stopped cooperating and began *competing*.

At least no one had been killed or injured when they started scavenging from other construction elements to complete their own. And at least the damned things hadn't gotten into the equivalent of fistfights over who a particular girder belonged to! But they had managed to gut quite a bit of already completed construction before the shift supervisor realized what was happening and hit the manual stop button.

"The good news is that we've demonstrated it works," Massengale continued. "Maybe not *perfectly*, this time, but anything you learn from is valuable. And they *were* awfully efficient when they started taking things apart."

That was also true, MacQuarie acknowledged. In fact, it was the main reason they'd managed to do so much damage before Samantha Twain shut them down. The drones in question had been ripping the platform apart at well over twice the speed their original Hegemony systems architecture would have permitted. Once they got their minor bug fixed and they started working *together* again, that would probably be a Very Good Thing. It was just a little hard to cling to that thought at the moment.

"Okay," he said after another second or two, "I'm going to go ahead and finish the flyby. Why don't you see if Tiffany can meet with us when Sheila and I get back to the barn? Oh, and see if Sang-wei can join us, too. I want to touch base with her on the new shielding protocols for those mining collector hub habitats."

"Sure, sure! You go have fun and leave me to do all the drudge work. That's all right. I'm used to it by now."

"And so damned cowed, too." MacQuarie shook his head and grinned at McIlhenny as the major chuckled again. "I can see I've been applying exactly the right amount of iron fist."

"Tyrant!" Massengale said, then laughed. "I'll set up the conference. You want Sang-wei to join you in the wardroom, or can she remote in? I'm not sure, but I think she's on the *Argus* platform right now."

"Remote will be fine. *Tiffany*'s going to be remoting in, after all! And at least there wouldn't be as much transmission lag for Sang-wei."

"True," Massengale conceded. "I'll get on that, then. Ping me when you head back in."

"Will do," MacQuarie agreed, then turned his head to smile at McIlhenny.

"I believe that's your cue to do what you pilots do," he said, waving one hand at the bottomless vista beyond the cockpit, and McIlhenny shook her head.

"You have so little respect for the mysteries of my profession, Sir," she said mournfully as the workboat accelerated.

"Nonsense! I have plenty of respect for them—I just don't *understand* them very well."

McIlhenny laughed, and MacQuarie sat back in his flight couch and watched the clutch of powered-down construction drones slide rapidly to one side as the small craft pulled away from them. It never ceased to fascinate him, since McIlhenny was accelerating at a leisurely twenty gravities. The Hegemony's inertial compensator could handle up to sixty gravities with no apparent acceleration, and the only sense of movement he had was the visual cue as the drones shrank rapidly from sixty-foot globes to sparkles of reflected sunlight.

Even at their current acceleration rate, it would take them two minutes to reach Refinery Five, almost six hundred kilometers from their starting point. Five was due to go online sometime in the next seventy-two hours, and the first four refineries were already in full production. The first-tier plan for *Invictus* called for a total of ten, each feeding a cluster of ten printer platforms. Once that was all online, *Invictus* would be rechristened *Invictus Alpha,* and one Roger MacQuarie would move on to building *Invictus Bravo.* Ultimately, there would be at least ten nodal control platforms—*Invictus Alpha* through *Invictus Juliette*—each with its brood of refineries and printers, located here at the L5 Lagrange point, equidistant from Earth and the Moon. That meant a hundred refineries feeding a thousand printers, each effectively its own assembly line capable of producing the equivalent of fourteen Greyhound buses per minute. That came to a combined equivalent of nine thousand "buses" a minute, or just under 7.4 billion per year, for the entire complex. Given the world's post-invasion population, that amounted to 3.7 Greyhounds for every surviving man, woman, and child. Put another way, the entire world's pre-invasion total production of motor vehicles of all types had come to just over 97 million per year—less than two percent of that. Now, admittedly, the world had manufactured a lot more than just cars, trucks, and buses. For that matter, *Invictus* wasn't making *any* actual buses. It was making things like *Starlanders,* emergency shelters and heaters, LENR reactors, contra-grav cargo lorries, and a bazillion other things Earth desperately needed. But a member of his planning staff had used the bus example in one of her briefings to help conceptualize the sheer scale of production, and for some reason, MacQuarie couldn't get it out of his head. Maybe because buses were so much more familiar than alien-designed, human-redesigned transatmospheric craft the size of a pre-invasion missile cruiser?

And that was at current productivity levels, he reminded himself. And from only the *Invictus* complex. *Provocatio* would double that output, and if his people could tweak production rates the way their projections said they *should* be able to, the results could be . . . impressive.

McIlhenny decelerated smoothly to rest relative to Refinery Five and rolled the workboat on its gyros to give her boss a better angle to the massive construct. Three more refinery platforms were bright marbles of reflected light from their new position, and her radar showed her a quartet of incoming colliers. Each of them was over a kilometer and a half in length, capable of carrying almost two million tons of cargo from the asteroid belt and the Jovian subsystem to feed *Invictus'* insatiable appetite.

She looked out from her own side of the cockpit at one of the ungainly-looking platforms, each somewhat larger than one of the U.S. Navy's CVNs had once been, which made up the ten-platform constellation known as Printer Five and marveled yet again at what their newfound technology could do. Mac-Quarie insisted on calling them "printers," which was how they were listed on the official manifest, and was actually the best description of what they did. Unlike pre-invasion human 3-D printers, however, these platforms printed on the *molecular* level, and so long as their materials banks were fed, any one of them could produce anything—anything at all—whose plan was in its memory. And it was probably inevitable that the official name for them should be challenged by the one most of McIlhenny's fellow pilots and drone supervisors applied. After all, what they did was a hell of a lot more like a Trekkie's replicator than any "printer" she'd ever seen!

She waited patiently while MacQuarie watched the construction drones putting the finishing touches on Refinery Five and wondered yet again what new roads *Homo sapiens* would explore in the years to come. It was hard enough to wrap her mind around how far her species had come in less than two years. Trying to visualize where they might go in the next century or two was more than she could even begin to imagine.

Except for one thing, Sheila McIlhenny thought, watching the growing muscle and sinew of planet Earth's industrial might. *One thing I know for damned sure is that the miserable bastards who sicced the Puppies on us aren't going to like it one frigging bit.*

Which, when she came right down to it, was all she really needed to know, now, wasn't it?

· XIX ·

Y ou wanted to make an entrance," the pilot said over the intercom as the
massive *Starlander* touched down on the wadi in northeastern Nigeria.
"I think it's safe to say we have."

The ramp in the back of the craft came down, and Abu Bakr bin Muhammed
el-Hiri could see dozens of men swarming around the craft. When the ramp hit
the sand, he strode down it, and, almost as one, all of them pointed their rifles
at him.

"Don't worry," Jasmine Sherman stage-whispered behind him. "If they
shoot you, I'll make sure I avenge you."

Abu Bakr raised an eyebrow at her over his shoulder. "I'm not sure what good
that will do *me*," he replied. "But I do thank you." He regretted, for a moment, not
accepting the "gift" of vampirism that had been offered him when Longbow had
been converted. While a huge part of him had wanted to cross over to the other
side, so that he could more fully harry the Shongari and drive them from Earth,
he'd decided his eternal soul was worth more to him in the end.

"No," he'd said. "This is *not* the way for me. This . . . this is a cheat. While it may
seem like a gift, I believe this is a gift from Satan so he can steal our souls." He'd
shrugged. "Maybe it's Allah's test—I don't know. Either way, though, while it
appears to give us what we want—the power to defeat the alien heathens—it
takes away that which is most important to me—my eternal soul." He'd shaken
his head with his final pronouncement. "No," he'd said, "if you do this to me,
you'll do it against my will, and I'll fight you tooth and nail to keep you from
turning me into one of . . . you."

"That's okay," Longbow had said. Abu Bakr had never seen his comrade in
arms as serious as he had been that day; even when surrounded by the Shongairi, Longbow had always remained upbeat. "I've got this one, Bro," he'd said.
"My soul doesn't mean all that much to me, in a lot of ways. I know yours does,
to you, and *one* of us should come out of this as the man he once was." And so
Longbow had nodded once, gone off with the vampires, and come back as one
of the soulless ones. Abu Bakr didn't love him less as a vampire—he'd fought
by his side too long to give him up that easily—but deep down, he believed the
vampires were . . . something *less* for having taken the easy way out.

Abu Bakr sighed, sure he'd made the right choice, even if it was the more dangerous one, and continued down the ramp towards the jeering men. Jasmine reached the ramp's midpoint behind him and sat down while he continued to the bottom.

"*Allahu Akbar!*" the only man without a rifle greeted him as he stepped off the ramp. "God certainly *is* great, for he has brought us this giant craft that we may use to spread our message anywhere we choose!"

All the men within hearing waved their rifles as they cheered his pronouncement.

"Have you come to join the cause?" the man asked.

"No," Abu Bakr replied. "Quite the opposite. I've come to bring you back to the path. Boko Haram was once a positive movement for our religion, but it is no more. Now it is just a force for terrorism—for giving *you* access to the pleasures of the flesh—and no longer for the betterment of the Faith."

"You talk about the pleasures of the flesh—our leaders have for too long known these vices. When leaders sin, it is the duty of Muslims to oppose those leaders and depose them. We have done so, and we continue to work towards a better world."

"By stealing schoolgirls and ransoming them or forcing them into marriage or worse? By using children for suicide bombings? By destroying villages and killing everyone who lives in them?"

The man shrugged. "Obviously, if they were not for us, then they were against us and off the path of the righteous. They needed to be destroyed. It is as Allah wills it."

"No, that isn't what Allah wills, nor is it what is right. I fought against the alien heathens to get our world back—a *world* of righteousness—and you are despoiling it with your actions. We—my government and I—are working to build a better world, where aliens from the stars can never come and make us their slaves, ever again."

"You are from the government, then?" the man asked. He turned to the other men. "He is from the government!" he exclaimed. "He will bring us a great ransom!"

"No." Abu Bakr didn't say it loudly, but he said it with such conviction the Boko Haram leader turned back to him.

"What did you say?" he asked in an evil tone.

"I said 'no'; you won't take me hostage, nor will you ransom me."

"And who will stop me? You?" The man laughed. "Your government?" He laughed harder, and was joined by many of his men. "We own the government here. In fact, we *are* the government. They pay us."

"No," Abu Bakr said, shaking his head. "I'm not going to stop you." He nodded up the ramp. "She is. Just as she'll stop you and anyone else who would seek to hold young women against their wills."

"Maybe we'll take her hostage and ransom her, too!" The men cheered. "Maybe we won't ransom her—maybe we will just use her and then kill her when we're done with her." The cheering grew even louder.

Abu Bakr smiled for the first time. "I'd really like to see you try."

"What? You don't think we will?"

"No; I don't think you *can*."

The man stepped back and nodded to two of his followers. "Akin, Mobo, go up there and bring her to me."

"With pleasure," Mobo said.

The two men handed their rifles to their neighbors and started up the ramp, grinning. Jasmine watched them with an expression of mild interest until they came within about two meters, then she flashed forward.

Akin and Mobo fell over backward, their torn-out throats fountaining blood. Jasmine seated herself on the ramp once more before most of the men even noticed she'd moved. She looked down at her right hand, then fastidiously wiped away a crimson stain.

And smiled.

There was a vast, ringing silence, and Abu Bakr stepped to the side to avoid the rivulet of blood working its way down the ramp.

"Those were your best warriors?" He shook his head. "You're going to need better ones than that, for my cause is pure and just, and my warriors will destroy *any* who oppose us."

The leader stepped up to Abu Bakr, and a knife appeared in his hand. He pressed the point against the American's neck.

"And what of you?" he asked in a harsh whisper. "What if I destroy you, first?"

"Oh, I think not," Abu Bakr replied calmly.

"And why n—"

Jasmine stood next to Abu Bakr, not a hair out of place, as the leader fell backward, his own knife buried in his chest. The crowd of men went silent as the man's corpse hit the ground. A flash of motion caught their eyes, and three more women appeared, standing where Jasmine had been sitting.

"What is your name, Holy One?" one of the men asked, going to a knee.

"My name is Abu Bakr bin Muhammed el-Hiri."

"I will follow the Wildcat, wherever he leads!" the man exclaimed.

"The Wildcat!" The rest of the men yelled, going to one knee. "Lead us!"

"Well," Abu Bakr said, turning to Jasmine with a smile. "That was easy."

· XX ·

REGINA, SASKATCHEWAN, CANADA

First, let me thank you again for agreeing to host our meeting, Mr. Prime Minister," Judson Howell said, looking around the polished table in the conference room that overlooked Legislative Drive. It was snowing again—or perhaps the word Dave Dvorak really wanted was *still*—and despite the conference room's warmth and the hot cup of coffee at his elbow, he was certain he felt a subliminal chill as icy wind roared softly across the Legislative Building's roof.

"You're most welcome, Mister President," Jeremiah Agamabichie replied gravely, then smiled. "And letting you borrow our facilities here seems reasonable enough, since it's your reactor in the basement powering the entire building!"

"No, it's yours. Or perhaps I should say *ours,* given the nature of our meeting. And while I'm thanking people, I especially thank you, President Garção. Not just for coming all the way from Bahia, but for the much appreciated gift you brought with you, as well." He touched the coffee cup at *his* elbow and smiled. "Secretary Dvorak and I had both been experiencing withdrawal symptoms—or, even worse, drinking *instant* coffee—before your arrival. I cannot begin to tell you how much getting the real stuff means to both of us." Chuckles circled the room, but then Howell's smile faded. "Seriously, I truly appreciate your coming to meet with us in person. I know it was a long flight."

"I suppose some might consider it so." Fernando Garção's English was excellent, although heavily accented. "It seemed less so in the *Starlander* you provided, however. I had not anticipated such comfortable accommodations. And the flight profile made it much shorter."

Which was true, Dvorak reflected. The *Starlander* was subsonic in atmosphere and it was almost six thousand miles from São Salvador to Regina. An atmospheric flight profile would have taken nearly eight and a half hours. But the same *Starlander* was capable of Mach 7 on a reentry profile, and its counter gravity could take it beyond atmosphere in less than seven minutes, so the actual flight time had been about forty-five minutes—less time than it had taken him to fly from Greenville to Atlanta back when Delta had still been hauling passengers.

"We've only diverted two of them to diplomatic duties," Howell said. "We really need more, but I hate pulling anything else out of the humanitarian lift effort." He shrugged. "As far as the 'accommodations' are concerned, at least it doesn't take the printers appreciably longer—or use up any more resources—to build a 'luxury model' to haul our august persons around."

"No doubt." Garção nodded. "It was a pleasant journey, however."

"I'm glad. Especially since I imagine all of us are about to find ourselves dealing with a lot of significantly less pleasant information. In fact, I'm afraid it's time for Secretary Dvorak to start sharing some of that less pleasant information with us."

Garção nodded again, his expression bleaker than it had been, and Dvorak drew a deep breath, rose, gathered up his coffee cup, and walked around to the podium at one end of the conference room. A proper Secretary of State, he supposed, would've had an appropriately senior flunky deliver the briefing. He saw no reason to be *that* proper, however, and with the IT services which were now available, the only excuse for having a flunky—for this briefing, at least—would have been to prove his own importance.

"Thank you, Mister President," he said, setting his coffee on the handy shelf built into the podium. "And allow me to add my own thanks to both you and President Garção, Mr. Prime Minister."

Agamabichie made a small waving away gesture, although all three heads of state knew the true reason they were meeting in Regina and not Greensboro. Assuming their efforts bore fruit, Greensboro—or some other location in the U.S.—would almost certainly become the future capital of their Continental Union. At this point in the process, anything they could do to undercut the inevitable protests that the U.S. had reassumed its habitual role of international puppet master with indecent speed was eminently worthwhile. Hopefully, holding this meeting in Regina—and, later, issuing the proclamation they intended to draft in São Salvador—would underscore the fact that Canada and Brazil were *partners* in the effort, not simple client states.

Yeah, lotsa luck with that one, Dave, he reflected dryly, even though the original suggestion had been his.

"Turning to the business at hand," he continued, removing his phone—and that was, indeed, what people had ended up calling them—from his pocket, "I'd like to begin with a few bits of *good* news."

He opened the phone and tapped the display, and the computer obediently dimmed the conference room's lights and activated the three-dimensional holographic projector which a crew of U.S. technicians had installed in the conference room's ceiling. A breathtakingly realistic view of the Earth appeared above the conference table, rotating slowly. The beautiful, cloud-banded blue gem was just under three feet in diameter, and a sense of awe which had not yet become routine flowed through him. He touched another icon, and the areas of the United States of America, Canada, and the Republic of Brazil superimposed themselves on the rotating planet in a sea of gleaming green light. That light covered eighty percent of North America, just over half of South America, and—altogether—over two thirds of the total land area of both continents.

It did not, however, cover *any* of Central America.

Yet, at least.

"The Continental Union's charter members, Gentlemen," Dvorak said. "Obviously, it's still early days and there are all sorts of legislative hurdles yet to be cleared, but I believe we can consider this what we in the United States call a 'done deal.' We're obviously still working on the exact wording of the new Constitution, but that seems to be going well, and Mister McCoury, Mister LaCree, and Ms. Araújo will submit a draft version this evening. It's been a . . . lively process."

All three heads of state chuckled.

Kent McCoury, who'd become Dvorak's Under Secretary for Political Affairs—and, God help him, he'd realized he actually *needed* one of those—was a few years younger than Dvorak himself. He was also a cross-grained, often ornery mountain boy from Johnson County, Tennessee. He was wiry and sharp featured, with black hair, a close cropped beard which somehow always seemed about to escape control, and a double doctorate in history and political science. He took a certain almost childlike delight in stepping on other people's political corns just to see how they'd react, and he cultivated an air of cynicism, but that cynicism was an imperfect mask for how deeply he actually cared.

Eduarda Araújo, Edson Soares' Assistant Minister of Foreign Affairs, was as dark-haired as McCoury, with almost equally sharp features, although they looked better on her than they did on him. She was very dark complexioned, only about five feet three, with a fiery temper. She was also fiercely proud of the job her president had done and determined that no one was going to step on *her* country. One would have expected that to make her a natural ally for Adam LaCree's efforts to build in every possible safeguard to prevent the U.S. from totally dominating the proposed Continental Union, but Brazil's ninety-eight million citizens would be a far better match for the estimated 110 million surviving U.S. citizens. In fact, Brazil was clearly the second most powerful of the three nations currently involved. On the other hand. . . .

"Another bit of potentially *very* good news," Dvorak continued, "is that even though King Henry decided he couldn't leave Bristol at this time, his Government—and especially Foreign Secretary O'Leary—has been in close communication with Prime Minister Agamabichie and President Howell. And while Bristol isn't ready to announce it just yet, three other Commonwealth nations have indicated that they're prepared to join us: the U.K. itself, Australia, and New Zealand." He tapped the face of his phone again, and the three nations he'd named pulsed a lighter shade of green. "He believes most of the rest of the

Commonwealth will be inclined to join in the future, but at the moment, none of the other member states have sufficiently intact national governments. The situation is particularly bad just now in the Indian subcontinent and South Africa."

Any hint of levity disappeared with his last sentence.

What the Shongairi had done to India had been bad enough. New Delhi, Mumbai, Calcutta, Bangalore, and Hyderabad had disappeared in the first wave of KEWs, taking almost ninety million Indians with them. Staggering as that total was, it had represented little more than seven percent of India's total population, but it had dealt a savage blow to the union government . . . and it had been only the *first* blow. According to the Shongairi's own records, the sheer numbers of humans in India had frightened them, given the rate of attrition their occupation forces were suffering elsewhere. That had become especially true after the organized uprising in China, however, and no one had ever accused the Puppies of excessive restraint. They'd apparently decided it would be a good idea to prune back India preemptively, before it followed China's example. The resultant second wave of KEWs had been devastating . . . and then, with both nations' central governments destroyed, what was left of Pakistan and what was left of India had apparently decided to settle their longstanding, pre-invasion animosities once and for all. And just to make a horrific situation still worse, it turned out that both India and Pakistan had possessed nuclear gravity bombs the Shongairi had missed. Two of them had been trucked into India from Pakistan and taken out Amritsar and Ludhiana.

That had *truly* alarmed the Shongairi. True, the humans were using them on each other, but nothing guaranteed things would stay that way, so they'd applied yet *another* layer of KEWs to the entire subcontinent. The third wave had eliminated every urban agglomerate—indeed, virtually every individual city with a population above a hundred thousand—and pretty much finished off anything like cohesive government—or society—in the region.

It was fortunate that so much of the Indian and Pakistani population had been rural, but not even that had been able to prevent unspeakable death tolls, especially when religious and ethnic 'cleansing' became part of the horror show which had engulfed one of the most populous areas on the face of the planet. Bangladesh had essentially ceased to exist, and by their current estimates, the population of the shattered region which had once been India was no more than two hundred million. That was a huge number by the standards of most nations, but it represented less than fifteen percent of the pre-invasion population. And Pakistan had suffered even more heavily at Shongair hands, partly because it had possessed a higher percentage of urbanization, which had put a higher proportion of its people into the first-wave KEWs' crosshairs, but mostly because the Shongairi had realized the origin of the Amritsar and Ludhiana bombs and paid the country special attention in its third wave of strikes. Perhaps as many as twenty-three million of Pakistan's pre-invasion two hundred million citizens were still alive.

And, as if to prove that nothing was so horrible that it couldn't be made still worse, the Shongair strikes had savaged the urban, richer, better educated, and more tolerant sectors of both countries. Too many of those who remained—especially in the mountains of Pakistan, where survival rates had been highest—could scarcely have been *less* tolerant, and fanatics on each side blamed the *humans* on the other side for all of their agony.

The Shongairi's withdrawal had only made bad worse by removing the occupying force which had gone after any concentration of armed humans, regardless of whether those humans were shooting at them or at other humans. Even that restraint had disappeared now, and there were still plenty of weapons available for humans determined to slaughter one another in the name of God or simple vengeance.

Every person in that conference room felt a desperate need to intervene—to do *something* in the face of such slaughter—but the carnage was too widespread, too bitter, and too deeply ingrained. There were literally thousands of individual leaders and warlords—far too many for even Pieter Ushakov and his vampires to find a vital individual or group to neutralize. It would have taken an army of vampires to make a dent in the madness, and they had less than a hundred of them, all told. God only knew where the carnage was going to end, how long that would take, or what would be left when it finally burned itself out.

And then there was South Africa.

The Shongair bombardment had destroyed all three South African capital cities—Pretoria, Bloemfontein, and Cape Town—in the initial wave. Fortunately, then-Prince Harry and his family had been in Johannesburg that day, and their security detail had gotten them out of the city before the second-wave KEWs arrived. In all, South Africa had lost perhaps a quarter of its fifty-six million citizens in the first week of the invasion, and, much as in India and Pakistan, the massive casualties had exposed the ugly underside of the ethnic and racial animosities the country had worked so long and so hard to resolve. Tribal, as well as racial, hatreds had driven the bloodshed and largely finished off the authority of any surviving national government. It looked as if calmer heads were finally starting to prevail, however, and there were indications that the bloodshed had burned out—or, perhaps, burned *up*—the most hate-filled elements. It would be a while before South Africa as a nation was prepared to join any new world governments, yet if the current trend lines held, that might very well change within the next year or so.

Australia and New Zealand, on the other hand, had taken far lighter losses from the Shongairi, at least in absolute terms. Canberra, Sydney, Melbourne, and Adelaide were lost in the first wave of strikes, taking with them nearly half the total Australian population, but there'd been very few secondary strikes, and New Zealand had escaped almost unscathed. Between them, they still mustered almost seventeen million citizens, which was a higher percentage of their pre-invasion populations than almost anywhere else on the planet.

Despite that, unfortunately, the Shongair decapitating stroke had been even more successful in Australia than most places outside the United States. The prime minister, his cabinet, and the governor-general had all been in Canberra, trying to cope with the implications of the unprecedented, world-wide computer hack which had been the first phase of the Shongairi's attack. Parliament had been in session, as well, while the Joint Committee for Intelligence and Security pondered the same information, which had put all of the federal government neatly into a single crosshair. The good news, such as it was, was that the state and territorial governments had survived much closer to intact, and the Shongairi had seemed content to let the huge island stew in its own juices until they had secured control of the rest of the planet. As a consequence, Australia was reassembling itself even more rapidly than the United States and needed less outside assistance than most while it did so.

Malaysia should have been an even brighter story.

It wasn't.

Kuala Lumpur, Seberang Perai, and George Town were part of the grim totals of the first-wave KEWs, but the best estimates were that twenty-two million—almost seventy percent of its pre-invasion population—had survived the strikes. There'd been an unfortunate tendency to slide into warlordism among the survivors, however, and long-simmering religious tensions had flared into ugly, violent life. The death rate was lower than that in the subcontinent, but that was about the only good thing to be said of it. No one knew how long it was going to take for something like stability to return or what that stability was going to be like. No one expected it to return anytime soon, however, and some of the early indications suggested the emergence of an even stricter and less tolerant variety of Islam. In particular, many of the imams were demonstrating a strain of Luddite thinking, casting the Shongairi as Allah's punishment on Western ways and technology, which scarcely seemed promising for the future. Worse, the same sort of conflict had spilled over into Indonesia—especially on Borneo—and the southern Philippines. All in all, the situation didn't look good, and given the poisonous religious component in the strife, inserting *vampires* into that mix seemed . . . strongly contraindicated, just at the moment.

Dvorak shoved that thought back into its cubbyhole. He was sure it would crawl out again—probably when he was trying to get to sleep—but for now he had more pressing matters.

"According to Foreign Secretary O'Leary, it's very likely the Republic of Ireland will be joining along with the rest of the U.K. In fact, we should end up with all of Great Britain, although she says some of the Scots are being—I believe her exact words were 'bloody difficult'—about it." He quirked a brief smile, then sobered again. "We already knew the U.K. had been hit badly, but I'm afraid it was even worse than we'd thought. Foreign Secretary O'Leary estimates the current population at no more than twenty-seven million."

Someone inhaled sharply, although, to be fair, that was about forty percent of the pre-invasion population, which was a higher percentage of survivors than in other places . . . like China and India.

Or, for that matter, the United States of America.

"On the other hand, the Foreign Secretary's informed us that the King believes it might be wiser to delay any announcement that the U.K. or Australia and New Zealand intend to join the Union." President Garção's eyebrows rose in surprise, and Dvorak shook his head quickly. "I don't think there's any doubt about his ultimate intentions. It's more a matter of timing, and, frankly, I think he's right."

Garção frowned slightly, and Dvorak understood at least part of what was probably bothering him. The Brazilian, Howell, and Agamabichie all agreed that the Continental Union had to hit the ground running, and adding three more nations to the original ratifiers of the Union Constitution, especially spread so broadly around the globe, would have to help in that direction.

"The King's feeling is that while our ultimate goal has to be to create a *planetary* union, and while there's a great deal to be said for striking while the iron is hot, there's also a great deal to be said for growing the ultimate union as . . . organically as possible. For letting it, as Foreign Secretary O'Leary put it, coalesce out of the chaos rather than take on the form of something imposed upon the world. And, as the King pointed out to the Foreign Secretary, Australia, New Zealand, and the U.K. are all primarily English-speaking nations who, despite the vast geographic distances between them, are generally perceived as part of the white, Anglo-Saxon world. To be blunt, it's King Henry's view that it will be far better for us to begin as the *Continental* Union President Howell first envisioned, with as many of our South American neighbors onboard as possible, before 'overloading' the new edifice with those same white Anglo-Saxons. If India and South Africa—even Nigeria—were better positioned to ratify the new Constitution at this time, it might make sense to move directly towards the Planetary Union. As it is, I think His Majesty has a pretty fair point."

And, interestingly enough, it would seem that it was, indeed, *His Majesty's* point. Dvorak very much doubted that Prince Henry Charles Albert David had ever expected to become King Henry IX, especially after his and his wife's decision to remove themselves from the U.K. and "step back" from their royal duties, but now that he had the job, he intended to do it. He'd returned to Bristol as quickly as he could, sneaking back onto the island by small craft while the Shongairi were still interdicting air travel, and judging by the firm, no-nonsense approach he'd taken where warlords and looters were concerned, he clearly hadn't wasted his time in the Army. He'd been forced to walk a fine line between restoring local order and provoking a Shongair intervention, but he'd managed to keep his balance. In terms of organized, functional infrastructure, North Carolina was still well ahead of the U.K., but Great Britain was making up for lost time under the King's energetic leadership. And, given the way most citizens of the U.K. had come to regard the youthful monarch who'd done so much to bring some sort of order out of chaos, it seemed likely the Crown was going to be rather more actively engaged in shaping British policies than it had been.

It sure as hell had been this far, at any rate.

President Garção's frown had eased as he digested Henry's reasoning. Now he nodded, but his expression remained troubled.

"As the president of one of those South American neighbors, I heartily approve," he said. "The problem is which of my fellow South American countries we nominate."

"Venezuela is . . . not a promising prospect," Dvorak replied, and Garção's nostrils flared. The arrival of the Shongairi—and the destruction of Caracas, Maracaibo, and Barquisimeto—had finished toppling "the Sick Man of South America" into a black hole that appeared bottomless. "The situation there has spilled over into eastern Colombia, as well, but despite that, it appears Colombia is probably a more promising proposition. Unfortunately, they're still trying to put their national government back together, and we haven't had much luck getting into contact with it at this time. Peru took an awful pasting along the coast, and it was the middle of their winter when they got hit. President Izquierdo is making a lot of progress, and we're providing as much humanitarian aid as possible, but it's going to be at least another eighteen months before he could even consider something this significant. Ecuador and Bolivia are in better shape than Peru physically, but politically—" He shook his head. "We don't have anyone in either of those countries who can speak for more than a few thousand people, and this has to be something that's done on a national basis if it's going to have any legitimacy going forward."

All three heads of state nodded gravely at that. That was another reason *they* were the ones beginning this.

More and more local governments in the shattered United States were acknowledging Howell's legitimacy as president. It would be entirely too long before the nation's physical infrastructure could catch up with its political infrastructure, but something that was still recognizably the United States of

America was emerging from the ruins. There were still places where anarchy governed, and it was likely military force would be required to sort out quite a few of them, but no one seemed to doubt any longer that they *would* be sorted out.

Agamabichie and Garção had smaller populations, but both of them had been the legal successors—through a somewhat strained procedure in Agamabichie's case, perhaps—to their dead heads of state. That gave them a degree of legitimacy that was simply lacking in places like Bolivia or—even worse—Venezuela, where it was very much a matter of every man for himself, bullets counted far more than ballots, and God help the hindermost.

"We're not sure about Argentina," Dvorak continued. "Ancieta Montalván seems to have some serious reservations about how close she wants to get to us. That could be a problem."

"How great a problem?" Agamabichie asked.

"Well, as Vice-President and President of the Senate, she was clearly President Salcedo's legal successor when Buenos Aires got hit, so she's got a lot of legitimacy," Dvorak replied. "And so far as we can tell, she's doing a damn good job of putting things back together. They're down to about sixteen million people, and it's taking her longer than I'm sure she'd like to reestablish the federal authority, but starvation was never a big problem for them. They had more problems with the winter weather, frankly. But Jorge Medrano—he's the Navy commodore who's become Minister of Defense—doesn't much like or trust the United States, and it sounds like he has a lot of influence with her. Hopefully, that's not going to be an insurmountable problem in the long term, but at the moment, it clearly is. The good news is that we think he's an honest, forthright fellow who just doesn't like us very much, so we're hoping we'll be able to change his mind in that regard in time. Or that's the way it looks from here, anyway."

"I met President Montalván before the *demônios,* although I'm not certain she would remember it," Garção said. "She is a determined woman, and one who thinks for herself. I very much doubt that anyone's influence with her would be strong enough to overcome her own judgment."

"That's our feeling as well, Mister President. It's just that like too many of us, right this minute she has a little too much on her hands to be worrying about new supranational constitutions."

"And then there is Mexico." Garção sighed.

Mexico had become, in many ways, the Americas' South Africa, although for rather different reasons. The cartels had seen their opportunity . . . and taken it. The Cartel de Jalisco Nueva Generacion had actually negotiated a deal with the Shongairi, acting as the Puppies' local enforcers in Colima, Guerrero, and Michoacán. None of the others had been quite as blatant as the CJNG, but all of them had possessed copious stores of military-grade weapons, and they'd seen the invasion primarily as an opportunity to increase their own power. With the collapse of the Federal authority after the initial KEW strikes, Mexico had disintegrated into feudal territories ruled over by the druglords who ran the cartels.

"Yes, there is, Mister President," Dvorak agreed. "The good news is that in part because of the CJNG, Mexico's total casualties were actually lower than they might've been. The Puppies had more pressing problems elsewhere, so they were content to let the cartels—who, unlike Pakistan or India, at least didn't have nuclear weapons—finish off the last vestiges of the Federal authority. After all, the process simply divided the country into smaller, more readily digestible bites under the control of humans who'd at least indicated they were willing to 'be reasonable' by Shongair standards.

"I rather suspect—" his thin smile was remarkably unpleasant "—that they eventually began to realize that the cartels' 'submission' was just a *bit* less genuine than they'd thought, but it did mitigate the death toll. And while conditions in Mexico are pretty horrible just now, at least there are still a lot of people living there. We estimate there are around sixty or seventy million Mexican citizens, and they took over half their total casualties in the initial kinetic strike. So once we can . . . neutralize the cartels, we should be able to find Mexican partners who can help us both reconstitute their country and turn it into another South American candidate for the Continental Union."

"No one could be happier than I if that were to prove possible, Mister Dvorak," Garção said, but his expression was profoundly doubtful. "Unfortunately, the one thing the cartels and the *traficantes* have proven over the years is how extraordinarily difficult to 'neutralize' they are."

"You're quite right about that, Mister President," Dvorak agreed, but his smile had turned even thinner and more unpleasant. "On the other hand, no one else ever sent them a . . . negotiating team quite like the one *we're* planning to send."

GREENSBORO, NORTH CAROLINA,
UNITED STATES

Longbow walked into the conference room and sighed as he looked around, then took a seat at the very back of the room. Several generals already sat around the main table at the front, and he avoided making eye contact with any of them. Having already spoken with some of the staffers, he knew what the meeting was about; he also knew there were things he would probably be asked to do that he wouldn't—no, that he *couldn't*—do. He expected the meeting to be contentious, at least from his perspective, and he would have skipped it . . . if President Howell hadn't asked him to be there.

A minor clamor announced the arrival of the official party, and everyone stood as the President and General Landers entered and were seated at the table.

"Seats, please, everyone," President Howell said, and Longbow fell back into his chair. The President waved for the young lieutenant at the podium to begin, and the man pressed a button on his panel.

A tridee hologram illuminated, displaying his presentation, and the lieutenant cleared his throat before beginning.

"Good morning, Mister President. This presentation will cover our recommendations for the creation of the Continental Union Armed Forces. Despite the plural noun 'forces,' what we're actually recommending is a single, unified force structure. Unlike the separate services we had in the past, a single chain of command will administrate all of our military efforts. We simply don't have the time, resources, or even the personnel to waste on internecine arguments. A single decision-maker—the Chief of Staff of the Armed Forces—will oversee the operations of this unified force structure, and he or she will ensure the effective and efficient allocation of resources across the entire force.

"Underneath the Chief of Staff, there will be a number of components, each of which will oversee their respective domains. The combat components will be: the Continental Union Ground Force, Continental Union Air Force, and Continental Union Navy.

"The Ground Force, led by the Commanding General of the Ground Force, will be responsible for sustained combat on planetary bodies," the lieutenant said. "Obviously, at the moment that means Earth, but eventually it will extend to other system bodies, such as Mars, or the Moon. Essentially, wherever a piece of ground needs to be defended, it will be Ground Force's responsibility."

He flipped a slide.

"The next component," he continued, "the Air Force, led by the Commanding General of the Air Force, will fly and fix fighters and bombers. Period. Unlike the Air Force of old, it will no longer have to transport people or worry about ground-based combat systems, like the old ICBMs. It just flies combat aircraft, whether those are air-breathing, operating from planets, or exo-atmospheric, operating from bases or ships in space."

He flipped another slide.

"Those exo-atmospheric ships will be operated by the Continental Union Navy, under the Commanding General of the Navy, with the missions of controlling space and transporting the other services through space to where they're needed. It hasn't yet been determined whether the command of orbital or deep space defensive installations will fall under the Navy or the Ground Force. There are arguments in favor of either, but the critical point is that the Navy no longer has aircraft or terrestrial ships; it has spaceships."

The lieutenant paused, looking at the President, and Howell nodded in understanding of the distinction.

"You'll notice I said, 'Commanding General of the Navy,' Mister President," the lieutenant said then. "In the interests of standardization and harmonization with other nations' militaries, we've done away with the previous naval-based rank names. There will be a single set of ranks, from the highest 'General' to the lowest 'Private.' That also lets us standardize a variety of uniform devices and insignias. The fewer things we have to print, the faster we can get them into operation so we can concentrate our energies on the things that really matter—protecting our new nation and, ultimately, our entire world."

"Makes sense," the President said with another nod.

"Within the Ground Force, there will be two subcomponents," the lieutenant went on. "We considered separating them completely, but decided that they would require commonality of equipment and basic training doctrine, although with rather different emphases. The first, the Defense Force, is exactly what its name implies: the defensive component, oriented towards protecting our own territory, possessions, and populations. The second is the expeditionary force. In fact, that was its original designation, but after a certain amount of internal discussion, we are *provisionally* suggesting that it be called the Space Marines, instead."

The lieutenant looked less than delighted by that, for some reason, Dave Dvorak reflected, managing—with difficulty—to hide his glee behind an attentive, focused expression. Damn. He'd always known Rob was stubborn, but still. . . .

"The Space Marines," the lieutenant continued, with only the slightest grimace, "are the subcomponent that takes things from our enemies, whether those are bases on their planets or ships in space. They will form an aggressive, expeditionary assault force that operates its own combat assault shuttles. If we want to hold on to an enemy's territory afterward, that will be a job for the Defense Force, which will operate bases that control territory. While the Defense Force can also capture territory, its primary mission isn't forced entry; that falls to the Marines. Both the Defense Force and the Marines operate under the orders of the Commanding General of the Ground Force—again, to ensure commonality of training and equipment—but each will have its own commanding general, reporting to the Commanding General of the Ground Force.

"The glue that holds all this together is the first of two new support services: Supply. The Commanding General of Supply is responsible for the effective utilization of resources in our printers and the distribution of products and personnel throughout the other services. Supply also operates the shuttles that carry those things—exclusive of the Expeditionary Force's assault shuttles—which removes the logistics missions of both the Air Force and the Navy by combining them into one."

"What about the wet-navy?" the President asked. "You said the Navy controls the ships in space. Who controls the terrestrial ships?"

"No one," General Landers replied. "Quite simply, they aren't needed. As the Puppies demonstrated, they're a concept that's out of date. When the Shongairi arrived, they destroyed every warship operating at sea. Every single one. Submarines lasted longer, but eventually they had to surface, and then they were targeted by KEWs. The subs that attempted to launch nuclear missiles were the first to be destroyed, right after the missiles they'd launched. If you hold the planet's orbitals, you can control their seaborne forces. There's no need to go down to their oceans to do battle with them."

The lieutenant giving the presentation held up a hand, and the general acknowledged him.

"We foresee that there will still be a need for a small, planet-based Coast Guard that does customs enforcement and antipiracy, but we're envisioning that as primarily a law enforcement function. Anytime they need a big stick, they can call it down from the forces in orbit; they won't have to provide it themselves."

The President nodded, and the lieutenant continued.

"The other new support service, Training, will be responsible for the indoctrination of new personnel. There won't be a need for huge training bases as in the past; with the Puppies' neural educators, it will be more a matter of finding and selecting the appropriate training modules, and then applying them during the indoctrination process.

"In order to make this work, ensuring a recruit's ability to be neurally educated will be a large part of the recruitment process. In the past, some personnel were excluded from military service due to physical limitations like being color blind; part of the new physical will be to ensure recruits are able to use the neural educators. Those recruits who aren't able to be neurally educated will be excluded from military service."

The President turned to General Landers. "Is it wise to exclude people who want to serve, simply because they aren't able to use neural educators?"

"We may, in the future, relax that requirement somewhat," Landers replied, "since there are some tasks that don't require a high level of technical knowledge; however, we feel it's important to implement that restriction at least for the time being. It's a simple matter of expediency—there aren't many pre-invasion military people left, and we need new personnel who are quickly trainable, and who can be quickly retrained to fill new positions that come up unexpectedly. One of our biggest needs right now is pilots, and using a traditional training approach is infeasible—we don't have the time, personnel, or resources required. We need them *now,* without having to spend two years instructing them on trainer aircraft we'd have to divert resources to build, using flight instructors who currently don't exist. Using the educators, we can also give our recruits training in secondary skills they may need to better fulfill their primary mission areas."

"That makes sense," the President replied. He nodded to the lieutenant. "Please continue."

"That leaves the final service," the lieutenant said, "the Special Forces."

Longbow sighed. This was the topic he'd been dreading.

The lieutenant continued, "This service will have the missions of doing the things the other forces can't, and assisting in the assault of enemy positions, ships, and planets. While there will be normal personnel operating within this component, Major Torino and his . . . forces will be a second branch within it."

"No," Longbow said, shaking his head. He didn't raise his voice, particularly, but somehow it sounded very, very loud. He didn't much like what he knew was coming, but he simply couldn't force himself to accept that tasking, no matter how much he tried, and he *had* tried. But despite his dedication to the U.S. Air Force and to his country, despite the fact that he knew he *ought* to accept it, he couldn't. Not anymore. Just being inside a formal command structure raised his hackles, and that bothered him, because he didn't understand why. In the end, though, "why" mattered a lot less than "what."

"We've been through this," he added as all heads turned in his direction. "The vampires won't be part of this. Vlad left us here to assist the President, not to be subsumed into the military."

"While the Jones girls aren't military, per se," General Landers said, turning to stare pointedly at Longbow, "you and Captain Ushakov quite specifically *are* military members, *Major.* For that matter, so is Petty Officer Sherman. Are you saying your oath is no longer valid, and that you'll no longer follow the orders of the officers appointed over you?"

While some part of Longbow's psyche wanted to follow those orders, that part seemed a distant memory—something ephemeral—while the rest of him wanted—no, the rest of him *needed*—to protect and do the bidding of the President.

"I'm sorry, Sir," he said after a moment of introspection, "but what I'm saying is that my loyalties are directly to the President, not to the military chain of command, and I need to follow his direction."

The President looked at Longbow, his brows knitting.

"While that's nice," he said after a moment, "and it certainly makes me feel secure, the military needs your services more than I do." He held up a hand to forestall Longbow when he started to speak. "I'm not saying I won't need them in the future, but for now, you're one of the few surviving military officers on this planet. I need you to help rebuild and realign the military."

The President waved towards the presentation, then continued, "There will be people who are . . . reluctant to make the changes the Lieutenant just briefed, and you'll carry a lot of weight with folks like that. I imagine *any* vampire would be . . . a fairly convincing spokesman, but you're also the guy who made ace in a single afternoon shooting down Puppies in air-to-air combat. You think that won't weigh on a few minds if *you* sign off on all this?"

Longbow frowned. He always felt ambivalent when someone brought up what the resurgent news services had dubbed "the Battle of Virginia." Especially when they gave him all the credit for it, as if none of his other three pilots had even been there! Damn it, they were the ones who'd died, and—

"I need you to rejoin the military and help General Landers implement these changes," the President continued. "You've proven your worth time and again, and I know that if I need you, I only have to call." He held up one of the new phones. "With this, I can reach you at a moment's notice, and with the new Shongair landers we're building, you can be anywhere on the planet in a matter of hours to take care of whatever needs to be handled. Until that time, though, my orders are for you to assist the General in implementing the new service."

Longbow suddenly felt as if a weight had been lifted from his heart—as if the restraints keeping him from doing what he thought right had been suddenly removed.

"Okay," he agreed. "In that case, I guess I'm able to participate in the new Special Forces. I'll warn you, though—I may have been on the ground during most of the war, but my experience is primarily in flying fighter aircraft, not conducting Special Forces missions."

"That won't be a problem," the general said, tapping his forehead. "We have some of the finest neural educators around that can get you up to speed in a number of areas, very quickly. You'll also have a staff of experts who can give you advice going forward and help you adjust to your new duties."

"Staff?" Longbow asked, sensing a trap.

"Of course," General Landers replied. "Didn't anyone tell you? I'm recommending you for promotion and then to fill the position of Commanding General of the Special Forces. It will only be a brigadier general's position, at first, but there will be an opportunity to expand the position once we begin to fill out the ranks."

"Commanding General?" Longbow asked. His shoulders slumped at the number of meetings and presentations implicit in that tasking and the hundreds—no, the *thousands*—of hours of paperwork entailed. All he could hope for was that something, somewhere—*anywhere!*—would get out of hand so he could get out of the office for some fieldwork. Although he didn't particularly feel any great urge to kill people, despite what the vampire legends said, after that much paperwork, he might be willing to make an exception. "I'm just a fighter pilot, Sir . . ."

"Oh, don't worry, General," Landers replied, "It won't be as bad as all that."

"It won't?"

"No," Landers said with an evil grin. "It will probably be worse."

"Ugh."

"Still . . ." The general's smile warmed slightly as he took pity on the younger officer. "There *will* be opportunities to try out the new space fighters we'll be implementing . . ."

"Fighters?" Longbow's head popped up and his eyes brightened. "I wouldn't mind getting my hands on one of those."

The general nodded. "Yes, we'll need space fighters . . . eventually. We really don't need fighters—or bombers, by the way—at the moment, though; we need transports, and as many of them as we can print."

"Oh," Longbow said, sighing as his gaze fell to the floor.

"That said," General Landers noted, his smile widening, "we *will* have to print out a few of the models to see what works best for us, and we're going to need some test pilots to run them through their paces. Since test pilots are in short supply right now—especially ones who're nearly indestructible—there just *might* be some additional work for an enterprising former fighter pilot in the days ahead. . . ."

Longbow squared his shoulders and sat up straight. "Okay, Sir, I'm in."

"Now that that's settled," President Howell said, "who are the Jones girls you mentioned?"

"They're one of the . . . intervention teams," Longbow said, reluctant to discuss them in front of the group. "They were brought over by Vlad in the final days of the war. They were . . . dancers, shall we say, in Las Vegas before the war. When the KEWs started falling, they tried to work their way east, but got picked up by a Puppy patrol and incarcerated. They were used for some experimentation by the Puppies and were slated for extermination, but Vlad got there first. And since Vlad is big on redemption, he brought them over."

"They're good at their jobs?" President Howell asked.

"Yes, Sir," Longbow said. "They worked together, before, and they're very much a team, even if one of them needs watching . . ."

· XXII ·

MANZANILLO, COLIMA, MEXICO

Iván López Cervantes, head of the Cartel de Jalisco Nueva Generacion, looked up from the movie playing on his computer as a voice began yelling loudly in the outer office. Happily, the video was between the interesting parts, and the dialogue wasn't what he was watching it for, anyway. The yelling ceased suddenly, with the sound of an open-handed slap, and Cervantes went back to the movie, sure the matter had been handled appropriately.

The picture quality was getting to be quite good, Cervantes saw, since they had hired the new producer from Los Angeles. He didn't know where his men had found the producer, nor how the sniveling *bribón* had survived the upheavals in California after the aliens' arrival, but the man knew how to direct a film. Some of the camera angles he used were nothing short of stunning.

It didn't hurt, of course, that the movie had some of the prettiest actresses Cervantes had ever seen, and this one was more flexible than he would have thought humanly possible. He shrugged; it never ceased to amaze him how far some people would go to get their next hit of crack. Regardless, he was sure the woman's family would pay great sums of money to make sure the movie never surfaced, and that the movie would make even more once it was released anyway after the payment had been received. People like that idiot Ercilla could say what they wanted about how useless money was after what *los Cachorros* had done to the world, but there were certain immutable truths which had never failed Iván López Cervantes, and one was that there would always be *something* to be used for money. In fact, from all reports, the *norteamericanos* were putting their country back together again. That would be nice. They would certainly see to it that *their* money regained its value . . . and they had always been the cartels' best customers.

On the other hand, Ercilla had a point about the way market conditions had changed. The pool of crackheads and junkies north of the border had been pruned back badly, and there was practically no demand for cocaine, heroin, or even meth these days. But that was all right, too. First, because *norteamericanos* were *norteamericanos,* which meant demand for the cartels' traditional products would recover with time. And also because another of those immutable truths was that product of *some* sort would always flow north and money would always flow south, and that was the way it should be. One simply had to find the proper product at the proper time.

Diversification. It was the wave of the future and how he intended to not only grow the CJNG's business in Mexico, but throughout the entire southwest of the North American continent. *Los Cachorros* had been stupid enough to actually take out the leadership of some of the other cartels to improve Cervantes' "loyal ally" position here in Mexico. Now that they'd departed to the stars once more, though, leaving a total vacuum in their wake, the possibilities for a man who controlled his own well-trained army were limitless.

Before he could get back into the movie, a rap sounded on the door.

"Come in!" he called in English, recognizing the knock.

"Sorry to interrupt, Sir," James Lohrman said, coming into the room, "but there's been a sighting." The former British SAS member stood an inch over six feet, with dark hair and a physique women loved and normal men didn't have the time, energy, or discipline to acquire. Cervantes had always regarded his decision to hire the special forces operator away from the Sinaloas as one of his better decisions. And he'd been even more convinced of that since the other cartel leaders had begun to go missing. As someone who'd specialized in anti-hijacking and counter-terrorism operations as a member of the SAS' special projects team, Lohrman knew how strike forces thought when trying to apprehend—or kill—their targets, which made him the perfect choice to figure out how to counter any such effort targeting Cervantes.

"A sighting?" Cervantes asked.

"Yes, Sir," Lohrman replied, emphasizing the last word the way the British military did. "One of the Shongair shuttles just set down about a mile away."

"A Shongair shuttle? I thought *los Cachorros* left?" Cervantes asked. "Have they returned?"

"No, Sir. We believe that someone—perhaps the United States, which seems to have acquired several of them—is using them to deploy their forces. We had word that one was sighted just prior to the takedown of the Tijuana Cartel. A Shongair shuttle was seen in the vicinity of their headquarters . . . and then nothing was heard from them again. A nearby farmer says he heard what sounded like a major battle, and when he finally went to check later, everyone in the compound had been slaughtered."

"And you're not going to allow that to happen here."

"No, Sir, I am not." Cervantes appreciated the certainty in the British man's voice, although with some skepticism—how do you know for sure, until you see the nature of the enemy?

"That's what you hired me for," Lohrman added. "If you'd like to bring up the closed circuit TV on your computer, we can follow along." He crossed the room to look over Cervantes' shoulder and caught a flash of the movie before Cervantes could switch the monitor to the security camera system. "Nubile little minx," he added.

"Focus," Cervantes growled.

"Yes, Sir," Lohrman replied. He cleared his throat. "If you would bring up Camera One, Sir."

Cervantes switched the monitor to the indicated camera and was given a view of the road leading to the hacienda. Since he'd hired Lohrman, the road had been bulldozed and repaved to make the last half kilometer of blacktop a straight line into the compound, with the foliage cleared off ten feet on either side. The sun had just set, but the monitoring system's low-light capabilities were top of the line, and the sky wasn't yet fully dark; he could easily see the military-style truck about a quarter of a kilometer from the hacienda's gates.

"Are you expecting visitors?" Lohrman asked.

"No," Cervantes replied, the first bits of doubt worming their way up his spine. "I don't have anyone coming tonight."

"Permission to engage?"

"Yes!" Cervantes exclaimed. "Do it!"

"Take it out," Lohrman said into his microphone.

The men at the watchtowers had obviously been prepared for the order—less than two seconds later, two missiles blasted through the camera's field of view, their rocket motors momentarily blinding the camera. Before the image could clear, the missiles hit the truck, detonating in a bloom that completely whited-out the screen.

"What was that?" Cervantes asked.

"LAHAT," Lohrman said. "Israeli laser homing antitank missiles. My lads and I brought a few along when you engaged our services. One of the few tank rounds you don't need a tank gun to operate. You can shoot them out of a 105-millimeter recoilless rifle, which is what my men just did. They're supposed to have a ninety-five percent probability of kill."

"Not a hundred percent?"

"That's why we used two," Lohrman said with a smile. "Just to be sure."

After a few moments, the fire engulfing the truck began to die down, and the camera returned to semi-normalcy, although the center remained a solid mass of white.

Which made it easy to see the three figures walking towards the hacienda as they silhouetted themselves against the fire behind them.

"Your missiles killed the truck, but it doesn't appear they were completely effective against its passengers," Cervantes noted.

"They must have jumped out right before the missiles hit," Lohrman said. "That's the only way they could have survived that." He shook his head. "Still, they don't look injured . . ." He leaned over Cervantes' shoulder to get a closer look at the monitor. "They almost look like women."

"They must have been hiding in the bushes," Cervantes scoffed. "There's no way anyone survived that explosion." He shrugged. "Still, we have enough junkies at the hacienda for tonight's activities; we don't need any more. Kill them, just in case."

"You're the boss," Lohrman said, with zero remorse. Cervantes smiled at the reply; he didn't like being second guessed. Lohrman muttered into his microphone, and Cervantes could hear the big .50 caliber machine guns in the watch towers firing, even through the main building's thick walls.

The women kept walking—sauntering, really, Cervantes thought—despite the tracers zipping past them on the monitor.

"Who trained your men?" he demanded. "Darth Vader? Even Imperial storm troopers should be able to hit three women just walking towards them!"

"*I* trained them," Lohrman said, his voice grim. "They're better shots than that. Something's fucked up." He muttered into his com system, then asked, "Could you switch to Camera Two, please?"

The women reached the gate and three of his men stepped out of the guardhouse just inside it to meet them. The leader—Carlos Melzi, Lohrman's second-in-command—held a pistol on the dark-haired woman in the middle, while the other two aimed Tavor assault rifles at the group. The women walked up to the gate, blurred for a moment, then continued strolling casually forward . . . *but now they were inside the chain link fence!*

"Shoot them!" Lohrman yelled at the screen. He pushed his microphone button and yelled it again.

The three women reached Melzi before the man could fire, and the middle one reached out, grabbed him by the throat with one hand, and lifted him from his feet.

That broke him out of whatever fog had possessed him, and he shoved his pistol against the side of her head and began squeezing the trigger frantically.

Just like the men with the machine guns, though, he seemed to miss her with every shot. Then her hand twitched, Melzi's neck snapped to the side at an unnatural angle, and she opened her hand. He hit the pavement like so much dead meat.

That seemed to free the other two men, who blazed away with their assault rifles. The leader frowned at them a second, then the other two women *blurred* and materialized abruptly next to the *sicarios*. They grabbed the rifles, reversed them, and shot their previous owners. Lohrman had never seen anyone move that quickly. They didn't seem to move so much as disappear from one place and appear at the other.

He shook his head, disbelieving, as the .50s started up again. The woman in command flicked a hand at her fellows, then at the machine guns, and both her companions disappeared from the camera's field of view.

After a second or two, the machine guns fell abruptly silent.

The woman looked up at the camera and blew it a kiss, then pulled out a pistol of her own. She aimed it at the camera and smiled, and the picture dissolved into static.

"Camera Four, please," Lohrman said.

He didn't seem quite so confident anymore, Cervantes noted, which was totally understandable, since Cervantes was shaking and about to piss his pants. Scared didn't do his feelings justice; he could barely get his shaking finger to toggle the system to the correct camera. He flipped Five on first—there was nothing going on in the game room—then managed to get Four as the brunette woman walked towards the porch of the main building.

A ball-shaped object flew into the picture to land next to her, then she disappeared in a fiery ball of smoke and dirt as the grenade exploded. She walked straight through it, unfazed, then frowned again as the men on the rooftop opened up with automatic weapons. She waved to someone outside the camera's field of view and first one weapon, then the other, went silent. She shook her head and walked up the stairs to the main entrance.

"Where . . . where are the rest of your men?" Cervantes asked. "Sh—shouldn't we be leaving or . . . or something?"

"It's too late," Lohrman muttered, almost to himself. He shook his head as if to clear it, then added, "I have a squad outside the door. I don't know how the others didn't do it, but these are my best men. They'll stop her."

The woman on the monitor opened the mansion's front door and was met with a torrent of bullets as the two men stationed in the foyer emptied their magazines on full automatic. She blurred and vanished. The rifle fire stopped.

"Who else is between us and . . . her?" Cervantes was afraid he knew the answer, but found he had to ask anyway.

"No one," Lohrman said grimly as ten rifles fired. They were in the outer office, just beyond the closed door, and the slab of wood did nothing at all to soften the weapons' staccato thunder.

Cervantes clapped his hands over his ears to block out the cacophony . . . then pressed even harder to block out the screams. Cervantes had heard plenty of men—and women, too—scream in fear, but these were different. These wrapped every ounce of terror and horror in the screamer's soul—*and then some*—into one final breath. One by one, they were snuffed out. Something hit the door, and a narrow stream of red oozed under it to puddle on the brilliantly burnished hardwood floor.

The sudden, total silence was even more terrifying than the screams had been.

Cervantes lost control of his bladder and felt the warm fluid running down his leg. He would have run if he'd had control of any of his muscles.

"What . . . what . . ." he mumbled. He wanted to know what the outcome had been, but he was physically unable to form words.

"I don't know," Lohrman said, somehow understanding. He squared his shoulders and exhaled explosively. "But it's time for me to go find out."

He drew his pistol as he walked to the door and threw it open. The arm that had been propped against it—no longer attached to its original owner—fell into the room to splash in the puddle. A woman—a rather attractive woman, actually, with dark hair—stood in the middle of a slaughterhouse. She was untouched, although the walls behind her were shredded with bullet holes, and huge patches of plaster had been blasted away, and the floor—what was visible of it, anyway—was littered with spent cartridge cases. Bodies and pieces of bodies filled the room, and the walls were coated in splashes of scarlet. In fact, the only thing not painted in crimson was the woman, who didn't have a drop on her. The stench of rent bowels wafted into the room, and Cervantes' stomach voided itself, too.

"Oops," the woman said. "I seem to have gotten something on my pants."

"Don't. Fucking. Move."

Despite what he had to be feeling, Lohrman managed to put some steel into his voice as he stepped forward into the outer office. Cervantes looked up to see the Brit still pointing the pistol at the woman, although it was anyone's guess where the bullet would go, as badly as he was shaking.

"Me? Move?" the woman asked. "I really don't think I want to, dahling." She looked around her feet, and her upper lip curled back. She pointed to the floor. "I might slip on some of his guts and ruin this new top."

"How?" Lohrman asked.

"Could you be a little more forthcoming?" The woman licked her lips. "There are many things I am, but a mind reader isn't one of them." She cocked her head. "Not yet, anyway."

"How . . . how—?" Lohrman waved his free hand at the gore, although he was obviously trying very hard not to look down at the dismembered parts of his squad.

"It's simple, dahling," the woman said. "I'm a vampire."

"Vampires don't exist."

"Why do they always have to say that?" a new voice asked. Cervantes' head twitched, and then he swallowed as one of the other women—the blonde—stepped out of the hallway to join the brunette. "Can't we just skip through this part and kill them? It's so boring, and I need to get back for a nail appointment. I seem to have broken one somewhere along the way." She shrugged. "Or, maybe I didn't break a nail, and I'm just bored and ready to be done here."

A redhead walked in to stand by the blonde, but she didn't say anything. Her silence was even creepier than the blonde's nonchalance.

"Vampire's don't exist," Lohrman repeated, like a man willing it to be true.

"Boring," the blonde noted.

"Cecilia," the first woman said, "could I trouble you for your pistol?"

The blonde pulled a pistol from a small-of-the-back holster and lobbed it to brunette, who put it to her temple and fired. It sounded like a cannon going off, and the bullet slammed into the wall on the other side of her. Another piece of plaster fell.

Lohrman looked back at the woman; there was no visible mark on her. His jaw fell open, but he wasn't quite done yet. As she turned to lob the pistol back to the redhead, he dropped his own weapon, grabbed the broken chair next to him, tore off one of its wooden legs, and dove forward to stab her with it. He slipped in some of the gore, though, and only succeeded in driving it through her stomach.

He jumped back up, covered in blood, and retreated, holding up his fists defensively.

The woman looked down at the chair leg in her stomach and sighed. "Seriously? Bullets didn't work, so now you're going to kill me with a chair leg?"

"I thought driving a stake through a vampire killed it," Lohrman said. "Killed you, I mean."

"It's supposed to be through my *heart*," the woman replied with a sigh, pulling the chair leg from her stomach. There wasn't a trace of blood on it, a corner of Cervantes' brain noticed. "It's supposed to go here," she added, pressing against her chest. "Like *this!*"

She drove the chair leg through her chest, and all three women gasped as she fell to her knees.

Then all three started laughing as she stood again, pulled out the wooden piece, and cast it aside.

"Sorry," she said, "but that's just too cliché. And, as you can see, it doesn't work, either." She shrugged. "As it turns out, neither do crosses, garlic, or anything else along those lines." She smiled. "I know, because people have tried all of them on me, and I'm still here."

Lohrman's mouth moved several times before he could get his voice to work.

"Why . . . why do they say they work then?" he finally asked.

"Probably to give you breathers some hope," the blonde said. "Unfortunately, there isn't any." She smiled, and her incisors grew down over her lower lip. "You're mine." She blurred, and Lohrman was slammed backward into the wall. A bolt of incredible agony went through his chest, and nothing in his body seemed to work as he slid to the floor. The last thing he saw as his vision grayed out was the blonde, holding his heart. She quirked an eyebrow at him and dropped it to the floor, her hand still a virgin white. There wasn't a drop of his blood on her, he realized almost calmly, and he carried that thought with him down into the darkness.

"Always have to go for the dramatic, eh Cecilia?" the dark-haired woman asked.

The blonde shrugged as she waded back through the ankle-deep shredded bodies, and the brunette turned to look at Cervantes. "There are certain things we'd like to know," she said. "I don't suppose you'd like to be reasonable about this, would you?"

XXIII

FORT SANDERS, NORTH CAROLINA,
UNITED STATES

Well, this should be fun."

First Sergeant Quintrell Robinson's sour tone and equally sour expression might have suggested to some that his sentiment was less than genuine, Major Robert Wilson decided.

"Gosh, aren't you a little ray of sunshine?" he inquired as he gazed at the LZ through his binoculars. "Get a lot of invites to emcee kids' birthday parties, do you?"

"What I do every weekend, Sir." Robinson hawked up a glob of phlegm and spat it out. "Right after I get done stealing all their candy."

Wilson chuckled without lowering the binoculars. They weren't like any he'd had before the invasion—he thought of them as his present from Luke Skywalker—and they were even better than his Hegemony-level contacts. At the moment, they were showing him a razor sharp, incredibly detailed view of . . . nothing in particular. It was, in fact, an empty, pine tree–surrounded field on the grounds of what had once been Fort Bragg and was now Fort Sanders, North Carolina.

Although, to be fair, it wasn't *really* empty.

Or the pines weren't, anyway.

The day was gray, drear, and humid, and a raw, cold wind sighed around his ears while heavy cloud cover rolled in from the west. The temperature had fallen four degrees in the last hour and the weather satellites promised heavy rain, turning into freezing sleet and then snow late tonight. For the moment, though, nothing was falling out of the skies on him, and he considered that a plus.

"And here I thought you were a fine, upstanding Marine," he told Robinson.

"Oh, but I am, Sir. Or I was, anyway, when I was an honest Gunny. Don't know about this new 'Space Marines' crap, though."

"You and me both, Top," Wilson sighed. "You and me both."

Robinson was nine years younger than he was, but Wilson understood the other man only too well. Robinson had been an active-duty E-7, otherwise known as a gunnery sergeant, when the Shongairi arrived. Wilson had been long retired by then, but even after he'd made master sergeant, he'd always thought of himself as a "gunny." Now he was a major, and that was just . . . wrong, in *so* many ways.

It wasn't that he'd objected to going back into the Corps. Not really, although as Robinson had just pointed out, it wasn't the "Corps" in which he'd served for twenty-plus years. It was that Wilson was a *noncom,* not a frigging officer. He'd never been an officer, never *wanted* to be an officer, and was totally unqualified to *become* an officer. He'd been very clear about that. Indeed, he'd fought the good fight with all his might.

Unfortunately, neither President Howell, nor General Landers—nor Dave Dvorak, damn his traitorous, black heart—had seemed to care what *he* thought about the whole idea. Worse, he never had learned how to say no when someone uttered the fatal words "the country needs you."

He had to work on that.

He had managed to wring at least one concession out of the pushy bastards before he went down to defeat, though. And so one-time Master Sergeant Wilson found himself not simply Major Wilson, but also CO (designate), 1st Battalion, 1st Brigade, *Space Marines,* Continental Armed Forces.

The man beside him had never learned to say no either, he thought now, which was how one-time Gunnery Sergeant Robinson found himself First Sergeant Robinson, and about to become *Sergeant Major* Robinson and the senior noncommissioned officer of the aforesaid 1st Battalion, 1st Brigade, Space Marines, Continental Armed Forces.

Assuming the Continental Armed Forces in general—and the Space Marines, in particular—ever got themselves up and organized, that was.

You're being unfair, Rob, he told himself. *Under the circumstances, Landers' boys and girls are actually doing a good job. Not as good as they* think *they are, maybe, but good. And their screw-ups aren't really their fault, either. Too damned many of them are making it up as they go along. Hell, all of us are making it up as we go along*!

Truman Landers had grabbed every surviving military vet he could find—and who could be spared from civilian jobs in the massive reconstruction effort—to staff his CAF. It was just Rob Wilson's bad luck to have been within easy reach when the grabbing started.

"Seriously, Sir," Robinson said, "this here's gonna be a cluster fuck."

"That pessimism isn't helpful, Sar'major," Wilson pointed out.

"Hell, Sir. Calling it a cluster fuck's being *optimistic*!"

Wilson snorted, but Robinson probably had a point. And he'd certainly earned the right to express an opinion. He'd spent most of the invasion in his home state of Alabama, picking off Shongair patrols. He was only about five-five, with skin a shade or two lighter than Wilson's friend Alvin Buchevsky's, but he was built like the proverbial fireplug. He'd spent several years as a DI at Parris Island, and Wilson couldn't imagine the recruit who hadn't crapped himself the first time Robinson got in his face for real.

At the moment, though, what bothered Wilson the most was his certainty that Robinson was right and that Landers' bright and shiny new planning officers were wrong. Or maybe it would be better to say that they were way, way, *way* too optimistic. He hoped he was about to be wrong about that. The possibility, however, struck him as . . . remote.

Hard to blame 'em, I guess, he thought. *The neural educator's still a bright, shiny new toy. That almost has to make them overestimate it, all by itself. And the fact that they really need it to work as well as they think it will only makes that worse. Course, most of 'em haven't spent nearly as much time with it as I have, now have they?*

Well, it was time to see if—

"Here they come," Robinson said in a suddenly much more serious voice, and Wilson nodded as the Black Hawk helicopters pretending to be *Starfire* assault shuttles swept in over the North Carolina pines with Lieutenant Palazzola's 1st Platoon and Lieutenant Samuelson's 3rd Platoon.

They didn't have real *Starfires* because none had been built yet, and they didn't have a *Starlander* they could use instead because they were all too busy on rescue operations. But that was fair, because they didn't have any real powered armor yet, either. The "Space Marines" aboard those helicopters had been outfitted with rudimentary exoskeletons which would duplicate many of the capabilities of the armor being designed as part of Project Heinlein—where movement was concerned, anyway—and the visors and backpack sensor pods they wore were designed to give them at least a rudimentary version of the ultimate armor's HUD and sensor suite. By the same token, they carried modified M-16s fitted with laser training units instead of the notional railgun rifles still being designed, but that was fine. Today wasn't really about the *equipment*; it was about the *training* with it in small unit tactics, and simulators would work just fine for that.

Aleandro Palazzola, commanding the "assault force," had exactly zero experience as a Marine or even an Army puke. He was only twenty-five, and he'd been a North Carolina state trooper for less than two years before the invasion. Jeff Samuelson, a Raleigh city policeman before the Shongairi arrived, was only a year older than Palazzola, with no more military experience than he had. Both of them were, however, very, very smart, and their lack of previous military experience was rather the point of today's exercise, because not one of their troopers had *any* formal pre-invasion military training. Like them, every one of their men and women had been neurally educated for their new duties.

Unlike 1st and 3rd Platoons, Lieutenant Elinor Simpson's 2nd Platoon was already on the ground, prepared to provide the "hostiles" for the exercise under the direct supervision of Captain Brian Hilton, Alpha Company's CO.

Hilton was the only person involved today who'd actually been an officer before the invasion—in his case, a lieutenant in the South Carolina National

Guard, who'd spent the invasion working in tandem with Sam Mitchell. While Mitchell supplied weapons and coordination over the entire state, however, Hilton had led one of the most effective guerrilla bands making the Puppies' lives miserable in the ruins of the Downstate.

In Wilson's opinion, that meant Hilton was probably better qualified than *he* was to command the battalion (assuming they ever got it stood up), but he was also barely thirty years old. His experience fighting the Puppies made him the perfect person to command Palazzola's "op force," however, and Simpson— like Sergeant First Class Consuela Curbelo, Hilton's senior NCO—was actually a vet. Curbelo, a tough-as-nails little Texan who described herself as "Tex-Mex and meaner'n a snake," had been an E-4 and a Marine, whereas Simpson had been an E-5 and Army, but they obviously liked and respected one another. Unlike either of them, Staff Sergeant Jacqueline Walsham, Simpson's platoon sergeant, was another Space Marine with no prior military experience. She'd been a first-grade teacher, of all damned things. Until, that was, the Shongairi shot up a fleeing school bus that failed to stop at one of their early roadblocks. They'd killed almost all of her students that afternoon . . . and turned her into their worst nightmare. She'd become the best bomb-maker her resistance group had, and she'd also been their interrogation specialist.

For some reason, every prisoner she'd ever spoken to had told her exactly what she'd wanted to know. Eventually.

By the standard of any pre-invasion infantry platoon, Hilton's op force was definitely top heavy with females, Wilson thought, but that was just fine with him. Once the Heinlein armor was up and running, all the old arguments about upper body strength would become thoroughly moot. Besides, he'd known plenty of tough, competent military women even before the invasion, and all three of these had fought under Hilton's direct command *after* the invasion. The three of them had needed a lot less neural education to get a handle on their duties, which was the other reason Wilson had picked 2nd Platoon as the opposition force.

Might be you've stacked the deck just a bit, you think? he reflected now, as the Black Hawks raced closer, and then snorted in amusement. Of course he had, and for damned good reasons, too. If this whole NET approach had any bugs, better they find out about them early.

The helicopters swept overhead, then flared and settled into a ground hover, and the men and women of 1st and 3rd Platoon vaulted out of them.

The first bit went well, Wilson thought. Of course—

. . . . .

"GO!" ALEANDRO PALAZZOLA snapped over the platoon's com net, and watched the men and women of the assault force bound directly away from their landing points towards the pine forest surrounding the clearing. They should have looked clumsy in their bulky exoskeletons, but they didn't. Their biofeedback skin suits activated their synthetic "muscles" almost as smoothly as if they'd been naked.

He and Staff Sergeant Cunningham were perfectly placed at the midpoint between the expanding semicircles of 1st Platoon and 3rd Platoon as the helos lifted away. His people raced outward, moving in the two-man "wing" fire teams the new doctrine specified, then went to ground, covering a three-hundred-sixty-degree perimeter from prone firing positions, and he nodded in satisfaction.

"So far, so good," he murmured to Cunningham over their dedicated link.

"Tempting fate, there, Sir," Cunningham muttered back. The staff sergeant—two inches shorter than Palazzola, with a thin mustache and a scarred right cheek—took a perverse pride in his role of platoon pessimist. "Always room for something to—"

The explosion was less than eight feet behind Palazzola.

It wasn't actually all that violent an explosion, he realized later. In fact, it was no more powerful than the "flash-bangs" he'd used himself when he'd run the NC Justice Academy's Regional SWAT In-Service Training program before the invasion. It was, however, totally unexpected, and he lurched forward, going to his knees while red damage codes flickered at the corner of his visor's HUD.

The backpack sensors flashed an identifier in his visor. A mortar round?! What the hell were the defenders doing with a frigging *mortar*?!

"Mortar!" Corporal Niedermayer announced . . . rather unnecessarily in Palazzola's opinion.

"Where's it coming—?" Palazzola began, then winced as a second "mortar bomb" exploded. This one was only about *three* feet away, and it felt as if someone had just clubbed him across the back of the head.

More codes flashed on his visor. Someone in Project Heinlein armor would be effectively invulnerable to something as feeble as a legacy, pre-invasion mortar, but that didn't mean the armor itself was impervious to damage. Nothing short of a direct hit was likely to knock it out, but enough near misses could degrade its capabilities—especially its sensor capabilities—badly. Not to mention that even an armored Space Marine this close to a genuine 120-millimeter mortar bomb would be shaken up at least as badly as the flash bangs were managing to disorient Palazzola.

"*Find* the fucking thing!" Cunningham snarled while Palazzola tried to uncross his eyes and sort out his platoons' icons on the HUD. They showed him exactly where each of them was, but at the moment, they were a little harder to follow than usual.

Shouldn't have surprised us this way, a tiny corner of his brain reflected while the rest of it was still unscrambling synapses. *Our sensors should've picked up anything the size of a frigging mortar, however hard Hilton tried to hide the damned thing!*

Except that they hadn't *looked* for one. They'd been briefed to go after a group of lightly armed guerrilla fighters. No one had actually said anything about who those guerrilla fighters might be supposed to represent, although Palazzola had a few suspicions. But the briefing officer had been clear that they had reports only of legacy small arms, maybe a couple of squad light machine guns, but no heavy weapons. And a 120-millimeter mortar was about as heavy as an infantry unit's support weapons came! So where the hell—?

The third and fourth bombs began walking their way across the clearing, and what the hell was taking so long about back-plotting the incoming? Their sensors should make pinpointing the incoming fire's point of origin child's play! They'd all run through the processes without a hitch after the NET download sessions.

But they'd been in a quiet classroom at the time. And what had been easy enough in a classroom was a lot harder out in a wet, mucky clearing, surrounded by dense pine trees, while someone dropped those nasty, *disorienting* flash bangs on top of them. It was so hard to *think,* to sort through the implanted knowledge. It was like trying to scroll through a drop-down menu in a pickup truck racing down a potholed road.

Rounds five and six landed, and the status window at the bottom of Palazzola's HUD indicated a twelve percent loss of function on his simulated armor.

"Got it!" Corporal Justina Fredericks, one of Jeff Samuelson's wing leaders barked finally, and the mortar's coordinates and bearing appeared in yet another corner window on Palazzola's visor. It was on 3rd Platoon's side of the clearing.

"Watson, Briggs—flank left! Jeffers, you and Francotti take right!" he heard Samuelson snap, sending four of his five "wings" sweeping out to flank the mortar position. "Jake, you and Bourbeau on me!"

He headed straight down the middle with Staff Sergeant Jacob Tyson and the fifth wing.

"Timmons and Jolson, you hold what you've got," Palazzola ordered, detailing the pair of his own wings farthest from the mortar bearing. "The rest of you, reorient to support Third Platoon."

His people started moving—two or three of them considerably more slowly than they had when they first exited the helicopters as their own exoskeletons reacted to the theoretical damage their theoretical armor had sustained. They moved with something less than textbook precision, as well, which didn't surprise him one bit, but at least they were moving.

"Wish to hell they'd included some of those frigging drones they say they're working on!" Cunningham growled over their link.

"Or just bothered to tell us about the goddamned mortars!" Palazzola snarled back.

"Just slipped their minds, you think, Sir?" Cunningham said.

"Oh, *sure* it did! And if you believe that—"

"*Shit!*"

It sounded like Jeff Samuelson . . . because it was, responding to the sudden, blinding glare his visor had just blasted directly into his eyes to simulate the impact of an M72 LAW's four-pound shaped-charge rocket. His exoskeleton locked instantly, sending him crashing to the ground, and Palazzola swore viciously as he realized where the "rocket" had come from. Someone less than two hundred meters away on Samuelson's left—which would put him just inside the pine trees—had been waiting for the assault team to charge the mortar . . . and offer a perfect flanking shot. And he wasn't alone. Four more of the damned "rockets" came scorching in. Fortunately, they weren't very accurate against individual, moving, human-sized targets at that sort of range, but they managed to take down Corporal Frank Barbeau, another of 3rd Platoon's Marines.

"Keep moving!" Staff Sergeant Tyson barked, but the speed of his own advance faltered as he and Kyle Boyd, Barbeau's wing, tried to link their "armor" systems now that each of them had lost his original partner.

It should have been almost instantaneous, Palazzola knew, but once again there was a minor difference between executing a simple function in a classroom and in the midst of howling chaos.

"Parker, you and Michaels cover left!" he ordered. "Try to find the bastards, but if you can't, at least keep them pinned down!"

"Roger," Corporal Parker acknowledged, and Palazzola finally heard return fire ripping back at *someone*. From his own HUD, he figured that Parker and his partner, Jadiel Michaels, were firing blind, but despite the mortar and despite the LAWs, he was damn sure there wasn't any Heinlein armor out there in the bushes. So they might just get lucky. They damned well deserved to get lucky about *something*, anyway!

"Got 'em!" Ollie Watson announced suddenly, and Palazzola's HUD was suddenly even more complicated as the tac window switched from a single icon indicating the mortar's predicted position to an entire cluster of icons, showing the mortar tube and its five-man crew.

Watson and his wing, Declan Buck, never stopped moving as they opened fire on their tormentors. At least part of the simulation worked perfectly, probably because it required no conscious input from the operators. The training lasers fitted to their M-16s synced with their visors, and precise aiming points flashed before them. They took down the mortar crew in a handful of seconds, and Palazzola allowed himself a deep breath of relief. Now, all they needed was—

"Oh, *fuck*," Cunningham groaned over the command link as the *second* mortar opened fire from the other end of the clearing. "What the hell *else* are they gonna do to us?!"

And why didn't you think to look in the other *direction, too, rocket scientist?* Palazzola asked himself harshly. *If you* had, *then maybe—*

A crimson visor code flashed as Elliott Timmons took a direct hit from the third incoming "mortar round." Unlike Simpson and Barbeau, he was technically still alive, but the computer monitoring the exercise had decided to completely disable his armor. And a moment later, two more LAWs took down Declan Buck and Mariah Johnson. According to the computer umpire, Buck was still alive, although badly wounded. Johnson's exoskeleton locked as she became a fatal casualty.

That was five out of the two platoons' combined starting strength of twenty-four. Palazzola doubted that a twenty-one percent casualty ratio against legacy-armed opponents was going to look very good in the after-action analysis. And they weren't done yet.

"Found the bastards!" Ryan Murphy, Timmons partner, announced, and Palazzola heard more outgoing fire. His visor showed him everything, relaying the tactical feeds from each of his people currently engaging the enemy, which he suddenly discovered was not a good thing. There was simply too much data on too small a display. He needed to reduce it, switch back to a display which showed only the cursors of his own forces, but yet again, he had to stop, think his way through the command steps, and while he was doing that, Corey Lawson and Guillermo Jolson joined the incapacitated list.

At least the platoons' survivors managed to take down the second mortar and both of the remaining LAW ambush parties while he was trying to sort things out. Unfortunately, that accounted for less than half of Brian Hilton's op force, and neither Elinor Simpson nor Jackie Walsham were among them. That meant Palazzola's battered and chastened Marines had to go find *them*, too, and—knowing those two redoubtable ladies—the worst was yet to come.

For some reason, Aleandro Palazzola found that thought less than exhilarating.

"Christ, I am *so* not looking forward to hearing from the Old Man about this," he moaned to Cunningham over their private link as the single reorganized, oversized platoon he had left headed with exemplary caution into the pine woods.

"Gotta get better, Sir, right?" Palazzola looked at his habitually pessimistic platoon sergeant in disbelief, and Cunningham shrugged. "I mean, we're already so screwed our efficiency curve has to go up from here, doesn't it?"

"As in from 'total cluster fuck' to simply 'screwed the pooch,' you mean?"

"Exactly." Cunningham actually grinned, and Palazzola shook his head.

"You're always such a comfort to me, Ezra."

"What I'm here for, Sir. What I'm here for."

• • • • •

"SO WE ROUNDED up the prisoners and made it back to the LZ for recovery," Lieutenant Palazzola said, six hours later.

A steaming mug of coffee sat on the table in front of him, he had a dry towel wrapped around his neck, and his hair was still slightly damp from the shower. The promised rain and sleet pounded the high-tech Quonset hut—that was how Wilson thought of it, anyway—drumming on its domed roof, but it was toasty warm inside.

He suspected Palazzola and his bedraggled Marines were even more grateful for that than he was.

To Palazzola's credit, there hadn't been any complaints about "cheating" where the mortars were concerned. Possibly because he'd ended up losing just under two thirds of his people—dead, wounded, or combat ineffective because of armor damage—and he wasn't about to sound like he was making excuses to cover his ass. He wasn't that kind of officer. More probably, though, it was because he'd already digested one of Wilson's little lessons.

Plainly, it had never occurred to any of the assault force's innocent souls that their designated battalion commander might not have been fully forthcoming with them when he structured their pre-op intelligence briefing, but that was scarcely his fault. The battalion S-2 had even stressed that their intelligence was incomplete, but they'd made the mistake of assuming that anyone equipped with Hegemony-level recon assets would have to be pretty much on the money. Which meant they'd forgotten that from the day he'd finally agreed to be a—*shudder*—officer, Rob Wilson had hammered away at the fact that the one totally expectable thing about combat operations was that something *un*-expectable was bound to happen.

Apparently, they hadn't thought he meant it, he reflected dryly. Or possibly they just hadn't realized what a nasty, sneaky SOB he truly was.

That's what happens when you take a devious old master sergeant and turn him into an officer, he thought.

"All right." Captain Bratton Mills, the company XO who'd conducted the immediate after-action analysis, glanced down the length of the table to Wilson and raised his eyebrows. "Any comment, Sir?"

"Actually, yeah," Wilson replied. He paused to take a long sip from his own coffee mug, then set it on the table in front of him.

"Good news first. You accomplished every one of your mission objectives. If the Heinlein armor turns out to be as good as projected and the simulation was accurate, it's going to be harder than hell to actually kill one of our people.

Unfortunately," he smiled slightly at Palazzola, "that's about it on the positive side. On the negative side, killing one of us isn't going to be outright impossible, and you lost over sixty percent of your people, either dead or mission killed, *despite* the armor. That's not what people usually call a 'sustainable loss rate.' Now, it would be fair—if perhaps unwise—of you to point out that no one warned you about the mortars, but even with them, if the full capabilities of your 'armor' had been used properly from the outset, Brian and Elinor wouldn't have had the advantage of total surprise, which would almost certainly have affected the final outcome.

"However," he leaned forward, laying his forearms on the table and cradling his mug between his hands, and his expression was suddenly very serious, "the real point of the exercise was exactly that—to test not just the capabilities of the 'armor' but to test your ability to utilize them. The fact that you accepted the intelligence brief at face value was a big part of what went wrong, too, of course. I'd like to think that if it had been an actual combat op you would've been at least a little more hesitant about accepting just how comprehensive its accuracy truly was, but we can discuss that aspect of it later. The point right now is that you and your people went in relying on your NET, and it let you down. Not because it didn't give you the skills and the information you needed, but because you'd been . . . inadequately drilled in using those skills and that information."

He turned his head slowly, letting his gaze travel around the officers and senior noncoms seated around the table.

"I deliberately put you in a position where you'd need to react quickly, instantly—instinctively—with the skill set you'd been given. And that skill set failed you, because it isn't really 'yours' yet. My brother-in-law's fond of saying that it's like looking something up on a wiki page before the war. It's all there, but it's like a nested series of drop-down menus. When you're not under pressure, when nobody's actually shooting at you, you can click right through it to what you want. Not as quickly as you think you're getting through it, but pretty damned quickly.

"The problem is that when you're under pressure, you don't think shit through, people. The worst mistake someone can make is to hope that when the shit hits the fan, his people will rise to the occasion. That's not what happens. What *happens* is that instead of rising, they *sink* to the level of their training. They respond with the skills and the reactions which have been drilled so deeply into them they don't *need* to think the shit through. They just *do* it. That's the reason you make training problems as demanding as you can. Why you train harder than you expect to have to fight, if you can. And that's why the NET concept let all of you down. It assumed you'd rise to the demands of the occasion and quickly and accurately access all the 'book learning' you'd been given. And you didn't, because nobody could have. You made some mistakes that didn't have anything to do with how automatic your skills had become, but they probably wouldn't have mattered when it was time to dig your way out of the hole if you'd been able to use the capabilities of your armor the way we should have *trained* you to use them. So I have to say that the fact that you actually accomplished your mission objectives despite the curve I deliberately threw you and all of the training issues actually speaks very highly of you all. Probably doesn't feel that way right this minute—" he sat back and flashed another smile "—but I'm not just blowing smoke up your collective ass on this one. So go find yourselves a hot meal—I understand they've got beef stew waiting for you—and write up your formal reports. I'm a nasty old SOB, but I'm *your* nasty old SOB, and I'm actually pretty proud of you all."

He looked around their faces one last time, then picked up his mug and waved it in dismissal.

"Go, my children, and sin no more," he said.

XXIV

SÃO SALVADOR DA BAHIA DE TODOS OS SANTOS, BAHIA, BRAZIL

One nice thing about Hegemony technology, Dave Dvorak thought, was the lighting it made possible. The flag-draped podium on the raised stage at the end of the studio was as brilliantly illuminated as any producer or director could have desired, but without the radiant heat traditional studio lighting would have produced.

He checked his watch again, but it persisted in telling him the same thing, and he leaned back against the wall, concentrating on staying out of the way of cameramen, sound technicians, and lighting specialists as they ran their final tests and made their final preparations. Like the studio's illumination, the "cameras" in question were products of the steadily expanding orbital infrastructure. They were both smaller and lighter than pre-invasion cameras would have been, and each of them floated on its own independent countergrav unit, obedient to joysticks on the control panels of the "cameramen" to whom they answered. They moved with completely independent motion and rock-steady smoothness in all axes, and the system was configured to generate three-dimensional imagery for the limited number of tridees in service while simultaneously feeding a signal to all the remaining pre-invasion TVs which had been returned to service.

He watched them, and as he did, his thoughts drifted to the city outside this quiet, coolly air-conditioned studio's soundproof walls.

His first visit to Salvador had been sobering, after the devastation and ruin he'd seen throughout so much of the United States and Canada. Or the devastation much of the rest of Brazil had suffered, for that matter. The city and municipal area were astoundingly intact, aside from several sections which had burned in the civil unrest before Judson Howell's assistance reached President Garção. Greensboro was even less badly damaged, of course, but Salvador's pre-invasion population had been ten times that of Greensboro, and returning refugees—drawn by the restoration of order—had swelled its original population by as much as twenty or even thirty percent. That made it the largest surviving city in the world, and it was also far older than Greensboro—by a mere, oh, three hundred years or so—with a panorama of architecture which appealed to his historian's soul.

That combination of population and history was one of the reasons he stood in this studio, waiting so impatiently and nervously, but it wasn't really the most important one. No, the most *important* reason he was here was that São Salvador da Bahia de Todos os Santos was the capital of a *South* American nation.

He checked his watch again. Another two minutes had ticked past. That was good. There were only thirteen more to go now, and he pulled out his "phone" to punch up the text of the formal statement. It was far too late to make any editorial changes, but he and Sarah Howell had sweated blood over the wording and rereading it was another way to eat up some of the remaining time. Of course, with his luck, he'd find something that absolutely needed to be changed now that they couldn't change it. At least he wasn't the one who had to present it, though. That was something. In fact, it was one hell of a lot. Besides—

"Relax, Dave," a voice said, and he looked up quickly. "It's fine," Judson Howell told him. "And if it isn't, there's nothing either of us can do about it at this point. Besides," he grinned quickly, "I'm the one history's going to blame if you got something wrong."

"Oh, *thank* you," Dvorak replied. "You've made me feel *so* much better, Mister President!"

"One of the things I'm here for," Howell assured him with another smile. Then his expression sobered, and he gripped Dvorak's shoulder. "Really, you've done fine. All I could have asked for. Tonight is as much your work as anyone else's."

"Nice of you to say so, anyway," Dvorak said.

"Only said it because it's true."

Howell squeezed his shoulder—the one Hosea MacMurdo's nanites really had fixed "good as new" . . . finally—and continued across the studio to join Fernando Garção and Jeremiah Agamabichie at the podium. Dvorak watched the three of them shaking hands while he thought about what Howell had said. Maybe there was *some* truth to it, he reflected, and it was true he'd seen the need for something like this even before Howell recruited him. But it was Judson Howell's vision and passion which had driven the entire process. No one would ever accuse Garção or Agamabichie of weakness or timidity—not after what the two of them had endured and achieved over the last eighteen months. Yet either of them would have been the first to acknowledge that this day was the result of Howell's imagination and focus. And of his willingness to genuinely compromise, coupled with a steely refusal to yield a single inch on the core principles for which he'd first reached out to the other two men on the soundstage with him tonight.

Did the man find his moment, or did the moment produce the man? Dvorak wondered, not for the first time. And the truth was, it didn't really matter how it had happened. All that mattered was that it *had* happened, and that he'd been privileged to be on the inside. To see history being *made,* not just study it, and that was worth—

He twitched as the alarm on his watch chimed.

"Places, please, gentlemen," the floor director said, and Howell, Garção, and Agamabichie looked up from their conversation. If any of them were nervous, it didn't show, and they shared another smile, then moved so that Garção stood directly behind the podium with Howell at his right shoulder and Agamabichie at his left. He and Howell were within half an inch of the same height, but Agamabichie was only an inch or so shorter than Dvorak, which made him the next best thing to five inches taller than either of the presidents. The flags of the United States and Canada flanked the flag of Brazil behind them, and Dvorak's throat tightened as he looked at them, thought of the struggle and the blood and the refusal to lie down and die those bits of colored fabric represented, and wondered what the hell *he* was doing caught up in such a moment.

"And everyone else, please," the floor director continued, and a color guard marched smartly into place in front of the podium's raised stage. It consisted of four uniformed military personnel from each of the three countries represented here, each armed with his or her nation's service rifle. But there was also a thirteenth man, bearing a staff with a cased flag tightly furled around it, and he wore a uniform no one had ever before seen: a space-black jacket with sky-blue facings and dark green trousers. The first twelve formed into three short ranks of four, forming three sides of a hollow square before the soundstage as they found their marks on the studio floor, and the thirteenth man moved into the open space between them, directly in front of the podium.

The floor director eyed them critically, then nodded in satisfaction.

"Ninety seconds," he warned everyone and stepped back.

A digital display on a side wall flickered steadily downward while Howell, Garção, and Agamabichie focused their attention on the 3D "teleprompter" display floating behind the cameramen. Then it reached zero, and the floor director pointed at Garção and nodded sharply.

"Good evening," the President of Brazil said clearly. "For those who do not already recognize me, I am Fernando Garção, the President of Brazil. I am speaking to you tonight from the capital of my country, but I do not speak simply as a Brazilian. No. Tonight I speak to you as a citizen of the planet every one of us calls home."

His expression was grave, his tone measured.

"In the course of the past year and a half, our home has suffered enormous damage and almost unimaginable loss of life as a consequence of the unprovoked attack of the Shongair Empire. I scarcely need to list all of the crimes and atrocities the Shongairi inflicted upon us in the name of conquest. Nor, for that matter, is there sufficient time to complete that terrible catalog of barbarisms tonight. What many of you watching and listening to me may not yet realize, however, is that their final decision, when they concluded that they would never be able to compel us to truly submit, was to utterly exterminate the entire human race."

He paused, letting that settle in, then resumed.

"Our surviving militaries and untold numbers of our private citizens fought valiantly against the invaders, spending their life's blood in our defense, yet our defeat—and destruction—was both certain and inevitable. Until, that was, allies of Governor Judson Howell of the state of North Carolina, in the United States of America, successfully boarded our enemies' starships and captured them in hand-to-hand combat. Most of those allies have now departed for the Shongair home systems in those same dreadnoughts to teach our foes—our would-be murderers—that humans are not to be attacked with impunity. Before their departure, however, they also captured the highly capable industrial base the Shongairi had brought to our star system to support their invasion, and they left that capacity in the charge of Governor Howell, to be used for the benefit of all humanity. Millions of you listening to me have been directly touched by Governor Howell's rescue efforts, enabled by that technology. More millions of you will be in the months to come, and I can tell you now that ever more advanced technology will become available to our entire world in the next few years.

"It will become available to our world because it must become available to all of us. Partly because simple decency dictates that it must not become the prize of any one nation, any one group. But, even more importantly, we must all have access to it so that we may use it in one united effort, because the stars are not yet done with us and—to borrow the words of a famous political philosopher of the United States—if we do not hang together, then, assuredly, we will all hang separately. And it is in token of the need for that unity that we appear before you today. It is my pleasure to present to you Governor—and now President—Judson Howell, of the United States of America, and Prime Minister Jeremiah Agamabichie, of Canada. President Howell has been chosen as our spokesman, but he speaks for all three of us."

He paused once more, gazing into the cameras, then stepped back from the podium with a courteous bow to Howell.

"President Howell," he said.

"Thank you, President Garção," Howell said, stepping up to the podium. "And thank you, Prime Minister Agamabichie."

He nodded to both his companions, then squared his shoulders as he, too, looked into the cameras.

"As President Garção's said—and as all of us know from bitter personal experience—our world has been mauled and mangled by an alien species whose technology far surpassed our own. We've learned a great deal about the Shongairi since their defeat, however, and we intend to share that information with the entire human race as rapidly as we can. I expect that most of you listening to me will be astounded by just how 'rapid' that process will be, yet even so, it won't happen overnight. So for now, I will simply summarize by saying that the Shongair Empire is only one member of a vast, multi-species political unit styling itself, as nearly as any earthly language can translate the term, 'the Galactic Hegemony.' The Hegemony is enormous, not simply in terms of the volume of our galaxy it controls and the number of star systems it has colonized and conquered, but also in terms of its sheer antiquity. It has been in existence longer than *Homo sapiens* has walked the face of our planet, my friends, and it prizes stability—the status quo—above all things.

"It was because of the value it sets upon stability that the Hegemony's ruling body agreed to permit the Shongairi to conquer us. It felt we were too bloodthirsty and savage—too likely to *de*stabilize their comfortable societies—to be allowed to attain an interstellar level of technology of our own. I rather doubt the Shongairi's defeat will change the Hegemony's opinion in that regard. Even more dangerously from our perspective, however, it's become evident from our study of the captured history of the Hegemony and its member races, that while they found our . . . pugnacity ample reason to throw us to the Shongairi like a scrap of bloody meat, they had no grasp—then—of our sheer inventiveness. We have advanced our own technology, however primitive it might currently be by Hegemony standards, far more rapidly than any of the Hegemony's member races ever advanced theirs, my friends, and their survey crews had no clue of how our fascination with the new and the better, with ways in which the status quo can be *improved* upon, empowers and drives us in that regard. The same drive which compelled an almost hairless biped, with neither fangs nor claws, to master an entire planet drives us still. It is our greatest strength . . . and it is also our greatest danger, because the day must ultimately come in which the Hegemony's masters *do* understand that. And when they do appreciate those qualities within us, there is no shadow of a doubt that they will find them far more disturbing than they found our perceived bloodthirstiness. They will view us as a mortal threat to the stability, the technological stasis, they hold so dear, and they will take steps to complete the extermination the Shongairi were prevented from carrying out. I tell you this in all sincerity, and the captured records, database, and technology we will make available to all of you will tell you precisely the same thing when *you* peruse them. For all intents and purposes, our planet is under sentence of death, for the crime of being *human,* and that sentence will be carried out as soon as the Hegemony realizes how we endanger its . . . peace of mind."

He paused, and the utter stillness of the studio was like an echo of the stillness spread across an entire world as those words sank into the minds and marrow of every man and woman listening to him.

"The time has passed when we can afford to fight with one another," he resumed, his voice quiet, his brown eyes dark. "As President Garção just said, if we cannot work together—if we cannot find a way to rise above those things which separate us and to embrace the survival imperative which must *unite* us—we, our children, our grandchildren, and our entire species will cease to exist.

"Even if we can unite, we are but a single planet in a single star system. In the wake of the horrendous casualties our world has suffered, the entire human race is no more than two billion strong. We've been reduced to the population of the 1920s, and there are literally *thousands* of other worlds beyond our skies, claimed by the Hegemony, which will decree our destruction the instant it learns the Shongairi have failed. The odds against us are, quite literally, astronomical.

"The good news is that it takes many years—often centuries—for starships to voyage between the stars. It will be at least a hundred years before the Hegemony can learn what happened here, and even longer before they could send fresh forces against us. We believe we should have a minimum of between one hundred and fifty and two hundred and fifty years before that can happen, and we possess now the entire knowledge base of the Hegemony. We are in a position to advance our own civilization's technological capabilities by thousands of years in a single generation, and—" he smiled for the first time; it was a remarkably thin, cold smile "—we *are* far more inventive than they. We must use those years to build upon that platform, the technology of which they are currently capable, so that when the time comes for us to meet them once again, the technological imbalance will favor *our* species, and not theirs. In short, we must become so dangerous that the cowardly, risk-averse species which comprise the 'Galactic Hegemony' will be too frightened to attack us again. And so dangerous that if they *do* attack us, in the end, they will find the outcome no more to their liking than the Shongairi have.

"That's what we must do, but we *cannot* do it as a separate, divided people. We can do it only when we speak and act as one. Yet the one thing of which I am totally certain is that human beings cannot be *driven* into that unity. The very characteristics which make us what we are, make us something the Hegemony fears, mean we cannot be regimented into one people against our will without our individualism driving us to rebel against our fetters. It's true that we must become one, but it's equally true that we must speak as a harmony—as a grand chorus of all our voices, joined *as* one but recognizing that we are many, with each of us finding our own note within that chorus.

"And that is why President Garção and Prime Minister Agamabichie and

I are speaking to you tonight. My own nation, the United States of America, still has much rebuilding to do, but the member states of our Republic have reconstituted our Congress and a special election has confirmed my Presidency. President Garção and Prime Minister Agamabichie were the legitimate, legal successors to their own heads of state when those were murdered by the Shongairi. Now the three of us have joined together to announce the creation of the Continental Union of the Americas, which will consist—for the moment—of the former Brazil, the former Canada . . . and the former United States of America.

"I say 'the former,'" he continued calmly and steadily, "but neither Brazil nor Canada nor the United States of America have ceased to exist. We remain what we have always been, proud of our histories, mindful of our pasts, true to our own institutions. The Continental Union will consist of sovereign states, each with local autonomy within its own borders so long as its domestic laws enshrine the human rights provisions of the Union Constitution. But they will be sovereign states within the framework of a federal republic, subject to the federal laws and provisions of a supranational government and judiciary to whom their citizens shall jointly elect representatives and senators. This isn't a trade association, not a union of independent states, but a *nation* which will enact laws, regulate our commerce, provide for a common military defense, and administer the scientific and technological cornucopia which has come into our possession in such a way as to guarantee equal access to it for all of our citizens.

"President Garção, Prime Minister Agamabichie, and I have initialed the draft of our new Constitution in the names of our own countries. The provisions of the Constitution—all of them—will be available on the Internet beginning at nine o'clock tomorrow morning, Brazilian time. We invite all of you to read it for yourselves so that you can understand precisely what we've undertaken in the names of our nations. Three months from tonight, referendums will be held simultaneously in the United States, in Canada, and in Brazil. It is our hope that those referendums will ratify this Constitution and bring the Continental Union of the Americas into formal existence.

"We have been in contact with President Izquierdo of Peru and President Montalván in Argentina, and we've invited them—as we intend to invite every other state of the Americas, as they, too, rise from the ashes—to join us in this endeavor to create a new Republic which, in time, will become truly representative of every citizen of North, Central, and South America—a nation which will reach from Antarctica to the Arctic Circle. And in token of that, we have created a flag for our new nation which partakes of none of our individual nations' flags."

He nodded, and the color guard snapped from Parade Rest to Present Arms as the single standardbearer un-cased the flag which had been furled so tightly about the staff in his hands. He turned to display it, and its image filled the viewers' screens as the cameras zoomed in. Its field was blood red, with a space-black canton adorned by a single, mini-spired golden star. The field was dominated by the western hemisphere of Earth—not a stylistic representation, but the planet itself, as seen from space, in brown, blue, and the white of ice caps. The areas of Canada, the United States, and Brazil had been superimposed upon that globe in green with each nation's borders outlined in a gleaming thread of gold.

"We present to you the banner of the Continental Union of the Americas," Howell said quietly. "It bears not the Stars and Stripes of the United States, nor the Maple Leaf of Canada, nor the Diamond and Southern Cross of Brazil. Its charge is our *world,* because that is what it has been formed to protect and to preserve against all threats.

"Creating the Continental Union, navigating the immense changes before us, and protecting our world will not to be easy tasks, but they must be achieved. The great Simón Bolívar was not especially fond of my own country." Howell smiled again, almost impishly. "I believe he said that 'The United States appears to be destined by Providence to plague America with misery in the name of Liberty,' and I'm forced to concede that, historically, there's been a great deal of truth in that. But that wasn't all he had to say." The smile disappeared, the eyes went dark and intent once again. "He also said, 'Do not compare your material forces with those of the enemy. Spirit cannot be compared with matter. You are human beings; they are beasts. You are free; they are slaves. Fight, and you shall win. For God grants victory to perseverance.' He spoke of human adversaries, and the adversary *we* face is far more powerful, its forces far more numerous, than anything he confronted. Yet his words remain true. We *are* human beings, we *are* free, we *will* persevere to the bitter end, and we will *not* be the slaves or victims of powers from beyond the stars who would take that from us, make us less than we are, or simply destroy us for daring to be *who* we are."

Those hard brown eyes looked out of tridees and televisions across the width and breadth of his home world, and they might have been forged from iron as the man behind them met the moment for which he had been born.

"It will not be easy," Judson Fitzsimmons Howell said from behind those eyes, "but Bolívar spoke truly, my friends—my fellow citizens of Earth. And to paraphrase another great revolutionary leader of history, 'Here we *stand*. We can do no other.'"

RENAISSANCE

SOL
SYSTEM

YEAR 15 OF THE TERRAN EMPIRE

SPACE PLATFORM *BASTION,*
L5 LAGRANGE POINT

The view was spectacular.

It wasn't actually a viewport, but he'd configured the smart wall to make it look like one, and the tridee made the illusion breathtakingly realistic. From his vantage point, the Moon was an incredibly bright, white nickel and Earth was a gorgeous cloud-banded sapphire the size of a quarter. The starscape receded into infinity—literally—and the space about *Bastion* was alive with a busy, hectic, seemingly random pattern of sunlight-gilded spacecraft. Looking at it from the outside, the only term that really came to mind was helter-skelter, yet he knew there was a carefully planned pattern buried in the midst of that confusion. The traffic control computers and their human supervisors managed it with the polished, almost offhand precision which came from ten or twelve years of constant—and constantly hectic—practice.

Most of the spacecraft visible through that "viewport" were employed continuing the expansion of *Bastion*'s already stupendous hull. Not only did the space platform house the federal government of the Planetary Union, it also housed the Terra House, the president's official residence; the Senate; the House of Representatives; and the steadily growing city for the people who made all of that work. It was also home to the Citadel, the Planetary Union's equivalent of the long-vanished Pentagon which had once served the United States' military. Since *Bastion* had been built for the specific purpose of putting the federal government's capital outside the borders of any earthly nation, it only made sense to put as many as possible of the federal organs in the same place.

The Citadel controlled a steadily growing military which dwarfed anything the United States of America might ever have contemplated, yet it ran with a fraction of the staff the Pentagon had required. Part of that was the result of an intentionally Spartan manning policy aimed at avoiding the bloat which had afflicted the American military bureaucracy. *All* military bureaucracies, to be fair, really, he supposed. But that bloat was something the Continental Union of the Americas had been unable to afford, and which the *Planetary* Union of Earth could afford even less.

At least as big a part of the reason was simply that the cyber support available to the Planetary Union was a staggeringly effective efficiency multiplier. There were still distinct limits on how much a single human brain could carry around and keep track of, but the computers aiding that human brain were something else entirely, replacing bevies of assistant project officers, clerks, accountants, and God only knew what else.

And it didn't hurt a damned thing that there were no defense contractor lobbyists knocking on office doors or taking senior officers out to five-martini lunches. That was because there *were* no defense contractors, which had come as quite a shock to the human race in general. On the other hand, it looked like most of humanity would adapt quite handily to the radically new "economy" which had engulfed them. Not all, of course. There were losers as well as winners in any paradigm shift, and this had been one hell of a shift.

None of that impinged directly upon him, however. Not at the moment, anyway. He still had plenty to do, and *his* headaches remained focused on something that *hadn't* changed in the new paradigm: human nature.

He leaned back in his sinfully comfortable chair, reading the latest correspondence from the display projected directly onto his cornea. As was not unusual when some new bit of technology was added to his person, he'd felt a few qualms when they explained that they were going to surgically implant his very own computer monitor to replace the contacts he had been using. Hosea had walked him through it (the way he'd walked him through quite a few things by now) and explained that the procedure was really no more intrusive than a cataract operation. And, oh, by the way, while they were about it they would give him roughly 40/20 vision, the equivalent of a really good built-in compound microscope, lowlight optical capability, *plus* infrared, all controlled by his personal computer. He could configure the new capabilities to deploy themselves automatically or override the autonomous software whenever he chose.

Doctor MacMurdo, he had concluded yet again, should have been a used car salesman. But he'd been right—yet again—and by now Dave Dvorak took the astounding capabilities of his vision completely for granted . . . until something startled him into remembering what it had been like for his first forty-odd years.

The thought flowed somewhere under the surface of his concentration on the report's far from amusing content. Sometimes it was difficult to remind himself how much better off the world was these days. Or how much they'd actually accomplished.

He paused the current file and leaned forward to slide his cup into the dispenser slot. His nostrils flared appreciatively as the fragrance of the elixir of life came to him in a tendril of steam. Thank God Brazil had survived! And Fernando Garção, who'd resigned as President of Brazil to become *Senator* Garção on the day the first countries outside the Americas joined the Continental Union and transformed it into the *Planetary* Union, had done a lot to educate Dave Dvorak's palate where coffee was concerned. He'd introduced Dvorak to a *Brazilian's* idea of what coffee ought to be, and Dvorak had become a devotee of a Bourbon Santos 2 blend from Garção's cousin Mateo's *fazenda* which had survived the Shongairi intact.

The cup finished filling with the tiny hint of cream he preferred, and he leaned back again, cradling the cup—it was an outsized mug, really—in both hands while he inhaled the rich, strong aroma. Then he sipped slowly and sighed in contentment.

All right, he told himself as the temptation to luxuriate in the moment rolled through him. *You haven't earned an all-up coffee break yet, Mister Secretary of State. You've got the better part of a meg of reports, analyses, and proposals to review before Tuesday, and you're leaving early tonight, so get cracking. You can take your cup with you.*

He snorted and un-paused the current report, and his brief spurt of humor disappeared as the grim analysis and even grimmer projections rolled across his corneas. Despite every effort to understand and appreciate other worldviews, he *still* couldn't wrap his mind around how—

A musical chime sounded, and he looked up in surprise.

"Yes, Calamity?" Like most humans he tended to anthropomorphize his personal AI. It was, perhaps, fortunate that AIs didn't recognize or care about the implications of the names some humans—especially ones named Dvorak—hung on them.

"You've got a visitor," the AI told him in his daughter Maighread's voice, and he blinked as Maighread's face at age twelve appeared on his suddenly cleared corneas. He'd programmed Calamity's avatar to rotate randomly between all three of the kids, and he smiled as "Maighread" wrinkled her nose at him in her patented mannerism.

"Who? There's no one on the calendar until my oh-nine hundred tomorrow with Patrick and Kasey."

And there'd damned well better not be anybody trying to change that, he added silently. He'd worked hard to clear the time to go home this evening, and—

"It's Uncle Rob," the AI said, and Dvorak laughed as the avatar rolled its eyes. His daughter Morgana had decided to opt for a career in psychology, but she also had a far better hand at cybernetics than her dear old dad ever would. She was the one who'd worked out the avatars' facial expressions and other mannerisms for him, and "Maighread's" current expression reminded him of just how well Morgana knew her twin.

"How'd he get clear to my office without anybody warning me he was coming?"

"Don't know. Should I find out?" Calamity offered.

"No." Dvorak shook his head. "I'm sure he'll tell me—probably with great gusto. Tell him to come on in."

"Yes, Papi," Calamity said—this time in Morgana's voice, accompanied by a wink—and Dvorak snorted as it disappeared from his corneas. Damianos Karahalios could continue to call their existing cyber systems "expert programs" rather than "artificial intelligence," and Dvorak believed him. They sure did give a much better impersonation of intelligence than any other software he'd worked with, though.

"Rob," he said, leaning even farther back in his chair and waving negligently at the matching chair on the far side of his desk. "How nice to see you. Did I miss the email telling me you were coming?"

"Must have," his brother-in-law replied, strolling across the spacious compartment to the indicated chair. He paused halfway there to examine the family portrait which dominated one paneled bulkhead. In an age of electronic media, it stood out as a hand-painted oil of Dvorak, Sharon, and their children, and the artist had captured their personalities perfectly in their expressions.

"This is new," he said, looking over his shoulder at Dvorak. "Nene?"

"Yeah." Dvorak nodded. "Steven dropped it off as a surprise gift for Sharon's birthday. I've been keeping it stashed up here to keep old Eagle Eye from spotting it." He shook his head. "It is nice, though, isn't it? I'm just glad they weren't in Oklahoma City when the KEW dropped."

"Agreed."

Wilson continued to his chair and flopped inelegantly into it. Dvorak regarded him for a moment or two, then shook his head mournfully.

"What?" Wilson challenged.

"Oh, I'm just thinking back to those treasured days of yore and your many pithy, pointed, one might even say pungent, comments on the difference between people who worked for a living and officers."

"And exactly whose fault is it that I'm not still a respectable noncom?" Wilson demanded. "Who was it who kept beating on me to 'accept the offer'? Who twisted my arm into a pretzel? Who enlisted my baby sister—even my nieces and nephew!—to make my life a living hell until I did? Who—"

"Lord, you're melodramatic!" Dvorak shook his head, eyes sad. "Poor, pitiful little baby. Was da big mean bwother-in-law mean to you, bugga cake?"

"I salute you," Wilson said. "Here."

He raised one hand, second finger extended, and Dvorak chuckled.

"Actually, you look pretty good, Colonel Wilson."

"I am a courageous and valiant Space Marine, which means I no longer shudder in horror whenever someone calls me that," Wilson replied. "And I miss my dress blues, dammit! I mean, this monkey suit isn't *bad*, but—"

He rolled his eyes, and Dvorak chuckled again. The uniform of the Continental Union Armed Forces had been adopted by the Planetary Armed Forces, although the Space Marines had adopted the scarlet "blood stripe" trouser seams of Wilson's beloved USMC. And the truth was that the black jacket and dark green trousers looked good on him, especially with the three stylized golden planets on each shoulder. Both of them had received the antigerone treatments which had become available as Hegemony medical tech was progressively adapted to humans. As a result, they were physically at least five years younger than they'd been before the Shongair attack, and the lost mobility which had forced Wilson's original retirement from the Marine Corps had been as completely repaired as Dvorak's shoulder.

And despite his lingering, honor-of-the-flag, pro forma bitching, Dvorak knew his brother-in-law was proud of the new service he was helping to build, and the fact that he was "only" a colonel didn't mean as much as it once might have, since the Planetary Armed Forces remained absurdly small, from a manpower perspective, compared to any pre-invasion military. The Space Marines remained the smallest of the services unified under the PAF command structure, although they were slated to begin growing as soon as the first of the human-built starships under construction completed its trials. For the moment, the Marines didn't have anyone to take stuff away from because humanity remained limited to a single star system.

That was due to change sometime in the next decade or so. The PUNS *James Robinson,* lead starship of the Planetary Union Navy—he tended to doubt that the implications of that service's acronym had occurred to its non-native English speakers until it was too late—was slated to enter service within seven or eight years, and Dvorak looked forward to her formal commissioning ceremony. He was also looking forward to Wilson's reaction when he found out that Colonel Wilson was about to become *Brigadier* Wilson.

"About that email I didn't get about your arrival?" he said out loud. "Would it happen I didn't get it because you never *sent* it?"

"Oh, I suppose that's possible," Wilson conceded. He waved one hand in an airy gesture. "Those highfalutin procedures and protocols are beyond the grasp of a mere Marine."

"Yeah. Sure!" Dvorak shook his head and crossed his arms. "Would that happen to be why you haven't talked to your sister for—what? Three months now?"

"Has it been that long?" Wilson quirked an eyebrow. "Funny how time flies when it passes in restful silence."

"You are so going to regret that when I tell Herself about it," Dvorak said. "And don't think for a moment that I won't!"

"Throwing me under the bus again to save yourself?" Wilson shook his head. "Sad. So sad to see someone so terrified of a mere female."

"Dead man walking," Dvorak said, trying to picture Sharon Dvorak in the role of "mere female." His imagination wasn't up to it, but he discovered that he *could* picture her dancing on her beloved brother's head for five or ten minutes.

"Only if you tell her, and I know you have a tender heart. You wouldn't want me on your conscience."

"Oh, my 'tender heart' can take quite a lot where some people are concerned."

"I'm not afraid. I'm a *Space Marine,* and we're fearless! Says so right in the Manual. So there."

Dvorak laughed and shook his head.

"Seriously, it's good to see you, Rob. Should I assume that the fact you're sitting in my office means you're back from those maneuvers?"

"You should."

"How'd they go?"

"Let's just say they went a *hell* of a lot better than the first ones did," Wilson said fervently, and Dvorak grunted in sour understanding.

"So, if you're back from Mars, could we possibly expect you to grace us with your presence for supper at the cabin tonight?"

"Only if *you're* cooking." Wilson shuddered. "I've had Sharon's boiled water, you know."

"You've already given me enough ammunition to get you shot twice. You really want to give me enough to get you shot *three* times?"

"Just your word against mine, and I'll lie," Wilson assured him.

"Yeah, you would." Dvorak shook his head, then cocked it to one side. "Should I go ahead and pencil you in for supper?"

"I expect I can find room for it on my crowded social calendar. Besides, unless my memory is in worse shape than usual, tomorrow's Crazy's birthday."

"Well, there's the ammo for the third shot," Dvorak said dryly, and it was Wilson's turn to laugh.

"If I didn't give her a hard time she'd think I didn't love her anymore," he said.

"True," Dvorak conceded. Then he let his chair come upright. "Should I assume you're here for more than just Sharon's birthday?"

"Sort of." Wilson shrugged. "I'm scheduled to head up the evaluation of our most recent exercises. I'm pretty sure my people and I have that nailed down, but General Cartwright wants us to include a section on ways in which the capabilities we've been perfecting might have short-term applications right here on Earth. So, since I always like to use real-world examples whenever I can, I thought I'd just drop by and pick my favorite brother-in-law's brain on the current situation dirtside."

"*Favorite* brother-in-law, is it? Thanks a whole heap!"

"Even if I had another one, I'm *sure* I'd like you better," Wilson assured him soothingly. "So, what can you tell me?"

"Well, overall we're in pretty good shape," Dvorak said in a considerably more serious tone. "Not perfect, you understand, and Afghanistan and Pakistan are looking ugly."

"*Quelle surprise,*" Wilson said sourly, and Dvorak's snort was harsh.

The Continental Union of the Americas had officially become the Planetary Union five years after its creation, with the admission of Australia, New Zealand, the United Kingdom, Spain, Italy (both Italys, actually; the various separatists had successfully split the pre-invasion Repubblica Italiana into the Repubblica di Padania in the north and the Repubblica Siciliana in the south as part of the process of reconstruction), Portugal, and Romania. A lot of other nations had joined since, including a reorganized India and South Africa, although it looked like there were going to be a few holdouts. Switzerland, for example, was still talking about "associated status," although President Howell wasn't going to give them that. As far as he was concerned there were only two statuses: "IN" and "OUT."

And then there was Southwest Asia, the subject of the very report he'd been reading when Wilson arrived.

"You know, I actually thought Ormakhel might turn that around," Wilson continued after a moment, and Dvorak shrugged.

"He might have, although he wasn't exactly a poster child for religious tolerance himself. Of course, that was before Ghilzai's coup."

"Shame on you, Dave! You know you shouldn't call that orderly transfer of government a *coup*! Are you seriously questioning the impartiality of the Supreme Jirga? How parochial of you!"

"What kind of self-respecting Space Marine even knows what words like 'parochial' mean?" Dvorak asked suspiciously.

"Stop changing the subject." Wilson smiled briefly, but his blue eyes were intent. "So, are the stories I've heard about Ghilzai—both Ghilzais, really—accurate?"

"Only if they're pessimistic."

Dvorak sighed and pinched the bridge of his nose.

India might have pulled itself out of the wasteland of sectarian and tribal violence and become a member in good standing of the steadily growing Planetary Union. The Islamic Republic of Pakistan had not, and the main sticking point was the Pakistani refusal to accept the fundamental human rights clauses of the Planetary Constitution. There were other issues, but that was the one that really mattered, and Prime Minister Ghilzai wasn't about to yield an inch.

Imam Sheikh Abbas Ghilzai, a Pashtun from the rugged mountains between

Afghanistan and Pakistan, was the founder and head of Altreg al-Jadid elly Alamam, the New Way Forward Party, although "new way" and "Abbas Ghilzai" really didn't belong together in the same sentence.

He was six feet tall, which made him enormously tall for a Pashtun, with dark hair, a fiercely hooked nose, a commanding presence, and the full beard and fiery eyes of a genuine zealot. A supporter of the Tehrik-i-Taliban Pakistan (the Taliban Movement of Pakistan) before the Shongair invasion, Ghilzai had risen to senior military command during the tribal and religious warfare which had wracked Afghanistan, Pakistan, and northwestern India in the wake of the Shongairi's devastating response to the nuclear attacks on Amritsar and Ludhiana. His title of *Imam* was self-awarded, although it had come to be accepted by his followers—and used even by those who *weren't* his followers, if they knew what was good for them—and his party, the AJA, had arisen out of his vision of Islam. A lot of the AJA's platform made ISIS look moderate, and no one who'd ever read one of Ghilzai's manifestoes could doubt that he meant it.

Unfortunately, according to the Supreme Jirga of Pakistan—the council of tribal elders which had emerged as the new national government following the destruction of most of the country's "Westernized" aspects—Imam Sheikh Abbas was also the "democratically elected" prime minister. What he was, in fact, was a totalitarian dictator who'd returned Islam to a Dark Ages mentality and converted Pakistan into *his* version of an Islamic Republic.

His cousin, Ghayyur Ghilzai, was the commanding officer of the rebuilt Pakistan Army and the Sheikh's right hand man. He carried the official rank of field marshal, but was more commonly known as Ghayyur Kahn. He was also at least as intolerant and probably even more brutal than Abbas, and he'd spent the last couple of years systematically purging the military of any potential opponents or rivals.

The previous prime minister, Tariq Ormakhel, was another Pashtun. The Spīn Ghar Mountains which formed the natural frontier between Afghanistan and Pakistan had offered their protection to their tough-as-nails inhabitants against the Shongairi, just as they had against every other invader. As a consequence, Pashtuns had gone from representing around fifteen percent of Pakistan's pre-invasion population to representing over *seventy* percent of its current population, which meant any non-Pashtun prime minister was . . . unlikely to succeed.

Ormakhel was no sweetheart in his own right, in Dvorak's opinion. He, too, hewed to a very repressive and fundamentalist interpretation of the Quran, but he'd been at least a little more open to what passed for pluralism. Non-Muslims were nonpersons in his eyes, but he'd been prepared to allow an actual discussion within Islam—to a certain extent and inside tightly proscribed limits—about its ultimate character. More to the point, he truly had been as democratically elected as anyone could have been in Pakistan following the carnage wreaked upon it by both the Shongairi and the Pakistanis themselves, and he'd recognized that whether he liked it or not, the Planetary Union was there to stay and Pakistan must accommodate itself to that reality.

That had been the kiss of death, of course. Ghilzai's supporters had accused him of "Western corruption" and of being soft on blasphemy, and the Supreme Jirga had removed him, ostensibly on its own initiative. Actually, as Patrick O'Sullivan's analysts at the Planetary Intelligence Agency had realized at the time, the Jirga had acted in obedience to Ghilzai as part of his move to reshape Pakistan. At the moment, Ormakhel was living in exile in Morocco—the hardliners in Iran had fared . . . poorly in the wake of the invasion, and he'd been as unwelcome in Afghanistan as in Pakistan—while the Ghilzais governed Pakistan from the rebuilt capital of Naya Islamabad.

A capital Ormakhel had rebuilt largely using Hegemony-level technology made available to Pakistan free of charge by the Planetary Union Ghilzai excoriated in his near-daily harangues.

"The truth is that Pakistan's busy backsliding, and that's gathering speed," Dvorak said, lowering his hand from the bridge of his nose to look levelly at his brother-in-law. "Ghilzai's obviously serious when he says he's determined 'to preserve the purity of the Islamic Republic' by remaining outside the PU and that horrible, corrupting human rights code of ours. That's his legal right, and nobody here on *Bastion* disputes it. But he's also using police state tactics to prevent anyone who wants to leave his Islamic Republic from doing so, and those tactics include 'disappearing' dissidents and persecuting—hell, *lynching*—'blasphemers.' Then there's *Sif al-Nabi*."

"'*Sif al-Nabi*'?" Wilson repeated.

"That's as close as I can come to pronouncing it. Roughly translated, it means 'the Prophet's Sword.'"

"*That* doesn't sound good."

"You think?" Dvorak shook his head, his expression disgusted. "It's a new paramilitary organization with no official connection to either his government or the AJA, but Pat Sullivan's people know damned well Ghilzai's subsidizing them and personally directing them. They're really good at killing people he doesn't like."

"Well shit." It was Wilson's turn to shake his head. "Nothing's ever so bad some asshole can't make it worse, is it?"

"Not much," Dvorak agreed.

"Does sound like a good 'what if' for me to use in a potential training scenario for Cartwright, though. Unless that would be contraindicated for political reasons?"

"Well, listen to you!" Dvorak laughed. "'Contraindicated' from my brother-in-law the Marine?"

"Allow me to salute you once again," Wilson said, raising his hand a second time, and Dvorak laughed harder. Then he shook his head.

"I don't know whether it would be contraindicated or not. Let me think about it. If I can get a few minutes of Judson's time at tomorrow's cabinet meeting I'll ask him about it, too. It probably wouldn't matter one way or the other, as long as your memo to Cartwright didn't leak. On the other hand," he continued thoughtfully, "I can see some possible upsides to making sure it *did* leak."

"My, how Machiavellian of you," Wilson murmured. Then grinned at his brother-in-law's expression. "Yes, you heard it here! Two consecutive sentences—well, interrupted by my salute—in which I used multisyllabic words!"

"And you didn't drop dead from brain sprain or *anything*!" Dvorak marveled.

"Nope, Marines are tough. But you were saying—?"

"I was saying there's a limit to the pressure we can exert on Ghilzai, for a lot of reasons. One thing both the President and the Senate are what you might call adamantly opposed to is nation-building through military intervention. There's probably a majority in the House that would be perfectly happy to do it that way, if it would just get the process over with. Quite a few of our Senators' countries have experienced that themselves, however, and they're not really eager to do it to anyone else. And even if they were, Judson's smart enough to know it won't work. You can't *build* another nation through coercion."

"Strange." Wilson tilted his head. "I seem to recall quite a few instances in which Pieter and Longbow and their friends exerted quite a bit of coercion."

"But to individuals, not entire societies, Rob," Dvorak said very seriously. "The vampires can convince almost any individual to . . . embrace enlightened self-interest in order to survive, you might say. You can't do that to an entire societal template. And in this particular instance, the guy at the top certainly appears to be a true believer. He might actually embrace the opportunity to become a martyr, and his denunciation of the vampires as unclean, accursed servants of Satan really resonates with his supporters. As I say, I think his beliefs are sincere, but it's obvious that he also recognizes the tactical value of demonizing—you should pardon the expression—our most potent 'special forces' weapon in the eyes of all Pakistanis.

"On the other hand, this is a guy who sees military force and terror as standard go-to tools, and who's probably just as paranoid about us 'Westerners'— even if we do have an awful lot of Muslim senators helping to formulate PU policy—as he says he is. For that matter, most of our Muslim senators would *love* for him to have a tragic accident. They hate his version of Islam more than almost anyone else I know, partly because they abhor its repressiveness on a personal level and partly because they know how a regime like his plays to the prejudices of Western bigots who lump every Muslim on the planet together under the label 'Islamic extremist.' So I expect he probably does spend the odd hour here or there worrying about a PAF descent on Naya Islamabad. Not much chance we'd actually *do* it, you understand, but *he* sure as hell would in our place, which means that wouldn't keep him from sweating the possibility. So if General Cartwright were to structure a purely hypothetical training exercise around the seizure and neutralization of an unnamed city in the foothills of an unnamed mountain range somewhere in an unnamed country in Southwest Asia and word of that were to find its way to Naya Islamabad. . . ."

"Never let it be said that I passed up the opportunity to be helpful to my favorite brother-in-law," Wilson said virtuously.

"Just make sure it *doesn't* leak unless the President signs off on it!"

"It won't."

"Good." Dvorak nodded, then checked the time and pushed up out of his chair.

"Well, your timing's good," he said. "Morgana and Maighread are both coming home for their mom's birthday. They're getting in early enough to spend the night, too, and I'm catching the six o'clock shuttle back to Greensboro so I can get home in time to fix supper." He grimaced. "I spend too many nights right here on *Bastion,* and Sharon's been giving me a hard time over it lately. She's fond of pointing out that for a *Starlander* at sixty gravities, it's only about a half-hour flight."

"And she thinks you should close up shop for the day thirty minutes earlier—like, I dunno, only an hour or two after everyone else does?—just so you can get home, sleep in your own bed, and relax a little." Wilson shook his head. "Damn. I knew she was unreasonable, but *that—*!"

"All right—all right!" Dvorak waved both hands in the air. "I know. And I really do try. I sort of suspect she got the girls to come home early just so they could bat those big brown eyes at me and *make* me come home. And Malachi's home on leave until the end of the week. I'm sure all three of them will be delighted to see you, too. It'll reassure them that space elves haven't stolen you after all."

"Dave, the twins are twenty-two now and Malachi's a commissioned officer in eight more months! Well, okay, a third lieutenant's more of a larva than an actual *officer,* but the principle's the same. Somehow I'm pretty sure none of them believe in space elves anymore!"

"No, and they haven't seen you in so long that they aren't sure they believe in *Uncle Rob* anymore, either," Dvorak riposted.

"Ouch." Wilson shook his head. "Point taken," he conceded, and Dvorak snorted.

"Come on. It's a ten-minute slidewalk to the shuttle terminal, and we have to assemble my security detail." He grimaced. "They don't like me wandering around alone, for some reason."

· II ·

AURORA, MINNESOTA,
UNITED STATES

No, you're being shortsighted," Simon Douglas, the Head of Strategic Planning, said to the meeting of Aurora's Planning and Development Department—the PDD. "Haven't you seen the estimates?"

"Yes, I've seen the figures!" Susan Clifford, the head of Zoning Innovation and Historic Preservation said. "But why do we have to build another one so *close*? We've already blotted out most of the original downtown area! If you build this one, too, we might as well just pretend the old Aurora never existed!"

Mayor Lewis Freymark sighed as he looked surreptitiously at his watch. Clifford was one of those people who always talked in exclamations, regardless of the topic. This time, he understood her frustration, though, and he could see she actually had reason to be upset. The "this one" they were discussing building was the third residential tower in downtown—yes, there really was a downtown now—Aurora. So far, they'd only built "small" ones, with the tallest of them "only" about fifteen hundred feet high. They could have built taller ones . . . but humans still had an innate distrust of technology, and many people didn't want to live that high. Whether it was the fear of having a fire, the lift breaking, or "Oh, my God, *what if it fell!*" he hadn't been able to get agreement from the PDD on anything taller.

Even at fifteen hundred feet, though, they were magnificent—each had a hundred or so habitable floors and somewhere around two million square feet of residential area. Nearly eight hundred families inhabited each of the two previous towers, which also had several floors of "local" shops, boutiques, and restaurants. It was hard to believe that only fifteen years ago, he would have killed—literally, *killed*—to have an infinitesimal fraction of that space to shelter his family. And now they were worried about changing the local character of the town. *How times had changed!*

Freymark especially liked the restaurants and would have given his approval for the third tower solely due to the fact it brought more of them to Aurora. Early on in the reconstruction, the engineers in the *Invictus* and *Provocatio* space stations had printed in-atmosphere refiners and printers, and—locked in another brutal winter—Aurora had been one of the first cities to get them. It was a dubious distinction, at best, as the refiners could produce nourishing—if not appetizing—food out of all sorts of biological waste materials. While that had been a major factor in reducing worldwide starvation deaths and had gotten Aurora through the winter, eating something you had just flushed a few hours ago took a level of hunger he hoped to never have again. Ever.

The new, improved hardware which had followed since that first, dreadful winter was considerably more capable, and the engineers had actually considered the human taste bud, which the original refiners . . . hadn't. Several people who'd tried their output swore to him that it actually tasted good, but he was prepared to take that on faith without putting it to the test.

The department head for the Transportation and Mobility Division cleared his throat. "We've looked at a number of places for it, but it just makes sense to put it there. Until we can get more of the public transportation network set up, a lot of people will still need to walk to get to work, shop, or get their neural education."

"But there's a historical marker there where John Davidson shot his moose in 1897!" Clifford whined. "That's an important piece of our history! That's what made him decide to settle here!"

"Let's face it," Freymark said, getting antsy. "The rest of the mayors and I have talked, and it's increasingly likely that Aurora's going to become the new capital of the state. We've recovered enough that the state needs one, and Aurora is the furthest along into reconstruction. We have the best shuttle landing area—" the old school on the southeast of town and about two square miles of forest had been leveled for that, over Clifford's protests "—and the best transportation network. We aren't centrally located, it's true, but we also don't have the tangled mass of scrap that's in the Twin Cities. We may move the capital back there . . . sometime . . . but in the meantime, it's us. We'll need to look at where we want to put the facilities for the new state capital at our next meeting."

"More construction!" Clifford wailed.

"Yes, more construction," Freymark confirmed. "And we need it soonest, too. We'll also need to enlarge the spaceport again and continue work on the transportation grid."

Janice Westfield, the head of the Office of Yes! looked up from her notes with a smile. "So, we *are* going to call it a spaceport?"

Freymark nodded. "We are. It's not like it's a big reach or anything. Half the *Starlanders* that touch down at the field go exo-atmospheric on the way here. Calling it a spaceport is forward-looking. Our future is in the stars, and we need to establish a link to them. By being the first to have a no-kidding spaceport, we set ourselves up to service the space industries and keep our town relevant moving forward."

"Great!" Westfield was positively beaming now, and Freymark smiled back. Personally, he found the name of her office a bit ironic. He'd inherited the "Office of Yes!"—an import from Detroit—along with his job as mayor when the new city charter was set up. He'd thought it was a silly, chirpy sort of name at the time, especially since its official purpose was "to support the efficient and cost-effective operations of PDD, including management of the Department's operating budget, grants and contracts; its partnerships with key vendor, foundation and university partners, and its large-scale community communications, meetings and workshops." In other words, it was the city's bean counters. Fortunately, Westfield was an enthusiastic and *helpful* bean counter. Her predecessor hadn't been.

"What if we don't want to be relevant to moving forward?" asked Fred Novack, head of the Citywide Initiatives Division.

"Then you're in the wrong business or the wrong city," Freymark replied, his eyes sweeping down the table to take everyone in. "We stand at a crossroads—not only for Aurora, but for humanity in general—and we need to determine where we're going to go as a race. I intend for my children to take *their* children—and our race—to the stars, and I'm going to help them. We need to be ready for the aliens when they return, because they're going to be ready for us." He raised a hand when he saw Clifford's mouth open to complain.

"I'm not saying we need to completely break from all our history and traditions. Someone once said that those who forget the mistakes of history are doomed to repeat them, or something like that, and I don't want that to happen here." He nodded to Clifford. "Your marker is an important part of Aurora's history . . . however, is it absolutely necessary that it stay *precisely* where it is now?"

"What do you mean?" Clifford asked. Freymark could tell from the tone of her voice she was suspicious and sensed a trap—and, based on previous meetings, she was probably right to do so.

"What I'm asking is if the marker resides *exactly* where he shot the moose, or is it just in the general vicinity? Did John Davidson mark the precise spot where it happened?"

"Well . . . no," she hedged, seeing where the conversation was going, "but we know it was *close* to there!"

"Well, that's perfect then," Freymark said as he smiled beatifically. "We can move the marker two blocks to the east to accommodate the new tower, and we can change the wording to 'Just to the west of this marker . . .' That will work perfectly and still allow the construction of the tower. All in favor?" Most of the hands in the room went up.

"All opposed?" he asked. Clifford's hand went up, along with the head of the West Design Region, who wanted the tower in her region.

"Okay," Freymark said as he spoke over Clifford's continued objections. "Sorry, I'm late for another appointment, so I can't continue the debate. The proposal to locate the new tower is approved, and the meeting is adjourned.

We'll meet back here on Monday to discuss the plans for the new Aurora Space-port and the capital facilities. Good day, everyone!"

Before anyone could grab him, he stood and strode towards the door, ignoring Clifford's continued pleas to be heard.

. . . . .

FREYMARK RACED INTO the Aurora Regional Medical Center, asked for directions, and sprinted to the indicated room, looking at his watch the entire way. "I'm not late, am I?" he asked as he burst into the room.

He drew to an immediate halt, the target of three very disapproving glares.

"No," his wife, Janice Freymark, replied with that particular level of scorn a wife has for a husband who has erred and wasn't where he was supposed to be, when he was supposed to be there. "You aren't late, yet, although you pushed it really closely."

"I'm glad you made it," her daughter Camila Rodriguez added, more prone to forgiveness. She doubled up as a contraction hit her, and her husband, Miguel Rodriguez, took her hand, wincing slightly at the pressure she applied.

The door opened, and a robot rolled in. "I am sorry to inform you, but the doctor will be a little late," the robot said.

"See?" Freymark said, smiling. "I wasn't late—"

"She regrets the inconvenience caused by the extra thirty seconds," the robot added.

Janice frowned, and Freymark found a nice piece of the floor to look at.

At almost exactly thirty seconds later, the doctor arrived with another robot in tow. While the first one's torso had been humanoid in shape, rising from the cylindrical column of its ball-mounted base, this one was large and blocky—it barely fitted through the door—with tracked wheels and a number of appendages. It rolled to the end of the bed and pulled out the stirrups that were an integral part of the bed, then it picked up the leads from Camila's monitors and plugged them into ports on its side.

"Hi," the tall, blond woman who'd followed it through the door said as she washed her hands in the sink and pulled on a set of gloves. She moved like she knew what she was doing and gave off an air of competency. "I'm Doctor Freitag. I'll be observing the operation today."

"Observing?" Freymark asked. "Uh . . . aren't we going to the operating room?"

"Camila would have gone over this with you if you'd been on time," Janice said, The Tone still present. "The robot is going to handle the operation; the doctor's here in case of any unforeseen issues."

"Right," the doctor agreed. "The medical robots have been adapted for human use, and they're incredibly efficient. Still, we like to be here, just in case.

There may come a time where we aren't needed . . . but that time hasn't arrived yet." She smiled. "I'm also here because they aren't great conversationalists yet, either, and most people like a human touch." She winked and passed out masks. "Please put these on.

"Okay," the doctor said as she put her own mask on and stepped up next to the robot. "Does everyone want to watch, or would you like a privacy screen?"

"Well—" Freymark started.

"I want to watch," Camila said. Her tone ended all discussion.

"Then let's begin," the doctor said.

The robot rolled up Camila's robe, and Freymark went to stand with his wife at Camila's head. He hadn't seen that part of his daughter in quite some time and—despite the circumstances—was somewhat uncomfortable looking at it now, especially from that angle.

An appendage passed over Camila's pregnant stomach, which was larger than he remembered Janice's ever being, and a fine mist sprayed down from it. "That's the antibiotic nano-spray," the doctor said. "It creates an antiseptic area to operate." The sprayer made a second pass. "And that's a local anesthetic that's more efficient than anything we had in our pharmacopeia prior to the arrival of the Shongairi. It also adds a suppleness to the skin and will help preserve it for the next few minutes."

Freymark wanted to ask a number of questions and opened his mouth to do so, but a look from his wife caused him to shut it again. The whole process seemed—at least to this point—as if the doctor considered it a trivial procedure. But it wasn't trivial—*people died in childbirth!* Didn't they?

An appendage with what looked like a pencil at the end hovered over Camila's stomach, and a beam of light came from it. Freymark couldn't help himself. "Is that . . . is that a laser?"

"Yes," the doctor said, without looking up from the procedure. "We've had medical lasers for a long time. We just haven't had the precision this one has."

The robot cut a large patch, then folded it off to the side. That was all Freymark had to see, and he turned away for fear of losing his lunch all over the proceedings. He glanced at the others in the room. His wife and daughter appeared engrossed in the process and watched with wide-eyed looks of wonder as the robot continued with the operation. Even his son-in-law didn't seem as disturbed as Freymark would have been if a robot had been cutting on Janice.

"And there's your new baby daughter," the doctor said, as a wail broke the near silence.

Freymark risked a glance as the robot handed the crying baby to the doctor, who stood waiting with a blanket. The doctor swaddled the baby, wiped off her face, and handed her to Camila. "Congratulations, Mom and Dad!" the doctor announced.

The robot reached into his daughter's stomach again, and Freymark had to look away again when his stomach spasmed. He concentrated on the wall in his effort to keep lunch down. "And here's your son!" the doctor announced as a second wail joined the first.

"Wait!" Freymark said. "Twins?"

"Yes, Daddy," Camila said. "We've known all along that we were going to have twins—the new medical technology is wonderful—we just wanted to keep it a surprise. We know you're kind of old-fashioned that way. Surprise!"

"Oh, my," Freymark said. He joined his wife at the top of the bed where Camila held one of the babies, while Miguel held the other. He looked at the two babies in awe—it had been a while since he'd been part of a delivery—and he felt as if his heart would break from joy. He was a grandparent! Not once, but twice! Seeing those two tiny, scrunched up, *beautiful* faces, he swore to do everything possible to ensure they had long, healthy, and alien-free lives . . . no matter what anyone on the planning board wanted. They would build and prepare, then they would build and prepare some more. They *would* be ready.

Movement caught his eye, and he looked down at his daughter's stomach. The robot had closed the patch of skin—everything was remarkably bloodless—and sprayed the edges of the incision. His eyes went wide as the cut joined together and the skin reformed as if it had never been apart.

"How is . . . how is this possible?" Freymark asked. Even he could hear the awe in his voice.

"Nanobots," the doctor replied. "Microscopic machines operating at the cellular level."

"I know what nanobots are," Freymark said. "I just . . . I just never saw this before. It's . . ." his voice trailed off, searching for a word. "It's miraculous," he finally said, although he found the word didn't do his feelings justice. He looked at his watch. Only ten minutes had passed.

"I'll probably do twenty-five of these today," the doctor replied. "It's not a miracle. It's just science."

· III ·

FORT SANDERS, NORTH CAROLINA, UNITED STATES

What should I be looking for out there?" Elias Favre asked as he scanned the terrain whipping past the window of the low-flying helicopter. The tall, dark-haired representative from the suburbs of what was left of Geneva had already shown himself to be inquisitive and extremely interested in the exercise going on in the fields and forests beneath the racing UH-60 helicopter. An ex-member of the Swiss militia, he also had a good grasp of military hardware and tactics.

"Over there, you can see one of our new tank companies massing for an assault on the enemy positions by that sandy area farther to the left," Colonel Russell Clayton replied, pointing out the left window of the Black Hawk. Although Clayton would rather have been down on the ground, commanding the troops, the President—*the no-kidding President of the Planetary Union*—had called him and asked him to take care of the two representatives, so here he was, giving them the dog-and-pony show.

"You mean those tanks over there?" Luca Gerber could have been specifically designed as a contrast for Favre. While Favre looked the part of a military man—tall and aristocratic—Gerber, a professor from Universität Bern, was the direct opposite, short and extremely stocky, with hair as fair as Favre's was dark. He represented an area that was the economic, educational, and health care hub of central Switzerland, and his support was crucial to moving the nation in the right direction.

"Yes, Sir," Clayton replied. "Those targets are what *used* to be our top-of-the-line tanks—like the ones Colonel Alastair Sanders' battalion used to defeat the Shongairi in Afghanistan during the Puppy Invasion."

"That's what I don't understand," Gerber said. "If we destroyed the Shongair armor with our old tanks, why do we want to use the inferior Shongair models now?"

Clayton gave him a hunter's grin.

"Those tanks—we named them the Sanders, after the Colonel, as a matter of fact—may *look* like what he faced in Afghanistan, but they're definitely *not* the same. As it turns out, the Shongairi had access to much better technology than they brought here; they just didn't field any of it. We have!"

Gerber's eyebrows knitted. "But that doesn't make any sense. If they had better technology, why didn't they use it?"

"It appears that, in all their previous conquests, they never needed anything more sophisticated and capable than what they brought, and they weren't expecting us to have advanced as far as we had. The last time they were here was in 1415, and the longbow was the king of battle then. The equipment they brought would have been very effective against troops wielding longbows. . . ."

"But we had advanced to tanks," Favre finished.

"Exactly." Clayton nodded. "They were unprepared for how far we'd advanced. And according to the history we captured from them, they were probably no more advanced than we were by the end of World War Two, say, when they fought their last war against a true peer opponent. So even though they had lasers mounted on their counter-grav tanks, they weren't optimized for use against enemies whose tech matched their own—they were bottom-of-the-line weapons. They would have completely overwhelmed the forces being fielded during the Hundred Years' War, or the Napoleonic Wars, or even World War One or World War Two, five hundred years later. But their vehicle-mounted energy weapons were unable to penetrate the frontal armor of an Abrams tank with a single hit.

"What's more interesting, though," he added, warming to the subject, "is the fact that once they found out how far we'd advanced, they didn't appear able to adapt to our new capabilities. The time window wasn't wide enough for them to have made any major changes to their hardware—their industrial modules were still spinning up when the vampires took them out, so it hadn't been physically possible to put new designs into production, even if they'd tried to—but they should have been able to figure out how to use what they had far more effectively once they found out what they were actually up against. Only they didn't. It was as if they were so used to bullying technologically inferior races that when we stepped up and punched them in the mouth, they didn't know what to do. Their only response was to call in strikes from orbit. We don't expect them to be so unprepared next time; we have to be ready."

"Are we?" Representative Favre asked. "Are we ready for them?"

"Let's find out." Clayton switched to the radio. "Control to all forces, advance and destroy the enemy armor."

The helicopter went into a hover, and Clayton pointed out the window as the tanks leapt forward on their counter-grav fields. The helicopter had moved a little closer to the tanks now, and Clayton could see their rectangular-shaped barrels move as they quested for targets. The hover tanks were about seven miles from the targets, with a small rise between them. As the tanks cleared the hill, they fired.

"A dud!" Gerber said. Unlike the older 120-millimeter smoothbore guns on the M1A2 Abrams, there'd been no enormous fireball when the new tanks fired. In fact, it was singularly unimpressive for anyone accustomed to pre-invasion artillery. There was a clearly visible cloud of *something* directly in front of the tank, however, and then four pieces of something else arced out of the cloud to land only a fraction of the way to the target.

"Just watch!" Clayton said, but before he could finish, two of the tanks on the range exploded.

"What . . . what the hell was that?" Gerber asked. "Lasers?"

Clayton shook his head. "We could have used lasers—they're in the printers' technology base—but we went with a railgun instead. It's affected less by weather and can handle a wider variety of ammunition types. It also lets us use the tanks for a number of different missions. The cloud you saw wasn't from propellant; it was just dust being kicked up by the atmospheric shockwave. And the black pieces you see aren't the actual rounds—those are the shoes that go around the rounds like sabots; they're discarded after the rounds clear the barrel.

"In fact, the railgun on the Sanders is a scaled-up version of the personal weapons you'll see in a bit," Clayton explained. "It has a muzzle velocity on the order of about thirty-four hundred meters per second, which is twice the average muzzle velocity of the Abrams' main gun. At that velocity, its ballistics closely approximate those of an energy weapon at the ranges it's likely to be used. It might as well be a laser . . . except that it hits with a *lot* more force."

"But the rounds can't be very big, if they come packed in a sabot we can see from here, can they?" Gerber asked. "How does something that small carry enough explosives to do the job?"

"The anti-tank rounds don't use *any* explosives," Clayton replied. "They're actually kinetic energy weapons, which, like a bullet, use only their kinetic energy to penetrate the target. Once a round forces its way through the armor, the heat and spalling it generates while it's going through destroys the target. The idea of a penetrator isn't new—our Abrams tanks used something similar—but now, with the railgun, we're able to generate a *whole* lot more force."

"I don't get it," Gerber said. "Why doesn't the round just bounce off? Isn't that what tank armor is supposed to do? Make rounds bounce off it?"

"Well, yes, that's what a tank's armor is for," Clayton said, reminding himself that Gerber was an academic, not an experienced military officer. "But this type of round has so much energy it pierces the armor, rather than bouncing off." Clayton turned to the representative to make eye contact. "Basically, energy is a function of a projectile's mass and velocity, right?"

Gerber nodded.

"In order to maximize the amount of energy we apply to the target, we increase the mass as much as possible, by using materials as dense as we can find.

For the Abrams, that was depleted uranium; what we can produce now is a lot denser even than that, so we can really dial the mass up. Then, we minimize the diameter of the final projectile, so all the energy is focused on as small an area as possible. In the Abrams, we encased it in a full-caliber sabot, basically a shoe to carry it down the barrel, because the sabot's base was wide enough to get the most velocity out of the powder charge. Then the sabot was discarded as the projectile cleared the barrel, and the penetrator continued to the target, with a *lot* less air resistance and a lot more kinetic energy than a full-caliber round would have experienced.

"The railgun still uses a shoe to engage with the magnetic field and stabilize the penetrator on its way down the barrel, but it doesn't have to be anywhere near as big as the Abram's sabot was. Basically, we make a *really* heavy arrow, then we shoot it at an *extremely* high velocity, and it hits in such a small area that it smashes straight through, rather than bouncing off. As it goes through, it pulls along pieces of the armor it touches, then it shoots all of that stuff into the tank's interior at nearly the same speed. Between the shrapnel and the over-pressure, the interior of the tank isn't survivable."

"Ouch," Favre said.

Clayton nodded. "As a former tank guy, I agree a hundred percent. The key, however, is to do it to them before they can do it to you."

"And these new tanks will allow us to do that?"

"Yes, they will."

"Why not just drop something on them from orbit, so they can't hit you back?" Gerber asked.

"Certainly, that's an option in some cases, especially if the enemy's out in the open, but what if you're trying to take a city? There's a reason the Army didn't just ask the Air Force to demolish entire towns and cities in Iraq and Afghanistan. You *can* level a half dozen city blocks to destroy a tank hiding there, but it's awfully hard on the local townspeople. You can't win the hearts and minds of an enemy population if you kill all the civilians while you're taking out their military—there won't be any of them left."

"Makes sense, I guess," Gerber said with a shrug.

Clayton nodded back out the window. Even from the helicopter, it was apparent the target tanks had all been destroyed.

"Let's go down and take a look at how the new technology translates to the common soldier."

. . . . .

"THIS IS A company from one of the other battalions in my brigade," Colonel Clayton said proudly as they approached the firing range near where the helicopter had landed. The company in question was just finishing and loading up into several counter-grav trucks. "The brigade has four battalions—the armor unit you already saw, a mechanized infantry battalion, a drone battalion, and an antiaircraft battalion—and attached engineering and heavy weapons companies. Altogether, we have about forty-five hundred personnel, which includes our own supporting logistics folks, engineers, cooks, medics, and other staff."

"That sounds like a well-rounded package," Favre said.

"It is, especially when you see the capabilities of the personnel involved."

Clayton led them to the end of the firing line, where the brigade's sergeant major stood at attention along with a corporal.

"Good morning, Sergeant Major."

"Good morning, Sir!" The noncom turned to the two representatives. "Good morning, Gentlemen! I'm Sergeant Major Jenkins, and Corporal González and I will be showing you the capabilities of the new M-1 Strike Rifle. Corporal González!"

"Good morning, Gentlemen," González said with a smile and a touch of an Andalusian accent. Clayton nodded—the Spaniard had been chosen because he was able to be highly professional, while being simultaneously open and engaging. "As the Sergeant Major said, I'll be showing you my new best friend, my M-1."

He raised his rifle to port arms and opened it for inspection so the two representatives could see it. The weapon had the high-tech, shiny look of a prop you'd see in the movies. Although Clayton hadn't expected the rifle's finish to hold up once it was put into his soldiers' hands—if you want to find five new ways to break something, give it to a soldier—but the finish had defied his expectations, and his battalion's rifles all looked the same as the day they'd arrived from the printers. Whatever alien composite they were made of was *tough*!

"The M-1 is a ten-millimeter, air-cooled, capacitor-operated, magazine-fed railgun," the corporal continued. "The M-1's receiver is made of an aluminum alloy, its barrel, bolt, and bolt carrier of a lightweight alien alloy, and its handguards, pistol grip, and buttstock of an alien composite.

"The M-1 is a little heavier than some of its predecessors at eleven-point-two pounds with a loaded forty-round magazine; however, the ten-millimeter round it fires is much larger than its predecessors. The earlier 5.56 round was approximately half its diameter, with a bullet that weighed less than four grams. Even the old 7.62 mm round is only three-quarters the diameter of the M-1's, and it weighs less than ten grams. The bullet fired by the M-1 weighs almost *twenty* grams, yet its weight is proportionally smaller than it would have been if we'd simply scaled up an existing round to ten millimeters. In fact, the sub-caliber penetrator is only six millimeters in diameter, smaller than the old NATO 7.62; the greater weight is possible because it's made of alien composites, like the new tank rounds. Despite its much larger size, the entire sub-caliber penetrator round—cartridge and penetrator—only weighs about forty-five grams total, and the explosive round only weighs about forty. Of note, that's only about ninety percent and seventy percent more, respectively, than the standard NATO round, but it puts out a hell of a lot more punch."

The sergeant major glanced at the corporal, who caught the look.

"Oops, sorry, Gentlemen," González said with a half grin, "I mean, it puts out a *heck* of a punch."

Gerber chuckled. "I'm familiar with the vernacular. What I'm not familiar with is what a sub . . . a sub penetrator is. Is that what you called it?"

"It's a sub-caliber penetrator, Sir," González explained, back on track. "Just like the tank rounds you saw earlier, the bullet fired by the M-1 is actually forty percent narrower than the diameter of the barrel it's fired through. The bullet sheds its sabot petals after it emerges from the barrel, and the super-dense projectile proceeds the rest of the way to the target. That lets it focus the kinetic energy on a smaller target area."

"Just like the tank round," Favre said with a nod. "Got it. Still . . . with a bullet that heavy, the muzzle velocity has to be fairly low, doesn't it? While I can see how it would have a lot of stopping power, wouldn't a lower muzzle velocity significantly shorten the rifle's effective range?"

"You're right," González said, nodding. "It takes a hel—a heck of a lot of energy to propel the new round, and if we tried to do that with a traditional powder charge, like in our legacy ammunition, it either wouldn't work, or it would kick a soldier's shoulder out of joint when it fired. The M-1 is a modified railgun, though—it doesn't have any powder at all. It uses an electrical charge to propel the bullet down the barrel."

González showed the men end of the rifle, which was a rectangle of composites with the barrel in the center. "You'll notice the rifle's forestock goes all the way to the muzzle. That's because the forestock holds the electronics and magnets that propel the bullet. All of this is powered by a Hegemony-level capacitor that's included in each of the bullet cartridges. Unlike the bullets of old that had 'powder' in the cartridge, our new bullets have 'power' in them." He smiled.

Favre looked thoughtful. "The question is, though, is it enough?"

"Absolutely!" González exclaimed. "Our old rifles had a muzzle velocity of just over nine hundred meters per second. These new rifles have a muzzle velocity of right at twenty-one hundred—that's more than our old tanks had. And when you apply that kind of energy to a three-hundred-grain bullet, you get a muzzle energy of over thirty-two thousand foot-pounds—uh, around forty-three kilojoules. That's over twice that of the old Barrett .50 caliber rifle, and it's a lot easier to carry around than the Barrett! Plus, it'll take out anything you want it to!"

Clayton chuckled. "Despite Corporal González' enthusiasm, that kind of energy caused some huge problems during the design phase, because the recoil force has the same energy as the round does leaving the muzzle. Unabated, the recoil from a bullet leaving at Mach six would have broken the corporal's shoulder, if it didn't knock it off him entirely.

"I'm told the problem drove the designers to distraction, and they almost gave up on this design several times before they figured out a series of mitigation features. In addition to some low tech options like recoil springs made of alien composites, they also incorporated some cutting-edge Hegemony tech, and they finally made it work. The whole assault rifle system is really cool."

He pointed to the rifle's barrel.

"Really heavy rifles—like the Barrett—sometimes used muzzle brakes that captured some of the expanding gases that propelled the bullet and ejected them to the rear. It was sort of like using a rocket venturi to pull the rifle forward at the same time the recoil drove it backward. Since we no longer have those gases, this rifle uses a variation on the same principle. The M-1's inner barrel has some range of motion, and as the bullet traverses the barrel, the recoil force creates an electric potential in the outer sleeve. As the inner barrel surges backward, the same magnetic field that drives the bullet 'grips' the barrel liner and damps a lot of the recoil force, and the springs absorb most of the rest of it. In effect, the inner barrel functions like a hydraulic piston as it pulses backward and then returns to its original position as the force damps out. The motion eliminates nearly all the recoil force—there's still more than there was with the M16, but less than with something like the old M1 Garand—and the system provides an added benefit in that the inner barrel charges a capacitor-type device the way a regenerative braking system stores energy, so the rounds don't have to hold quite as high a stored charge.

"That's what the manual says, anyway. There's a ceramic tube that clamps onto the barrel that you have to pull off so you can clean the connector. If you don't, it sparks like crazy when you fire the rifle."

"Ceramic tube?" Favre asked.

"Yeah, it's got some sort of mesh in it. You don't want to mess with it." Clayton shrugged. "We could talk about it all day," he added, "but a demonstration would probably be a lot more informative. Corporal, why don't you show them how it works?"

"Yes, Sir! If you'll follow me, Gentlemen?" González led the men to the firing line.

"Damn!" Favre muttered as he looked out across the range. A little louder, he added, "Aren't those targets a little far? What's the distance?"

González smiled. "Well, yes, they probably are farther than what you might be used to, but that's because we had to move them back a bit to make it more of a challenge. It used to be that in order to qualify, you had to hit at least twenty-three out of forty pop-up targets at ranges from five meters to three hundred meters. Turns out, with the integrated ballistic computer, sensors, laser ranger, and the new scope system that comes standard on the M-1, they're like firing a laser for distances out to over half a mile—wherever you aim, that's where the bullet's going to go. Even without the scope, you still ought to be able to put at least thirty into a target at five hundred meters."

"Is that right?"

"Yes, Sir," González said. "The problem we had wasn't hitting the target; it was keeping the bullets on the range. With even a little bit of extra elevation, you could easily toss a round off base. The first day we had the new rifles, we put five rounds into people's houses and cars where they're rebuilding Fayetteville outside Fort Sanders. Thankfully, no one got hurt, but we had to put in a new rifle range that was longer and had higher backstops. And buy up all the land beyond it for about ten miles." He gave them a bashful grin. "It was kind of a mess."

"I guess so," Favre agreed.

"Okay, González, assume a good prone position," Sergeant Major Jenkins said.

"What about hearing protection?" Gerber asked, looking around somewhat frantically. "Don't we need some?"

"These rifles aren't that loud," Jenkins replied. "I can get you some if you want, Sir, but generally, we no longer use them for normal range operations. Most militaries were pretty fanatical about that, using the old-style firearms, and we still use them if someone's going to be firing for extended periods or we have a lot of weapons on the firing line. But normally, they aren't necessary for something like this."

"If you think it will be all right. . . ."

"You'll be fine," Clayton reassured Gerber as he handed each representative a set of binoculars. "If you'd like to step back a few paces, please feel free."

Gerber looked uncomfortable, but when Favre stepped up to where González was lying on the firing line, Gerber took a step closer, although he still stayed ten feet behind the trooper.

"Lock one magazine of forty rounds and load," Jenkins ordered. González snapped a magazine into the rifle and worked the bolt manually to charge it.

"Ready on the right?" Jenkins asked. "Ready on the left?"

"Ready," González said as the two representatives looked around.

"The firing line is ready," Jenkins noted. "Place your selector lever on semi-automatic, scan your sector, and commence firing."

After a couple of seconds, González fired, and the rifle made a *crack!* The sound was sharp, but not as loud as a conventional military rifle. In fact, it was less noisy than most .22 target rifles.

"That's it?" Favre asked. "That's not so bad."

"No, Sir, it isn't," González said with a smile. "But the Bronto's bark is still the crack of doom . . . for the enemy, that is."

One of Favre's eyebrows went up. "The Bronto?"

Clayton sighed. "Yes, that's the slang name some of the soldiers have given the rifle. As you may have noticed, the rifle itself is fairly silent; the noise it makes when it fires is the crack of the Mach six bullet breaking the sound barrier as it leaves the rifle."

Favre nodded. "But, 'the Bronto'?"

"As it turns out," Clayton said, "there's a debate among paleontologists about the brontosaurus. Some of them believe the bronto could snap its tail as a weapon, the same as the triceratops used its horns or the stegosaurus used its tail spikes. If you think of a fifty-ton bronto cracking the whip with its forty-foot-long tail, some paleos think it would have been able to break the sound barrier, and it would make a *crack!* similar to what the round makes as it leaves the rifle. One of the troopers—"

"Jim Beall, Sir," González interjected.

Clayton continued over the interruption. "One of the troopers was a dinosaur enthusiast, and he said the rifle made a similar noise to the bronto whipping its tail, and the name kind of stuck."

He shrugged. "As we already discussed, the mass of the projectile affects the rifle's recoil; the sound it makes is affected by its cross-section—the wider it is, the more noise it makes breaking the sound barrier because it creates a larger shockwave. The actual round the rifle fires is smaller, like a needle, so the round is loudest right at the muzzle, while its still in the sabot, but it's a lot quieter downrange after the petals discard."

"That makes sense," Favre said.

Clayton looked at González. "If you would finish the demonstration, Corporal?"

"Yes, Sir!" He continued firing. After a few shots, there was a hole in the bull's-eye large enough to be seen without the binoculars. By the time he finished the magazine, he'd shot out all of the bull's-eye.

"Cease fire," Jenkins ordered. "Lock and clear your weapon."

"Wow, that's impressive," Gerber said. After five shots, he'd gone to stand next to Favre so he could see better. He'd still jumped every time the rifle fired, but less and less with each successive shot.

"No," Clayton said, "that's just really cool. *This* is impressive." He turned to the sergeant major. "Give them three rounds of full-caliber explosive in a three-round burst."

"González, lock one magazine of three full-caliber explosive rounds and load," Jenkins ordered.

"Yes, Sergeant Major, it would be my pleasure," González replied. He pulled a small container from a cargo pocket, loaded three cartridges from it into the magazine, and locked it back into place. He charged the rifle and got back into his firing position.

"Ready on the right?" Jenkins asked. "Ready on the left?"

"Ready," González said.

"The firing line is ready," Jenkins noted. "Place your selector lever on burst, scan your sector, and commence firing."

Crack! Crack! Crack! The three rounds fired within less than a second, and the ground around the target erupted in three large fireballs. *Boom! Boom! Boom!*

As the smoke cleared, Clayton couldn't find any evidence of the target. He smiled.

"Those are the full-caliber explosive rounds," he explained. "Basically, they're like ten-millimeter grenades. They fire at a lower muzzle velocity than the penetrators, only about Mach five, because they don't need the same degree of penetration to be effective. They're just as accurate, though, and the M-1's onboard ballistic computer adjusts the sights or scope automatically. For that matter, its sensors can detect and measure changes in gravity—the difference between ours here on Earth and on Mars or the Moon, for example—and factor that information in right along with wind, humidity, and atmospheric pressure . . . if any."

The colonel smiled at Gerber's expression.

"The grenades themselves are formed out of an explosive compound hard enough it needs no case, unlike conventional grenades," he continued. "In the standard U.S. forty-millimeter grenade, the explosive filler accounted for less than twenty percent of the total weight of the round and maximum effective range was only about three hundred and fifty meters—and it wasn't very accurate at that sort of distance. *This* round is effective to over three times that range, with a very high degree of accuracy, and it delivers ninety percent of the forty-millimeter's explosive payload by weight. Since the explosive compound is about forty percent more energetic than anything we had before the invasion, it's actually about thirty percent more powerful than the forty-millimeter at only a quarter of the old grenade's diameter. That means we no longer need the under-barrel grenade launcher; all we have to do is put in a new magazine and rock and roll."

Both representatives stared at him, open-mouthed. Favre started to ask a question, but Clayton held up a hand, silencing him, as three young female corporals approached. One of the soldiers, an Indian woman, carried a small table, which she set up on the firing range. The second, who looked Hispanic, carried a chair she set next to the table. The third, a tall, lithe Caucasian, carried a set of goggles and an integrated keypad and joystick. Without a word, she sat in the chair, pulled on the goggles, and began tapping on the keypad. As she sat, the group could see she also had on a backpack, from which a thin sliver of metal projected.

"I would ask you to turn your attention back to the range," Clayton requested. "In the back left of the range, there are three tanks. Do you see them?"

"Yeah," Gerber said, confusion coloring his voice.

"I see them," Favre replied in a firmer tone.

"Good," Clayton said. "Now, if you look above it, you can see four things flying there. If you look closely, you'll see that two are a little larger than the other two."

"You mean those little specks?" Gerber asked. "What are they?"

"They're drones," Jenkins replied. He nodded to the blond woman sitting at the table. "Corporal Adamescu will be controlling them for the final demonstration of the day."

Clayton cleared his throat. "Corporal Adamescu, when you're ready, you may begin."

"Yes, Sir," the woman replied, although her voice was hollow, as if her concentration was elsewhere.

"You'll want to focus your attention on the tank to the left," Clayton noted when the two representatives continued to stare at the corporal.

The two men refocused their attention in time to see a pair of the drones dive towards the tank. The drones fired—although it was impossible to tell exactly when, since there were no muzzle flashes or other indications—and explosions danced on top of the tank, with a few other misses nearby. After two seconds, and numerous hits, the tank exploded. The two drones raced off and were quickly lost to sight.

The other two drones dove on the center tank of the group. These drones were larger, and carried missiles of some type, which could be seen as they launched. The missiles appeared to accelerate all the way to the target, and detonated on impact. They obviously penetrated the tank, as its turret blew off in the resulting explosions. The second pair of drones, although larger, also disappeared quickly.

"Is that it?" Gerber asked.

"No," Clayton replied. "Keep your eyes on the last—"

The third tank exploded.

"Wha . . . what was that?" Gerber asked.

"Mini-drone," Jenkins replied. He held out his hand, and a small drone came and hovered over it. The drone was an ovoid about three feet long and two feet in diameter at the midpoint. He caught it with both hands and brought it over to show the two representatives.

"When we were watching the tanks," Clayton said, "you may remember I said the key was to do it to the enemy before they could do it to you. This is one of the ways we can. This is one of our stealth drones, which can operate over an enemy battlefield, or any other high-value target, for a surprisingly long length of time. A controller like Corporal Adamescu can control a small fleet of them, since they're fairly autonomous and usually don't need much more from the controller than permission to fire."

Clayton smiled.

"Although the Puppies didn't arm their drones—they only used them for reconnaissance and as communications relays—we've altered their designs somewhat. The one Sergeant Major Jenkins is holding has a laser that can be used to take out high value targets, usually without anyone knowing, as its re-active camouflage makes it extremely hard to see. The one issue we have with it is that, due to the size of the counter-grav unit, there isn't a lot of space for armament. We've been able to reduce that—a lot—from the Puppies' original design by stripping out redundant components, but it's still the major squeeze on the drones' internal volume. Because of that, each mini-drone can only fire three or four shots, so they aren't as good against troops or large concentrations of vehicles; for those targets, we have the drones you saw earlier . . . which are now located behind you."

The representatives turned to find the other four drones—each about three times the size of their smaller, laser-armed cousins—had come in and landed on the firing line behind them, *and they'd never heard them coming!*

The two men turned back to Clayton with their mouths open. "I thought . . ." Favre said. "I thought counter-grav gave off some sort of . . . vibration, or some-thing, so you could tell when a counter-grav unit was operating nearby."

Clayton nodded. "That *used* to be true; however, we figured out how to damp the vibration. Like much of the Hegemony technology, the Shongairi *could* have fixed it, but they never saw any reason to, since they were far less sensitive to it and it apparently never occurred to them that they might need stealth to fight us primitives."

They gawked at him, and he smiled, but then he beckoned to Corporal Adam-escu and Corporal González.

"Gentlemen, that will conclude our demonstration for today," he said as they came to stand at attention alongside Sergeant Major Jenkins. "As you can see, the Planetary Union's Brigade of the Future has the capability to go anywhere and conduct a wide variety of combat operations. Unfortunately, we weren't able to show you our Project Heinlein armor or our antiaircraft folks today—the people of New Fayetteville *do* get kind of worried when planes start falling from the sky—but I can confirm our new antiaircraft technology is comparable with everything else you've seen today."

"Now," Clayton said, moving to stand next to his troops, "what questions can we answer for you?"

IV

NAYA ISLAMABAD, CAPITAL TERRITORY, ISLAMIC REPUBLIC OF PAKISTAN

There they go," Captain Henry Frye said as the third *Starfire* assault shuttle broke off from the formation and began to spiral down.

"Copy," Colonel Rob Wilson said from where he stood at the back of the flight station. "Do we have stealth engaged?"

"Yes, sir," the weapons operator, Lieutenant Chris Solice, said from alongside him. "We've been invisible to anything they have since we formed up. Our wingman is, too. As far as anyone down there knows, there's just the one shuttle inbound with the delegation."

Wilson took a last look out the cockpit canopy, but the third shuttle was already out of sight. He let his breath out slowly. *Go with God, Abu Bakr,* he thought. *Your Allah, my God—I hope* Someone *is watching over you right now.*

He shook his head once—it was out of his hands now, at least for a while. Hopefully, everything would go well, the team would deliver their message, and they'd leave peacefully. He had a bad feeling, though. Ghilzai had rebuffed every Planetary Union effort to bring Pakistan into the fold ever since he'd taken over, and then suddenly—out of the blue—he said he'd allow a delegation to land in Naya Islamabad.

Had he changed his mind? From the outside, there didn't appear to be any cause or justification for a change of heart, which left a very bad feeling in the pit of Wilson's stomach. He'd recommended sending a complete team of vampires—including a vampire flight crew for the assault shuttle—but he'd been overruled. Ghilzai hated vampires and refused to conduct any negotiations with them. Wilson's superiors had allowed him to pre-position his forces overhead, but the shuttle was going in with precious little defense for its lead negotiator. Not that three vampires couldn't put a hurting on anyone that wanted to do Abu Bakr ill . . . but great as they were on offense, offense wasn't called for in this situation.

And they couldn't stop Abu Bakr from eating a bullet in any event.

Although the Planetary Union *had* to send a mission to talk with Ghilzai and see what he wanted, something seemed very wrong, and Wilson would have bet his retirement that his force was going to get the call before this was all over. He nodded, looking at the weapons officer's screens. Lieutenant Solice had a crystal clear picture of the compound, with all of the weapons emplacements located. He hadn't locked any of his own weapons on them—yet—but it would take only seconds for him to have them targeted and missiles on the way. The flyboy was ready; it was time for Wilson and his troops to get ready, too.

"I'll be in the back getting suited up," he said to the pilots. "Let me know when things start falling into the crapper."

Captain Frye looked over his shoulder. "You think they will, Sir?"

Wilson nodded. "Count on it."

· · · · ·

"REMEMBER," ABU BAKR said as the *Starfire*'s aft ramp cycled down, "this mission isn't about killing Ghilzai or any of his followers, and *especially* not about killing his cousin, no matter how much of an asshole he may be to me or any of you. We're here to *warn* Ghilzai, not to make a martyr out of anyone. Got it?" He looked at his team of "negotiators," of which he was the "lead negotiator." It consisted of the three "sisters," who seemed to be inseparable—Jill, Cecilia, and Susan. While they were all *extremely* accomplished at getting the attention of any petty warlord who overstepped his or her boundaries, the sisters' missions more often than not ended up with all of the warlords dead. Their second in command (or third, or fourth—whoever was still alive by that point) was usually very tractable (having just seen their bosses die horribly in front of them), but Howell and Dvorak had made it *exceptionally* clear that Abu Bakr was *not* to leave a trail of bodies in his discussions with Ghilzai.

"Yeah, we know," Jill, the tall brunette who led the group, said.

"Obviously," Susan added. Although the redhead was the group's number three, she was probably the smartest of the lot and radiated intelligence. "The asshole would like nothing more than to have a few martyrs he could point to."

Abu Bakr looked pointedly at Cecilia, who said nothing. The blonde looked steadily back at him until he raised an eyebrow at her. She nodded, once, a minute twitch of her head.

"What does that mean?" Abu Bakr asked, already tired of dealing with her.

"I know," she said.

"What do you know?" Abu Bakr asked. "I want to hear you say it."

"You didn't make them say it," she noted.

"No, I didn't, but they also didn't give me shit, nor do they make a point of killing people just for the sake of killing them."

"I don't kill people without reason," Cecilia said, turning up her nose. "Everyone I've killed deserved it, for one reason or another."

"I've seen the reports," Abu Bakr replied. He could feel his temperature continue to rise. "I think many of the bystanders might have disagreed with some of your reasons. I want to hear you say it."

Cecilia looked down the ramp at the security forces massing there. Abu

Bakr watched her eyes narrow; she looked like a wolf selecting which sheep it intended to cull from the herd.

"Damn it, Cecilia," Jill said. "We don't have all night. We're supposed to get in and out before the sun comes up, and people see us here. Just tell him what he wants to hear."

Cecilia sighed theatrically and turned to Abu Bakr. "I heard you. We're not supposed to kill any of these assholes, no matter how much they might deserve it. Okay?"

Abu Bakr nodded once. "Don't forget it." He turned from the vampire and took a deep breath to calm his nerves before he went to meet Ghilzai. He hadn't wanted to bring the sisters, and he *definitely* hadn't wanted to bring Cecilia. He would rather have brought Jasmine in place of the entire group—he knew he could trust her—but her presence was required on *Bastion* as part of some meeting, and he'd been saddled with the sisters, instead.

He understood that. Which wasn't remotely the same as saying he *liked* it.

Nor did he like his view of the compound's grounds. Located within the heart of Naya Islamabad, the "Prime Minister's Palace" resembled nothing so much as an updated medieval castle, complete with the ten-foot wall that surrounded it. Instead of turrets in the corners, though, it had large automatic machine-gun mounts, with excellent fields of fire, not just outside the palace grounds but within them, as well. Abu Bakr could see one of the mounts, and if it wasn't pointed *at* the shuttle, it was very close. An antiaircraft mount was also located near each of the machine guns; if they had to leave quickly, it might get dicey.

The shuttle was surrounded by members of the *Sif al-Nabi*—the Prophet's Sword—the paramilitary organization run by Ghilzai. The pre-mission briefing he'd seen had noted the organization was "good at killing people Ghilzai didn't like," which did nothing to calm his nerves. All the men—there were no women to be seen—were armed, although the man who waited at the bottom of the ramp still had his pistol in his holster. The rest of the men were armed with rifles, which, like the machine gun, weren't pointed directly at him . . . but weren't very far away from him, either.

He glanced behind him. The vampires had formed up behind him and looked ready to go. If they were nervous, they didn't show it. He couldn't match Cecilia's bored expression—nor did he want to, as lead negotiator—so he put on his warmest smile as he led them down the ramp.

"*As-salāmu 'alaykum*," the man with the pistol said. Like the pictures Abu Bakr had seen of Ghilzai, the man was tall and dark. "Peace be upon you. I am Colonel Zimri."

"*Wa 'alaykumu s-salām*," Abu Bakr replied. "And peace be upon you. I am Abu Bakr."

Zimri's eyes widened. "You speak the language of the Faithful."

"Of course," Abu Bakr said, simply.

"If you are a member of the Faithful, why did you bring *them*?" He nodded towards the vampires, but didn't look at them.

"I would have come without them," Abu Bakr said, meaning it, especially in the case of Cecilia, "but, unfortunately, my leaders required me to bring them."

"They must stay here. They are not allowed in the Prime Minister's presence."

"That's not going to work—" Jill said, but Abu Bakr held up a hand and silenced her.

"They go where I go," he said. "Either they're allowed in the Palace, or I get back in the shuttle and leave."

"As you will," the man replied, waving a hand as if it didn't matter. Obviously the Pakistanis must have expected the response, because the man neither looked flustered, nor did he have to call and ask for instructions. "If you would follow me."

Colonel Zimri led them into the palace, which looked as much like a castle on the inside as it had on the outside, although Abu Bakr soon realized there was something missing—there were no decorations to be seen. He smiled as the realization hit him—they'd entered via the servants' entrance and were using the corridors the servants used. He was sure it was meant as a snub, although it amused him far more than it annoyed him. *The games some people played.*

Eventually, they were led to a stairwell, and Abu Bakr's stomach clenched as Colonel Zimri started down.

"*Control, this is Wildcat,*" he subvocalized on the radio he'd been given prior to the mission.

"*Go Wildcat, this is Control.*"

"*We're being taken down into the basement, and I have a bad feeling about this.*"

"*Understand you're—*" A burst of static followed, and then nothing.

He looked back over his shoulder at Jill, who shook her head. She hadn't heard any more of the reply than he had. Control had heard their initial transmission, but their descent had apparently cut the link. Something in the castle walls had blocked their reception, which meant the team would be unable to summon help if things went wrong. He could only hope they'd heard enough to know where to look for his body if—when—things went badly.

Colonel Zimri led them down three flights of stairs and then down a wide, unmarked corridor lined with blank doors. Aside from a lack of bars on the doors, the level had the feel of a cell block, with concrete floors and walls. Zimri opened the door at the end of the corridor and held it open for them.

"You have an interesting concept of how to treat a guest," Abu Bakr said as he entered the room.

Imam Sheikh Abbas Ghilzai waited for him within, along with ten armed members of the *Sif al-Nabi*. The room was huge—nearly fifty feet by eighty feet—and appeared to be the entrance hall for a complex of underground rooms, as several passageways led off from the other side of the space. Abu Bakr wasn't sure what purpose the warren of underground rooms served—*perhaps an underground bunker complex for when the PAF ultimately bombed him?*—but he could easily tell what this particular room was for. The padding on the walls to prevent ricochets—complete with rust-covered stains—and the drain in the center of the room gave him a pretty good idea that he was on the front line of Executioner's Row.

Abbas Ghilzai stood on the other side of the *Sif al-Nabi*, arrayed in what appeared to be a firing line, along with his cousin, Ghayyur Ghilzai. Both men were cast from a similar mold—tall and thin, with dark hair and full beards. Where Abbas had the fiery eyes of a fanatic, though, Ghayyur had the cold, dead eyes of a shark. Ghayyur was a killer, and Abbas was a man not afraid to turn the killer loose. Neither appeared happy to see Abu Bakr.

"I wasn't expecting a full state dinner," Abu Bakr added as Zimri closed the door behind him, "but some simple refreshments after my journey would have been nice. And hospitable." A glance behind him showed that Zimri hadn't followed them in; a *click* as the bolt on the door was thrown from the outside of the room added to the air of foreboding.

"I have heard tales of your demons," Abbas said with a shrug, "and I didn't want to put myself in a position where they might be able to get close and kill me."

"That's certainly not our intention," Abu Bakr said, "and I've given instructions to my team that you aren't to be hurt in any manner. Our purpose here is to find out what you wanted when you contacted the Planetary Union government and to pass on some messages from our government."

"You have messages for me?" Abbas asked with a grin that could only be called "evil." "And what would these messages be?"

"Just as you keep tabs on us, the Planetary Intelligence Agency obviously does the same for you, and President Howell is worried about a number of things he sees going in the wrong direction."

"And those things are?"

"While it's not his intention to tell you how to manage your country—"

"As if I would listen to his pathetic mewlings," Abbas interjected.

"—he is, however, very much interested when those things spill out into other countries that are either already in the Planetary Union, or who are deciding whether or not to join. The safety and security of the world at large is not enhanced when you send out terrorists to assassinate and cause dissent."

"And this is what he sent you here to tell me?"

"That's part of it, certainly. While we're distressed that you continue to move Pakistan away from the twenty-first century, much less the future, that's Pakistan's business. But we cannot—and will not—abide it when you attempt to foment rebellion in other parts of the world. For example, we're aware of your assassination attacks on the more moderate imams and political leaders of Afghanistan and Iran, as well as your vengeance attacks in India. We also know you're heavily involved in the unrest in Malaysia."

"Your president thinks I am responsible for unrest in places like Malaysia, which are far from our borders? How exactly does he think this is possible?"

"Actually, Mr. Prime Minister, he *knows* you're behind the unrest in the countries I mentioned, and my mission is to ask you to cease and desist these activities."

"And if I refuse?"

"Then I'm instructed to warn you that there will be consequences if you continue in this manner. While we don't like what you're doing to your own people, we're willing to let that work its way out on its own, within reason; however, we will not tolerate continued attacks on other countries."

"Oh, really? And what might those consequences be? A return visit from your pet demons?"

Abu Bakr heard a growl from behind him and turned to give Cecilia a warning glance. He looked back at the prime minister.

"Actually, our response might be anything from economic sanctions to a military response by the Planetary Armed Forces to a return visit from the rest of my team. Trust me, you don't want that. These three ladies might be more devastating than an Armed Forces assault."

"I'm sure they're very scary for the great masses of unbelievers," Abbas replied, waving a hand as if the threat were inconsequential, "however, I have faith. I have faith in a number of things. First, I have faith that it is my duty, from Allah, to preserve the purity of the Islamic Republic. Thus, my country will never join your Planetary Union, and I will do everything possible to keep other Islamic countries from joining it, too. If that means removing imams or others who do not have the same level of faith, so be it. I will do as I must.

"I also have faith that none of your threats—your so-called consequences— will have any effect on either me or my country. We will weather your sanctions, like we have ignored them in the past. If you want to send forces, feel free! We will fight you, and we will make every step you take so costly that you will drown in an ocean of your own blood. And as for these . . . these things you have with you, they have no soul. They are faithless demons, and I am not afraid of them. We've prepared for them, and we will destroy all the ones you send!"

"I'd like to see you try!" Cecilia said, taking a step forward. "I live to kill arrogant breathers like you!"

Abu Bakr turned and put a hand on her chest, stopping her from advancing any further.

"Step. Back," he said. "Right now." The whites of her eyes had gone scarlet, and he realized how close she was to going over the edge. It was only his own anger that allowed him to speak forcefully to her.

"Take your hand off me," she said, her eyes snapping from Ghilzai to Abu Bakr.

A shiver went down his back as her eyes met his; her gaze made it abundantly clear why people feared the night. After a moment, some of the red left her eyes, and he removed his hand, happy to not have to do anything else to restrain her.

As the stress of controlling her faded, he realized Abbas was laughing, as was his cousin. Even the members of his guard force were smirking.

"Stop!" Abu Bakr ordered. "You have no idea what you're doing!"

While he'd wanted—at some point—to show the Pakistanis how dangerous the vampires were, he'd envisioned it as a controlled demonstration. If they continued to goad Cecilia, though, there was sure to be bloodshed.

"See?" Abbas asked his cousin. "This is what you get in the decadent West—men who can't control their women. Not only can't he control *her,* he presumes to tell us how we should manage our country, and how we should follow the directives Allah has given us."

He turned to Abu Bakr.

"I laugh at you and your arrogant Crusader demands that I keep my missionaries at home, rather than have them spread the word of Allah abroad. And the idea that you could come here and tell me how to manage my own country or people? Ludicrous.

"I called you here to show the world exactly how the Planetary Union operates—how it forces itself on countries who don't want to be members, and how it threatens them with sanctions, warfare, and even releasing its pet demons on them if they refuse to kowtow to its wishes."

He pointed to the corners of the room. "I've been broadcasting this meeting live the whole time! The veil has been removed from your heavy-handed political maneuvering, and now the world can see what the Planetary Union is really about—the complete eradication of Islam from the world! Muslims around the world, unite! Do not stand for it! Do not let them pull the wool over your eyes! Stand up for your rights! Stand up for your religion! Stand up for your God! Kill them! Kill them all!"

The guards leveled their rifles at Abu Bakr's team.

"I will lead the way!" Abbas Ghilzai shouted. "They came here to kill me, but I will beat them to it! My guards have silver bullets in their rifles—watch what happens to their pet vampires now! *Fire!*"

. . . . .

"COLONEL WILSON," CAPTAIN Frye's voice came over the intercom. "Can you come to the flight station? You're going to want to see this."

Wilson looked up as he snapped the last latch on his Project Heinlein armor. "Uh, I'm kind of busy at the moment," he said. "I just finished putting on my armor, and I'd have to take it off again to come up there. Have we heard anything from the team yet?"

"No, we haven't, but this is about that," Frye said. "Stand by a second." After a couple of moments, the screen next to the intercom came on with a picture of Abu Bakr. The vampires were standing behind him, and he could see that Cecilia's eyes were bright red.

"Oh, shit," he muttered. "That's not good."

Although he said it softly, the microphone obviously picked it up and transmitted it to the cockpit, because Frye added, "If you think that's bad, wait 'til you see this!"

The picture changed, and the camera view shifted to one from behind Abu Bakr's group. Abbas and Ghayyur Ghilzai stood on the other side of them, behind a row of gunmen. Abbas appeared to be exhorting the watchers and was totally into the moment. Spittle flew from the corners of his mouth as he gestured at the Planetary Union team.

Muttering broke out across the shuttle's cargo bay as the rest of his squad watched the video.

"What the hell's that from?" Wilson asked.

"It's being live-streamed," Fry said. "The weapons officer just picked it up. Apparently, there are several cameras streaming different views from the room."

"Do we have audio?"

"Just a second."

With a click, the audio source shifted, and Abbas Ghilzai's voice came through the speakers. "—came here to kill me, but I will beat them to it! My guards have silver bullets in their rifles—watch what happens to their pet vampires now! *Fire!*"

"*Fuck!*" Wilson exclaimed as the men opened fire on the group. "Get us down there—*now!*"

. . . . .

SOMEONE HURLED ABU Bakr to the side as the men opened fire, and the vampires charged them. By the time he'd bounced off the wall and the floor and looked towards the firing line, most of the riflemen were already down. Two had arms torn off, one had his rifle shoved through his stomach, and the others sported a variety of blood-spouting claw and bite wounds. The vampires seemed to go for arteries, and the spray of blood around the room was . . . mind-bogglingly horrific.

None of the vampires appeared injured in the slightest.

This was not going to play well on the tridee, and it was exactly how the meeting was *not* supposed to go. "Kill—" he coughed, trying to catch his breath, then took a breath and shouted louder, "Kill the cameras!"

Susan heard and raced to the corners of the room, destroying the cameras while Jill finished off the men with rifles. Cecilia, on the other hand, leapt over one of them to grab Ghayyur.

"Hi, Big Boy," she said, looking into his eyes as her fangs extended.

Ghayyur screamed as she leaned in to his neck, but it was cut short as she pulled back, ripping out most of his throat. She dropped the body, blood drooling thickly down her chin, and turned to Abbas as the prime minister aimed his pistol at her.

"Don't kill him!" Abu Bakr yelled as Cecilia walked towards him.

Abbas fired, but the bullet had no effect. He fired again, and again—faster and faster—as she approached, but each bullet passed through her without her even noticing it. His eyes grew with each shot, until his pistol clicked empty.

Cecilia reached forward, grabbed the pistol out of his hands, and tossed it away. "Now, what were you saying about me?" she asked.

"No!" Abu Bakr yelled. "Don't kill him!"

"Don't do it, Cecilia!" Jill said as she threw aside the remains of the last gunman. "The team lead said not to kill him."

Cecilia glanced at Jill. "Who cares?" she asked. "He's just another breather." Her hand flashed towards Abbas, and returned with his heart. She looked into his eyes as she held it up in front of him.

"Whose heart do you suppose this is?" she asked, her tone light and sweet. She shrugged. "Must be yours, since I don't need one anymore." She dropped it and stepped aside as Abbas fell to his knees then forward onto his face. She spat on his back. "Asshole."

Abu Bakr turned in time to see Susan destroy the last camera. *All of that had been on camera.*

"Damn it!" Abu Bakr exclaimed. "I told you not to kill him, you idiot!"

In a flash, Cecilia was in front of him, and she grabbed him around the throat with one hand and lifted him from his feet.

"You ungrateful *bastard*!" she screamed, her eyes blazing. Abu Bakr made a strangled noise as he grabbed at her hands and struggled to break free. "I saved your *life*!"

Jill appeared next to her. "Put him down, Cecilia," she said.

"I'm tired of his shit!" Cecilia said with a snarl. "I just saved his life—Ghilzai was going to kill him—and I just want a little bit of gratitude from him!"

"We don't have time for this," Jill said. "We need to get out of here."

"We will, just as soon as he says it."

"Wha—" Abu Bakr asked as he choked.

"I want to hear you say you're sorry. Say it."

Abu Bakr tried to say something, but it didn't make it past the hand strangling him.

"He can't talk with you holding him by the throat," Susan said, coming to stand on the other side of Cecilia.

"No, he can't, can he?" Cecilia asked with a smile.

"Cecilia!" Jill said. "Drop him, *now*!"

"Fine!" Cecilia exclaimed, and threw Abu Bakr to the floor.

"Damn it," he said with a grunt as he struggled back to his feet. "We still could have saved this mission, if you hadn't killed him, you stupid bitch!"

Cecilia hit him in the chest, hard enough to lift him from his feet. He flew through the air and slammed into the wall five feet away. As he slid down it, he realized something inside him was broken. Not just the ribs—he'd heard them shatter—but then the rib shards must have speared something else inside him. He looked up from the floor, unable to catch his breath.

Before he could say anything, or even try, Cecilia was in his face.

"Stupid bitch? How'd you like getting your ass kicked by a stupid bitch? Now you're going to find out what it's like to get *killed* by a stupid bitch." Her fingernails lengthened into claws and she drew her hand back to strike.

"No," Jill said, grabbing her arm. "You can't do this."

"Stay out of this, Jill; it's none of your business." She tried to pull out of Jill's grasp. "Let go of my arm!"

"It *is* my business, and you need to back off."

"She's right," Susan said as Abu Bakr coughed weakly. "You *do* need to back off. And we need to get out of here. It sounds like you damaged him pretty badly."

"After I kill him, we can leave. The cameras are all out; no one will know." She spun away from Jill and succeeded in pulling her arm out of the other vampire's grasp.

Jill and Susan stepped together, blocking her away from Abu Bakr.

"Move!" Cecilia ordered. "I'm not asking; I'm telling you. *Move*!"

"Or you'll do what?" Jill asked. "You'll kill us, too?"

"If I have to!"

"You can't," Susan said. "We're sisters. Let's get out of here, and we'll work it out once we get back."

"After I kill him."

"No," Susan and Jill said simultaneously.

Cecilia struck without warning, her claw aimed at Jill's face.

Jill flinched away, unable to block the blow in time, and Cecilia's claws ran across her cheek, digging furrows into it that closed nearly as quickly as they were opened. She struck back, but Cecilia blocked the blow.

"Hey!" Cecilia yelled as Susan punched her in the head from the side, and she staggered away from the other two vampires. "So this is how it's going to be, huh?"

"If you intend to kill everyone you meet," Jill said, "then yeah, this is how it's going to be."

"Fine!" Cecilia launched herself at the other two vampires, throwing punches and kicks, and clawing for all she was worth.

Jill and Susan, equally fast, blocked all of Cecilia's strikes. The more blows Cecilia threw, the more frustrated she became. Finally, she stepped back and glared at them, fangs out, the red in her eyes a glowing scarlet.

"I'm done with you," Cecilia snarled. "I'm done with you both!"

Jill shook her head. "It doesn't have to be like this—"

The door at the end of the room slammed open.

"There they are!" someone yelled as half a dozen men poured through it. "Kill them!"

Jill and Susan leapt forward and killed all six of them. Only two managed to get off a shot, but when the two vampires turned around, Cecilia had disappeared down one of the other passageways. Jill returned to Abu Bakr, whose eyes were closed, and checked his pulse.

"We need to get him out of here," she said.

"I know," Susan replied. "The only problem is carrying him. I'm not sure that's the best choice, especially since we're likely to face more of these idiots on the way out."

"Well, we can't leave him here. He looks like he's about to die."

"I know," Susan repeated, "and we can't have that, either. You guard him, and I'll go get the cavalry."

"I guess I don't have to warn you to be careful?"

Susan smiled. "I don't think that will be an issue."

· · · · ·

"GET US DOWN there—*now!*" Wilson called from the back of the shuttle.

"Are we cleared to fire?" Lieutenant Solice, asked.

"Yes," Wilson replied. "Clear us an LZ!"

"Roger that," Solice said, and armed the system. His view tilted as the pilots dove for the compound. He'd already targeted the four antiaircraft positions in the compound's corners; he quickly reconfirmed the targeting and pulled the commit trigger on his joystick. "Firing!" he warned the pilots.

Four missiles raced off the *Starfire*'s rails and leapt ahead of the shuttle. With them en route, he moved the targeting reticle for the main gun over the first of the machine-gun nests. The alarm had obviously been given in the compound, since people were scurrying everywhere throughout the courtyard. The crew's orders had been to not kill anyone they didn't need to . . . but they'd also been told to interpret that loosely. If the defenders "could" be a threat, they were to be taken out.

The machine guns were manned and pointed at the shuttle in the courtyard. While they probably weren't a threat to it as long as it was buttoned up, they would definitely be a threat when the team made it back out. He pulled the trigger as one of the missiles destroyed the antiaircraft position next to it, and a five-round burst of 20 mm high-explosive rounds turned it—and its crew—into a finely divided red mist. Like the new infantry rifle, the gun mounted on the chin of the assault shuttle was a railgun, but the shell was twice as large and four times as heavy. When Solice released the trigger, there was nothing left.

He switched to the next machine gun, but had to ease back on the zoom—the pilots were coming in hot, and he had less time than he'd thought. Another brief burp of 20 mm rounds, and there was nothing left of that position, either. There was motion at the antiaircraft position next to it so he triggered a few rounds at the men there. The motion ceased.

Solice ripped the other two positions apart as the militia forces began firing at the shuttle in the courtyard, and he could see tracers ricocheting from the *Starfire*'s armored skin.

"SAM, right, three o'clock!" Captain Frye called. After a pause, he added, "Not tracking."

The weapons officer let out the breath he'd been holding as he searched for the missile launch site. Sure, they'd been told the sites wouldn't be able to target them . . . but you never knew what would happen once the missiles started flying. He found the launcher and fired one of his remaining missiles at it; the launcher detonated spectacularly, with a good secondary explosion as one of its own missile warheads exploded.

"Five seconds to touchdown!" Frye said over the intercom. "Ramp coming down!"

Solice ripped the targeting cursor back to the courtyard. Any additional launches would have to be taken care of by the other shuttle that remained in overwatch above them at twenty thousand feet. He had more immediate concerns, like the two groups of guards charging across the courtyard towards the grounded shuttle, and he pulled the trigger as he dragged the cursor across both groups.

The consequences were unspeakable.

"Courtyard clear!" he called.

The shuttle touched down with a barely noticeable bump, and Solice launched two of his drones to provide overhead air cover. He switched his targeting camera to the first drone in time to see Wilson's company of troopers charge down the ramp, firing periodically as they went. Solice smiled; the men and women looked like badass cyborgs in their Project Heinlein armor, and he was happy to not be on the receiving end of their attack.

The powered armor had started with the best personal defensive equipment the Hegemony printers had in their databases, but the wizards on the platforms had adapted it further. A *lot* further. It was an exoskeleton which was also a set of articulated plate armor, worn over a haptic suit that sensed the operator's movements and moved the armor accordingly. After a period of calibration, the armor moved and functioned as a second, ultra-protective skin which made the soldiers virtually invulnerable to most light-and medium-caliber projectile weapons and chemical explosives; defeating it required a serious anti-armor weapon.

In addition to the armor that protected the trooper, the suit also gave the soldier many times more strength and incorporated an arsenal of weaponry. All the troopers Solice could see carried handheld weapons, but most of them had shoulder-mounted railguns, as well. The weapons were synched to a targeting system in the soldiers' helmets, which allowed them to keep their hands free for other activities while destroying everything around them. An ammunition feed tube led from the weapon to a drum on the soldiers' backs.

About the only thing the armor didn't have installed yet were the jump jets, which were still "under development." They would ultimately give the troopers the ability to jump over obstacles and shorter buildings, but Solice had heard the performance of the first models had been less than satisfactory. The suits had been tremendously unstable in the air, which had resulted in "non-successful landing evolutions." Basically, the troopers involved had gone "splat" in some fairly painful ways . . . including one poor guy whose jump jets hadn't cut off, and he'd basically been a missile that flew along the ground, slamming into things, until the juice ran out. While the armor had protected him from the worst of the collisions, the sudden stops had been traumatic, to say the least. Like being in seventeen car wrecks, one after the other. Solice had seen the tri-dee video someone had leaked, and it confirmed he'd made the right decision when he'd chosen aviation.

The suits were nothing if not effective, though, and Solice had trouble finding targets with the drones as the troopers spread out—the enemy troops were eliminated by the Heinlein-suited troopers as quickly as they showed their faces. With the main compound weapons already eliminated, the PAF soldiers advanced quickly. While three of the company's ten-trooper platoons spread out to provide security from the walls and hold the compound's entrances, the fourth raced across the courtyard to the palace. The first trooper kicked in the door, and they charged into the building.

With no targets remaining in the courtyard, Solice parked one of his drones in overwatch above the shuttle, while he watched the courtyard's main entrance with the other. If reinforcements arrived, he'd be ready.

Something blew up a couple of blocks away in the periphery of his drone's field of view, and Solice sighed. With the other shuttle orbiting overhead, he suspected he wouldn't get the chance to do much more than await the colonel's return.

· · · · ·

"GO!" WILSON COMMED over the squadnet.

Sergeant James Ramirez kicked in the door, his muscles augmented by the Heinlein suit. Two members of the Prophet's Sword had been hiding behind the door, and they went flying down the corridor along with it. Before they came to rest, Ramirez' shoulder mount fired, and both of the militiamen disintegrated—literally—as they were hit with a three-round burst of point-blank railgun fire that could have taken out a legacy armored personnel carrier.

Private Sekiguchi Kokan, Ramirez' "wing," leapfrogged him to lead the way as the platoon charged into the palace's front hall. The scope was overwhelming—a massive, open space with a huge staircase leading up to the next level, and hallways that ran off in a number of directions.

A scream came from one of the side hallways, then a group of militiamen charged them. The squad turned, nearly as one, to meet the attack as the militiamen ran towards them, yelling at the tops of their lungs.

"Fire!" Wilson ordered, and the ten troopers' combined fire cut the militia down. In fact, the torrent of railgun fire pretty much *vaporized* them, he thought with a grimace.

"That was weird," Ramirez said. "None of them fired at us."

"Maybe they saw the video from when we landed," Corporal Patel said. "Maybe they were trying to get close enough they might penetrate the suits before they fired."

Wilson shook his head. Now that Ramirez mentioned it, the attack had been strange. He scanned the massive entryway, searching for additional enemy forces, as he replayed the assault in his head. As he went through it, he realized that some of the Pakistanis had been looking behind them—not at the troopers they were charging. It was almost as if they were running *from* something, not into—

One of his soldiers fired a burst as a figure materialized in the corridor the militiamen had come from, and he spun to face the new threat.

A woman—the red-haired vampire from Abu Bakr's team—stood in the hallway. A massive cloud of dust billowed behind her, rising from where the rounds had reduced a swathe of wall to gravel, but she appeared unharmed as she frowned at the man who'd fired at her.

"Do I look like *any* of them?" she asked with a sigh.

"Uh, sorry, Ma'am," Corporal Andersson said. He turned towards Wilson and added, "Sorry, Sir. She just kind of materialized there, and it spooked me."

"Next time, make sure you ID your target *before* pulling the trigger," Wilson growled. The soldier nodded, and he turned to the redhead. "Sorry about that, Susan," he said. "He meant well."

"If you say so, Rob," she replied a tad sourly—justifiably so, in Wilson's opinion. "Good thing I'm not a breather anymore, though."

"Shit," one of the troopers said at the revelation. A couple of the others were more colorful.

"I may be fine," she continued, "but Abu Bakr isn't. There was an . . . accident, and he's pretty badly broken up. He needs medical assistance and immediate evacuation."

"That won't be a problem. Our medic's right here with us. Just take us to him."

"Follow me." The vampire started back the way she'd come, but then turned back to Andersson. "And don't shoot me again, or you'll make me angry. And you *won't* like me when I'm angry."

Her tone sent a shiver down Wilson's back; he was glad it hadn't been directed at him.

"Uh . . ." Andersson said, obviously even more taken aback. "Yes, Ma'am. I *will* be careful, Ma'am."

She turned and raced down the hallway, clearly unworried about the possibility of running into any additional militiamen, and Wilson shook his head as he charged after her. He knew the militiamen's rifles weren't going to bother *her*—she had, after all, just survived a burst of railgun fire at close range—but he hoped to hell she didn't lead them into an ambush that might cost him some of his people.

She led them into a stairwell and down several flights of stairs, then yanked open a door. The thunder of gunfire filled the stairwell as she flung it wide—clearly, a pitched battle was underway in the hallway beyond it—and she charged forward to join the fray. It took Wilson a second to realize that the "battle" was between a company of militiamen and Jill, who appeared to be trying to keep them from entering a doorway. A number of the men shot at the vampire, but hit their comrades as often as not.

"What do we do?" Ramirez asked. "We can't shoot into that, but we have to help them!"

Wilson seriously doubted they needed assistance, but he was too much of a gentleman to leave the women to fight at those odds.

"Draw swords, and *charge!*" he yelled.

The alloy sword blade snapped out and down on his right arm as he ran forward to join the melee. As fast as Susan was, though, there was only a little bit of hallway available for his troopers to fight in as she dodged back and forth, attacking nearly the entire rear rank simultaneously. Blood flew from a number of the militia troops as she flitted between them, moving almost too quickly to see. It was a slaughter.

"Screw this," Wilson muttered. He'd seen enough death for one day.

He retracted the blade as he ran down one edge of the hallway. Reaching the scrum, he leaned in, grabbed one of the Pakistanis, and threw him back over his head.

"Disarm him and send him on his way," he ordered over the com as the yelling militiaman landed.

Ramirez joined him, and they waded into the melee, throwing people out of it. Wilson triggered his rear view as he grabbed the next man. The militiamen seemed *delighted* to be out of the fight and sprinted away from the PU troopers as soon as they were released.

The battle was over in a few seconds, with nearly half the militiamen bleeding out on the floor. The vampire they'd just "rescued" frowned as she saw the last of the militiamen running away down the hallway past Wilson's troops.

"Probably should have killed them all," she noted.

"I don't think they'll stop running until they reach Afghanistan," Wilson said, "and we need to get Abu Bakr and get out of here. There's already going to be hell to pay."

"You saw the broadcast?"

"Yeah, right up to when Cecilia ripped out Ghilzai's heart. I don't think that's going to play well. Where is she, anyway?"

Jill shrugged. "I don't know. We argued and she ran off. You're right, though, we need to get Abu Bakr to a hospital." She motioned at the doorway. "He's in there."

"Santos!" Wilson called.

"On it!" the company medic, Sergeant Sophia Santos, said as she pushed past and entered the room.

Wilson followed her in and found the room he'd seen on TV, complete with Ghilzai lying face-first on the floor at the far end.

The floor drain was doing box office business, a corner of his brain reflected, and he was glad his helmet protected him from the stench.

"What's wrong with him?" Santos asked as she knelt next to Abu Bakr. "I don't see any visible injuries."

"Chest trauma," Susan said, kneeling next to the medic. "He was punched, really hard, in the chest. I know his ribs are broken, and there are probably internal injuries."

Santos looked up to Wilson as she readied an injector. "His vital signs are really low," she said. "I may be able to keep him alive, barely, but we'll need to fly directly to the closest hospital." She pushed the injector into Abu Bakr's chest and pressed the button. Medical nanites flooded his chest cavity. She repositioned the injector and triggered it again, then pulled off her pack and hauled out the collapsible stretcher. She had it set up and Abu Bakr ready to transport in under a minute.

"Andersson, help Santos with the litter," Wilson directed. "Everyone else, let's go!"

"Why don't you let us lead?" Susan asked. "We know the way and we can handle any opposition. Especially Cecilia. If she's still running around here, you might not enjoy meeting her without us."

Wilson nodded.

"Go ahead," he said. It burned him, a little, that his brand-new combat suits had to play second fiddle to women who were—essentially—unarmed, but he was damned sure *he* wouldn't want to take one on, even with a squad of Heinlein-suited troopers. In fact, he was pretty sure all of them together wouldn't be enough to kill Cecilia if she showed back up. For the moment, he decided to just concentrate on how happy he was to have the other two on his side. Cecilia would have to be brought in at some point, he knew . . . but that was for another day, and would—hopefully—be someone else's problem.

Although the stairwell wasn't built for the passage of a stretcher, his squad managed. Having the suits certainly made it easier. Within a couple of minutes, they were back in the courtyard and loading into the assault shuttle. He surveyed the courtyard as he called back the other platoons. If there was any of the militia left, they'd decided not to challenge the PU troops any further.

Wilson didn't blame them. Between the shuttles' combination of passive and active defenses, they'd been able to land unscathed, and then control the battlespace—against all comers—in the middle of the enemy's capital. He could see a number of fires burning outside the compound—it was obvious the Pakistanis had tried to reinforce the installation—but forces in the air and on the walls had completely denied them the ability to do so. He chuckled as he realized the Shongairi could have had access to the same equipment his troops were using. If they'd bothered to design and deploy it, they could have wiped humanity out; there might even have been something in their tech base to deal with vampires. He dwelt on the possibility for a couple of moments and decided he'd have to pass that thought on to Dvorak when they returned, since it appeared they might need something along those lines.

"Sir!" Santos called on the squad net as the last of his troops raced towards the shuttle. "Abu Bakr wants to talk to you."

Wilson squeezed through the crowded bay to where Abu Bakr's stretcher had been secured.

"I told him he needed to rest," Santos said, "but he said he needed to talk to you first."

Abu Bakr turned his head and looked up at Wilson. "Did you—" He coughed, and red spittle wet his lips. "Did you find her?" he asked.

"Who?" Wilson asked. "Cecilia?"

Abu Bakr's head moved in a minute nod.

"No, sorry, she got away, and I'm not going to stay here looking for her," Wilson said. "She can find her own way home. This mission is fucked up enough as it is. We killed the one person we weren't supposed to, and we've wiped out a large chunk of the capital's downtown area. I'm not losing any of my people looking for that crazy bitch. I'm already going to get reamed for this when we get home—and none of it was my fault."

Abu Bakr gave another small nod, then turned away from Wilson. The Project Heinlein audio pickups were just good enough for the colonel to hear him mutter, "We never should have brought her."

V

PRESIDENTIAL BRIEFING ROOM, SPACE PLATFORM *BASTION*, L5 LAGRANGE POINT

Man, did Sharon have a point, Dave Dvorak thought as he walked into the briefing room with his phone in his left hand and a coffee mug in his right. *I swear I didn't expect the gig to last* this *long!*

It was true. He *knew* it was true, and it cut absolutely no ice with his loving wife. Her response was that if he hadn't realized what was going to happen, then he'd probably been the only surviving human dumb enough not to. Of course, a lot of her protests were pro forma these days. She could hardly let him get away with it unscathed, but with all three kids off and launched on careers of their own, and her own hectic schedule as the United States of America's representative on the revamped and restored USO's board of governors—now the *Planetary* United Service Support Organizations—she was hardly in a position to give him too much grief.

Not that it stopped her for a moment. And not that he really would have wanted it to, for that matter. But still. . . .

He genuinely hadn't envisioned becoming Secretary of State to the entire flipping planet. For that matter, he'd fondly imagined that once the planet had been unified, it wouldn't *need* a Secretary of State. True, it wasn't entirely unified just yet, even after closing in on two decades of effort, which was rather the point of the current meeting. But surely once the deed was done, once there were no more diplomatic deals to negotiate, the Planetary Union wouldn't need a top diplomat anymore. So he could go home again, right?

Not on your life. He'd forgotten Judson Howell's habit of thinking in terms of the larger picture, which was why—in the moments when he wasn't pissing on forest fires like the one in Naya Islamabad—he was immersed in the study of the Hegemony's notions of "foreign policy." Not so much against the day when humanity once again had to confront the Hegemony, although that was important, too, but because Howell fully intended for humanity to mount its own interstellar expansion. And unlike the Hegemony, he intended to offer alliances and assistance to other pre-interstellar species which might find themselves in the Hegemony's sights and choose to stand against it at the human race's side. Which meant that one Dave Dvorak got to write the instruction manual for humanity's eventual first contact teams.

Oh joy, oh joy.

Although, if pressed—in fact, without any pressing at all—he would have admitted that he would far rather have been working on that instruction manual than heading for the current meeting. He should've put his foot down and overruled the mission planners, and he'd *known* it, damn it. But had he? Of course not! And because he hadn't, the whole—

He chopped that thought off—again—and nodded to Bill Taylor, one of Howell's Presidential Security Detachment agents.

"Morning, Bill," he said.

The Secret Service still protected the President of the United States, but the PSD had responsibility for the Planetary Union's chief executive, and Taylor had obviously arrived to secure the briefing room before any of the official attendees arrived. It was unlikely, to say the least, that space orcs might have infiltrated it, but as Joyce Eckerd, the head of Dvorak's own security team was fond of saying whenever *he* complained, "You never know . . . Sir."

It was amazing how much like his third-grade teacher that little pause made her sound, despite her pronounced Boston accent. She even had the same way of looking at him with her eyebrows at half-cock, too. Unfair, that's what it was.

"Good morning, Sir," Taylor replied. "Early again, I see."

"What I get for having my office right down the corridor." Dvorak shrugged. "I assume the others are inbound?"

"Yes, Sir. In fact—"

Taylor broke off as the briefing room door slid open once more and Jessica Tallman walked through it. Like Dvorak himself, the onetime State Secretary of Administration and then Secretary of Federal Management had followed her boss into the executive suite of the Planetary Union. For that matter, so had Fabienne Lewis, Patrick O'Sullivan, and Kacey Zukowski. The other members of his PU cabinet were drawn from other member states, chosen both for ability—which was uniformly high—and to make sure no one thought the PU was simply the U.S.A. under a new label. The U.S.—for that matter, the State of North Carolina—was still more heavily represented than any other Planetary Union member state, but given who'd organized it and who'd been elected its first president, most of the planet was prepared to live with that.

Not all of it, of course. Human beings were still human beings. There were times that was irritating as hell, but taking everything together, Dvorak found it immensely reassuring.

"Good morning, Jessica," he said.

"What's good about it?" the normally affable Secretary of Management half-snarled. "Do you have any idea—?"

She chopped herself off with a visible effort, then inhaled deeply.

"Sorry, Dave. If anybody on the platform has 'any idea' about this crap, it's you. And Kacey and Pat, of course. So let's try this again. Good morning, Dave."

She smiled a bit wanly and held out her hand. Dvorak set his coffee mug on the conference table with the caution its contents deserved in order to shake hands, then chuckled. She cocked her head at him, and he shrugged.

"I'm jest a boy from th' mountains, Ma'am, but I kinda 'spect you'ins ain't gonna be th' only b'ar with a sore tooth this here mornin'."

"God, I hate that hillbilly impersonation of yours," she said with an unwilling smile. "The only thing worse is when you start punning."

"Don't challenge me to trot out the big puns," he warned, and she raised both hands in quick surrender.

"No more! I'll be good!"

He smiled, and the two of them settled into their accustomed places at the conference table, chatting with each other while the meeting's other attendees trickled in.

Secretary of Health Doctor Charles Musset, a stocky New Zealander who'd been one of his nation's best thoracic surgeons, was the next to arrive. He joined their conversation, and then Dvorak looked up as Secretary of Housing Cao Ming, the fine-boned Chinese who was the youngest of President Howell's cabinet secretaries by several years, walked into the briefing room in earnest conversation with Secretary of Transportation Lyadov Denis Yermolayevich. Cao was the sole survivor of her family, which had died with the rest of Chengdu's fourteen million inhabitants when the local Party leadership obeyed the injunction for a simultaneous mass uprising against the invaders. Her father, a senior Party official in Sichuan Province, had been instrumental in making that happen ... which was why Cao Ming was as virulently anti-Communist as it was possible for a human being to be. She was also one of the founders of the Republic of Sichaun, one of the four successor states which had rebuilt themselves out of the ruins of Earth's most populous country. They didn't represent the totality of China—there were still half a dozen splinter "republics," including one whose Party leadership had survived and which considered itself the sole legitimate successor to the People's Republic of China—but they accounted for over eighty percent of China's total land area. All four of them together had perhaps twenty percent of the People's Republic of China's pre-invasion population, and all of them were just about as anti-Party as she was. It was rather difficult to blame them, when the Party-inspired uprising had gotten somewhere in the near neighborhood of 520 million Chinese killed in less than half an hour.

She and Lyadov—a former CEO of MEZHTRANSAVTO, one of the largest transport companies of the Russian Federation—greeted Taylor and Dvorak affably enough, but then dived back into their own quiet conversation. Ägrid Furstenfeld, the former CEO of Deutsche Bank's Corporate and Investment Bank Division, who'd become the Secretary of the Treasury, was hosting a conference of member state treasury heads and would be unable to attend, but Fred Tanner, one of his assistant secretaries, walked in behind Cao and Lyadov.

Secretary of War Zukowski and Secretary of Planetary Security O'Sullivan arrived together, accompanied by General Landers. From their expressions, they looked forward to the day's gathering about as enthusiastically as Dvorak did, but they were at least polite as they found their chairs.

The last to arrive were Howell and Vice President Jolasun Olatunji. At five-ten, Howell wasn't exactly short, but Olatunji was almost four inches taller than the president. He was also broad shouldered and black-skinned, a Christian Yoruba from southwestern Nigeria with broad, powerful cheekbones and a blade-like nose. He'd been a fanatic soccer player—only he called it "football," of course—in his youth, but he was sixty-five now, and he'd given it up. Until the antigerone treatments kicked in, at least. Now he'd returned to the soccer pitch, and the PSD agents assigned to him had been known to bemoan the fact that he hadn't taken up something like golf.

Or possibly chess.

"Good morning, people," Howell said, settling into his place at the head of the table while Olatunji took the facing chair at the opposite end. "I'm sorry Jolasun and I kept you waiting, but there's always something to get in the way. And—" he grimaced "—to be fair, I don't suppose I was any more eager for this than the rest of you."

A murmur of agreement ran around the table, and Howell tipped his chair back and nodded to Zukowski, O'Sullivan, and Landers.

"This is more in your bailiwick than anybody else's, except maybe Dave's, Kacey," he said. "So why don't you and the General get us up to speed? And after that, Pat, I guess we need to hear anything the PIA has to share with us about aftermath." He grimaced again, less cheerfully this time. "I don't imagine we're going to be happy to hear any of it."

"Of course, Mister President," Zukowski said. "We brought along the video, if anyone really needs to see it." Howell snorted harshly. Virtually every human being on and around the planet Earth had seen that live-streamed video by now. "Since I assume no one will," she continued, "I think it would be simplest to just let General Landers begin. Truman?"

"Thank you, Ma'am." You could tell Landers was a soldier, Dvorak thought; there wasn't even a trace of sarcasm in his courteous tone as he thanked her for what he knew would be a thankless task. "Yesterday, at approximately nineteen hundred hours, local time, our diplomatic mission landed in Naya Islamabad, as I'm sure all of you already know. Initially, it appeared that—"

Dvorak tipped his own chair back, eyes half shut while he listened.

. . . . .

"AND YOU DON'T have any idea where this . . . Cecilia is now, Mr. O'Sullivan?" Cao Ming asked twenty minutes later, when Landers and the Planetary Security secretary had finished their presentations and invited questions.

"No, Ma'am." O'Sullivan clearly didn't like admitting that, but his expression was unflinching, and he went on steadily. "To be honest, it's virtually certain that we won't find her until she decides to find *us*." He shrugged ever so slightly. "We've been working with the vampires for fifteen years now, and we've never been able to track them, even with Hegemony-level sensors."

"*Zamechatel'no*," Lyadov muttered in a disgusted tone. The neural educator had taught Dvorak Russian when Larissa Karpovna and her kids came to live with his own extended family, and he snorted. "Wonderful" was one way to describe it, he supposed.

"That's definitely something we need to be concerned about, but it's also something we can't do very much about," Vice President Olatunji observed in musically accented English. "I'd like to ask Secretary Dvorak if his read on the . . . consequences of this is as bad as my own?"

"That depends, Mister Vice President, on how bad you think it is," Dvorak replied bitterly. "Because the truth is that I haven't found a single upside. Well, that's not entirely true. If anyone's paying attention, Abu Bakr did his damnedest to keep her from killing Ghilzai, so I suppose we should get at least partial credit for that. Of course, it's offset by the fact that it only proves that not even we can control the 'monsters' we've set loose on the world."

"Ease up, Dave," another voice said. Dvorak turned towards the head of the table, and Howell leaned forward to tap an index finger on the polished surface for emphasis. "It's bad, yes. But it's not a *total* disaster, and if your brother-in-law and the vampires weren't mixed up in this, you might be able to recognize that. Hell, you *did* recognize it in the hot wash analysis your people wrote up for Jolasun and me!"

"That may be so, Mister President," Dvorak began, "but—"

"But me no buts," Howell said sternly. "Stop feeling like this is somehow your fault and hit the high points for us. The *good* ones, as well as the bad ones."

"Yes, Mister President," Dvorak said after a moment. He sat for a handful of seconds, composing his thoughts, then straightened his shoulders.

"The bad points. Our 'diplomatic mission' killed the prime minister and the commander-in-chief of the armed forces of a sovereign nation, on camera, streamed live to the entire world. Hard to see a plus in that. Maybe worse, if anyone actually listens to the sound, they'll realize Abu was doing his damnedest to stop Cecilia every step of the way and that she totally ignored him. And anyone who watches her and the other two in action, will realize that nothing the Pakistanis had could have hurt any of the three of them in any way, so except from the perspective of protecting Abu, it's hard to argue they *had* to kill anyone in self-defense. Anyone who's predisposed to view the vampires as uncontrollable, demonic, soulless, accursed, undead monsters just got confirmation of all his phobias on live tridee, and the religious zealots—especially the Islamic fundamentalists, but quite a few of their Christian counterparts, as well—who look at this, watch it, listen to the way Cecilia talked to Ghilzai as she ripped out his heart and held it in front of him, are absolutely going to buy into that narrative. And let's face it—where Cecilia and her actions are concerned, they'll have one hell of a lot of justification.

"Those are the diplomatic and political downsides. Oh, I'm sure there are others, but my people and I are in agreement that those are the big ones.

"Now, as the President's reminded me, there are a few upsides. First, most of the people who'll be enraged and frightened by this and try to use it to beat on us are people like the Pakistanis themselves—holdouts against joining the Planetary Union. For them it will justify their resistance. People in nations that have already joined the PU are likely to be upset, disquieted—even frightened— but they're already invested in membership in the Union, and it won't change their minds. I also doubt that it's going to change the minds of any fair-minded, reasonably well-educated people—like the Swiss—who are still in the process of deciding whether or not they want to join.

"There are a couple of reasons for that, but the biggest one, to be honest, is the fact that Ghilzai had obviously intended to murder Abu and the vampires from the outset. He made that abundantly clear himself, before Cecilia killed him. And Abu is *not* a vampire, which means the silver bullets that didn't kill the other three certainly *would* have killed him if they hadn't prevented it. That means their initial attack on the firing squad was totally justifiable, although I think it's probable that they didn't have to actually *kill* everybody in sight. In a situation like that, though, the primary objective is to completely incapacitate the aggressor. Dead is about as 'incapacitated' as someone gets, and their responsibility was to Abu, not to the murderous bastards who'd planned to kill all four of them."

He paused looking around the table. No one seemed prepared to dispute that, and Landers nodded firmly in agreement.

"Some of the allegations hitting the news services and—especially social media—about Colonel Wilson's rescue mission are way out of line, in my opinion," Dvorak resumed levelly, "although I expect that's pretty much inevitable. As the President's just more or less pointed out, I have a personal stake in seeing Colonel Wilson's actions in the best possible light, so I deliberately took myself out of the loop when my analysts evaluated his actions. General Landers' people weighed in on that, as well. In fact, Truman—?"

He looked across the table at Landers, who shrugged.

"Aside from being what might be considered a trifle . . . overexuberant in the way his assault shuttles dusted off the landing zone for him, my people haven't found a single thing in Colonel Wilson's conduct to criticize," the general said flatly. "Even that was well within the scope of his mission brief and instructions, given the quantity of air defense weapons Ghilzai had mounted to cover the Presidential Palace, and I don't think any reasonable person could legitimately second-guess his people after they breached the Palace to rescue Abu Bakr. We've reviewed the footage from the drones, from the satellites, and from the troopers' individual cameras, and it all confirms that, with the single exception of a group of hostiles who were apparently running away from one of the vampires, the members of his team did not engage a single individual who wasn't already engaging them. And under the circumstances, when a group of men charge out of a corridor at you with guns in their hands, I believe you might be reasonably justified in assuming they have hostile intent. The truth of the matter is, though, that by the end, Colonel Wilson's people were actually *saving* Pakistani lives by hauling militiamen out of the melee before the vampires got around to ripping their throats out."

"That's approximately what my people concluded, as well," Dvorak agreed. "Expecting people who already don't like the Union to recognize that would be more than a little unrealistic, however. And we've already heard from a couple of our own 'human rights' critics that it's obvious the Heinlein armor made our Marines as effectively invulnerable as the vampires themselves. So, *obviously,* there was no justification in utilizing lethal force against people who were only *trying* to kill them."

He couldn't quite stop an eye roll of disgust, and Howell snorted in bitter amusement. It never ceased to surprise Dvorak that there were still people capable of putting forward that particular argument with a straight face, despite everything the Shongairi had done to humanity. Most of the human race had rather significantly reconsidered how and when one should turn the other cheek to those bent on homicide; they hadn't. Their most frequent response when someone quibbled with their viewpoint was "But we're supposed to be *better* than the Shongairi." Dave Dvorak couldn't argue with that point, and he supposed he preferred people who didn't want to wade through any more blood than they had to, but he'd found his own exquisite sensitivities somewhat realigned since someone had dropped by and murdered the majority of the human race.

"That's well and good," Tallman said, "but there's another issue here. What the hell *happened*? I mean, we know *what* happened, but *how* did it happen? I've watched that footage several times now, and there's no question about it. She was in a full-bore, Hollywood monster-level, killing frenzy. For that matter, she was determined to kill *Abu Bakr*! And as far as I can tell, this is the first time—ever—that we've actually seen a vampire's eyes turn *red*. So what the hell is going on?"

She looked very pointedly at Dave Dvorak, and even as he returned her gaze steadily, he felt his heart sink. He was the Cabinet's resident expert on vampires—for his sins—and he'd known someone was going to ask the question. The problem was that he really, really didn't want to answer it.

On the other hand, better it should be him than someone else. In fact, that was why he'd made certain Jasmine Sherman wouldn't be here today to field Tallman's questions. Nor had that been solely his own idea.

He looked away from the Secretary of Management to glance at the other person who'd signed off on his decision, and Judson Howell didn't look any happier than Dave Dvorak felt. The President's nostrils flared, but then he shrugged.

"Go ahead, Dave," he said, but then he held up a hand, pausing Dvorak. "What Dave is about to tell you is, for obvious reasons, as classified as information gets. And before any of you ask, Dave and his brother-in-law—and Pieter Ushakov and Major Torino—made sure that I got this information within a day or so of when Dave himself became aware of it. In other words, this isn't something that either he or the vampires attempted to conceal from me."

That was just a *tad* overly generous of the President, Dvorak reflected, recalling how reluctant Ushakov and Torino had been to share that information with him in the first place. It was accurate enough to be going on with, though, so he only nodded and looked back at the others.

"According to Pieter and Longbow," he began, "a certain small percentage of vampires . . . go off the deep end. It doesn't happen to very many of them, it sometimes takes quite a while to develop, and there's no way to know ahead of time who it's going to be true of. The behavior Cecilia displayed in Naya Islamabad is a textbook example of what they were talking about, I think, and it's probably the basis for a lot of the more horrific legends about vampires in general. You're right, Jessica—she was in a frenzy, and from what Pieter and Longbow had to say, once you fall off that curb, there's practically never any coming back."

"Well, isn't that just peachy," Tallman said. "So what the hell do we do about it?"

"*That* is more than I can say," Dvorak admitted. "From what Abu said and from everything Colonel Wilson's said—for that matter, from what Jill and Susan had to say—they couldn't hurt her any more than we could. They could get between her and Abu, they could keep her tied up trying to get past them, they could physically intercept her to keep her from finishing him off, but they couldn't hurt her, and they damn sure couldn't kill her."

"If they can't, who *can*?" Tallman asked, and this time there was an edge of genuine fear in her voice.

"All I can tell you, is that Pieter and Longbow have assured me they'll 'deal with her.' They haven't told me how, but as far as I know, those two men have never lied to any of us about anything. If they say they can 'deal' with her, it's because they genuinely believe they can."

"I agree with everything you've just said," Secretary Mussett said, "but that rather brings up a point I think all of us have been dancing around for a while now. The truth is that we've learned a lot about the Hegemony's medical technology. For that matter, we've already tweaked its effectiveness in several ways, and we've learned to apply a lot of it to human physiology. But we still don't know a damn thing about *vampire* physiology. Well, we know that *apparently* they subsist on directly absorbed energy, not the blood diet of legend. In fact, that's the only way you can tell one of them is around if he doesn't introduce himself. They don't show on any of our other instruments, but they make a sort of . . . hole in the electromagnetic spectrum about them. If the Puppies had known what to look for, that *might* have let them detect, maybe even track, Vlad's strike teams when they assaulted their ground bases. It might not have, too; it's just the only possibility we've been able to come up with. But that's it, the sum total of our 'knowledge' about them.

"Leonard Gillespie and Nancy Kaufman and I were talking about this even before what happened in Pakistan. We've been dropping hints for over fifteen years now, and somehow none of the vampires have ever submitted to any sort of medical exam. Well, obviously they don't get sick and they don't get hurt, so they don't need doctor's care. And they've always had a dozen places they had to be at any given moment, so it's understandable that they don't have time to sit around in labs right at the moment we ask. But after *fifteen years,* I expect they could've found the time if they really wanted to."

"I understand what you're saying, Charlie," Dvorak said sharply. "But I also understand the entire human race would be *dead* without them. The only reason we're around to be worried about the fact that they're not letting us treat them like lab rats is because they damned well saved our lives. And they haven't asked us for a single damned thing in return—not one! They've cooperated with us, they've helped put the world back together—hell, they've actually put themselves into the formal military chain of command so that the President can *order* them to do things! Have you really thought about what that means? That these creatures—these *people*—who can pour themselves through key holes, disappear into a cloud of smoke, walk through a solid wall of bullets, and who don't need a single frigging thing from us—not even *food*—are willing to take *our* orders and fight *our* battles."

He realized his voice had risen, and he sat back suddenly, shaking his head.

"Sorry." He raised both hands. "Sorry, Charlie! Didn't mean to sound like I was ripping anybody's head off. And it's not like I haven't had some of the same thoughts. But still—"

"But still, we're talking about a massive invasion of their privacy and, at least potentially, about their allowing us—*helping* us, really—determine if they have any vulnerabilities we might capitalize on," Howell completed his sentence quietly. Dvorak looked at him, then gave a choppy, unhappy nod.

"Believe me, Dave, I understand what you're saying," the President continued. "In fact, that's why I've stayed out of this. I knew about the hints that were being dropped, and I knew Longbow and Pieter were deflecting every one of them. And because of how much we owe them, and because of how much I respect them—and because of how much I *trust* them—I was willing to leave it at that. But now that Cecilia's gone rogue, I don't think we can do that anymore. I don't like it, and I don't expect them to like it, but the time's come when we're going to have to insist."

"And if they refuse, Sir?" Dvorak asked quietly.

"Then we have a problem," Howell replied, equally quietly. "To be honest, I don't expect it to happen, but if it does, then it does, and we'll have to deal with it when we get there."

Their eyes held, then Dvorak nodded again, heavily.

"All right, Mister President. I'll contact Pieter and pass the message."

· VI ·

VILLA DACIANA, ARGES MOUNTAINS, ROMANIA

The night air was unseasonably chill for late summer, even for the mountains of Romania. It was certainly too dry and cold to create fog over the Arges River Valley. Even if that hadn't been true, the small patch of fog drifting steadily—and rapidly—northeast had oddly well-defined borders . . . and it was moving *against* the wind.

There were no human eyes to see it, yet it traveled in its own little pocket of silence. The nightly rustlings of the virgin forest—the twittering of small birds, the grunt of wild boars, the grumbling snuffle of a bear—all went still as the fog sailed past, quiet as an owl. It floated under the trees, winding its way up a babbling stream, ghostly pale when a shaft of cool moonlight broke through the tree cover, invisible in the dark.

It reached a road. Not much of one, but one which shouldn't have been there, according to the maps. The fog stopped there, and it seemed to *quiver* somehow, if a motionless patch of vapor could be said to do that. Then it moved back the way it had come, but only for a few feet before it stopped once more. It hovered there in the moonlight, radiating—if there had been any eyes to see—a sort of *stubbornness,* perhaps.

But then, finally, it moved once more, drifting along the roadbed towards the half-seen walls of a mountain villa. It slowed even further as the villa's walls loomed before it. The villa—more of a fortified château, really—was tucked away in a steep-sided mountain valley, surrounded by ancient trees growing close against its walls. It had a look of permanence, as if it had been there for centuries, but it wasn't exceptionally large. Nor did it show any visible lights, and a suspicious individual might have wondered why it had been built so deep in the valley's depths, where it had no view of the surrounding mountains and was all but invisible even from directly overhead.

The fog stopped again, and this time it definitely swirled with an inner agitation. When it moved once again, it drifted back and forth across the roadway, as if leaning back against an invisible leash, but every movement ended with it closer to the villa than where it had begun.

· · · · · ·

THE VILLA WAS larger on the inside than it appeared from the outside. It wasn't simply set against a valley wall; it was cut deep into the mountains' rocky bones. The library at the foot of the magnificent sweeping staircase looked as if it should have been lit by candles, not by the modern fixtures which filled it with clear illumination. The floor was marble, in intricate geometric patterns of bright, contrasting colors, and its shelves were densely populated by meticulously cataloged books, many of them obviously ancient.

A tall, blond man sat at one of the ornately carved reading desks. If that desk was a genuine antique—and it was—it would have been worth a not-so-modest fortune before the Shongair invasion. The book open before him would have been worth even more—a hand-copied, beautifully illuminated fourteenth-century Bible, its covers crusted in gems and precious metals—and he looked up at the soft sound from the head of the curved stairs.

"Good evening, Cecilia," he said.

The soft sound stopped, and the ticking of an antique clock seemed deafening in the stillness.

"Come down, Cecilia," he said, and it was a command, not an invitation.

The stillness lingered a moment longer, and then a woman stepped out of the darkness at the top of the stairs. She sauntered down them with arrogant, insolent grace—her head high, her shoulders back, her lip curled. But there was something else in her body language. Something more sensed than seen, perhaps. That arrogance was a mask for something else, and her eyes flitted around the library as if seeking some avenue of escape.

"I'm pleased you finally got here," Pieter Ushakov said, closing the Bible with the care and reverence it deserved as she reached the bottom of the stairs.

"Really?" Cecilia's voice was hard, defiant, and the red tinge flowed and flickered across her eyes.

"I've been waiting for you," he said, leaning back in his chair. "You have much to answer for, and we have a great deal to discuss."

"And what makes you think I give a damn what you want to 'discuss'?" Cecilia sneered.

"I don't really care whether you do or you don't. We're still going to have the discussion. Or do you think we aren't?"

His voice was calm, cool. Courteous, but with an iron note of authority, and the red in her eyes blazed higher. Her weight shifted, as if she were leaning back against a powerful wind, but then—manifestly against her will—she took a step. Not away from him; *towards* him.

"Fuck you!" she snapped, stopping as she forced her rebellious body to obey her once more.

"Somehow, I'm not surprised you feel that way," Ushakov said. "But surely you've realized by now that you *will* obey me?"

"Like hell I will!" she snarled defiantly, but she took another step towards him even as she spoke, and there was desperation under the defiance.

Three weeks had passed since the massacre in Naya Islamabad. Three weeks in which she had at first headed for the mountains of Afghanistan, where she could hide from the breathers and their vampire lickspittles and find an abundance of those ignorant, holier-than-thou religious fanatics who thought they were so tough, so strong, to prey upon.

But it hadn't worked out that way. Something—some . . . force or power she didn't understand—had frozen her each time she found a new toy to amuse her. She'd quivered in place, fighting its compulsion, hungry to rend and break, but she couldn't. And then she'd realized she wasn't truly looking for a hiding place, either, not really. She was *going* somewhere—somewhere specific—and she'd had no idea what her destination was.

When she'd realized that, she'd stopped. She'd found a mountain cave, hidden deep inside the rock. She'd told herself it was her imagination, that nothing was really affecting her but her own desires. Yet she'd found out differently, pacing the confines of the cave like a trapped animal, snarling at the comforting dark around her, as something picked and prodded and whispered and gibbered so deep in her brain that she couldn't lay mental hands on it. It was there—she knew it was—but she couldn't isolate it, couldn't make *sense* of it.

For two full days she'd hidden in that cave, fighting to understand, trying to resist whatever it was. Yet in the end, she'd been unable to do either . . . then. Step-by-step, against her will, fighting it every inch of the way, she'd left the cave, transformed herself once again into a cloud of mist, and gone drifting westward towards the setting moon once more. And gradually, in the days that followed, as she'd waged her losing struggle against the compulsion, she'd realized that she recognized the voice she couldn't quite hear in her brain.

And a part of her had also realized where she was bound, even though she'd never been there before.

"Get the hell out of my head!" she growled now, glaring at Ushakov.

"As Longbow would say, that is so not going to happen," Ushakov replied with a thin half smile, half grimace. "Trust me, I don't enjoy being there, but I have responsibilities."

"Oh, I know all about you and your *responsibilities.*" Her sneer made the noun a curse. "And you know what, *Captain* Ushakov? I don't give a flying fuck about you *or* your responsibilities. I am *done* taking orders from breathers. They're *cattle.* No—they're *worse* than cattle. They think they're so special, that they should be able to tell *us* what to do? Well, I've got news for them—and for *you,* too. They can't tell me *shit* anymore! Without us, they'd all be dead, and the universe would be better off without them!"

"I should have seen this coming sooner," Ushakov said. "No, that's not really true. I *did* see it coming; I simply closed my eyes to it because I didn't want to acknowledge it. But it's here, now, Cecilia, and it has to be dealt with, one way or the other. We aren't superior to the 'breathers.' Not really. Oh, we can do things they can't, and if Vlad is any example, it's possible we're truly immortal, now. But they can do things *we* can't, as well, including building something that can break the Hegemony when the time comes. And I remember what the Hegemony cost me. I remember my wife, my sons and my daughter, my entire family— all those *breathers* the Shongairi slaughtered. I admire and respect immensely those 'merely mortal' breathers you speak of with such contempt. I admire their refusal to lie down and die and their sheer, raw determination. And, when the time comes, they're the ones who will give my dead the vengeance they *deserve*. I'll go every step of that journey with them—like Vlad, and Stephen, and Longbow, and all the rest of us—for that moment, and I will protect them. I will protect them from *anything* . . . including our own kind."

"Words? You're going to use *eloquence* against me? *That's* your secret anti-vampire weapon?" Cecilia's laugh was a brittle silver icicle. "I don't know how you made me come here, but I'll bet you've been sitting on your ass in this library—and where the hell are we, anyway?—the entire time. Little hard to walk and chew gum at the same time, is it, Mr. I'm-So-Fucking-Holy? So knock yourself out. I've got plenty of time, and if you want to spend the next couple of centuries sitting here under this pile of rocks while we just look at each other, that's okay with me. Because you're not going to be doing any of that 'protecting' from anything else if you have to spend all of your time just sitting on me!"

"Which is why I have no intention of doing anything of the sort," Ushakov said.

"Well, I ain't going anywhere I don't fucking well *want* to go, so you're shit out of luck on that front, Jack!"

"One of us is, at any rate," Ushakov told her.

"Oh, yeah? And why's that, asshole?"

"For the same reason you had no choice but to come to me here. Vlad left me in command, with Longbow as my deputy. I am not yet as old and as strong as Vlad is, but I hold his authority, and you have no choice but to yield to it. Wherever you go, my mind can reach you. You can't hide from me, and you can't defy me—not for long. But I knew you'd try to, and that's the true reason I decided to summon you here, to Villa Daciana."

"And what's so special about 'Villa Daciana'?" Cecilia demanded.

"This is the home Vlad built for himself five hundred years ago, Cecilia, when he first mastered his own change. He named it for his first wife, who died by her own hand at the siege of Poenari Castle, barely ten kilometers from here, rather than face Turkish captivity. Poenari was one of Vlad's principal fortresses, although it lies in ruins now, of course. But the villa has served him in much the same way over the centuries, and he designated it as our . . . HQ when he left. So it seemed wisest to bring you here, where we could have this discussion in privacy."

"And what 'discussion' would that be?" Her tone dripped contempt.

"The one in which you agree to turn away from your madness."

"Like hell I will!"

"Yes, you will. Unless you wish to force me to resort to harsher measures."

"Ohhhhh, I'm so *scared*!"

"I suppose that in many ways this isn't really your fault." There was a sort of stern compassion in Ushakov's tone. "This is the madness Vlad warned Longbow and me about. We're fortunate, actually, that you're the only one of us in whom it's manifested . . . so far, at any rate. But I won't permit you to play with the breathers around you as if they existed only to be your toys."

She snarled wordlessly at him, and he shrugged.

"You're the only one who can defeat your madness, Cecilia. I can't do it from the outside. Not even Vlad could . . . cast out your demon. That, as Stephen or Dave would say, is 'on you.' It *can* be done, by someone with sufficient strength of will, sufficient determination. Vlad himself faced it and won. You can, too, I believe, and if that's what you choose to do, I'll help you in every way I can."

"Go to hell! I *like* it just the way it is. I am so sick and tired of having to worry about what other people think, or care about, or need. And you know what? None of that matters a single good goddamn to me anymore, and I'm *glad*. It shouldn't matter to you, either, but if you're so frigging stupid, so holy, then you go right ahead. But me? I am fucking *out* of here!"

"No, you aren't. Because under this villa there are not simply cellars, but dungeons . . . and crypts. And in one of those crypts, in a lead coffin, is where you'll await Vlad's return if you choose to continue to defy me."

Her eyes blazed scarlet, her hands curled into talons, and her fingernails extended into knife-edged black claws, but he only regarded her calmly.

"You'll take no harm. You'll simply sleep—hibernate, perhaps—until Vlad awakens you to deal with the situation. He's much stronger than I am, so perhaps he'll be able to get through to you. If not, I'm afraid he'll move to the final option."

"Oh, goody!" She rolled her eyes. "I'm so glad we're finally getting to the *final* option. Maybe when you're done going on and on, I can get out of here. So go ahead. What's the 'final option,' oh fearless leader?"

"The final option is to kill you," Pieter said levelly.

"*Kill* me?!" She laughed incredulously. "You think you can *kill* me? Do you have any idea how many *bullets* have gone right through me in the last fifteen years? Hell, I've even let some of the breathers stick knives into me, just so I could watch their faces when they realized it wasn't going to do them a damned bit of good! What makes you think *you* can kill me when none of *them* have been able to?"

"I don't 'think' I can, Cecilia. I know I can."

He reached into a drawer of the reading desk. His hand came out of it with a *khukuri,* the traditional weapon of the Gurkhas. The curved blade was razor-sharp and sixteen inches in length, with a chill, steely gleam under the library lights as he stood at last.

"A knife." Cecilia shook her head, her expression almost pitying. "Weren't you *listening*? I've had plenty of knives stuck into me already."

"Not by me, you haven't."

He stepped around the desk to face her. She tried to move back, away from him. Instead, she took a step towards him before she could make herself stop, and her eyes were the color of blood.

"I don't care who you think you are." Her words were slurred by her growing fangs. "It doesn't matter. Jill and Susan and I went at it in that stupid basement in Pakistan, and none of us could hurt the other one any more than the breathers can. You're no different."

"Cecilia, please," he said. "I *am* different, and I *can* kill you. I don't want to, but I can, and I will if you force me to it. What you've done—what you've *become*—has to end, and it will. One way or the other, it ends right here, tonight."

"You really mean that, don't you?" The tension in her body eased slightly. "You really think you can kill me, and you really don't want to."

"Yes, I can, and no, I don't want to."

"Well, in that case, maybe—"

It happened so quickly that a "breather" wouldn't even have seen her move. Her voice was calmer than it had been, reasonable, almost soothing, and then she lashed out from a relaxed, manifestly nonthreatening posture with those lethal claws, going for his throat with a viper's speed.

But fast as she was, she was still too slow. The *khukuri* in Ushakov's hand flashed in the light as the curved edge, shaped to maximize the force of the blow, slashed into the side of her neck.

Cecilia had been right about the number of knives she'd faced and laughed at. About the bullets, the blades, even the chair legs, which had completely failed to harm her or any of the other vampires. But that cold steel in the hand of Vlad Drakulya's deputy was unlike any other blade she'd ever encountered, and her hungry snarl ended in a shocked grunt as sharpened steel clove completely through her neck.

Her head flew, the scarlet eyes wide in disbelief. It hit the library floor and rolled, and for just a moment, those eyes blinked up at him from the marble while her decapitated body stood upright, frozen. And then, as silent as smoke or drifting snow, she simply . . . dissipated into dust and vanished.

Pieter stood for a long, still time, looking at the space she'd occupied. Then he drew one of the deep breaths he no longer truly needed, shook his head, and replaced the *khukuri* in the desk drawer. He laid one hand on the closed Bible for a moment, then squared his shoulders and drew his phone from his pocket.

"Dvorak," he told it.

"Contacting David Dvorak," the phone replied. He stood waiting.

"Pieter?" Dvorak's voice said from the phone.

"It's finished," Ushakov said. "She was . . . unreasonable to the end. She will no longer be a problem."

"I'm sorry," Dvorak said quietly. "I'm sure that was . . . difficult for you."

"In many ways. But—" Ushakov shrugged "—in other ways, her attitude made it much easier than it might have been."

"Do you think we're going to see any more like her?"

It was like Dvorak to come straight at the question, Ushakov reflected.

"I don't know," he replied. "From what Vlad told us before he left, it's unlikely many more of our kind will react as Cecilia did. Not at this late date. If we were going to, there should have been signs earlier, as there were in her case. But I'd be lying if I told you I can guarantee that."

"About what I thought," Dvorak said. "And I know you don't lie, Pieter. But I also have to tell you there was some discussion about this point at the Cabinet meeting right after the Ghilzai fiasco. I'm sure you'll understand why what happened in Naya Islamabad has a lot of my fellow secretaries' knickers in a wad. There's a lot of concern, and Charlie Mussett mentioned that—"

"That Longbow and I have been . . . less than eager to submit to examination?"

"That's exactly what he mentioned." Ushakov could almost hear the shrug at the other end of the phone. "Howell stood up for you guys. He had your backs—exactly the way you frigging well deserve for *all* of us to have them. But it's been fifteen years, Pieter, and most of the 'breathers' don't know you guys the way Rob and I do—the way Howell does. Cecilia's made them . . . nervous."

"Of course she has." Ushakov let his friend hear an audible sigh and shook his head. "And rightly so. And Doctor Mussett has a point. We *have* been avoiding him on this."

"I know," Dvorak said quietly.

"I won't pretend I'm pleased by the notion of . . . complying with Doctor Mussett's request. That seems to be a general characteristic of vampires."

"Really?" Dvorak's tone was desert dry. "I wonder why that could possibly be?"

Ushakov snorted in amusement and shook his head again.

"As I'm sure you understand, Vlad has always avoided anything remotely like a scientific exploration of his nature and capabilities. Of course, up until very recently—by his standards of 'recent,' at any rate—that 'examination' probably would have been carried out by, oh, the Church authorities, and the consequences if *they* had determined a way to destroy vampires would have been . . . less than desirable from his perspective, shall we say?"

The slight but unmistakable emphasis he'd placed on the word "they" was not lost on Dave Dvorak.

"Pieter—"

"There's no need for explanations or apologies, Dave," Ushakov said gently. "I would vastly prefer, even now, to avoid what Vlad described as 'exquisitely polite vivisection by the breathers,' but the reason he described it that way was because he knew this moment would very probably come. As he says, we've all 'come into the light' now. The existence of vampires has been scientifically demonstrated and recorded for posterity, and it will never be possible for us to simply disappear again. More than that, Vlad understands that a technological, scientific age will want answers, and that which we fear the most is that about which we know the least. And much as we all hope there will be no more Cecilias, we can't know that, nor can we know there will always be another vampire at hand to restrict the damage another Cecilia could do. So I suppose it's not simply understandable that you 'breathers' want to comprehend our nature but morally indefensible for us to refuse to share that information with you when just one of us in Cecilia's state could wreak so much carnage."

"I hate it, but you're right," Dvorak said after a moment. "And as much as I hate it, I can't tell you how grateful I am you've reacted this way."

"It would do me very little good to react any other way," Ushakov pointed out with a slight smile. "Besides," the smile vanished, "Vlad left me and the others here to *protect* humanity. I can scarcely fulfill that directive by refusing to help humanity understand us . . . and learn how, if necessary, to protect themselves *against* one of us. Holy water, crucifixes, wooden stakes, garlic, and communion wafers seem unable to do the trick. Who knows? Perhaps science will discover a weapon religion has not."

· VII ·

S o you've decided which one you want?" Lewis Freymark inquired, looking
at his daughter Jacqueline across the supper table.

"Really?" Janice Freymark smiled at their next to youngest. "Finally!"

"Don't pick on me," Jacqueline replied with a smile of her own. "It wasn't an
easy decision with so many makes and options to choose from. Besides, it's my
very first car, and I'm buying it with my own money, so I have a perfect right to
spend however long I want to thinking about it."

"Yeah, but do you have to take *months*?" her younger brother asked. Lewis
Alexander Freymark was only thirteen, nine years younger than Jacqueline. He
hadn't experienced the Shongair invasion firsthand, for which his parents were
profoundly grateful. And he had every iota of the typical kid brother's attitude.

"I have *not* taken 'months,' pipsqueak." Jacqueline's tone was repressive, but
her eyes twinkled. "I've only taken about *one* month. Well, okay—one and a
half, if you're counting. Which I'm not."

"Gee, Dad always said you weren't great at math, but I thought for sure you
could *count*!"

"You are so going to regret that one," Jacqueline promised.

"Come on! Admit I got you!"

"I shall do nothing of the sort." She elevated the pert nose she'd inherited
from her mother with an audible sniff, and Freymark pointed a finger at him.

"Don't expect me to sympathize when she starts looking for somewhere to
hide the body, young man," he said. "Although," he lowered the pointing finger
and grinned as he extended his fist across the table for a fist bump, instead, "you
did get her."

"*Riiiight!*" Lewis Alexander said with a huge, infectious grin of his own
that sent a fleeting jab of pain through his father as Freymark remembered the
brother Lewis Alexander would never know.

"So, what did you pick?" he asked, turning back to Jacqueline with a smile
that hid his own flash of grief.

"I'm going with Franklin's Rapier with a second-tier upgrade option," she
said.

"Going to be a little pricey," he mused, and she nodded.

"Really wish I could go first-tier, but I don't think I can quite swing it now that I'm out on my own." She shrugged. "And second-tier is still gonna be great!"

"Yeah, it is," he agreed.

The horrible days of reconstruction immediately after the invasion were a thing of the past, not just here in Aurora but pretty much around the world. There were still places that wasn't true—like Pakistan, which had actually managed to get worse following the demise of the Ghilzai regime—but anywhere the Planetary Union's writ ran, the pre-invasion distinction between the "First World" and the rest of the planet had become a rapidly receding image in people's rearview mirrors. The standard of living only a minority of nations had been able to afford before the Puppies' arrival was now the baseline, the starting point, for the invasion's survivors and their children. In fact, they'd actually achieved something very like a true post-scarcity economy.

There'd been some changes in how the economy worked along the way, of course. For example, prior to the invasion, Freymark was one of the people who would've had serious reservations about total government ownership of the principal means of production. Under the new economy, however, that was the basis for the planetary currency. In one of his few nods to U.S. chauvinism, Howell had decreed that the new currency would be called the planetary dollar. He'd also decreed that it would be backed by something a lot more concrete than the notional value of a fiat currency, though. And what backed it was the fact that the planetary government owned the deep space infrastructure, including all the Lagrange point printers and the entire resource extraction infrastructure. That was a concrete, quantifiable asset and the amount of dollars in circulation was pegged to its extent and expansion.

Every adult citizen of the Planetary Union was entitled to free education and free healthcare—a lot more practical with post-invasion medical tech than it would have been previously—and a monthly stipend to pay for other needs, like food, housing, or anything else they chose to spend it upon. The MS was pegged to a basket of commodities provided by the private economy and was more than sufficient to maintain someone in relative comfort with access to public entertainment. It was not, however, sufficient to finance something like Franklin Motors' Rapier. Anyone could save up for a major purchase by economizing in other areas of his life, but the majority of people had jobs to bring in extra income. An awful lot of them—like Jacqueline, actually—were employed in the booming virtual-reality field. Given the uptick in leisure time and income, entertainment was in greater demand than ever before, although the majority of the PU's member states had enacted legislation limiting the total number of hours per week any of its citizens could spend in VR. Most of them allowed people to "bank" hours—up to a point, at least—but there'd been some nasty experiences when post-invasion level virtual-reality became available.

Another huge chunk had jobs in the public sector, working directly for the PU, one of its member states, or a local municipality. Others were self-employed consultants, fashion advisors, physical fitness coaches, or provided any number of personal services to a human race which was far more affluent than it had ever been before. But there was also, somewhat to Freymark's surprise, a robust manufacturing sector.

It wasn't quite like any manufacturing sector he'd ever imagined before the invasion, however. Instead, companies—or individuals—created copyrighted designs for consumer goods and either rented printer time from the government or owned their own private printers—many of them in near-Earth orbit, but more of them conveniently located on the planet's surface. The only physical limiting factor on production was printer speed, really, and something like Jacqueline's Rapier could probably be printed out in no more than an hour or so, so most of the entrepreneurs involved followed the same pattern as Franklin and printed only after an order had been placed and paid for. Managing production flow so that someone didn't get tired of waiting an entire two or three *days,* sometimes, could be a little tricky, but the real battle was in marketing. In finding the tweak that would appeal to the broadest customer base and then convincing those customers that they really, *really* needed your product and not some other inferior piece of junk.

Before the invasion, Freymark had been accustomed to auto manufacturers beginning design of the next year's model even before this year's had hit the showroom floors. Now things like the Rapier were individually customized to the buyer's requirements—for a suitable upcharge, of course—and "next year's models" were being introduced on a daily basis, literally. And quite a lot of "*last* year's models" were being traded in for their reclamation value when the latest, newest, best, brightest, shiniest version became available, and someone just *had* to have it.

He didn't know how the system would ultimately evolve, but he'd been more than a little surprised by how well the human race in general appeared to be adapting to it. By any pre-invasion standard, there was an awful lot of conspicuous consumption going on, but apparently the need to be productive truly was hardwired into the human psyche. It might be that fifteen years simply wasn't long enough to eradicate a "need" which had been created by grim necessity, but he didn't think so. He thought it went deeper than that.

And then there was the never-forgotten threat of the Hegemony, the Sword of Damocles hanging over humanity's collective head. A certain froth—normally he preferred the term "scum"—had floated to the surface, arguing that simply because the Shongairi had been nasty, genocidal monsters, there was no reason to *assume* the Hegemony as a whole would feel the same way. He didn't have a lot of patience with that viewpoint. In his opinion, a lot of them were from the side of the mental tracks which just had to prove its superiority by adopting a contrarian position. That, after all, demonstrated their intellectual fearlessness and willingness to think outside the box. On the other hand, in his more charitable moments, he acknowledged that as yet Earth had no firsthand experience with the Hegemony as a whole. The Shongairi might not be as typical as most folks assumed, and it was possible—*possible*—that the critics of the anti-Hegemony viewpoint *might* have a point. That, however, was the sort of mistake one only got to make once, and as his father had said, the one virtue of pessimism was that any surprises would be pleasant ones.

For the vast majority of human beings, the threat of the Hegemony was taken as a given, and that focused a great deal of creative effort on ways to help mitigate that threat. Quite a few engineering and research firms had sprung up, offering both collaborative and competitive designs to the Planetary Armed Forces and building prototypes using their own printers or rented government printer time, and recruiters for the PAF itself had pretty much as many volunteers as they could use.

"So, which of the second-tier mods are you planning to add?" he asked his daughter now.

"I'm going with the Apollo package and adding a full VR HUD plus the level six counter-grav and the full manual control option."

"You really think you need transatmospheric capability, Honey?" Janice Freymark asked, raising her eyebrows.

"I probably don't *need* it, Mom, but it'd be handy to have. For example, that convention on the Othello Platform. Next time, I'll be able to hop into my own car, scoot up to orbit, and have it available once I get there instead of having to use public transport or carpool. And it's only another thousand bucks or so."

"*I'm* a little more leery about that manual control option, especially with the counter-grav you're talking about, young lady," Freymark said. "That kind of acceleration and velocity can get away from you in a hurry if you're flying by hand and relying on the Mark One eyeball."

"Oh, *Dad!*" Jacqueline's eye roll reminded him of a much younger daughter. "First, I'm a really good driver—you know that as well as I do. Second, that's why I want the full VR HUD. I don't have any intention of flying by eye! Besides, Franklin won't sell a manual control without a mandatory backstop AI override."

"That's true," he acknowledged. "On the other hand, wasn't it just last week some idiot boy child managed to hack around his backstop and kill his fool self?"

"That was a *boy* child," Jacqueline pointed out, ignoring a rude sound from Lewis Alexander. "And I believe you were the one who pointed out to me years ago that one of the few immutable rules is that stupidity is ultimately its own punishment."

"Yes. Yes, I did." He smiled at her, then shrugged.

"Your money; your car; your decision," he said. "I assume you've at least taken your design for a test drive, though?"

"Only in VR, so far, but Franklin has an option. For an extra two hundred, they'll print the car and let you drive it for a month while you decide whether or not it's what you want. If you decide it isn't, they'll take it back, no questions, for reclamation, and you can swap it for another model of equal value, if you want to. Or even upgrade the one you already bought by paying the difference. Not a bad deal."

"No, it isn't," he said thoughtfully, and looked at Janice. "Weren't you looking at one of Franklin's designs last week, Honey?"

"The car I've got is perfectly fine, Lewis."

"Didn't say it wasn't, but your birthday's coming up. So, weren't you looking at one of them?"

"Well, yes. I was looking at the Cirrus. It's not as flashy as the Rapier, but it's nice. And it's got some nice mod packages."

"In that case, why don't you and I hop into the Net tomorrow and take a test drive? If you decide you really like it, then maybe I've got your birthday covered early!"

"Way to surprise somebody with a gift, Dad," Lewis Alexander pointed out.

"Silence, undutiful child!" his mother said sternly. "Don't interrupt your father when he's giving me exactly what I want for my birthday!" She glowered at him for a moment, then relented and looked around the table. "So, who's ready for dessert?"

· VIII ·

Hi, Uncle Pieter!"

Pieter Ushakov looked up from the book reader as Maighread Dvorak—*Doctor* Maighread Dvorak now, actually—walked into the comfortable, if sterile, waiting room. She'd changed a lot from the huge-eyed nine-year-old he'd met in the North Carolina mountains, he thought. She was never going to match her father's or brother's towering inches, but she was five inches *taller* than her mother and she moved with a springy, athletic grace. She was twenty-four now, he realized, although she'd begun the antigerone treatments early enough that she looked like someone scarcely out of high school, and according to rumors, she and her sister—both avid soccer players— were more than capable of holding their own on the soccer pitch against Vice President Olatunji. Now she crossed to him with rapid strides and threw her arms around his neck.

"It's *so* good to see you!" she said, hugging tightly.

"Hello, Maighread," he replied, just a bit less effusively, and put one arm around her to hug back.

"Not too crazy about this, are you?" she asked sympathetically, standing back with her hands still on his shoulders.

"I believe one might reasonably put it that way." He quirked a smile at her. "Still, if I must submit to being poked and prodded, at least there will be a friendly face involved. How are you?"

"I'm fine, Uncle Pieter." She squeezed his shoulders briefly, then stood back and shoved her hands into the pockets of her traditional white lab coat. "I hope you've marked your calendar for the wedding?"

"I will most assuredly be there," he said, smiling more broadly. "That is, I'll be there unless you think the fearsome vampire's reputation will frighten off your young man?"

"Ray doesn't exactly scare easy!" Maighread chuckled and shook her head. "He and Malachi are both Southern boys, and if counter-grav hadn't come along, they'd probably have both been busted for drag racing. Of course, that wouldn't have been as much fun as illegal aerobatics, now would it? And putting the two of them into the same chain of command—" She shook her head.

"Honestly, I don't know what the Marines were thinking when the Corps put both of them into the same company!"

"Perhaps you should take that up with your uncle?"

"Oh, that'd be a wonderful idea!" She snorted. "You do realize they're both just like Uncle Rob, don't you? Or rather, he's just like them. Trust me, *he* doesn't see anything wrong with giving an overgrown pair of juvenile delinquents matches and then turning them loose in the dynamite plant!"

"Matches?" Ushakov repeated quizzically, and she snorted again, harder.

"What would you call making them junior project officers on Project Heinlein *and* giving them the first two suits fitted with the new, improved booster system to play with? Trust me, it's a good thing we noble healers can put almost anybody back together these days, no matter how thoroughly they've managed to shatter the bits and pieces!"

"Oh, my!" Ushakov shook his head. "*Malachi* is playing with the new boosters?"

"No, Malachi and *Raymond* are playing with the new boosters. I expect to see my beloved brother and fiancé rolled in here on matching gurneys any day now."

"I'm sure you're unduly pessimistic," he reassured her. "The Heinlein suits are really very good at protecting people, you know."

"*Nothing*'s good enough to 'protect' my baby brother when his enthusiasm's fully engaged."

"Perhaps you're right. But, as you say, modern medicine can do wonders." He cocked his head at her. "And, I'm sure modern medicine has many questions for me. It was very kind of Hosea and Doctor Kaufman to let you come in and put me at my ease first, but they're probably getting tired of standing in the hall."

"Actually," she acknowledged, "they're sitting in Hosea's office down the hall until I give them the high sign. So, have I succeeded in putting you at your ease?" She grinned. "To be honest, I'm the one who suggested letting me handle the greetings, but it wasn't because I was worried about your state of mind. It was because I haven't seen you in a while, and it probably would've seemed unprofessional to run up and hug you in a more . . . structured setting."

"Perhaps," he replied. From her body language and her pulse—which his hearing detected easily when he focused on it—she was being truthful with him, not just diplomatic. Mostly, at least.

"It probably is time we were getting started, though," she said, "so, if you're ready to face the Inquisition, I guess we should go." She tucked one arm through his as he stood and leaned her head briefly against his shoulder. "I know you don't want to do this," she said more quietly, "and I don't blame you any more than Dad would. And I really do want you to be sure you're among friends while it happens."

"Trust me, *Lyubyy,*" he said, "I know that. I knew it even before you walked in to hug me. So, let's go get this done."

．．．．．

"WELL," HOSEA MACMURDO said, "this is mildly irritating."

He and Doctor Nancy Kaufman stood at one end of the large examination room which contained the comfortable chair in which Pieter Ushakov sat.

"Nothing?" Kaufman asked, green eyes narrow.

"Not a damned thing!" MacMurdo thumped the microscope—which looked very little like a traditional human microscope—disgustedly. The tridee display above the microscope housing showed a hugely magnified view of a hollow rod. The actual "rod" was an extremely thin needle, although the casual observer might have been excused for not realizing that from a glance at the display.

"That doesn't make any sense," Kaufman protested.

"You think you're telling me something I don't already know?" MacMurdo retorted just a bit caustically.

"Is there a problem?" Ushakov asked mildly, looking up over his shoulder at Maighread Dvorak where she stood behind his chair, one hand on his shoulder, while she gazed at the senior physicians with a quizzical expression.

"Well, yes." She sounded a bit amused, he noticed. "You know that tissue sample they were taking?" He nodded. "Well, apparently it's not there."

"Indeed?" He frowned. "That seems . . . odd."

"One way to put it, I guess," she agreed. "On the other hand, they're trying to conduct a physical exam of a *vampire,* Uncle Pieter. Not too surprising if we hit a few bumps in the road."

"You're very like your father, you know," he observed. Then he pondered for a moment. "And like your mother, too. God, I hadn't realized what a frightening thought that could be!"

"You're just saying that because you're jealous of my good looks, wit, and charm."

"*Very* like your parents," he murmured, his own eyes going to MacMurdo and Kaufman. "I don't understand why they didn't get their specimen, though."

"Neither do they, obviously." Maighread shook her head, then raised her voice. "Doctors?"

"Umph!" MacMurdo looked up from his conversation with Kaufman. "Sorry, Maighread—and you too, Pieter. It's just that we're a tiny bit baffled."

"Why?"

"Because there ought to be a sample of your tissue in this needle, and there isn't."

"I see. How is it supposed to work?"

"Well, the biopsy needle that we inserted actually has two main parts." He lifted the device in question from the tray at his elbow as he spoke. A long, thin needle protruded from an ergonomic grip with a button on its end. "It's a bit fancier than anything we had before the invasion, but it still works basically the same way. This outer shaft is the guide needle. It's hollow, and normally we'd insert it through a small incision. Incisions don't work very well on vampires, though, so we had to forgo that, just like we had to forgo anesthesia. Fortunately, you don't feel pain, so—"

"That's not precisely correct," Ushakov interrupted in a polite tone, and MacMurdo paused.

"It's not?" the doctor asked, one eyebrow raised.

"Our nervous system seems to work just the way it used to in terms of our ability to see or feel or smell," Ushakov said. "Unless we choose for it not to, that is."

"'Choose' not to?" MacMurdo repeated.

"Yes. It's a conscious decision on our part."

"So that's why it doesn't hurt when you get shot?" Kaufman asked, frowning intently.

"I suppose, although there appears to be a certain degree of automatic response involved there. The handful of times someone has shot me when I wasn't expecting it, it . . . stung, I suppose, is the best way to put it. It's a very brief sensation, which leads me to conclude that some subconscious instinct shuts down the pain sensors. I have not—" he smiled dryly "—attempted to overrule that instinct, if it exists, in order to experience the full pleasure of being shot, you understand, so I'm not positive I've described what happens correctly."

"That's interesting," MacMurdo mused. "I never realized you could still feel things normally. Or, if you could, that you could choose *not* to feel them."

"Actually, we can boost sensory data, as well," Ushakov told him. The doctor's other eyebrow joined its raised companion, and Ushakov shrugged. "The purpose of this examination is supposed to be the exploration of my abilities and nature. There are many questions we haven't been asked, and a number of self-observations we haven't previously shared with you. In fact, I can hear your pulse beat quite clearly, Hosea."

"You can?" MacMurdo frowned. He was over six meters away from Ushakov at the moment. "You can hear something that faint from that far away? And even separate it out of the ambient noise?"

"I can isolate *anything* I choose to focus upon," Ushakov said flatly. "Nor, before you ask, does it have to be an organic sound, as I suppose might be appropriate in a predator. Wind, sleet—even snowflakes." He shrugged. "The symphony about us is quite lovely if you can truly hear it all."

"Fascinating," MacMurdo murmured. He stood in thought for a handful of seconds, then shook himself. "That really is fascinating, Pieter, but getting back to the biopsy. The guide needle is actually the shaft down which an even thinner core needle travels. When I push the button here," he pointed at the button on the end of the sturdy housing, "the core needle extends from the end of the guide shaft. There's a section cut out of it to create a channel in its side, and when it retracts into the guide shaft again, that channel is supposed to carry a specimen with it. You could think of it as a thin strand of tissue, sort of like a very thin strand of angel hair pasta."

"Now there's an appetizing simile," Maighread murmured, and MacMurdo gave her a quick smile.

"Just trying to put it into layman's terms, Maighread."

"And this particular layman appreciates it," Ushakov said. "But, obviously, it failed to work that way in my case?"

"According to the microscope, yes," Kaufman said.

"Interesting." Both of them looked at Ushakov, and he shook his head quickly. "I have no more idea why it failed than you do, Doctors."

"Well, if you don't object, I guess the next step is to try again," MacMurdo said, and Ushakov nodded.

· · · · ·

"OKAY," MACMURDO SAID thirty-five minutes later. "I think I've gone from 'mildly irritated' to 'acutely pissed off.'"

"I assure you—" Ushakov began, but MacMurdo's waved hand cut him off.

"Not at you, Pieter! At *this*." He jabbed a finger at the microscope. "It's not your fault, but if we can't even take a tissue sample, this examination of ours isn't going to get very far."

Maighread Dvorak stood with one hand shoved into her lab coat pocket while the other held her long braid. Her hair fell almost to her hips when it was loose, which meant that braid was long enough she could nibble on its end to help herself think. It was a habit she'd had since childhood, despite her parents' every effort to break her of it, and at the moment, she was thinking rather furiously.

Every attempt to take a needle biopsy had failed. After the sixth attempt, MacMurdo had suggested—and Ushakov had agreed—that they might take a small sample with a scalpel. That had failed, as well. The scalpel passed through the tissue easily, but the cut closed behind it instantly. There was never time to actually take the sample, and examination of the scalpel blade under the microscope showed that none of Ushakov's cells—assuming vampires still *had* cells—had adhered to the blade on its way through. After that, they'd attempted a vacuum biopsy, with a powerful vacuum sucking the tissue sample through a hollow needle. That had failed, too. In fact. . . .

"*I'm* out of bright ideas," Doctor Kaufman sighed. "I suppose we can just stick Pieter's hand under the microscope, but that's only going to give us a topical examination, and we've already done that."

She tapped the magnifying lenses she'd laid aside. They weren't as powerful as the microscope, although they were considerably more powerful than a pre-invasion human would have judged looking at them. All they'd demonstrated, however, was that Ushakov's skin, hair, and nails appeared completely normal.

"We haven't looked at the cellular level, of course," she continued, "but I'll be very surprised if—"

"Um, excuse me, Doctor Kaufman," Maighread heard herself interrupt politely. Kaufman paused, head cocked, and looked at her. "I've just had what my dad would call a sort of crazy, off-the-wall thought."

"Which is?" MacMurdo asked with the wary expression of someone who had experienced his fair share of *Dave* Dvorak's "crazy, off-the-wall" thoughts.

"Well, Pieter says he has control over his nervous system. Over his ability to feel sensations and hear sounds. What if he has control over more of his body? And what if there are even more of those 'subconscious' prompts of his at work?"

"Where are you taking this, Maighread?" Ushakov asked, gazing at her intently.

"We're trying to take tissue samples so we can analyze them," she said. "Now, what if there's a . . . call it a survival mechanism, for want of a better word, built into a vampire. The same sort of survival mechanism that lets bullets only sting briefly on their way through your liver or lungs, for example. If I were a secretive creature of the night, and if that meant the human beings around me might want to know more about me and maybe even figure out how to kill something *like* me, I don't think I'd like them being able to take samples of my tissues. What if there's something like that at work here? Something working on a deep enough level that you're not aware of it yourself, Pieter?"

"I suppose that's possible," Ushakov said slowly. "I've never actually considered it, but Vlad did say—and it matches my own experience—that the very thought of being examined was enough to make him acutely uneasy. He couldn't define precisely why, although he certainly had any number of *conscious* reasons to avoid such an examination, and neither can I. My Dasha—" his eyes darkened briefly as he spoke the diminutive form of his murdered daughter's name "—was always afraid of needles, of being poked and prodded. But I never was. Until now, when it can't possibly hurt me. That does seem . . . odd, doesn't it?"

"That's one way to put it," Maighread agreed. "But what if that's because something deep inside you is . . . resisting exposure? Wouldn't that explain it?"

"It might," Ushakov acknowledged.

"But you said you can override the sensory cutout when it happens automatically," Maighread went on, brown eyes intent. "What if you tried *that* while Doctor MacMurdo tries to take a specimen?"

"You mean concentrate on the fact that I consciously wish for him to succeed?"

"Exactly!"

"I don't see where it could *hurt*," MacMurdo said with a shrug. "We've certainly tried everything else!"

"Very well," Ushakov said. He sat back, eyes closed, frowning faintly in concentration.

"Try now," he said in a slightly distant voice, and MacMurdo inserted the core needle again. He withdrew it, crossed back to the microscope, and slid the needle into the viewing receptacle. He looked up at the display, and smiled suddenly.

"Worked!" he said exuberantly. "At least this time we got something." He tapped a control, zooming the image even farther. "In fact, it looks like—*Jesus Christ!*"

. . . . .

"YOU'RE JOKING," JUDSON Howell said.

"No, I most certainly am not, Mister President," Hosea MacMurdo said from the smart wall tridee. "There's no question. And I had Warren's people backcheck me on this." He twitched his head at Warren Jackson, who stood next to him in his own office. "There's no question," he repeated.

"Jesus," Howell said, looking across his desk at Dave Dvorak and Jolasun Olatunji. "Nanotech? Vampires are built out of *nanotech*?"

"Not 'just' nanotech, Mister President," Jackson said. "This is really advanced stuff. It's more nano*bots* than nanites, actually. We're only just starting to scratch the surface, but I can already tell you this is a lot more advanced than anything we've found in the Hegemony tech base as of yet. As nearly as we can tell—of course, like I say, we're at a very early stage—these nanobots are completely . . . labile, for want of a better word. In essence, they're Captain Ushakov's cells, and that's how tiny they are, but they aren't programmed to be a specific *sort* of cell. When you manage to separate them from the rest of him, they go . . . blank. They seem to be transparent, clear as water, and completely quiescent. Until you put them back, at least. We've actually put Captain Ushakov's hand under the microscope and returned the sample by applying it to his skin, and the instant the sample comes in contact with him, it changes from its transparent state. In fact, in the brief window in which we can continue to observe it, it seems to transform into additional skin cells."

"Shades of *Terminator 3*!" Howell muttered, and Johnson chuckled.

"Not really that bad a simile, Mister President. It's too early to say this for certain, but based on what we've been able to observe so far, I'd guess these nanobots can configure themselves into whatever kind of cell he needs them to be—skin cell, hair cell, bone, cartilage."

He shrugged.

"It gets even better, Mister President," MacMurdo put in. Howell looked at him, and the surgeon shrugged. "After we began to realize that things were even weirder than we'd expected, we got Pieter to agree to turn himself into smoke for us while we watched. Under sufficient magnification, *what* he does is apparent now, although figuring out *how* he does it is likely to take a little longer. Those 'nanobots' of Warren's . . . disassociate themselves. It's like they transform into a dispersed array of some sort, but even dispersed, Pieter's completely conscious and has complete control over where that array moves, and it moves using what *appears* to be something like counter-grav but doesn't register on our sensors."

"That sounds ridiculous," Howell said slowly.

"Maybe not," Dvorak said, and there was something very odd about his voice. And about his expression, Howell realized, when he looked at the Secretary of State. In fact, he'd never seen quite that expression on Dvorak.

"What do you mean?" he asked.

"I've been digging even more deeply into the history, and especially the diplomatic history, of the Hegemony ever since you shared your brainstorm about contacting other species," Dvorak said. "And the deeper I've dug, the more I've become aware of the holes in the *historical* record, not just the scientific record. It's not anything I can pin down, you understand. It's more of an itch I haven't been able to scratch. A sense that somebody's not telling me *something,* if you know what I mean. I've told myself it was only my nasty, suspicious imagination, because if I'm right about that, it's not something that could've happened by accident. Not on this scale. Whatever they aren't telling us was carefully expunged from the record. Or, at least, from the record the Shongairi had. I don't know what might be in the Hegemony's 'secret Vatican archives,' you understand."

He paused, eyebrows arched, and Howell nodded.

"Okay, I'm with you so far. I think. But where are you going with this?"

"Doctor Jackson, you said this is more advanced than anything we found in the Hegemony's database, yes?" Jackson nodded on the smart wall. "And Hosea said that these 'nanobots' use a form of counter-grav that we can't detect?"

"I'm not prepared to say it *is* counter-grav, actually," Jackson said. "I don't see what else it *could* be, you understand, but if I can't even detect it, I'm not prepared to categorize it yet."

"Granted. But, either it's a form of counter-grav we can't detect, and as far as we know the Hegemony couldn't produce something like that, or else it's something else entirely, using some principle the Hegemony doesn't know anything about. Either way, it sounds like it's clearly outside the Hegemony's technological capabilities, at least in so far as those capabilities are laid out in the data we captured from the Shongairi. Would that be fair?"

"It's certainly one way to describe it," Jackson said slowly.

"You're suggesting that what we actually acquired is the . . . export version of the Hegemony's technology?" Howell's expression was troubled, to say the least, and he frowned heavily. "They gave the Puppies a downgraded version, not their cutting edge tech? We don't have a handle on their *actual* tech capabilities at all? No yardstick?"

"I didn't say that, Mister President," Dvorak said quickly. "I mean, that *may* be the case, but I don't think so. And you might think about when Vlad was first transformed into whatever this stuff really is, too. At that point, the Hegemony didn't know a thing about us, didn't have any record of humanity or our planet at all. So how would he have gotten exposed to Hegemony tech?"

Howell's frown segued from unhappiness to confusion.

"It *has* to be from the Hegemony, doesn't it?" he asked almost plaintively.

"Except for the fact that it *can't* be," Dvorak replied. "Unless we're going to assume that every word of all the data we acquired from the Shongairi was deliberately 'cooked' before it was handed to them, and from the records we have, the tech base we captured from them predates any mention anywhere in the Hegemony's records of us or the planet Earth. That suggests to me that if the tech base was doctored at all, it was done before the Hegemony knew anything about us or our planet. So I don't think this is theirs."

"You're suggesting *another* bunch of aliens?" Howell asked skeptically. "Vlad Drakulya had a close encounter of the third kind with some other group of interstellar travelers six hundred years ago, and they beamed him up to the mothership for experiments?"

"Not exactly," Dvorak said dryly. "But I need to go run a different search—a more focused one—on the historical data. Because there are a couple of places—only a couple, you understand—that I've come across in which there's a sort of . . . truncated reference. All of them are from the very early history of the Hegemony, and there could be other explanations. But on the basis of what Hosea and Doctor Jackson are telling us, I have to wonder if they aren't *redactions.*"

"What kind of 'redaction'?" Howell asked intently.

"I don't know, frankly," Dvorak admitted. "And I don't want to talk myself into any theories the evidence doesn't support. Or, worse, to decide that the evidence *does* support a theory when it actually doesn't. But if we're looking at a nanotechnology more advanced than anything the Hegemony has now and Vlad was exposed to it less than sixty years after the Hegemony's first scout ship ever discovered us, then that sure as hell suggests it came from somebody else. I don't have any clue who the . . . call them the 'Other Guys' for now, might be, but if there are redactions in the historical record, and if they occur as early as they seem to, then one hell of a wildcard's just been dropped into the game."

· IX ·

SPACE STATION *INVICTUS*,
L5 LAGRANGE POINT

Really something, isn't it?" Rhonda Jeffries murmured.

"Could say that," Alec Wilson agreed. He was technically head down in the microgravity as the two of them gazed through the workboat's viewport at the improbable geometry of the Planetary Union Navy's first true shipyard.

The "building slips"—immense, widely dispersed, openwork frames of krystar, a synthetic alloy far stronger than anything Earth had ever dreamed of—were enormous, but they weren't big enough to build entire ships. Not the size of interstellar vessels. Instead, they used the modular technique, with each slip building one component of the starship-to-be. The one they were examining at the moment was Golf Section, the seventh of the fifteen sections which would be assembled into the core hull of the starship PUNS *James Robinson*, the lead dreadnought of the Planetary Union. The entire slip appeared to be rotating on its axis, but that impression was false. Actually, their workboat was the one moving relative to it as they kept station on the slip's rotating hub, but it did give them an opportunity to appreciate afresh the sheer size of the project. Golf Section was basically a circular slice of thickly armored hull, life-support sections, environmental and power runs, and everything else that went into creating an artificial, inhabitable world . . . that just happened to be as broad as five and a half nuclear aircraft carriers laid end to end.

And it was "only" three quarters of a kilometer thick and just under two kilometers across. When completed, the core hull would be a cylinder 11.25 kilometers long and 1.9 kilometers in diameter. Of course, the final dimensions of the finished ship would be substantially greater than that.

"It'll be even more impressive when we're done, though," Wilson pointed out now.

"Yah," Jeffries agreed. She was from Minnesota, with straw-blond hair, blue eyes, and a strong nose. She was also three inches taller than Wilson.

"Well, I suppose we should get to it," he said now, reaching up and securing his helmet. His suit's gloves extruded from its sleeves as Jeffries donned her own helmet, and he tapped a key on his sleeve pad. "Com check," he said.

"Five-by-five," Jeffries replied. "All systems green."

"Here, too," Wilson confirmed, and tugged on a bulkhead handhold to send himself drifting into the workboat's airlock.

As he stepped out into the bottomless void, Alec Wilson found himself reflecting on how far from home he was. Earth and the Moon were equidistant from his current vantage point, and his wildest dreams—pre-invasion, anyway—had never included his becoming an astronaut. At the moment, however, the "astronaut" program had been broadened quite a bit. At least ten thousand men and women worked aboard the *Invictus* platforms alone, and *Bastion* boasted a population of over twelve thousand.

And those numbers were only going to grow. It was inevitable.

"Any more word on that problem last night?" he asked as he and Jeffries activated their suit packs and sailed across the half-kilometer gap between the workboat and the slip's hab module.

"Sounds like it was human error this time," Jeffries replied. He could almost see her shrug, even though she was behind him at the moment. "One of the foremen got his work orders confused. He sent the bots the wrong coordinates, so they went where they were told and then just stood there when there was nothing for them to do. Cost us about five hours."

"I thought we caught it after about two and a half," Wilson said.

"Sure, but while they were standing there doing nothing, they were blocking the bots that were *supposed* to be working that part of the site. So we lost two and a half hours in both places. That's five, in my book."

"I suppose so," Wilson sighed, and suppressed another sigh—this one of relief—as his boots touched down on the module's landing stage and adhered. The module's rotation reasserted a sense of up and down, although the apparent gravity was only about half of the one he'd grown up in. He couldn't help how vastly comforting he found that, but whatever his forebrain might understand, his hindbrain couldn't quite seem to grasp that he wasn't really plunging to his doom down an endless, bottomless chasm whenever he went EVA. Some people, like Jeffries, said they enjoyed the experience. He found that difficult to understand, but he believed them. After all, putatively sane people had enjoyed jumping out of perfectly functional airplanes for a long time. Still, he did cherish a few doubts about exactly how *much* they enjoyed it. However convenient the humans and bots actually out working on Golf Section might find microgravity, even Jeffries seemed to prefer a firm sense of "up" and "down" while she worked.

The hatch in front of him cycled, and he and Jeffries stepped into an airlock which could have comfortably accommodated at least a dozen people. Hegemony-tech techniques for evacuating and pressurizing airlocks were as advanced as any of the rest of the technological cornucopia humanity had acquired. Given what they did, the "monkey boys" from Earth, as Wilson's

Uncle Dave was prone to call them, had done far less tinkering with the software which controlled those techniques, too. Screwing up an airlock was something someone only got to do once.

The pressure stabilized, the inner hatch irised open, and they stepped through it into the master control room for building slip *Argonaut Seven*.

"Well, look who's here! And an entire—" Marsail MacAmbrais looked ostentatiously at the bulkhead clock "—*seven minutes* early! My God. The millennium has come!"

"Yeah, yeah. We love you too, Marcy." Wilson snorted. "And, trust me, if I'd realized we were running that early, we'd have finished our pinochle game before we came across."

"I know. I know!" She shook her head, then climbed out of her float chair to shake hands with him as his gloves vanished once more into his vac suit's sleeves. "Lazy, idle layabout that you are."

"That's me," he agreed, gripping her hand firmly. "Anything else interesting happen after the little snafu last night?"

"Don't be pushing that black mark off on me," MacAmbrais told him with a grin. "And, no. Once we got Mister Friedman straightened out, everything went smoothly. And I'll have you know that we're still ahead of Echo, Juno, and Lima."

"Oh, I see. But, excuse me for pointing that out, isn't that another way of saying that we're coming in *twelfth*?"

"If you want to be picky about it, I guess."

"I'm pretty sure the *Navy's* keeping track, whether you are or not," he pointed out. "On the other hand, all of us are ahead of projections, so I don't suppose they're going to be collecting heads anytime soon. If they do though, I'm nominating you as our donor."

"You're always so good to me," she said with a chuckle. "And are you and Jess coming to dinner Tuesday or not?"

"Sure, as long as you promise not to cook. I mean, I like haggis as much as the next sane person."

"Oh?" MacAmbrais cocked her head, her Scottish accent abruptly more pronounced. "Ah wisnae gang tae bring it oop, ye wee nugget, boot that kedge ye fed us fer brakfast—'grits,' did ye ca' thaim?—wisnae sae guid."

"It must be something about living on an island surrounded by sheep," Wilson mused with a smile. "It's so . . . so . . . so *insular*. You just never get the opportunity to develop a taste for the finer things in life."

"Yer an eejit," she told him, then laughed. "I promise it won't be haggis. In fact, Frank was in Argentina last week. He brought back some really nice beef."

"In that case, we'll be there," Wilson assured her.

"Thought so." She nodded with a trace of complacency, then rounded up her partner, Oliver Woods, with a nod of her head. "Chariot's waiting, Ollie."

"Yeah, and I got a hot date with a third-grade choral presentation," Woods said.

"It's all yours," MacAmbrais continued, turning back to Wilson. "Boards are all green, and aside from Friedman's little mishap, the shift went perfectly. Try to keep it that way."

"Show off," Wilson muttered, and she chuckled. Then she patted him on the shoulder, collected her helmet, and led Woods into the airlock.

"See you guys tomorrow," she said, then settled her helmet over her head and checked the seal. Wilson could see her lips move as she went through the communications test with Woods. Then she waved one hand, and the inner hatch closed.

"Well, I guess we should get to work," he said then, and Jeffers nodded. She settled into the chair Woods had occupied and started running quickly through the standard checklist. Wilson waited long enough to collect a cup of coffee, then took MacAmbrais' chair and began his own checks.

It didn't take long, not with the computer support they enjoyed, and then he tipped back, crossed his legs, and held his coffee cup in both hands as he gazed at the panoramic view screens showing every phase of Golf Section's construction.

He never would have expected to end up here, either, before the invasion. He'd worked for GE, a specialist in turbines, which at least meant he'd been accustomed to thinking in terms of what had then represented both high-tech and the manufacturing sector. That hadn't really been appropriate training for his present duties, but off the top of his head, he couldn't think of anything that would have been. The pre-invasion experts in spacecraft design had suffered heavily when the Shongairi's KEWs went after Earth's technological sectors. Even if they hadn't, as advanced and esoteric as their knowledge had been, they'd been natives paddling around in dugout canoes compared to humanity's current projects. Most of them were in really senior positions, like Claude Massengale, anyway. So the nuts and bolts of building Earth's interstellar fleet fell to people like Alec Wilson and Rhonda Jeffers and their NET training.

And they were doing it. They were actually *doing* it. The familiar wonder of that thought went through him as he looked at those view screens, thought about what those hundreds of robotic carpenter bees and their human supervisors were actually creating. *Robinson* would be the first Earth dreadnought; she wouldn't be the last.

And the Hegemony's not going to like them one bit, he thought with somber satisfaction.

Fleet Commander Thikair's dreadnoughts had been about half the size of *Robinson*, with a third of her armament, and fifty percent slower in phase-space. And the *Robinson* class was only humanity's first stab at building an effective capital ship. Wilson had seen some of the design teams' discussions about ways in which even she could be improved, and the thought of where they might be in another fifteen years—or fifty, or a hundred—was . . . mind-boggling.

When completed, *Robinson* would consist of an outer war hull, a geodesic basket weave krystar cage, wrapped around a heavily armored core hull. Power generation, life-support, all of the control systems, and manned parasites would be carried in or limpeted to the exterior of the core hull, which would form a spin section to create a comfortable single gravity. It would rotate on friction-less magnetic "bearings" in a normal flight regime. When docked, or going to battle stations, it would be mechanically locked in place and the crew would fight their ship in microgravity.

The outer hull mounted the phase-drive nodes, but it also carried missile launchers, magazines, energy weapons, and defensive systems, all run by auto-mated, self-repairing systems so efficient that the entire ship could be operated by a crew of only thirty-five under emergency conditions.

It would've been really neat if they'd been able to give *Robinson* shields, to go with all those other goodies, but not even the Hegemony had tech that would do that. Wilson was certain some of the theoretical teams would be diving down every rabbit hole in sight to figure out if the "monkey boys and girls" could find a way to do it, but he wasn't going to hold his breath waiting for them to succeed.

In the meantime, the outer hull was designed to suffer major damage without losing structural integrity, although the best defense of all was to not be hit in the first place. In pursuit of that, she was lavishly equipped with electronic warfare systems and antimissile defenses. There wasn't much they could do about stop-ping energy weapon hits, but even Hegemony effective ranges for energy fire were no more than a few hundred kilometers, thanks to physical limitations on the focusing mechanism. They were quick firing and required no magazines, which made them ideal for missile defense, but the true killers were the missiles.

The launchers were basically enormous railguns, launching self-guided homing missiles with an initial velocity of right on 25 KPS. The recoil effect of launching such heavy projectiles at such high velocity meant that even some-thing as enormous as *Robinson* couldn't fire a lot of them in a single salvo, which limited the density of the patterns she could throw. On the other hand, those launchers could spit out one missile every five seconds, which would turn her fire into a continuous stream of incoming destruction.

Each missile massed right on thirty metric tons, which meant each of them would hit with just over the energy of an eight-hundred-kiloton explosion. Dis-couraging something like that when it had locked onto its target took a lot of energy delivered really, really quickly, which was what lasers were good for, but there were also the last ditch "autocannon." Wilson thought of them as railgun Vulcans. Although their rate of fire per barrel was only two rounds a second, they were mounted in quads, giving each mount a firing rate of almost five hundred rounds a minute, and each of their eighty-kilo "slugs" would meet the incoming round with a closing velocity of just under 50 KPS . . . and four megatons of kinetic energy. They would drill through any missile ever built like a hyper-velocity awl, shedding energy as they went. Not *all* of their energy, of course—not in the microsecond or so their passage would take—but enough. The material they vaporized and displaced on their way though would radiate outward and thoroughly shatter their target from the inside out. But hitting a bullet with another bullet was always a chancy proposition, especially when the incoming bullet could dodge and would be doing its best to avoid being hit. Hence the light-speed lasers as the outer defense zone, designed to kill the incoming missile's guidance capability. If it didn't cause the missile to miss entirely, it would at least eliminate or impair its ability to evade its target's defensive kinetic fire.

If *Robinson* did take damage that got through to the core hull, it was massively armored in five meters of what the Hegemony had called choham armor. Humanity had renamed choham "battle steel," because the Hegemony's name for it had struck someone as too close to "Chobham," a purely terrestrial armoring system which had been in use for over half a century even before the invasion. Wilson was actually a bit surprised they hadn't just gone ahead and called it Chobham, since it was very similar conceptually to the original Chobham. It consisted of multiple, thin barriers of tysian sandwiched between much thicker, and incredibly tough, layers of spun krystar and ceramic strands. Krystar all by itself was far more resistant to both kinetic and directed energy weapons than any purely Terran material had ever been, but its primary function was to absorb and channel damage, not to actually stop it. That was the task of the tysian, an even tougher alloy whose molecules had been partially collapsed. Its density was many times that of osmium, the highest-density stable element known to pre-invasion humanity. In fact, it weighed so much that only something the size of a starship could use it. On the other hand, a one-centimeter plate of tysian would have laughed at a sixteen-inch shell.

Under the circumstances, he supposed, sixteen feet of that sort of armor might be considered adequate. In addition, however, parasite hangars and service facilities formed the next layer in, followed by the crew's personal quarters, all wrapped around the essential power and environmental systems. In short, it would take a *lot* of damage to drive her out of action, and she would be pounding the everliving shit out of whatever was shooting at her in the meantime.

Plus, of course, the fact that she could outrun—and run away *from*—anything the Hegemony had.

Alec Wilson sipped coffee, watching the enormous ship growing before his very eyes, and thought about that. And the more he thought about it, the deeper his satisfaction grew.

· X ·

SPACE PLATFORM *BASTION*,
L5 LAGRANGE POINT,
AND COLD MOUNTAIN,
TRANSYLVANIA COUNTY, NORTH CAROLINA,
UNITED STATES

I'd like to open today's session," Warren Jackson said, "by pointing out the way this just gets more . . . frustrating as we go along."

"And what brought that up this time?" Trish Nesbitt pushed her counter-grav float chair back from her console and turned to give him a quizzical look. "I mean, aside from supervisory grumpiness."

"I'm not even sure what 'supervisory grumpiness' *is*." Jackson gave her a suspicious look.

"It's the way you get when something is bugging you, and you decide to share it with the rest of us. Usually at great length," she told him with a smile.

"Should I bring this back up the next time—in, oh, like seventeen minutes from now or so—when *you* go off at these idiots? Trust me, this one—" Warren twitched his head at the holo display over his own console, which showed a dense spread of text and equations "—is a doozy, even for them."

"What have they done now?" Chester Gannon's hologram asked in a re-signed tone as he tipped back in his own chair. Unlike Nesbitt and Warren, the former Lawrence Livermore physicist was ensconced in his "home office" back in North Carolina, attending their twice-a-week conference remotely, which imposed a light-speed delay of just over one second in the conversation loop. All three of them were accustomed to that by now, however, and Warren and Nesbitt didn't begrudge him the comforts of home. He was the Assessment Team's lead expert on the Hegemony's power systems, but he'd actually begun consulting with Judson Howell and Fabienne Lewis well before the team had been formally set up under Jackson's leadership. He'd been offered the lead position, in fact, but he'd turned it down. He had many strengths; administration and patience were not among them, and he knew it.

"Well, I was actually following up on something Trish pointed out a long time ago," Jackson said.

"Something *I* pointed out? So whatever has a bee in your bonnet or a hair up some other portion of your anatomy is *my* fault?"

"Exactly." She made a rude gesture, and he laughed. "Truthfully, you did start my mind—such as it is—along its current trajectory way back when you were pointing out the way the Hegemony fail-safed its counter-grav so that it couldn't reverse polarity and suddenly start *generating* a gravity field."

"So this is from *that* long ago?"

"Please." He gave her a quelling look. "It's not like we haven't all had other things on our minds between then and now. But I was looking at something else last week—the tweak the PAF wants to make to the *Starfires'* counter-grav—when I hit one of my old notes from our initial conversation about it. So *this* week I've been poking at it in my copious free time and I started by going back through your memo on the original counter-grav's . . . superabundance of fail-safes, shall we say?"

"Oh." She cocked her head. "In that case, I don't suppose I should feel too wary about this, should I?"

"Only if it blows up in my face. Again."

"Wonderful! In that case, why don't you go ahead and share your current 'Why I hate the Hegemony' with us?"

"Well, I've figured out why they were worried about somebody doing it. Reversing polarities, I mean. It's because it's possible after all."

"Really?" Gannon frowned, then shook his head a second later when Jackson's raised eyebrow reached Earth. "Oh, I agree it was probably inherent in the math, but I'd have thought that even the Hegemony would've followed up on it if it was really possible. Or practical, at least. Out of curiosity, if nothing else."

"The one thing we've learned is that 'curiosity' and 'the Hegemony' don't belong together in the same sentence, Chester," Jackson pointed out, and Gannon snorted.

"Fair enough," he acknowledged. "But in that case, you've probably just answered my question about why they didn't."

"Actually, I think there might be a couple of reasons," Jackson said more thoughtfully. "One of them is their fabled lack of interest in anything outside the existing status quo. The other is that if they got too carried away with it, it looks like they could actually generate an artificial black hole, which could be sort of unfortunate for anything around them. Of course, doing that would have presented its own nontrivial challenge—one that's probably more up your alley than mine, really, Chester."

"In what way?" Gannon frowned, then raised a hand before Jackson could reply. "Never mind. I was having a dim moment. Power requirements, right?"

"Absolutely." Jackson nodded vigorously. "If I'm reading this right, they'd be pretty much—you should pardon the term—astronomical at the other end of the scale."

"Still be interesting as a purely theoretical exercise, though," Gannon said thoughtfully, running one hand through his sandy brown hair. "Assuming we *could* come up with the power, at least."

"Oh, if we could, I think it could be a lot more than a theoretical exercise," Jackson said.

"You've got a planet you want to suck into a black hole somewhere?" Nesbitt inquired.

"I'm sure there are a couple of planets somewhere in the galaxy that no one would miss, but, no," Jackson told her. "It's just that one of the reasons I'm so frustrated with our super cautious Hegemony counterparts is that the model I'm looking at right this minute suggests that a black hole might just crack the interface between normal space and phase-space without a phase-drive."

"Excuse me?" Gannon sat up straighter.

"I don't know if it would do any good," Jackson said with a shrug. "But it could be sort of interesting to find out, don't you think?"

"I can see how that kind of concentrated gravity well would weaken the wall between n-space and phase-space, but you'd have to kick it with something more than just a black hole." Gannon thought about that for a moment, then grimaced. "Did I just say 'just a black hole'?"

"Sounded like it to me," Jackson said with a smile.

"Hmmmm." Nesbitt frowned thoughtfully. "You know, a phase-drive uses up a lot of volume—and mass, for that matter."

"That may be true, but even assuming it was possible to crack the wall without a phase generator—and actually cross it in the process, I mean, instead of just making a really spectacular explosion—we're not talking just a little difference in power requirements here. The phase-drive's an energy hog, but this would be literally, not just figuratively, orders of magnitude worse than that. So, unless you've got a small star tucked away in your hip pocket somewhere—"

Jackson shrugged, and Nesbitt chuckled appreciatively. Gannon didn't, though, and Jackson frowned at the physicist's suddenly thoughtful expression.

"Chester?"

The other man just sat there, staring at something only he could see.

"Chester?" Jackson repeated rather more loudly, and Gannon twitched.

"Sorry," he said, "but I just had a thought."

"We noticed," Nesbitt said dryly.

"Well, it was sort of wild. But there might just be something to it."

"To what?" Jackson asked.

"Why is the phase-drive so big?" Gannon asked in reply.

"This is a trick question, right?" Jackson said, frowning at the *non sequitur*.

"No, I'm serious." Gannon waved one hand. "The real reason the phase-drive is so big is that it needs so many nodes. It has to rupture the p-space wall simultaneously across the entire surface of a three hundred sixty-degree sphere big enough to enclose a starship, right? And each node actually creates only a conical rupture zone. So, it's not really just the power requirements that make it such a mass hog. It's the fact that you need so many nodes—literally hundreds of them, for one of their dreadnoughts—spread around the hull. Right?"

"I suppose so. But isn't that sort of an inseparable part of the engineering?"

"Sure, for the phase-drive. But if what you're saying about black holes and the wall holds up, then we wouldn't need all those nodes."

"No, you'd only need somewhere around . . . oh, ten or twenty thousand times the dreadnought's power supply. I would imagine that many antimatter plants would tend to compensate for any savings in nodes," Jackson pointed out.

"Sure, but p-space is essentially an energy state, looked at the right way. A very *high* energy state; one of the functions of the phase-drive is to protect a ship traveling through it. And each successive 'layer' is a higher and even more intense energy state."

"Sure." Jackson drew out the single syllable and looked quizzically at Nesbitt, who simply shrugged, watching Gannon intently.

"Well," he said, "assume that somehow a hole opened in the phase wall. What would that look like?"

"Probably a vest pocket quasar," Nesbitt replied after a moment.

"Exactly!" Gannon beamed at her.

"And what, precisely, besides a Really Big Explosion, would that give us?" Jackson asked skeptically.

"I'm glad you asked!" Gannon beamed even more broadly. "As it happens, I have a theory about that."

· · · · ·

"YOU'RE JOKING, RIGHT?" Dave Dvorak asked across the table.

Fabienne Lewis and her husband, Greg, had joined the Dvoraks for supper in their suite aboard *Bastion*. It was a family gathering—discussing, among other things, plans for the upcoming wedding between Maighread and Raymond Lewis, not "business"—but, Dvorak being Dvorak and Lewis being Lewis, what their respective spouses referred disrespectfully to as "shop talk" had been bound to rear its ugly head.

"No, I'm not," she said, shaking her head.

"Gannon *seriously* wants to build this thing?"

"Yep. I pointed out that things would get just a little lively if his numbers were off."

"I suppose that's one way to describe a several megaton explosion."

"Oh, *lots* worse than that, really. He's talking about a cascade system."

"Cascade?" Dvorak picked up his beer stein. "What kind of cascade?"

"Dave," Sharon said warningly. He looked at her quickly, and she raised an accusatory index finger.

"Just because you're the cook doesn't mean you get to drag us all off into the weeds." She gave him a stern look. "Now that Malachi's off with the Space Marines, I've finally got a break from the dinnertime history discussions. You are *not* going to replace them with 'shop talk.' I thought we'd had that conversation?"

"And you thought that because you had that conversation it actually wouldn't happen?" Greg Lewis shook his head.

"Anyone's aspirations should always exceed the achievable," she replied. "And if I use a big enough club, I might actually make some progress."

"Not this time." Greg grinned. "Besides, if I have to put up with Fabienne bringing this home and pounding my ear over it, I don't see why you shouldn't, too. Misery loves company, and all."

"Yeah, sure! 'Pounding your ear.' Like you weren't just as bad is she is." Sharon rolled her eyes. Before the invasion, Greg had been a senior aerospace engineer with Lockheed, and he'd been up to his hip pockets in the design of the Planetary Union's spacecraft from the beginning.

"Some truth to that," he conceded. "But I really think you should make an exception to the no shop talk at the table rule."

"Or we could just adjourn to the living room and get away from the table," Dvorak suggested.

"Don't you dare!" Sharon shot back. "I am *not* leaving without my crème brûlée!"

"I think that's what Dad's counting on, Mom," Maighread said with a chuckle. Her father was an excellent cook, but he wasn't a very good baker, and his desserts tended to be very . . . basic. Which was why *she* had prepared her mother's favorite dessert in all the world.

"Devious, underhanded, unprincipled, *evil* diplomat that he is," Sharon said darkly. Then she sighed. "All right. I recognize defeat when I see it, and I have no intention of rushing my enjoyment of Maighread's handiwork. So go ahead. Go ahead!"

"Thanks, Honey." Dvorak smiled at her, but there was genuine gratitude in his tone, and he blew her a kiss across the table before he looked back at Fabienne. "You were saying something about a 'cascade system,' I think?"

"Yep. What he seems to think he might be able to do is to design a—well, call it an energy siphon, for want of a better term. The basis would be something like the current phase-drive, but with a unidirectional 'node' designed as a sort of phased array. It's not my area, by any means, but the way I think of it is putting together a concentric series of nodes. The outer ring would break the phase wall; the next ring in would break the wall between alpha and beta phase-space;

the next would break into gamma, and so forth. Theoretically, there's no limit to how high he could go—assuming his model holds up and he wants to build the damned thing big enough."

"My God." Dvorak took another swallow of beer and shook his head. "I'm assuming he does understand what would happen if he could manage something like this?"

"You mean if he lost control of it?" Fabienne snorted. "Oh, I think you can assume that. I figure we could build it in, say, Ganymede orbit. I mean Jupiter's got a lot of moons, so it probably wouldn't miss just one of them too much. On the other hand," her expression turned much more serious, "he's right about the kind of power source it could represent."

"And it's sure as hell something that would never occur to the Hegemony," he said thoughtfully.

"I'm inclined to say that it's something that would never occur to anyone who's sane," Fabienne said wryly as she picked up her coffee cup.

"Sure, but Chester's from North Carolina."

"Excuse me?" Fabienne looked puzzled.

"Beneath all that polished, sophisticated surface of his, he's a Southern boy, Fabienne. Hell, Trish Nesbitt's a Southern *girl*!"

"And your point is?"

"My point is that the Hegemony is so cautious and cowardly it makes itself stupid in a lot of ways. Round these parts, *we* do stupid in a whole 'nother way. I can't quite decide whether our people's motto should be 'Hey, y'all! Watch this!' or 'Somebody hold mah beer!'"

Fabienne laughed so hard she spilled a little coffee, and Sharon shook her head, blue eyes twinkling despite her martyred expression.

"Actually," Fabienne said after a moment, mopping up coffee with her napkin and an apologetic expression, "there's probably something to that."

"And I think maybe we aren't really the first species to think that way," Dvorak said, and his tone and expression were both much more serious.

"What?" Fabienne cocked her head.

"I've been running those data searches I told Judson I would," he said, "and I think I've come to the conclusion that there was something to my initial suspicions. The Hegemony's historical record *has* been edited."

"Edited, Dad?" Maighread asked, watching her father's face.

"Edited," he repeated with a nod. "Whoever did it did a really good job, but we've found six what you might call 'highly suspicious' references. Not much out of a hundred and fifty thousand years of recorded history, but I don't see how they could be accidents."

"What kind of references?" Sharon asked, forgetting her designated martyr role and looking at him just as intently as their daughter.

"Officially, the Hegemony was founded by four species: the Kreptu, the Liatu, the Hexali, and the Bokal. All the records agree on that. *Except* that we've found two references to the *five* founders. The other four . . . anomalies we've found are rather less obvious than that, but the shared implication seems to be that once upon a time, long, long ago, there really was a fifth founding member of the Hegemony. Somebody the rest of the family doesn't talk about anymore."

"You're serious," Greg Lewis said after a second.

"As death and taxes." Dvorak nodded. "I probably wouldn't have thought much about it if not for what Hosea, Nancy, and Maighread here—" he twitched his head at his daughter "—have turned up about the 'vampires.' I mean, it's possible that what we've found in the histories represents the equivalent of typographical errors. In fact, on the face of it that's a lot more likely than some sort of—you should pardon the expression—galaxy-wide conspiracy to suppress the truth. But then you look at these nanobots. They don't match anything we've seen in the Hegemony's tech base, and, frankly, they're not something the Hegemony *could* build, given our understanding of their tech base."

He ended on a slightly questioning note, and Fabienne shook her head, her expression as troubled as it was intent.

"No," she agreed.

"Well, in that case, assuming that I'm not completely out to lunch about what I've been thinking of as 'the Other Guys,' what if *they're* the ones who built whatever turned Vlad into what he is? I've been thinking about that, too. And look at it from his perspective as a good fifteenth-century Transylvanian: What other conceptual model is he going to have for what he got himself turned into? Of *course* he's going to assume he's been cursed with vampirism, and, frankly, given some of the things he did before that happened, he probably saw it as an appropriate punishment!"

"So he's spent the better part of seven hundred years thinking he's a member of the accursed undead when he's actually the result of some kind of industrial accident?" Greg said.

"More or less. I mean, that's clearly *what* happened to him even if my 'Other Guys' isn't a good explanation for *how* it happened. But think about everything we've seen in the Hegemony's record base. These are a bunch of people who are super-cautious and in love with the status quo. If there'd been someone around that long ago who'd been capable of producing tech the Hegemony *still* can't—or won't—produce, wouldn't they have to be seen as a really, really significant threat? And we know that the Hegemony was perfectly prepared to use the Shongairi to eliminate us before *we* became a threat, if for somewhat different reasons."

"You may be right about all of this," Fabienne said thoughtfully. "But whether or not your 'Other Guys' are responsible for Vlad and the others, you're definitely right about the difference between 'Southern boys and girls' and somebody like the Kreptu or Liatu when it comes to running and finding things out. Warren's team isn't the only one turning up some interesting possibilities inherent in their existing tech base. I use 'interesting' in the sense of the old Chinese curse, you understand."

"Such as?" Dvorak leaned back, wondering what fresh rabbit hole had just opened up.

"Marcos Ramos' project," she said. "Or, rather, Brent Roeder's part of it, anyway."

"What project would that be?"

"You do occasionally speak to your daughter—I mean your *other* daughter—don't you?" Fabienne asked quizzically.

"Sharon and I had lunch with her yesterday, as a matter of fact," Dvorak replied just a bit repressively. Maighread's twin had also gone into the health profession, but in her case into psychiatry and not surgery. She was just as smart as her sister, though, and she'd become one of Marcos Ramos' personal assistants.

"And she didn't mention Roeder to you? Repeatedly? With a martyred expression? I'm amazed."

"And just why should she have mentioned Mister Roeder to me?" Dvorak demanded, trying not to smile at Fabienne's tone.

"It's *Doctor* Roeder, actually. And he's driving Marcos crazy. Him and Damianos Karahalios both."

"I'm in favor of driving Karahalios crazy," Dvorak said sourly. "But I kinda like Marcos. So what's this Roeder doing to them?"

"Being obsessed with the notion of a neural computer interface."

"I can see why that could be a good thing."

"Of course it could, and it should *probably* be possible. After all, we have NET, which means we already have an interface that lets us directly record and implant knowledge—experiences and memories, really—and it runs a checking process during an education session, which requires a two-way loop. So we already know how to send what you might call mental data files back and forth. There's a bit of a difference between that and figuring out how to actually neurologically—*cognitively*—link the human mind to a computer, though. We've already produced tech that will let us control external systems through a neural link—we're incorporating it into the next-generation Heinlein suits—but that's a matter of what you might call physiological response. We can train our brains and the link to perform functions the same way that we train our hands or our fingers. But you don't actually have intense mental soliloquies with your pinky. And that's what Roeder wants to do."

"He actually *wants* to 'talk to the hand'?" Dvorak asked innocently, then jerked in his chair.

"Ouch!" he said, reaching down to the kneecap his beloved wife had just kicked under the table.

"One more like that, and you'll need Hosea to give you new knees, not just a shoulder," she said, shaking that deadly warning finger at him again.

"I'll be good!"

"For *now,* maybe." She gave him one more glower, then looked back at Fabienne. "So this Roeder that Morgana didn't tell us about wants to go a step farther?"

"He's positive it's possible. Nobody's actually cognitively aware of the information she's receiving during a NET session. We just sort of blank out while the information is recorded in a convenient corner of our brain. It's only when we have to 'find' the new knowledge that we actually begin thinking about it or interacting with it. Roeder is focused on what happens during that blanked out period. He's been likening it to a dream state we simply can't recall when we wake up, and he wants to experiment with what happens during his hypothetical dream."

"Doesn't sound like such a terrible idea to me," Dvorak said thoughtfully.

"There are certain risks attendant upon it," Fabienne said dryly.

"What sort of risks?"

"I'm not the expert on this that Morg is, Dad," Maighread said, "but I can think of a few. For example, I know there are about a bazillion safety interlocks built into the neural educators to prevent significant neurological damage." She grimaced. "One of the reasons the Shongairi first exposed Base Commander Shairez' human 'subjects' to neural education was to see whether or not the existing safeties would prevent it from frying *our* brains. Apparently the Hegemony's had some bad experiences with that."

"Exactly." Fabienne nodded. "Roeder's fully aware of that, too. But he wants to push forward with human experimentation anyway, and he's . . . sort of bouncy."

"Bouncy? You just seriously called one of your lead researchers 'bouncy'?"

"Of course I did, Dave. Why, in a great many ways, he reminds me a lot of *you.*"

"Well, if he's *that* brilliant, then obviously you should be listening to him," Dvorak said, and lifted his beer stein in salute as his wife covered her eyes with both hands.

· XI ·

FORT SANDERS, NORTH CAROLINA, UNITED STATES

The *Starfire* assault shuttle fell to the Earth like a meteor, a trail of smoke behind it as some of the ablative coating on its wings burned off. Just when Abu Bakr was sure the shuttle's journey would end in a fiery impact, it pulled up in an exhibition of G-force loading that would have been suicidal twenty years earlier. The shuttle came to a hover three feet above the ground, then settled to the earth, its ramp already in motion.

Heinlein-suited troopers poured from the craft before it touched the ground, and the company of troops established a perimeter that expanded as a second shuttle touched down and disgorged its troopers, followed by a third, then a fourth. The empty shuttles scattered in different directions—anywhere but straight up—and in under a minute, one hundred and twenty troopers were in place. They used their jumpjets to bounce over obstacles as they continued outward, with the scouts bouncing even higher so their sensor suites could find and categorize targets.

The first of the gigantic *Starlanders* touched down as the soldiers reached two hundred meters from the debarkation point, almost completely filling the area behind them. Like its smaller brethren, the *Starlander*'s ramps were already down, and troopers poured from its forward ramps—one on each side. Eschewing the ramps, they rode their jumpjets to the ground as massive vehicles of war hovered down the *Starlander*'s enormous rear ramp in a stream two vehicles wide.

Tanks led the first wave, their massive railguns locked at full elevation to keep from digging into the ground as they went planet-side; as soon as they were off the ramp, the barrels unlocked as their targeting systems searched for enemies. The tanks joined the men as they enlarged the perimeter, although they stayed in the "safe" lanes marked out with their blue force identifiers. Similar to the "blue force trackers" of the pre-Shongairi U.S. military, the blue force identifiers not only kept the tanks from firing at known-friendly units, but kept them from driving over them, as well.

A variety of other vehicles followed the tanks off the *Starlander*—antiaircraft systems, drone carriers, and infantry fighting vehicles for the follow-up forces—until the massive craft was empty. Nine minutes after the first trooper stepped off the first assault shuttle, the *Starlander* lifted and was replaced by two more, the circle having been reinforced and expanded to a diameter of over six hundred meters. More personnel and weapons of war poured from the two transports, which were pointed in opposite directions to facilitate dispersal.

"Impressive," Colonel Rob Wilson said from where he stood next to Abu Bakr on the observation platform. "Isn't it?" He pointed to the impact area, fifteen kilometers away, where two simulated KEWs had landed. Although built to mimic the flight profile of a full-size KEW, they hit with a tiny fraction of the energy. While that distinction was a moot point to anyone who happened to be under an errant one—they wouldn't be around to care—it did help minimize the clean up after the rounds landed on the target range, as well as the number of resulting forest fires that had to be put out.

Two of the new transatmospheric fighters zipped past the observation platform on their way to drop their ordnance on the target range. Abu Bakr noticed they avoided the mushroom cloud the KEWs created.

"Impressive?" Abu Bakr asked. He shrugged, more worried about the implications than he was the display of military strength and prowess. "Sure, it's neat that we can do this . . . that we have this kind of power. We've come a long way in the past couple of decades; we may even be able to take the fight to the Hegemony at some point in the future."

"I hear a 'but' coming," Wilson said, looking at him quizzically. The two of them had known each other since the invasion, but they'd become close friends in the five years since Naya Islamabad.

"You're right. But just because we *can* do this—put forces ashore on some far-flung planet—doesn't necessarily mean we *should*." He shrugged again. "I take it that you support this? Going to other worlds and looking for new allies?"

"Absolutely," Wilson said. "Very much so."

Abu Bakr turned to look at the Marine.

"I'm sure you do," he said with a smile, "but I have a couple of . . . issues with the plan. First, President Howell wants to go out and look for allies among the systems the Hegemony hasn't explored. That's great . . . but what if we go somewhere and find out there are worse things than the Hegemony? Aliens bent on conquest and destruction? Ones that make the Shongairi look like plant-eaters? And what if they're more powerful than the Shongairi, and they don't even try to negotiate? What if they just try to wipe us out from the start?"

"Well," Wilson smiled and flexed a bicep, "first we send in the Space Marines."

"You do realize that not everyone even right here on Earth has a positive response to the words 'send in the Marines,' don't you?" Abu Bakr inquired with a crooked smile.

"Sure, I guess," Wilson acknowledged, recalling Abu Bakr's pre-invasion attitudes and political activism. "I'll even grant that some of those people have a valid reason to feel that way. But after the Puppies, I don't think anybody's going to object to a little proactiveness on our part."

"Maybe not," Abu Bakr said. "But what if we send in the Space Marines, and even their fancy Heinlein suits and their tanks with their enormous guns aren't good enough?"

"Then I guess we send in the vampires." Wilson's eyebrows knitted momentarily. "Hey, weren't you offered 'the vampire transition'? You could do that, and then you wouldn't need the little 'ol PAFSM folks to protect you."

He smiled as he pronounced the acronym. It came out "paff-sim," and the Space Marines' native English speakers found the pun amusing as hell, since anything less pacifistic than a Space Marine in Heinlein armor was impossible to imagine. Abu Bakr flashed a brief answering smile, but his expression segued into a frown as he recalled an unpleasant evening in Naya Islamabad.

"Not that it matters to you," he said, after a moment, "but yes, they did offer to turn me into a vampire."

"And you turned them down." It wasn't a question.

Abu Bakr nodded.

"I did. I didn't feel that was what Allah wanted from me. I show my worth by doing good deeds—by doing the *hard* deeds—and being a vampire obviates all of that. Where's the value of the struggle, if there *is* no struggle? No danger? There's no virtue in attacking the infidel, if the infidel can't possibly hurt you. Nor do I particularly want to live forever. I'd like to go to heaven at some point . . . although I'm hoping it won't be anytime soon.

"Besides," he continued, "if what they say is true, being converted to a vampire would mean giving up my soul. Do nanobots have souls? I don't know . . . but I suspect they don't. Thank you, but I'll hold on to mine for a while longer yet."

"Okay, I understand that, but there are people who'd like to be vampires and, more importantly, people who already *are* vampires. If the Space Marines can't do the job, the vampires certainly can. I'm not aware of *anything* that can take one of them down."

"If they're nanobots, then they're machines, and there's something that can defeat them; we just don't know what it is yet. I don't care how well shielded they are; I'll bet a strong enough EMP will cause them to disassociate, or something."

Wilson smiled. "I'm sure you're trying to confuse the Marine with big words, but, as a military person, I'm passingly familiar with weaponry, and I'm pretty sure that dropping a nuke on a vampire to stop him is contraindicated if the people you're trying to save are anywhere close to the vampire."

"There is that, I guess." Abu Bakr shrugged. "Regardless, let's just say I have 'reservations' about going into the big, uncharted black looking for potential allies to help us stand up to the Hegemony. On ancient maps, they put 'Here there be dragons' on the areas they hadn't explored . . . and if it comes right down to it, I'm worried about what we might find."

"Well, that point'll be moot pretty soon. We've already started building starships, and President Howell intends to send them out."

"I know. He's asked me to be on one of the initial diplomatic teams."

"I see," Wilson replied. "So the question of how we're supposed to defend the diplomatic teams on an alien planet hits close to home for you."

"It does, especially after Naya Islamabad, thank you very much." The two men smiled at each other, but then Abu Bakr shrugged. "But, to be honest, that's my second concern. While all of this—the tanks and orbital KEW fire support—is awesome, the purpose of the mission is supposed to be diplomacy, and it's hard to develop alliances when your first greeting card is a spread of KEWs that levels their cities and announces your presence with authority." He shrugged and waved towards the deployment site. The *Starlanders* had lifted and a veritable army of robots was assembling the first buildings. "That's not how you develop a friendship."

"Well . . . no, not really," Wilson was forced to admit.

"However," Abu Bakr said, "there has to be *some* sort of military support to the diplomatic teams, despite what some of Howell's advisors are advocating."

Wilson rolled his eyes. "Yeah, I see where you're going now, and I agree. You should hear Dave when *he* gets going on the re-emergence of professional arm-chair diplomats and political scientists. I guess that applied to him, too, when he got started, but it's been twenty years now, and he's worried that the influx of folks who've received all their knowledge from books or their neural educators—who've never gone anywhere or done anything—is going to put us in a bad place."

"It isn't *quite* that bad," Abu Bakr pointed out. "As you say, it's been twenty years—but, looking at it another way, that's *only* twenty years. It's going to take a while for the human race to forget what happened when the Shongairi came to call, so I'm not saying anyone's going to object to our developing the capabilities you're demonstrating right here." He nodded in the ongoing exercise's direction. "But it is true that the bureaucracy's growing and that a certain type of personality is beginning to reemerge."

"You mean the 'Oh, military people don't belong on the teams!' crowd? The ones who're all 'They're all ignorant savages who don't have any understanding of the finer nuances of inter-species communication! Only *enlightened* people belong on the teams!' That bunch?"

"Yes, I see you know exactly what I'm talking about, and you could probably even guess who," Abu Bakr said with a chuckle. "For that matter, it's not a bad thing to have that viewpoint represented. You do remember my earlier comment about 'sending in the Marines,' I hope? A little restraint on military exuberance can save a ton of trouble down the road, Rob. I'm fully aware that if we go out to the stars, we *will* want to have this capability—" he waved at one of the tanks that had stopped nearby as a static display for the visitors "—but it's not exactly the best possible way to introduce ourselves to potential allies. That's really where a lot of the discussion is right now. I'm in the group that believes we'll need military professionals to accompany the diplomatic teams and provide security for them. Will the teams include vampires? Yes, probably, but they need to have some flesh and blood personnel as well, regardless of what any of the progressives in the administration might say. And the security to go with them needs to be enough to protect them but something short of landing a full-fledged invasion force."

"So you'd prefer to leave the heavy backup in orbit, but you wouldn't object to having a few Space Marines looming ominously in the background?"

"As long as they didn't loom *too* ominously." Abu Bakr shrugged. "My father always used to say that in a negotiation, you needed to bargain from a position of strength. I'd hate to go somewhere and have an alien society view us as so weak that they tried to capture our team."

"I'd hate that, too," Wilson said. When Abu Bakr's eyebrow went up, he added, "Especially since I'm lobbying to command the 'away team,' and I've got what they call friends in high places, so I'll probably get it."

"I see. And, frankly, I'm glad to hear it." Abu Bakr smiled. "You did fairly well in Naya Islamabad, I guess." Wilson snorted, and Abu Bakr's smile broadened. The situation in Pakistan was about to change, and both of them had been briefed on it only yesterday. Then Abu Bakr's expression sobered as he reflected on what that was going to mean in human terms. Wilson saw the darkness in that expression, recognized the awareness, but, after a moment, the Muslim shrugged and looked him in the eye.

"Seriously, I'd feel a little better about the mission with you along." he said. "I doubt you'd allow your supporting cast to be . . . undermanned."

"No, I won't." Wilson said as he returned the smile. He paused and then added, "There's one other thing to be said about going to other systems looking for friends."

"Oh, what's that?"

Wilson pointed to the mushroom cloud above the impact area from another mini-KEW strike.

"I don't want us repeating the Shongairi's mistakes, but if we go to someone else's system and find out they really are worse than the Puppies were, we can always do that to them, there. It beats the hell out of them coming and doing it to us here."

· XII ·

A re you getting all of this up front?" the weapons operator, Captain Chris Solice, asked from his position in the back of the *Starfire* assault shuttle's cockpit.

"Yeah, we see it on the tridee," the lead pilot, Major Henry Frye, replied as he indicated the display on his instrument panel to his co-pilot. "Looks like there has to be what? Three or four thousand people down there?"

Solice snorted. "More like twenty thousand. Watch."

The display broadened as Solice zoomed the camera back out, showing more of the crowd that had gathered around the prime minister's palace below them. A lot of things had changed since "The Death Seen Round the World," as the tridee press had dubbed the death of Imam Sheikh Abbas.

The compound still resembled a medieval castle with its surrounding walls, but now, instead of turrets in the corners, it had heavy magnetic accelerator cannons that Ghilzai's successor had acquired on the black market and installed. Frye had heard the supplier had been found by one of the vampires and euphemistically "put out of business"; however, the weapons were already inside Pakistan and the Powers That Be had decided not to violate the country's borders to recover them. Although the weapons were antiaircraft mounts designed to point up—to fire at incoming shuttles like the one he was flying— the way they'd been installed, their gunners could also use them to sweep the crowds gathered outside the walls. Developed to penetrate an assault craft's armor, there was no telling how many people a single round would go through. No doubt, quite a few. Frye was happy to be sixty thousand feet above the compound, stealthed, and not outside the walls of the compound with those cannons pointed at him.

Members of the "new and improved" *Sif al-Nabi* manned the walls. There had been a purge after Ghilzai's death, which had included the deaths of any of their members who'd been at the palace "that night." The remaining members were highly motivated to protect the new prime minister, and there was no doubt in Frye's mind about whether they'd fire on the crowd—they would; it was only a matter of how long they'd shoot at the fleeing protestors once they started to run away. He shrugged. *Probably until the gunners can't see 'em anymore.*

Apparently, President Howell thought the same way, and Frye had heard, off the record, that the prime minister, Baseer Badrashi, had been given a new "line in the sand." If he used the advanced technology weapons against his own people, there would be consequences. Frye's crew, orbiting overhead the palace square, were the consequences if the prime minister chose to do so. Like his predecessor, Badrashi had proven remarkably immune to common sense, though, and the PU intel staff had every expectation that he would use them as a show of force. After all, what was the point of having advanced weapons if you didn't get to unveil them periodically?

The scene below the orbiting craft was reminiscent of the Arab Spring uprisings that had embroiled the Middle East prior to the arrival of the Shongairi. Just as Cairo's Tahrir Square had become the focal point for protesters in Egypt demanding the end of the thirty-year autocratic rule of President Hosni Mubarak, crowds had been gathering around the palace all week, demanding reform and entry into the Planetary Union. The size of the crowds had grown to the point that the PU had authorized an overflight of today's event—although the shuttle was to stay high and out of sight.

The Arab Spring uprisings were the first popular revolutions in which social media allowed people to bypass the tightly controlled, state-run news outlets to share information, and their legacy was apparent in the crowds gathered outside the prime minister's palace. Although the new phones everyone in the PU carried had been outlawed by the government—and it was a death penalty offense to have one in your possession—from Frye's viewpoint above the crowd he could see a number of people using them. Unlike Voice of America and Radio Free Asia that broadcast information to the masses inside the nation— and which could be jammed or denied to the citizens by cutting off Internet access—the phones bypassed all of the central government's measures and allowed people to talk unmonitored to anyone they wanted to, both within the country and outside of it.

Frye had heard—anecdotally—that large numbers of the devices had been made available—i.e., given—to traders in the area, to the point that the PU had completely flooded the market. They were so available inside the country that they could be picked up, even on the black market, for very little cost . . . beyond the danger of being caught with one. While he knew what the PU government hoped would happen—exactly what was going on below him—he knew there was going to be a large price paid in blood. And soon. The *Sif al-Nabi* were well armed. Enough to stop twenty thousand people? Not if the members of the crowd were extremely well coordinated or willing to take horrific losses, but certainly well enough to *inflict* those losses.

Now that the populace of Pakistan had access to news from outside the country, the fuse had been lit. It wasn't a matter of whether the country was going to blow; it was only a matter of when. As Solice pulled the camera farther back, he could see more people streaming towards the square, along with defensive units—tanks and APCs—responding to the gathering.

It was going to be soon.

. . . . .

"OH, SHIT," SOLICE said two hours later. "Take a look at this."

"What have you got?" Frye asked. The armored vehicles had made it to the square and taken up positions, leaving a trail of dead bodies along the way when people either could not, or would not, get out of the way. The road was also littered with the bodies of people who had thought they could stop the tanks by sitting in front of them in a line. The tanks had rolled right over them without stopping, leaving little more than a line of red stains to commemorate their protests.

Several fire engines with water cannons followed the tanks into the square. When they arrived, they opened fire on the crowd, working together to divide the people and drive them off. Frye had just decided that today wasn't going to be the day the revolution occurred, after all, but as he viewed the tridee, he saw he'd been wrong. The monitor showed people passing long scaling ladders from second-floor windows to a large group of people in the alley below.

"Where's that?" Frye asked.

"About a block away from the Palace," Solice replied. He pulled the camera back to give perspective. "It's also here . . . and here . . . and here, among other places." He zoomed in the camera to show the other locations. "Those are just the ones I saw in a quick scan. There may be more."

"Radio back to base and let them know it's happening," Frye ordered.

"I'm streaming all the video back," Solice replied.

"Good. I want you to make sure they're actually *seeing* this—this shit is going down *today*! Make sure we're authorized to fire."

"Think they'll authorize us to go full offensive and help the revolutionaries?" Lieutenant James Turbot asked.

Frye shook his head. "No, I don't think they will; the locals will have to—generally—do it themselves." He turned and gave his co-pilot a predator's grin as the authorization came over the radio. "But the Prime Minister's troops are going to have to do it without their MACs.

"Speaking of which," Frye continued, turning in his seat to look at the weapons systems operator. "We ready, Chris?"

"Yes, Sir. Drones are out, positioned, and targeted. As you noted, we're cleared to fire if they use the MACs on the crowd, but only on the MACs."

Solice scanned the camera back to the square. Although the water cannons were driving off the people in front of the fire engines, people were clustering behind them, as well as behind the tanks and IFVs that ringed the square. A large number of people seemed to be sheltering along the walls of the palace, as well.

"Hey, Chris?" Frye asked as the camera zoomed in on some of the people along the wall.

"Yes, Sir?"

"What's the temperature down there?"

"It's expected to be about thirty-two degrees Celsius today—so about ninety degrees. Why?"

"Isn't that kind of hot to have on *bishts*?"

"What the hell are *bishts*?" Turbot asked.

"They're those long outer cloaks they wear over the Muslim robes. It looks like nearly everyone along the wall has them on, as well as quite a few people in the crowd."

"Now that you mention it, yeah," Solice replied. "I wonder why—"

He stopped as nearly half the people along the wall, as one, pulled lighters from under their robes and held them under the rags that protruded from the bottles the other half of the people removed from under *their* robes.

"Molotov cocktails!" Frye yelled as the people began throwing them up and over the walls towards the MACs mounted in the corners and the other machine guns scattered around the top of the wall. "It's on! Watch the MACs!"

Solice zoomed out to show more of the action, and the crew could see other people lighting and throwing firebombs at the tanks, APCs, and even the fire engines. Other members in the crowd pulled out weapons and began firing; still others ran away from the chaos as if their lives depended on it . . . which they obviously did. Flames and smoke choked the square.

One of the MACs on the front wall went up in a sheet of flames as several fire-bombs hit it near-simultaneously. A member of the other crew, though, swung wildly at a Molotov cocktail headed his way and succeeded in knocking it back over the rampart and into some of the people along the base of the wall. Their robes caught immediately, and they ran, like blazing embers from a crackling fire.

The ladders arrived at the same time the second round of firebombs were thrown, and the operational MAC opened up on the crowd in front of the pal-ace complex. A tremendous spray of red mist blossomed above the square as the hyper-sonic rounds blew people from their feet. Designed to penetrate armor, they had no problem going through multiple unarmored humans when they were in a row, and lines of death were cut from the crowd as the MAC gunner fired mercilessly into it. The other MACs on the back wall began firing as they realized they were under assault as well.

"Light 'em up!" Frye ordered. "Kill the MACs!"

"Arming and . . . firing!" Solice replied, his voice slightly distant as he controlled the drones.

Nearly as one, the four MACs, including the one already on fire, disappeared in a hail of explosions. Solice had targeted all of them with his drones and gun system, and the HE rounds destroyed both the weapons and their crews.

The battle still raged in in front of the palace as the remaining militiamen on the ramparts fired into the crowds with their machine guns.

"Base says we are not cleared to engage the others," Solice noted, his voice louder. "We are to let the revolutionaries do it themselves, unless things go badly."

It was soon apparent, though, that the attacking force wasn't going to need any additional support, as snipers appeared on the roofs of nearby buildings and began picking off the militiamen. Several realized they were under attack from above and tried to fire on the snipers, but they were quickly put out of action. Other members of the *Sif al-Nabi* ran for the safety of the palace, and a few made it, but then the attacking force made it over the walls and dropped into the courtyard, cutting off their escape.

Several of the attackers pulled out coils of rope, looped them around crenellations and tied them to the militiamen's appendages, then pitched the bodies over the side to dangle in the sun.

Other members of the attacking force opened the front gates, and additional forces streamed into the courtyard, while others continued to scale the walls. A group of nearly one hundred, all with rifles and pistols, grouped up at the palace, then kicked the doors in. Several were immediately shot by militiamen from the interior, but the attackers threw in grenades and then followed them into the building.

"Holy . . ." Turbot's voice trailed off as if he were at a loss for words to describe it.

"Yeah," Frye replied. "Revolution isn't pretty, is it?" Although he was sickened by some of the things he saw the attackers doing to the corpses—and sometimes still-living members—of the *Sif al-Nabi*, he found he was unable to look away. It was necessary for progress . . . but it was appalling to watch.

"Holy shit," Turbot finally muttered after a particularly gruesome death. He made gagging noises as he stumbled from his seat towards the craft's small bathroom facility.

Frye hoped his co-pilot didn't lose it; he was sure he would join him if he did. After a few minutes, the people who had gone into the building came out—far fewer in number—along with what looked to be the prime minister's corpse.

"Looks like they got him," Solice said in a small voice.

Frye didn't know how Solice felt, but he felt dirty. Just watching had been enough to sicken him. Frye wasn't sure what he wanted to do first when he got home—throw up or shower. Maybe he'd save himself the trouble and just throw up *in* the shower.

"So I guess the revolution is over," Solice added.

Frye reached up and turned off the tridee monitor.

"No," he replied. "It's just beginning."

SPACE PLATFORM *BASTION*,
L5 LAGRANGE POINT

No," Damianos Karahalios said flatly. "We're not going to discuss this again."

"But the possibilities—" Brent Roeder began.

"Are fascinating, exhilarating, and potentially extremely important," Karahalios finished for him in a cutting-off-the-conversation tone as he waved one hand. "I understand that. Believe me, *everyone* understands that, Doctor Roeder. Most of us even agree with you. What you're proposing, however, is scarcely what anyone could call a controlled experiment."

"I wouldn't go that far," Roeder said a bit stiffly.

"Because it's *your* experiment," Karahalios' tone was even tarter than it had been, and Roeder bit his tongue rather firmly, reminding himself to avoid any phrases about pots discussing kettles' complexions. He also decided against mentioning any little inequities in how time was assigned . . . and to whose projects.

"That's true," he said instead. "That doesn't invalidate my reasoning or diminish the potential returns. And *my* calculations indicate the risk factor is substantially lower than the assessment committee's analysis."

"Perhaps because they're *your* calculations?" Karahalios suggested, although, to his credit, this time his tone was almost sympathetic.

Almost.

"My models all indicate—"

"I said we're not going to discuss this," Karahalios said firmly. "So, I want you to save all your data, all your notes, and put away all your bits and pieces. I promise we'll come back to this at some point. Right now, however, there are more pressing—and less risky—projects that need your attention. Is that clear?"

"Yes," Roeder sighed.

"Good." Karahalios held his gaze for a second or two, then smiled slightly. "I know you've got a lot of material, so go ahead take the rest of today and tomorrow to tidy up. But starting Monday, I have another assignment for you."

"Understood." Roeder actually managed an answering smile, and Karahalios nodded once, then turned and left the younger man's workspace.

Roeder gazed after him glumly, then turned back to his computer display and the modified NET headset on his bench. It looked pretty much like any

NET gear, at least externally. For that matter, the *hardware* changes were minimal, mainly confined to the neural receptors which error-checked NET downloads. He'd had to modify them to give them both more sensitivity and greater bandwidth, since the basic system had been designed to minimize peripheral data eddies and strip away unwanted "sideband" elements when an experiential file, as opposed to simply a direct data transfer, was initially recorded and uploaded to the system. Nobody wanted the possibility of someone else's trace memories or emotions wandering around inside his own head.

The majority of the changes were to the software, however. Like every other Hegemony program, the ones controlling the NET process were loaded down with tons of safety features, most of which, in this case, were specifically designed to prevent what Roeder wanted to accomplish. He understood the potential risks, whatever Doctor Ramos and Doctor Karahalios might think. But the possibilities were so boundless!

He activated his virtual keyboard and "tapped" its insubstantial keys, bringing up his latest software tweak and gazed at it pensively. He hadn't dropped this one into the system yet. In fact, there were half a dozen he'd carefully tucked away on his individual workstation. Partly because he'd been doing them on his own time, and partly because most of them had been wild, off-the-cuff, blue sky, high-risk approaches. He'd never intended any of them as serious proposals—in fact, he'd been looking at the most extreme iterations he could come up with, in no small part to *avoid* them—but he'd rather doubted Ramos and Karahalios would recognize that if they ever saw them.

The truth was, he conceded, that he truly had made himself a pain in the ass over this. By this time, both of his superiors were not unreasonably convinced that he was at least borderline irrational on the subject. So he'd decided it would be a good idea to keep the really crazy stuff to himself.

Not that it had saved his project in the end, he thought glumly.

He opened the most recent file and ran back through it moodily. It wasn't as far off the reservation as most of the others. In fact, its risk factor was substantially lower, according to the models he'd run. But that also meant it was probably less likely to succeed. Unless. . . .

His eyes narrowed as a sudden thought came to him. It had never occurred to him before, and it was undeniably off the wall. In fact, it was *way* off the wall. But at the same time, if there was anything to it. . . .

He jumped out of the file and into a detailed schematic of the NET hardware. If he boosted the inductance a smidge, then loaded the mod he'd just been looking at, reduced the data transfer rate just a bit, opened the gate a tiny bit wider where those unwanted "peripherals" were concerned, and then. . . .

He sat there, looking at the schematic, lips pursed in a silent whistle as he thought about it. He knew exactly what Karahalios or Ramos would say, especially if he suggested something this outlandish. In fact, Karahalios had just finished saying it. So it wasn't like the idea was going anywhere. After the weekend, he'd be doing something else—no doubt valuable, but nowhere near as interesting as this—and that was that. But still. . . .

Several minutes passed. Then he straightened in his chair and began tapping more keys.

· · · · ·

"—SO I UNDERSTAND the potential advantages, Mister President," Edson Soares said, "but I must confess that I still cherish some reservations." He shrugged with a thin smile. "Perhaps the problem is that I am too well aware of how hard it is to understand some *humans*. It does not fill me with optimism where understanding *aliens* is concerned."

Dave Dvorak chuckled and shook his head, smiling at the Brazilian across the conference table. Soares had continued to serve as Brazil's Foreign Minister until about five years ago, when he'd finally transferred to the Planetary Union's Department of State. If he'd known what he was letting himself in for, he probably wouldn't have. He'd ended up the Under Secretary of State for Human Rights, a thankless post which left him to deal with the remaining trouble spots—places like, oh, Pakistan, Afghanistan, the portions of the old China which had resisted inclusion in any of the new successor states, and the lingering meltdown in Malaysia—which remained outside the PU and didn't give much of a good goddamn about "human rights." If anybody in the solar system had enjoyed ample experience of human irrationality, he was the man.

"That's one way to look at it," Kent McCoury conceded, his Appalachian twang a sharp contrast to Soares' Brazilian accent. "But we're going to have to talk to other species sooner or later, Ed, and at least you and I have had lots of practice right here at home."

As Under Secretary for Political Affairs, he and Soares worked closely together, since at the moment, those trouble spots were the only remaining foreign powers with whom the Planetary Union was required to interact.

"To be honest, this is why we even have a State Department these days," McCoury continued. "As far as our remaining idiots here on Earth are concerned, we all know we're basically just marking time. Eventually, they'll either have to sign on the dotted line—which will mean satisfying your people on their human rights record—and join up, or else get so egregiously out of line the PU's voters demand that we send in the troops and just get it over with."

"I'm not in a tearing hurry to intervene militarily," President Howell said mildly from his seat at the head of the table. "I'm perfectly prepared to exert as much external pressure as we can *short* of that, but I believe history demonstrates that it's a lot easier to shoot people than ideas. Dave?"

"I'm not sure we're up against ideas as much as bigotry, intolerance, hatred, personal ambition, and megalomania," Dvorak replied in measured tones. "Of course, history also demonstrates that it's a lot easier to shoot people than any of *those* things, either." He shrugged. "In any case, unless we want to 'make a desert and call it peace'—which, I will admit, has a certain appeal when I'm most frustrated with the idiots—I don't think military intervention's the way to go. Not, at the very least, until there's a genuine, identifiable, grassroots, *indigenous* resistance movement like the one that's finally emerging in Pakistan. That's why your and Ed's people are doing every damned thing we can think of to generate exactly that, Kent."

"I know." McCoury nodded. "I'm just saying that I think we'll reach a point where public opinion will demand that we step on the cockroaches and just get on with it. We're already seeing that tide rising. People's reaction to Pakistan's a good example of that, as a matter of fact."

"Maybe," Howell acknowledged.

The president's tone was just a bit repressive, and Dvorak resisted the urge to shake his head. Public opinion hadn't moved quite as far in favor of intervening in Pakistan as McCoury's last sentence suggested. It was certainly moving in that direction, but the situation was still . . . fluid, to say the least, and the original move to oust Baseer Badrashi's government was busy breaking down into a nasty, multi-sided internal dogfight. All the Resistance's factions had been united in hating *him*; now their competing agendas were duking it out, and it was obvious that many of the elements which had united against Badrashi weren't a lot fonder of each other than they'd been of him. Some of their supporters had taken to the streets against their recent allies, and there were still a lot of weapons floating around.

Under the circumstances, Dave Dvorak heartily endorsed the president's decision against trying to pick winners and losers in that kind of internecine bloodfest. But although Howell had never said so in so many words, Dvorak suspected he'd had more motives to avoid military interventions in general than he'd ever actually enunciated. Not that the ones he'd given weren't fully sufficient to justify his position. For example, he was right about the Sisyphean nature of any attempt to impose outside solutions. And from the very beginning, he'd insisted that any nation-state's decision to join the Planetary Union had to be internal. He would *not* increase the PU's mandate by force of arms lest he undermine its ultimate legitimacy, and military intervention to impose a PU-sponsored local government was all too likely to do precisely that. But places like Pakistan had also provided handy horrible examples to remind people who had joined the Planetary Union of some of the alternatives, and the PU's patience with such obviously outlaw regimes could only encourage faith in the federal government's promise to respect the local sovereignty of the

Union's member states. In the end, there was no doubt in Dvorak's mind—or in the minds of any of the other three men present, he was sure—that sanity would break out even in the remaining lunatic asylums. When it did, Howell would support the opposition to the hilt, and at the end of the day they would know that they'd rebuilt their own nations when they decided to seek PU membership.

"Getting back to the topic at hand," Dvorak said now, "Kent's right about having to talk to them eventually. And if we need to do that, then obviously the Sarthians are the place to begin."

"Do we really want to start with a Level Three civilization?" Soares asked soberly. "I know there are many arguments in favor, but would it not be better to begin with the Calgarths or the Ranthors?"

"They'd make a safer test case, possibly," Dvorak said dryly. "I suppose our own reaction to the Shongairi could be considered an argument in favor of that conclusion."

The Calgarths and Ranthors had been the other two species on Fleet Commander Thikair's list before he bloodied his nose on Earth. The Calgarths were a Level Five culture on the Hegemony's classification system, which meant they were basically at a 16th-century level of technology. The Ranthors were a bit more advanced, probably on the border between Level Five and Level Four, with a very early steam-age level of technology but not yet into anything much more sophisticated than the telegraph. Of course, those were the levels they were projected to have attained based on their capabilities at the time they were surveyed, somewhat longer ago than Earth had been surveyed, so no one knew how accurate those ratings actually were. Humanity was proof that the Hegemony's projections could be just a *bit* off. On the other hand, humanity was also a sharp exception from the rule of the Hegemony's hundred-and-fifty-millennia experience, so they were probably right about both the Calgarths and Ranthors.

The Sarthians, however, were projected to be at Level Three, roughly equivalent to Earth's capabilities in, say, 1940 or 1950. Because of that, they'd been protected by the Hegemony Constitution, which mandated that species at that level be left to develop to interstellar capability—or not—on their own. They were also omnivores, which had made them even more of a hands-off proposition for the Hegemony. Unlike carnivores, who were confidently expected to exterminate themselves before they got loose among the stars (the Shongairi were the only unfortunate exception to that rule), omnivores were considered much stronger candidates to make the cut. Some of them could be just a little . . . edgy by the standards of the Hegemony's herbivore majority, however, and the Sarthians seemed to fall into that category. That meant they were more likely to react poorly to the Hegemony's attitude towards other species, and also that they'd probably attained a level of technology which could be much rapidly improved upon without quite as much utter dislocation as the introduction of Hegemony-level tech would produce on a 16th-century world.

It also lent rather more point to Soares' concerns about how they might react to visitors from another star. They'd be considerably more capable of doing something about it if they reacted . . . poorly. However—

"I'll agree there's a higher potential risk factor with the Sarthians," Dvorak continued. "I think that's outweighed by the potential pluses of where we expect them to be about now. More to the point though, they're in range."

Soares frowned, but he also nodded.

Upon occasion, in the not-too-distant past, some Terran astronomers had asserted that the binary 61 Cygni star system possessed massive planets, only to have those claims debunked by later observations. But what the debunkers had not been able to detect prior to the invasion was Sarth, orbiting 61 Cygni A at roughly 56,000,000 kilometers—about 0.38% of Earth's orbital radius.

More importantly for the purposes of this conversation, 61 Cygni was less than eleven light-years from Earth, whereas Calgarth, otherwise known as 26 Draconis, was forty-six light-years away and Ranthor, listed as Eta Corona Borealis A in Earth's catalogs, lay just over sixty from Earth. Humanity had managed to tweak the phase-drive as it had so much of the Hegemony's technology, but not as much as in other instances. By accepting a greater possibility of failure (all the way up to once in every eleven hundred years of operation), the first human starships—which were well advanced in construction—would be capable of just breaking into the beta bands of p-space. That would allow them an advantage of better than seventy-five percent over the Hegemony's best apparent interstellar speed, but that was still only eleven times the speed of light. Which meant that even a mission to 61 Cygni would require a voyage of almost a full year each way. Calgarth's round-trip time would be almost eight and a half years, however, and Ranthor's would be almost eleven.

"Assuming we actually have several centuries before the Hegemony gets back around to us, that probably doesn't really matter all that much," Howell observed. "From the perspective of human beings who aren't accustomed yet to thinking in those sorts of terms, though, I think finding out within a couple of years whether or not our first mission succeeded has a lot to recommend it."

"Agreed." Soares nodded. "I suppose—"

Howell's phone chimed. His eyebrows rose, since his day was always tightly scheduled, and people knew better than to interrupt him for anything short of crisis-level events. But then it chimed again, and the eyebrows which had risen lowered as he recognized the priority of the tone, and he raised one hand, halting Soares.

"Friday, identify incoming caller," he said.

"Secretary Lewis," his phone replied.

"I see." He glanced at the other three men, then shrugged. "Put her through. Public view."

"Public view," the phone acknowledged, and Fabienne Lewis and Damianos Karahalios appeared above the conference table as the phone linked to the ceiling-mounted HD unit.

"Fabienne. Doctor Karahalios." From Howell's courteous tone one might have assumed he was equally happy to see both callers.

One would have assumed incorrectly.

"I understand you wouldn't have interrupted unless it was for something important, Fabienne," the president continued, "but I have another meeting scheduled in only about twenty minutes."

"Yes, Sir. I know. I checked your agenda before we called. But I think you're going to want to hear about this."

"About what?"

"First, let me show you a short video clip," she said, and he nodded a bit impatiently.

"Go ahead."

"Yes, Sir."

Lewis and Karahalios disappeared, replaced by the image of a youngish looking, brown-haired man in what was obviously one of *Bastion*'s labs. Howell and his secretaries watched as he settled a NET headset onto his head. Then his right index finger moved, clearly hitting a key on a virtual keyboard projected onto his contacts.

For an instant, nothing seemed to happen. Then his entire body spasmed, his head slammed back, and he shuddered like someone experiencing an epileptic seizure. It went on for several seconds—almost a full minute—and then, just as suddenly, he stopped shuddering as abruptly as he'd begun.

The HD zoomed in on his open, staring eyes and the burnt skin under the headset's contacts. It held there for a moment, then his image disappeared, replaced by Lewis and Karahalios.

"He's alive," Lewis said. "Well, the body is, anyway. There's no brainwave activity, though."

"What the hell did he do to himself?" Howell demanded.

"Let me guess," Dvorak said grimly. Lewis glanced in his direction. "Brent Roeder, right?"

"Got it in one." Lewis nodded, then turned back to Howell. "Doctor Roeder was one of the cyberneticists working with Doctor Ramos and Doctor Karahalios' team. He was especially interested in creating direct neural interfacing with our computers. He believed it would not only be a huge step forward in interface efficiency but that it might well prove the first step toward achieving genuine, self-aware AI. That if human brains could communicate directly with the existing AI, they could learn from *us,* instead of the one-way street we have now with NET."

"And that's what he was working on when this happened?" Howell waved one hand at the space the accident's imagery had occupied.

"Not anything he was *authorized* to be working on, Mister President," Karahalios put in. "In fact, we were going to assign him to an entirely different project." He shook his head, his expression sadder than Howell had ever seen it. "I'm afraid that's what pushed him to this . . . rashness."

"I'm sorry to hear that Doctor Roeder's dead, of course," Howell said, "but what makes this tragic accident so important that you brought it directly to me?"

"Because that's not exactly what happened, Sir," Lewis said. "The NET didn't kill him."

"It sure looked like it. And you did say that there's no brainwave activity," Howell pointed out. "Isn't that the definition of 'brain-dead'?"

"Well, yes." Lewis nodded. "But let me show you something else, Sir." She raised a tablet into Howell's field of view. "We've set up an interface with Doctor Roeder's lab computer."

"Why?" Howell sounded just a bit more impatient.

"To show you this, Sir." She tapped the tablet. "Go ahead," she said.

"What?" Howell asked.

"Not you, Mister President," she said. "I meant—"

"She means me, Sir." The voice was male, a bit deeper than Karahalios', although the speaker was nowhere to be seen, and Howell frowned.

"And you are?"

"Mister President, I'm Brent Roeder. This isn't the way I imagined meeting you, but it's what I've got right now."

For an instant, Howell looked confused. Then his lips tightened.

"A recording?" he asked. "What kind of joke is this?"

"No—" Lewis began, but the other voice cut him off.

"No, Sir. I'm really here. This is me. Well, I suppose I'm not really *there*, since I'm still in the lab—"

"What the hell are you talking about?" Howell demanded in exasperation. "I'm down to ten minutes till that next meeting, and I'm not finished here. So could you please get to the point or talk to me about this later?"

"I'm sorry, Mister President," Roeder said. "But this really is important. It seems that now I'm *in* the computer, not just connected to it."

Howell's eyes went wide, and he looked back at Lewis and Karahalios.

"You mean—?"

"Yes, Mister President," Karahalios said, and for once the arrogant, detail-obsessed scientist sounded almost awed. "We may not have AI, but we do appear to have computer intelligence."

Howell sat back, eyes narrowed, and stared at them for a few moments.

"Friday," he said.

"Yes, Mister President?" his phone replied.

"Cancel my appointments for the rest of the day. No, wait. Not the appointment with General Landers. When he gets here, send him straight to the conference room. Tell Angelo to reschedule the others."

"Cancel all appointments for the rest of today, except for General Landers, who is to be sent directly to the conference room when he arrives from *Citadel*," the phone said. "Inform Mister Christopherson that you wish him to reschedule all of the canceled appointments."

"Correct."

"Very well, Mister President."

Howell laid the phone back down on the conference table, tipped back in his chair, and gazed intently at the hologram.

"Fabienne, I think you can assume that you and Doctor Karahalios and—especially—Doctor Roeder have my undivided attention."

· XIV ·

"All system monitors report go, Doctor," Vivian Osterbeck announced.

"Good!" Chester Gannon replied with a vigorous nod.

He sat in a comfortable chair at the center of an only moderately large control room at the heart of the *Prometheus* Platform in Ganymede orbit. Prior to the Shongair invasion, that control room would have been enormous, filled with dozens—or even scores—of highly trained, highly skilled scientists and technicians. They would have monitored their vast array of displays, funneling reports to team managers, and through the team managers to the project managers, and there probably would have been several of those *project* managers, all making their own decisions in their assigned spheres but reporting to the one person who bore ultimate responsibility for the *entire* project.

Today, there were exactly twelve people present, without a single physical display in sight.

Of course, each of those twelve people commanded an information flow which was incomparably broader and deeper than any of them could have processed in real-time under those long-ago, primitive conditions. An entire bevy of AIs—and, yes, Gannon was a scientist, he knew they weren't really self-aware, but, dammit, they *were* AIs—reported to the visual displays and keyboards projected onto the corneal implants each of them had received. And each of those AIs controlled a host of subsystems which, in turn, ran and monitored every cubic centimeter of the multi-million-ton platform.

Then there was the *thirteenth* person.

"You concur, Brent?" Gannon asked him.

"Yes," a voice replied in his earbud.

Brent Roeder was, in many ways, the ultimate backup for the entire program. It had taken a couple of years for him to really get a handle on his radically changed environment, and it was evident to the psychiatrists and psychologists working with him that that changed environment was also changing him. All of them—and Roeder—were committed to understanding *how* it was changing him, but the process was obviously a slow one. As he himself put it, "I'm just not as *interested* in things as I used to be," and that was growing gradually worse.

Clearly, it worried him, yet he'd never allowed it to affect his work, nor, so far as Gannon knew, had he ever complained. The closest he'd ever come to it in Gannon's presence was the day he'd remarked "I kinda wish I'd at least written down what I was doing. At least that way, someone else could've learned from my mistakes. But whatever else happens, so far it's been a hell of a ride!"

In the meantime, he'd recorded a complete copy of himself in a computer core identical to the one he inhabited. As a test, he'd "awakened" his alter ego and confirmed that it was just as self-aware—just as much *him*—as he was. And after talking it over, Roeder II had been the one to suggest that he should be powered back down to serve as the backup for Roeder I in case whatever was changing him proved fatal in the end. That said a great deal about his mental toughness, in Gannon's opinion. It was yet another reason he'd come to both like and admire the impetuous young man who'd become something so very different.

And Roeder's changed circumstances made him extremely useful on projects like this one. It wasn't really his field, but all of the working files and research data were literally an extension of his own personality and mind. Interestingly, he didn't seem to be able to "think" any faster than he had as a corporeal human being, but if his data retrieval speed wasn't actually instantaneous, it was damned close. It took him just as long as it ever had to combine information and concepts after they'd been retrieved, but "just" the difference in retrieval time meant he came up with answers to even complex questions very, very, *very* quickly and that he had the ability to monitor a vast array of subsystems. Although he was carried on Project Prometheus' books as a "backup," the truth was that the human personnel in Gannon's control room were *his* backup more than he was theirs. They all understood the theory and the science better than he did, but his reaction time if something went wrong would be astronomically faster than theirs, and all of them knew it.

"All right, then!" Gannon clapped his hands together and smiled as the rest of his people turned and looked at him. "If all of you say we're ready, and if Brent agrees, then we're damned well ready! So I'd say we're go for the Alpha test."

"Yes, Sir," Osterbeck agreed. "Seems a pity we have to do it by remote, though."

It would have been unfair to call Vivian's tone "wheedling," Gannon thought . . . but not very, and he understood. That wasn't the same thing as saying he sympathized, however, although a teeny-tiny part of him did.

"It may be a pity, but it's also the way it is," he said firmly. "Secretary Lewis was very clear about that."

"I know, but—"

"And *I* know what you're going to say," Gannon interrupted with a smile which took most of the sting from his words. "And, I repeat, it's the way it is. Right?"

"Of course, Sir."

Osterbeck matched his smile with one of her own that was perhaps a bit more tart than his had been, and he nodded to her.

As the head of Prometheus—and despite his own opinion of his shortcomings as a team leader, he'd been the inevitable choice—he was delighted with the progress they'd made so far, and he thoroughly understood the rest of his team's . . . ego involvement, perhaps, in those accomplishments. For just one example, they'd demonstrated that it was, indeed, possible to create an artificial gravity field which would ultimately make the spin sections built into long-endurance spacecraft and platforms obsolete. Power requirements were still an issue, but he and his team were confident those could be solved using currently mature tech. Other applications and uses had spun off of their basic work as they went along, as well, and other human R&D teams had pounced on them.

But Prometheus was still after Leviathan. He'd proven elusive, but they were closing in on him now, and he was twins. The possibility of producing an FTL drive faster than was possible with any conventional phase-drive was one prong of that Leviathan, but the other was the possibility of effectively limitless energy. Energy in magnitudes no human physicist would even have dreamed of harnessing as little as four years ago, far less before they'd acquired the Hegemony's tech base. And since all of modern technology, especially on the macro level, was about using *energy,* really, when one came down to it, if Prometheus worked—

"Okay," he said briskly. "Everybody out of the pool!"

Several people, including Osterbeck, chuckled, but they also climbed out of their chairs and filed obediently towards the control room hatch. Gannon waited to come last, then followed them out.

Actually, there wasn't any reason they had to have a "control room" at all, he reflected. They could just as easily have stayed in their own living quarters and used the platform's infonet to run everything and communicate with one another in a virtual control room. Eventually, he felt sure, that would become the new norm. The younger generation, growing up with Hegemony-level technology already did it, and he supposed it was a logical extension of remoting in from home. But the old farts like him still wanted that sense of a communal presence in the flesh.

Idiot, he thought wryly. *You're already in a "virtual" control room sitting there with your implants and your earbuds. Just be grateful they're willing to put up with a dinosaur like you!*

He chuckled, yet it was true, and he knew it. Just as he knew he was going to break down and get one of the cochlear implants most of his youthful team already had, so he wouldn't need even earbuds.

That thought carried him down the passage to the lift shaft. The lift car was ample for just twelve human beings and carried them swiftly to the docking bay. The airlock was open when they got there, and Commander Quyền was waiting to personally greet them as they arrived.

"Looking good, Doctor Gannon!" she said, raising her right hand.

"It is, indeed, Thoa," he agreed, raising his own hand to high-five her.

Commander Quyền Bảo Thoa was about fifteen years younger than he was, and there were dark places behind those brown eyes of hers, just like there were behind the eyes of most of the people who'd survived the invasion. She was also diminutive, attractive, prone to practical jokes, and one of Project Prometheus' charter members. Although she herself was a commander in the Planetary Union Navy—and, despite all of the initial good intentions, the Squids of the world had succeeded in reasserting the traditional naval ranks in all their confusing glory—her command wasn't technically a unit of the Navy. PUS *Andromeda* belonged to the Department of Technology, and she was the mobile home of Brent Roeder's computer core. It didn't really matter to Roeder where his computer "body" was located, and putting him aboard *Andromeda* made it practical to dispatch him to places like Ganymede, where he could interface with the local computer net without crippling light-speed delays. That wasn't the only thing *Andromeda* did for the Department, but in many ways, it was arguably the most important.

In this case, one of those "other things" was to serve as a safe, remote aerie from which the results of the Alpha Test could be monitored. And however much it might irk Vivian Osterbeck, Chester Gannon was perfectly all right with that. Even assuming the test went perfectly, they were still dealing with an energy density roughly comparable to the heart of a thermonuclear explosion. He was just fine putting a little prophylactic distance between him and his brainchild while they found out how well it worked.

"Well, come on aboard," Quyền told him. "I have *got* to see how well this works after all this time and effort."

"So do I," Gannon said as they entered the lock together. "On the other hand," he tossed out his traditional caveat and sheet anchor, "a real scientist learns more from experiments that fail than he does from the ones that succeed."

Quyền snorted and the lock closed behind them as they swam the boarding tube to *Andromeda*.

·　·　·　·　·

"ALL RIGHT," GANNON said forty-five minutes later, settling himself into the chair on *Andromeda*'s bridge and securing the restraints to keep him safely out of the way in the bridge's microgravity. The ship was two light seconds from the

Prometheus Platform, and Jupiter was a huge red marble in one corner of the visual display. But only for a moment. Then "Big Red" disappeared as the display zoomed in on Ganymede and the orbiting platform they'd left behind.

"Brent, I think the honor is yours," he continued. "Please initiate the Alpha Test."

"Of course, Doctor Gannon!" If Brent Roeder thought he was "losing interest" in the world around him, it certainly didn't show in his tone today, Gannon thought. "Initiating Alpha Test in thirty seconds."

A digital timer appeared one corner of the complex display on Gannon's corneal implant, and he sat back, arms folded across his chest, watching it.

"Five . . . four . . . three . . . two . . . one . . . initiate!"

Roeder's voice counted down the last five seconds, and then the timer vanished as a waterfall display began climbing. Other readouts flickered and changed, as well, but it was the waterfall that really interested him, and he watched as it continued rising for several seconds, then slowed and stopped.

"Stage One, successful," Roeder announced. "Initial black hole activation confirmed."

Someone smacked a celebratory hand on a console. It wasn't Gannon. They'd reached this stage twice before, from this same bridge.

The real reason the platform was so big was to provide sufficient space for the antimatter power plants required to create an artificially produced Gravitationally Completely Collapsed Object. Personally, Gannon agreed with Wheeler that it was a lot easier to say "black hole" rather than "GCCO," every time they spoke of one. Of course, Wheeler had come up with quite a few other neat bits of terminology—Gannon had always been especially fond of "quantum foam"—and someone of his stature could call things whatever the hell he wanted. But whatever someone wanted to call it, producing today's version of it had required as much energy as a dreadnought's phase-drive devoured. According to his team's calculations, they should be able to reduce that significantly as they continued to refine their understanding and control. For now, though, it was an incredible energy hog.

But that, of course, was for the *initial* black hole, wasn't it?

"Stage Two, please," he said.

"Initiating Stage Two."

Nothing changed for a moment. It took Roeder's commands two seconds to reach the platform, after all. Then the initial waterfall began rising once more and a second appeared beside it.

"Phase wall successfully breached," Roeder reported, and this time there was a spatter of applause. So far as any of them knew, this was the first time anyone had penetrated into phase-space without a phase-drive. Of course, there was a downside to that, and the second waterfall began shooting upward as the higher energy state of phase-space started "draining" into what humans and the Hegemony fondly called normal-space.

"We're ten percent above projections," Vivian Osterbeck announced unnecessarily. Gannon had already seen that, and he frowned slightly. Their base calculation had always been a range, not a hard number, and they were still well within that range, but Osterbeck was right. The power density at this stage was significantly higher than their best models had projected. On the other hand, everything else was almost exactly where it was supposed to be.

"The system's handling it," Tony Furman, another of the team's plethora of PhDs, pointed out. "Still plenty of margin at this point."

"Agreed," Gannon said. "Brent, initiate Stage Three."

"Initiating Stage Three," Roeder confirmed. Again, there was a momentary delay. And then the second waterfall shot upward again and a *third* appeared beside it.

"Beta wall breach confirmed," Roeder said, and the third waterfall soared with explosive speed.

"Twenty percent above calculations! "Osterbeck exclaimed. "Thirty! Thirty-six!"

"Losing containment!" Furman shouted. "Estimate failure in ten seconds!"

"Shutting down," Roeder said, his "voice" far calmer than either of the others, even before Gannon could give him the order. "Shutdown in—"

He stopped, and Gannon felt his jaw muscles clench as the bridge visual display flared with sudden, eye-watering brilliance.

It wasn't an explosion. It was too intense to call it that. The entire platform simply vanished in a blinding flash that was far larger than the platform itself had ever been. In fact—

"Oops," someone whispered from behind him.

·　·　·　·　·

"YOU REMEMBER HOW I told you I was going to put Chester Gannon and his merry crew out in Jupiter orbit, don't you?" Fabienne Lewis asked as she and her husband settled into chairs in the Dvorak dining room aboard *Bastion*.

"Excuse me?" Dave Dvorak blinked at her for a moment, then finished setting the bowl of mashed potatoes with red and gold bell peppers on the table. That was scarcely what he'd expected as opening table talk at Sharon Dvorak's dinner table, and it took him almost fifteen seconds to rummage around his memory for the two-year-old conversation. Then he nodded.

"Yeah," he said, glancing warily over his shoulder at the door through which his beloved spouse would be arriving momentarily with the roast beef.

"Well, it turns out it was a good thing I did."

Her tone was almost whimsical, but her eyes weren't, and he looked at her sharply.

"Why?"

"Because Ganymede isn't there anymore."

"I . . . beg your pardon?"

"I said, Ganymede isn't there anymore." Lewis shrugged. "Well, actually that's not fair. There's still some debris that *used* to be Ganymede. Our initial estimate is that as much as twenty or even thirty percent of it's left. And I might point out that Ganymede's the eighth largest orbital body in the entire solar system. It's—or, more precisely, it *was*—about half the size of Mars, bigger than Mercury. You know, a fairly *substantial* piece of real estate?"

"Jesus." Dvorak sank onto one of the other dining room chairs as astonishment pulled the single word out of him. Then his eyes narrowed. "Was anybody hurt?!"

"No, thank God." Lewis shook her head. "*Andromeda* was a couple of light seconds clear at the time. I sort of insisted."

"And a damn good thing, too!" Dvorak shook his head. "They blew up the whole damned *moon*?"

"Well, they did enough damage to *shatter* it, so I guess that counts." Lewis shrugged again. "I've watched the imagery. Really impressive, especially when you slow it down."

"I'm sure it is." Dvorak grinned wryly. "I started to say 'I can imagine,' but fortunately, I stopped myself in time. Because I'm pretty sure my imagination would come up short."

"Probably. In fact—"

Lewis broke off as Sharon appeared, carrying the roast beef. The suddenness with which she interrupted herself raised a copper-colored eyebrow over one blue eye.

"Should I assume someone was talking politics, or maybe history, before we even got to the salads?" she inquired sweetly.

"Not guilty, Honey!" Dvorak raised a solemn right hand. "But that said, I have to admit that what Fabienne *was* talking about is . . . pretty impressive."

"Impressive enough I'm going to have to put up with it while we eat?" she asked just a bit ominously.

"Well, that depends," her husband said. "I mean, only if you *want* to know why we don't have a Ganymede anymore."

"Excuse me?"

"I said we don't have a Ganymede anymore. You know—Ganymede? Jupiter?" Her husband shook his head. "Not there anymore. But that's okay, just put the roast down and I'll carve. We can talk about it later."

"You unmitigated bastard," she said, lips twitching despite herself.

"What?" He looked at her innocently, eyebrows arched. "I said put it down, I'll carve. No need to do any of that nasty old shop talk while you eat."

"Later tonight, don't ask me why it happened," she said.

"Why what happened?"

"It'll be a surprise," she said sweetly. "You'll recognize it when it comes around, though."

"I'm sure I will," he chuckled. "Should I take it that constitutes permission for us to go on talking about it while I carve?"

"*This* time," she sighed.

"Thank you, Babe," he said with genuine gratitude, then looked back at his daughter's mother-in-law as he picked up the carving knife and fork. "You were saying, Fabienne?"

"Well, it all went fine at first. But then—"

· · · · ·

"IT'S A GOOD thing we don't worry about funding levels as much as we used to have to," Dvorak said, much later that evening, as Sharon finished shuffling the cards and began to deal.

"Thinking about the investment in the *Prometheus* platform, are you?" Lewis asked, picking up her cards and sorting them.

"Yeah. That was a nice piece of hardware."

"It was," Greg Lewis agreed, sorting his own cards. As usual, he and Dvorak were partnered against Sharon and Fabienne. "Hardly a blip on the federal budget, though, these days."

"True," his wife said. "But downrange, it's going to turn into something a heck of a lot bigger than a 'blip,' Greg. You should know that better than anyone else at the table."

"Why?" Sharon asked. She had no issue with "shop talk" over Spades. In fact, anything that distracted her husband from counting trump was a plus, in her opinion.

"Because it's very likely that eventually, we're going to scrap all of our existing blueprints and start designing starships all over again, from scratch," Greg said.

"Why?" Sharon repeated in genuine surprise.

"We were already looking at a major redesign once Gannon and his boys and girls figured out how to generate artificial gravity," Greg told her. "We're not at that point yet, because we're still dealing with the power requirements, but it's on the horizon and probably not more than another couple of years out. When that happens, we won't need spin sections anymore, which will hugely simplify design constraints. It'll inject some of its own, you understand, but overall we'll be able to design a lot more efficiently and probably significantly reduce vulnerability in the process.

"But assuming Gannon gets a handle on this thing—and he already 'has a theory about' what went wrong," all of them chuckled at Gannon's trademark phrase, "he's just done two things. One is to give us a power source, if we can figure out how to use it without blowing up any planets in the vicinity, that dwarfs anything the Hegemony has. Trust me, as an engineer—and, especially, as an engineer who's spent the last several years working with *warship* designs—energy, power, is undoubtedly *the* most critical element in balancing the factors of a successful design.

"That's probably not the biggest single reason we'll be redesigning, though, because he successfully breached both the phase wall *and* the beta wall before everything went to hell. If he can do that in a mobile application, and there's no reason he shouldn't be able to, and *if* his 'phased array' approach works, it will simultaneously produce a faster-than-light drive that's *significantly* better than anything the Hegemony has and actually give us the power to make the damn thing work!"

He paused to finish sorting his cards, then looked back at Sharon.

"The key element's going to be how successfully he can work out the control systems on this monster. I mean, in a lot of ways it's like trying to bottle a nova and stick it in your back pocket. As long as it stays bottled, you're fine. If the cork pops—"

He shrugged, and Sharon nodded soberly.

"But if it *does* stay corked—" he began.

"If it stays corked, then Gannon just gave us one hell of a trump card where the Hegemony's concerned," Dvorak interjected.

"Exactly." Lewis nodded. "This is all still speculative, and even assuming we hit the most optimistic development schedule imaginable—and don't blow up any more moons—we're years away from actual hardware. I don't think it would make any sense to delay the Sarth mission waiting for it."

"Neither do I, I suppose," Dvorak said a bit glumly, looking at his wife.

"It'll only be a couple of years," she said, blue eyes softening. "And if you took me along, that'd be pretty unfair to everybody else who can't haul along their spouses."

"But it's not just me," he said softly.

"Well, at least Maighread will still be here. She and I can cheer each other up."

"Greg and I will chip in on that, too," Fabienne promised. "Lots of 'girls night out' stuff while they miss you and what's-his-name."

"His *name* is Raymond," her husband said severely. "And I cannot believe

you just used such a sexist term. '*Girls* night out?' The X chromosome con-
tingent at this table would have committed physical violence if Dave or I had
ventured—*dared!*—to use such language!"

"Darned right," his wife told him with a twinkle, then looked at Sharon. "I'll
bid three," she said.

AGE OF EXPLORATION

YEAR 26 OF THE TERRAN EMPIRE

·I·

CITY OF DIANZHYR, REPUBLIC OF DIANTO;
AND CITY OF KWYZO NAR QWERN, QWERN EMPIRE,
PLANET SARTH

W hat I'm telling you, Qwelth, is that as big a pain in the excreter as Solkarn was, there were a lot of downsides to losing him," Swordsman Consort Bardyn ShoKymBar said. The Republic of Dianto's Director of Intelligence ran a four-fingered hand over his cranial down and closed his nasal flaps in an expression of disgust. "It's like Juzhyr's decided it's ous job to . . . I don't know, *avenge* Solkarn, I guess." Bardyn was tall and broad shouldered, even for a male, which always made his shrugs impressive, but today's was something special, Prime Director Qwelth QwelSynCha reflected wryly. "Sometimes, I think ou thinks that stupid crash was our fault! Ou's out for our reproductive equipment, at any rate!"

"It's not quite that bad, Bardyn," Mynsaro MynQwerDyn said in a milder tone. "I'm not saying it didn't affect oum; losing a spouse will shake any triad. Chelth knows we all know that! But Juzhyr never really needed any more reasons to dislike us. The entire Republic's been on Clan Qwern's shit list for the last thousand years."

"Which doesn't invalidate a single thing I just said." Bardyn's response was just a tad more acerbic than most males would use addressing a neutro, but he and Mynsaro had known one another for over seventy years. They were close friends, even if they did have occasionally . . . energetic discussions during meetings of the Directors.

"No, it doesn't," Qwelth intervened, "but Mynsaro has a point, Bardyn. Oh, you do too, but it's a matter of degree, not a change in kind."

"That's fair enough," Bardyn acknowledged after a moment. "But I'm more worried about it than I've been in quite a while because of what our station chief has to say about old Erylk's health."

Now there, Qwelth conceded to ouself, Bardyn probably had a point. Erylk ErGarzHyn nar Qwern, the Flock Lord of Dyrzhyba, was not only Chancellor of the Qwern Empire but the bearer-in-law of its current ruler, and ou was a tough old daurysaki. But ou wasn't getting any younger. The old neutro was still a force to be reckoned with in the Ministries, but ou was clearly less energetic than ou had been. Which was potentially very bad news indeed. Erylk was no fonder of the Republic than any other Qwernian, but at least ou had always been realistic about it, which had made oum a moderating influence.

"I don't see them getting adventurous anytime soon," Jartyr LysJarKyn put in. Qwelth turned to her and arched one nasal flap, inviting the second lord of war to continue. "Nothing's changed on the military front," Jartyr pointed out, and raised both nasal flaps to grin at Bardyn across the table. "I know it's your job to worry about things, but I don't think there's any way the Qwern Alliance is rolling tanks through the Nahsyr Gap next day-half, Bardyn!"

"Probably not. I'm more worried about where they're headed diplomatically, though," Bardyn replied. "Just look at their talking points at the last Nonagon session. Mark my words, Jartyr—Myrcal's picking up the influence Erylk is losing."

"I don't think there's any doubt of that," Qwelth agreed. "And I agree it's worrisome, too, but none of the other Eight seemed too impressed by the Empire's arguments."

The Nonagon was the closest thing Sarth boasted to an authoritative international body. To be sure, that wasn't saying all that much, but at least the majority of multinational conferences and negotiations were increasingly held under its auspices. The last plenary session had been . . . fractious, to say the least, though. If the Qwernians really meant to revert to the sort of adversarial relationship their Nonagon delegate's recent language seemed to embrace, things could get—

The door to the Directors Room opened without warning, pulling Qwelth out of ous reflections. Ou turned in ous chair, both nasal flaps wide in surprise, and then ous eyes narrowed as ou recognized the sheer shock in ous aide's expression.

"Prime Director, I—" The aide paused, and Qwelth realized he was actually shaking. "I wouldn't have—I mean, I'm sorry but—"

The aide paused again, and Qwelth stood and reached out and up to lay a steadying hand on the taller male's shoulder.

"What is it, Fyrdak?" Ous reasonable tone seemed to steady the young male, who swallowed and closed both nasal flaps tight, then exhaled.

"I apologize for interrupting, Tysan," he said then, in a tightly controlled tone, "but we're receiving a transmission."

"A transmission?" Qwelth cocked ous head. "What sort of transmission? From whom?"

"We don't know, Tysan."

"What do you mean 'we don't know'?" Bardyn demanded sharply. "Where's it from?"

"Sir," the aide turned to the intelligence director, "we don't really know *that*, either. But whoever it is, they're transmitting to every nation on Sarth on every radio frequency and in every Sarthian language. And it looks like they're doing it from orbit!"

· · · · ·

"WHAT DO YOU mean, *'aliens'*?" Clan Ruler Juzhyr XI demanded irritably as ou stalked into the communications center. Ou disliked having ous afternoon nap interrupted. Ou was a night chyrn who did ous best work when all the world was asleep outside ous study windows. Unfortunately, ou'd discovered ou needed more sleep than ou once had, and ou had to make up for it somewhere. Of course, ou thought grumpily, settling the lenses onto ous muzzle ridge to peer through them at the note ou'd just been handed, ou'd been a lot younger when ou developed those work habits.

"That's what *they* say they are, Clan Ruler," the young Air Force gauntlet who had the Palace communications watch said. From his expression, even he had trouble believing that.

"And they just happened to be speaking perfect Qwernian?" Juzhyr grunted skeptically.

"And also Diantian, Wynokian, and Deltaran, Clan Ruler. That we know of." Juzhyr looked up at the gauntlet, and he twitched his nasal flaps. "We've copied the same broadcast in all of those languages," he said. "And, as you can see, they said—"

He waved a hand at the message form, and Juzhyr scowled. Then ou tossed the paper onto one of the desks and gestured at the banks of radio consoles and the personnel manning them.

"I assume we recorded this?"

"Of course, Clan Ruler!"

"Then play it back and spare my eyes."

"Yes, Clan Ruler!"

The gauntlet turned to the senior noncom of the watch and snapped both thumbs on his left hand.

"Spool it up for the Clan Ruler, Thirty-Six."

"Yes, Sir!"

Juzhyr waited rather more patiently than ou felt while the thirty-six rewound the wire recorder to the right time chop. The clan ruler refrained from pointing out that the gauntlet should damned well have ordered the noncom to have the recording ready to go long before Juzhyr actually got to the radio room. As a general rule, the clan ruler tried to avoid biting off officers' heads in public, partly because having the ruler of the largest empire on the planet scream at one didn't do wonders for one's self-confidence. Juzhyr could have lived with that—sometimes a good kick to the self-confidence (or some other portion of the anatomy) was what someone needed—but ou refused to undercut an officer's authority by berating him in front of his subordinates. Besides, it was beneath ous dignity to misuse the authority of the crown to score a petty victory over someone who couldn't possibly respond in kind. Even if it hadn't—

"We're ready, Clan Ruler," the thirty-six said respectfully.

"Then play it, Thirty-Six, please." That was another thing ous bearer had taught oum. Inferiors might not expect courtesy from their superiors, especially when the gulf between them was vast, but they certainly *remembered* it.

"Of course, Clan Ruler."

The noncom flipped the PLAY switch. For a moment, there was only the quiet hiss of blank wire passing through the heads. Then a voice came from the speakers in—as the gauntlet had said—perfect Qwernian.

"Greetings, people of Sarth," it said. "We come in peace. My name is David Dvorak—" Juzhyr's nasal flaps twitched at the bizarre sounding name "—and I am speaking to you on behalf of my government, the Planetary Union of Earth. We have traveled many light-years to speak to you and to warn you. There is a grave danger waiting in the stars, and as our presence in your star system indicates, it is closer than I fear any of your scientists may yet suspect. My government wishes me to warn of that danger and to seek allies who would stand against it with us.

"I come not to speak to any single nation, or any single alliance of nations, on your world. I come to speak to all Sarthians: Sarthian neutros, males, and females alike. It is my intention to seek contact with the Nonagon in the next few days to establish an interface through which our two species may communicate openly and clearly. I think it must be obvious that our visit portends a time of potentially great change for your planet. My own species has endured a great deal of change itself since we were attacked by those against whom we would warn you, and we know it is not an easy thing. But your world belongs to *you*, and the conditions under which we speak—the amount of change you choose to embrace—must ultimately be up to you. We will not seek to dictate, to coerce, or to seek private arrangements with one of your nations at the expense of the others, yet time is precious. I therefore request that all the nations of Sarth, not just the members of the Nonagon or those who have official observer status, send delegates to Lyzan to meet with me and with my colleagues.

"My people realize that no Sarthian could have expected this contact, and we wish to disrupt your societies no more than we absolutely must. Yet there is much we can teach you, much we can share with you, and much we can learn from you, and we look forward to beginning that journey.

"I will speak to you again soon."

PUNS *OUTREACH,*
SARTH PLANETARY ORBIT

Weird looking buggers, aren't they?" Brigadier Rob Wilson mused, leaning back in his chair and nursing his beer as he and Dave Dvorak watched the take from one of the stealthed drones hovering ten kilometers above the city of Dianzhyr, capital of the Republic of Dianto.

Other drones had been deployed to every other national capital on the planet, and smaller ones zipped quietly about, closer to the planetary surface. Unlike the drones the Shongairi had brought to Earth with them, these drones' counter-grav units were undetectable even by humans with sophisticated sensors looking for signatures that no one on the planet Sarth had ever heard of. They'd been scurrying around Sarth for three months now, updating the sadly out of date data in the Hegemony's survey files. It wasn't as *far* out of date as it would've been for a bunch of humans, but the Hegemony's last visit had been more than a thousand Sarthian years—almost three hundred Earth years—ago, and there'd been definite changes.

"We don't need any species-centric prejudices around here," Dvorak scolded.

"Didn't say a derogatory word about them as a species," Wilson replied with a grin. "Hell, they may be a perfectly nice species! But, from a human perspective, they *are* sorta weird looking. Tell me they aren't!"

"To be fair," Dvorak said in a more serious tone, "I agree they're going to take some getting used to, but there's a certain . . . I don't know, grace to them."

"Sorta like velociraptors from *Jurassic Park*?"

"Actually, that's not too shabby a comparison, for a mere Space Marine."

"I try not to let my knuckles drag on the deck *too* obviously."

"Trust me, most people never even notice. And those of us who do are far too polite to mention it."

"Oh, *thank* you. But getting back to my original point, these really are weird beasties in a lot of ways."

"You've got a point," Dvorak conceded. "The hardest part for me's been wrapping my brain around the gender distinctions. And that's something I'm going to need to be really careful about in my role as suave, sophisticated, cosmopolitan, interstellar diplomat and all."

"If anybody can carry it off, you can," Wilson said, bracingly. "Trust me. I wouldn't lie to you about something like this. The mere fact that your fragile ego might require shoring up to permit you to function in waters so far beyond your depth could never induce me to exaggerate my respect for your ability to deal with this situation."

Dvorak raised one hand, second finger extended, without ever taking his eyes from the holo display.

To call the Sarthians "weird beasties" was putting it mildly in some ways. They were bipeds, and they walked upright, and that was about the only thing their physiology shared with that of humanity.

They were shorter, on average, than humans, but that wasn't apparent just by looking at them, because they were built on much more of a "long and lean" model. In fact, Wilson's comparison to the velociraptor wasn't that far off, in a lot of ways, because to a human, they looked distinctly "saurian," and they were toe-walkers. Their limbs were jointed differently from humans', as well, providing a subtly different arc of motion, and their hands and feet were long and narrow compared to humanity's. That was largely because they had only four digits, but to make up for that, two digits on each of their hands were mutually opposable and opposable to the two middle fingers, as well, which gave them an awesome level of manual dexterity.

Although they bore living young and lactated, making them closer to Earth mammals than anything else, the saurian simile was inevitable. The fact that they were scaled contributed to that, but what made it *truly* inevitable were their heads. As bipeds, they carried those heads very much as humans did, with a very similar range of motion, and the eyes were together on its front—the binocular vision of a predator, not the "widescreen" vision of an herbivore—but they also bore a pronounced crest, very like the one which had earned the dinosaur Lambeosaurus the description of "hatchet-crested." That crest rose a good twelve to thirteen centimeters above the cranium, as much as seven or eight percent of a typical Sarthian's total height, and ran all the way down the back of the rather long and slender (by human standards) neck to the shoulders, tapering as it went. It was also the only part of their skin which wasn't scaled. Instead, it was covered in a fine, almost feathery down whose color was gender-linked. They had no ears; instead, the crest contained an acutely sensitive bony structure which extended their hearing to frequencies the human ear simply couldn't detect. In fact, he'd wondered if that audio acuity of theirs might not let them "hear" the counter-grav humans no longer could, but there was no sign that they were able to detect it, either.

Their facial structure rather resembled Lambeosaurus', as well, aside from the eye placement, and they had no real equivalent of human facial muscles. What they did have were prominent nostrils with broad, highly mobile flaps, and they used flap placement in ways which were just as expressive as any human smile or frown. Of course, *Dvorak* didn't have any nasal flaps, which was likely to make face-to-face negotiations interesting. On the other hand, he had a databank full of Sarthian expressions, and the translating software they'd acquired from the Hegemony had been tweaked right along with most of the rest of the Hegemony's software. It now included a function which could be enabled or disabled that injected expression of tone into the translation, flowing both ways. So far, it had worked perfectly with every human language group, but they hadn't had the opportunity yet to see how well it would work for a nonhuman species. Hopefully, the emotion-reading add-on would cover his ass if the tonal interpretation turned out to be less than perfect.

Facial expression wasn't the only anthropomorphizing landmine he'd have to look out for, however, because Sarthians were tri-sexual, and that had a profound effect not simply on their language but on ways in which their entire societal construct had formed. So while there were useful parallels between human societies and those of Sarth, he had to be careful about pushing any of those parallels too far.

Two of the Sarthian sexes produced gametes, but they required the third sex to combine them into a zygote. Externally, there was no structural difference at all between the gamete-producing sexes; even their genitalia were identical, since both of them had to be capable of impregnating the *third* sex, which actually gestated the zygote. Fortunately, there *was* one external differentiator, and it was fairly obvious: the color of their crest down and the matching scale colors and patterns which covered the backs of their necks. Actually, the patterns ran down as far as their shoulder blades and across their chests, as well, and Sarthians defined genders in terms of those colors. "Males" bore red and black scales in a diamond pattern which reminded Dvorak of a terrestrial rattlesnake and had red crest down. "Females" were scaled in yellow on black, but with a distinctly different pattern of bands, more like a coral snake than a rattlesnake if he was going to stick with serpent similes, with yellow crest down, while the third gender was scaled in white-on-black chevrons with *white* down.

The existence of that third gender colored every Sarthian attitude and had a profound effect upon their languages. For translation purposes, the software used the masculine for the Sarthian male, the feminine for the Sarthian female, and—somewhat to Dvorak's surprise—the Old English "ou" for the third gender. It took some getting used to, since every Sarthian noun or pronoun was gendered, and hearing "ou" instead of "he" "she," or "it," for example—or "oum" for "him" and "ouself" instead of "herself"—still sounded decidedly odd to his ear, although he'd immersed himself in the process for the last couple of months.

There were a lot of other implications. Humans tended, by and large, to think in binaries where parenting was concerned, whereas Sarthians, for obvious reasons, thought in triads. The third gender—the translator software had assigned the Latin "neutro" to it—was also referred to as the "bearer" by the Sarthians themselves, especially in terms of procreation, and Sarthian births were almost always multiples. In fact, less than ten percent of Sarthian births were single-tons, and a full eighteen percent of them were quadruplets. The neutros not only bore the young, but they also nursed them, and their hormonal balance changed radically during gestation and lactation. From what Dvorak could see, and with all due respect to his beloved wife and the mother of his children, even the most pronounced mood swings a human woman experienced during those processes were only a shadow of those a Sarthian bearer experienced. Fortunately, given the size of their "birthings," most bearers produced only one or two birthings in ous lifetime, at least in more technologically advanced so-cieties. Which was probably a good thing in a lot of ways. Producing that many young had almost certainly been a useful survival mechanism for the species as it evolved, but it could have rapidly led to catastrophic overpopulation once the child mortality rate declined and average lifespan increased.

Also fortunately for the poor bearers, Sarthian young matured quickly. Their "baby teeth" came in in only about six Earth months, at which point they transitioned rapidly to solid food and any of the three parents could—and did—take on "mommy duties." The gestation period was about forty-two Earth weeks long, so the entire process from conception to weaning lasted only about seventeen Earth months, although Dvorak suspected it seemed far longer to the bearer and ous long-suffering spouses.

One thing he found especially interesting about Sarthians was that while the neutros had enjoyed something like the protected role of the female in the Sarthian equivalent of chivalry, they'd never been restricted to "hearth and home," even in preindustrial societies. In fact, in many ways their social posi-tion was more dominant than either of the other two genders. For example, the bearer was the "anchor member" of any Sarthian marriage. Sarthian surnames combined the first syllables of each member of the triad's first names, and in every single Sarthian nation, the bearer's name always provided the surname's first syllable whereas the male and female names were added in the order in which they'd joined the triad.

There seemed to be a lot of reasons for that, despite the fact that bearers were significantly smaller and more delicate than males or females (there was no sexual dimorphism between those two genders). For one thing, males' and females' normal hormonal balances made them significantly more aggres-sive, and the neutros had always occupied the role of arbiter between them. For another thing, almost all Sarthian societies had practiced primogeniture, but the inheritor was the eldest *neutro*. As on Earth, primogeniture had been abandoned for most purposes by more advanced Sarthian societies—the Sar-thian equivalent of the "Third World" still clung to it—but titles of nobility continued to pass through the neutro even in their First World nations, and neutros tended to be elected to the higher political offices, probably as a reflection of their historic "arbiter" role.

A lot of that had been part of the initial survey data from the Hegemony, although there'd been significant social evolution, hand-in-hand with the technological advances Sarth had achieved, over the past three Earth centuries or so. What hadn't been part of the survey data was how the geopolitical situation on Sarth had developed during that same stretch.

The planet orbited its K5v primary at approximately fifty-six million kilometers, which was only about 0.374 AU, but the system's stellar components orbited their common barycenter in 659 years with a mean separation of eighty-four AU, so 61 Cygni B's closest approach to Sarth was well over twelve billion kilometers, close to four times the distance from Earth orbit to Neptune. Which was handy, because 61 Cygni B had a considerably more active flare cycle than its more sedate sister.

The planet's radius was actually about fifty kilometers greater than Earth's but its gravity was only about 0.85 as strong, which argued for a considerably less dense planet. That made sense around a K-type dwarf, and the fact that its mass was so much lower than the giant exoplanets whose existence had been confirmed in other star systems prior to the Shongair invasion was probably the reason no one had spotted it from Earth. Despite how closely it orbited its primary, its mean temperature was only about eighteen degrees Celsius, three and a half degrees warmer than Earth's. In addition, its axial inclination was only about eight degrees, around a third of Earth's, and eighty-two percent of its surface was water, with multiple smaller island continents, both of which had a profoundly moderating influence on its seasonal variations.

Its orbital period was just over a hundred Earth days, but it had a rotational period of sixty hours. That meant a Sarthian year lasted only about forty-two *Sarthian* days. For obvious reasons, they used a base-eight numerical system, and they divided each day into more manageable day-quarters and day-halves. The local version of chlorophyll—it wasn't chlorophyll, but it did the same thing—was considerably darker than Earth's, and Sarth's vegetation was a dark green-black that produced leaves and grasses which were almost velvety looking.

By far the most advanced of the planet's continents was Sanda, and Sanda was also the source of a geopolitical rivalry which was almost comfortingly familiar to a pugnacious primate, despite the distinctly Sarthian variations which had been rung on the theme.

The wealthiest and arguably most advanced single nation on Sarth was the Republic of Dianto, a classic thalassocracy which had originated around the Gulf of Dianto in southeastern Sanda. It was, in many ways, Sarth's Athens.

And, predictably, if there was an Athens, there had to be a Sparta. That role had been taken by the Qwern Empire, on the other side of Sanda, beyond the Yaluz Mountains in southern Sanda and the Cruel Peak Mountains to the north, and whereas Dianto was a thalassocracy, the Empire had evolved out of the steppe nomad tradition of mounted warriors. The modern Republic was heir to a tradition of global maritime exploration, trade, and occasional conquest; the Empire was heir to a tradition of nomadic raids, overland expansion, and *frequent* conquest.

If Sanda was Sarth's First World, most of the Second World was composed of daughter nations of Dianto or indigenous nations which had embraced an industrial age in competition with their Diantian-descended neighbors. Those indigenous nations tended to acquire their military hardware from the Qwernians and aligned their foreign policies much more closely with the Empire than with the Republic, which produced quite a few . . . uneasy relationships, and there'd been several messy proxy wars, although none in the last twenty Earth years. Border incidents, yes; outright wars, no. Dvorak wasn't sure if that was a good sign, or a bad one.

Sarth's patterns of expansion and nation-building were also inextricably linked to its concept of clan. Like humans, Sarthians didn't fit precisely into the Hegemony's neat psychological groupings, although Dvorak had to admit the system fitted Sarth much better than it had Earth. But whereas the Hegemony's herbivores and omnivores tended to think in terms of herd to define social relationships and most of the carnivores the Hegemony had encountered tended to think in terms of pack, Sarthians were an interesting intermediate step between the Hegemony's "herd" species and humanity's focus on the individual family unit, because Sarthians thought in terms of clan, although that included rather more than just the familial relationships with which humans imbued the noun. It also embraced geographic and territorial connotations, and it was central to any Sarthian's sense of identity.

Throughout Sarthian history, the pattern had been for weaker clans to be absorbed by more powerful neighbors. Quite often, that had been by intermarriage and gradual amalgamation, but the more frequent pattern had been conquest and military defeat. After such a defeat, the conquered clan simply ceased to exist. That didn't mean its members had been systematically slaughtered by the victor—although that *had* happened upon occasion—but rather that the defeated clan, in a mechanism which resonated with the Shongairi's concept of submission, disappeared into the identity of its conqueror. There was usually quite a bit of cultural appropriation involved in the process, but the defeated clan's name and identity were relegated to history. Indeed, every Sarthian nation was named for its dominant clan.

Except one.

The Republic of Dianto was the only nation state on Sarth which was named for a geographic feature, the gulf around which it had originally taken shape, rather than for its dominant clan. And that was because in Dianto, clans didn't disappear into their conquerors' identity. Oh, once upon a time they had, but the clans of Dianto had outgrown that centuries—*Earth* centuries, not Sarthian ones—ago, choosing to cooperate with one another and to maintain their separate identities. It gave them a rather more fractious body politic, but Dvorak suspected it also had a lot to do with the Republic's role as one of the—indeed, probably the single most—influential nations on the entire planet.

It was certainly the wealthiest one, by a substantial margin, which was one of the many bones the Qwern Empire and its allies in Western Sanda had to pick with the Republic and its allied Kingdom of Shanth, in East Sanda. Over the years, the Empire had attempted to settle accounts with the Republic militarily more than once, but without success. Both nations had effectively expanded up to their natural frontiers along the mountainous spine of the continent they shared, and every pass through those mountains was covered by fortifications which would have turned André Maginot green with envy. The thought of butting one's head against those sorts of defenses was undoubtedly . . . unattractive to even the most belligerent general, and while the Qwernian Alliance was considerably more populous and had a much stronger land warfare tradition, the Diantian ability to dominate the seas and the amphibious doctrine which seemed to come naturally to it, coupled with astute diplomacy, had kept the Empire in check for the last eight hundred Diantian years.

It would be interesting, to say the least, he reflected, to see how humanity's intrusion into Sarth's long-standing international rivalries played out. He hoped devoutly that it would work out well for all concerned, but he was too much of a historian to even begin taking that for granted. His instructions had been formulated on the basis of what the Planetary Union could extrapolate from the Hegemony survey data, and he expected them to be generally applicable to the actual situation. There were going to be spots that needed tweaking, however, and as he looked at those images and thought of the task before him, he couldn't avoid wondering if Earth's diplomatic mission—which meant *him,* when all was said and done—would end up being the best thing that had ever happened to Sarth . . . or the worst.

III

CITY OF KWYZO NAR QWERN, QWERN EMPIRE,
PLANET SARTH

"Stop!" Clan Ruler Juzhyr XI thundered, ous nasal flaps tightly closed in anger. Ous nasal flaps stayed closed as ou glared at ous ministers. "I asked you here to discuss the arrival of the aliens, not to run around like syldaks with your heads cut off. If you can't control yourselves, I have no need of your advice. Now either sit down like rational Sarthians *or get out!*"

Silence reigned in the chamber as the ministers looked at the floor or the ceiling—anywhere but at Juzhyr—and those who had launched themselves from their chairs sat back down.

"Now," Juzhyr said once everyone was seated and the silence had gone on for several *very* uncomfortable seelaqs, "I would like to get your thoughts on what the arrival of these—" like the majority of the Sarthians, ou had trouble pronouncing the aliens' race "—these 'Earthians' means to us. Erylk?"

Chancellor Erylk ErGarzHyn nar Qwern, Flock Lord Dyrzhyba, shook ous head in acknowledgment. As Juzhyr's senior minister, ou had the privilege of speaking first. Ou also had the right to speak *last*, letting ous colleagues expose their arguments to ous fire first, and ou often exercised that right. Ou was, however, Juzhyr's most trusted advisor, and Juzhyr, obviously wanted to hear from oum first.

"I would urge caution, Clan Ruler, before we make too many assumptions," ou said. "We've only just been contacted by them, and we don't know anything about them. We need to find out more about their intentions before we make too many long-term plans."

"I would also counsel raising the alert level of the military," Myrcal MyrFarZol nar Qwern, Flock Lord Hantyr, added. "We know they *say* they come in peace; however, that doesn't necessarily mean they truly have peaceful intentions. All anyone needs to do is look at Dianto if they doubt the common sense behind that—Prime Director Qwelth keeps talking about how all Dianto wants is peace, but look at the alliance ou's assembled! Dianto has ally nations across the entire globe!"

"I agree that would be wise, Clan Lord," Flythyr MuzTolFlyth nar Qwern, Flock Lord Consort Pantyl, added. "I've already put our forces on a higher alert footing in case they're needed. We might also want to activate some of our reserve forces—especially our special operations forces. They may eventually be needed, and we'll want to have them in place, if they are."

"Yes, yes," Juzhyr replied, shaking ous head at the Minister of the Army in vigorous agreement, "it makes sense that we should do so." Ous eyes moved on to take in the other ministers. "What I'm more interested in, though, is how we can put ourselves in a position of advantage, and what opportunities there are for us in these negotiations."

"If nothing else," Chancellor Erylk noted, "we're on an equal footing with Dianto with respect to the aliens when we meet with them at the Nonagon. They've made it plain they're here to talk to everyone, so for once we don't have to worry about Dianto and its allies subverting the process—they won't be able to use their vassal states to block us the way they do at most Nonagon meetings."

"Regarding opportunities," Herdsman Stal StalTarChal nar Qwern said, "I feel we need to take advantage of everything the aliens offer us." The Minister of Industry raised both nasal flaps to smile at Juzhyr in obvious anticipation. "Given that they've crossed space to get here, their level of technology has to be much higher than ours. This represents opportunity.

"The more we can learn from them," ou continued, "the more we'll strengthen our position here on Sarth, as well as with the aliens. I would counsel that our answer be 'Yes!' to any offer the aliens make. Myrcal isn't wrong in counseling that we keep our eyes open to ensure they are indeed what they say they are, but I feel we need to be open and accepting of any opportunities."

"I agree," Juzhyr said. "Not only ones that are offered in formal negotiations, but especially those we can broker out of sight of our enemies."

"Especially any military opportunities," Flythyr interjected. "We can't allow Dianto to get any of the alien technology we don't."

"Agreed," Juzhyr replied. "But I don't want to focus solely on opportunities with military application. As Stal noted, the aliens crossed the stars to get here. It's impossible to know what technology they have that will give us an advantage. Not every military victory comes through force of arms. Perhaps there will be a resource they need—like oil—which we have and Dianto doesn't. Trading with the aliens might give us an economic advantage over the Diantians. Perhaps in return, the aliens will give us new technology that we can turn into military hardware."

"That should definitely be part of our approach," Myrcal agreed. "They say they've come here to find allies. Obviously, they need those allies badly or they wouldn't have come such a vast distance to get them, and if we could acquire the new technology Stal and Flythyr are talking about and use it to gain supremacy over the Diantians, we could negotiate with them as first among the nations of Sarth. Given how sorely they seem to need allies, they might well welcome that sort of simplification of our planet's politics. Especially—" ous nasal flaps smiled cynically "—if they don't have to bring it about themselves!"

One or two of ous colleagues' nasal flaps seemed more dubious than ous did. The clan ruler's did not, however, and Chancellor Erylk shook ous own head in at least conditional agreement.

"It's agreed, then," Juzhyr said. "We will attend the meeting at the Nonagon, and we will be on the lookout for all opportunities which may come our way. Especially those which don't involve the Diantians."

· · · · ·

HERDSMAN CHOLKYR CHOLANGEN nar Qwern, the Qwern Empire's Minister of Agriculture, nodded ous head slightly as ou followed the rest of the ministers out of the room. No one noticed oum except during periods of famine and crop failure, and then it was only to make oum the scapesorqh and target of abuse. Ous opinions on matters often ran counter to those of the others, as well, which ou knew also didn't help oum in the long run.

Sure, the Diantians and their treaty partners had amassed a large number of allies across Sarth, but was that because they really wanted to bully Qwern, or was it that they were responding to the threat of the Qwern Empire as they perceived it? They were merchants, after all, rather than the proud descendants of warriors, so it was more likely they'd rather have the smallest military they thought they could get away with—traders only looked at the price tag, didn't they?—and militaries were expensive! Cholkyr was *very* familiar with the cost of feeding one; ou saw the figures on ous desk every day.

Cholkyr couldn't voice that opinion in front of Myrcal, though—the other neutro was xenophobically suspicious of anyone from outside Clan Qwern, as well as anyone who stuck up for them. Mentioning that possibility would only get Cholkyr a massive amount of abuse from Myrcal—and probably Juzhyr, as well—and ou knew from past experience that no one would jump in to support oum. *Why bother mentioning it, then?*

Similarly, no one saw—or was willing to mention, at least—the logical fallacy buried in their proposals to "get ahead of the Diantians." Yes, the Earthians clearly needed allies badly, but they'd also said they wanted to disrupt Sarthian society "no more than they had to." Assuming they were being truthful about that, it struck Cholkyr as unlikely they'd be giving either side technology that could be used to gain supremacy over the other. Myrcal and his ilk could plot and plan all they wanted, but ou didn't think it would work out the way they hoped, and ou was worried about what they'd do when that happened.

IV

THE NONAGON, CITY OF LYZAN, RYZAK ISLAND, PLANET SARTH

Yerdaz NorYerDar nar Qwern, Charioteer Consort Zyr, reminded herself to watch her nasal flaps as she stood on the front steps of the Nonagon with far too many other Sarthians. She felt especially crowded because there was no one at all in Accord Square, the vast plaza in front of the Nonagon. That enormous sweep of colorful pavement lay bare and gleaming under the sun, without even the kiosks for food vendors or the scattered, welcoming clusters of dining tables which usually dotted its expanse. She knew why it was clear, but that didn't make her any happier. She didn't much care for being surrounded by a rabble which included so many commoners at the best of times, and given the ancient Qwernian tradition—no one would *possibly* do that now, of course—of resolving interpersonal problems with a discreet assassination, she felt particularly nervous surrounded by so many who wished the Empire such scant good fortune.

That reaction was a throwback to days long past, and most of the time she knew it. Today wasn't "most of the time," however, and she concentrated on looking suitably impassive and unimpressed as she and her fellow diplomats—and every other Syraq, Shyk, and Shydo who could find an excuse to be there—awaited the "Earthians'" arrival. Not that she was likely to fool anyone, but a noble of Clan Qwern was supposed to remember who she represented.

"Four kysaqs out," someone murmured. Her head twitched, but she suppressed the reflex that would have looked in the speaker's direction.

"I don't see anything," someone else replied.

"Me neither," the first speaker agreed. "That's what somebody just said, though."

"Well, doesn't look like they know anything more than we do. In fact—"

"Look!" another voice intruded. "There!"

As directions went, "there" wasn't especially useful, Yerdaz reflected irritably. Not, at least, when it wasn't accompanied by a pointing digit or *something* to give it what those in the diplomatic community liked to call "context." The tart amusement of the thought—and of how unmercifully her spouses would have teased her over it—did more to relax her than she would have believed possible at a moment like this. Still—

Despite her earlier resolve, her nasal flaps flared as sunlight glinted far above.

It was more nearly directly overhead than she'd anticipated, although perhaps that shouldn't have surprised her. It *was* coming from outer space, after all.

She craned her neck, shading her eyes with one hand as she gazed at the rapidly growing sparkle of sunlight as avidly as any mud-footed peasant. Part of her really wanted to look away, if only to emphasize her poise, but she couldn't. She truly *couldn't,* and as she gazed, she suddenly realized one of the reasons she couldn't.

Yerdaz NorYerDar was an accomplished pilot. In fact, Lance Yerdaz had been a major contributor to the Imperial Army Air Force's development of close support doctrine when she'd been on active duty, back before Flock Lord Hantyr had lured her away to a diplomatic career. She was licensed in both single and multi-engine aircraft, and she'd helped write the IAAF's syllabus for dive bombers. She was intimately familiar with what aircraft could and couldn't do . . . which meant that unlike many of the sorqhs around her, she knew they couldn't do *that.*

That . . . vehicle—she wasn't prepared to call it an "aircraft" at this point— wasn't circling as it descended, wasn't losing altitude as it approached. It was simply coming down. *Straight* down, like an elevator, and a tiny, irrational part of her insisted that meant it was about to crash. Only it obviously wasn't doing *that,* either. Instead, it was simply sliding smoothly down that invisible elevator shaft in an obviously controlled descent. And as it got closer, she began to realize just how enormous it actually was. She'd thought it was at a much lower altitude, but it just continued to grow and grow and grow.

The biggest combat aircraft the IAAF owned—the twin-engined Haruk bomber—was less than two cherans long. Even the mammoth four-engined Great Starth transport was only a bit *over* two cherans. But this thing—this "*shuttle*"—was stupendous. In fact, she realized with a sort of numb disbelief as it slid into a smooth—and impossible—hover directly overhead, its length was within a couple of tyrans of the Diantian Navy's Hydak-class dirigibles, the biggest aircraft ever built on Sarth. But this was no dirigible, no lighter-than-air ship with its gas cells filled with hydrogen. Just one of its wings was as long as two Great Starths laid end-to-end! And as she stared at the preposterous monster, she wondered why it even *had* wings, since it obviously didn't need them.

. . . . .

"THINK THEY'VE ABSORBED the message, Dad?" Captain Malachi Dvorak asked with a grin, looking out the *Starlander*'s window at the throng of Sarthians below.

"I know not this message of which you speak." His father gave him his best innocent look, and Malachi snorted. He had his mother's coloring and, Dave Dvorak thought sadly, her obvious lack of respect for his own august dignity.

"The message where we hover overhead like the hammer of doom," the youthful Space Marine said helpfully.

"Like I told them, we come in peace," Dvorak replied. "And I hardly think you can call an unarmed shuttle the 'hammer of doom,' Malachi."

"I'll give you 'unarmed' in terms of bombs, ground attack missiles, and things like that," his undutiful offspring said. "I see that you somehow managed to miss mentioning the *Starhawks,* though. For that matter, if any of them try shooting at us they're going to find out that things like point defense autocannon do a damn good job of strafing, too."

"There was no need to mention the *'Hawks* to them. They can't see them with anything they've got, so it's like they were never even there. Unless we need them of course. And I'm sure we won't. Says that right in the mission plan somewhere."

"What was that Burns poem you always liked to recite to us when we were kids? Something about ganging agley, I think?"

"Disrespectful young whelp, that's what *you* are!" his father said with a grin, although Malachi had a point.

This wasn't a standard *Starlander,* and there was plenty of room to hide things like retractable point defense systems in a six-hundred-foot-long fuselage. And the quartet of *Starhawk* transatmospheric fighters flying top cover— mere minnows, almost fifty feet shorter than an old jumbo jet—could have turned the entire city of Lyzan into a parking lot.

Not, as he'd told his son, that they had any intention of letting something like that happen.

"Just doing my job, Mister Ambassador Plenipotentiary, Sir. Mom told me to keep you humble. And my point stands."

"The one about messages?" His father joined him, looking down on the beautifully manicured grounds of the Nonagon, and shrugged. "Probably. Couldn't hurt anything, anyway."

"I'd feel a lot better if you'd let me bring my Heinlein." Malachi's tone was more sober than it had been, and his father looked at him. "Mom also told me to be sure you get home in one piece," his son said. "She said something about the last time she let you and Uncle Rob out of her sight unsupervised."

"Damn. She is *never* going to let me live that one down, is she?"

"Not after you scared the shit out of her that way, no. Not so much. Or not until twenty-three minutes before the energy death of the universe, at least."

Dvorak snorted, but a part of him agreed Malachi had a point. On the other hand, the whole notion of "coming in peace" might seem just a tad undercut if his son accompanied him to the first meeting wearing the equivalent of a main battle tank. And there was no way to disguise someone in Heinlein battle armor as anything but what he was: the most lethal individual soldier in the history of humanity. On the other hand . . .

He glanced over his shoulder, and Jasmine Sherman smiled blandly back at him. There was security, and there was *security*, he reflected, and returned her smile before he turned back to the window again. He gazed out it for several more seconds, then inhaled sharply and looked at the Navy commander standing beside him.

"Tell Lieutenant Theodore she can go ahead and set us down, Commander. I'm sure she'll be happy about that."

"Yes, Mister Secretary." The commander came briefly to attention, then keyed his personal com link. "We're authorized to land, Lieutenant."

No one else could hear the pilot's response, but the *Starlander* resumed its smooth descent, and Dvorak turned back to the window once again.

The *Starlander* was capable of vertical takeoffs and landings, especially with its improved and more efficient counter-grav, but most pilots preferred to make an airfoil approach. That was why they had wings, after all, and even with human-engineered counter-grav, a *Starlander* could carry twice as much cargo on an airfoil flight profile as it could relying solely on counter-grav. Cargo weight wasn't really a factor this time around, though. There were barely sixty people in his entire entourage—he *liked* that word: entourage. It carried such implications of pompous importance!—so there was plenty of reserve grav lift for the vertical approach he'd decreed. And while he himself would never have been so crude as to use phrases like "hammer of doom," Malachi had grasped the essential purpose behind his decision.

Sarthians were accustomed to dirigibles, so in one sense "lighter-than-air" might not be all that impressive to them. But they weren't accustomed to *heavier*-than-air aircraft that could simply hover above them, and it wouldn't hurt a thing for them to have a visual reminder that the aliens about to land among them weren't the sort of people you really wanted to piss off.

In a lot of ways, he agreed with his brother-in-law and Abu Bakr that a more armed-up initial contact might have been a good idea. Malachi and his Heinlein would have been a very reassuring presence at his back this afternoon. But they were supposed to be making friends with these people, and the mission brief had been very clear on the point that he was supposed to concentrate on talking softly and not flourish any bigger sticks than he had to. Philosophically, he was totally onboard with that, but the last thing they needed was to send any messages of weakness, either. So perhaps his son's "hammer of doom" analogy was well taken, after all.

· · · · ·

"HOLY EXCREMENT," QWELTH QwelSynChar murmured as ou watched the stupendous aircraft settle towards Accord Square. The vast concourse could accommodate thousands . . . and was barely big enough for that monster to find a footing. No wonder the aliens had requested that it be kept clear!

"From your lips to Chelth's crest," Zhor ZhorSalDyr said. "Although, I'm not sure that's exactly the sort of prayer Ou likes to hear. It does sort of sum things up nicely, though."

"Thank you." Qwelth curled ous nasal flaps ironically. "Tell me *you* aren't as . . . impressed as I am."

"I'm hovering somewhere between impressed and scared excrementless," Zhor replied.

"I imagine that's pretty much what they had in mind. Smart of them, really. I imagine a lot of our esteemed colleagues are busy digesting the message."

"Those that aren't thinking about ways they can steal the technology," Zhor said.

"Well, in that case, it's your job to see to it that they don't. Or that they don't get their hands on any more goodies than we do, at any rate."

"*My* job? I'm just a lowly foreign minister. You're the Prime Director around here!"

"And I intend to rely heavily on your expertise. And to blame you for anything that goes wrong, of course."

"Oh, of course."

Qwelth chuckled, but ou also looked across the width of the Nonagon's enormous portico at the Qwernian delegation. Ou wasn't all that fond of Yerdaz NorYerDar, although ou had to admit the Charioteer Consort of Zyr was less mindlessly anti-Republic than many of her colleagues. Unfortunately, that just made her more dangerous. Opponents who thought about things made far more formidable foes than those who simply charged in.

In a lot of ways, ou wished Juzhyr had come in person. Ou and the clan ruler had only met one another four times during Qwelth's sixty-year tenure as Prime Director. It was a pain in the excreter, because ou'd always thought they might have been able to iron out at least some of their nations' differences if they'd only been able to talk face-to-face instead of through bevies of diplomats, each of whom inevitably shaped the discussion. But the clan ruler's dignity had to be protected at all costs. That was an essential part of Qwernian psychology, and it also meant the clan ruler always had the option of renouncing anything ous representative said as having been unauthorized or garbled in transmission. Even more to the point, perhaps, Qwernian notions of proper behavior . . . differed from those of the Republic. The rule of custom was far more important to the Empire than the rule of law, which was one of the most frustrating things about negotiating international compacts with it. But while the clan ruler's diplomatic corps was totally free to lie, cheat, steal, and connive with the best of them, *ou* wasn't. If Juzhyr gave ous word, ous own people would damned well expect oum to keep it.

That was why ou went so far out of ous way to avoid any situation in which ou might do that.

Qwelth, on the other hand, was a simple prime director, not a crowned head of state, and a commoner, to boot. Normally that meant ou was far down the pecking order, at least in the eyes of the Empire. But it also meant ou could attend any gathering ou chose in person without worrying about protecting ous dignity or who might think that ou'd given ous personal word about something.

Which was why ou got to be here in person, watching with ous own eyes at what was undoubtedly the most momentous event in the entire history of Sarth.

· · · · ·

YERDAZ NORYERDAR STOOD in her place of honor behind Gyrdan FarSylGyr nor Howsyn, the current Speaker of the Nonagon. Gyrdan was also Sword Lord Consort Symkah and deplorably Diantian in his general outlook, but, as was an unspoken tradition at the Nonagon, he was neither from the Republic nor the Empire. In fact, he was from Desqwer, one of the two Diantian-descended nations of the continent of Deltar. The other Diantian daughter state of Deltar was Synchanat, and the pair of them shared one of the nine voting seats on the Nonagon. The indigenous nations of Deltar—Andryth, Chayzar, Serdian, and Ryzh—also shared a seat, and while everyone pretended not to realize it, the indigenous nations were firmly in the Empire's sphere of influence, since the Qwernian military had supported them in more than one border clash with their "foreign conqueror" neighbors. They'd been handed their reproductive members on each occasion, unfortunately, but that was fine with the Empire. The clan ruler and ous bearer had bought a lot of goodwill replacing the tanks, guns, and rifles they'd managed to lose.

As Desqwerians went, Gyrdan wasn't that bad, and he always scrupulously honored the letter of the diplomatic code. Yerdaz would have felt better with a fellow Qwernian in the Speakership, but Gyrdan would do, she supposed.

She glanced from the corner of her eye at Prime Director Qwelth. This morning had been as carefully choreographed as any moment in Sarthian history, allowing for the fact that they'd had barely two days to set everything up. And, as always happened at formal moments, the Nonagon's permanent staff had been careful to put at least three other delegates between Yerdaz and Qwelth. The two of them would have to make nice at the formal dinner tonight, which would be tedious but part of the normal political theater. They might actually have something to discuss this time, although both of them would obviously be watching their words very carefully.

The stupendous aircraft—although it would probably be more accurate to call it a spaceship, Yerdaz supposed—sat there, gleaming in the sun. Then a hatch opened far up on its side and a disk of what appeared to be metal a couple of cherans across floated out of it. There was no visible means of support, although the disk was the better part of a ran thick, so gods only knew what sort of alien technology might be hidden inside it. Whatever was holding it up, it was clearly rock steady—a point it demonstrated as half a sixteen of . . . beings stepped out of the hatch onto it and it didn't even bobble.

It stayed where it was for a moment, then slid silently to the multi-hued pavement, and Yerdaz heard a collective sigh of indrawn breaths as Sarthian eyes finally beheld the aliens who'd crossed the stars to reach them.

They wore an awful lot of clothing, was Yerdaz' first thought. Rather than the simple trousers or kilts of Sarth, they appeared to favor a wide variety of garments. Including ones that covered their entire torsos, which seemed . . . bizarre. And their cranial down seemed to come in an incredible profusion of shades. She could see at least four just looking at them, so with their scale patterns covered and such a bewildering palette of down, how did they recognize genders?

Some of them wore headgear which hid most of their down, as if they were deliberately making that recognition even harder. Maybe that was some kind of species modesty taboo? And how could they hope to hear anything with their crests covered that way?

Only they didn't *have* crests, she realized with a sense of shock. And they had repulsively—or possibly exotically—flat faces, with no muzzle at all and what looked like feeble little jaws that would have trouble chewing anything. At least their eyes were in roughly the right place, although she wondered what the flaps on the sides of their heads were for.

Then their hovering platform reached the ground, and Yerdaz swallowed as she realized another thing about the aliens. Even standing flatly on their wide, spatula feet, they were *huge*! Oh, a couple of them were no taller than a tall male or female, but most of them—!

The platform settled. Most of the Earthians stood in what were probably respectful poses as one of them stepped off onto the pavement, and Yerdaz swallowed again. At just over one and a quarter rans, she was tall, even for a female, but this alien—this Earthian—would have towered over her. She—or he; something that size simply *couldn't* be a bearer—was over two full seqrans taller than Yerdaz, and the Earthian's shoulders were at least half again as broad.

The alien stepped forward, moving with a flat-footed, undeniably ponderous-looking stride, to where Gyrdan waited alone to greet the visitors.

. . . . .

DVORAK KEPT HIS eyes resolutely on the single Sarthian waiting to greet him. What he wanted to do was to gawk at the crowd at the Speaker's back. The color palette of their kilts was an armed assault on a human's optic nerve, which only emphasized the fact that Sarthian eyes and human eyes didn't see things the same way, to put it mildly. Fortunately, there wasn't a whole lot of clothing in evidence. Sarthians experienced very little temperature variation, given their planet's lack of axial inclination, so standard daytime wear consisted only of the bare minimum—his lips twitched in a totally inappropriate smile at his choice of adjective—to modestly conceal their reproductive organs.

Unlike the Sarthians, he'd at least spent months watching them on tridee, so their appearance wasn't coming at him cold, the way his must be coming at them. But there was a distinct difference between watching images and seeing them in the flesh. For one thing, their diminutive size was much more apparent now, and so was the peculiar, fluid grace of their stride. They really did move a lot like Jurassic Park's velociraptors, he thought, although without quite as much "bounce."

He reached the waiting Speaker and raised both arms, forearms crossed before him in the formal Sarthian salute between equals to whom one had not yet been introduced, and the Speaker—Gyrdan—returned it. Then Dvorak lowered his arms and cleared his throat.

I will not *say "Klaatu barada nikto," whatever Rob wants!* he reminded himself. Although, he admitted, the temptation was great. Once the Sarthians discovered human movies, though, they might be less than amused. Not that his chosen phrase would be all that much better if they decided to take it that way. Still, he had to say something, so best to proceed as he'd already begun.

"Greetings, Speaker Gyrdan," he said, his translator converting the words to the Desqwerian dialect Gyrdan had grown up speaking. "My name is David Dvorak, and I have the honor of serving as the Planetary Union of Earth's Secretary of State. On behalf of my President and all the people of Earth, I greet you.

"We come in peace."

THE NONAGON, CITY OF LYZAN, RYZAK ISLAND, PLANET SARTH

I t was nice to see that humans weren't the only species that did things its own way because . . . well, because That's the Way Things Are Done, Dave Dvorak reflected. He'd offered to give every delegate to the Nonagon his/her/ous own human-made earbuds (except that they were actually a very narrow headset designed to fit over the Sarthian crest) to translate into every Sarthian language simultaneously. But the Nonagon's staff had politely refused. So, instead, they had him speaking to all of them in Speaker Gyrdan's native tongue while an entire staff of Sarthian translators murmured over *Sarthian*-made headsets which were far bigger and clunkier than the hardware he'd been prepared to provide. He couldn't quite figure out why a native Sarthian's translation of a Sarthian translation of English was superior to a direct translation, but it wasn't his planet.

The enormous Hall of Nations, the Nonagon's official meeting chamber, was packed. The delegates and their staffs were seated at ornate podium-like desks, and the spectators' gallery was standing room only. Those desks were rather taller, proportionately, than humans would have preferred, but then Sarthian torsos were longer and their shoulders and elbows were jointed differently. Their thighs were proportionately shorter than their calves, as well, which gave their chairs a contour that was distinctly odd by human standards. He didn't think he'd be very comfortable perched in one of them for long. Worse, none of the Sarthians he'd met so far came as high as his shoulder, so he was pretty sure he'd feel like he was sitting at the kiddie table, anyway.

And isn't that a splendid example of thinking about inconsequential nonsense to pretend I'm not about to pee myself up here?

He snorted and couldn't quite suppress the grin that thought evoked. Fortunately, Sarthians didn't have a clue how to read human expressions yet. Still, there were standards to be met as his species' top diplomat, he reminded himself sternly as Gyrdan finished his introduction.

"And so, Members of the Nonagon," the Speaker concluded, "it is my responsibility and my honor to yield the podium to Secretary of State David Dvorak."

The title he actually assigned Dvorak was *chirzahlk*, which didn't translate *exactly* as "Secretary," but came close enough. On the other hand, he absolutely butchered the pronunciation of "Cavid Dcorak," although Dvorak was confident the Sarthian had come closer to getting it right than he could have come to pronouncing Gyrdan's name and title without cybernetic assistance. Then the Speaker stepped back, crossing his forearms, and bent his head slightly as he invited Dvorak to take his place.

The human stepped up to the podium, which—predictably—was far too short for him. There was no equivalent of the teleprompter a pre-invasion human diplomat or politician would have used, but that didn't matter.

"Bring it up, Calamity," he murmured so softly no one could possibly have heard.

"Yes, Papi," the AI replied in Maighread's voice, and the text of his remarks suddenly appeared before him, floating in midair as the computer projected them onto his corneas. Not that he really needed them.

"Thank you for introducing me, Speaker Gyrdan," he began, turning to give a human-style bow to the Sarthian. He was careful to move slowly, making certain that his audience would recognize that it was a formal gesture on his part. The fact that Sarthians nodded their heads when they disagreed and shook their heads when they agreed was something he'd have to bear in mind.

"And I would like to thank all of the Nonagon's members for permitting me to address you," he continued, turning back to the crowded chamber before him. "It's a great honor to be the first representative of my species to speak to you here, on your home world, in your own chamber. It's also exciting, because you are the first non-human species we've voluntarily contacted. This is the sort of thing that someone gets to do for the first time only once, and I think it's inevitable that all of us will be going down in our own species' history books."

He paused to let that settle in . . . and for the merely mortal Sarthian translators to do their jobs. Then he straightened and squared his shoulders.

"Exciting as this moment is, however," he said in a more somber tone whose weightiness he hoped his audience would recognize, "we did not come all this way just for the adventure. We came to warn you. And we also came because, frankly, we're seeking allies."

He watched the stir rustle through the Hall of Nations, and the translation software threw a faint orange overlay across his vision. The translator had been loaded with Sarthian body language and micro-expressions, culled from literally decades of the survey footage in the Hegemony's data base, then run through sophisticated analytical algorithms. It had apparently never occurred to the Hegemony's psychiatrists to do that, which was fortunate for the human race. Dvorak hated to think what would have happened to Judson Howell if the Shongairi had possessed the equivalent of a lie detector every time he spoke to one of them!

Human psychs had used micro-expression analysis for decades, however, and they'd seen the possibilities almost instantly. The legal system had moved promptly to limit their use in both marketing and court testimony—which Dvorak thought was an interesting juxtaposition—but the new software could read human emotions with devastating accuracy. It could also parse them with a subtlety which would have been almost useless in most conversations simply because of information overload, so the psychiatrists and the programmers had come up with a color-valued system which used the six basic emotions Paul Ekman had identified in the middle of the last century: anger, disgust, fear, happiness, sadness, and surprise.

If Dvorak had wanted to, he could have set the software for a detailed analysis of emotions presented in text format, projected onto his corneas. Trying to read and digest the information would have been a nightmare, however, so the default setting tied each emotion to a specific color. Then the software overlaid them on an individual's face—or, as in this case, on a large group of people—with a weighted intensity reflective of the depth of the emotion in question, blending them into distinctive hues. It had taken him a while to get used to it, but he'd practiced diligently on his human companions on the long voyage from Earth, and (always assuming the people who'd analyzed *Sarthian* emotions had gotten their sums right) what he was seeing now was a combination of surprise's red and an edge of fear's yellow projected across the delegates as a group.

Could really have used this playing Spades all those years, he thought, waiting for the motion to subside once again.

"My people were attacked, without warning or provocation, by a species which calls itself the Shongairi," he continued then, his tone steady and level. "We were at a somewhat more advanced level of technology than Sarth has yet achieved, but they were far, far more advanced than we were. Fortunately for us, however, they were grossly overconfident when they attacked us. The Shongairi think of themselves as a warrior race, but they discovered we were better warriors than they were. Their technology was vastly superior to ours, but they hadn't applied it to war-fighting as thoroughly as we had applied ours. It also helped that they'd expected us to be at a much more primitive level than we'd actually attained. In the end, we proved too much for them to digest. Indeed, in the end, we captured their ships and gained access to their entire tech base. The species which came to conquer and enslave us ended up giving us the stars, instead."

Just as well not to mention little things like "vampires" at this point, Dave, he thought dryly as he paused once again to let that sink in. *Always time for that later, if we need it. And I agree with Rob and Abu. Longbow was right when he suggested we keep their capabilities in reserve.*

"Our people had developed advanced versions of the 'analyzers' with which Sarth has been experimenting," he went on after a moment. "We call them 'computers,' instead, but they evolved in much the same way your analyzers have. Indeed, much of the original impetus for them came from our military, just as it has from yours, as we developed fire control systems for our warships. Ours, however, had advanced beyond the point of simply performing numerical operations to systems which also used and stored data and information. Like a wire recording, but in much greater detail and with text and visual images, as well.

"Just as our pre-invasion computers were more advanced than your present analyzers, however, the Shongairi's computers were far more advanced than ours. In fact, they contained not simply the scientific and technological data-base of a vast, interstellar civilization which calls itself the 'Galactic Hegemony,' but its entire history, as well. And it also contained the documentation of how and why the Hegemony had authorized the Shongair Empire to conquer and enslave us. It was because it deemed us dangerous primitives who would per-haps upset the status quo the Hegemony has maintained for over half a million of your years. Because it feared—rightly—that humans would never stop asking 'why' or seeking answers to the endless questions the universe itself represents. Because anything—and anyone—the Hegemony believes might pose a threat to that sacred stability, that *stasis,* must be crushed, and its ruling Council fully intended for the Shongairi to crush *us.*"

He paused once again, turning his head to make eye contact with as many of the delegates as possible, and wished they'd taken his offer of translator earbuds so that the software could have translated his tone into its Sarthian equivalent for all of them and not just the Nonogon translators. Although, now that he thought about it, the software was certainly adding that tone when it trans-lated his English into Desqwerian. Anyone out there who spoke that language needed no translators . . . and all of them were probably hearing the emotional overtones the software was inserting into it.

"I tell you this in part because the reason we've come to Sarth is that we found your planet and your star system in the Hegemony's records." Another, sharper stir ran through his audience, and the overlay was far more yellow than orange this time. "They have been observing you, at widespread intervals, for a quarter million of your years, and just as they evaluated us, they've evaluated *you.*

"Honesty compels me to admit that they don't seem to find your people quite as . . . unsettling as they found mine. From their files, they do find Sar-thians disturbingly violent, prone to bloodshed, and generally less than de-sirable as interstellar neighbors, but not to nearly the extent they applied that same judgment to my own species. And at the moment, your civilization falls into a category which enjoys at least limited protection under their law—as, indeed, ours ought to have been protected when the Shongairi arrived in our star system. The Shongairi chose to ignore the protections written into the Hegemony's fundamental law, however, and they did so because they were confident that was precisely what the rest of the Hegemony wanted them to do."

He paused once again for the translators.

"I believe they were correct about what the rest of the Hegemony wanted from them," he said then. "The Hegemony's rulers felt far more strongly about the Shongairi than they currently feel about Sarth, but the Shongairi attained interstellar flight out of their own resources, at which point the Hegemony's Constitution required the other member races to grant them at least provisional Hegemony membership. As you, we hadn't yet achieved that, although we were much closer than you presently are. Yet they felt even more repugnance and fear in our case than in the Shongairi's, and so they chose to use the Shongairi to neutralize the threat to their peace of mind that we represented. And if neutralizing that 'threat' required the extermination of our entire species, that would have been quite acceptable from their perspective. Especially since they could have blamed it upon the 'bloodthirsty' Shongairi, rather than their own highly moral races."

He hoped the software—and the Sarthian translators—had communicated the savage irony of his last sentence.

"As I say, at this moment, you would be classified by the Hegemony's surveyors as a Level Four civilization, which enjoys certain protections, but not those which apply—or are *supposed* to apply, at any rate—to a Level Three or Level Two civilization, such as ours was when the Shongairi arrived. You would still be considered in or on the very fringe of primitivism by their evaluators, because you have not yet achieved what we call fission, fusion, advanced electronics, an orbit-based communications system, or the other technologies which form the necessary steps to independently attaining interstellar flight. As such, the Hegemony Council could still decide to authorize your conquest or destruction.

"In honesty, it's unlikely they would do that in your case. Indeed, it was unusual for it to happen in *our* case. Generally speaking, the Hegemony operates on the theory that truly bellicose species will probably destroy themselves once they acquire sufficiently advanced weapons, which means the Hegemony doesn't have to step in and do it for them. And again, in fairness, that's generally been what's happened.

"Earth's experience, however, demonstrates the Hegemony's willingness to give self-destruction a little help whenever that seems best to its member species. From my own study of their historical record, I believe they've done that rather more often than even the Shongairi realized. And I'm afraid there's no guarantee they won't come to the same decision in your case, the next time one of their survey ships orbits tracelessly beyond your atmosphere and discovers just how much more technologically capable you've become since their last visit.

"The people of my planet are just as rambunctious, truculent, and determined to forge our own destiny as the Hegemony feared we were, and their actions have pushed us even farther in that direction, at least where they themselves are concerned. They killed three quarters of our entire species. We don't intend for them to kill any more of us. Nor do we think, having reviewed the Hegemony's records of its previous visits here and our own study of your world over the space of one of your years, that Sarthians would take kindly to the role of domesticated animals, forced to renounce innovation, change, and *freedom of thought* lest you disturb the sacred interstellar status quo. And that's why we've come to you. To warn you, and to tell you our story. To *show* you our story in visual records of the Shongair invasion and what it cost us. To show you what we've achieved already, the ways in which we have not simply acquired the Hegemony's technology but significantly improved upon it. And to offer you friendship, alliance, and access to that same technology if, after hearing what we have to tell you, you freely choose to join us in our stand against an interstellar tyranny so absolute that it considers the eradication of entire intelligent species acceptable collateral damage if it preserves the stasis it has embraced."

The vast Hall of Nations was silent as he paused, letting that sink fully home. Then he straightened his spine and raised his head.

"You don't have to listen to us. We won't attempt to compel you in any way. And it's likely—far from certain, but *likely*—that rather than their destroying you, Sarth would simply be absorbed, willingly or unwillingly, into the Hegemony on the day you achieve independent interstellar flight. The choice is yours, but we've come to *offer* you that choice. To give you the option to be something other than one more cog in the Hegemony's enormous machine. To remain Sarthians, with your identity and your institutions, your hopes and your aspirations—your entire way of life—still intact. Still *yours,* to do with as *you* choose. Those are your possible futures. We've come to tell you that, and to offer you our aid if you, too, choose to remain who you are.

"But I warn you, and you must understand, that that choice is not the choice of safety. The Hegemony is enormous, far vaster than you could even conceive without viewing its own records, and so far, we're a single star system and a single planet whose population will need at least three of your centuries to recover from the billions of deaths we've suffered. We're like a buzzing insect around a starth's ears, in many ways. But this insect has a dangerous sting already, and we intend to become far more dangerous still before we meet the Hegemony again at a time and a place of *our* choosing. They've tried to destroy us once. It's entirely possible they'll try again when they discover they failed . . . and this time, succeed. But I tell all of Sarth this: should they make that attempt, it will be the most terrible—and the bloodiest—mistake they have ever made."

.   .   .   .   .

"SO, WHAT DO *you* make of all this, Yerdaz?"

The charioteer consort looked up from the cup of hot terahk the server had just refreshed and quirked a sardonic nasal flap.

"And what, pray tell, makes you think that my opinion is going to be based on anything solider than everyone else's, Feltik?"

Feltik JohrShym shorak Weyrsol, the head of the Chayzarian delegation to the Nonagon snorted.

"I could say it's because you're so brilliant and insightful that I anticipate learning a great deal from your always pithy observations," he replied. "Or I could be more honest and say that it's because you have a lot more military background than I do, which means you're probably in a better position to assess what these Earthians have told us—so far—about the 'Shongairi' and the Hegemony bogeyman they're here to find help against. Or I could be even more honest than that and say that because you're Clan Ruler Juzhyr's personal representative, whatever judgments you do form—however brilliant and insightful they may or may not be—are going to carry a lot of weight, not just here at the Nonagon, but back home in Chayzar."

One thing about the Deltaran male, Yerdaz reflected. He didn't beat around the bush very much, and he did have a point. Several of them, in fact.

"Well," she sat back, nursing her terahk in both hands and opening her nasal flaps wide to inhale its rich, strong aroma, "I'd have to say that this . . . David—" she took her time to come as close to pronouncing the bizarre name correctly as she could "—is an impressive male, if only for his size."

"Size isn't everything," Kwysar HalSyn shorak Andryth put in from the chair beside Feltik's. Kwysar was the head of the Andrythian delegation, and he and Feltik were old friends and cronies. The two males had invited Yerdaz to an "informal" late dinner, and she'd accepted the invitation for several reasons. Partly because she'd known this conversation was going to happen and because Andryth and Chayzar were among the Empire's staunchest (if poorest) allies. And very reliable ones, too.

The Qwern Empire floated on a vast sea of oil, with the most extensive proven reserves on Sarth. In fact, the Empire sat on almost half of all known oilfields and, over the years, Clan Ruler Juzhyr and ous bearer had sought to use that bounty as a diplomatic tool against Dianto and its allies. Results had been mixed, especially where the Republic itself was concerned. The eastern half of Sanda was as petrochemical-poor as the western half was rich, which had always struck Yerdaz as a sign of divine favor, especially when the Republican

Navy took the high-risk step of converting its entire battle fleet from coal—of which it had immense quantities in the Krelk Mountains—to oil—of which it had virtually none. By rights, that ought to have made Dianto more receptive to policy proposals from the Qwernians, who controlled so much of the oil its navy and its merchant marine required. Unfortunately, New Dianto, the huge island in the middle of the Surifar Ocean, between Sanda and Deltar, was almost as oil-rich as the Empire. In absolute terms, its reserves were much lower; proportionate to its size, they were even greater, however, and its actual output was within a few percent of the Empire's.

And New Dianto was a member in good standing of the Diantian Commonwealth, Dwomo damn it.

Still, Qwernian oil remained a potent diplomatic weapon, especially with nations like Andryth and Chayzar which either had no substantial reserves of their own or lacked the ability to get at whatever petroleum they possessed. Oil purchases by those nations were heavily subsidized by the clan ruler, which bought a lot of political support when it was needed.

Feltik and Kwysar were as well aware of those realities as Yerdaz, but if they resented their Qwernian collars they'd always hidden it well. Mostly, she suspected, because they were diplomats and that was what diplomats did. But that wasn't the only factor. She'd known both males for a long time now, and they were personal friends, not just diplomatic allies. Of course, the diplomatic allies' part of their relationship trumped personal friendship, and all three of them knew it.

"No, size isn't everything," she agreed now, with a slight, teasing twitch of her nasal flaps. She was no dwarf, but Kwysar was a couple of kyrans taller than she was. That made him a virtual giant for Chayzar, yet the Earthian male was at least two and a half seqrans taller than him. Of course, whether or not the Earthian truly was a male was a debatable point. The notion of a species which possessed only two sexes made Yerdaz feel . . . uncomfortable. There was something almost perverted about it, although she kept reminding herself that the word she really wanted was "alien," not perverted.

"On the other hand," she went on with a more serious expression, "David is impressive for more than just his size or even how . . . bizarre all Earthians look. I listened to his speech directly, not through the Nonagon translators, and assuming that whatever magical technology was translating his words into Desqwerian did a decent job of reflecting his actual tone, he was a lot less nervous than I would've been in his place."

"Probably a little easier to be calm when you have a technology advantage as great as the Earthians'," Feltik said just a bit sourly.

"Assuming they're telling the truth about it, at least," Kwysar qualified.

"I think we can assume they've been fairly truthful in what they've told us so far." Yerdaz' tone was dry. "Just for starters, they've crossed interstellar space to reach us, and we still haven't gotten beyond our own atmosphere. And despite how hard we've looked, neither our radar nor visual observation has seen a single sign of their ships yet, either. Not unless they *want* us to, anyway. I'd say that's a pretty fair indication they can do all kinds of things we can't. Yet, at least."

"That's definitely a valid point," Kwysar replied. "But we still don't know how accurate those images they showed us are, or how truthful they are about sharing all the information they 'captured' from their adversaries."

"Oh, be reasonable, Kwy!" Feltik said. "They've only been on the planet for a single day-half or so. That hasn't given them a lot of time to go into detail."

"I know. But something about their story just strikes me as . . . odd." Kwysar's nasal flaps were taut, and Yerdaz cocked her head at him.

"What do you mean, odd? I mean, beside the fact that we couldn't possibly have produced those images the way they did!"

"That was impressive," Kwysar conceded with generous understatement. "In fact, it may have been even more impressive than you two realize! Believe me, I know."

The other two shook their heads in agreement. It had been readily apparent even to them that the Earthians' ability to re-create moving, three-dimensional images put the best Sarthian cameras and talkies to shame. But Kwysar had relatives in the talkie business. In fact, he'd been involved as a producer on at least a half-sixteen of feature-length talkies, and he knew firsthand what Sarthian special-effects editors were capable of. It wasn't just the images, either; good as the sound effects specialists were, they would never have been able to match the fidelity of the Earthians' "tridee's" sound quality. And they'd been able to display an apparently infinitely scalable image, floating in mid-air, using a single unit no bigger than a Sarthian's head.

"To be honest," he continued, "the fact that they could show us what they showed us in the *way* they showed it is a pretty fair indicator that their technical capabilities, however they got them, are one hell of a lot better than anything we've got. But you're the ex-soldier around here, Yerdaz. What did you think about the way the Earthians' pre-invasion weapons stacked up against their opponents'?"

"*Please!*" Yerdaz fluttered her nasal flaps in mock horror. "Soldiers spend their time down in the mud. I was an *aviator*. We're much more sophisticated people."

"I understand, but my question stands. What did you think about it?"

Kwysar's expression was serious, and Yerdaz sipped terahk while she considered the male's question.

"I was impressed," she said finally, recalling the images of the sleek, propeller-less aircraft—the "Raptors," David had called them—and their unbe-lievable speed and maneuverability. Assuming those images hadn't been doc-tored, she suspected that an Earthian pilot could handle much tighter, faster turns than a Sarthian before passing out. And their weapons! No Sarthian air force had yet contemplated using rockets in air-to-air combat. Certainly no one had ever dreamed of a weapon which could launch, then track its target and maneuver to strike it.

She was less viscerally aware of the degree to which the Earthians' ground combat equipment outclassed its Sarthian counterparts. A tank was a tank, as far as she was concerned. From her perspective, it was basically a target. But she suspected that her ground combat counterparts would have been just as impressed by the huge "Abrams"—whatever an "Abram" might be—and its massive cannon as she had been by the Earthians' aircraft.

"I could see what the Earthians were talking about in terms of how much more effectively they'd applied the technical capabilities they had to their hardware," she continued. "Those Shongairi landing craft should have been a lot more difficult to take down than they were, and anyone who could travel between the stars should have been able to build tanks more effective than the ones the Earthians could put up against them. It took a lot of courage for the Earthians to fight back at all, Kwysar, especially after the Shongairi's initial bombardment destroyed virtually every organized military force on the planet before the Earthians even knew they were there! The fact that they fought so effectively for as long as what was left of their armed forces lasted says a lot."

"Agreed. But does it say *enough*?"

"What do you mean, 'enough'?" Feltik asked, gazing at the other male in-tently.

"It's just that as brave as the Earthians were, and as capable as their weapons were, how did they win?" Kwysar regarded his table companions intently.

"Well, mostly by catching the Shongairi by surprise, I imagine," Yerdaz said. "And it probably helped that the Shongairi must be dumber than rocks." She twitched her nasal flaps derisively. "They obviously didn't do a very good job of extrapolating what the Earthians' weapons could do to them! Surely if they had, someone with their tech advantages should have been able to come up with counters for them ahead of time."

Feltik waggled his own nasal flaps in amusement, and even Kwysar twitched a brief smile, although, Yerdaz thought, what she'd just said was self-evidently true. And it was something the Earthians should bear in mind if it turned out that their purposes here on Sarth were less benign than they'd so far implied.

The Shongairi might have been caught by surprise when it came to the Earthians' combat capabilities, but it was obvious from the Earthian account that the initial *strategic* surprise had all been on the Shongairi's side. The

attackers' pre-invasion bombardment had destroyed virtually all of the Earthian organized combat forces, leaving only fours and eights of Earthian aircraft
and tanks intact. If they hadn't, if the Earthians had been left with anything
like the combat strength they'd had prior to that bombardment, the initial
Shongair landings would have been a bloodbath. It was probable that someone
who controlled orbital space would still have won in the end, but the initial
price would have been exponentially higher. Indeed, it might have been high
enough to leave the Shongairi with the choice of bombarding the Earthians
back to the Stone Age out of simple vengeance or turning around and going
home to come back and try again later.

Sarth knew about Earthians. Sarth knew there were starships no Sarthian
could see in orbit around their home world, or perhaps hiding behind one of
their moons. And because Sarth knew that, virtually every Sarthian military—
even that of the oh-so-pious Diantians—had gone to a high state of alert and
dispersed its combat power as widely as possible. Which meant the Earthians
would find it much more difficult to do to Sarth what the Shongairi had done
to them. No doubt, like the Shongairi, they could still carry through to victory, assuming they were prepared to pay the price in blood and lives, but her
impression was that they wouldn't be. Judging from their reaction to what the
Shongairi had done and what was probably a completely reasonable unwilling-
ness to absorb enormous casualties after what had already happened to their
entire species back home, they wouldn't have the stomach for it. No doubt some
of her fellow Qwernians would put that down to cowardice or despise Earthian
timidity, but Yerdaz was less chauvinistic than that. It wouldn't be cowardice or timidity; it would be a rational evaluation of cost-versus-benefit. And at
least they seemed less likely to simply destroy Sarth in a petulant rage than the
Shongairi probably would have been.

In fact, the more she thought about it, the more like the Diantians the Earthians seemed. They preferred negotiation to conflict, they seemed to believe in
the "rule of law" about which the Republic bleated so constantly, and so far, at
least, it seemed unlikely that they would attempt to *compel* Sarth to accept their
offers. That was the good news. Well, that and the fact that, again so far at least,
she'd seen nothing to suggest they were liars. Not that she'd had a great deal of
time to prove that one way or the other. But if the fact that they were unlikely to
resort to coercive measures to force Sarth into agreement was a good thing, the
fact that the same attitudes would almost certainly make the Republic a more
congenial partner for them than the Empire was a very *bad* thing. Potentially,
at least.

"I agree that surprise was a major factor in their favor," Kwysar said once
his nasal flaps stopped quivering. "That wasn't my point, though. You're talking
about how they won some of the battles; I'm trying to figure out how they won

the *war*. Airplanes and tanks are all very well on the ground and in the air, but how did they capture invading *spaceships*? No matter how hard they fought, by their own admission, they were beaten on the ground, yet in the end, they won everything. So what turned that around? What let them defeat the Shongairi?"

"I don't have any idea," Yerdaz admitted after a moment.

"Neither do I," Kwysar said. "Maybe they'll get around to telling us that, but in the meantime, I have to wonder if there's anything *else* they haven't mentioned yet."

VI

I appreciate your willingness to meet with me, Councilor Arthur," Yerdaz NorYerDar said as one of her aides escorted the Earthian into her office. He was at least three or four kyrans shorter than Secretary David—Yerdaz was making a conscientious effort to learn how to pronounce the outré Earthian names—but even so, his disturbingly flat head was dangerously close to the chamber's ceiling. The Earthian-style chair Yerdaz had procured was similarly outsized, taking up much of the private office's floor space.

"I was honored by the invitation," the Earthian replied. His lips didn't match the shape of the words, but Yerdaz was relieved to hear them in perfect Qwernian. She'd worried about not using her own translator, but she'd decided that relying upon the alien's mysterious translating "software" would be a way of demonstrating her trust.

"Our entire planet is honored—or at least considerably taken aback—by your people's arrival," she countered.

"I can understand that," he acknowledged, his lips moving in one of the still incomprehensible expressions of his people. Of course, with no nasal flaps, they had to make do as best they could, poor things. And the lines of down above their eyes seemed impressively mobile for such a limited facial feature. She simply hadn't had time to figure out what all the wiggling around meant.

"It occurred to me that formal settings aren't the best way to get to know one another," she continued. "And I think it's especially important for the representatives of nations to have a direct and personal understanding of one another."

"The Secretary and I could not agree more with you about that," the councilor said with another of those weird lip movements. "Obviously, formal addresses are all very well in their place and serve a vital function, as do meetings between actual heads of state. But it's also crucial for there to be understanding at the lower levels of the process." He started to nod, then stopped himself and shook his head. Yerdaz had noticed the Earthians doing that several times.

"You're too kind," she said, and she meant it as he equated his own rank with that of a mere delegate.

"Not at all," he disagreed.

"At any rate, I thank you," she said. "And I must say that it's been my experience, speaking as a Sarthian diplomat, that it's possible to speak more frankly when one speaks face-to-face rather than through the interface of a formal body like the Nonagon."

"Earthian diplomats have always found it that way," he said, shaking his head once more. "At most major multinational diplomatic sessions, the real work gets done in committees and side meetings because the heads of the delegations have too many formal duties. And—" those lips moved again "—frankly, there's always the concern that the head of a delegation may inadvertently say something he didn't mean to say, or be misunderstood to say something that he actually *didn't* say. When that happens, it can confuse the other delegations as to what they can reasonably expect. Underlings, such as you and myself, can speak without that concern because we lack the authority to commit our superiors."

"Exactly!" Yerdaz shook her head vigorously.

Thank Dwomo! After almost a double-eight day-halves of listening to Secretary David, she'd been coming to the conclusion that Earthians were even more like the Diantians than she'd feared. Everything David had said sounded exactly like those rules-worshiping sorqhs. She'd hoped, without a great deal of optimism, that that was mostly a concession to the Nonagon's atmosphere and forms, and that was what she'd reported to Minister Myrcal. But clearly Councilor Arthur understood how practical diplomacy truly worked.

She reminded herself not to read too much into a single conversation, but, really. When Secretary David's councilor said something, it clearly had to be taken very seriously, indeed.

"My Clan Ruler has charged me, as ous representative here at the Nonagon, to assure you of ous understanding of the enormous opportunity, and also of the potential risks, your visit to our world entails," she continued. "Ou is most interested to learn more of the nature of this 'Hegemony' and also about the wonders of you Earthians' technology. Obviously," she waggled her nasal flaps in a knowing smile, "you aren't going to want to tell us *too* much at this point— not until you've been able to reach the understanding you've come so far to gain. Before my assignment to the Nonagon, however, I was a pilot in our Army Air Force, so I'm sure you can imagine how awed I was by the arrival of your craft!"

"I'm a diplomat, not a military man," Councilor Arthur replied. "That isn't really my area of expertise. However, I'll readily acknowledge that our current capabilities are pretty astounding even for us, given how rapidly and how far they've advanced in just ninety or so of your years."

Yerdaz shook her head politely as the councilor skillfully deflected her probe, although the notion that the Earthians had made such huge strides in such a short period of time was, frankly, a little frightening. She couldn't conceive of any Sarthian education system that could have made that much new information available to an entire planetary population in such a brief interval! But perhaps the Earthians hadn't done that. Perhaps the full breadth of their acquired technology had been imparted on an emergency basis to a smaller group of scientists and scholars while the rest of their population acquired it more gradually. How many engineers would it have taken to *design* something like their "shuttle"? The laborers building it didn't have to understand the principles involved; they only had to know how the parts went together. How many Sarthians really understood what happened inside a rotary aircraft engine, after all?

"I can readily see how someone in your position would have less need to understand the nuts and bolts that an ex-aviator such as myself would be interested in," she said. "I would be fascinated, however, by anything you could tell me about your people. For example, your family life. I'm sure you can understand how it would be very difficult for a Sarthian to visualize a child with only two parents!"

"I doubt that that's a lot more difficult than it is for us Earthians to visualize a child with three biological parents," the Councilor said with another of those lip movements. Yerdaz was beginning to suspect it was the Earthian equivalent of a smile, although she reminded herself not to allow herself to be too wedded to the notion. "To be honest, we find the difference between Sarthian and Earthian biology to be fascinating, Delegate Yerdaz. Although there are huge numbers of different planetary ecologies and biologies in the Hegemony's records, this is the first opportunity we've had to actually see one firsthand. For many of our centuries, Earthians believed we were the only intelligent life in the universe. Most of us realized how statistically unlikely that was, but it took a great deal of time to wean us away from it. Now, of course," the Earthian made a soft sound, almost like a cough, "we've had entirely too much empirical evidence of just how wrong we were!"

"So I understand," Yerdaz said. "But, tell me, Councilor. Among Earthians, is one of your genders primarily responsible for child rearing?"

"Well," the councilor said after a moment, "in many ways, that depends upon the particular Earthian culture one is speaking of. You see—"

VII

CITY OF KWYZO NAR QWERN, QWERN EMPIRE,
PLANET SARTH;
AND PUNS *OUTREACH*,
SARTH ORBIT

I don't like it, Flythyr," Myrcal MyrFarZol nar Qwern growled. Ou and Flythyr MuzTolFlyth, the third ranking member of the Qwern Ministries sat on the balcony of Myrcal's favorite restaurant as the sun slid slowly towards the horizon. Watching it, Flythyr thought, it was hard to believe just how completely Sarth had been changed in so short a time. The Earthians had been on Sarth for barely a double eight day-halves, yet their arrival had overturned every Sarthian political and diplomatic calculation.

"Which part of it, in particular, Tysan?" Flythyr asked. Technically, Flythyr was a flock lord, just like Myrcal, but Myrcal was ous title bearer, whereas Flythyr was simply a flock lord *consort*. More to the point, Myrcal was a bit of a stuck-up prig in Flythyr's considered opinion. A very smart, very dangerous-to-cross stuck-up prig, but still a prig. Ou did like the occasional honorific— possibly even a little discreet groveling—from ous social inferiors. And the truth was that Flythyr didn't mind giving ous ego an occasional stroke.

"Any of it!" Myrcal stood, strode angrily to the balcony's railing, and stared out into the heart of the setting sun as it poured molten copper down the heavens. "I don't like *any* of it! We have enough purely Sarthian problems without adding this kind of excrement to the dung heap. And we only have their word for how badly they intend to 'disrupt' our society, now don't we? I don't trust them, Flythyr. I don't trust them a single seqran. Not without some way to corroborate what they're telling us.

"'Aliens' would be enough to require the strictest possible skepticism—and security procedures, for that matter—at the best of times and even assuming they'd turned up armed only with offers of technological uplift. But these aliens—these *Earthians*—didn't do that, did they? They came to us with these tall tales about tyrannical interstellar governments out to crush all innovation. And then they told us that they actually managed to defeat those cruel, technologically advanced monsters somehow, despite the inferiority of Earthian technology. And now they want us to join them as allies against their enemies. Wouldn't you say that sums things up pretty well?"

"*I* can't think of anything you left out, Tysan," Flythyr said frankly.

"I'd be happier if I detected a little more skepticism in Yerdaz' cables," Myrcal muttered. The charioteer consort was one of ous favorite and most trusted envoys. She had a good head on her shoulders, and she was skeptical about anyone's altruism. In this instance, though, ou suspected she'd been caught up in the stupid, fluttering, commoner enthusiasm for this "pivotal moment in history."

Ou closed ous nasal flaps in mingled disgust and self-anger. The truth was, ou ought to have gone to the Nonagon ouself, and ou hadn't. That had been a mistake, if only because it meant ou hadn't seen the Earthians' initial presentation ouself. Ou had to rely on other people's reports, and from Yerdaz' cables, ou suspected she'd been almost as overwhelmed by the Earthian David's appeal as all the rest of the sorqhs. True, she had passed on Kwysar HalSyn's suspicion that there was something the Earthians weren't telling them, but she'd also pointed out that the aliens hadn't had all that much time to tell them anything. Or perhaps what she'd really meant was *everything*. But it struck Myrcal that explaining exactly how they'd managed to defeat such an overwhelming foe was a fairly critical piece of information. It was definitely something ou wanted to know before ou recommended climbing any farther into bed with the Earthians. And instead of being in Lyzan to press for more information, ou was here in Kwyzo nar Qwern protecting ous dignity.

Unfortunately, ou could scarcely climb on a dirigible and head for the Nonagon now without underscoring ous initial absence. Besides, ou'd never liked the damned Nonagon. The Empire had resisted its creation in the first place because it was based on paper laws, not the laws of blood and custom that truly counted. Unfortunately, Clan Ruler Juzhyr's bearer had felt compelled to bend to the force of "international opinion" in ous efforts to play nice with the self-fertilizing Diantians. And the Republic had been using it to break the Empire's knees ever since. That was why Myrcal had made it a point to *avoid* the Nonagon from the beginning of ous tenure as Foreign Minister. Ous view, and the Empire's official position since ou'd assumed office, had been that the Nonagon was a purely consultative body and that any agreement had to be signed at the foreign ministers' level—and finalized through the traditional diplomatic channels custom had hallowed over the centuries—to be binding. So how—

Ous question broke off in mid thought. Yes, the Nonagon was the end-all and be-all of the sorqhs who allowed themselves to be herded by the Republic, but the Empire and its allies and client states had always been more resistant to that view. Perhaps it was time to remind the rest of Sarth about that.

· · · · ·

MYRCAL STEPPED INTO the audience chamber, glanced at Chancellor Erylk ErGarzHyn nar Qwern, and raised a questioning nasal flap. "I thought, Clan Ruler, that perhaps I might have a moment of your time . . . alone?"

Juzhyr nodded firmly. "Anything you need to say, you can say in front of the Chancellor. Ou has my utmost confidence."

"As you wish, Clan Ruler." Myrcal closed ous nasal flaps and took a moment to steady ouself. "I wanted to discuss the most recent cables I've received from the Nonagon, and propose a way forward."

"So we've received fresh word from Lyzan?"

"We have, Clan Ruler, and I must say it's . . . unsettling."

"Why is that?" Juzhyr asked. "Are the Diantians getting ahead of us in the negotiations?"

"No," Myrcal replied, nodding. "It's nothing like that at all—if anything, the Earthians have been *too* even-handed in their dealings with us. Our envoy there has yet to find an opening where we might be able to advance our cause."

"What's the problem then?"

"The problem is, I don't believe they're telling us everything. Yerdaz doesn't think they're lying to us, but she does mention that there are things they haven't been completely forthcoming on with us."

"Like what?" Erylk asked.

Myrcal turned to the Chancellor and raised both nasal flaps.

"The Earthians still haven't told us how they—who were admittedly inferior in most ways to their enemies—were able to drive them from their planet . . . or even how they were able to get *at* the Shongairi in their spaceships," ou said. "I—along with Minister Flythyr—find this somewhat disturbing. Did their enemies make a mistake . . . or are the Earthians hiding something from us? Some military capability . . . or maybe some dark side to this offer of theirs?"

Both of Erylk's nasal flaps opened wide in surprise, as Myrcal had expected—the old bearer's over-cautious nature was too predictable—and ou turned to Juzhyr.

"This *is* worrisome," the Chancellor said. "I believe continued caution should be exercised with the Earthians, Clan Ruler, before we make any long-term agreements with them. It would be prudent to find out what they're hiding first."

"That course does seem to be indicated," Juzhyr agreed, shaking his head slowly. "But I don't want Qwelth or any of ous sorqhs using our reticence as a means to get ahead of us in the negotiations, or to get something from the Earthians that we don't get, ourselves."

"Yes, Clan Ruler, I will so advise Yerdaz." Ou paused a moment as if considering Juzhyr's orders, and then jerked as if an idea had just come to oum. "There might be something else we can do, too, Clan Ruler."

"What is that?"

"Well, I was just thinking that there are three issues here: our lack of knowledge of the Earthians, our lack of faith in the Nonagon process, and our desire to crush the Diantians. What if we could come up with a plan that solved all of them simultaneously?"

Juzhyr raised a nasal flap. "And you have an idea which will do so?"

Myrcal shook ous head. "I believe so, Clan Ruler. What if we invited the Earthian representatives to bring a delegation to Kwyzo nar Qwern? That would give us greater access to them and would allow our scientists to study the Earthians more closely, and in a number of situations. Not only would it be helpful in understanding the Earthians better—and maybe we can get them to divulge information the Diantians won't have access to—but it will also help us show the Nonagon for what it really is—unnecessary frippery and window dressing."

"The Diantians will never go for that," Erylk said. "If we get access to the Earthians like this, they will want something similar."

"And that's fine," Myrcal replied, alternately wagging ous nasal flaps in a shrug. "As long as we get this Secretary Dav . . . Davi—as long as we get access to their ambassador, we'll have the key to winning the Earthians over to *our* side."

"And if the Secretary refuses to choose a side? What if he decides to remain at the Nonagon?"

"Then invite one of his assistants. Our observers say he looks to an Earthian named 'Abu' whenever he seeks approval for what he is saying. We can invite Abu; he appears to have the Secretary's ear."

"That would give us an opportunity to learn more about them firsthand," Juzhyr mused. "I would also be able to take a look at one of them myself." He considered it a moment, then asked, "Do you think we can get the Earthians to go along?"

"I believe so, Clan Ruler. We can couch this as a matter of hospitality and let them know we would consider it rude if they didn't come. Then—if they are really here, looking for allies, as they say—they wouldn't be able to say no and risk offending us." He raised both nasal flaps in a smile.

"But what if the Diantians oppose us?" Erylk asked. "What if they try to keep the Earthians in Lyzan?"

Myrcal kept control of ouself through a supreme effort of will, despite the chancellor's constant questioning. The bearer was really past ous prime, and Myrcal realized it was time for oum to be replaced with someone younger and more aggressive. Someone a lot like Myrcal, if the truth was known. He allowed ouself another smile, although ou made it seem as if it was a response to the chancellor's question, not ous internal monologue.

"Nothing could be easier, Chancellor," ou replied. "It won't be difficult to have our allies and clients back us in this proposal. In fact, we will phrase it so the Earthians have to send people throughout all of Sarth, which will give our spies the ability to watch them in a variety of environments." His nasal flaps wiggled in amusement as he warmed to the idea. "In fact, if we spread the Earthians far enough, they'll have to draw on some of their junior diplomats, who might be a little more approachable or more likely to let something slip that one of their senior officials might not have. Yes . . . I think this would kill a number of krats with a single arrow."

"I like this plan," Juzhyr said. Myrcal noticed ou didn't look to Erylk for confirmation and smiled to ouself. "Contact our representatives throughout the Alliance and let them know what they need to do to assist in bringing it to fruition. Make sure they know it was my idea, and that I will be most displeased if they fail to assist in this endeavor."

· · · · ·

"WHAT DO YOU make of Myrcal's brainstorm?" Dave Dvorak asked, looking around the conference table aboard PUNS *Outlook*. Silence answered for a moment, then Abu Bakr shrugged.

"On the one hand, I don't much like it. I'd really prefer to stick with your original game plan and run all negotiations and all contact through a single interface. You were right from the get-go when you said that was the best way to avoid misunderstandings. On the other hand, it gives us an opportunity to be more hands-on with Sarthians in general. As long as we don't step on our swords, I think the opportunity to have contact teams out in as many locations as possible would probably help overcome any xenophobia these people might feel."

"Of course, there is that bit about not 'stepping on our swords,'" Alex Jackson put in.

Jackson, Dvorak's senior aide, was only about a third of Abu Bakr's age, although that didn't mean as much as it once had now that humanity had acquired the Hegemony's antigerone technologies. He was also a very strong-willed, no-nonsense sort of fellow who'd lost his entire family to the Shongairi.

"Expand on that, Alex," Dvorak invited, although he was confident he knew where the younger man was headed. Sometimes he thought they thought a bit too much alike, that he might have needed someone a bit less likely to see things the same way he did, like Arthur McCabe, for example.

"It's just that despite everything in the Hegemony database, despite everything we've seen since we got here, we're still dealing with *aliens*, Mister Secretary." Jackson was always careful to observe formal courtesy in public. "We have—or we ought to have—a lot better window into how they think, how they're likely to react, than they have for us, but we're still a hell of a long way from really understanding them the way we might other humans. If that's true for us, it's got to be ten times as true from their side. And we're already tending to anthropomorphize them; what happens when they start . . . I don't know, *sartho*pomorphizing us? That's bound to happen, and if we're spread out all over the planet, they'll have a lot more opportunity to do it. And to make exactly the same kinds of mistakes *we* might make doing it to them."

"There's some truth to that, Mister Secretary," Arthur McCabe said.

That was the way the "special advisor" usually addressed a remark he intended to disagree with, Dvorak thought wryly. He was only in his thirties, only a year or two older than Dvorak's son, Malachi, and he'd grown up in Raleigh, where he'd been protected from the worst aspects of the Shongair invasion. He'd been attached to the mission at the strong urging—it would never have done to call it "insistence"—of a small but growing coterie in the Senate who were concerned that the "first-generation" leadership might be so blinkered by its traumatic experiences that it had developed tunnel vision. It would have been a gross exaggeration to call McCabe "soft" on the Shongairi or the Hegemony, but he belonged to the group which pointed out—correctly, Dvorak conceded—that the only actual contact humanity had ever had with the Hegemony was through the Shongairi, and that the Hegemony's own records made it clear that the rest of the Hegemony regarded the Shongairi as barbaric and bloodthirsty. Perhaps it might be wiser to remember how that sort of hideously traumatic experience might be shaping their interpretation of the Hegemony as a *whole* and driving their assumption that it had to be automatically hostile to humanity when they finally met once more.

Personally, Dvorak didn't think there was a chance in hell they'd misinterpreted anything about either the Shongairi or the Hegemony, but he recognized the need for countervailing viewpoints. The last thing the people responsible for leading the human race in any confrontation with something the Hegemony's size needed was to live in a damned echo chamber. Too many politicians had done just that, and in the process forgotten that they were supposed to be statesmen first and politicians second.

"At the same time, however," McCabe continued, right on track, "we do know a lot more about the Sarthians and Sarthian psychology than they know about us. And, courtesy of the translating software, any of us can be completely fluent in conversations with them and be confident we're not going to make a wrong word choice. That doesn't mean they can't misinterpret something we say, anyway, but it's not going to be because of a language barrier. And we have a significant advantage in the computers' ability to read their body language and expressions.

"It's entirely possible that what Alex is worrying about could turn around and bite us, but the bottom line is that it would provide a *major* increase in our ability to interact with them and learn more about them firsthand. I believe I understand Yerdaz much better now, after our personal conversations, for example. In fact, I can't help wondering if that's not part of the reason they're suggesting this. And in relation to that, we need to remember that while the Empire may have proposed this, it has solid support among all of the Qwernian allies and client states. That's somewhere between a third and half of the entire planetary population. If we ignore the request, then we risk alienating—" his lips twitched slightly at his own choice of verb "—that part of Sarth."

"True," Abu Bakr said. "I can't dispute a single word of that. At the same time, though, I'm not comfortable allowing the Sarthians to dictate the terms upon which we'll have access to their political leaders. And I especially don't like the thought of finding our mission tangled up in purely Sarthian international politics and power rivalries."

"With all due respect, Mister Bakr, it's their planet," McCabe pointed out. "If we want to convince them to join us as allies, don't we have to respect their wishes about how they conduct their political business on their world?"

Abu Bakr frowned. Dvorak knew he wasn't one of McCabe's greatest admirers, and he'd made it quietly—and privately—clear that he had reservations about the advisor's personal contacts with the Qwernians. On balance, Dvorak was tempted to agree with him, but Yerdaz had been quietly insistent on meeting with the younger man, and openings were too precious to be passed up. And every word of their conversations was recorded by McCabe's personal computer for later replay, so it wasn't like he could accidentally commit them to anything without their knowing it. But Abu Bakr was obviously less than fully onboard with McCabe's last comment.

"That's certainly true within limits," the secretary of state observed now, before his second-in-command said something unfortunate to his special advisor. "The converse of that is that we're the much more advanced civilization— technologically, at least—which is offering to share that technology with them. That means we have a right to set limits and conditions on the way in which we go about that. And I watched the Diantians and their allies pretty carefully while Yerdaz was presenting Myrcal's 'proposal.' They didn't say so in so many words, but unless the software was way off the reservation reading their expressions and body language, they weren't at all happy about it. I think they and *their* allies and clients would very much like to maintain a single point of contact at the closest thing to a neutral site they've got."

"That's because the Republic is a politically more mature system, Sir," Jane Simmons, Dvorak's third in command on the civilian side, said. She was only a few years older than Dvorak, but she'd been a State Department attaché for the United States in several Third World countries before the invasion.

"I've seen a lot of this in purely human terms," she continued. "The extent to which national leaders can approach domestic and international politics like responsible adults is governed by the ability of their own political system to absorb that kind of behavior. One-party nations, or nations where political chicanery in elections is routinely expected, aren't exactly noted for producing moderate leaders. And if you couple that sort of problem with a sense of inferiority or victimhood—even if, or perhaps *especially* if, a nation has truly been victimized—you produce a policy and diplomats who are defensive and passive-aggressive at the best of times. The Republic has a many-generational tradition of open debate, representative politics, the art of learning to accept compromise, *and* the importance of a rule-of-law system which is binding on all parties. My read is that the Qwernians aren't there yet, and that's part of what this is about. They don't trust anyone else not to be cutting secret deals with us at the Nonagon, so they want to spread out points of contact, if only to give themselves and their allies the chance to cut secret deals of their own. Assuming, of course, that any secret deals are being cut in the first place.

"The Diantians have a lot more faith in the process through the Nonagon, partly because they have that domestic tradition, but also, frankly, because they figure they can game the situation better than the Qwernians can in the Nonagon's environment. It's more congenial to them, and they expect to be able to dance circles around the Empire because of that. So there are a lot of factors in play here, on both sides."

Dvorak nodded soberly. He always known Simmons was a smart cookie. And, of course, the proof was that she pretty much agreed with his reading of the situation, he thought sardonically. Maybe he wasn't quite as free of that echo chamber–friendly thinking as he liked to pretend he was?

"I think there's a great deal to be said on both sides," he said finally. "The bottom line, though, is that the Nonagon is going to vote on the proposal in a couple of days. If the decision is to accept Myrcal's proposal, then our choices are to go along with their desires as our hosts or to tell them to pound sand, which is unlikely to endear us to them. So either we'll be staying with the arrangement we have, or we'll be forced to split up our mission between national capitals. I think we can legitimately insist on limiting the number of individual missions we're prepared to staff, but however we slice it, we'll be spread a lot thinner than anyone envisioned when we set out. Right this minute, I'm thinking that we insist that our primary mission—our formal embassy—will remain at Lyzan and continue to work through the Nonagon, and that that will be my point of contact as Secretary of State and our senior ambassador. I think we have to do that to avoid the appearance of taking sides by assigning me to any single nation."

He paused, looking around the conference table, until a wave of sober nods had answered him.

"To be honest, I'm hoping the proposal fails, but our remotes are all suggesting it's more likely to pass, although the margin looks like it'll be thin. That being the case, I think it behooves us to start some contingency planning now.

"Abu, much as I hate to say it, I think that as a sop to any potential Qwernian passive-aggressiveness, you'll have to head the mission to the Empire. Jane, I'd like to have you in Dianto, but the truth is I need that 'Third World' experience of yours, so I'm thinking you'll probably end up on Deltar, in Synchanat or Chayzar. Jefferson," he turned to Jefferson Davidson, Simmons assistant, whose name had been the source of endless bad jokes, "I think that means you get Dianto. We haven't presented any kind of formal hierarchy to these people, and I don't intend to, so neither the Empire nor the Republic should be able to think it got the more senior representative.

"Now, in addition to deciding how many missions we'll staff, we have to give some serious thought to our ability to provide security over such a widely dispersed area without dusting off that big stick we're not supposed to be waving under the Sarthians' nostril flaps. I'll be sitting down to discuss that with Brigadier Wilson and Admiral Swenson this evening after dinner, but my initial thought is—"

・ VIII ・

SOKYR CHELSO'S RECTORY, CITY OF MYRCOS,
AND PRIME DIRECTOR'S OFFICE, CITY OF DIANZHYR,
REPUBLIC OF DIANTO

haymork take it!" Sokyr ChelSo nor Chelth snarled. "Taysar sear them all!"

Trygau HyrShalTry nor Ganyth bent his head in agreement and deference as Sokyr stalked around the stone-walled chamber. The priest was in a truly foul mood, and from Trygau's expression, it was obvious he was in full agreement with oum.

"Even that godless apostate Qwelth should see where this has to lead!" Sokyr continued. "Ha! It's not a case of *should*—of *course* ou sees. It's where ou's always wanted to go anyway! But ous soul will pay a mighty price for this, Tryagu. Mark my words! Ou will burn in Hell *forever,* because there's no possible excuse for ous actions! Even ou has to recognize that! The Book clearly states that Chelth created Sarth and all that lives upon it out of nothingness. We're Ous people and the work of Ous hand, and the Book says nothing about Ous having created other worlds, other people! These aliens, these Earthians, may claim whatever they choose, but they *cannot* be the work of Ous hand. Yet they come to us with this preposterous tale of other murderous aliens among the stars. And why?" Ou whirled to face Trygau, jabbing an accusatory digit at him. "I'll tell you why! They're here to drive those godless, secular policies which have controlled the Sitting for far too long! They're going to tell us all about those *awful* 'Shongairi' and warn us of all the changes we have to make if we hope to survive, and all the while they're simply Shaymork's talons, reaching into the world to finish off the one true religion. And it's the cleverest thing Shaymork's done yet, too, because it plays directly into those atheists' prejudices and blind faith in 'science'!"

"Of course it does, Bearer!" Trygau said. "I realized that the instant the news broke, and every word their accursed leader's said only underscores my fears."

Sokyr's nasal flaps flared angrily, and ou jerked a headshake of agreement. The truth was that ou normally found Trygau's fervency a bit trying. Or, rather, that ou found the way the male expressed that fervency a bit too sycophantic. Sokyr never doubted the strength of Trygau's faith, but ou doubted the male had ever truly *thought* about their shared beliefs in all the ten years since he'd joined Sokyr's Chelthists. That was what better educated brains—like Sokyr's—were for. And he would follow to the end without ever once questioning or testing his faith the way The Book of Chelth urged Ous worshippers to do. But those very qualities suited him especially well for his role in the Chelthite struggle. He'd amply earned his position as the leader of Sokyr's action teams, and this day-half his unquestioning agreement with anything Sokyr said was both soothing to ous fury and fuel for ous rage.

"You can bet that's not what that gutless wonder Mykair is going to say, though," the priest grated now. Ou stamped over to the window and glared out into the evening day-half's rain. "Ou's going to fall right into line behind ous good friend *Qwelth*."

Sokyr's tone made the prime director's name a curse, and Trygau shook his head in fervent agreement. Sokyr clenched ous nasal flaps tight and suppressed an urge to spit out the window. Mykair ChelMyk nor Chelth was the anointed high priest of Chelth, at least according to the "mainstream" Chelthian church. Sokyr and ous followers knew what Mykair truly was, however. And the apostate traitor's lifetime friendship with ous old school friend Qwelth QwelSyn-Char only made oum even more willing to trample the deity ou supposedly served into the dust.

Sokyr gripped both hands together behind ouself as ou stared out into the slowly gathering dark, watched the raindrops glitter in the wash of light from the lamps which flanked ous front door. Why, ou wondered, not for the first time. Why had ou been born only to see the final downfall of God?

Not so very long ago—indeed, barely two centuries ago—that question would never have crossed ous mind. No one would have dared to suggest anything like this . . . this foul, evil, heretical apostasy could possibly come to pass! But all those other pantheons, all those other minor, all too often totally *false* deities and their blinded followers, had been jealous of Chelth's position as the Republic of Dianto's patron deity—the one true God, before whom all others bowed. And so they'd waged their vile campaign in the Sitting, buying one vote after another, until they finally had enough to pass their never-to-be-sufficiently-accursed "Freedom of Religion Act." *Freedom!?* Freedom to turn their backs on the God who'd given all of them life in the first place! That was what *they'd* meant by "freedom," and Qwelth—yes, and especially Mykair—were their spiritual heirs, sworn to complete the destruction of Chelth and all Ou had ever stood for.

It was also what the Band of Myrcos had been formed to oppose. The Band's political arm continued the struggle in the Sitting, yet it had become little more than a bad political joke, retaining barely an eight of seats. That was why Sokyr had been drawn to the Band's extralegal arm so many years before. Ou had fought the good fight with every ounce of strength, yet even as ou'd fought, ou'd felt the flame of hope flicker ever more weakly.

And now Shaymork had sent these demons, these *Earthians,* disguised as a beneficent alien species, and Qwelth and Mykair saw their opportunity to snuff that flame completely. To stamp out the last flickers of the once mighty blaze of Chelth.

Not on my *watch,* the cleric thought grimly, staring into the rain. *Not on my watch, and not while there's a breath within me.*

· · · · ·

THE SERVER WITHDREW, and Qwelth QwelSynChar picked up the carving knife and fork.

"I assume that, with your usual greed, you're going to insist on a drumstick?" ou said, nasal flaps waggling in amusement.

"You know me entirely too well, my nata," his guest said solemnly. "Alas, that you should consider it *greed,* however. I prefer to regard it as the possession of an exquisite palate for the finer things in life which impels me to constantly seek them out."

"Like ou said—greed," Syntevo QwelSynChar put in. She nodded her head sadly, eyes laughing at their guest. "It's no use trying to fool any of us, Bearer Mykair! We've known you far too long. Besides, Qwelth and Charkyno have told me all about what you were like in school, before you fell into the clutches of the church."

Mykair ChelMyk nor Chelth chuckled and waved a digit at her.

"I did not 'fall' into the clutches of the church, my daughter," ou said solemnly. "The incentive package was simply too good to pass up. Think of it! A lifetime warrant to poke into other people's lives, dictate the way they're supposed to live, and lay down my own opinions as the very law of Chelth. Who could possibly have passed that up?"

All three of ous hosts laughed, but Charkyno QwelSynChar, Qwelth's other consort, nodded his head far more somberly than Syntevo had nodded hers.

"All very well to joke about it, Mykair," he said. "But that's not that bad a description of the way the hard-core Chelthists see the church's role."

"If I don't joke about it, I'd have to weep, instead, Char," the primate of the Church of Chelth replied. "The good news is that the hard-core, as you put it—personally, I prefer 'lunatic fringe'—is slowly but steadily dying out."

"And getting increasingly militant as they feel their numbers shrinking," Qwelth put in, beginning to carve the roasted, stuffed syldak.

"Exactly," Charkyno said, darting a look of agreement at oum.

"Unfortunately, you both have a point," Mykair acknowledged. Ou picked up ous wine glass and sipped, then set it down with rather more precision than usual beside ous plate. "Would it be reasonable of me to suppose that the reason for this convivial evening is for the three of you to pick my brain about how the Band is likely to react to the Earthians' arrival?"

"You wound me, old friend," Qwelth said, looking up from ous knife and fork. "How could you possibly suppose we would have any such ulterior motive?"

"The fact that I've known you for more than a century, perhaps?"

"Well, there *is* that," Qwelth conceded.

"I suppose that if you hadn't invited me here to ply me with syldak, wine, and conviviality, I would've had to make an appointment to discuss it with you in a more official setting," Mykair said with a sigh.

"I know, but it's been too long since we had you over for dinner, too, so it struck me that we might as well combine business and pleasure. I barely had to twist Charkyno's arm at all to get him to agree to tolerate your presence."

"I truly appreciate your willingness to endure my visit, birthmate," Mykair said solemnly as Charkyno fluttered his nasal flaps derisively. Charkyno had met Qwelth and Syntevo, who'd already paired, when they'd spent several days visiting with his and Mykair's parents while Qwelth and Mykair were still in upper school together.

"It's difficult, but I bear up under the weight of it as best I can," ous sibling replied with equal solemnity.

"I'm sure. But, getting to the meat of your concerns," Mykair said, returning ous gaze to Qwelth, "I'm not sure how the Band's going to react. Not yet. I'm afraid the odds aren't in favor of sanity, though. They seldom are where the Band is concerned."

Sorrow had replaced ous earlier humor and ou nodded ous head sadly. Ous role as the leader of the Chelthian Church brought oum all too frequently into conflict with the Chel*thists*, the self-proclaimed "holy warriors" out to restore Chelth to Ous "rightful place" as the acknowledged supreme ruler of the Universe. They seemed unaware of the fact that Chelth was perfectly capable of accomplishing that goal Ouself if that was what Ou wanted. Or of how their own intolerance and willingness to embrace violence must grieve Oum.

"I think it would astonish some of the truly fanatic Chelthists to discover how deeply I sympathize with them on many levels." He sipped more wine, then set the glass down again. "But the law is the law, and The Book of Chelth has always recognized the primacy of *freedom* of belief. That freedom can't be extended solely to those who already follow Oum. It must be extended to all, or it becomes meaningless for any. There's no way the Band can admit that, however, and I'm already hearing rumbles about 'demons.'"

"*Demons?*" Syntevo repeated. "That's absurd!"

"To anyone with an open mind, of course it is," Mykair agreed. "But I believe we're talking about the Band here, aren't we, my daughter?"

"Point taken," she replied. "But still—*demons?*"

"A sufficiently narrow reading of The Book can support almost any bigotry, Syntevo," the priest said sadly. "Of course, one has to twist the words totally out of context, but that's never a problem for any true zealot. Indeed, it's the essential core of Chelthite thinking, and I'm quite sure the Band's position is going to be that whatever else they may be, the Earthians cannot be Chelth's children. And if they aren't Chelth's children, what else could they be?"

"That's what I was afraid you were going to say," Qwelth said, putting the syldak's fat drumstick on Mykair's plate. "I'm sure you'll do everything you can to tamp that down, Mykair. I just wish I felt more confident you'll be successful."

"As do I, Qwelth. As do I." Mykair nodded ous head again, nostril flaps drooping. "I *will* do all I can, I promise. I'm very much afraid, though, that in the end it's going to be up to you and the police, because I'm equally afraid it would be impossible to overestimate these people's ability to do something outstandingly stupid."

T hese people are beginning to piss me off," Dave Dvorak said sourly. "Two and a half months—*their* months, not ours—" the Sarthian month, called a triad, was forty-two of their long days in length, which came to fifty-three Terran days "—we've had delegations scattered to hell and gone all over the frigging planet, and aside from the Republic, Desqwer, and Synchanat, we're getting nowhere really, really slowly."

He glowered around the compartment, as if daring someone to dispute his assessment. An assessment, he knew, which sounded . . . well, for want of a better word, *petulant*. But damn it!

"With all due respect, Mister Secretary, you *are* attempting to negotiate an alliance with an entire planet."

Admiral Francesca Swenson's tone was mild, and her blue eyes twinkled— undeniably, they *twinkled*—at him across the conference table, and he hunkered down in his chair, resisting an urge to cross his arms and pout. Aside from the fact that she was eight inches taller, the red-haired Swenson reminded him a great deal of a somewhat younger version of his wife.

"And your point is?" he growled, then raised his left hand and waved it. "I know—I know! But if we hadn't gone along with the Qwernians and scattered delegations everywhere, I'll bet you we'd be a lot farther along than we are now."

"They aren't really 'scattered everywhere,'" Abu Bakr said. Dvorak turned a betrayed gaze upon him, and Abu Bakr snorted. "Well, they aren't. They are, perhaps, spread over-broadly, but there aren't really all *that* many of them."

"They are spread broad enough to make me a little uneasy, though," Brigadier Wilson said. Abu Bakr looked at him, and he shrugged. "Look, Benjamin and I—" he twitched his head in the direction of Captain Benjamin Bertrand, the commanding officer of PUNS *Troy* "—have an entire brigade up here. If we could stack up every Sarthian army in one place, we could probably polish them off in an hour or so. But they aren't stacked up in one place, and if we have to start dropping relief forces over such a broad area, it's going to spread my people pretty thin."

"Well, there are always Longbow and *his* people," Abu Bakr said.

"Of which we have precisely six," Dvorak pointed out before Brigadier

Torino could open his mouth. "And, deploying them would be the one thing we don't need in Dianto."

"I agree it could be . . . problematic, Sir," Torino said. "On the other hand, there is that old saying about 'Needs must when the Devil drives.'"

"You had to go and mention devils, didn't you?" Dvorak asked in a disgusted tone, and several people chuckled. Not that there was anything especially humorous about it, the secretary of state reflected. But sometimes all you could do was laugh at the universe's curveballs.

Dianto and its daughter states were coming along nicely. If he'd wanted to, he could have signed a bilateral alliance with them tomorrow and let the rest of the planet stew in its juices. In fact, he was tempted to do just that, and he knew Prime Director Qwelth and the members of ous Directorate were beginning to get a little impatient themselves. But the decision before his mission ever left Earth had been that the Planetary Union wasn't going to be dividing up any of the planets it contacted. The mere fact that they'd contacted Sarth was bound to be traumatic for its existing societies. It couldn't be any other way, when such a huge shift in their understanding of the galaxy and their place in it had been imposed upon them, and when the Terrans began actually introducing cutting edge technology, that could only get worse. The last thing anyone back home—or Dvorak, for that matter—wanted to do was to Balkanize the planet or create a situation in which power groups which were both theoretically allied to Earth used their new technology against each other! The idea was to find allies, not destroy existing cultures.

Yet, much as he liked Qwelth, and as much as he'd come to admire the accomplishments of the Republic, Dianto wasn't without a few prickly spots of its own.

The worst of them, almost inevitably, he thought sourly, were its religious nuts.

As a Methodist lay servant, although his certification had lapsed—something to do with not having enough hours in the day—Dvorak was very much a person of faith. He was also, however, a historian, which meant that he fully understood how often religion could be a negative force, usually (although not always) because its tenets had been twisted to serve secular need or ambition. Because of that, one of the many things he'd come to admire about the Republic was its ecumenicalism, which had spread to New Dianto, Desqwer, and Synchanat, as well. No other nations on Sarth, including the Republic's ally, the Kingdom of Shanth, had adopted a constitutional amendment guaranteeing freedom of religion and prohibiting the establishment of any official state religion.

The downside was that, once upon a time, Dianto *had* had a state religion. The pantheon of Myrcos, one of the original founding clans of the Republic, had been recognized as the preeminent religion of the entire Republic, and its chief deity, Chelth, had been the recognized patron of Dianto. Nobody had questioned that for a long time, but eventually the adherents of other gods had begun to feel marginalized. So the Sitting had amended the Constitution to make all religious beliefs equal.

The vast majority of Diantians thought that had been a good idea. The ones who didn't think it had been a good idea, thought it had been a very *bad* one, and some of them were perfectly willing to resort to force in an effort to turn back the clock and reestablish Chelth's supremacy.

Did the Diantians really have to be that *much like us?* Dvorak thought in exasperation.

"It's mostly that idiot Sokyr, Mister Secretary," Alex Jackson said.

"And if it was *only* Bearer Sokyr and his parishioners, that would be one thing," Dvorak replied. "Unfortunately, he's not the only Chelthist running around the planet, and not even Bearer Mykair seems to be able to shut him down. I wouldn't mind so much if he just didn't *like* us, but his insistence that we're 'demons' is a genuine pain in the ass. Especially where the vampires are concerned. You don't think turning your people loose would validate what he's been saying, Longbow?"

"Actually, I don't think it would, for anyone with a genuinely open mind," Torino said after a moment. "On the other hand, I don't know how many minds down there are genuinely open, and I'd rather not find out the hard way that I'm wrong."

"Listen," Wilson said, "I'm totally willing to put in the vampires if that's what it takes, but Space Marine though I may be, I do understand the need to do 'subtle' from time to time. You can't always fix things just by breaking them into tinier pieces. My problem is that since they don't know about you guys, and since they've never actually seen any of our hardware in action, and since we haven't gone down and staked out an extraterritorial enclave where we could *display* our hardware to them, some idiot down there—like, oh, one of Father Sokyr's nut jobs—is going to come all over stupid and try something. If that happens and it's an isolated incident, we'll probably be okay, aside from whatever damage we might take in the initial incident. But if it's not a one-off—if it happens in multiple places—we'll have to bring the hammer down. That's why I'd like to have our people in closer proximity to one another, not spread hundreds or even thousands of kilometers apart."

"I understand your concerns, Brigadier. I truly do," Arthur McCabe said. "And I agree with you that the Qwernians, in particular, are being . . . frustrating, Mister Secretary. But we're still learning more about this species every day, and I actually think it's especially important for us to have as much contact as possible with the Qwernians simply because we find them so much less . . .

compatible, or sympathetic to our own natures, than the Diantians. If we're going to conclude an alliance with the entire planet, we have to have an awareness of and a sensitivity to the differences between the people who live on it."

Dvorak nodded, albeit grumpily, because McCabe had done nothing but voice his own thoughts in that regard.

And your biggest problem is that you're not exactly the most patient person in the universe, he reminded himself. *Sharon's mentioned that to you often enough. Which is sort of rich, coming from the* next *most impatient person in the universe. But just keep remembering the solution to something that isn't coming together fast enough to suit you isn't always to reach for a bigger hammer.*

"All right, Arthur—and Francesca," he added, nodding to the admiral on the other side of the table. "Point taken. But I really would like to see this move off dead center where the Empire's concerned."

"I can suggest to Myrcal that we'd like to move forward," Abu Bakr said. "I'd be cautious about making that too explicit, though."

"Wiser words were never spoken," Dvorak agreed, shaking his head. "I swear to God, it's like talking to Napoleon III when he thinks he's Otto von Bismarck!"

"No doubt I'll understand the reference after I do a little research," Abu Bakr said in a martyred tone, and Dvorak laughed.

"I imagine you will, but you're right. The one thing we really don't need is somebody down there getting clever and—what was it you said, Rob? 'Coming all over stupid,' I think. So if you see any sign Myrcal and Juzhyr might be heading in that direction, let me know."

"Don't worry, I will." Abu Bakr shook his head. "So far, I think they've impressed themselves more with their cleverness than they've impressed me, but I'm reminding myself not to underestimate them because of that. The problem is that Jane was right when she said the Republic is a more mature political system. The Empire's still thinking in imperialistic terms, and there aren't a lot of checks and balances."

"And they'd like to cut their own secret deals with us," Alex Jackson pointed out.

"Oh, I'm sure they would!" Abu Bakr agreed. "So far, they haven't come right out and said so, and I'm not exactly encouraging them to. But I'll be astonished if they don't get around to it."

"Well, if they do—" Dvorak began.

"I'll cut them off at the knees," Abu Bakr interrupted, shaking his head again. "I may not agree with every single aspect of our mission orders, but they got that part exactly right. We spent too many centuries killing each other back home to have any part of creating a situation where the Sarthians start doing that because of *us*!"

"Exactly," Dvorak said. "Exactly."

· X ·

KWYZO NAR QWERN, QWERN EMPIRE,
PLANET SARTH

Myrcal's nasal flaps smiled as one of the Palace staff brought Abu Bakr out to join oum on the veranda overlooking the royal gardens. "Welcome, Ambassador Abu," Myrcal said, dismissing the minion with a shooing motion of one hand. "Please have a seat."

Ou indicated the two chairs overlooking the gardens. They were different in shape as Myrcal had commissioned one of the local craftsmen to build an Earthian chair, similar to the ones they used at the Nonagon when they were going to be in lengthy discussions. Although the object didn't look like a real "chair," the Earthian folded himself down onto it and seemed relatively comfortable. Myrcal knew from experience it was actually a torture device, though—ou had tried it and had only lasted a kysaq before ous legs and back had begun screaming.

Abu looked out over the garden, then back to Myrcal.

"Thank you for the invitation," he said. "The view is beautiful."

"It is." Myrcal shook ous head in agreement. "The Clan Ruler has had the best and brightest plants brought here from all over Sarth. Ou finds its beauty comforting when ou is . . . troubled, and I thought it might be a pleasant venue for us to talk."

"I see," Abu said, his lips turning up at the ends. "I take it you find yourself . . . troubled also?"

"I do," Myrcal said, happy the Earthian had caught on. "There are a number of issues I'm working on from a purely Sarthian perspective, and then there are the issues brought about by your arrival, which don't seem to be resolving themselves as quickly as we—all of us—might hope."

"And I suspect you're hoping I can help you resolve some of these issues, just between the two of us?"

The Earthian cut straight to the crux of the matter, Myrcal thought. *I can appreciate that.*

"Yes, exactly," Myrcal replied. "In fact, it's one of the main reasons we wanted you to come to Kwyzo nar Qwern, if truth be told. We wanted a chance to get to know you better and to chat with you without the Diantians prattling on and on about their laws and treaties and such."

"I see."

"Do you?" Myrcal asked.

"Yes," Abu said. He nodded his head momentarily, then shook it, leaving Myrcal somewhat confused as to whether he was indicating assent or disagreement. The confusion must have showed on his nasal flaps, because Abu's lips turned up again and he added, "I think I understand quite well why you wanted us here; you're looking to make a secret agreement with us that will be to your advantage."

"I would never do such a thing," Myrcal replied. "My intentions were just to discuss with you how we—the Qwernian Empire—might be of benefit to your society. Whether those benefits exceed what the Diantians are able to provide, of course, is a matter for you to decide . . . and if it led to any agreements, that would also be up to you. Besides, if we were to agree on anything, any 'deals' we made would have to go through the Clan Ruler, too, of course."

"I notice he isn't here to greet me," Abu said.

"Yes, I'm sorry, he's very busy at the moment. I hope he'll be able to join us later, but I am unsure whether that will be so."

"I see." The Earthian twitched his shoulders. "So what is it you wanted to discuss?"

"As I said, I wanted to discuss how the Qwernian Empire could assist you." Myrcal took a moment to center ouself; this was the opportunity ou had been waiting for.

"You came a long way to talk to us," ou began. "Truth?"

"Yes," the Earthian replied. "We did."

"That tells me your need is great," Myrcal said. "Otherwise, you wouldn't have made this journey. The resources tied up in the trip here—both personnel and equipment alike—are staggering from our perspective. Your need must be great in order for you to do so.

"And, in fact, you've said it, yourself," ou continued, warming to the topic. "Secretary David has told us that you're alone against this Hegemony, which is made up of hundreds of races, spread out over thousands of star systems. You're vastly outnumbered and are, as you said, in need of allies."

Ou wagged ous nasal flaps in a shrug. "You also say your allies-to-be will be treated equally and brought up to your standards, although you've given us no indication of how that will be accomplished. This is just one of the key pieces of information you haven't given us. There are many others. In fact, what you *don't* tell us seems to say more than what you actually do. With that said, though, I really do believe that you're in need of people to join your cause. I also believe your need is dire."

"You do?" Abu asked. "Why is that?"

"As I said, you came here, investing your resources to do so. Then, when you got here, you didn't bomb us and force us into submission, despite the fact that you very easily could have done so."

The Earthian shook his head slightly, which Myrcal took as conceding the point, and continued, "To me, this suggests the need is dire. Not only do you need our assistance, but you need our *willing* assistance. You don't have time for anything other than our best efforts. You're scared of the Hegemony and what it could do to your species.

"That point alone should tell us to avoid you. If hundreds of races want you destroyed, the odds are that they'll be successful in that effort. Adding our planet of substandard—to you—troops wouldn't make a difference in that effort. As far behind you as we are, we're even farther behind the Hegemony. Our help won't make the difference in direct battle with them."

Abu shook his head again, once.

"Where we *can* make a difference, though, is in your recruiting effort. You found us, and you've said there are other systems like ours in your records. If we join you—and do so willingly—we'll serve as advertisements for the next race you contact, and the ones after that. We can say, 'Yes, join us. These Earthians are exactly what they say. Join us, and help us conquer the galaxy.'

"You need us to help you recruit others. Perhaps in time, you can bring us up to your standards, but it will indeed *take* time—time you may not have. You need us on board with you, and soon. You need us with you, doing what you say. You need able-bodied tryzhans who—"

"Excuse me," the Earthian said, raising one hand in what Myrcal had learned was intended as a polite gesture of interruption.

"Yes?" ou said, lifting one nasal flap invitingly.

"You just used a word our translator didn't recognize," Abu said. It wasn't the first time that issue had arisen, and it was probably because the words in question had emerged in Sarth's languages between the last visit by the Hegemony's surveyors and the Earthians' arrival.

"Tryzhan?" Myrcal asked, and, after a very brief hesitation, the Earthian shook his head in agreement.

"Yes," he said. "Could you define it for the translator's vocabulary?"

"Of course," the Foreign Minister agreed, then closed ous nasal flaps in a brief expression of distaste. "It isn't actually a Qwernian word, you understand. It goes back to the days when the Diantians were sailing all around the planet planting colonies and conquering everyone in sight. When they reached Deltar, some of their great trading companies established trading posts. In fact, they carved out entire enclaves on the Deltaran coast in what are now Synchanat and Desqwer. They needed the wherewithal to defend those enclaves, and they had no desire to invite their government back home to take over their assets in Deltar, so they raised and armed troops locally. Deltaran troops who owed their loyalty to the companies who paid them. They were called 'tryzhans,' and in the end, they proved more loyal to their employers than to the rest of Deltar.

Indeed, the tryzhan regiments formed the backbone of the Synchanatian and Desqwerian armies when they rebelled against the Republic many, many years later."

"I see," Abu Bakr said, obviously remembering to shake his head this time in agreement. "I believe you're describing something very much like what we would call a 'sepoy.'"

"Perhaps." Myrcal, flipped both nasal flaps in a shrug. "Tryzhans are what you obviously need, though—troops who will do as we're told, like the members of our Alliance follow our lead. You need us—the Qwernian Empire—which has troops and allies that follow orders and do what they're told, not the Diantians, for whom everything is a matter of debate and discussion. Before they can do anything, they have to debate the topic to death, and may very well miss the opportunity to act.

"Not so, the Qwernian Empire. When our troops are told to attack, *they attack*! When our citizens are told to do something they do it *immediately*!

"Who is the better ally for you? The one who understands what it's like to be a tryzhan—and who is happy to follow your lead—or the nation that dithers and debates when danger is near? There is only one logical choice—the Qwernian Empire. And, luckily, the Qwernian Empire would like to be your ally. We would be happy to serve you. Is this not what you want and need?"

The Earthian looked at Myrcal for a moment, then took a deep breath and let it out slowly.

"Those are fine words," he said finally, "but what are we to do with the Diantians?"

"I'm sure their agreement can be arranged," Myrcal said. "All that would be necessary would be for you to leave us some of your advanced weapons and take word of our alliance back to your planet. When you return, all of Sarth will rejoice at your return and be willing to serve you."

"You're going to kill the Diantians?"

"That would be a waste of resources," Myrcal replied, "and it's already been noted that resources are at a premium. Let us just say that the Qwernian Empire will . . . reorder our society to accommodate our inclusion into an alliance with you."

"And we should sign this deal now?"

"If you would prefer to do it now, I'm sure an audience with the Clan Ruler can be arranged and an agreement concluded."

The Earthian blew out his breath and laughed as he stood.

"I'm sure your Clan Ruler would finally show up for an event like that; unfortunately, it's not going to happen. Even if I *was* empowered to make a deal with you, I would never make one that included the suppression of half your planet's people. Nor would anyone in our delegation. Good day."

"Wait," Myrcal called after him. Abu turned and looked back. "Can you at least tell me how you were able to beat the Shongairi when they outclassed you so badly?"

Abu turned and left without another word. When Myrcal called out to him again, he neither stopped nor looked back.

. . . . .

"AND HE DIDN'T look back, Clan Ruler," Myrcal related later.

"What do you suppose that means?" Juzhyr asked.

"I'm starting to wonder. Based on what we've seen from Lyzan, as well as the other countries that have Earthian delegations, and now this . . . it seems the Earthians are far more favorably inclined to the Diantians than us."

"Do you suppose that's because their race is more like Dianto than the Empire?" Erylk asked. "If so, that would make them more predisposed to offer them the choicest morsels on the table."

"It may be," Myrcal reflected. "But if that's so, it's only a predisposition. . . ."

"What are you saying?" Juzhyr asked.

"Nothing is firm yet in the Earthians' minds, Clan Ruler, and no decisions have been made. There are a number of things we can do to help the Earthians reconsider just how good a partner the Republic might be. I spoke with Flythyr earlier, and she said the special forces are on standby 'for anything they're needed for.' She also said that her people have all of the pieces in place for Operation Thunder, should you decide to go forward with that, but that the window of opportunity for it is rapidly closing."

"Operation Thunder is a high-risk option, Clan Ruler," Erylk pointed out, and Myrcal suppressed a nasal flap curl of frustration. The old bearer's obstructionism had become more and more wearing over the past several full-days. "If it fails. . . ."

Ou let ous voice trail off, and Myrcal shook ous head in false sympathy with ous point.

"That's always a valid concern," ou acknowledged. "But from Ambassador Abu's attitude, I fear they're drawing steadily closer to the Diantians. If that's true, we have to find a way to reverse it. I believe Operation Thunder may be our best way to do that, but if we're going to move forward with it, we may have to do it soon. . . ."

XI

THE NONAGON, CITY OF LYZAN, RYZAK ISLAND, PLANET SARTH

D ave Dvorak gazed out over the enormous nine-sided chamber.

Over the months, he'd become more of an everyday sight for the Sarthians, especially here in Lyzan where he had established Earth's official embassy. His appearances before the Nonagon hadn't been all that frequent, but they'd been frequent enough that the incredible crowding which had packed the Hall of Nations solid for his first address had eased a lot.

Not so much today, though, he thought dryly. Well, that was fair. He'd made it clear that today would mark a major policy statement on the Planetary Union's part, and journalists and reporters from every Sarthian nation had jockeyed furiously for position. Apparently, Sarth had no equivalent of the concept of a "press pool." He didn't think anyone had resorted to outright violence to secure a place, but he wasn't willing to risk money betting on that.

Sword Lord Consort Symkah completed his introductory remarks and stepped back, offering the raised dais to his Earthian guest, and Dvorak bowed deeply as he rose from the human-style chair. He stepped up onto the dais and hid a smile as the podium from which Gyrdan had introduced him rose smoothly on hidden electric motors to a more suitable height. He rested his hands lightly on it and surveyed the chamber for several seconds in silence. Then he squared his shoulders and inhaled.

"Thank you for that introduction, Speaker Gyrdan," he said first, turning his head to give the Sarthian a human-style smile, and then turned back to the rest of his audience.

"Gentle folk of the Nonagon, I'm happy to say that we've made a great deal of progress during our time here on Sarth," he began. After all, one had to be polite. "Not all of our diplomatic missions have been able to report equal levels of success, but in general, we've established what I believe are excellent relations with our hosts and I believe our understanding of one another has grown enormously.

"It's partly because of the way in which that understanding has grown that I asked Speaker Gyrdan for permission to address you this day-half.

"As you know, we've maintained our official embassy here in Lyzan in order to emphasize that our mission is to your planet as a whole, not to any single Sarthian nation. I've made flying visits to the individual capitals of every member of the

Nonagon and had the opportunity to meet personally with virtually all your heads of state, and in each of those meetings I have, again, emphasized that we are here to negotiate with your world as a whole. Obviously, when Sarth has no official, worldwide government, as we do in the Planetary Union, that means we must speak to—and listen to—all of your nations individually, and that's what we've been doing over the last Sarthian year or so.

"During that time, we believe we've reached better understanding with some of your nations than with others. That's probably inevitable, since we have different levels of contact and access, and since most beings interface most comfortably with those most like themselves. We work very hard to keep that in mind from our side, because one of the great lessons of our own often violent past is that assuming the other side of a dispute thinks and understands things the same way you do is an excellent way to create the sort of misunderstanding which leads to bloodshed and destruction. It's true, however, that what one might call . . . compatibility is always a factor in the success or failure of negotiations.

"In our case, we are, frankly, more comfortable dealing with those of your nations whose governments most closely resemble our own. I would add that in forging the government we now have, it was necessary for many nations with very different traditions and forms of government to reach understanding and acceptance of the Constitution we ultimately adopted for our planet. As such, we fully understand that it isn't always—or even often—a matter of governments which are superior or inferior; it's simply a matter of governments which are *different* from one another. As I say, we work very hard to keep this in the forefront of our thinking, and we ask you of Sarth to do the same where we're concerned.

"I say this because it's become clear to me that there's been some misunderstanding about the fashion in which we approach Sarth."

He paused to let that settle in and allowed his eyes to circle the chamber while he waited. He deliberately didn't look at the Qwernian delegation, but he didn't have to, either. The Terran cameras which had been mounted to cover the Hall of Nations with the Nonagon's approval took care of that for him, and his personal computer projected a window into the corner of his vision, showing him Yerdaz NorYerDar's reaction. Judging from the dark-tinged red and yellow overlay, she knew exactly who he was talking about. Well, that was good. He had no intention of naming names or specifically singling out and embarrassing Minister Myrcal or Clan Ruler Juzhyr, but it was important for both of them to understand why Abu Bakr had reacted as he had . . . and that Dave Dvorak was in complete agreement with him.

"We've presented you with an extraordinarily complex problem," he continued after several seconds. "We're aware of that, and it is not our purpose—never has been, and never will be our purpose—to destabilize your world. Above all, we have no intention of inflaming existing national rivalries, and backing one Sarthian nation or alliance against another is not part of our mission to you. One of our great healers once said that a physician's first responsibility was 'to do no harm,' and that's how we approach Sarth. Much as it would grieve us, we would make none of our technology available to any Sarthian if we cannot make it available to all Sarthians.

"Moreover, we have learned the hard way—at the cost of countless wars and millions of human deaths—that binding international agreements must be openly arrived at. It took us far longer than it ought to have taken rational beings to learn that lesson, just as it took us far too long and far too much blood to grasp that binding international agreements which contain no effective enforcement mechanism are useless. If there is no effective enforcement mechanism, then rather than regarding the agreement as solemn, binding international law, it is regarded as something by which to abide only so long as it is expedient to do so. That, unfortunately, is a fundamental aspect of human thinking, and from our observations here on Sarth, I would say that it's one of the things our species have in common.

"Please understand that I would never deny that the parties to a negotiation have every right to speak to one another in conditions of confidentiality. If one is to reach an understanding acceptable to all parties, then all parties to that understanding must have the right to express themselves fully, freely, and frankly without worrying about how their words might be twisted, taken out of context, misinterpreted, or used against them in some public forum. This has been part of our fundamental approach to these talks from the very beginning."

He glanced at the window showing the Qwernian delegation. Yerdaz at least appeared to have herself under better control, and he hoped she'd caught his pointed emphasis that neither he nor any member of his delegation had any intention of running to the Diantians to tattle on Myrcal's bald-faced bid to conquer the Republic in the Planetary Union's name.

"We welcome and invite continued conversations—conversations which will not be communicated to any other party without permission and previous consultation—as our mission here moves forward," he continued. "Any terms which are ultimately accepted, however, will be disclosed openly and completely here, on the floor of the Nonagon, where all of Sarth can witness everything which has been agreed upon. There are no other terms, no other basis, on which final agreement can be reached.

"Gentle folk of Sarth, we came to you because we believe we face a common threat. We've asked you to assume the risk of joining us in alliance against that common threat. For that alliance to succeed, it must be firm. It must stand upon bedrock, and that bedrock can only be created on the basis of mutual understanding and mutual trust. Moreover, that understanding and that trust must be strong enough to stand in the face of hurricane and earthquake. It cannot be—none of us can afford for it to be—based upon anything short of openness and honesty, because we can all be assured that if there is any weakness, any flaw—if at sometime in the future any member of that alliance discovers that it was ever lied to or betrayed by its other members—that alliance will crumble. We will all discover that it rested not on bedrock, but on sand, and the consequences will be a disaster for all of us.

"It will be far, far better for Sarth—and for us—to arrive at no final treaty of alliance than to arrive at one forcibly imposed from outside or reached by betrayal from within.

"Our missions will remain in your capitals, serving as our interfaces with all of your nations, but understand that they will take no binding position that isn't openly disclosed here, before the Nonagon. We wish you to continue to speak with us frankly, assured that you speak in confidence, and I pledge to all of you that nothing any Sarthian nation says to any human representative will be disclosed without the prior consent of that nation, but no agreement will be final until it has been disclosed to all of your neighbors.

"I thank you again for the opportunity to speak to you, and to clarify our position in this regard. Believe me, we understand the . . . complexity of the situation you confront, but it is our imperative responsibility to be as open, above board, and honest as we possibly can.

"If we cannot give you those things, then any other 'gift' we might give you would be worse than offering you food and handing you poison, and the bedrock of our mission is 'to first do no harm.'"

He let that fade into the stillness, then drew himself up and bowed slightly.

"Thank you," he said again, and stepped back from the podium.

XII

PRIME DIRECTOR'S OFFICE, AND HIGH BEARER MYKAIR'S OFFICE,
CITY OF DIANZHYR, REPUBLIC OF DIANTO;
CITY OF KWYZO NAR QWERN, QWERN EMPIRE;
AND SOKYR CHELSO'S RECTORY, CITY OF MYRCOS,
REPUBLIC OF DIANTO,
PLANET SARTH

W hat do you make of it, Zhor?" First Director Qwelth asked, nasal
flaps half-closed in obvious unhappiness.

"I'm not exactly an alien mind reader, either, Qwelth," Zhor
ZhorSalDyr pointed out. The foreign minister didn't look a lot happier than
the first director, but ou managed to put at least a little humor into ous tone.
Qwelth looked at oum, and ou waggled ous nasal flaps. "It sounds to me like
somebody got caught trying to sneak into the syldak coop. And, if I had to
guess who it was, it was probably Myrcal. Or ous *idea*, anyway."

"But Secretary David—" Qwelth had learned to do much better with the
Earthian name "—didn't say anything about the Empire."

"Of course he didn't," Zhor replied. "That's not the Earthian way. He's trying
to save Myrcal's face while simultaneously sending the message that the Earthians genuinely aren't going to be signing any secret side deals with anyone."

"I wish they'd sign one with *us*," Swordsman Consort Bardyn muttered.
Qwelth glanced at him, and the intelligence director's nasal flaps grimaced. "I
don't trust Myrcal—or Juzhyr, for that matter—as far as I can spit. This 'illness'
of Chancellor Erylk's comes at a really bad time from our perspective. All our
sources agree ou's completely out of the equation for now, and that leaves Myrcal
in the driver's seat. We all know what *ou's* like . . . and whatever else is going on,
their military's up to something."

"What?" Qwelth asked sharply.

"If I knew what they were up to, I wouldn't have called it 'something,'" Bardyn
retorted. "We don't know. But we do know they've been passing a lot of signals
lately. In fact, if I were a suspicious fellow—which Chelth knows I'm not—I'd
say all the signal activity started about the time something apparently pissed
off Secretary David."

"You don't think they're planning an attack on the *Earthians*?" Foreign
Minister Zhor demanded in a tone of considerable alarm.

"I doubt even Myrcal's that stupid," Bardyn replied. "The Earthians have

390 DAVID WEBER and CHRIS KENNEDY

been awfully careful about not waving weapons under our snouts, but you know they didn't come without a lot more security than they've shown us so far. For that matter, I've been talking to some of the Fellows of the Academy. If they wanted to, they could just drop rocks on us."

"Rocks?" Qwelth repeated blankly.

"Rocks. Or you can call them what we call them when one of them falls on us without anyone helping it along: meteorites. We still haven't actually detected any of their ships, not even visually, but we know they have to be in orbit around the planet. That means they're at the top of the 'gravity well,' and all they really have to do is drop something from that altitude to hit with more power than the biggest bomb we've ever built. According to the Academy, just one 'kinetic projectile' traveling fast enough could wipe out Dianzhyr completely."

"*Chelth*," someone whispered.

"More like Taysar's lightning," Bardyn said. "I don't know if Myrcal and Juzhyr have had the same sort of conversation with their academics, but even if they haven't, anybody smart enough to raise his kilt before he takes a piss should realize they don't want to tangle with someone who can travel between stars and has landing ships the size of one of our battleships. If that's how big their passenger craft are, I don't think we even want to think about what their combat aircraft are like! To be honest, that's what worries me. If the Qwernians are contemplating some sort of military action, I don't think it could be directed against the Earthians. Which leaves only one other target, so far as I can see."

"But why would they attack *us*?" First Sea Lord Hyrthah asked. "Now, I mean," ou clarified when all of them looked at oum.

"I don't know," Bardyn admitted. "The only semi-plausible scenario I've been able to come up with is that they might hope for a lightning victory which removes us from the table as a potential rival for the Earthians' affections."

"I don't think David would stand for that," Qwelth said.

"I don't think so either," Bardyn agreed. "Unfortunately, what we're talking about is what *Myrcal and Juzhyr* think. They may have misinterpreted David's emphasis on not choosing sides or getting involved in local political squabbles to mean he'd regard any . . . changes on the ground as a purely Sarthian affair and none of his business. I think they'd have to be out of their minds to believe that he and the other Earthians would go along with their plan, but that doesn't mean they aren't thinking that way."

"Wonderful," Qwelth muttered. Ou glared balefully at Bardyn. "All I can say is that you damned well better be wrong. But, in the meantime," ou turned his attention to First Director of War Mynsaro, "you'd better put our frontier formations on alert. But for Chelth's sake, do it quietly! The last thing we need is to be adding any fuel to whatever bonfire Myrcal's decided to light."

. . . . .

"I THINK IT'S time for a letter to Bearer Sokyr," Mykair ChelMyk said to Nykar ChelNyk nor Chelth, ous senior secretary. The high bearer's expression was not amused, and Nykar lifted one nasal flap in question.

"A letter, Holiness? Ah, what sort of letter did you have in mind?"

"What sort did you *think* I had in mind?" Mykair asked tartly.

"Well, Holiness, I was fairly sure it wasn't to wish him happy natal day."

"Such a mind reader, you are," Mykair said in a slightly more amused tone. "And, no, it's not a happy natal day card."

"Of course, Holiness," Nykar said in a much more serious tone. "Do you wish to dictate it, or do you want to give me an idea of its content and have me run up a rough draft for you?"

"I'll dictate it personally." Mykair curled ous nasal flaps. "But, before I do, I want you to pull all of my previous correspondence with oum. And then I want you to bring me the file folder on all those Chelth–damned 'manifestoes' ou's been strewing about. *All* of them, mind you. I want to review them and I want to be properly pissed off when I get around to actually addressing oum."

"Of course, Holiness," Nykar said, but her nasal flaps showed her own satisfaction clearly enough. She was barely half Mykair's age and only an underbearer, but she'd been with oum almost half her own life, and she was fiercely devoted to oum. More than that, she'd had a front row seat to watch Sokyr and the rest of the Chelthists inflict their misery upon oum. Upon the rest of the Republic, too, of course, but Nykar was of the opinion that the rest of the Republic could look after itself. It was her job to look after *Mykair*.

"Don't worry, Nykar," the high-bearer said, reaching up to lay one hand lightly on her shoulder. "Our friend Sokyr is about to find out that even my patience has an end."

"Good, Holiness." Nykar didn't even try to hide her satisfaction, and Mykair's nasal flaps smiled at her.

She bent her head respectfully and withdrew, and despite the fact that she'd made no effort to conceal her satisfaction from Mykair, none of the other clerics and clerks she passed on her way to her own office could have guessed her elation from her expression. The High Bearer's decisions were none of their business until ou chose to make them public, and Nykar took that seriously.

But inside, behind that expressionless exterior, vengeful approval sang a hymn of victory. She'd waited *so* long for the High Bearer she served—and loved—to give Sokyr ous just deserts! The bearer had mistaken Mykair's patience and sense of Chelthian charity for weakness, and it was long past time ou discovered how mistaken ou'd been.

Nykar had no doubt what had brought Mykair to decisive action at last. She could have guessed that even without ous request for the manifesto file. Sokyr and ous circle of sympathizers and sycophants had waxed more and more virulent in their denunciations of the Earthians as demons and agents of Shaymork. It was as if they'd realized their opposition to any "accommodation with evil" was doomed and the realization only fueled their desperation. It had been bad enough when Sokyr was simply thundering anathemas and calling down colorful curses, but over the last several day-halves, ou'd been straying into increasingly less subtle calls for "direct action."

Nykar doubted that the mutinous bearer commanded more than a few sixteens of followers, so it wasn't as if they could do much damage even if they heeded him. But that didn't mean they couldn't try, and Mykair took ous responsibility to protect the Earthians seriously. And, on a perhaps less lofty note, the High Bearer wasn't about to let a bevy of Chelthist lunatics humiliate the Church of Chelth by demonstrating their stupidity and bigotry for all Sarth to see.

Which was just fine, with Nykar ChelNyk nor Chelth.

. . . . .

"IT'S NOTHING SHORT of an outrage, Clan Ruler!" Myrcal MyrFarZol nar Qwern exclaimed, ous nasal flaps closed tightly in anger, as ou stormed into the conference room.

"What is that?" Juzhyr asked. While Myrcal *had* had a lot to be upset about recently, Juzhyr was also well aware the foreign minister lived ous life on the edge of perpetual outragement and tended to view events from that perspective. Sometimes ous outbursts had to be taken with a grain of yden.

"The latest cable just arrived from the Nonagon, Clan Ruler. The head Earthian requested and received permission to address the entire assemblage. His whole purpose in this address was to issue a backhanded rebuke to us!"

"Slow down, Myrcal, and begin at the beginning. A rebuke for what purpose?"

"David took the podium with one message and one message only—that the Earthians won't make any secret deals with anyone."

"Yes," Juzhyr replied, shaking ous head slowly. "But that isn't a new message. They've said that all along. That was even Abu's message to us when you approached him about one here in the gardens."

"But to call a special session of the Nonagon, for the sole purpose of reiterating this message, Clan Ruler? It will be obvious, even to the dim-witted Diantians, that there had to be a *reason* for him to do so. Obviously, something happened to make him feel he needed to address the entire Nonagon. And what will happen when the Diantians query all their diplomatic staff and find out none of them were responsible for proposing such an agreement? It will be plain that *we* were the ones to do so. It will be plain that *we* tried to make a secret deal with the Earthians, and that it was rebuffed. David's making this proclamation in so obvious a manner is a tremendous loss of face for us."

Juzhyr's nasal flaps closed tightly as ou followed Myrcal's line of reasoning to its logical conclusion. The Qwernian Empire—and by extension, Juzhyr, ouself—had definitely lost face with David's pronouncement. *And it was neither right nor diplomatic for them to humiliate the Empire so obviously and flagrantly.*

Juzhyr found ouself wishing old Erylk was here even more strongly than usual as that thought ground through oum. Unfortunately, the chancellor's physicians doubted ou would ever be able to take up ous duties once more. Ous absence left Myrcal as acting chancellor as well as foreign minister, and part of the clan ruler's mind reminded oum it could be dangerous for any one minister to have too much influence. The problem was, Myrcal was obviously right, and Juzhyr tried to bite back on ous own anger.

"Why do you suppose David felt the need to make this pronouncement?" ou asked.

"I don't know, Clan Ruler, but I can guess." Myrcal ran a hand down ous crest and closed ous nasal flaps in disgust. "We've long wondered why no progress has been made over these long triads. What if . . . what if progress *was* being made, but it was the Diantians the Earthians were making it with? What if the Earthians decided they had more in common with the Diantians, and they've been making secret plans with *them* . . . and this pronouncement is nothing more than a sham to make us lose face and give them the reason they need to make their backroom dealings with the Diantians public? By humiliating us, they can say, 'Since you broke the rules, we've decided to work foremost with Dianto.'"

"Do you think this is the case?" Juzhyr asked. Ou could feel the blood pooling in ous crest and had to resist the urge to strike out at Myrcal—to strike out at anyone or anything—in ous anger.

"Unfortunately, I do, Clan Ruler. In fact, David's own words damn him. In his speech to the Nonagon, he said, 'In our case, we are, frankly, more comfortable dealing with those of your nations whose governments most closely resemble our own.' That's a direct quote from his speech. We know for a fact that they aren't dealing with us . . . so who *are* they dealing with? There can only be one answer—they're secretly dealing with the Diantians!"

"David really said that? Those words, exactly?"

"Yes, Clan Ruler; those were his exact words. Not only that, he also said the Earthians would only give their technology to us if we all agreed—they wouldn't give it to just *some* of our nations."

"So? What does that mean?"

"I think it means they're setting us up to assume a position of subservience to the Diantians. They're trying to humble us so that when they announce the agreement with the Diantians, we have no recourse but to go along with it. If we don't grovel at their feet, they'll take everything away from Sarth and go back to their own home world, leaving us with nothing! They've put us in an untenable position, Clan Ruler! When their secret agreement comes out, we'll either have to kowtow to it or be known as the nation who refused to be a party to the agreement and drove the Earthians—and all their incredible new knowledge—away from Sarth for all time."

Juzhyr shut ous nasal flaps tightly and tried to think. While there were times where a display of anger was appropriate to help motivate ous subordinates, this wasn't one of them. What they required was a plan. They needed . . . they needed the Earthians to go in a new direction. But what was the best way to show the Earthians that a new direction was needed, when they'd already shown themselves to be disinterested in the Qwernian Empire's needs and desires? When they'd thrown Myrcal's advances back into Juzhyr's own face? A new direction could only come from one place—the highest level of their delegation.

"Perhaps it's time the Earthians had a change of leadership," Juzhyr said slowly. "They could obviously use someone a little more open to the way diplomacy is supposed to be conducted." Ou thought for a moment, then asked, "If Secretary David were to have . . . an unfortunate accident, who would replace him?"

"According to Yernaz, Councilor Arthur is their second, and she believes she has a special understanding with him."

"Interesting," Juzhyr said, arching a questioning nasal flap. "How does she define this 'special understanding'?"

"She's met privately with him on a number of occasions, Clan Ruler, and found him to be someone more open to our way of thinking. And someone less likely to be blindly led about by the rules-worshiping Diantians. She believes he understands how diplomacy works, and would be far more open to our advances if he were in charge."

"And you say he's second to only David? If he's so important, why does he stay at the Nonagon? If he's truly their second, why isn't he here, talking with us? Or even talking with the Diantians, if they're the Earthians' golden children?"

"He's undoubtedly staying in Lyzan for the same reasons David is—that's what diplomacy requires. Just as you wouldn't want senior members of your Ministry inadvertently committing you to a course of action, I'm sure the same is true with David. That can be the only reason he keeps Arthur close by—David doesn't want him committing the Earthians to a plan of action that David would later have to publicly disavow. If Ambassador Abu says or does something wrong, his actions are easily dismissed as the incorrect ramblings of an underling."

Juzhyr shook ous head, fluttering ous nasal flaps derisively at the mention of Abu Bakr. "That makes sense," ou said. "I wouldn't want to be tied to the actions of someone who so obviously doesn't understand diplomacy or negotiation, either." All the pieces lined up in ous mind. Ou'd long wondered why it was taking so long for agreements to be signed. If there truly were this "Hegemony," and it was as bad as the Earthians said, why would they delay as long as they had? They obviously wouldn't delay—they would want to come to a conclusion as quickly as possible so they could move forward. An agreement with the nation that most resembled their own. David's own words damned him. They *were* working with the Diantians.

They were also obviously nearing what they thought was an agreement if they were trying to humble the Qwernian Empire. David's speech to the Nonagon was nothing more than a transparent message to Juzhyr that ou had lost; the Earthians were moving forward with the Diantians, and they were putting oum in a position where ou was forced to accept it. They'd put Juzhyr in a position where ous back was against the sea; there was no further retreat and only one option remained.

"It's time, Myrcal. The Earthians have done it to themselves. Initiate Operation Thunder."

· · · · ·

"DID YOU GET the latest manifesto to the printer, Trygau?" Sokyr ChelSo nor Chelth asked as the leader of ous action teams entered his office.

"I did, Bearer," Trygau replied, bobbing his head deferentially.

"Good!"

Sokyr rose and stalked to the window, gazing out into the twilight of the late second day-half. Ous shoulders were tense, ous nasal flaps tight, and ous entire body radiated fury and outrage. And, perhaps, fear. Ou could feel everything in which ou believed slipping through ous fingers. The tighter ou closed ous grasp, the more quickly it trickled away, and there was nothing ou could do about it.

That was what truly tormented oum. It was ous duty, ous *responsibility,* to restore Chelth to Ous rightful place, and ou couldn't do it. They weren't *listening.* All those Sarthians out there, all those children of Chelth, simply refused to hear Ous voice in Sokyr's words. They ignored oum. They *laughed* at oum, so fascinated by the wonder and the false promises of the accursed Earthians that they didn't even *care* about their immortal souls.

Ou'd done ous best. Ou had—ou truly *had*! Ou'd argued, ou'd excoriated, ou'd begged, and none of it had worked. Oh, ous band of Chelthist warriors, pledged to shed their own life's blood—or anyone else's—in Chelth's service had grown. There were almost three sixteens of them now! But that was only a syldak's egg to throw against the looming granite cliff of the Earthians' hypnotizing songs, especially with First Director Qwelth and High Bearer Mykair singing in harmony! If ou thought that taking up the sword in Chelth's name could change the blasphemous epiphany ou saw racing towards all of Sarth, ou would have done it in a kysaq.

But it wouldn't. All it would accomplish would be to get ous faithful followers, Chelth's last true servants, hunted down and killed by the apostate authorities. They couldn't stop what was coming. They could only brand themselves as murderous fanatics in the eyes of all those blind, misled, ignorant, *uncaring* Sarthians so eager to be seduced by the aliens from beyond the stars. And because it would do no good, there was no point in—

Sokyr ChelSo nor Chelth's thoughts shattered as the garrotte went around ous neck from behind. Ous hands darted up, fingers and thumbs ripping at the thin wire, twisting frantically as it sawed still tighter. Ou felt blood spilling down his throat, hot and slick as the wire sliced its way through scales and flesh. Ou gurgled, fighting desperately for air, but there *was* no air, and ous eyes bulged as they slowly, slowly dimmed into the final darkness.

Trygau HyrShalTry nor Ganyth—whose real name was Gauntlet Sydar HynSyTar nar Qwelth—looked down on the corpse and prodded it with his toe. It was odd, but he'd expected to take more satisfaction out of eliminating the insufferably smug cleric. And in some ways, he had. In other ways, though, he thought he might actually *miss* Sokyr, although he had no intention of admitting that to his superiors.

Always assuming he ever had the opportunity to admit *anything* to his superiors.

Sydar wasn't about to question his orders, and he'd worked for almost eleven Sarthian years to position himself to carry them out, but he had few illusions about the efficiency of the Diantian security forces. If he managed things perfectly, they'd probably spend the next several years chasing the original Trygau while he slipped away home to the Empire. Given that the suitably weighted records clerk who'd managed to lose that Trygau's death certificate was at the bottom of a flooded granite quarry three minrans outside Myrcos, it was unlikely they'd ever find him.

Or Sokyr, who would be joining the clerk shortly.

· XIII ·

PUNS *OUTREACH*,
SARTH ORBIT

D ad, are you sure this trip is necessary?" Captain Malachi Dvorak
asked.
"It may not be strictly 'necessary,' but I'm not going to cancel it, if
that's what you mean," his father replied. "Is it?"

"Well . . . maybe," Malachi said.

"Why?"

"Because my nose itches."

If most people had said that, Dave Dvorak would have asked them what the
hell it had to do with the subject under discussion. Malachi, however, wasn't
"most people," and he wasn't talking about his physical nose. He was talking
about what his mother had always referred to as his "nose for trouble." She
hadn't meant it as a compliment the first time she'd used it in response to a
typical thirteen-year-old's flippant backtalk. Nor had the typical thirteen-year-
old in question enjoyed her reaction to it. But while the experience might have
made him more wary, it hadn't made him any less flippant—hard to see how it
could have, given his parentage—and he'd adopted the term himself to describe
something very different.

Dvorak didn't know how it worked, and it was far from infallible, but he
had to admit Malachi had predicted trouble before it arrived with a statistics-
defying accuracy ever since adolescence. Morgana had actually hauled him in
to test for any evidence of extrasensory perception, although both of them had
regarded it as more of a joke than anything else. Needless to say, the tests hadn't
found anything. But—

"Do you have any idea why?" Morgana asked. She was the mission psychology team's number two—it made the entire mission more of a Dvorak family
firm than her father sometimes wished, but Marcos Ramos had insisted she
was the one for the job—and now she looked at her brother intently.

"You mean aside from the fact that the Chelthists have been preaching fire
and brimstone about us demonic Earthians? Or the fact that Diantian intelligence claims that Qwernian military radio traffic is twenty percent above normal? Or the fact that we don't really know what their military traffic's total
volume is because so much of it goes by cable? Or the fact that it's obvious from
the way Myrcal canceled his scheduled session with Uncle Abu last day-half

that the Qwernians don't appreciate the way Dad tried to save face for them? You mean aside from that?"

Dvorak snorted, but he had to admit Malachi had a point. And he also had to admit that a good bit of it was his fault, although he still didn't see any other way he could have responded to Myrcal's blatant attempt to cut a secret deal. He'd had to react to that, one way or another, and he'd tried his damnedest to avoid bludgeoning the Empire over the head with it. But while the Terrans' penetration of the inner workings of the various Sarthian nations remained far short of what it could have been if they'd only had an Internet to be hacked, it was clear that Myrcal was the most xenophobic of the foreign ministers involved by a substantial margin. With Erylk out of the picture—with an "illness" which had quite possibly been helped along by Mrycal—the foreign minister was effectively chancellor, as well. And according to Alex Jackson and Arthur McCabe's latest analysis, ou was probably going to carry the can if the Empire's diplomacy went completely south on it. Given all of that, it was hard not to wonder just how desperate ou might be feeling.

On the other hand, ou was only a minister, not the clan ruler. Ous authority was limited. For that matter, if Clan Ruler Juzhyr decided Myrcal had blown it, the influence and authority ou'd managed to accrue would probably evaporate.

Which could only add to any sense of desperation ou might be feeling, damn it.

"Look, Malachi," he said after a moment, "you're right about all the crap going on down there. I'm the one who kicked the fire, though. That means I have an even greater responsibility to carry on with my normal schedule. To be as 'business-as-usual' as I possibly can."

"Excuse me, but *you* didn't kick any fires," Malachi retorted, his eyes hard. "That asshole idiot Myrcal kicked one; all you did was try to stamp out the sparks!"

"And there wouldn't have been a fire to kick in the first place if we hadn't poked our nose into their planet." Dvorak reached across to squeeze his son's shoulder. "We knew we were going to disrupt their society the instant we approached them, Malachi. So, yeah, Myrcal's the one who screwed up most spectacularly, but we're the ones—and since I'm head of mission and Secretary of State, that means *I'm* the one—who gifted oum with the opportunity to be outstandingly stupid."

Malachi glared at him stubbornly, but he was no longer thirteen years old, and after a moment he nodded curtly.

"So that means I have to do whatever I can to pour water on the coals. If Myrcal hadn't decided to show ous ass and refused to meet with Abu or even accept the note Abu was supposed to present, I'd probably be going to Kwyzo nar Qwern in the next couple of day-halves, too, and I'm sure you'd hate that even more. But Prime Director Qwelth did accept my self-invitation, and I can't cancel it from my end without explaining why. And I don't really think it would make Myrcal and Juzhyr feel any calmer if I said, 'Sorry, I can't come because the Qwernians are being assholes.' I mean, I *could* be wrong about that, but I don't think so."

"I'm sure you're not wrong about that, Papi," Morgana said. "On the other hand, I really wish we had a better handle on their psychology. Part of the problem is that some of them really are a lot like us, especially in Dianto. But the Qwernians have a different mindset in a lot of ways. What I'm saying is that while I'm sure explaining publicly that you really wanted to visit their capital and they refused to even listen to the invitation would be seen as a slap in the face, I'm not sure *not* explaining it—as diplomatically as possible—might not be even worse."

Her father looked at her, and she shrugged.

"It's obvious they're already in 'We are officially offended' mode. There's no other reason for Myrcal to refuse to sit down with Uncle Abu, especially if ou was interested in repairing the damage ou'd obviously done to the Qwernian position with us. So it's not likely they'd be a lot more offended, and it might be a way to do an end run around Myrcal's belligerence."

"I always knew you were a smart one," Dvorak said, smiling at her across the breakfast table.

"Hey! What about *me*?" Malachi demanded.

"Do you really want to discuss your geometry grades?" Dvorak asked. Even with NET, Malachi had had a dreadful time with geometry, for some reason.

"Not particularly," Malachi replied. "But you've got to admit, she and Maighread never cared about *history* at all."

"Stop trying to suck up to Dad," Morgana told him with a twinkle.

"Not gonna work, anyway," Dvorak said. "Sorry, Malachi, but she's got an unfair genetic advantage. Daddies are programmed to be suckers where their daughters are concerned."

"Damn betcha, Skippy!" Morgana said, and Dvorak laughed at one of her mother's favorite comebacks.

"In this case, though, she also has a point," he continued. "I went back and forth over that same point with Alex, Trish, and Jane for the better part of an hour yesterday. We even got McCabe involved. And the answer we came up with is that it's a crapshoot. It might help a lot, and it might throw everything farther into the crapper. So, since Myrcal avoided ous last meeting with Abu on the basis that ou had 'a scheduling conflict' and rescheduled it for day-half after next, we decided—no, *I* decided—that I'll go ahead with the trip to Dianzhyr as scheduled and Abu can explain to Myrcal that he had instructions to request clearance for me to visit the Empire at the same time we were requesting clearance for me to visit the Republic. That way we can slap oum on the wrist and hopefully inspire oum to be a little more reasonable without risking ous feeling further *publicly* humiliated. Frankly, if ou feels a little *personal* humiliation, that's fine with me. Ou damned well ought to understand how diplomacy works, and if ou wants to run with the big dogs, then ou'd better figure out that the sun doesn't rise and set on ous exquisite sensibilities."

Morgana nodded, but she also darted a look across the table at her brother when her father turned his head and reached for the coffee pot.

Malachi looked back and shrugged. They loved their dad, and they both thought he was one of the smartest people they knew. But he *did* have a temper, however successfully he hid it from most people, and it was evident that Myrcal MyrFarZol had hit his "I am *pissed* with you" button. Neither of them could argue with his analysis of the political equation, and both of them agreed that Myrcal needed to smell the terahk. But it sounded to them like this had turned personal for Dave Dvorak, as well. Their father, in irate mode, was capable of accomplishing a great deal in a very short interval, but there *were* times when it made him just a tad less empathetic and forgiving than he normally was. When, as their mother had put it upon occasion, he didn't really care where the chips were falling as long as the damned tree got cut down.

Dvorak finished pouring coffee and looked back at his children, and Malachi shrugged again.

"You're the boss, Dad," he said, "and if the job were easy, they could've given it to someone like me, God help us all. So, if this is the way we're going, it's the way we're going. Uncle Rob's called a brief of all the battalion and company commanders for oh-nine-thirty, and we'll be going over contingency plans then. But, unless you want to object—and I really don't think you do, unless you want us reporting it to Mom when we get home—guess who's going to be in command of your protective detail?"

"Don't have a clue," his father said innocently.

· XIV ·

Hannibal," Captain Malachi Dvorak said to his phone, "communications check."

"All coms optimal," the AI replied, and Malachi nodded in satisfaction. It was not *unflawed* satisfaction, given the itch still plaguing his nose, but he and his people were as prepared as they were going to get for whatever might happen.

Which would have made him feel a lot better if it hadn't been his father's safety he was worrying over.

"Hawk One," he said, cuing the AI to connect him to the pair of heavily stealthed *Starhawk* fighters providing top cover, "Ground One, ready to roll."

"Ground One," Captain Isidor Berarroa, the lead *Starhawk* pilot, replied, "Hawk One copies; ready to roll."

Malachi nodded again, then glanced at Corporal Mbarjet Celaj, his driver, who just happened to also be his wing.

"Move us out, Margie," he said.

"Moving." The Albanian-born Celaj was a woman of few words, at least on duty. *Off*-duty, now . . .

Their vehicle rose on its counter-grav, floating a rock-steady thirty-eight centimeters above the pavement, and headed for the ring road. Malachi closed his eyes to concentrate on the imagery projected onto his corneal implants as the rest of the convoy followed in their wake.

The Airaavatha was only lightly armored . . . by the Planetary Union's standards, at least. Its frontal and side armor was proof against a direct hit from a pre-Invasion main battle tank's main gun, however, and it was capable of speeds approaching five hundred kilometers per hour in ground effect and fifteen hundred KPH in flight. Normally, it was armed with twin-mount thirteen-millimeter railguns, but he wasn't allowed to operate it in "normal" mode, so it wasn't armed at all at the moment. It retained its defensive ECM and antimissile defenses, but all of that was pretty much concealed inside armored hatches. Personally, he was in favor of showing the baddest-ass guns available, but he'd been overruled. Apparently older and better-paid heads than his own—including, he acknowledged, his father's—had felt that trundling around the capitals of sovereign nations in vehicles capable of annihilating the heaviest tanks their hosts might possess would be in poor taste.

Which is a piss poor reason to get someone—including my father, bless his thick skull—killed, he reflected grumpily. *Of course, if I had my way, we wouldn't be making this trip on the ground at all.*

He decided not to dwell on that particular irritation. It wasn't like dwelling would do him any good, and at least some of the arguments against it had a fair degree of applicability. Fwerchau Field, the Republic of Dianto Navy's main dirigible base, was the only open spot handy to the capital that was big enough to land a *Starlander,* and it lay on the western outskirts of Dianzhyr. So whenever Terran diplomats visited the Sitting, perched atop its steep hill in the middle of the city with a magnificent view of the harbor, they had to land at Fwerchau. He understood that; where he parted company with those older and better-paid heads was that he would have made the trip from the dirigible base to the Sitting by air. Unfortunately, there was no flat, open spot convenient to the Sitting, either, and his father, in his infinite wisdom, had ruled that as a matter of courtesy to their hosts, they would travel using surface roads, just like any other diplomat. From Malachai's viewpoint, that was a . . . less than inspired decision. They could easily have used those same surface roads to land someplace much closer to the Sitting, without crossing half the city at ground level, but, no. His father had insisted.

Damn, but that man could be *stubborn.*

At least they'd gotten his obstinate posterior into a modified Airaavatha command car rather than accepting the Diantians' no doubt sincerely meant offer of a Sarth-built vehicle. Of course, he'd insisted that the upper deck armor had to be replaced with something less military looking, so the krystar armor had been removed and clear crystoplast had been fitted in its place. That was what they'd told his father, at any rate. Actually, it was two centimeters of considerably tougher armorplast which was proof against anything short of a Sarthian bazooka.

Malachi Dvorak took considerable satisfaction from that particular deception.

Now the convoy—Malachi's command vehicle, followed by a second Airaavatha, then his father's "limo" and two additional Airaavathas as chase cars—moved down the ring road towards Fwerchau's eastern gate at a sedate sixty kilometers per hour. Each of the other Airaavathas carried two wings—four Space Marines— from Alpha Company's 1st Platoon, while the *Starhawks* drifted overhead, invisible at four thousand meters on their own counter-grav. His Marines weren't in Heinleins, unfortunately, but he was reasonably confident of their ability to handle anything any Sarthian threat might throw at them.

"*Troy,*" Malachi reported to the orbiting assault transport as the gate came into sight, "Ground One is leaving Fwerchau with the Secretary."

"Ground One, *Troy* copies." Malachi's lips twitched as he recognized his uncle's voice. "Try to keep him from doing anything . . . outstandingly unwise."

"Ground One copies, *Troy.*"

· · · · ·

"I'M NOT SURE how much longer the package will last," the operative reported over the phone.

"Don't worry," Gauntlet Sydar HynSyTar nar Qwelth replied. "It's almost time." All of their communications were being conducted by landline. Sydar knew the Earthians had monitored their radio communications prior to making themselves known, and he knew the Diantians had the capability to monitor radio communications as well. "The Earthian ship has already landed, and they'll be heading out soon."

"I hope so," the operative said. "We secured it in place as best we could, but it's so big it's blocking the normal flow. At some point, someone's going to notice the blockage and come looking, or the water pressure is going to rip it from its moorings."

"It'll be fine," Sydar responded. "Leave the area before you're seen."

Sydar looked out the window and watched as the Diantian who'd been babysitting the "package" left a building across the street at the other end of the block. It had taken the better part of a Sarthian full-day for Bearer Sokyr's devoted followers to smuggle the "package's" contents into the sewers, one knapsack load at a time in obedience to "Trygau's" orders, but they'd managed it without detection. Religious fanatics they might be, but Sydar had at least seen to it that they were *well-trained* fanatics. Now the babysitter, equally well trained in fieldcraft, vanished into the foot traffic, indistinguishable from any other local going about his business.

The phone rang again. "Yes?"

"They're coming," a voice said.

"Good," Sydar replied. He broke the connection and looked out the window again. There was nothing in view which could hinder their plans. His nasal flaps rose in a smile.

· · · · ·

"GROUND ONE," CAPTAIN Berarroa's voice said in Malachi Dvorak's cochlear implant, "Hawk One sees construction work on Qwyrk Street, three blocks north of Shyrdyn Street."

"Ground One copies construction work," Malachi replied. "We were informed that the city was making repairs."

"Not on my brief, Ground One."

"That's because they were supposed to finish up yesterday, but something's wrong in the main storm drainage system. They haven't located the fault yet, but they're keeping us advised of their progress. I thought it had been added to your brief, but I admit I didn't double check."

"As long as it's all good," Berarroa said.

· · · · ·

ANTRO TAMANSYL, THE lowest ranking member of the road crew, crawled slowly from the sewer. She nodded her head, while the other members of the crew moved upwind and a couple of paces farther away. The smell was bad enough from where the sewer overflow had generated the complaint they were there to investigate; Antro, however, reeked.

"Something's blocking the sewer," she reported, "but it isn't from anything we did yesterday. The blockage is farther down the line. I went downstream as far as I could, but I couldn't find it."

"I was afraid of that when you didn't come right back up," the team leader, Zhal ZhalBalFen, replied. "So I sent Samyk to check the flow in the other storm drains to find out how far down the blockage is."

The group waited for Samyk to return, staying well away from where Antro dripped on the paving stones. After a couple of kysaqs, he could be seen running towards them.

"I found it!" he exclaimed, puffing heavily as he tried to catch his breath. "I found the blockage. Or its location, anyway."

"And?" Zhal asked, impatiently. "Where is it?"

"The drains below Shyrdyn Street are dry as bones, but the one immediately above it's flooded just like here. So the line has to be blocked somewhere under Shyrdyn."

"Well, we'd better get to work quickly, then," Zhal said, ous nasal flaps shut tightly against ous junior team member's continued stench. "That's the route the Earthians are taking, and we can't have it smelling like Antro as they go by."

· · · · ·

"JUST REMEMBER WHAT you told us all before we headed down," Trish Mc-Gillicuddy told Dave Dvorak.

"Which would be what?" he asked innocently.

"That we aren't giving the store to anybody, on either side," she said with a severe look, and he smiled.

Despite the fact that she had blonde hair and gray eyes, McGillicuddy reminded him a great deal of his own daughters. She was a bit stockier than they were, but she moved with a quick grace, and she was one of the smartest people he knew. She was also very attracted to Arthur McCabe, for some reason, although in Dvorak's view, McCabe wasn't remotely in her league. She clearly thought some of his personal beliefs were naïve and believed humanity couldn't afford to buy into the "the Hegemony may not be all *that* bad" mindset, but aside from that the two of them got along very well.

"I know not of what you speak," Dvorak replied. "I have no stores, and, more importantly," his tone turned a bit more serious, "I'm not giving anything to anybody today. We've got to get the Qwernians at least talking to us again, and I'm dead serious about the need to reach an agreement that covers the entire planet equitably."

"I know you are," she said with a fond smile. "I just don't want you appearing so effusively glad to see Qwelth and Sword Master Zhor that Myrcal and Juzhyr decide the Republic has us in its pocket." Dvorak arched an eyebrow at her, and she snorted. "Boss, the problem is that you *like* people, and it shows. It's one of the things that make you so effective. But just this once, you need to dial it back, at least in public. Alex told me to be sure I reminded you of that."

"Yes, Mom." Dvorak sighed in a credible imitation of his offspring in their teens. "I know—I know! You and Dad will ground me if I'm out past curfew."

"You know, you really can be a pain, Boss." The severity of her tone foundered on the chuckle in its depths, and she shook her head at him. "In fact, I think—"

. . . . .

SYDAR'S NASAL FLAPS rose in a grin as the first of the Earthian vehicles rounded the corner and came into view. The procession had followed its announced route, and the first vehicle floated up the street as if its driver didn't have a care in the world, followed by a second and then a third.

The grin became a smile of satisfaction as the occupants of the third vehicle came into view. The Earthians hadn't even bothered to hide which one their leader was in! Sitting in the third vehicle, exposed to view, was Dvorak himself! The others were armored, but Dvorak had chosen to ride in one protected only by a layer of glass. Sydar nodded his head in disbelief.

Two more vehicles followed Dvorak's, but they were of no importance. Sydar waited a couple of seelaqs longer—until the middle one was over the sewer lid—then dove to the side as he pushed the button.

. . . . .

THE WORLD BLEW up.

Malachi Dvorak's Airaavatha skidded insanely sideways on its counter-grav as three and a half Terran tons of high explosive detonated. The shockwave slammed the IFV like an enormous fist, driving it across Shyrdyn Street at an angle that smashed it into and through a plate glass storefront.

The second Airaavatha, caught in the fringe of the actual explosion, tumbled end-over-end to slam down on its nose with sufficient force to crumple even its armored hull.

It was luckier than the two chase Airaavathas.

The IED's location had been chosen with care, utilizing a portion of the storm drain system which ran under Shyrdyn Street at an acute angle, and both of the IFVs were in the footprint of the shaped-charge explosion that ripped an elongated, forty-meter-wide gash through its paving stones. They rocketed upward, tumbling in the blast wave as their counter-gravs shredded and they lost all ability to control altitude or direction. One of them landed upside down and slid a good fifty meters before it ground to a halt. The other was thrown into the second floor of a nearby office building, killing over twenty Diantians as the stonework disintegrated and the Airaavatha's twenty-ton bulk smashed its way through interior walls like Thor's hammer.

And the last Airaavatha, the one carrying Secretary of State Dave Dvorak, flew out of the heart of the blast like a mangled tin can.

· · · · ·

SYDAR ROSE FROM the floor slowly, the glass from the shattered widow falling from his back—the shards that weren't embedded in his back, anyway—to make a tinkling noise on the floor. He could barely hear it, though; the concussion of the blast had damaged his hearing, as well as stunned him. He pulled himself to the window.

He hadn't trusted anyone else to do the job, and he wasn't disappointed in the results. Most of the street had been transformed into a vast, gaping crater, he noted at a glance. The building fronts had been shattered, fires raged throughout its length, and only four of the Earthian vehicles were visible. He waggled his nasal flaps in amusement as he found the fifth; it had been blown into the second floor of the office building across the street.

The detonation must not have been instantaneous, the professional side of his mind noted after a moment; although the last three vehicles had been destroyed, the first two had survived relatively unscathed. He'd intended to destroy the middle three to be sure Dvorak's was in the center of the blast.

He turned his attention to the center vehicle and realized another error. Although the canopy of the aircar *looked* like glass, it was obviously made of something far stronger; it had withstood the blast nearly intact. The vehicle as a whole, had not taken it so well, however. It lay on its side, shredded and crushed, and easily beyond repair. Although some of the Earthians were running towards it, he couldn't see any movement from within, and a liberal amount of the Earthians' red blood painted the not-glass in large splotches. As wrecked as it was, everyone in that vehicle *had* to be dead.

He staggered to where the phone lay on the floor and picked it up. He re-seated the receiver, paused for a kysaq, then picked it up again. Dwomo be thanked, there was a tone, and his nasal flaps rose in a smile as he dialed the number of the cutout.

"Chyltak's Bakery," a voice said on the other end.

"I got your shipment," Sydar replied, "but it was damaged in transit. It looks like it was subject to severe damage. I haven't opened it yet, but I don't see how anything could be intact."

"We're sorry," the voice said. "We'll send a replacement as soon as we're able." The line went dead.

Sydar replaced the receiver on the phone, then dropped it to lie amid the rubble. He looked out the window once more—the Earthians appeared to be having an issue with a natural gas line that was burning merrily nearby, hampering their recovery efforts—then he hobbled towards the door and left as quickly as his battered body was able.

. . . . .

"DAD! DAD!"

Malachi Dvorak didn't remember dismounting his Airaavatha. He ran to-wards his father's demolished vehicle, left arm raised to shield the side of his face against the bellowing demon of flame gushing from the ruptured natural gas line, and as he ran, he realized Mbarjet Celaj was right behind him. Unlike him, however, she'd unlimbered her Bronto.

"Oswald!" he heard Captain Berarroa announcing over the com net. "Oswald! *Troy*, we have an explosion!"

"*Troy* copies." Rob Wilson sounded almost obscenely calm in Malachi's implant. "Ground One, I need a report from you," he continued, and this time Malachi heard the edge in his voice.

"*Troy*, three of the Airaavathas are down," he heard his own voice say, and he didn't recognize it. He could feel it gusting and flickering with terror for his father, but there was no sign of it in the words actually coming out of him. "I say again, three Airaavathas down. And the Secretary's vehicle is—" he heard a quaver at last "—badly damaged."

"Rescue and medical personnel are en route," Wilson said. "ETA ten minutes. I say again, ten mikes."

"Understood."

Malachi slid to a halt beside the shattered Airaavatha. It lay crazily canted on its left side, rent and torn, despite its armor, by the force of the explosion. He opened the cover, grabbed the emergency override latch for the starboard hatch, and heaved, but nothing happened.

"*Shit!*" he snarled and dropped back down to the belly hatch. The latch cover was buckled and twisted, and he rammed his fingers under its warped edge, wishing desperately for his Heinlein's exoskeletal strength. He heaved with all his might, but it didn't even bulge.

"Margie!" he snapped.

"Right here, Boss." Her voice was amazingly calm as she slapped him on the shoulder. He looked around, and his eyes widened as she handed him the krystar prybar she'd had the presence of mind to snatch from their vehicle before she followed him.

He grabbed it from her with a look of profound thanks even as he cursed himself for not remembering the same thing, then shoved the end of the bar under the cover's lip and threw every one of his eighty-four kilos of muscle and bone against it. Nothing happened for an instant, and then metal screeched in protest as the cover yielded.

He reached in, yanked the handle, and almost sobbed in relief as the belly hatch, despite its surface damage, opened. He had to heave it fully open, and then his heart seemed to stop.

None of them had been strapped in.

Patricia McGillicuddy lay on her back, head twisted at an impossible angle, surprised gray eyes open and staring at something she would never see again, and the interior was drenched in blood. The driver's corpse was still at the controls, virtually decapitated by a flying sliver of armorplast spalled from the inside of the canopy, and much of the blood coating every surface had to have come from her. Her wing hadn't bled as badly, but he was either unconscious or dead, and David Dvorak—

Malachi's vision blurred as he took in the unnatural angle of his spine, the blood pooling under him, and tried to access his phone. There was no signal, so Malachi leaned in through the hatch and made himself touch his father's limp wrist. For an endless moment he felt nothing at all, but then something fluttered faintly against his fingertips.

"*Troy*, Ground One," someone else said with his voice. "We have at least two dead, but Secretary Dvorak is alive. I don't know for how much longer. He's unconscious; I estimate his spine is broken, and he appears to be bleeding heavily. I can't tell how badly because he's lying face down on top of the wound."

"*Troy* copies. Can you move him?"

"*Troy*, I'm afraid if I try to move him and his back *is* broken I'll kill him." An icicle went through Malachi as he said the words.

"Ground One, I understand. But medical is still six minutes out. If he's bleeding as badly as you say he is, we may lose him."

Malachi Dvorak closed his eyes, then he inhaled deeply and opened them again.

"I understand, *Troy,*" he said, and crawled in through the belly hatch. He looked back out at Celaj, his eyes dark. "I'm going to need another pair of hands, Margie."

"Right here, Boss," she said gently. "Right here."

· XV ·

CITY OF SHALTAR, DESQWER;
CITY OF SYRZHYR, REPUBLIC OF NEW DIANTO;
CITY OF KWYZO NAR QWERN, QWERN EMPIRE;
AND 50 KILOMETERS NORTHWEST OF
THE CITY OF KWYZO NAR QWERN, QWERN EMPIRE,
PLANET SARTH

This is how we assemble our latest aircraft," Terkyr TerJarGen said over the noise, extending a hand to indicate the production line below the catwalk on which they stood. Darkness had fallen outside, but the work continued; Terkyr had already mentioned the factory ran all sixty hours of the insanely long Sarth day.

James Ivanov nodded as he looked down, realized his mistake, and shook his head. He smiled as he listened to the familiar pounding—it wasn't too different from the way Russia had assembled its aircraft back in his younger days. Quality control was always an issue, so the people in the assembly line would put the next piece into place and beat it into position with a ball-peen hammer if it didn't fit. He still probably had a few calluses after the years he'd spent doing exactly the same thing.

He surveyed the line with a practiced eye. Although the Sarthians were very different in their looks and attitudes, there were still a number of similarities between the two races. The form of the cockpit was different due to the Sarthians' physiology, but the aircraft was easily identifiable as a fighter, and he was curious how it would have stood up to similar craft from World War II back on Earth.

Lost in his reverie, it took a second for the scene below him to register on his conscious mind as one of the Sarthians on the line pulled a pistol from its pocket, turned towards the guard standing at the base of the catwalk, and shot him through the head.

The report from the pistol was louder than the hammering, and the background noise ceased as the workers turned to see what had caused the unexpected sound. By then, the Sarthian with the pistol was already charging up the catwalk's steps towards Ivanov, and he was pushed to the side as the two members of his security detail moved to intercept the gunman. Both humans fired nearly simultaneously, and the Sarthian was thrown backward down the steps. As the body hit the floor below, Ivanov could feel the vibrations of many feet pounding along the catwalk, running towards him, and he turned to greet them.

"It's—" was all he was able to say before he saw the barrel of the pistol pointed between his eyes. Several other Sarthians rushed past towards his security detail, but they were no more than a blur as Ivanov's eyes focused entirely on the pistol's muzzle.

Which meant he had a great view of it as it fired.

. . . . .

IT WAS RAINING hard in the city of Syrzhyr, New Dianto. Kelsyr FirKelMel nor Surak heard it drumming on the kitchen roof as she turned and motioned her followers forward with her free hand.

The kitchen staff lay dead behind her. Only one of them had managed to find a weapon—even in a kitchen where knives were handy—before her team put them down. They'd even captured one of the serving staff and stripped her of her uniform kilt before killing her; Kelsyr now wore that kilt as she led the assault team towards the dining room where the negotiations were being held.

Kelsyr approached the double doors and looked through the crack between them. It was as she'd been briefed to expect. All the delegates sat at a long table that ran the length of the room. The intermixed Sarthians and Earthians sat talking to each other animatedly. At the far end of the table, seated in the position of highest rank, sat Representative Jane Simmons, her target.

She turned back to her team. "She's here," she said, shaking her head. "Give me five seelaqs."

They shook their heads in agreement, and she took a deep breath. Releasing it, she turned back to the doors and pushed through them, careful not to spill her tray of beverages. Smiling with her nasal flaps, she walked the length of the table, acknowledging various requests from the Earthians and the members of the New Diantian Sitting.

As she reached Representative Jane, she heard a sudden buzz from the far end of the table and knew without looking that her team had entered the room with their weapons drawn. She tossed the tray of drinks aside and pulled her other hand out of a pocket, her pistol already set to fire.

The tray hit the floor as the members of her team began firing. Out of the corner of her eye, she saw the door behind the representative swing open as she pulled the trigger. The woman in the doorway blurred, and Kelsyr was catapulted into the air to crash down on the table as the slaughter continued.

. . . . .

MELTAU FIRKELMEL WAS the last of the group to enter the room. As the junior member of the team, his duty was to stand guard at the double doors and ensure no one made it out. His mate, Kelsyr, would perform the same task at the other end of the room once the representative was dead.

He watched as Kelsyr cast aside the tray in a fountain of spilled drinks and started to smile as her pistol came out and pointed down at Representative Jane. Kelsyr was exactly where she was supposed to be, her moves were flawless, and her timing was perfect.

But that was as far as the perfection went.

From his position at the end of the table, he had a perfect view of the door at the other end of the room as it swung in with enough force to shatter the wall with its entry knob when it slammed back, revealing a tall Earthian with long, dark hair.

The female—he'd seen her several times while spying for the group and knew the Earthian was female—moved faster than any being he had ever seen; if she hadn't been coming straight at him, he doubted his eyes could have kept up with her. She had nearly a cheran to cover in the time it took Kelsyr to pull the trigger—it was an impossible task, but she nearly made it; she struck the barrel of the pistol just after the bullet had left it, and then hit Kelsyr with enough force to catapult her through the air.

Shocked by the Earthian's speed and power, Meltau froze, unable to move, as the female raced down the length of the table, chopping the necks of his team members faster than they could react to stop her. *Pop! Pop! Pop!* The bones breaking sounded like the reports from the team's pistols just seelaqs before.

She circled around to the other side of the table in a blur of motion, killing the rest of the team. Meltau's mate struggled weakly on the table, and the Earthian raced towards the movement. The Earthian took Kelsyr's head in her hands, looked into Kelsyr's eyes, then brutally twisted Kelsyr's head around in a complete circle to the crunch of her shattering spine.

"No!" Meltau cried, his pistol finally coming up, seemingly of its own accord.

The Earthian turned towards him and the corners of her mouth turned up slightly. She took a step towards him.

He fired, and she took a second step. He didn't see how his first bullet had missed, but he fired again. She took another step, and the corners of her mouth rose higher. Before he could fire a third time, she blurred again and appeared right in front of his pistol. Her hands reached towards his head, and he fired again.

The bullet passed through the Earthian without any effect at all. Her hands touched the sides of his head, and he had a moment to mouth a quick prayer to Chelth as he realized to his horror that the Earthians really *were* the demons that Sokyr ChelSo had declared them to be. Then his neck snapped, and he didn't worry about it anymore.

· · · · ·

ON THE OTHER side of the planet, Theodore Berke dove through the door into the café's storeroom and Flock Lord Consort Pantyl slammed it behind him. Berke cued his AI to access the military's tactical operations command and control net. "*Troy,* this is Representative Berke in Kwyzo nar Qwern! Come in! I need help!"

"Representative Berke, this is *Troy.*" The voice sounded bored. "You know you don't have authorization for this circuit, correct?"

"I know, damn it, I know! But I'm being attacked, and I need help!"

"Roger. Understand you're being attacked." The voice sounded much more interested and professional this time. "State the nature of the assault and what assistance you need."

"I'm at a café in the city where I was having lunch with one of the Qwernian ministers. All of a sudden, a group of Sarthian gunmen attacked us!"

"Understood, Representative Berke. I am sending assistance. Drones and forces en route. Say status of your protective detail?"

"I don't have a protective detail!" Berke wailed. "Abu Bakr took the duty section when he went out with Minister Cholkyr. Flock Lord Consort Pantyl brought along several of her soldiers and told me she'd provide security! I didn't think I'd need anyone else!"

"Understood. Relief force ETA five minutes. Drones in three."

"Hurry!" Berke transmitted. The sounds of gunfire continued from outside the door. If anything, they were louder now. "I think they're getting closer!" He looked down and realized he'd wet himself, but couldn't remember that happening.

The clock ticked slowly. He could hear Flythyr MuzTolFlyth firing from the other side of the door; the terrorists—or whatever they were—were close, if they'd gotten past the flock lord consort's bodyguards. Berke found he couldn't stop shaking, and it was all he could do to keep his bowels from letting go, too.

Then he jumped as the voice from *Troy* came back.

"Drones overhead," it said. "It looks like there are five people shooting from the street into what may be a café of some sort."

"That's us!" Berke couldn't contain his excitement. "We're on the inside!"

"Roger. Firing."

Berke didn't hear any firing, but the ground jumped from several explosions close by. There was no more firing from Flythyr in the stillness that followed; Berke had no idea whether that was because Flythyr no longer had any targets or because she'd been killed.

"Targets neutralized," the voice said. "Troopers inbound."

If the sensation of the earlier explosions was a jolt, the next round of explosions was an earthquake. The ground shook with the detonations, and smaller, secondary explosions followed immediately. There was a pause, then crashing sounds took the place of the previous gunfire. At a guess, it was tables being turned over or thrown aside. There was a tremendous clatter, then an augmented voice commanded in Qwernian, "Drop the pistol and step aside."

Additional crashing followed, and Berke had just begun to worry about the building's structural integrity when the door to the room was torn off its hinges, revealing a trooper in Project Heinlein armor. The trooper bent over—the doorway was sized to Sarthian standards—and looked into the room.

"Representative Berke?"

"That's . . . that's me," Berke said. He found he had a hard time finding his voice; the cyborg-looking trooper was incredibly intimidating, even when you knew it was on your side.

"Follow me!" the trooper ordered. He turned and stalked towards the front of the building, weapons at the ready, and Berke followed. As he exited the room, two things were apparent. The last crashing sounds he'd hear had been the trooper tearing up the ceiling of the passageway so the armored suit would fit, and that Minister Flythyr was wounded. Blood flowed from a couple of wounds.

"Wait!" Berke called. "We need to take the Minister with us!"

"My orders don't include her," the trooper replied, scanning the remains of the dining area and the street immediately outside the café. Three other troopers were on guard in the street, and Berke could see the bodies of the troopers Flythyr had brought with them. They were behind tables and benches where they'd died, defending him.

"We need to . . ." Berke replied. He had to pause as he was overcome by the gore in the restaurant. In addition to the dead soldiers, a number of civilians had been killed, and blood was everywhere. "We need to help her. She's a minister . . . and she's wounded. Wounded defending *me*! We can't leave her here—our mission will suffer if we do!"

"Sir," the trooper replied, "my orders are to retrieve you, and that's what I'm going to do. You can either get on the *Starfire* yourself, or I'll carry you aboard. The choice is yours."

Berke looked back at Flythyr, who was following at a cautious distance. The Qwernian had a noticeable limp and blood dripped from her left leg. "No," Berke said, coming to a halt. "You need to at least call your superiors and tell them I said we need to bring her."

The soldier muttered something, but then said, "Okay," and came to a halt. He continued to scan the area around them while he called for clarification.

"You got your wish," the trooper said after about thirty seconds. "She can come with us, but we need to get out of here *now*!"

"You got it," Berke said, willing to be gracious now that he'd won the point. He turned back to the Army Minister. "Come with us," Berke said. "We'll get you to safety."

Flythyr shook her head and moved forward, so Berke turned and picked his way through the café, trying to dodge the piles of entrails and pools of blood. The assault shuttle waited across the street, hovering over the remains of the building which had previously stood there. He understood the earlier explosions now; the shuttle's flight crew had destroyed the building to make room to get into the narrow street. The shuttle's ramp was down, and it almost reached the street.

Berke looked back and saw Flythyr was slowing, so he went back to the minister. He bent over slightly and pulled Flythyr's arm over his shoulders, then he hurried the minister across the street to the shuttle, helped her onto the ramp, and climbed aboard himself. The troopers boarded right behind him, and the *Starfire* streaked towards the heavens before the ramp had even come up.

. . . . .

SHERDYS NORHANSHER LAY very still at the bottom of the shallow hole. The hole was much longer than it was wide or deep, and not just so that she could fit into it. At almost ten seqrans, she was far and away the tallest and strongest member of the team, which was why she'd drawn the most critical role. It was also why she was all alone in her miserable hole, and she closed her eyes to whisper another prayer to Chelth's crest for the male she loved.

She shifted very carefully under the concealing, sod-covered tarpaulin stretched over her hide to check her watch and her nasal flaps tightened. Six more kysaqs. Only six. Less than an eight.

Her mind spun back to the long journey which had brought her and Hansyn and their sworn companions to this spot in the middle of a miserable grain field deep inside the Qwernian Empire. It wasn't where she'd ever expected to die for God, but the place didn't really matter. Chelth would know Ous own wherever they fell in Ous cause.

She remembered the last time she and Hansyn would ever embrace Norsuyl. Ou had longed to accompany them on their journey, but ou was pregnant with the children she and Hansyn would never see, never have the opportunity to hold. The tears had flowed, but there'd been pride with the anguish in Norsuyl's eyes as ou hugged ous beloved mates one last time.

Then the long train ride, crossing the Empire's frontier, the suspicion of every Qwernian police officer they met, and the final bus ride to the small hotel where Nyrtag HalNyrShar had reserved their rooms.

And now this.

She checked her watch again. Two more kysaqs. She ran one hand down the hard, reassuring length of her weapon. Hansyn had loaded that for her before he tugged the tarp over her hide and covered it with the squares of sod they'd cut and removed before they dug it. His final wedding gift, he'd said, nasal flaps trying to smile as she stared up, watching the tarp hide his face from her one final time. They'd trained as a team, but there was little point pretending they'd have time for a second shot, and so he'd taken Nyrtag's place in command of the rest of the team, determined to buy her the time to make that shot count.

She wondered exactly how Nyrtag had gotten Diantian weapons across the border, given how difficult it had been just to get the members of their own armed team past the beady shyrmal's eye of the Qwernian customs agents, but the merchant was a veritable sorcerer. He'd made all the travel arrangements, gotten them into position, and somehow gained access to the critical information they needed about their target's travel schedule. Yet in many ways, she was most grateful of all for the familiarity of those weapons. They were identical to the ones she and her team had trained with. They knew them like they knew their own hands, their own mates' faces, and at this moment, that mattered.

She'd told Nyrtag that and seen the mingled pride and sorrow in his nasal flaps. Pride at having given them the tools they needed; sorrow because he'd been forbidden at the last moment to accompany them. But however deeply he'd longed to be with them, he'd had no choice. The message from Trygau HyrShalTry had been inflexible, and it had borne Bearer Sokyr's personal signature. The Bearer had decreed that as a respected expatriate in the Qwernian business community and the male who'd been able to put the entire mission together, Nyrtag the merchant was too valuable to become Nyrtag the martyr leading that mission. At least he'd live to serve Chelth again. That mattered, too. Ou needed warriors of Nyrtag's ability. In fact, Sherdys wondered if—

The field radio at the end of the hole clicked three times as someone keyed the transmit button, and Sherdys NorHanSher breathed one last prayer to Chelth, gathered the rocket launcher—a full three seqrans longer than even her height—and waited for the first shots.

. . . . .

"SIR!" CORPORAL JOHN Williamson exclaimed. "Please get into the vehicle, right now!" He put a hand on Abu Bakr's shoulder and attempted to guide him into the Airaavatha.

Abu Bakr shrugged it off. "Why?" he asked, raising a hand of his own to indicate the field of . . . whatever grain it was that Cholkyr CholAnGen nar Qwern had asked him out to the countryside to see. "We just got here."

"I need the Minister to get back into his vehicle, too," Williamson replied. "*Now!*"

As an accomplished one-time freedom fighter—if not a soldier, per se—Abu Bakr recognized the tone of a soldier who was acting on immediate, "danger close" orders, and he jumped back into the car through the side hatch. He left it open and watched Williamson guide Cholkyr back to the second vehicle while the other member of the protective detachment, Private Jim Pascoe, moved to stand in front of Abu Bakr's door, his Bronto at the ready.

"What's going on?" Abu Bakr demanded through the opening.

"There's been an attack on the Secretary of State!" Pascoe replied, never taking his eyes off the fields surrounding them. "There have been other—"

CRACK!

Sarthian rifles, Abu Bakr discovered, sounded exactly like old-style Earth firearms. And so did a rifle slug whizzing in to ricochet from the Airaavatha's armor.

Pascoe's rifle snapped to his shoulder as Abu Bakr turned in the direction the Space Marine was facing and saw armed Sarthians popping up out of the grain field as if by magic. The Bronto barked its far quieter snap, and one of the Sarthians' torsos disappeared into a cloud of red mist, but there were at least ten more of them.

Every one of them had a rifle, and the sound of bullets slamming into the armored vehicle was suddenly a pounding downpour.

．　．　．　．　．

DESPITE HER ANTICIPATION, despite her determination, Sherdys NorHanSher jerked as gunfire shattered the pastoral silence. If Chelth was truly good, that torrent of rifle fire might just do the job for them, but Shaymork worked Ous evil in the world, as well. That was why her role was critical. She waited one more heartbeat, then rolled to her knees. She came upright in the hole, leveling the weapon across her shoulder as her eyes sought out her target.

．　．　．　．　．

ANOTHER SARTHIAN APPEARED suddenly, well separated from the attackers engaging Abu Bakr's security detail. The part of Abu Bakr which had fought the Shongairi recognized the tactic instantly, especially when the new apparition leveled what looked like a World War II bazooka—*a no-kidding bazooka*—over her shoulder. She was barely sixty yards from the Airaavatha, and Abu Bakr's nerves tingled as he realized he was looking straight into that gaping muzzle.

There was no way Pascoe or Williamson could possibly engage the new threat before the Sarthian fired.

．　．　．　．　．

SHERDYS' HEART FLAMED with triumph as she realized how good Chelth had been.

She was perfectly positioned on the Earthian vehicle's flank, and its hatch was *open*! She laid the launcher's ring and post sights on that beautiful, beautiful open hatch. The hatch that made any magical armor the Earthians' technology might boast meaningless. She heard her team's rifle fire dwindling. She knew what that meant, but they'd done their job, and she squeezed the trigger.

Nothing happened.

Her eyes flared wide, her right inside thumb pressed the safety, but the lever was already in the firing position, and she squeezed the trigger again.

Nothing!

But that was *impossible*! That—!

· · · · ·

ABU BAKR DUCKED.

It was pure instinct. His brain knew it was futile, but his body didn't, and he flung himself prone. Yet even as he dove for the Airaavatha's deck, he couldn't look away from the bazooka in the hands of his executioner.

But it didn't fire. For some reason, *it didn't fire*. Maybe the Sarthian had panicked, frozen when the moment came. Maybe there was some other explanation. But as Private Pascoe spun back towards the new threat, Abu Bakr bin Mohammed el-Hiri realized he'd never have a chance to ask her about it.

· · · · ·

SHERDYS NORHANSHER NOR Hyul, warrior of Chelth, opened her mouth to scream in furious denial as she squeezed the launcher's trigger yet again.

She never had the chance to make a sound. Her crested head exploded into a finely divided cloud of bone and brain matter as the Bronto round hit it at six times the speed of sound.

Two shots later, every other member of her team was down, as well.

· · · · ·

THE HATCH ON the other side of the Airaavatha opened, and Williamson jumped into the driver's seat while Pascoe climbed in through the door he was standing next to. Williamson jammed the accelerator to the stops and the counter-grav to full almost before Pascoe's hatch closed, and the IFV rocketed up and away.

"What about the Minister?" Abu Bakr asked.

"With all due respect, Sir," Williamson snarled over his shoulder, "screw the Minister! There've been a number of attacks, Secretary Dvorak may be dead, and my priority is to get you to safety!"

As the Airaavatha continued to climb, it finally dawned on Abu Bakr. If Dvorak was dead, he was now in charge.

· XVI ·

PUNS *VANGUARD*,
SARTH ORBIT

Y ou were lucky to make it out of there alive," Rob Wilson said grimly, then twitched a thin smile. "Especially without me or any of the vampires to drag your ass out of the line of fire this time!"

"I know." Abu Bakr gave him a smile of his own, one of shared memories, then shook his head.

The two of them stood in the flag briefing room aboard PUNS *Vanguard*, waiting for the rest of the attendees to arrive. Abu Bakr had arrived aboard less than ten minutes earlier, delivered by the *Starfire* which had picked him up from the Qwernian capital. Wilson had only just arrived in the briefing room, but he'd come aboard over an hour ago. The meeting wasn't supposed to begin for another quarter hour yet, and he'd had a niece who needed him more than his highly competent staff aboard *Troy* did.

"I know I'm lucky," Abu Bakr repeated more soberly, and raised an eyebrow at Rob. "Is Dave going to be equally lucky?"

"We think so," Wilson replied, blue eyes dark. "It was a damned near thing, even with modern medicine, though. Without it, he'd've been gone before the medevac team even got there. Hell, he looked worse than *you* did after Naya Islamabad!" He shook his head. "The docs aren't letting him out of the life-support tank for at least a week."

"A *week*?" Abu Bakr looked at him in shock.

"At least." Wilson shook his head. "Six vertebrae gone. A rib through his heart. Not one but *two* skull fractures. Left lung perforated in three places. Half his liver turned into hamburger. He damn near bled out completely, even with Malachi and Corporal Celaj right there. They got the sealant into the wounds and stopped most of the internal bleeding, then hit him with the nano blood expander, but—" his expression went very grim "—they aren't certain yet about his brain. He lost a *lot* of blood, Abu, but it's the bits and pieces of bone they pulled out of his cortex that really have them worried. So they plan on keeping him in the tank, total life-support, until the nannies have time to repair any neural damage. So that 'at least a week' is probably grossly optimistic. I'd say we may be looking at something more like three weeks. Maybe even a month."

Abu Bakr looked at him for a moment longer, then laid a hand on the Space Marine's right shoulder and squeezed hard.

"You and your Marines do seem to have a habit of pulling people's shot-up posteriors out of the fire, don't you?"

"A modest talent, but my own," Wilson acknowledged in a tone much more like his own, and Abu Bakr squeezed again.

"*Inshallah,* my friend," he said. "Dave is tough. Besides that, Allah has plans for him. He wouldn't have made him so irritating if He didn't still expect great things out of him."

"One way to put it," Wilson said, then chuckled. Abu Bakr raised another eyebrow, and the Space Marine shook his head. "He's got to make it. If he doesn't, I can't rat him out to Sharon for not wearing a seat belt. Idiots would've been fine instead of bouncing around the interior like frigging pinballs if they'd been strapped in. As it is, he's the only one who made it."

"Like I said, *inshallah.* On the other hand, Allah obviously has a sense of humor, too. After all, look who He's left in charge on the civilian side!"

"You're up to it," Wilson said encouragingly. "Besides, you've got Longbow and his people in your corner."

"Assuming we want to unleash them. I'm afraid I have somewhat . . . mixed feelings in that regard." Abu Bakr's tone was wry, and Wilson snorted.

"There's plenty—" he began, then broke off as the hatch opened to admit Admiral Swenson, Captain Jeng, and Captain de Castro. Commander Néhémial Routhier, Swenson's chief of staff, and Lieutenant Commander Penelope Quinlevan, her staff intelligence officer, followed them. Alex Jackson and Major Anthony McIntyre, Wilson's own S-2, came in with Routhier and Quinlevan. The brigadier looked a question at McIntyre, and the major nodded in reply.

Swenson walked towards the two early arrivals, accompanied by Jackson, and paused, looking at Abu Bakr. He looked back, wondering why she'd stopped. Then Jackson cleared his throat gently and twitched his head at the seat at the head of the briefing room table.

Abu Bakr felt perplexed for a moment, but then he nodded in understanding as his brain finally caught up. He'd been wrong—or at least not completely accurate—when he'd said he'd been left in charge "on the civilian side." As Dvorak's deputy, he'd just become the commander of the entire expedition.

It was not, he discovered, a comforting realization, and he wondered if he hadn't thought about it before because his subconscious hadn't *wanted* to.

"Admiral Swenson," he said, and she nodded back respectfully.

"Director," she replied, and waved her own hand at the conference table.

"Of course," Abu Bakr said.

He walked to the chair at the head of the table. Swenson crossed to her own place, facing him from its foot, then waited until he'd been seated before she sat herself. The others remained standing until Abu Bakr cleared his throat.

"Be seated, please," he said, wondering in a corner of his brain how Dvorak had become so apparently comfortable in the same role.

He waited while everyone else sat, then cleared his throat again.

"I realize I've just inherited Secretary Dvorak's position, at least until he's up and around again himself," he said. "I don't think we can organize any effective response to what's happened until we understand exactly what *has* happened, though, and I've been just a little busy for the last ninety minutes or so. So with your concurrence, Admiral, I think it would probably be a good idea for our intelligence people to bring us up to date on what we know so far."

"I think that would be an excellent place to start," Swenson agreed, and looked at Routhier. "Néhémial?"

"Of course, Ma'am. Ambassador." Routhier nodded politely to Abu Bakr, then cued his phone and brought up a three-dimensional map of Sanda, spotted with broadly scattered, glaring scarlet icons.

"As you can see," he began, "with the exception of the attacks on Mr. Berke and Director Bakr in the Empire, Ms. Simmons' assassination in New Dianto, and Mr. Ivanov's assassination in Desqwer, all of the incidents occurred in the Republic. About thirty minutes ago, a Diantian radio station received a 'manifesto' from a Chelthist organization associated with Sokyr ChelSo nor Chelth claiming responsibility for all of them, including the ones outside the Republic. We've had our own recon assets—including some of Brigadier Wilson's Scultator drones—looking for Sokyr ever since the attack on the Secretary, because given his past rhetoric we considered him a prime candidate for this from the get-go, but wherever ou is, ou's hidden ousself very successfully. We've had a single sighting of Trygau HyrShalTry, who appears to be ous tactical coordinator, in Dianzhyr, but he disappeared again before we could vector in the Diantian authorities or drop in on him ourselves.

"Commander Quinlevan's also run a search of all the Sarthian newspapers and broadcast news looking for either of them, and we've run a computer search of our standard recon imagery, as well. As far as we can tell, no one's even seen Sokyr in the last two local days. He's fired off a couple of manifestos, but he was due to be interviewed by one of the Myrcos radio stations day-half before last, and he never showed. That's not like him, and we only have a couple of recon hits on Trygau in the same period. That can't be just a coincidence, given what's just gone down. I don't think either of them know about the Scultators, but they obviously have a pretty good clue about orbital recon—probably because of the satellite pictures we've been sharing with their weather services and that search-and-rescue for the lost kids we helped with last month." The commander grimaced wryly. "We might want to go a little easier with that on the next planet we contact."

Several people chuckled, but then Routhier's expression sobered.

"I'm going to let Commander Quinlevan handle the details of what we've found—or think we've found—so far. Mister Jackson's been coordinating with the Diantians on the civilian side, and Major McIntyre's been liaising with their police and military. I think that at the moment we have a pretty clear picture of what the Diantians know—or *think* they know—but the truth is we're really just starting to put this thing together."

He paused and Abu Bakr nodded.

"Of course you are," he said. "Couldn't be any other way. So, why don't you go ahead and start, Commander?"

"Yes, Sir," Quinlevan replied. She was a tall, black-haired woman with a pronounced Galway accent, and she brought up her own phone's AI, producing a larger-scale map of Sanda, alone.

"What we know so far," she began, "is that in the space of less than thirty minutes, the people behind this were able to execute no less than sixteen attacks. They met with varying degrees of success, but we've lost a lot of people. That degree of coordination suggests much better planning than we or the Diantians had expected out of the Chelthists, which in turn suggests that we—and by 'we,' I mean specifically the mission's intelligence staff—significantly underestimated the threat."

She looked around the briefing room, gray eyes unflinching, and Abu Bakr waved one hand.

"You were hardly the only ones," he said. "Secretary Dvorak and I have been in constant contact with both the Diantians and the Qwernians, and neither of us—or any of our Sarthian contacts, for that matter—expected anything like this, either. What matters is that it's happened and how we decide to respond."

"Of course, Sir," Quinlevan replied, and cleared her throat.

"The first attack was the one on Secretary Dvorak's convoy," she continued. "We suspect that the terrorists, at least in the Republic, were in communication by telephone. All of the attack teams had to be in position ahead of time, but the sequencing strongly suggests that they were waiting until they could be notified by landline that the initial attack had gone off on schedule. The attacks in the Empire and in New Dianto had to have been timed, rather than the result of that sort of notification, however. We're still trying to figure out how they could have known the Secretary's schedule closely enough to carry those attacks out before we could tighten our security measures.

"So far, all weapons used were standard Diantian Army issue, and Major McIntyre is in touch with the police and military authorities who are tracking serial numbers to discover where and how they were diverted. I'm inclined to think most of the rifles were surplused rather than stolen, but we can hope otherwise, because if they were stolen for the Chelthists, it may lead us to someone we can squeeze.

"In terms of the damage inflicted, so far—"

Abu Bakr frowned in concentration, listening closely, and wondered how they were going to react to his own observation.

· · · · ·

"AND THAT'S ALL the hard data we have at the present moment," Commander Routhier finished the staff presentation twenty minutes later. "There's a lot of speculation down on the planet, of course, and filtering through that is going to take a lot longer. Until we've had time for that, none of us are prepared to make any hard and fast conclusions about how this all went down, but we're in agreement that so far—*so far*—" he emphasized, "nothing we have contradicts the Chelthists' claim of responsibility."

"Maybe it doesn't *contradict* it," Wilson observed, "but the timing outside Sanda damned well raises some interesting questions."

"I think so, too, Sir," Major McIntyre agreed. "At the same time," he continued in a respectful tone, "while I hate to say this, we may very well have made the whole thing possible by being so predictable—and open—with the Secretary's movements."

"Trust me, Tony, I'll be kicking myself over that for a long time." Wilson's reply was harsh, but everyone around that table recognized the true target of the anger in his tone. "But my point stands. No one outside the Republic's phone network could have known they'd gotten Dave—the Secretary—and Trish before they attacked Ivanov, Berke and Jane."

"They may have figured it didn't matter," Admiral Swenson said.

"Because the other attacks were going in whether or not they were able to attack the Secretary's convoy?" Abu Bakr asked.

"Exactly." Swenson nodded. "It's possible we're looking at this from the wrong end. I admit it seems unlikely, given how tightly sequenced everything was, but the attack on the Secretary may actually have been the fortuitous part. They did know his schedule, and in retrospect, that was clearly a mistake. But with all due respect, Rob, given the tech we had protecting him, the risk certainly seemed justifiable." She grimaced. "The lengths they had to go to get to him actually underscore that, when you get down to it. They had to blow up an entire damned city block! But they could have timed all of the attacks to hit around when they hoped to get him with the understanding that the others would go in, whatever happened in the capital. Even without succeeding there, the other attacks would've been a pretty damned emphatic announcement of their disapproval of our 'demonic' interference with Sarth."

"That's probably fair enough," Wilson said, after a moment. "I just can't quite get past how *tightly* sequenced it was. If we'd had everything in place, coordinating it would've been a snap for us, but no bunch of terrorists on Sarth have anything like the communications capability we've got."

"The Diantian intelligence people are making the same point, Sir," McIntyre said. "Swordsman Consort Bardyn's people in the Intelligence Directorate obviously think the attacks on the Sandian mainland, at least, *were* command-coordinated. Doing that long distance to the Empire wouldn't have been a piece of cake, but it would at least be possible. It's the ones overseas that have them stumped."

Abu Bakr nodded thoughtfully. The phone networks in both the Empire and the Republic were well developed, but they were all landline. The connections across the Qwernian frontier were subject to unpredictable delays and interruptions, however, and as yet there were no voice undersea lines at all. Sarthians were still limited to telegraphic cables when it came to direct, non-radio communication between continents.

He looked around the conference table for a second or two, then leaned forward slightly.

"I'm about to ask a question that's likely to sound like what Longbow would've called 'a little weird . . . even for you,' back in the day," he said, hiding a smile as Wilson snorted in amusement. The smile faded quickly, however. "What if this isn't the cut-and-dried 'religious fanatics' attack it looks like?"

The others looked at him, and it was his turn to snort at the expressions of some of the older people present. People who had clearer memories of pre-invasion Earth and the role of one Abu Bakr bin Mohammed el-Hiri. He'd never been an actual terrorist himself, but he had to admit that he'd kept some fairly dubious company during his career as an advocate for the Muslim community before the Shongairi's arrival.

"The Diantians have positively identified the bodies of the Desqwer attackers as Diantian nationals, Sir," Lieutenant Commander Quinlevan pointed out. "And three of them were known associates of Sokyr."

"And the Qwernians just informed us that the people who attacked you were all Diantians who entered the Empire within the last three local days," Major McIntyre added.

"I didn't say that the people who attacked us weren't religious fanatics," Abu Bakr replied. "I'm just wondering if there's another element involved."

"Why?" Wilson asked. The brigadier knew Abu Bakr better than anyone else in the compartment, and he was gazing at him very thoughtfully indeed.

"You remember when you said I was lucky to get out alive?"

"Yeah. You were. Unless you'd closed the damned *hatch,* at least!" Wilson shook his head. "An Airaavatha's armor would've laughed at a Sarthian bazooka. Even the armorplast on Dave's would probably have held. But if she'd popped that rocket *inside* on you—"

"You do have a tendency to dwell on people's minor lapses in judgment, don't you?" Abu Bakr said, and Wilson barked a short but genuine laugh.

"Leaving aside any critical observations by people who weren't there," Abu Bakr continued, "there are a couple of things about that entire attack that bother me. Besides the fact that they were trying to kill us, I mean."

"Such as?" Wilson asked.

"You and Longbow and I did a fair amount of ambushing aliens ourselves during the invasion," Abu Bakr said, looking at his old comrades-in-arms. "Would you say we were fairly successful at it?"

"I like to think so," Wilson replied. "Although now that you mention it, Dave managed to get himself half-killed doing *that,* too!"

"We all came close, one time or another. But, speaking from the perspective of that experience, they had us." Abu Bakr shook his head, brown eyes grim. "You're probably right about the Airaavatha's armor, but they couldn't have known that, and they *had* us, Rob. It was well-planned, and it was beautifully executed. Williamson and Pascoe didn't give me time to walk the ground afterward, but they had to have been in position hours before we got there. They were waiting in hides, perfectly concealed until the moment they came out of the ground and opened fire. And when the riflemen opened fire, they did *exactly* what they were there to do; they completely distracted Williamson, Pascoe, and Cholkyr's security detail from the one with the rocket launcher who was almost a hundred yards from the others. It was all designed to give her the shot . . . and enough time to be sure she found *my* vehicle before she fired."

He paused, and Wilson cocked his head, obviously running back through his Marines' reports. Then the brigadier's eyes widened, and Abu Bakr nodded.

"Excuse me," Swenson said as the pause stretched out, "but I seem to be missing something here."

"I was looking straight down the tube of that launcher," Abu Bakr said. "She had me dead to rights. Like Brigadier Wilson says, I even held the door open for her, and she had plenty of time to get the shot off before Williamson or Pascoe could engage her. She would've been just as dead in the end as the Sarthian who shot Jane Simmons, but she had more than enough time to kill me first."

"Except that she *didn't* get the shot off," Wilson said slowly.

"Exactly." Abu Bakr nodded, then held up his phone. "I thought, at first, that it was just that 'slow-motion' effect that sometimes sets in in a firefight. But I had Jibril—" like most humans, he had long since anthropomorphized his phone's AI "—here check the timing. There may have been some of that in my impressions, but Jibril says she had almost seven seconds from the moment *I* saw her, and I saw her before Williamson or Pascoe."

"Seven seconds?" Alex Jackson repeated, and Wilson barked a short laugh.

"Back in the day, Alex, I could empty a fifteen-round magazine, aimed fire—*and* reload—in about *eight* seconds. That's an eternity in combat. If she had a bead on Abu for seven seconds, she damned well should've fired."

"Unless she froze," Abu Bakr agreed. "I wondered if that was what happened, and it may be what really *did* happen, but it doesn't fit with any of the rest of our reports or, for that matter, with the rest of her team. They would've put their most reliable person behind the launcher, especially if the rest of the team planned to deliberately draw fire away from her. They probably didn't realize how good our equipment—or your Space Marines, Rob—actually is, but they obviously figured they *needed* to draw fire, which suggests they at least tried to allow for that in their planning. And she still didn't get the shot off."

"There could be all sorts of reasons for that, Sir," Quinlevan said respectfully, and Abu Bakr nodded.

"You're right. And I think we need to eliminate as many of those reasons as we can before we draw any hard and fast conclusions about what this was all about."

"I know I have a nasty, suspicious mind," Wilson said slowly, "but I'd really like to examine that bazooka." Swenson raised an eyebrow at him, and he shrugged. "The most reasonable explanation is a 'golden BB' for our side." Swenson's other eyebrow rose. "A freak accident that caused her launcher to malfunction at exactly the right moment for Abu. And the truth is, we might be due for one, given how badly we got hurt other places. But I really do want to get our hands on it so we can check it out ourselves."

"The Qwernians have secured the site, Sir," Major McIntyre said. "I don't know how good their forensic people are, and we don't have anyone eyes-on on the ground yet, either."

"Have we asked for access?" Abu Bakr asked sharply.

"Yes," Alex Jackson said. Abu Bakr looked at him, and he shrugged. "I asked for access to *all* of the attack sites as soon as we had Secretary Dvorak back on board. The Republic agreed to include any investigators we wanted to send almost immediately. There was apparently a snafu on the Qwernian side. I just got notification—" he touched his own phone to indicate how "—that Clan Ruler Juzhyr's personally directed that we be granted complete access."

"Juzhyr?" Abu Bakr repeated in a thoughtful tone. His security detail had rushed him out of the Qwernian capital—over his objections—before he'd had any opportunity to speak personally with Foreign Minister Myrcal, but he couldn't imagine why anyone had needed to buck the request all the way up to Juzhyr.

"Yes, Sir." Jackson nodded. "And there was another strange thing about it, too. The response wasn't directed to you, although they obviously know you got safely back to the ship and that Secretary Dvorak was badly injured. It was addressed to Arthur McCabe."

"*McCabe?*"

"McCabe," Jackson confirmed. "He copied it to me after Charioteer Consort Yerdaz handed it to him. I thought it was a little odd that they delivered it through the Nonagon rather than handing it directly to Fikriyah—" Fikriyah Batma was Abu Bakr's senior aide in Kwyzo nar Qwern "—but I figured they were probably in a bit of confusion down there, themselves. But it wasn't just delivered to him; it was *addressed* to him."

"Odd," Abu Bakr said after a moment.

"Might have been just courtesy on Yerdaz' part," Jackson said. "She and Mc-Cabe have established a pretty good relationship, and if they just sent her the clearance rather than a formal communiqué, she might've had to work out the wording herself. But you're right; it is a bit . . . peculiar in a communication that directly invokes Juzhyr's authority. They're usually really careful about how they handle anything like that."

"True," Abu Bakr replied. He sat for several seconds, rubbing his neatly clipped beard with one hand, then grimaced.

"It *is* odd," he said. "And the odds are that it doesn't mean a thing, and you're right about their being 'in a bit of confusion,' Alex. But I can't help thinking what Secretary Dvorak would have said at this point."

"I can think of *several* things he might have said," Wilson said dryly. "Which one did you have in mind?"

"'Curiouser and curiouser,'" Abu Bakr said. "I think there may be a few more things we need to find out before we start thinking about formal responses to this."

XVII

PUNS *VANGUARD*,
SARTH ORBIT,
AND KWYZO NAR QWERN, QWERNIAN EMPIRE,
PLANET SARTH

Bardyn ShoKymBar nor Garyth tried not to gawk.

He failed.

He sat in the Earthian chair, which had somehow magically configured itself to fit Sarthian body structure, and stared out the port beside him. The huge *Starfire* "shuttle"—only about a quarter the size of the even bigger *Starlander* which had delivered Secretary David to the Nonagon that first day—had lifted from the Fwerchau dirigible base in eerie silence, with none of the gradual acceleration of any fixed wing aircraft in which he'd ever flown. It really was more like one of the Navy's airships, except not even an airship could have climbed straight up—or as swiftly, or remotely as high. That had been awe-inspiring enough, but he'd never imagined the way the atmosphere had turned darker and darker blue before the blue faded into black and he'd realized he was the first Sarthian to ever move into the hard vacuum of space.

And now....

The behemoth waiting for them turned even a *Starlander* into a mere speck. A central hull, at least a minran in length and, more probably, even larger, rotated steadily inside an even bigger cagework of massive girders and bulky shapes whose purposes he couldn't begin to imagine.

"Impressive, isn't she?" Alex Jackson asked from beside him.

"That's certainly one way to put it!" Bardyn agreed. "But why is that big part of it turning?"

"To create a sensation of gravity."

"Gravity?"

"Yes. Once you get off the surface of a planet, there's no gravity. You're in what some people call 'freefall,' although 'microgravity' is a better term. Because, really, there *is* gravity; it's just so weak it might as well not exist."

"I don't feel any lack of gravity," Bardyn said.

"We can generate artificial gravity over fairly small areas, but the energy cost is . . . well, it's *extreme*, let's say. We usually don't bother with it, but it's built into the shuttles for times like this."

"Like this?"

"Times when we have passengers who haven't been trained in microgravity."

"I see." Bardyn's nasal flaps smiled wryly.

"The apparent gravity aboard *Vanguard* is a bit lower than Earth's, but it's pretty close to Sarth's, so we're hoping you'll be fairly comfortable, Director."

"I'm sure I will, and I must admit I'm looking forward to the experience . . . however much I regret the circumstances that bring me here."

"We all regret them, Director," the Earthian said quietly. "But *we're* looking forward to any information you have for us."

Bardyn shook his head in agreement, and then sat silent again, watching as the monstrous shape looming against the stars grew steadily huger.

. . . . .

"THANK YOU FOR coming, Director Bardyn," Néhémial Routhier said as the Sarthian followed Jackson into the compartment.

Bardyn was doing an impressive job of hiding his awe and wonder, and he probably would have fooled another Sarthian. Then again, no Sarthian would have had the advantage of the translating software's emotion-parsing capabilities.

"It was the least I could do," the swordsman consort said with quiet—and genuine—sincerity. "It's our maniacs who have done all of this. Anything we can do to help will be far less than you deserve of us."

"Sir, I'm afraid we Earthians have had ample experience with religious or political fanatics." Routhier grimaced. "For the last triple-eight or so of our own years, we've been focused on other threats, thanks to the Shongairi. But left to our own devices, we've been just as willing to kill each other over disagreements as any Sarthian."

"So Secretary David's said," Bardyn agreed with a curled nasal flap. Then his smile faded. "And, speaking of the Secretary—?"

"We're pretty sure he's out of the woods—I mean that he's out of danger," Routhier replied. "In fact, we're expecting him to make a full recovery." Which was true enough, aside from the lingering concerns about brain damage. "Even with our physicians, though, he's going to be out of action for a long time."

"That's very good to hear. That he can be healed, I mean. And I have to say you're very fortunate to have Ambassador Abu to stand in his place until he's fully recovered."

"We think so, too," Routhier said. "But, now, let me introduce my companions."

"Of course!"

"This is Lieutenant Commander Quinlevan," the commander said, indicating the tall, dark-haired, gray-eyed Earthian to his left. From the shape of Quinlevan's torso, Bardyn thought that she was almost certainly a female.

"This is Colonel Palazzola, Brigadier Wilson's chief of staff, and this is Major McIntyre, the Brigadier's staff intelligence officer."

Both of Brigadier Wilson's subordinates were probably males, Bardyn decided. Especially Major McIntyre. Earthian males tended to be taller than their females, he'd learned, and McIntrye was at least a kyran taller even than Secretary David!

"I'm honored to meet you all," he said, as the Earthians murmured polite greetings.

"Admiral Swenson and Brigadier Wilson are in conference with Ambassador Abu," Routhier said then. "They've asked us to share information with you and present them with a briefing in a secar or so. If we need longer than that, the briefing can be rescheduled."

"I don't think we'll need that long," Bardyn said, settling into the chair Routhier indicated and feeling it conform to his body shape as the one on the shuttle had. "I do have a couple of notes Prime Director Qwelth asked me to deliver to Ambassador Abu. One is from the Prime Director ouself, expressing ous and our government's profound regret and shame that this should have happened on Diantian soil. The other is from Bearer Mykair, expressing ous bitter grief and shame that anyone even purporting to act in Chelth's name could have been guilty of such heinous actions."

Routhier remembered to shake his head in acknowledgment. Bardyn's personal remorse was obvious, and he didn't doubt that Mykair's was even greater than the intelligence director's. For that matter, Qwelth was undoubtedly sincere, if only because the Prime Director had to be aware of how severely attacks by Diantian fanatics were likely to affect Terran views of the Republic, as well.

"The real reason I'm here, though, is to update you on our latest findings," Bardyn continued, laying his briefcase on the table and snapping the latch open. "We've been looking at all the information available, piecing together the bits and pieces, identifying the holes in what we think we know so far—" he continued, reaching into the case for the first of the fat folders it contained "—and we've turned up a few surprises, including one that's potentially significant. To begin with—"

· · · · ·

"SO, NÉHÉMIAL—" FRANCESCA Swenson tipped back in her chair, arching her spine, fingers interlaced against the back of her neck, as Commander Routhier and Colonel Palazzola entered the compartment "—what do we know?"

"Actually, Ma'am," Commander Routhier said, "we may know quite a bit more than we did."

"Really?" Swenson let her chair come upright as her chief of staff's tone registered. She glanced at Wilson, then leaned forward, folding her arms on the briefing room table.

"Really, Ma'am."

"Then enlighten us. And, by the way," Swenson added dryly, "may I ask where Penelope is?"

"She and Major McIntyre are headed down to Dianzhyr with Director Bardyn. He brought photographs of some of the physical evidence, but they want to take a look at it firsthand with our own instrumentation. More than that, though, they want to sit down with his investigators and get them to walk us through what Bardyn summarized for us."

"Which is what, Commander?" Wilson asked.

"First, let me say that all four of us were very impressed by the Diantians' speed and efficiency," Routhier said, and Palazzola nodded in firm agreement. "Their police and their analysts are topnotch, and they've really hit the ground running to turn up so much so quickly. Especially since it's obvious this came as just as much of a surprise to them as it did to us."

"Actually," Palazzola interjected, "I think it may have come as even *more* of a surprise to them because of how close an eye they've been keeping on the Chelthists. They've been watching those people closely, and like Néhémial says, they're *good*. They thought they had the situation pretty much nailed down, and the way they got blindsided's been really hard for them to process."

"That's a fair point," Routhier acknowledged. "In particular, they still haven't figured out how Sokyr managed to vanish so completely. On the other hand, I think Bardyn has a couple of interesting suspicions about that.

"His people have made some other significant progress, though. For example, they've been turning over every rock and beating every bush, and so far they've managed to identify all but two of the terrorists killed here in the Republic."

"They *can't* identify two of them?" Wilson asked with a frown.

"No, Sir," Palazzola said, and Wilson's frown deepened.

The Republic's ability to process biometric data lagged light-years beyond the Planetary Union's, but it was considerably more advanced in some areas than Sarth's general tech level might have suggested. In particular, they understood fingerprints, and while they couldn't match prints digitally the way Terran computers could, their fingerprint experts were very good. More to the point, every "First World" Diantian child was routinely fingerprinted when he, she, or ou began primary education.

"That's very odd," Swenson observed, then shook her head. "I'm starting to sound like Abu Bakr!"

"It's more than just 'odd,' Ma'am," Routhier said. "One of the two they can't identify has tin dental fillings." Swenson looked blank, and the chief of staff waved one hand. "It doesn't prove anything, Ma'am, but Bardyn tells us that modern

Diantian dentistry uses amalgam fillings—usually a mix of silver and copper. Some really old-fashioned dentists still use tin, but they're the dinosaurs. And they're also a lot rarer in the Republic than they are some other places."

"I see." The admiral glanced at Wilson, then turned back to the two chiefs of staff. "Go on."

"Yes, Ma'am. Bardyn also tells us that at least two of the attack teams used field radios that have been recovered. Obviously, they're a lot bigger and bulkier than ours are, but like the weapons they used, they're Diantian Army standard issue. No real surprises there. They've also turned up some evidence that confirms the attacks were, indeed, coordinated by phone, however. I won't say I find their evidence conclusive, but it's certainly suggestive. And one reason Bardyn pointed that out is that all landline communications across the frontier are monitored and logged."

"Excuse me? Without computers?" Wilson asked.

"Yes, Sir." Routhier shook his head, his expression wry. "In fairness, there aren't a lot of private phone conversations across the frontier. In fact, there aren't many conversations at all, and most of those that do occur are either business or diplomatic. More than that, there are only two exchanges that handle cross-border traffic at all. So, every originating number and every destination number is recorded for those calls. They don't exactly have the Fourth Amendment, either, and their intelligence people routinely listen in on conversations. Obviously, they can't listen to *all* of them, and the diplomatic lines are privileged—it's a severe violation of international law to listen to or record them—but they do listen to a significant percentage of all the other traffic, and Bardyn's people have pulled the records and interviewed all of the monitors. So far as the Diantians can tell, there are no unaccounted-for calls between the attack on Secretary Dvorak and the attack on Mister Berke. There might have been a couple before the attack on Abu Bakr, but we've got a very good time chop on the attack on Mister Berke because of when his call for assistance was logged in. In that interval, there were no civilian calls that went anywhere near the attack's location. And, of course, the attempt on Abu Bakr occurred in the middle of a farm, without a telephone within a kilometer of the actual attack."

Wilson and Swenson glanced at each other again. Then they refocused on Routhier and Palazzola.

"All of that is interesting, and possibly suggestive," Routhier continued, "but what really brought Director Bardyn up here is something one of his teams turned up in Myrcos. It seems that Bearer Sokyr's right-hand man, Trygau HyrShalTry, died in infancy."

For a moment, the two flag officers only looked at him. Then their eyes narrowed simultaneously, and Wilson's right-hand made an imperative "tell me more" gesture.

"Trygau is a bachelor, so he carries his parents' surname and there are no spouses or children in the picture," Routhier said. "He's lived a totally unspectacular life, all of it in Myrcos, and apparently he never held a regular job until he went to work as Sokyr's butler and general all-around office manager. He never even had any close childhood friends, as far as the Diantians can tell—certainly not anyone who actually remembers him as a kid. I mean, he's just a gray little fellow who's gone through life without leaving any significant footprints until he found his true calling as a religious nut and True Believer." The commander shook his head. "I imagine there are plenty of potential live-in-my-mom's-basement Brownshirts looking for a *Führer* to follow in any species, and that's exactly what Trygau obviously is."

"Why do I think you're being ironic, Néhémial?" Swenson asked.

"Maybe because I am," her chief of staff replied. "Not that we'd have any reason to think he was anything but that gray little fellow if one of Bardyn's investigators hadn't decided on a really deep dumpster dive into his history. He and his team ran every record they had on him, clear back to Day One, back through the wringer, and they turned up his birth certificate. But then—and I think this was as much the kind of 'luck' persistence and good investigative procedures generate as it was anything else—they found a death certificate, too. And according to it, Trygau HyrShalTry died when he was only four local years old."

"That isn't just 'odd' anymore," Swenson said flatly.

"No, Ma'am, and it gets better."

"What do you mean 'better'?"

"What the cops found is a *duplicate* death certificate, Ma'am. The one in the official registry is missing. They're all numbered sequentially for each registry office, but Bardyn says gaps in the files aren't all that uncommon, thanks to human—well, Sarthian—error. Certificates get numbered wrong, numbers get skipped sometimes, file copies don't get put in the right place—things like that. People don't usually think too much about it when they hit that sort of thing. But this death certificate was in the hospital records, not the official repository. And when they checked its number against the repository, they found a hole. The one before it and the one after it are exactly where they're supposed to be; this one's no place to be found."

"Jesus," Wilson murmured.

"Exactly, Boss." Palazzola's expression was hard. "Standard tradecraft. Find the birth certificate for a dead kid who would've been about the right age if he'd lived and step right into the identity. It looks like this time they even had someone pull the death certificate, which is a nice touch, really. They could only get away with it because the Sarthians are still stuck with paper records, but it shows somebody put at lot of thought into making sure their tracks were buried deep. And by an interesting turn of fate, the entire HyrShalTry triad and both of his surviving siblings were killed in the same house fire when our 'Trygau' would've been about twelve Earth years old, so there are no living family members to ask about it. Bardyn's people are hunting for his school records now, but by the strangest coincidence, the primary and secondary schools he attended were parochial schools, run by the Church of Chelth, on a shared campus. And—surprise, surprise—the administrative building burned to the ground twenty-three local years ago. About the time our friend 'Trygau' went to work for Bearer Sokyr, as a matter of fact."

"Well, how convenient."

"You might say that, Ma'am," Palazzola agreed.

"So everything else they've got—phone lines, monitored conversations, all that—is *possibly* suggestive," Wilson said thoughtfully, "but this—"

"Nobody could prove it in a court of law yet, but that doesn't matter," Routhier said flatly. "Whoever the hell 'Trygau' really is, he's not who everyone's *thought* he was, and none of us and none of Bardyn's people can see any reason why a genuine religious nut would have—or, for that matter, *could* have—gone to such lengths to create a false persona this detailed."

He shook his head, eyes cold.

"That's not the kind of thing religious terrorists do. It's the kind of thing *nation states* do, and I'm pretty damn sure it wasn't the *Republic* that did it in this case."

· · · · ·

FLYTHYR MUZTOLFLYTH, FLOCK Lord Consort Pantyl, eased into her seat at the table as Myrcal FarMyrZol entered. While she was in no danger of dying—not anymore, because of the Earthians' assistance—the doctors had advised her to take four or five full-days off to recover from her wounds. Unfortunately, current events didn't allow that.

Herdsman Consort Vistal Hyrkyl ShoHyrTo, head of the Imperial Intelligence Service, followed Myrcal into the conference room and raised his hands respectfully before his face to Clan Ruler Juzhyr. Then he closed the door quietly behind himself and found a chair at the foot of the table.

"I assume there's a reason you asked for a meeting of the senior ministries, Myrcal?" Juzhyr asked, ous eyes boring into the minister. "With the ongoing . . . events, there are many things that currently require my attention; I hope, for your sake, that your reason is a good one."

"I'm afraid it is, Clan Ruler," Myrcal replied. "Herdsman Consort Vistal tells me we have word from Dianzhyr." With Chancellor Erylk obviously dying now, the Intelligence Service reported directly to Myrcal, as senior minister. "I felt his report required your attention, but that you might want to keep it confined to just those of us present." He nodded to Flythyr.

"Fine," Juzhyr said with a single shake of ous head. "What information have we received?"

Myrcal closed both nasal flaps tight, then exhaled, and Flythyr could see oum steadying ouself.

"We have an asset on the staff of Bardyn ShoKymBar, Dianto's Director of Intelligence. He isn't one of Bardyn's senior officers, but he has access to much of Bardyn's correspondence and files. According to his latest reports, it appears they've found a copy of the death certificate for Trygau HyrShalTry."

"Trygau who?" Flythyr asked blankly, one nasal flap raised.

"He's Bearer Sokyr's right-hand male, Flock Lord," Hyrkyl explained for Myrcal. "We inserted him there some time ago. At which time—" he looked at the clan ruler "—we had the death certificate removed from the records."

"So how did they find it, then?" Juzhyr demanded.

"It appears there was a copy stored locally at the hospital where the original Trygau died, and that copy has resurfaced."

"I don't understand," Flythyr replied. "The Diantians found out about one of our operatives. That happens periodically—even *they* aren't stupid, after all. What's the importance of that, compared to dealing with these Chelthist attacks?" A bad thought occurred to her. "Unless . . ."

"Yes, Trygau was our male, and he's the one responsible for initiating the attacks," Myrcal explained. "Not only did the Intelligence Directorate learn of it, Bardyn also went to the Earthians' spaceship to talk with them about it."

"Just a seelaq," Flythyr said. "The operation is ours, and you didn't think it was important to brief me on it, especially when *I* was the target of one of the attacks?"

"*You* weren't the target of the attack," Juzhyr said. "Representative Theodore was the target."

"But still—I was with him! Why didn't someone warn me about the attack?" She pointed to her wounds. "I could have been killed! I nearly was!"

"We didn't warn you," Juzhyr said, "because we needed the attack to look genuine. We couldn't tell you about it in advance, because we didn't want it to appear staged. I *did*, however, advise you to take a half-eight of troops with you, which you did."

"But they outnumbered us by double!"

Juzhyr snapped both left thumbs dismissively. "The day the head of my Army, along with four handpicked troopers, can't defend themselves from ten religious fanatics, is the day I need to find a new head of the Army." Ou looked pointedly at Flythyr's leg. "And I very nearly did." Juzhyr shrugged. "Still, you served a purpose, and you *did* survive, so my confidence in you wasn't misplaced."

Ou turned back to Myrcal. "Now that that's settled, let us speak of this death certificate that's appeared. Does our agent on Bardyn's staff know what was spoken about on the Earthians' ship?"

Myrcal nodded in unhappy negation and beckoned for Hyrkyl to respond.

"He's not on one of the teams Bardyn sent to Myrcos, Clan Ruler," the herds-man consort said, "so he wasn't able to learn much about their findings, beyond the discovery of the death certificate, although he doesn't think they've found anything else significant. But thanks to him we at least know Bardyn made the trip, and I doubt he would have if he hadn't planned on laying their current findings on the table."

"This isn't good." Flythyr's nasal flaps closed tightly. "In fact, this is very bad."

"I'm afraid I must agree," Myrcal said with manifest reluctance.

"Why?" Juzhyr asked. "Because one operative's cover was blown?"

"Clan Lord," Hyrkyl said diffidently, "that may be only the first stone of an avalanche."

"Why?" Juzhyr repeated impatiently.

"First," Hyrkyl replied, with what Flythyr thought was remarkable courage, "the Diantians—and the Earthians with them—are going to realize Trygau was a plant. Second," he continued, counting on his fingers, "Sokyr is no longer around. It won't be long until they start to ask questions about where ou went. It's going to be obvious someone from outside the organization was planted there specifically to take it over, and, third, Bardyn is no fool. It won't take him long to figure out that he can't find Sokyr because 'Trygau' eliminated oum specifically to direct a series of attacks *attributed* to Sokyr, a Diantian religious hothead, as a way to make Dianto look bad.

"While *we* aren't afraid to do something like that to ourselves and then blame Dianto," Hyrkyl's eyes dipped briefly to Flythyr's wounds, "*they* would never have the fortitude to do so. And terrorist organizations don't have the foresight, plan-ning, or manning to get someone like Trygau into place so long before the opera-tion actually occurred; only nations do. And if Dianto wasn't responsible for the attacks, despite all of the equipment pointing the finger at the Republic—and the number of genuine Diantians committing them—then the next place Dianto and the Earthians will come looking is right here. Uncovering 'Trygau' won't *confirm* our participation in the attacks, unless they manage to capture him and he talks, but it will certainly cause them to wonder about us."

"This is your plan, Myrcal, and your blunder," Juzhyr said. "Not only has your incompetence put us into a very dangerous position with this operation, you also appear to be driving the Earthians into the Diantians' claws. Bardyn went up to the Earthians' spaceship? Next it will be Prime Director Qwelth going up to the Earthians' ship for long, moonlit dinners under the stars, then word of Dianto signing a treaty with the Earthians that doesn't include us! *How do you intend to* fix *this?*"

Myrcal was unable to meet the clan lord's eyes for a moment, then ous head came back up. "I will talk with the Earthians, and I will get the finger pointed back at the Diantians."

"And how do you intend to do that?" Juzhyr asked. "Councilor Arthur is still at the Nonagon and even Abu and Fikriyah Batma are back aboard their ship up in space!"

"Representative Theodore is still here, though," Myrcal said with a smile. He nodded towards Flythyr. "And, thanks to our somewhat unwilling head of the Army saving him, he owes us a favor."

· · · · ·

"THANK YOU FOR seeing me on such short notice," Myrcal said. "I hope you're doing well after your recent harrowing experience?"

"I am," Theodore Berke replied, turning away from the balcony and the royal gardens he'd been looking over. Despite the results of his last meeting here, Myrcal had been told the Earthians found the gardens relaxing and hoped for a happier ending this time. "Although I'm sorry your troops had to give their lives for me."

Myrcal shook his head slowly. "Yes, it is unfortunate; however, that's what troops are supposed to do—to give their lives—so that their country can move on to bigger and better things." He waved Berke to one of the two chairs on the veranda. "And that's what I'd hoped to talk with you about today."

"Certainly," Berke replied, sitting. "I'm at your disposal. What is it you wish to discuss?"

"Well, I had hoped to have this meeting with Ambassador Abu, but he doesn't appear to be coming back soon. . . ."

"No, with the injury to Secretary Dvorak, he's working through a number of issues aboard ship. It may be some time before he's able to return to the planet."

"I see . . ." Myrcal looked out over the gardens then returned his gaze to the Earthian. "Perhaps I should communicate directly with Councilor Arthur, then?"

The Earthian's eyes widened for a moment, then he shook his head.

"That won't be necessary, Minister. I can pass on any message through our channels here faster than it could go through Lyzan."

"Thank you. Would you please inform him that I would very much like to express my concern over the . . . impression, shall we say, presented by Bardyn ShoKymBar nor Garyth's trip up to your spaceship?"

The Earthian twitched back slightly; Myrcal had surprised him. Good!

"Um . . . yes?" the Earthian said after a moment. "What impression concerns you, Minister?"

"I'm worried about the precedent this sets," Myrcal replied, "and how our people will view it. It almost appears as if you Earthians are looking to reach secret deals with the Diantians, contrary to everything you've said previously. Taking a member of their government—and the head of their intelligence directorate, at that—up into space is a major event. Is there some reason we were excluded? Denied the same opportunity? Something we've done to deserve this slap in the face? Something we've failed to provide you with as we both try to deal with the attacks that have so recently plagued our country?" He cocked his head as he'd seen the Earthians do. "Do you believe *we* were behind these attacks?"

"No!" Berke exclaimed.

"And do you think Councilor Arthur agrees with you about that?" Myrcal tightened ous nasal flaps to show ous anxiety . . . and realized it wasn't entirely acting as ou waited for the Earthian's response.

"Art—I mean, Councilor McCabe—hasn't spoken directly to me about that," he said after a moment. His translating device's tone sounded almost surprised, and Myrcal's heart sank. If Councilor Arthur was keeping his views that carefully hidden. . . .

"But while there are many people, both from Sarth and Earth, looking into a number of possible causes," Berke continued, "there's no doubt in *my* mind that you weren't behind them. Heavens! I saw the aftermath of the battle—how your people gave their lives, and how even the head of your army was prepared to sacrifice her life to save mine. I know you're not behind it."

"Then can you tell me why you're taking Diantians to your *Vanguard*, but aren't interested in any information *we* may have uncovered?"

"I'm sure we're interested in what you've found, although I know there were some . . . irregularities the Diantians found that have people all astir up there. I'm not at liberty to talk about what they are, but I'm given to understand they're potentially damning."

"So what are we to do?"

"I'll liaise with my superiors and find out," Berke replied. "And I'll also reiterate my feeling on the battle I was a part of. I'm sure they'll contact you soon."

"Thank you," Myrcal said with a small shake of his head. "We greatly appreciate it."

As they got up to leave the veranda, Myrcal was aware of two things. First, although the Earthian in front of him believed the Empire wasn't behind the attacks, the Earthians in general were now leaning towards the conclusion that it was. And, second, ou had to do something major to bring the Earthians back into Clan Qwern's camp.

XVIII

PUNS *VANGUARD*,
SARTH ORBIT;
CITY OF KWYZO NAR QWERN, QWERNIAN EMPIRE;
AND CITY OF DIANZHYR, REPUBLIC OF DIANTO,
PLANET SARTH

What the hell do you think put the bug up Myrcal's ass?" Rob Wilson asked irritably.

"Oh, most probably the fact that ou sees Bardyn's visit up here as the first step in cutting the Empire out in the Republic's favor," Abu Bakr replied dryly.

"Oh, bullshit!" Wilson shook his head, expression irate. "Myrcal spends all ous time *looking* for things to be upset about. And if ou's feeling left out in the cold, exactly whose fault is that?" The brigadier turned away to glare out at the blue-and-white marble of Sarth through the observation deck's armorplast dome. "If the miserable son-of-a-bitch hadn't been playing political games and refusing to talk to you, Dave wouldn't have been in Dianzhyr that day in the first place! I care exactly *squat* about ous hurt feelings just this minute."

Abu Bakr looked at the other man's back with a faint, sympathetically sad smile. Wilson had come to the observation dome straight from having dinner with Morgana Dvorak, and Morgana was a doctor herself. She wasn't a neurosurgeon, but she did have a basic medical degree as part of her psychology training, and she'd been looking at the scans of her father's brain.

They were getting better, but. . . .

"I can't say I disagree with you, Rob," Abu Bakr said after a moment. "And remember, I'm the one who's had the indescribable pleasure of working with oum on a regular basis. And just between you, me, and the observation dome, I wouldn't trust oum as far as I could throw oum. The reason ou worries about us cutting deals with the Republic to freeze oum out is that ou was totally sincere when ou offered to make the Qwernians our sepoys to take over the entire frigging planet for us if we'd only cut everyone else out of any deals. And I'm pretty damned sure ou was already thinking forward to ous own version of the Sepoy *Mutiny*, too. But ou does have a point about appearances, if it should become publicly known that Bardyn came to call on us. Which, by the way, is one of the more interesting aspects of Berke's conversation with oum, actually."

Wilson turned back to raise one eyebrow above an angry blue eye, and Abu Bakr shrugged.

"*We* didn't tell anyone he'd been up to orbit, and the *Republic* didn't tell anyone that, but Myrcal knew about it anyway. How do you suppose that happened?"

"Obviously they've got someone inside the Diantian government." It was Wilson's turn to shrug. "There was some reason you thought they *wouldn't* have spies in the Republic?"

"No, I just find it interesting that Myrcal effectively confirmed it for us."

"Bastard probably figured it was so self-evident they'd be spying on the Republic—and vice versa, I'm sure—that there was no point pretending otherwise."

"Probably. But I think ou confirmed something else for us, too."

"And that would be . . . what, exactly?"

"That ou's worried—badly worried—about what Bardyn may have had to say to us."

"What? All ou complained about was what our own more despicable politicians refer to as the 'optics,'" Wilson pointed out. "Ou didn't say a word about any conversation we might've had with Bardyn once he was up here. Ou just complained about the fact that he was aboard ship to have it . . . and Myrcal wasn't."

"And as Sherlock Holmes once pointed out, the remarkable thing about the dog is that it didn't bark during the night."

Wilson blinked at him, then his eyes narrowed, some of the anger leaching out of them as his brain engaged fully.

"You're right," he said slowly. "Ou didn't ask about what Bardyn might have had to say, either, did ou?"

"No, and I've listened to ous conversation with Berke several times now," Abu Bakr said, and Wilson nodded. Berke's phone had recorded the entire discussion with Myrcal.

"I won't pretend I understand Sarthian psychology," Abu Bakr continued. "I expect Myrcal's is probably twistier than most, even if I did, too. But it's evident that ou took it as a given that whatever Bardyn said had pointed a finger at the Empire. That was the thrust of ous entire exchange with Berke, and the software's emotional overlays say ou was really worried about it, not just striking a pose to score diplomatic bargaining chips. Ou tried to hide it, but ou's genuinely concerned we think the Empire somehow orchestrated the entire thing. Which is pretty strange, when all the known attackers have been Diantians, the communique claiming responsibility was issued by a Diantian religious nut, and ou didn't even ask if Bardyn had offered any evidence that the Empire was pulling strings to make it all happen."

"Ou may just automatically assume that if Bardyn's pointing fingers at *anyone*, it would have to be the Empire," Wilson pointed out in his best devil's advocate voice, then chuckled harshly. "Probably a simple exercise in mirror-imaging. It's sure as hell what *ou'd* be doing in Bardyn's place!"

"Agreed. But first ou confirmed to Berke—which means to me—that they knew Bardyn had come aboard *Vanguard*. Ou didn't have to do that, and if ou was going to, there are a lot of things Bardyn could have been doing besides casting suspicions on the Empire—or on anyone else, for that matter. It's a matter of public record that Bardyn's directorate's in charge of investigating the Chelthist attacks, so he could very well have come up here to report a breakthrough on the *domestic* side of the investigation. We haven't said a word to suggest that we think this was anything except an assault by Diantian religious fanatics. We've been very careful to label it as the criminal action of private Diantian citizens without assigning any responsibility to the Republic's government, but we certainly haven't suggested that any non-Diantian might have been behind it. For that matter, we've never said a word to suggest we think *any* government's behind it. Yet Myrcal leapt immediately to asking Berke if we thought the Empire was responsible for it without even asking what Bardyn had said first. It's entirely possible that it was a simple passive-aggressive response to being excluded from any 'invitation' to visit *Vanguard,* but listening to oum, watching the software overlays of ous emotions, ou's obviously afraid we do think the Empire put this all together. And why would ou think we might have some reason to think anything of the sort?"

"If ous source in the Republic's high enough to know about the Trygau death certificate, that might explain it," Wilson said. "Ou may be figuring—and it wouldn't really be all that unreasonable of oum—that if we think it was a state actor outside the Republic, then the Empire and the Qwernian Alliance are the only logical suspects."

"Agreed," Abu Bakr said again. "But Myrcal's played the diplomacy game for a long time, Rob. Ou should damned well realize that the way questions get asked can compromise intelligence sources. Or, conversely, that how they're asked can shape the way an adversary interprets those sources. What ou *ought* to have done was to ask what Bardyn had actually said. If Berke had told oum about the death certificate and the forensic evidence the autopsies have turned up, ou could have presented counter arguments or a defense against them—even suggested that perhaps the Diantians were manufacturing evidence to get themselves off the hook—without giving away anything about what their source had told them. Obviously, Berke might not have told him that, exactly the way that Berke didn't tell him what has us 'astir,' but ou didn't even probe. Ou just went straight to 'how could you think that of us?' mode. Now, I know I'm probably more suspicious than most, especially after Naya Islamabad, but it seems to me that the fact ou didn't ask about what Bardyn had to say confirms that ous source *is* high enough ou already knew about it. That's a pretty high trump card to show us this early, especially if ou thinks there's a chance we may hand that information to Bardyn, but that's not the worst part of it. Potentially, at least."

"It's not?"

"No." Abu Bakr shook his head, his expression unhappy. "Whatever else I think of Myrcal, ou's been doing this long enough to know how the game is played. I don't think it's a good sign if ou's so nervous about what we suspect that ou's making that kind of careless, newbie mistake. It brings up that verse about the wicked fleeing when no one's chasing them and makes me wonder—it makes me wonder a *lot*, Rob—if there's some reason *ou* knows about that death certificate . . . and that it's only the tip of a really messy iceberg. One ou's afraid we and the Diantians might be about to dig up."

"Wonderful." Wilson's expression was at least as unhappy as Abu Bakr's. "I'll admit there's a part of me that would really like an excuse to kick Myrcal's ass up between ous ears, but I don't like where you're going with this one at all."

"I'm not too enthused about it myself. And I may be completely wrong, but once I got myself into 'suspicious as hell' mode, I realized there's another aspect of that entire conversation that strikes me as odd."

"What else?" Wilson eyed him with a certain trepidation.

"There's something . . . off about the way ou asked about McCabe."

"McCabe?" Wilson's surprise was evident.

"McCabe," Abu Bakr confirmed, and shrugged irritably. "I wish ou'd been talking to Fikriyah, not Berke. I wish I'd left her in Kwyzo nar Qwern instead of hauling her up here for that conference. She's sat in on enough of my conversations with oum to have a better feel for ous mannerisms and tone, and I think Berke missed something she might have picked up on and tried to clarify."

"Such as?"

"Such as I think Myrcal wasn't talking about sending a message to me through McCabe in Lyzan, the way Berke assumed ou was. I think ou was talking about sending a message *to* McCabe."

"Huh?" Wilson shook his head. "Come again? McCabe's an *advisor*. He's not even in the mission's chain of command!"

"I know that." Abu Bakr nodded. "And you know that. For that matter, Alex's spent enough time at the Nonagon with Dave for it to be obvious that he's Dave's senior aide, which means McCabe shouldn't even be in the running for the position. But I'll be damned if that isn't what it sounded like ou was saying. Is it possible for some reason that, whatever you and I may know, Myrcal *doesn't* know McCabe's not in a senior command position?"

"I don't know," Wilson said, turning back to gaze thoughtfully through the armorplast once more. "To be honest, you're a lot better with this 'people' stuff, even when the people in question are aliens, than I am. But assume you're right, that for some reason ou thinks McCabe's one of our actual policymakers. You think that's significant?"

"My turn to say 'I don't know,'" Abu Bakr admitted. "On the other hand, in this instance it's the things we don't know that could get a lot more people killed, so I think we should probably find out."

"Simplest way would be to just ask oum," Wilson pointed out.

"So speaks the simple-minded Space Marine." Abu Bakr's tone was dry. "If the Qwernians really are up to something—whether it's because they did have a hand in arranging all of this to begin with, or simply that they're fishing in troubled waters to take advantage of it now that it's happened—the last thing I want is to let someone like Myrcal MyrFarZol see any of my hole cards. And the way ou approached that entire conversation has me looking under the bed for bogeymen." He shook his head. "Maybe I'm just being paranoid because of what's already happened and because of how little I trust Myrcal to begin with, but I don't want to give oum any clue that ou's made us suspicious."

"You been hanging around Dave too long," Wilson said even more dryly. "He always makes my head hurt when he gets into double- and triple-think."

"I'm going to take that as a compliment, even though I suspect that's not how you meant it."

"Diplomat." Wilson actually chuckled, but then he cocked his head and looked at Abu Bakr quizzically. "But if you're not going to ask oum about it, then how are you going to figure it out?"

"I'm going to start by sitting down with Alex and all the rest of Dave's advisors—including McCabe—individually. I'm going to play the conversation for each of them and then ask him or her what *they* think Myrcal's up to and if there's any reason they can see for oum to be sending messages to McCabe."

"You don't think McCabe—?"

Wilson let his voice trail off, and Abu Bakr shook his head quickly.

"I don't agree with a lot of Arthur McCabe's philosophy, but he's not the kind to run around behind his superiors' backs or cut corners. If he knows any reason Myrcal might want to approach him, he'll tell me about it."

"And if no one can think of a reason?"

"Then either I'm seeing things that aren't there—which would probably be a good thing, really—or we need an outside opinion." Abu Bakr shrugged. "If they can't convince me I'm imagining things, I think I may ask Bardyn and Prime Director Qwelth to listen to the same conversation."

"That could be construed as a violation of Myrcal's presumption of confidentiality as a diplomat," Wilson pointed out.

"Of course it could, but we've just agreed that the entire conversation's evidence of the Empire's penetration of the Republic's government, and what-ever the Chelthists may have done, Qwelth and Bardyn—all the Diantian directors—have done their damnedest to get to the bottom of it. They're ab-solutely sincere about that, even if only because they realize how disastrous this could turn out for them if we decide they should've seen it coming and prevented it. I'm convinced of that, and so is the software."

He paused and Wilson nodded. Bardyn and Qwelth were either totally sin-cere in their shared desire to figure out what had happened and make sure it never happened again, or else they were the best actors ever born. The emotion-parsing feature of the translating software made that abundantly clear.

"I'm not going to lose any sleep over helping them figure out that the Qwernians have planted spies on them," Abu Bakr continued then. "As you say, they have to already know they've been penetrated at least to some ex-tent, if only because that's how things work. But that whole conversation about McCabe nags at me, Rob. It just . . . nags at me. It's like the terrorist with the bazooka—something just isn't right. And if none of our people can figure out what that something is, maybe we need a Sarthian viewpoint on it."

· · · · ·

MYRCAL'S EYES TRAVELED the length of the conference table in ous war room in the War Palace. Buried beneath cherans of dirt and concrete, the war room was the safest place ou could think of to hold the meeting. While it was possible the Dwomo–damned Earthians could still spy on their meeting—ou had no idea how their spy systems worked—there was no safer place on the planet. If they could spy on oum here, then the future of Clan Qwern in general—and ous future, in particular—was in serious jeopardy.

Ou beckoned for the male to ous right to begin.

"What do we hear from our sources?"

"According to Herdsman Consort Vistal, the investigation into Trygau con-tinues in the Republic," Jorhsal JorhFyrTol, ous chief of staff, replied. "While they haven't been able to tie anything to us yet, Bardyn's staff is almost unan-imous in their opinion that either the Empire or the Qwernian Alliance was responsible for the attacks."

"And they've reported as much to the Earthians?"

"We can't confirm that, but based on the lines of communication that ap-pear to be in place between Bardyn and the Earthians, we feel certain they have."

"If the Earthians decide we were the ones responsible for the attacks, what's their probable response going to be?"

"We don't know. The Earthians—aside from their displays of force in responding to the attacks—have been extremely reticent about showing us any of their capabilities."

Myrcal raised one nasal flap. "Why do you suppose that is?"

"Also unknown, Minister. Perhaps their capabilities aren't as much greater than ours as they want us to believe? Maybe they're worried we would attack them if we knew that?"

Tarquo StalTarChal raised her hand, and Myrcal arched a nasal flap for her to speak.

"Can we really assume that, though?" she asked. "They flew through interstellar *space* to get here, and they already defeated another starfaring race. They must have *some* capabilities beyond ours that we haven't seen yet."

"That can't be proven one way or the other," Gennyn CholAnGen replied. "While what you say is true, the capabilities they exhibited during the recent attacks—aside from their aviation assets, which are much more advanced than ours—weren't as far beyond ours as I would have thought they'd be. And besides, the Earthians never really did explain how they beat the Shongairi. Perhaps there was some sort of virus on the planet the Shongairi succumbed to, and the Earthians didn't do anything more than just steal their equipment once they perished? That would explain some of the holes in their story."

"All of this is conjecture," the chief of staff said in summation, turning back to Myrcal. "The truth of the matter is we don't know *what* their capabilities are, any more than we know what their true intentions are regarding us. The Earthians appear to say one thing, but then they do something else entirely, and most of the time, their methods don't make any sense!"

Myrcal shared a wry smile with ous staff.

"No one knows better than I the truth behind that statement," ou said. "I wish Dwomo had sent the Earthians somewhere else . . . but Ou didn't, and we have to deal with them. Worse, now that the Earthians seem to be beginning to suspect we had something to do with the attacks, we need to be prepared for the possibility they might decide that as a certainty. What are our options?"

"One thing we know for sure," Tarquo said, "is that they can drop things on us from space. Even if they're afraid to face us—soldier-to-soldier—for some reason, they can still drop asteroids or other bombs on us from their spacecraft if they decide we were responsible and choose to retaliate, and there's nothing we can do to stop them. They can do that with impunity, any time they wish."

"Then we need a way to prevent them from exercising that option," Myrcal replied. "You seem to have given this some thought. What would you recommend?"

Tarquo shrugged. "In order to make them come to us, we have to take away their ability to drop things on us from space. There are only two ways to do that—either we need to go up there and take away their ability to do so, or we need to take away their *desire* to do so."

"The first of those is . . . problematic at this moment," Myrcal said with a chuckle. "I suspect you have a way for us to accomplish the second option?"

"I do," Tarquo said, shaking her head. "The Earthians would be retaliating because of the attacks on their people and, especially, because of the Earthians who died. So the trick would be to create a situation in which they can't bomb us from orbit without endangering still more of their fellow Earthians. If we can create a situation like that—put Earthian lives in peril in the event of any attempt to bomb us from orbit—they would have to come down here to face us, instead. Assuming, of course, that they had the spiritual fortitude to do anything of the sort."

"So just grab a few of the Earthians and hold them hostage?" the chief of staff asked.

"No," Tarquo said with a smile. "I'd advise the Minister to grab *all* the Earthians we can that are currently resident in the Empire and the Alliance's member states. If we could capture enough of them, we could them put them in all the places we think might be targeted by the Earthians and use them as a de facto shield against anything dropped from space."

There was a collective intake of breath around the conference table at the sheer audacity of the plan. Not to just grab a few Earthians . . . but to grab *all* of them? Myrcal shook ous head slowly. Ou liked it. And the more ou thought about it, the more ou liked it. In fact, the plan was exactly what ou—what the Empire—needed. An exceptionally audacious strategy that hit the Earthians throughout all of Qwernian territory! Capturing *all* the Earthians would show the ones in space the lengths to which the Empire was prepared to go to achieve dominance over the Republic. And then, once they'd captured some of the Earthians, the others wouldn't be able to bomb them from orbit! They would have to negotiate with the Empire, but now, the Qwernians would be the ones in power. *They* would hold the cards for once, and the Earthians would have to come begging if they wanted their people back.

Yes, this strategy had real potential. Myrcal might have bungled ous first meeting with Abu Bakr, but this approach was *sure* to prove which nation on Sarth was most prepared to do—and most ruthlessly capable *of* doing—whatever it took to accomplish the next step towards the stars. The Earthians would probably be furious, at least at first, but ultimately they would realize it only proved that the Empire was their absolute best ally here on Sarth.

"You're right," ou said, smiling at Tarquo, then turned to ous chief of staff. "I endorse this plan. Have Hyrkyl instruct our operatives to begin planning the capture of the Earthians."

"But what about the Earthian soldiers and the armor they wear?" the chief of staff asked. "Surely, after the other attacks, the Earthians will be more on guard. Won't that preclude capturing their personnel?"

"Have we seen their soldiers wearing the armor in the last two day-halves?" Myrcal asked.

"No," Tarquo said. "Only the ones who came to assist Earthians under attack actually wore the armor. In the days since, none of them have been wearing it."

"Good," Myrcal said. "Make sure our operatives know to grab the Earthians and get under cover before any of those forces show up to assist. If there are other soldiers or guards in the area, they should kill them first."

. . . . .

"SIR, I DON'T have a clue," Arthur McCabe said from Lyzan, shaking his head in the com image projected onto Abu Bakr's corneal implants.

The younger man's expression was weary, almost haggard, and Abu Bakr felt a stab of sympathy. Apparently McCabe and Trish McGillicuddy had grown even closer then Abu Bakr or Dvorak had realized. Her death had hit him hard.

"I've never even spoken to Minister Myrcal," McCabe continued, "and I can't think of a single reason he'd want to talk to *me* now."

"Don't worry, you're not alone in that," Abu Bakr said dryly. "And in case you were wondering, no one thinks you've done anything to convince him you're more highly placed in our chain of command than you actually are." He smiled ever so slightly. "I've known a few weasels over the years, especially since the invasion, who wouldn't be above doing exactly that. One thing about fighting a guerrilla war against alien invaders is that you don't have to worry about careerist empire builders. I've seen plenty of them since I got shanghaied as a diplomat, though, and you're not one of them."

"I appreciate that, Sir, and I'm glad to know you don't think of me that way. But I still can't come up with a reason for Myrcal to single me out as important to the process. I mean, I have a fairly cordial relationship with Charioteer Consort Zyr here at the Nonagon. I like her and I respect her, and we've gotten into the habit of touching base over coffee and terahk every two or three day-halves. I've passed summaries of most of our conversations to Secretary Dvorak."

Abu Bakr nodded. All of the mission staff summarized any contacts with Sarthians for the mission data base, and actual copies of those contacts were on file from their translation software for review, if that seemed necessary.

"But however well she and I may get along," McCabe continued, "she's only their representative to the Nonagon, which isn't exactly a critical posting in the Qwernian diplomatic service." The sad-eyed young man quirked a faint smile. "I guess what I'm saying is she's not a whole lot farther up the Qwernian totem pole than I am on ours."

"I understand." Abu Bakr nodded. "I can't say you've been able to tell me anything I didn't already know, but, then, neither has anyone else!"

"Maybe not, Sir, but even if I can't think of a reason for Myrcal to think I'm important enough for oum to be officially communicating with me, I think I have to agree with you that that's exactly what he was suggesting to Ted. And I have to say, that worries me."

"It does?" Abu Bakr asked, eyeing him thoughtfully.

"Yes, Sir." McCabe shook his head again. "If the Qwernian Foreign Minister is misreading who's in charge now that Secretary Dvorak's down so badly that ou thinks I'm the one—or one of the ones, at any rate—ou needs to be talking to, then what *other* mistakes is ou making? And for that matter," those weary brown eyes turned remarkably dark and hard, "what other mistakes has ou already *made*?"

Abu Bakr nodded, slowly and thoughtfully. No one had shared the Diantians' evidence that the Chelthists might have been manipulated by someone outside the Republic with McCabe, but it would seem the same suspicion might already have occurred to him independently. That said some interesting things about him. Things Abu Bakr wouldn't have anticipated from a member of the "the Hegemony might not be all bad" crowd.

"I don't know the answers to those questions any more than you do," Abu Bakr said out loud. "Not yet, anyway. But just between you and me, I have an unhappy feeling they may be turning up soon."

. . . . .

"I HAVEN'T SEEN you in several day-halves, Myrcal," Juzhyr noted as ou started the meeting. "I hope that's because you've been planning something extraordinary to get us back in the good graces of the Earthians."

"I have, Clan Ruler," Myrcal replied with a shake of ous head. "My staff and I have been working on contingency planning, and we've come up with a strategy that will do more than just get us back in their good graces."

"And . . . it's going to work, *this time*?" Juzhyr's nasal flaps indicated irony . . . as if Myrcal hadn't been able to discern it from ous voice. "Perhaps you'd be willing to enlighten all of us?"

Myrcal nodded. "I think it's better if you aren't aware of it, Clan Ruler. There is some risk involved. I believe it's manageable, but I would prefer not to involve you in those risks. The plan is audacious, however, and it will show the Earthians exactly who on this planet is willing to do what it takes to be part of their clan. Perhaps, once the dust settles, they may even decide they want to be part of *our* clan, and not the other way around."

"And you're confident this plan will work?"

"Yes, Clan Ruler, we believe it will, or we wouldn't have put the pieces for it into place. With the failure of our last operation—"

"The fault for which has been laid almost entirely at your feet."

"—Yes, Clan Ruler. Because of its failure, though, I'm sure we became weaker in the eyes of the Earthians. By proving the Empire's ruthlessness and strength—*your* ruthlessness and strength, Clan Ruler—with this operation, we'll be able to convince the Earthians for all time that the Empire is a stronger and more efficient ally than the Republic."

"And it's going to work?"

"Undoubtedly."

"Let's hope so, then," the clan ruler said, ous nasal flaps closing menacingly. "For your sake, if nothing else." Ou smiled. "At least *my* hands are clean."

· · · · ·

"HOW IS SECRETARY David?" Prime Director Qwelth QwelSynChar asked, nasal flaps tight with concern, as the Earthians were escorted into the conference room.

"Actually," Ambassador Bakr replied, "the doctors' reports are a bit more optimistic than they were."

"Praise Chelth," Qwelth said, then froze, nasal flaps closing in dismay.

"Prime Director, don't worry about it," Abu Bakr said. Qwelth looked at him, and he shrugged. "Back on Earth, we have our own religious extremists, and some of them have been willing to kill thousands of their own species, not just a few dozen aliens from another world, in pursuit of their own brand of fanaticism. Quite a few of them share my own religion—or claim they do, at any rate—and a dozen or so of them did their very best to kill me several of my own people's years ago." He nodded his head. "Sarthians in general, and Diantians in particular, have no monopoly on people who commit acts their God would never approve of in His name."

"Bardyn told me that was how you'd reacted," Qwelth said, not even trying to hide ous relief.

"It wouldn't make any sense to react any other way." Abu Bakr shrugged. "Mind you, an awful lot of Earthians *have* reacted to our own religious extremists by deciding that anyone who shares the religion the extremists claim to follow is equally guilty of the extremists' crimes. That, unfortunately, is Earthian nature."

"And yet another way in which we're very alike, despite our physical differences." Qwelth's nasal flaps fluttered a sigh. Then ou waved at the massive Earthian-style chairs at the conference table. "Please, sit! I shouldn't have kept you standing."

Abu Bakr's mouth moved in what Qwelth had learned was the Earthian equivalent of a smile and he took one of the chairs. Alex Jackson took the one to his right, and Lieutenant Commander Quinlevan took the one to his left.

"Bardyn tells me you have a question about Minister Myrcal," the prime director said, settling into ous own chair and lifting one nasal flap in inquiry. "Obviously, anything I can answer, I will. I suspect, however, that your own means of gathering information is superior to my own."

"Commander?" Abu Bakr looked at Quinlevan. "Would you like to take that one?"

"Of course, Mister Ambassador," Quinlevan said, then looked at Qwelth. "Our means of gathering information are much more technically sophisticated than yours, Prime Director, but they aren't omniscient, and, to be honest, the Qwernians we especially want to eavesdrop on are taking surprisingly effective precautions." Her shoulders moved in an Earthian-style shrug. "We don't think they've been able to evaluate our actual capabilities with any degree of accuracy, but they appear to have decided it would be best to operate under the theory that we can work outright magic. Clan Ruler Juzhyr and ous senior ministers have retreated to the War Palace and locked the door behind them."

Qwelth's nasal flaps twitched in unhappy surprise. The War Palace was buried under three cherans of concrete underneath Kwyzo nar Qwern. Its armored steel doors were at least a kyran thick, and its ventilation system was designed to be proof against poison gas. Not that the Republic had ever threatened to use poison gas. The Qwernian Empire, on the other hand, had not simply threatened to use it but actually *had* used it in the past. So perhaps it wasn't totally irrational for Juzhyr to think it might be used against ous capital, although Qwelth didn't even want to contemplate the sort of mind which could have done that to *any* city, far less one Kwyzo nar Qwern's size.

"We can't get inside it without resorting to brute force," Quinlevan continued, "and the overburden's thick enough that we can't pick up anything through it, either. We have been able to eavesdrop on their radio traffic and many of their secondary command communication centers, but even that's of limited use. They're still broadcasting all over the copulating place—pardon my language, Prime Director—and they're using prearranged code phrases. We're pretty sure most of them are decoys, nonsense transmissions covering the real ones, but we don't have any way to identify which is which."

Qwelth shook ous head in understanding. The Qwernian Alliance's regular wargames had begun three day-halves before the attack on Secretary David. No one had worried much about it at the time; the training exercises were part of the Alliance's semiannual routine, and they'd been scheduled almost a full year in advance. But the Alliance hadn't demobilized in the wake of the Chelthist strikes. The official reason for that was to be sure the Alliance's military was positioned to respond to any future Chelthist attacks. An additional unstated—but clearly understood—reason was to discourage the Republic from taking advantage of the current crisis with some sort of military action of its own. And yet a third unstated reason—in this case, one everyone pretended didn't exist—was to prevent the Earthians from doing to the Qwernian Alliance what the "Shongairi" had done to the Earthians, should they be so inclined. In fairness, the Republic's military had remained at a higher readiness level ever since the Earthians' arrival, as well, and it, too, was even higher in the wake of the attacks. But even though most of those attacks had occurred inside the Republic, Dianto's readiness level remained considerably lower than the Alliance's. And as part of its continued mobilization, the Alliance's message traffic remained high. In fact, it was far higher than usual for training exercises.

"Despite the problems Commander Quinlevan's sketched," Abu Bakr said, his tone somber as he reclaimed the conversation, "we're strongly inclined towards the possibility that the Qwernians may be considering something . . . preemptive."

"I find that difficult to believe," Qwelth said, and nodded ous head when Abu Bakr looked at oum. "In all honesty, I don't want you thinking any better of Juzhyr and ous damned Alliance than I can help, but that would be outstandingly stupid. I mean, *outstandingly* stupid."

"The problem with 'stupid,' Prime Director, is that people who act that way typically don't realize they're being *stupid* until it's too late," Abu Bakr said.

"That's true, of course. But I do hope your suspicions about Juzhyr and ous ultimate motives aren't pushing *you* towards some sort of preemptive action." Qwelth looked at ous visitors frankly. "We haven't fought a war between first-class powers in generations, but we've seen plenty of smaller scale bloodletting. However much we Diantians may dislike—even fear—the Alliance, I wouldn't wish for the sort of casualties an all-out attack on their capital would have to inflict!"

"We have no intention of doing anything of the sort," Abu Bakr said reassuringly. "Unless, of course, they do something to force our hand."

Qwelth wished the Earthian hadn't added his second sentence's qualification, but ou shook ous head in unhappy understanding.

"In the meantime," Abu Bakr continued, "there are some gathering straws in the wind that concern us."

Qwelth's nasal flaps frowned. The Earthians' translator had obviously translated the Earthian literally, and ou had to think for a moment before ou realized what the expression "straw in the wind" might mean. Then he shook his head in understanding. It was actually quite an apt descriptor, ou thought. One well worth adopting as ous own.

"One of those 'straws,'" Commander Quinlevan said when Abu Bakr nodded at her, "is that they tell us the rocket launcher used in the attack on Ambassador Bakr has 'been lost.' That's after they sent us the wrong one, initially."

"The wrong one?" Qwelth repeated.

"Yes. They just got around to sending us even the wrong one last day-quarter, so Major McIntyre and I haven't had a chance to bring Director Bardyn up to date on that bit yet. They handed over the right *kind* of launcher, but we flooded the site of the attack with recon drones immediately after evacuating Ambassador Bakr. We got excellent imagery on the terrorists' weapons—and their bodies, for that matter—before the Qwernian police reached the site, and the rocket launcher used in the attack had the old-style sights." She shrugged. "Your Army retired that model ten or twelve of your years ago; the one they handed us was the current Diantian issue, though."

"I assume you raised that point with them?" Qwelth asked, and Quinlevan shook her head in agreement. "And their response was?"

"They apologized profusely. As you know, they've tracked the terrorist team back to the hotel where they stayed while waiting to launch the attack. Their search of the hotel turned up a much more extensive weapons cache, including four additional rocket launchers. Apparently the officer who had custody of the captured weapons simply assumed the terrorists wouldn't have used a semi-obsolete weapon when they had a more modern version of it available. Besides, ou doesn't *have* the actual weapon any longer. Apparently—" the Earthian seemed to be rather fond of that word, Qwelth noted, and their mechanical translator pronounced it with an edge of exquisite irony each time Quinlevan used it "—they managed to lose it somehow, which was another reason the custodial officer handed us the wrong one."

"And—forgive me if I seem less than sympathetic to my fellow Sarthians—they expected you to believe all of that?"

"We don't really know," Abu Bakr said. "We didn't speak directly to the custodial officer, and one of Minister Myrcal's aides called on Ambassador Fikriyah to personally deliver the message. So far as she could tell, the aide was obviously embarrassed—possibly even a little ashamed—but believed his own message. And while it does strike one as a bit suspicious, Allah knows Earthian investigators have lost enough critical evidence. On the other hand, these little coincidences do seem to be piling up."

Qwelth fluttered ous nasal flaps in derisive agreement, and Abu Bakr gave him an Earthian-style shrug in reply.

"The thing is," Abu Bakr continued, "we can't figure out what the Qwernian endgame might be, assuming all of this isn't, in fact, simply one unlikely but genuine coincidence after another. From a strategic perspective, it might make sense for them to make the Republic look responsible for the attacks, but that potential gain is hugely outweighed by the potential downsides. There's an Earthian phrase—'smart enough to pour piss out of a boot.' Is there a similar Sarthian phrase?"

"I believe we would say 'smart enough to raise ous kilt before ou takes a piss,'" Qwelth replied gravely, and Abu Bakr snorted.

"Well, assuming Juzhyr and Myrcal qualify under either of those, they should have been able to figure out exactly how Dave—Secretary Dvorak, I mean—would react if he figured out they'd done something like this. Obviously, the people who planted that bomb expected to kill him if they could detonate it at the right time, and they damned well nearly did. But killing him would only have put me into his place, which is exactly what happened when he was incapacitated instead of killed. And Myrcal and I have crossed swords enough that he should have been equally able to predict that *my* response to it wouldn't have been much better."

"But they—I mean, the terrorists, of course—attempted to kill you, as well," Qwelth pointed out. "If they'd succeeded, who would that have left in charge?"

"We're . . . not as convinced as we were initially that they really did try to kill me," Abu Bakr said.

Qwelth arched a nasal flap in question, and the Earthian shrugged.

"That's one of the reasons we wanted to examine that rocket launcher," he said. "But in answer to your question, Jane Simmons would have been next in the chain of command if I *had* been killed. Now it would be Fikriyah Batma. Beyond that—" he shrugged again "—I'm afraid Admiral Swenson would have had to nominate someone to take over."

"And they also killed Ambassador Jane," Qwelth mused.

"I know. We thought about that. Of course, we're not sure they really understand exactly how our command chain is organized. Which is actually what brings me to another of the things we wanted to get your input about."

"Yes?"

"Our Ted Berke had a conversation with Myrcal a full-day or so ago. Fikriyah was aboard *Vanguard* with me at the time, which left Berke as our senior representative in Kwyzo nar Qwern. Myrcal was quite upset about Director Bardyn's visit to the flagship. Ou seemed to feel that the Empire in general—and probably ou in particular—had been slighted. 'Slapped in the face' was the way ou put it. Ou wanted to be certain that ous unhappiness and 'concerns' were communicated at the highest level. But instead of asking Berke to pass the message to me, ou suggested that perhaps ou should take it directly to Arthur McCabe at the Nonagon."

"Well," Qwelth said slowly, nasal flaps pursed in thought, "the Nonagon *is* the official communications point. It does seem a bit out of character for Myrcal to be worrying about going through official channels at a time like this, but I can't see any other reason for oum to use Councilor Arthur as ous relay."

"The thing is that I'm not sure ou intended to use him as a 'relay' at all. I think it's possible ou meant that ou saw him as the proper *recipient* for ous message."

"Not you?" Qwelth's surprise was obvious, and Abu Bakr nodded his head in negation.

"The more I thought about it, the more bizarre it seemed," the Earthian said, "but that's certainly what it sounds like ou intended. To me at least. And most of our people who have listened to the recording agree that I might—and I emphasize might—be right about that. But we're not Sarthians."

He looked levelly at Qwelth, and the Prime Director cocked ous head.

"May I assume you'd like a native Sarthian's opinion?"

"I would. And I know Secretary Dvorak trusted your integrity, Prime Director. I don't know you as well, but if Dave trusted you, that's good enough for me. Of course, the entire exchange is in Qwernian, not Diantian."

"I assumed it would be." Qwelth's nasal flaps smiled wryly. "And I also assumed that, given your intelligence capabilities, you were already aware that I spent almost a triple-eight of years as our ambassador to the Empire. I assure you, my Qwernian is still excellent."

"I hoped that would be the case." The Earthian's mouth smiled back, and he reached into his pocket for his miraculous "phone." He opened it and looked down at it.

"Jibril, please play the audio of Minister Myrcal's last meeting with Theodore Berke."

"Of course," the phone's melodious baritone replied, and Qwelth leaned back, eyes closed, listening intently as the playback began. It certainly sounded innocuous enough. Of course—

"*Stop!*"

The Prime Director's eyes flared open and ou jerked upright in his chair.

"Pause, Jibril," Abu Bakr said sharply, and Qwelth found every Earthian eye focused upon him.

"What?" Abu Bakr asked.

"He called Councilor Arthur '*Councilor Arthur*,'" Qwelth said. "Why?"

Abu Bakr and his subordinates looked at one another, then turned back to Qwelth.

"Because that's his title," Abu Bakr said. "Like Alex, he's an advisor—a councilor—not an accredited ambassador."

"But that's not what Myrcal called him. He called him *Councilor*," Qwelth said.

"Because that's his *title*," Abu Bakr repeated. His confusion was evident, and Qwelth looked at him in matching perplexity. Then the Sarthian's nasal flaps flared wide.

"When I say 'councilor,' does your translator translate that as '*councilor*'?" ou asked slowly.

"Well, yes," Abu Bakr said after a moment.

"Oh, sweet Chelth," Qwelth said with soft, intense passion.

"What is it?" Abu Bakr leaned forward, eyes narrow, and Qwelth nodded his head in lingering disbelief.

"The first 'councilor' in my last sentence was the Qwernian word Myrcal is using; the second 'councilor' is the Diantian word *we've* been using as his title. Technically, they mean the same thing, but the Qwernian word has totally different connotations when used in reference to a political or religious official."

"How so?" Abu Bakr pressed.

"The Diantian word means 'advisor' or perhaps 'consultant.' In a political or religious context, the Qwernian word means 'deputy.' Or perhaps, because we're talking about a monarchy and not a republic, a better word would be 'vizier.'" Qwelth nodded ous head again.

"You were right, Ambassador Abu. Ou wasn't talking about passing a message to you *through* Councilor Arthur. Ou was talking about passing a message *to* Councilor Arthur . . . because ou thinks *Councilor Arthur* is Secretary David's successor in command of your entire mission."

· · · · ·

JORHSAL HURRIED INTO the war room as quickly as ous dignity would allow. "Minister!" ou called when ous eyes met Myrcal's.

"What has you in such a rush?" Myrcal asked.

"We just got the word," ous chief of staff said tautly. "The Earthians just met with Prime Director Qwelth."

"What? Where?" Myrcal asked. "Which Earthians?"

"Abu Bakr, along with two other Earthians, met with Qwelth. They're still in Dianzhyr, at their embassy there."

"Do we know what their agenda with Qwelth was?"

Jorhsal nodded. "All we know is that they wanted to talk about some questions they had, regarding some of the evidence. Our agent said they were very secretive about what their questions actually were, though. As close as they were to discovering our involvement before, I can only assume this means they've linked us to the Chelthist attacks."

Myrcal took a moment to consider ous options. "You said Abu is leading the delegation?" he finally asked.

"Yes," Jorhsal replied, ous nasal flaps indicating disgust.

"Oh, come now, he isn't *that* bad." The look on Jorhsal's nasal flaps indicated ous disagreement with Myrcal's statement, but ou didn't disagree aloud. Myrcal smiled. "Of course, Abu doesn't have our best interests at heart, and we've certainly . . . disagreed at times, but there are other Earthians who are far worse. That's why I didn't have him killed—better the Earthian you know . . ."

"Still, Minister, he isn't to be trusted."

"Of course not," Myrcal said with a smile. "He would, however, make an excellent hostage."

"You want to . . . you want to capture Ambassador Abu as part of the hostage grab? But he's in Dianzhyr."

"But what if we were to summon him here, asking for an accounting of his meeting with Qwelth? I believe he'd come . . . right here, into our clutches, before he goes running off to Councilor Arthur to report whatever suspicions or evidence they've found. That can be the trigger for grabbing all the rest of the Earthians, planet-wide."

"That's certainly bold," Jorhsal said, shaking ous head slowly.

"It *is* bold, which is what makes it so perfect," Myrcal said, "but what makes it even better is that—if we capture Abu here in Kwyzo nar Qwern—we'll be able to take him straight to the War Palace, where even the Earthians won't be able to find him. They'll *have* to negotiate with us!"

"That is indeed an inspired plan, Minister."

"It is. Now, I must go inform Ambassador Fikiryah that we'd like to have Abu come here to brief us on whatever he was discussing with Qwelth. While I'm gone, I want you to let all our operatives know that the time to act is at hand."

"It will be done, Minister."

"Good." Myrcal smiled again. "It's time to finally bring this to a conclusion."

· XIX ·

Well, I'll say this for Myrcal," Malachi Dvorak said sourly. "For a neutro, ou's got big brass balls. I have to wonder how much *brain* ou's got, though!"

"I detect a certain rancor," Abu Bakr observed from the Airaavatha's VIP passenger compartment, and the Space Marine snorted.

"You might say that, Sir."

Although Abu Bakr had been as much an "uncle" to the Dvorak kids as Daniel Torino and Pieter Ushakov, Captain Dvorak was always careful to observe military courtesy when he was on duty. He would have done it anyway, but his father's—and especially his mother's—reaction if he hadn't would have been . . . epic, Abu Bakr thought with a smile of memory. It was welcome, that smile, under the circumstances, but it was also fleeting.

"I won't say you're wrong, Malachi," he said, after a moment, "but there are rules. And whether or not we like it, we have to follow them."

"Tell me, Sir," Malachi asked, looking back over his shoulder, "did you ever see a movie called *Road House*? It's from all the way back in 1990, I think. Maybe even a little earlier." Abu Bakr raised an eyebrow, and Malachi shrugged. "Hey, it was one of my folks' favorite movies."

"I know." Abu Bakr shook his head. "Your father inflicted it on me several years ago. In fairness, it was actually pretty good. Should I assume you're thinking about Patrick Swayze's three rules for the bouncers?"

"That's exactly what I'm thinking about, Sir." Malachi smiled thinly. "I understand about the rules, and I understand we have to follow them, and I understand that we have to smile and be nice while we do. But the truth? The truth is I really, really hope Myrcal's going to give us a reason to *not* be nice."

Abu Bakr considered pointing out that it would be far better for all concerned if that didn't happen, but he decided not to. First, because he strongly suspected that it *was* going to happen, if not today, then soon enough. Second, because he had complete faith in Malachi Dvorak's professionalism. Whatever the captain might want, he wasn't about to engineer any reasons "to not be nice." Third, because Jasmine Sherman sat in the passenger seat behind his, prepared to be however "not nice" it took to ensure that nothing untoward happened to one Abu Bakr. But, fourth . . . fourth, because he understood precisely why Malachi wanted to kick the hell out of the people responsible for what had happened to his father.

And because, despite his own responsibilities, Abu Bakr felt exactly the same way.

"If Myrcal does do something stupid—something else stupid, I mean—I'm sure you and the rest of your uncle's Space Marines will convince him of the error of his ways," he said.

"Oh, yes, Sir. I think you can *rely* on that."

Abu Bakr nodded, and Malachi turned back to face forward again while the Airaavatha's icon moved steadily westward on the terrain map projected onto his corneal implants, boring through atmosphere at a leisurely six hundred kilometers per hour. They could have made the trip much more rapidly. For that matter, they could've used one of the *Starlanders* or *Starfires,* except that Abu Bakr had decided to make a point. If Myrcal wanted to "request" Abu Bakr's presence in Kwyzo nar Qwern "at his very earliest convenience," then Abu Bakr would come directly from Dianzhyr, underscoring where he'd been when the "request" came in. And he would take his own sweet time getting there, too. Whether or not the Qwernians would recognize just how leisurely he was responding to their summons was more than Malachi could say. Ostensibly, it was to permit the fighter escort the Qwernians had insisted on providing to keep pace with them, but Malachi could always hope Myrcal realized Abu Bakr's decision to make the trip in air-breathing mode was at least partly to rub ous nose in ous relative importance—or lack thereof—on the Earthians' current "Things to Do" list.

He smiled again at that thought, then closed his eyes to concentrate on his implants. After so many years, switching corneal projections was as automatic as breathing, and he flipped quickly through the status reports not simply from the units of his own command, but from *Troy*'s command center, as well.

At the moment, everything seemed to be exactly where it was supposed to be and doing exactly what it was supposed to be doing, on the Sarthian side as well as the "Earthians'." Of course, that could have been said of his father's last visit to Sarth, right up to the moment his vehicle blew the hell up.

Malachi's jaw tightened. Every hideous second of that day came back to him in nightmares, and he knew Morgana was right. Part of it was simple trauma, but part of it was his own belief that he should have been able to prevent the attack. That was his job. It was what he'd *been* there for. And he'd failed miserably.

His uncle—as Brigadier Wilson, not Uncle Rob—had taken him ruthlessly back through every single step, and Rob Wilson's conclusion matched that of his staff and of Admiral Swenson and *her* staff: Malachi Dvorak had done everything right that day.

Now if only *Malachi Dvorak* could accept that.

Oh, quit kicking yourself and concentrate... *at least while you're on the clock,* he told himself. *And you know Morg is right. You and Marge damned well saved Dad's life. Even if you did let him get blown up first.*

He gave himself a mental shake and told himself to take his own advice. And at least he was better equipped to keep Abu Bakr alive.

For one thing, the modified Airaavathas with the armorplast canopies were a thing of the past. The Sarthians had understood perfectly when their visitors decided to put safety in front of courtesy and appearances. If there were any who hadn't, Malachi Dvorak didn't give a good goddamn. So not only had they retired the diplomatic models, but they'd broken out the offensive armament to supplement the IFVs' defensive suite and re-embarked the gunners.

If the bastards wanted to try to kill someone else on his watch, they were welcome to bring it on, he thought grimly.

"Crossing the Danto border in two minutes, Boss," Corporal Celaj said. "'Nother hour or so to Kwyzno."

· · · · ·

"THEY'VE CROSSED THE frontier and the close escort's made contact, Tysan," Lance Swaygan KySwayHyr reported.

Myrcal MyrFarZol started to reply, then stopped ouself and shook ous head in acknowledgment, instead. Ou wasn't certain ou had adequate command of ous own voice at the moment.

Swaygan saluted and turned on a heel to march back to his own post at the center of the War Palace command post, and Myrcal's nasal flaps smiled faintly as ou watched the lance's back. Swaygan hadn't said so in so many words, but Myrcal knew he'd rather be in the field, commanding his regiment, and not cooped up here in the War Palace. For that matter, the foreign minister strongly suspected that Swaygan didn't really approve of the entire operation. Like so many of the Army's "professionals"—from Flythyr, who had strenuously opposed it, all the way down—the lance had trouble thinking outside the tightly drawn limits of conventional thought. He saw the potential downsides of Operation Whirlwind only too clearly. It was unfortunate that he was unable to recognize the enormous potential prize with equal clarity, but he *was* a professional, and that meant he'd do as he was told.

Myrcal shrugged that thought aside and crossed to look down at the large map table and discovered that Lance Swaygan's report, while accurate, had been incomplete.

The Earthians could have been invisible to Qwernian radar if they'd chosen to be, and ou reminded himself that there might well be Earthian aircraft up there which were doing just that. The air car bearing Abu Bakr towards his rendezvous with captivity, however, was a diplomatic vehicle, and there were niceties to observe where diplomatic vehicles were concerned. It was incumbent upon the Empire to clear airspace around it, and that meant it was incumbent upon the Earthians to be visible so that their hosts could know which airspace to clear. That made tracking it easy enough, and it hadn't actually crossed the Empire's frontier yet. It *had* crossed the frontier between the Republic and Yaluz, however, and Yaluz was a member of the Qwernian Alliance, so technically Abu Bakr was now in Qwernian airspace. But he was also on the far side of the Yaluz Mountains, still thirty-five minrans from the Empire's airspace and well over a hundred minrans from Kwyzo nar Qwern itself. At his current speed, the Earthian would take about half a minaq just to cross the *Empire's* frontier and about half a secar to actually reach the capital.

Ou stood, watching the progress as one of Swaygan's noncoms moved the token representing Abu Bakr slowly across the map in response to updates over his crestphones.

Soon, ou thought, anticipating the moment when Abu Bakr discovered how totally he'd been outthought and outmaneuvered and the Empire presented its terms to Councilor Arthur. *Soon. And we'll* see *who looks down on who when this is over.*

· · · · ·

"WHUPS. GOT SOMETHING here," Private Somogyi Fanni said suddenly.

"Got what?" Corporal Tomas Alvarado asked.

He and Somogyi were the wing assigned to ride herd on Doctor Yamazaki Motoshige. At the moment, they were parked at the end of the short hall which provided the only access to the lecture room in which Yamazaki was demonstrating the rudiments of modern medicine to an audience of Sarthian surgeons. Alvarado would've preferred to have either himself or Somogyi in the room with him, but Yamazaki had pointed out that there was no other way into the lecture room and suggested that a bodyguard standing around with an assault rifle might possibly distract some of the Sarthians from his presentation.

Alvarado rather liked Doctor Yamazaki, but he could be a little frustrating to the Space Marines charged with keeping him safe. Yamazaki was a stout, cheerful fellow who'd gone into medicine because of how much he liked people, and that extended to people who looked a lot like tailless velociraptors. Despite what had happened to Secretary Dvorak and half a dozen of his fellow diplomats, Yamazaki—who, to be fair, *wasn't* a diplomat; he was a doctor—clearly had trouble believing that even a religious fanatic could possibly want to harm *him.*

Alvarado, who'd spent a tour in Pakistan, had encountered quite a few religious fanatics. They continued to come out of the hills every so often in efforts to "restore the legitimate government" of Pakistan (this despite the fact that seventy-plus percent of all Pakistanis strongly supported the "degenerate Western travesty" the religious nuts in question opposed), and Alvarado had had more experience with them than he could have preferred. As such, there was very little he was willing to put past a religious fanatic whose fanaticism was fully engaged.

He just wished he could convince Yamazaki of the same thing. Unfortunately, he couldn't, and Yamazaki had a point about the only way into the lecture room.

"Not sure," Somogyi said in reply to his question. She was frowning as she reran the sensor anomaly. "Giselle is picking up something from Alpha Three."

"Like what? Talk to me here, Fanni!"

"Working on it," Somogyi said, and Alvarado grimaced. Giselle—Somogyi's phone's AI—could be occasionally cranky, but—

"Tom, she's calling it nitrocellulose," Somogyi said suddenly, interrupting his thoughts.

"What? On Alpha Three?"

"That's what she says. And—" Somogyi's tone sharpened "—she says it just turned up."

"*Mierda,*" Alvarado muttered, wondering if Giselle's crankiness was to blame for the reading. It seemed more likely than that the sensor they'd deployed in the shrubbery of this hospital wing's central courtyard should suddenly be picking up a nitrocellulose signature. For that matter, they *were* in a hospital, and a Sarthian one, at that. Cristo only knew what kind of chemical compounds might be floating around an environment like that! But Giselle was reporting that it had "just turned up"?

"Anything on visual?"

"No, but Alpha Three's pretty much buried in the bushes."

There might have been just a hint of criticism in Somogyi's tone, Alvarado thought. He was the one who'd chosen the positions for the Alpha sensors, and he'd been more concerned about keeping them concealed than about giving them the very best visual angles.

"All right," he said. "Hold one. Marcela," he cued his own AI, "Doctor Yamazaki."

"Yes, Tomas?" Yamazaki's courteous voice replied after a moment.

"We have a sensor anomaly out here, Doc. May be nothing, but we're going to have to check it out. You know the drill."

"But I'm coming up on a critical moment of the presentation," Yamazaki said.

"Sorry about that, Doc. And like I say, it may be nothing and you can get right back to it. But, right now, you need to start heading this way in case we need to cram you into the car and bug out."

"You're going to insist on this, aren't you?" Yamazaki's tone was resigned now, and Alvarado chuckled.

"'Fraid so, Doc. So, are you on your way?"

"Give me ten seconds to at least make my excuses."

"*Ten* seconds, Doc. Not eleven!"

"Slave driver!"

Alvarado chuckled again, then glanced at Somogyi.

"Doc's on his way. Once we've got him safely under our eagle eye, guess who gets to go beat the bushes?"

"Gee, thanks."

＊　＊　＊　＊　＊

"YES?" FIST WEYRKYN HarShulWeyr pressed the phone receiver to his crest.

"The Earthian is leaving!" the voice at the other end said.

"What do you mean, *leaving*?" Weyrkyn demanded.

"I mean he just told the doctors he 'has to go but he hopes he'll be back.'"

"Shit." Weyrkyn looked at the rest of his team. Aside from Starth Fyrmalyk JyrKholTarn, who Weyrkyn had just sent out to watch the courtyard, all of his double-eight of heavily armed special operations troopers were assembled in the spare doctors' lounge, looking at him, waiting for orders. But what did he do now?

There are only two of them, he told himself, closing his eyes in thought, *and they don't have their magic armor or anything else. And my people are* good. *But—*

Both the mission orders and the pre-op briefings had emphasized the need for the operation to kick off simultaneously, and he wondered which civilian genius had been responsible for that? Any *soldier* knew "simultaneous" was more easily ordered than accomplished. But the same orders that warned so sternly about the absolute necessity of waiting for the command code had also emphasized that it was essential none of the Earthians earmarked as hostages be allowed to escape capture. So what did he do—?

＊　＊　＊　＊　＊

"HERE I AM," Yamazaki Motoshige said, and Corporal Alvarado nodded.

"I'm genuinely sorry, Doc, but standing orders."

He shrugged, and Yamazaki nodded.

"Understood, Tomas. And I'm grateful you're taking such good care of me. It's just a tiny bit inconvenient."

"I know, but inconvenience—"

"'Is a piss-poor reason to get yourself killed,'" Yamazaki finished with a smile.

"Only reason I repeat myself so much is because I'm so right about that," Alvarado riposted with a broader smile. Then he nodded to Somogyi.

"Go check it out, Fanni."

·   ·   ·   ·   ·

"THE FEMALE'S HEADED for the courtyard," the voice on the other end of the telephone said, and Fist Weyrkyn swallowed a curse.

"The female is headed for the courtyard," he repeated to Leader of Thirty-Six Qwezyr as the noncom leaned closer. Qwezyr's nasal flaps frowned, and Weyrkyn didn't blame her one bit.

Fyrmalyk JyrKholTarn was young, and looked younger than her age. She was also slightly built, more like a bearer than a female, and looked about as threatening as a secondary student on her way to her graduation dance. Appearances could be deceiving, however, and the harmless looking starth was actually extraordinarily dangerous, whether with her bare hands or with the blade and automatic pistol in the thigh holsters under her hospital uniform kilt. And despite her lowly rank, Fyrmalyk was both smart and ruthless. Coupled with her innocuous appearance, that made her the perfect choice as Weyrkyn's forward picket. But she was on her own now. There was no way for him to communicate with her even to warn her of the Earthian's approach.

"How do you want to handle it, Sir?"

The thirty-six's voice was as low-pitched as Weyrkyn's had been, and the fist's nasal flaps grimaced.

"Get the team ready," he said. Qwezyr looked at him, and he shrugged. "I don't like it," he told her quietly, "and I trust Fyrmalyk's judgment, but who knows how Earthians think? I sure as Dwomo don't, and we need to be ready whatever happens."

·   ·   ·   ·   ·

FYRMALYK JYRKHOLTARN HAD never heard of "chemical sniffers," and she had no idea that the remote hidden in the landscaped courtyard's carefully shaped shrubbery had detected the propellant of the eight-millimeter automatic holstered under her hospital kilt. But she knew the female Earthian wasn't supposed to be wandering around the garden. She was supposed to be helping her partner keep an eye on the Earthian doctor until their scheduled departure.

The Earthian bodyguard's mirrored visor was lowered, hiding her face and her eyes. Her rifle was slung, but her right hand rested on the butt of a pistol which probably made Fyrmalyk's automatic look like a child's toy.

The special operations starth forced her nasal flaps to remain calm, but her heart raced. The last thing they needed was to have the Earthians changing up the schedule! No one had explained to her exactly why the timing was so critical, but she didn't need anyone to give her a map.

· · · · ·

"WHATCHA GOT, FANNI?" Tomas Alvarado's voice said in Somogyi Fanni's cochlear implant.

"Looks like just an orderly on her lunch break," Somogyi replied, taking in the small, slender Sarthian female, the crumpled paper bag on the bench behind her, and the half-eaten piece of some brightly colored local fruit in her right hand. The Sarthian stood on the far side of the courtyard, looking at her across the waist high—on Somogyi, not a Sarthian—fountain splashing at its center.

"Little early for lunch," Alvarado said thoughtfully.

"Might be *supper*, depending on her shift," Somogyi pointed out.

"Guess it could be," Alvarado agreed with a chuckle, but his tone remain serious. "You see anything that could have pinged the remote?"

"Negative. Think it's a glitch?"

"I think I'm not going to *assume* it's a glitch. Make a sweep. Let's make sure somebody didn't leave an explosive surprise under one of the benches."

"Roger that," Somogyi agreed with feeling and keyed her visor's multimode sensor function as she started forward.

· · · · ·

"GOOD MORNING." FYRMALYK put a careful note of shyness into her voice as she greeted the Earthian. "Can I help you, Sir? Or Ma'am?"

She let her nasal flaps flutter in obvious embarrassment as she deliberately "flubbed" the Earthian's gender. The innocent youngster was one of her better personae, and she knew she did it well. It was a little harder to remember that this time as the alien's head swiveled, and she found herself looking at that blank mirror of a visor.

"No, I'm fine, thank you," the Earthian said. Her translated voice sounded as normal as any Earthian's voice ever did, despite the closed visor. "Tell me," she continued, "have you been here long?"

"I just came out to eat on my lunch break," Fyrmalyk said.

"Has anyone else passed through in the last few kysaqs?"

"No," Fyrmalyk said cautiously.

"I see," the Earthian said, and Fyrmalyk drew an unobtrusive breath of relief as the alien shook her head in understanding.

· · · · ·

"**SOMETHING A LITTLE** weird here, Tom," Somogyi said quietly over the com.

"Define 'weird,'" Alvarado said tautly.

"Got a kid here. Seems like a nice enough sort. But the emotional overlay's . . . off somehow."

"What do you mean?"

"She seems polite, helpful," Somogyi replied. "Looks pretty relaxed, too, to me. But the overlay's reading an awful lot of anxiety. And the software says she's fibbing to me about what she's doing out here."

"Don't like that."

"Me neither," Somogyi agreed, moving casually farther into the courtyard. "Could just be that she's *not* on break. Maybe she's worried we'll tell her supervisor she's playing hooky from her job."

"You want to put any money on that?" Alvarado asked cynically, un-slinging his rifle.

"Not so much, no," Somogyi said. She moved another ten yards into the courtyard, sweeping the ornamental plantings with her helmet sensors and finding exactly nothing. Then she turned her head casually in the Sarthian's direction.

. . . . .

FYRMALYK WATCHED THE alien, wishing fervently that she had a better grasp—in fact, *any* grasp—of Earthian body language.

. . . . .

"GUN!" SOMOGYI SAID as her sensors picked up the unmistakable shape of a handgun under the timid young Sarthian's kilt.

. . . . .

FYRMALYK MIGHT NOT know how to read Earthian body language, but she'd kept her eyes unobtrusively on the hand resting on the butt of the Earthian's sidearm.

. . . . .

"PISTOL UNDER HER kilt and—" Somogyi began.

. . . . .

THE EARTHIAN'S FINGERS curled around her weapon.

It was the only sign she gave, and a corner of Fyrmalyk's brain recognized a fellow professional.

. . . . .

THE SARTHIAN VANISHED. Her knees buckled, and she dropped straight down, disappearing behind the solid bulk of the fountain, and Somogyi dove for the ground on her side of it even as her own sidearm cleared its holster.

"*Oswald!*" she snapped, and her phone's AI automatically shunted the transmission to the central command channels.

· · · · ·

"TALK TO ME, Fanni," Alvarado said, his voice tense. "What's going on?"

"The Sarthian made a move on me," Somogyi said. "I'm trying to catch her."

She worked her way around the fountain to where she'd seen the Sarthian go to ground, but the young female was gone. If she wasn't there, that meant—

CRAAAAACK!

Somogyi was halfway through spinning around to look behind her when the round hit her, and her left shoulder blade exploded in a white-hot ball of pain. The eight-millimeter bullet aided her spin, and she threw herself to the side. A second round ricocheted off the pavement next to her as the female's point of aim couldn't keep up with her sudden change of direction.

"I'm hit—" she called, but then she slammed into the ground and anything else she would have said was lost in a scream as her shattered shoulder crashed against the concrete.

"Hold on!" Alvarado urged. "Help is on the way!"

Somogyi knew whatever help was coming would be too late—for her, anyway—and rolled onto her back to face her assailant. Somehow, she'd held onto the pistol, and she tried to aim it, but the Sarthian was faster and fired again. Pain exploded in Somogyi's right leg, and she jerked as she fired. Instead of hitting the Sarthian in the chest area, the round went higher and through the young female's head, blowing off most of her crest as it exited.

· · · · ·

CRAAAAACK!

"Oh, *excrement!*" Fist Weyrkyn snarled as the unmistakable sound of a pistol shot exploded through the lounge's door.

CRAAAAACK!

"Go!" he barked. "*Go,* Dwomo dammit! Send Code White, Gersyl!"

"Yes, Sir!" the radioman acknowledged, and as Weyrkyn followed Thirty-Six Qwezyr and the rest of the team out the door, he heard Gersyl speaking into the microphone of the big backpack field radio.

"Code White. Team Razdyr, Code White. I say again, Razdyr is Code White!"

· · · · ·

"I'M HIT TWICE," Somogyi said with a grunt as she tried to sit up. "Shoulder and leg, but I got her." She took a look at her downed assailant. "She's dead."

Somogyi saw the fountain two meters away—it seemed much farther—and began pushing her way towards it. She could brace her back against it until the rapid response team arrived. She wouldn't be a hundred percent combat effective, but maybe she could be seventy percent . . . at least until she passed out from blood loss. Her leg was useless—the bullet had hit the bone and broken it—and it took all of her discipline not to scream again as she worked her way over to the fountain with one arm and one leg.

"Stay there," Alvarado said. "We're en route."

"No," she panted through her teeth. "Stay under cover. May be more of them."

"*Mierda!* You're right—there *are* more! I have motion on Alpha Three, Alpha Four and Alpha Seven. You're surrounded! I'm coming to help!"

Seven and Three were on opposite sides of the courtyard; if they were bad guys who knew she was there, she was trapped. It was possible the Sarthians were first responders coming to investigate the shots fired . . . but it was also very possible that the movement was from other members of the young female's team. Somogyi dropped the nanite injector she'd just pulled from her first aid kit and grabbed her pistol again. With her shoulder damaged, the rifle was impractical. Motion to her left made her spin in that direction, but it drove her damaged shoulder into the side of the fountain. Pain blossomed again, clouding her sight. Through the pain she could see rifles in the hands of the newcomers—*rifles that were aimed at her!*

She fired several times, and might even have hit a couple of them, but then another rifle fired from behind her. She barely felt the rounds that ripped through her chest.

· · · · ·

ALVARADO LOOKED AROUND wildly as a fusillade of shots crackled viciously outside.

"What?" Yamazaki asked. "What's going on?"

"I need someplace to stash you while I go help Fanni," Alvarado replied. He was faced with a corridor of closed doors, and, besides the one that led into the lecture hall, he had no idea what was behind any of them. Alvarado knew only one thing—he had to get Yamazaki somewhere safe!

A door opened behind him, and he spun around to find Sarthians pouring from the lecture hall. Most of them saw Alvarado and went running in the opposite direction, but some—probably seeing the wide-open passageway behind him—came running in his direction.

"Other way!" he yelled, leveling his rifle at the oncoming Sarthians. When they kept coming, he raised the muzzle of his rifle slightly and the corridor's ceiling erupted in a haze of dust as he fired a couple of rounds over their heads.

"Turn around, or I *will* shoot you!" Most of the Sarthians stopped and turned, but one kept coming. "I mean it!" he added.

"No!" Yamazaki yelled. "Don't shoot him!"

"If he doesn't stop, I'll have to!"

"No," a voice said in Qwernian from behind him. Something hard and metallic pressed into his neck below his helmet. "He was talking to me."

Alvarado turned to find at least eight Sarthians pointing rifles at him, along with a ninth who pointed a pistol at his face. While there was a chance his helmet visor might stop the pistol's bullet, with that many rifles aimed at him, from that close, he knew he had no choice. Besides, one of them also held a bead on Yamazaki's head, and Alvarado knew there was no way he could stop the soldier from killing the doctor.

He lowered his rifle, and the Sarthian with the pistol took it from him.

. . . . .

DR. YAMAZAKI SIGHED; his warning to Alvarado had been misinterpreted. He watched as the Sarthian trooper disarmed Alvarado, taking both his rifle and pistol, as the Sarthian who'd been fleeing towards them came to a stop next to Alvarado.

"Well done," the Sarthian, who had been sitting in the front row of Yamazaki's presentation, said. He reached up to unsnap Alvarado's helmet and removed it, then took the pistol from the trooper who was pointing it at Alvarado. The Sarthian doctor looked over at Yamazaki for a second, then put the barrel of the pistol to Alvarado's temple and fired.

Alvarado's head snapped back, and he collapsed to the floor. It only took a second for blood to begin pooling.

"Now," the Sarthian doctor said, "will you come along with us willingly, or will I have to shoot you, too?"

. . . . .

"IS IT REALLY necessary to leave this early, Ståle?"

Fikriyah Batma's tone was plaintive, but her black eyes twinkled at Sergeant Ståle Floden as she stepped out onto the spacious veranda of the palatial mansion Clan Ruler Juzhyr had made available for her on Diplomats' Row. They were barely two blocks from the Imperial Palace, which made it a very prestigious address indeed, but she'd been offered an even more prestigious one— Abu Bakr's old suite in the Palace itself. She'd turned the offer down, arguing that such prestigious quarters should be reserved solely for Abu Bakr, not his assistant. What had happened to other "Earthians" over the last few local weeks had nothing at all to do with that decision on her part, of course.

She'd only gotten back on-planet and into the mansion a few hours ago, and now they were leaving it again, thanks to Myrcal's demand that Abu Bakr—personally—return to Kwyzno nar Qwern. Could ou talk to *her*? Oh, no! Of course not! It had to be Abu Bakr, and she wished she could think that was a good sign. Unfortunately. . . .

"Well, I suppose how early we leave depends on exactly what you want, Ma'am." The towering Floden—the E-5 was a good thirty-two centimeters taller than Batma . . . and *she* was as tall as any Sarthian she'd ever met—never looked at her. Those icy blue eyes, the same shade as his native Norwegian fjords, were too busy scanning the peaceful street scene before them.

"Really? I get a vote?" she teased.

"Of course you do, Ma'am. You get to vote on when you want to arrive. *I* get to vote on everything else." He shrugged, those eyes still never stopping their steady sweeping motion. "You said you wanted to be on the ground to meet Ambassador Bakr. So—"

He waved one hand gently at the steps leading from the veranda to ground level.

"But he's not even going to land for another twenty or twenty-five minutes, and it's only *five* minutes to the airport," she pointed out.

"Yes, Ma'am, it is," Floden agreed, forbearing to mention that he'd told the Qwernian Army gauntlet—the equivalent of a Planetary Union major—who was the Terran diplomatic mission's official liaison that they'd be leaving only ten minutes before Abu Bakr's arrival. He didn't think Batma would have complained about his "misleading" the Qwernians (lying was such an ugly word) after the earlier attacks—she was a lot less trusting than some, like Theodore Berke, for example—but it was so much simpler to not find out.

. . . . .

"THE EARTHIAN FIKIRYAH is leaving early, Tysan," Lance Swaygan announced, and Myrcal MyrFarZol swallowed a curse.

"Is your team in position to seize her now?" ou asked sharply.

"We have an entire company in place—two platoons each in the mansions on either side of the Earthian's residence," Swaygan replied.

"So your team *is* in position to seize her?" Why was it the military could *never* give simple yes or no answers?

"Yes, Tysan. They'll have to emerge from their hides first, though, and if the Earthians are alert, they're bound to see them coming."

"That doesn't sound like very good planning on someone's part, Lance," Myrcal observed in a chill tone.

"It's not ideal, no, Tysan." Swaygan's nasal flaps were tight. "It's the best we could do, however. We had to breach the basements' walls and infiltrate our people in through the storm drains to avoid any Earthian aerial reconnaissance. We're actually lucky we were able to gain access at all."

Myrcal recognized the controlled anger in Swaygan's tone and ous nasal flaps rose in a placating smile.

"I didn't mean to sound as if I were criticizing, Lance," ou lied. "I suppose I'm feeling a few preshow jitters of my own."

"Understandable, Tysan."

"Will it make any difference in the end?"

"Probably not, Tysan. A lot depends on the timing, of course. If she's on the ground at the airport by the time Ambassador Abu arrives, they should both be in the open at the critical moment, and we have two full battalions earmarked for that."

Myrcal shook his head a bit impatiently. The notion of using Abu Bakr's honor guard to capture him had been *ous* idea, after all. Well, ous chief of staff's, anyway.

"It would certainly be less problematical to take both of them there than trying to overwhelm her escort in the city confines," the lance continued. "I'm sure we can do it. I'm just not sure how many casualties we'll take or how long we'll have before the Earthians' quick response teams arrive."

Myrcal shook ous head in understanding, hiding a fresh flash of irritation at yet more qualifiers. The military mind did have a tendency to cover its excreter, didn't it?

· · · · ·

"EIGHTEEN MORE MINUTES to Kwyzo nar Qwern, Sir," Malachi Dvorak said.

"Oh, joy," Abu Bakr responded.

"Hey, look at it this way," Malachi said. "If it's a pain for you, those poor bastards out there probably haven't enjoyed it very much, either."

He twitched his head at the passenger compartment's visual display. No one really needed it, since all of them could tie directly into the sensors' feed and watch it on their corneal implants, but humans—and especially humans who'd grown to adulthood before the invasion—liked more "conventional" displays. At the moment, that display showed the dozen Qwernian Army Air Force Shyrmal fighters accompanying the Airaavatha. The entire notion of an "escort" of air-breathing, propeller-driven aircraft was ridiculous, but the Qwernians had insisted that the Empire's honor required them to ensure their Earthian guests' safety against any threat.

The Shyrmal was a single-engine fighter that was actually fairly impressive for a prop-driven aircraft. Its cruise speed, however, was about twenty-five kilometers per hour slower than the Airaavatha's current leisurely—for it—pace. In fact, they were within twenty kilometers per hour or so of the fighters' maximum level speed, which had to be galling to their pilots. After all, they knew the Airaavatha was an IFV that maneuvered like a homesick rock compared to Earthian aircraft. Worse, at this speed, their maximum endurance was only about thirty minutes, even with auxiliary fuel tanks. The Airaavatha was on its second set of Shyrmals, and the current escort was due to be replaced in about five minutes.

· · · · ·

"CODE WHITE!" A communications noncom barked suddenly. "Team Razdyr is Code White!"

"*Excrement!*" Myrcal snarled. Couldn't these eight-thumbed idiots do *anything* right?!

Ous brain raced, but not for long. Dwomo knew the Earthians' communications were better than anything the Empire had, which meant it wouldn't take long to—

"Take Fikiryah now, Lance!" he snapped. "And send the immediate execution signal to all your other teams!"

· · · · ·

"CODE WHITE!"

The code phrase crackled over Gauntlet Lysal MorLysDyn's crestphones and her nasal flaps tightened under her oxygen mask as her flight of twelve Shyrmals sliced through the air towards the Earthian "personnel carrier."

Yeah, sure, a corner of her brain thought derisively. *"Personnel carrier." Wish to Dwomo's third hell we had "personnel carriers" like that!*

But it was only a corner of her brain. The rest was too busy responding.

"Drop tanks and follow me!" she ordered, and yanked back on the stick as her fighter's auxiliary fuel tanks tumbled away. Frankly, she didn't think they had a chance in hell of intercepting the Earthian representative—or doing much with him, if they did—but that was what her orders said to do under Code White, and by Dwomo, that's what she'd do.

Fortunately, they'd been close to the point at which her flight was supposed to relieve the current escort. She couldn't see the Earthian vehicle yet, but the escort's contrails were clear enough in the cold air, and she was almost a minran higher than the Earthians' cleared air corridor. So, if she was Ambassador Abu's pilot, and if she had any clue what was going on, what *she'd* be doing was—

· · · · ·

"OSWALD!"

The single word cracked over Malachi Dvorak's cochlear implants and a map of the Empire flashed in his vision with an icon labeled "Somogyi, F." superimposed on the city of Razdyr.

"Oswald!" he barked out loud. "Marge, time to go!"

"You got that right, Boss!" Celaj acknowledged.

"Where is it?" Abu Bakr demanded from behind them. "*Who* is it?"

"Razdyr and Doc Yamazaki," Malachi responded, looking over his shoulder. "And sit down and buckle the *fuck* in, Uncle Abu!"

. . . . .

"AMBASSADOR ONE," A voice said in implants. "Cheetah One sees Shyrmals coming from the west and climbing hard."

"Got them," Malachi acknowledged as the Qwernian fighters' icons dropped into his field of view. They must have started climbing even before Celaj had, and the dotted line of their projected vector passed close to the Airaavatha.

"My HUD—" it wasn't actually anything so crude as a Heads up Display, of course, but like "phone," the term had stuck "—shows you clear of their weapons on your current vector," Major Steve Douglass said. "How do you want to handle it?"

Malachi started to reply. There was no point shooting down primitive aircraft that couldn't even hope to intercept them, he thought. Besides—

Somogyi Fanni's light code turned blood red on the map of Razdyr. Seconds later, Tomas Alvarado's did the same thing.

Malachi Dvorak looked at those crimson icons of death where two more of his Space Marines had been, and his brown eyes were cold.

"Take the bastards out," he grated. "Every fucking one of them."

. . . . .

"CHEETAH FLIGHT, WE are cleared to splash all the Qwernian fighters. I say again, weapons red and free!" Major Douglass announced over his squadron com net. "Cheetah Two, you're with me. We'll take the twelve currently on station. Cheetahs Three and Four, you've got the ones that are just arriving. Splash them all!"

"Cheetah One, Cheetah Three. Copy all," the leader of the second section replied. "C'mon, Four, let's go kill the sons-of-bitches."

Douglass nodded as the second section of trans-atmospheric fighters pulled to the right and dove on the unsuspecting Shyrmals.

"Section," he said, cuing his AI to switch to the section frequency. "I've got the six closest to the Airaavatha," he continued without a break. "You've got the other six. Stand by to fire."

He designated the six targets to his weapons system. He allocated a

Lancer radar-guided missile to each of them as they started to break apart to chase the maneuvering Airaavatha. He'd still have two Lancers left in case he missed or any more showed up. And his heat seekers. And his gun, if it came to that.

"Targets designated," Lieutenant Simmons, his wingman reported.

Douglass took a last look as his display. All the targets were green—the system had radar locks with live missiles assigned to each.

"Roger that. Standby to fire. Three. Two. One." The bay doors opened, and the missiles leapt from the interior of the fighter. "Fox One . . . on all of them!"

. . . . .

MALACHI SCANNED THE tactical presentation on his cornea, pissed off that the Qwernians had actually been dumb enough to try it a second time. Even worse—for them—this time, the attacks lacked the precision of the first round. If he'd have been running them, the Shyrmals would have led off against the hardest target—the Airaavatha.

He shrugged. Now, the twelve oncoming Shyrmals would never be a factor— Corporal Celaj had maneuvered to leave them behind. The ones that had been "escorting" them were still relatively close by, but with the IFV's sudden change of direction, they would never be able to get within weapons range of it.

While the IFV was out of range of the Shyrmals' guns, though, the Shyrmals were *not* out of range of the Airaavatha, he saw with a smile. "Hey, Santos. If you can range on the Shyrmals, feel free to take them out."

"Sorry, Sir," Corporal María Fernanda Santos, his gunner said. "No can do."

Malachi spun around. "Why not?"

"Check your visual, Boss," Santos replied, and Malachi swapped his corneal display. A series of fire-cored black smoke clouds extended off into the distance to starboard, and even as he watched, another string of black puffs appeared on the port side, a little farther out.

"The *Starhawks* beat us to it," Santos said with profound satisfaction.

. . . . .

"DON'T MOVE!" THE Earthian ordered as Gauntlet Fuldan JelFulJar, along with three eights of troops, marched down Dwysyr Street towards the house assigned as Representative Jeng Hanying's quarters in the city of Tyrhaz.

Something was wrong—the two Earthians outside the door had been alerted somehow and looked ready for battle. There was very little cover outside the house—not entirely by accident—but one of them knelt behind the front steps' balustrade. And both of them had unslung their rifles . . . which were pointed at him.

Fuldan didn't much care for that.

He waved one hand unobtrusively at Fist Myrthan ShalMyrDyn, the platoon's CO, and raised one nasal flap at the senior Earthian.

"What's wrong?" he asked, trying to sound both innocent and offended.

"We've had assaults on our people all across the Empire," the Earthian said. "Now you show up here, armed, with twenty-five troops. Are we supposed to think you just happened to drop by?"

Fuldan sighed. He'd hoped to catch the Earthians unaware, but apparently something had happened and the Earthians' communications network was—sadly—faster than the Qwernian Empire's. How he *wished* they could build radios that small!

"I suppose not," he said after a moment, realizing the element of surprise was gone, no matter what he did. If anything, his admission made the Earthians even more tense, if that were possible.

"Turn around and leave," the Earthian said. "If you do, no one has to get hurt."

"Unfortunately, that isn't true," Fuldan said. "My orders are to take Representative Jeng Hanying into custody, and I'll likely be executed if I fail in my mission. So I, at least, would be hurt. But no one has to get hurt if *you* put down your rifles. Let us have him, and you can go about your business."

"Not happening."

Fuldan tapped his foot on the sidewalk.

"That's too bad," he said, tapping a second time. "I'd hoped—"

He dove to the side as his foot tapped a third time, which was the signal to attack, and his troops raised their rifles and fired into the Earthians. His people were well trained, and this was no time for finesse. They opened up, spraying bullets at the Earthians and concentrating their fire on spots the aliens' armor didn't protect.

That many weapons, firing on full automatic, couldn't all miss. The flimsy protection of the balustrade erupted in a cloud of cement particles, and both Earthians went down with bullets through their throats.

The Earthians, unfortunately, couldn't miss either, Fuldan saw as he stood. Both of them might be dead, but the brief bursts they'd gotten off as his troopers' rifles came up had been devastating. Over half his troops were down, including Fist Myrthan. Most were sprawled in heaps of ripped and torn meat, but others curled in agony around brutal, gaping wounds and the sounds of their screams burned in his crest. He looked at the mangled bodies and lakes of blood, listened to those screams, then tightened his nasal flaps and strode to the door while the medic worked to save who she could.

He reached it and nodded his head in resignation. It was locked . . . of course.

"Representative Jeng! Come out, please."

"Think that's going to work, Sir?" Leader of Twenty-Four Chastik TanSolChas asked.

"No, not really," Fuldan replied. "But it was worth a try if it got him out more quickly." He waited for another half-eight of seelaqs, then added, "However, it doesn't appear that anything's going to be easy for us today, and we're on a short timeline. Blow the door."

Chastik called forward the leader of eight who was the platoon's surviving explosives expert. In less than a kysaq, they were ready, and Fuldan shook his head once.

"Do it."

The leader of eight pushed the button, and the detonation blew in the door, destroying the door frame in the process.

Chastik raced to the room, but stopped in the doorway. She turned to Fuldan, her nasal flaps closed tightly, and waved him over. "Sorry, Sir," she said. "It looks like the Eight used too big a charge."

She moved out of the way, and Fuldan strode through the door to find Jeng Hanying on the floor in the center of the room. He'd apparently been trying to listen at the door, and when it blew, fragments of it had riddled his face and chest. If Fuldan hadn't known whose door it was, the Earthian would have been hard to identify.

Fuldan sighed one last time. Civilians. Any soldier would have known to stay the hell away from a door that was about to be breached, but not a Dwomo–damned civilian. And was anyone going to think about that? Of course not. His orders had allowed for a certain amount of destruction—and specified that the Earthian *troopers* were better dead than alive—but they'd been quite clear in that the representative was to have been captured alive.

"The Minister *is not* going to like this."

· · · · ·

"I SUSPECT MINISTER Myrcal's less than delighted by these curbside pickups," Batma observed as the Airaavatha came sliding down to the street in front of her mansion. A half dozen Qwernian police had halted regular street traffic, and the other three Marines of her double-wing security detachment formed a hollow, alert triangle around its landing space.

"With all due respect, Ma'am, my piles bleed for Minister Myrcal," Floden said dryly. She wrinkled her nose at him, but she didn't say anything. Myrcal was not popular with any of the Terrans who'd had the unfortunate honor of serving here in the Qwernian Empire.

"It does look suitably ominous, doesn't it?" she said instead, and Floden grunted in satisfied agreement.

The twenty-ton vehicle was long and lean, and the teardrop dorsal turret with its twin thirteen-millimeter HMG1s faired sleekly into its lines. It slid down the last few meters of sky with glassy smoothness and touched down neatly.

"Your chariot awaits, Ma'am," Floden said, and fell in alertly at her heels as she started down the steps.

. . . . .

"CODE WHITE!"

Double Fist Lyrquyn LyrGozHal had been watching the menacing-looking Earthian vehicle's arrival. Now ous head snapped around at ous radio operator's sharp announcement. Dwomo! It *would* happen at the worst possible moment, wouldn't it?

"*Excrement!*" Fist Prydyr HowPrySyn, the commander of Lyrquyn's first platoon, snarled, then shook herself. "Sorry, Tysan."

Lyrquyn only grunted, because ou knew exactly what was going through Prydyr's mind. The same thing was going through *ous* mind.

"Stand to," ou said out loud, trying to mask the sinking sensation in ous midsection. If this really was Code White, there was only one way it could go down, and when that happened—

"Execute Krylith, Tysan," the radio operator said, as if Minister Myrcal had read ous mind, and ou looked at Prydyr.

"You heard," ou said grimly. "Move out."

. . . . .

THE AIRAAVATHA'S STARBOARD hatch cycled open as Batma and Floden approached. The walkway through the mansion's large, beautifully manicured garden was a good sixty meters long, shaded by native trees with long, spatulate leaves that rubbed cheerfully in the gentle breeze. Colored pea gravel crunched underfoot, and the assistant ambassador drew a deep breath of flower-scented air. It really was a nice planet, she thought, despite the endless days and nights and the dim—by human standards—sunlight. Now if only the people who lived here were all as rational as the Diantians! She wouldn't mind an assignment—

"*Oswald!*" Floden snapped suddenly over the command net. "Move, Ma'am! *Move!*"

. . . . .

"OH, *FORNICATE!*" DOUBLE Fist Lyrquyn snarled as the three Earthians stationed around the grounded air car dropped suddenly to one knee and rifles snapped into the firing position. They couldn't have seen *ous* people yet, so it had to be—

It was. From ous position at the first-floor window, ou saw the incredibly tall

Earthian male bark something at Ambassador Fikiryah that sent her running towards the waiting vehicle.

This was going to be even uglier than ou'd thought, ou realized as the first of Fist Prydyr's special ops troopers came boiling out of every door and window of the mansions in which they'd been concealed.

· · · · ·

"OH *SHIT!*"

Batma was vaguely aware of Floden skidding to a halt and dropping into a kneeling firing position behind her. She started to slow.

"Get into the *jævla* Airaavatha!" he snarled at her, and she redoubled her pace as her security team's Brontos began to snap.

· · · · ·

LYRQUYN WATCHED IN shock—not really disbelief, but *shock*—as the Earthians opened fire. Ou'd never seen or imagined individual firearms that could do that!

The Earthians ripped off controlled bursts. They didn't just point and spray like too many soldiers did. Their fire discipline was at least as good as ous own troops', and their weapons hit with devastating power. Charging infantry didn't simply go down; all too often their torsos or limbs seemed to *explode,* and the same bullet could take down three or even four of them!

There were only four Earthians, while Lyrquyn had brought eight eights of picked troopers with oum, but it was a massacre.

And not of the Earthians.

· · · · ·

FIKRIYAH BATMA HURLED herself headfirst through the open hatch. Waiting hands caught her, hauling her fully into the IFV, and someone half-flung her into a seat.

"Package secure!" the vehicle commander announced over the communications net.

"Cover us," Sergeant Floden responded curtly.

"My fucking pleasure," the vehicle commander agreed. "You heard him, Gus. Weapons free."

"Rock 'n' roll time," the gunner acknowledged, and the dorsal turret came to life.

· · · · ·

LYRQUYN'S NASAL FLAPS clenched in dismay as the Earthian vehicle's dorsal turret suddenly trained out. It moved with precise, lethal speed, and then it opened fire.

. . . . .

THE LAST OF the Sarthian troopers poured out of the mansions in which they'd hidden. Whatever one might think of their mission, there was nothing at all wrong with those troops' courage. Of course, they hadn't had very long to realize just what the Space Marine's rifles could do to them.

They didn't live long enough to find out.

. . . . .

LYRQUYN LYRGOZHAL CRIED out in wordless horror as the twin Earthian machine guns ravaged ous remaining troopers. They didn't just explode, now; they *vaporized*. Ou'd seen what Sarthian heavy machine guns could do, and that paled to insignificance beside *this*!

. . . . .

"ALL ABOARD AND accounted for," Floden announced. "Let's get the hell out of here."

"Suits me," the vehicle commander acknowledged. "What about where they came from, though?"

"Object lesson time," Floden growled as the crimson codes of dead Space Marines from other locations spangled his corneal displays. "Burn the bastards out."

"Suits," the vehicle CO agreed. "Switch to explosive, Gus."

. . . . .

LYRQUYN WATCHED SICKLY as the alien vehicle lifted off the pavement in eerie silence, leaving the street literally running with Sarthian blood. As far as ou could tell, every single member of the assault force was dead. Ous entire company, gone. Just . . . *gone*. And ou was alive, untouched. How was ou going to *live* with that?

And then, as the alien craft hovered there, ou saw the turret training around in ous direction and realized ou wouldn't have to.

. . . . .

THE GROUND FLOOR of the first mansion disintegrated as the thirteen-millimeter twin mount hammered it with fourteen hundred rounds per minute of high explosive. That torrent of destruction gutted it within seconds, and then the turret swiveled to the second structure.

"Good?" the vehicle commander asked five seconds later.

"Good," Floden acknowledged. "Now get us the hell out of here."

. . . . .

THE AIRAAVATHA SCREAMED towards orbit, tearing a hole through the smoky air, as the first mansion simply collapsed downward onto its disintegrated ground floor.

· · · · ·

THEODORE BERKE LOOKED up as the door to his suite slammed open.

"Can I help you?" he asked the four armed soldiers who poured into the room, shut the door, and then began pulling furniture over to block it. "You, know? 'Knock, knock. Come in'?"

"Sorry, Sir," one of the soldiers said. He turned, and Berke recognized him—Sergeant Demir Noorani. "We just got the Oswald warning. Looks like the Qwernians are trying to grab humans across the Empire. I grabbed—"

The door shook as something slammed into it from the outside.

"What?" Berke asked. He'd seen the Oswald warning flash, but that was in *Razdyr*; it hadn't been local. Besides, he was in the *Palace,* where he was sure to be safe. He'd gone back to what he'd been doing. "They're attacking *here*? In the *Palace*?"

"Looks like it," Noorani said, waving the other soldiers over to grab Berke's desk. "They already grabbed Doctor Yamazaki and killed two of his guards. There are reports of other attempts going on across the Empire."

"What . . . what should I do?" Berke asked.

"Go into your bedroom," Noorani replied. He pulled his pistol from its holster, reversed it, and handed it to him. "Take this. If anyone enters without shouting 'Oswald' first, shoot them."

Berke took the pistol and looked down at it as the door reverberated with another crash.

"Go, Sir!" Noorani repeated. "We've got this. I don't want you getting hit with any stray rounds."

Berke nodded once, then went into his bedroom and closed the door. The slamming continued for another thirty seconds and then went quiet. Before he could ask if everything was fine, an explosion rocked the outer room, and he realized it wasn't.

Rifles fired, and someone screamed. The voice sounded human. More rifle fire followed, the bellow of Sarthian weapons burying the far quieter fire of the Space Marines' Brontos. Berke moved to the other side of the bed and took the pistol in both hands while the weapons thunder seemed to go on and on, endlessly. But then it ceased, and he aimed the pistol at the door. He wanted to yell out to the soldiers, but knew that their silence was all the answer he needed as to who had been victorious.

The door burst open, and he fired, but the round went wide and slammed into the door frame. He tried to control his shaking hands as a Sarthian filled the doorway, and he fired again. Success! He hit the Sarthian, and it fell back. Before he could congratulate himself, a flood of troops raced through the doorway. He was able to fire only one more time before several dove across the bed and tackled him to the floor.

. . . . .

HALF A DOZEN Qwernians dragged Berke down the broad palace corridor. His shoes left smears of blood on the marble floors. Some of it was human, but even more of it was Sarthian, and his captors were no gentler than they had to be.

Which wasn't very.

They turned a corner and his shocked brain realized they were approaching the clan ruler's personal suite. He'd never been in this section before, but he had little chance to appreciate the extravagant furnishings as he was hustled through it and to a set of stairs that led belowground. The dropdown hatch above them was propped open, but it looked like it could be sealed with very little notice. The locking mechanism he could see on the bottom of the hatch was impressive. Once it was down and locked, he doubted anyone would be able to get through it.

Myrcal was waiting at the bottom of the stairs.

"What . . . what's the meaning of this?" Berke asked.

Myrcal waved, and a soldier stepped forward and slammed the butt of his rifle into Berke's stomach. The representative collapsed to the floor, fighting to catch his breath and trying desperately not to spew out his lunch. After several seconds huddled in a fetal position, two of the bigger Sarthians grabbed him, pulled him to his feet, and held on to his arms.

Myrcal strode over, grabbed the collar of Berke's shirt, and pulled his face down to where ou could look eye-to-eye with him.

"I am in charge," Myrcal said, "and I ask the questions. Do you understand?"

"Yes . . ." Berke gasped. "Yes, I do."

"Good," Myrcal said with a shake of ous head. "Now, I know you have the ability to contact your people in orbit."

"I can't—" Berke started, but then a soldier stepped forward and slapped him in the head with an open palm. Berke saw stars momentarily, then gasped at the pain of the Sarthian's nails down his cheek.

"I hadn't asked for a response," Myrcal said with a nod. "You need to listen."

Berke stared at the minister, unsure whether to nod, shake his head, or say something. His head and cheek hurt, and he cringed inwardly as a drop of blood fell to the floor.

"I'll take your silence to mean you understand," Myrcal said after a few seconds. "Now, I want you to contact your people in orbit, and I want you to tell Councilor Arthur that I have an ultimatum for him."

. . . . .

BERKE COLLAPSED TO the floor as his guards flung him into the empty cell.

As he lay there sobbing in pain, he wasn't sure what he could have done any differently. He couldn't understand why the Qwernians thought *Arthur McCabe* had succeeded Secretary Dvorak, and he had no idea why Myrcal had reacted with such rage when he discovered who actually had. The truth had earned him a savage beating when Myrcal thought he was lying about who was in charge, but in the end the Foreign Minister had grudgingly accepted the truth and Berke had passed the message on to Abu Bakr, instead.

And then he'd been beaten *again* when he'd passed along Abu Bakr's response that "he'd get back to oum."

PUNS *TROY*, SARTH ORBIT;
KWYZO NAR QWERN, QWERNIAN EMPIRE,
SARTH

So," Rob Wilson said bleakly, "how pissed off are we?"

His blue eyes circled the Space Marines assembled in *Troy*'s command center and the viewscreen connected to the naval officers in *Vanguard*'s flag briefing room. No one spoke immediately, and that icy gaze settled on Abu Bakr.

"Personally, I'd say very," Abu Bakr replied after a moment. "Why?"

"Because I want to know where I start planning mission packages." Wilson showed his teeth. "Personally, I think it's time we demonstrated the error of ous ways to Minister Myrcal."

"I think there's general agreement on that," Admiral Swenson said.

"I know." Wilson nodded. "What I'm asking about is how *firmly* we want to demonstrate it."

"The most important thing is to get our people back intact," Alex Jackson pointed out.

"Those of them who *are* intact," Captain Jeng's voice was as bleak as Wilson's. His eyes were even colder, and Wilson felt a pang of sympathy. The flag captain had taken his nephew's death hard, and Wilson knew how he hated the thought of telling his sister-in-law Yuhan her youngest son would never return.

"Send in the vampires?" Jackson suggested.

"There aren't enough of us," Longbow Torino replied. "Not the way Myrcal has the hostages distributed. We could get to maybe a third of them before they realized what was going on, and if ou's serious about killing them if we try anything—"

He shrugged, and Wilson nodded. His quick response teams had retrieved just under a third of the humans scattered around the Qwernian Empire and Alliance before they could be grabbed. The others had been used as human shields by their captors to prevent further rescue attempts as they were hustled to obviously preselected locations. It reminded him forcibly of old footage he'd seen of the runup to Desert Storm, and he bared mental fangs as he considered how that had worked out for Saddam Hussein. In the meantime, though. . . .

"That's about the way I read it, too, Longbow," he said. "Mind you, I don't know if Myrcal's crazy enough to actually start slaughtering our people, but ou might be."

"What about Juzhyr?" Swenson asked. The others looked at her, and she shrugged. "We haven't heard a single peep out of oum. Myrcal's obviously ous front man—*expendable* front man—in all this. But do you think ou'd let Myrcal start killing Earthians?"

"He's already let them slaughter enough of our *Marines,* Ma'am," Colonel Palazzola pointed out in a voice like crushed gravel.

"I realize that, and I'm not trying to minimize anything here." Swenson's tone was sympathetic but unflinching. "But there's a difference between casualties inflicted during the actual take-down and the cold-blooded murder of hostages. For humans, at least. I'm wondering if Juzhyr's ready to cross that line with us. Especially after what happened to the Ambassador's 'escort fighters' and the bastards who tried to take Ms. Batma."

"Morgana?" Wilson asked, looking at his niece.

She looked back, her eyes dark and somber. Marcos Ramos had been speaking to a group of Qwernian psychologists when the attacks began. No one knew for certain if he was alive, but they knew none of his escorting Space Marines were. And his absence left her the senior member of the psychology team.

"I can't say for certain, obviously," she said. "And I think it's fair to say that I'm at least as pissed at these people as anyone else. I'm trying to allow for that in my thinking, but I'm pretty sure it's coloring my response, anyway.

"Having said that, Juzhyr's probable reaction depends on things we can't assess from orbit. Clearly, Myrcal, at least, thinks that if ou demonstrates sufficient fortitude and ruthlessness, we'll make the obvious calculation that Clan Qwern is the only clan on Sarth capable of conquering the rest of the planet for us. That represents a serious . . . misunderstanding of our entire mission here, and there could be a lot of reasons for oum to be that far off base. The one that worries me the most is that I think it's entirely possible that, in human terms, we're dealing with a sociopath. I don't think Myrcal has an internal value set of 'right' and 'wrong.' I think ou has an internal value set of 'useful' and 'use*less*.' By definition, anything that advances ous objectives is good; anything that fails to advance ous objectives is *bad*; and ou's probably able to deny anything ou has to deny to believe ou can win. I'd also say that, like most human sociopaths, ou has virtually no sense of empathy for anyone else, which means no one else is real for oum in the sense of having any intrinsic value or rights as a living, thinking being. Again, tool or obstacle—the only categories ou uses even for fellow Sarthians, far less aliens.

"The difference between the Qwernian view of custom and tradition versus the Diantian view of the rule of law has to factor into this, as well. I'm not the historian Dad is, and I don't have his gift for wrapping my mind around alien societies, but in some ways, Qwernian *society* is sociopathic where anyone who's not a member of Clan Qwern is concerned. For instance, I strongly suspect that in Myrcal's thinking, humans, by definition, can't fit into the category of clan member, and probably can't fit into the category of 'guest,' either. If we fell into either of those niches in ous thinking, Clan Qwern's own societal codes would require oum to *protect* us, not victimize us. But as soon as ou denies us that status, Qwernian custom justifies anything ou might do to us or with us to advance ous clan's objectives.

"And that's the point where Juzhyr's reactions become problematic, as well. Thanks to our remotes, we probably have more—and more current—data on oum even than the Diantian diplomatic people, but it's not enough for me to even hazard a guess as to whether or not ou shares Myrcal's attitudes towards Earthians. It's tempting to conclude ou must, if ou's going to authorize an operation like this. But there's that Qwernian tradition of the clan ruler's infallibility and inviolability. Ou may well genuinely believe that we're prepared to settle for Myrcal's head, the way a Qwernian would, rather than assigning ultimate responsibility to Myrcal's clan ruler, the way a Diantian would. And, if that's the case, then ou may be prepared to let Myrcal go just as far as Myrcal wants to go because ou thinks ou has a fallback position: handing over Myrcal."

"So the bottom line is that we can't know for certain, but there's probably—what? A fifty-fifty chance?—that ou *would* let Myrcal kill at least enough of our people to 'send a message,'" Swenson sighed.

"I don't know if the chance is that high," Wilson said, "but I know for damn sure that it's higher than I'm prepared to risk."

"And how do you propose to avoid it, Rob?"

From Abu Bakr's tone, he clearly suspected where Wilson was headed, and the Space Marine smiled coldly at him.

"I propose that we 'send a message' that's clear enough to damned well make *sure* Juzhyr doesn't let Myrcal do anything of the sort," he said.

• • • • •

"TOWER, DESHKYR ONE, requesting clearance to take off."

Leader of Seventy-Two Syltar SylAnTry scanned the airfield from ous observation post in the airfield's tower. All clear.

"Deshkyr One, Kwyzo nar Qwern Tower, you are cleared for takeoff, Runway Seventeen. Winds are from the south at two minrans per minaq."

"Deshkyr One is cleared for takeoff, Runway Seventeen."

The Shyrmal-3 fighter took the runway, ran up its engine, and started its takeoff roll.

Its wheels had just left the ground when it exploded.

"Seventy-Two!" Leader of Eight Mynsaro MynGenJar exclaimed. "Deshkyr One—!"

"I see it," Syltar replied, watching one landing gear bounce out of the cloud of smoke and fire which had once been a fighter. It bounded along the runway for another few cherans, trailing smoke, then skidded off into the grass. "Call out the crash crew and get an ambulance from the base hospital."

Ou didn't think there'd be a need for an ambulance, but someone would have to take the remains—whatever they could find, anyway—away.

Ou had just picked the microphone back up to suspend operations at the base when Mynsaro made an inarticulate sound and pointed frantically upward. The leader of eight's eyes were huge, nasal flaps gaping in horror, and Syltar's eyes jerked heavenward.

The skies above Kwyzo nar Qwern were a crisscross of white contrails where the capital air defense squadrons mounted a massive protective canopy. Syltar had serious doubts about the canopy's effectiveness after what had happened to the Earthian Abu Bakr's "escort," but ou'd decided to keep them to ouself. There were six squadrons overhead, stacked in three layers, at six serans, twelve serans, and eighteen serans, and ou felt his own nasal flaps widen in disbelief as he saw the first blossoms of flame.

They started with the high-altitude squadron, but they flashed downward like fuel igniting when a match was dropped into it. The explosions grew more visible as they came closer to the ground . . . and he didn't see a single parachute.

"*Dwomo,*" he muttered, and then a deafening roll of thunder snatched his eyes back down to the runways as a row of explosions ran down the ramp of Deshkyr One's squadron, Fighter Squadron 143. Syltar jerked back in involuntary surprise. The explosions weren't from a row of bombs—no! Every single aircraft in the squadron had spontaneously blown up! There had to be something wrong with their aircraft . . . or maybe . . . *Diantian sabotage!*

"We'll need more fire vehicles," Syltar said. "Call the city fire department as well—we're going to need everything they can spare. It looks—"

Ou stopped as every aircraft on Fighter Squadron 142's ramp exploded. Then every aircraft on Attack Squadron 34's ramp. Then Attack Squadron 36's. Then Attack 176's. Within seelaqs, every plane on the airfield was ferociously ablaze, deluging the ramps in a sea of roaring flame and seething black smoke.

Syltar was at a loss. It had to be enemy action, but ou had no idea what had just happened. Still, it was obvious the folks on the ramps would need every bit of assistance ou could send their way.

Ou turned to Mynsaro, but ou was staring out the window.

"Let's get a move on!" Syltar exclaimed. "Those troops need help."

Mynsaro didn't reply; instead, ou pointed out the window.

"Seventy-Two, what's *that*?" ou asked.

Syltar turned to find a . . . thing pointed at him. Although generally aircraft shaped, it wasn't an airplane, because it didn't have a cockpit and it was only about one-quarter the size of an airplane. And it didn't move—it simply hung in the air outside the tower, about three cherans away. Syltar didn't recognize much about the craft, but ou did understand one thing—the objects under its port wing looked an awful lot like the rockets the attack airplanes used. The object waggled its wings, then *flew backward* several cherans.

"*Run!*" Syltar yelled. "*Clear the tower!*"

. . . . .

CAPTAIN LLOYD SNIDERMAN smiled as he looked through the targeting reticle onboard the *Starfire* assault shuttle.

"Looks like you got their attention," his pilot, Captain Darlene Giannetti, said as the Sarthians began to run towards the one door visible in the tower. "Going to let them get away?"

"Nope," Sniderman replied. "Just wanted to let the bastards know it was coming." He squeezed the launch trigger, the Cunningham H-1 heavy attack drone's remaining two missiles roared off the wings, and the airport's tower facility was suddenly an expanding ball of flame.

. . . . .

"OUR TURN."

Double Fist Sodyr TamSoFly's voice crackled in Fist Stelyk SylStelRam's crestphones, and she grunted, standing higher in the hatch to wave to the other units of her platoon. Engines snorted to life, belching black exhaust clouds, and she settled back down into the turret.

The orders to move from the Kwyzo nar Qwern cantonment area had come in early that morning, and tanks had been deploying for the last several hours. Stelyk hadn't been told what had happened, only that she needed to get her tanks to the Palace ASAP to help defend the Clan Ruler from the Earthians. Although she'd heard they had armored suits, she couldn't see how that would stop a shell from her heavy tank. Nearly a seqran in diameter, the shell was sure to obliterate any Earthian stupid enough to try to take her on one-on-one.

"Rolling," Double Fist Sodyr announced over the radio, and Stelyk shook her head in satisfaction as her driver put the massive Myosark in gear. They moved forward, following Sodyr towards the gate as he led the way out of the cantonment area. His tank had just reached the gate when it exploded.

Stelyk's tank slid to a halt as the flaming wreckage of Sodyr's Myosark blocked the exit and she gawked at the roaring furnace which had once been her company commander and his crew. What the—?

Stelyk SylStelRam saw a blur out of the corner of her right eye. Her head started to turn in that direction, but then the missile hit her tank and it—and she—disintegrated.

· · · · ·

"WELL, THAT'S CERTAINLY impressive," Master of Lances Antryl AnHenKel noted as ou looked through the farseers from the top of the castle complex. Ou didn't need the vision enhancers to see the enormous Earthian spacecraft that had come down from the heavens to float over the river that ran through Kwyzo nar Qwern. A large ramp had deployed from the back of the craft and vehicles moved down it while individual troopers floated to the riverbank from openings in its side.

"I think that's an understatement," Flythyr MuzTolFlyth replied as she watched the vehicles float down the ramp and over the small beach area scrupulously reserved for the well-to-do. The Earthians didn't seem to care that they were trespassing, though, she thought with bitter humor.

The vehicles themselves were obviously tanks, but they didn't appear to actually touch the ground—they seemed to float above it, the same way the Earthian APCs did. She'd hoped their tanks might be too heavy for whatever magic supported the smaller vehicles and become mired in the soft sand, but it hadn't presented even a minor obstacle.

"We've made a big mistake," she added. "I told them not to do this, and now the krats have come home to roost."

"At least we were able to get some of our tanks out of cantonment before they began blowing them up," Antryl said. "Perhaps they'll make a difference."

Flythyr shrugged.

"I doubt it," she said. "We still don't know how the Earthians destroyed the rest of them, nor how they destroyed all of our aircraft. If they could do that, though, it suggests they don't *have* to come down to take us on on our own ground. That means they're here because they *want* to be here, so I strongly suspect they have the capability to destroy the tanks that made it out of cantonment, too."

The initial Earthian tank cleared the beach area and drove onto the main street, where it was engaged by two of the massive Myosarks. Both fired, and the armor-piercing shells slammed into the front of their Earthian opponent.

They bounced. Like a child's ball, they *bounced*, ricocheting wildly before their delayed action fuses detonated them.

The Earthian tank continued towards the Myosarks without slowing. If it had been damaged, it didn't give any indication. Then *it* fired, and one Myosark's turret blew straight up on a roaring column of exploding ammunition. The Earthian fired again—far more quickly, Flythyr knew, than any

Qwernian tank could have gotten off a second shot—and she actually saw the round go all the way through the second Myosark! The round—or spalling from it—set off something inside the tank, and it blew up, as well.

"You appear to be correct," Antryl said. "What are we going to do?"

Flythyr squared her shoulders. "We're going to do our duty. We're going to protect the Clan Ruler. We're going to fight the Earthians to the best of our abilities."

"And if that isn't good enough?"

"Then we'll die." Flythyr shrugged. "Come on; let's get to the command center."

· · · · ·

CAPTAIN ANIKA PRADHAN, call sign "Blue One," scanned her surroundings as her Sanders tank drove along the main thoroughfare towards the castle. A swarm of drones orbited overhead, their operators praying for a Qwernian stupid enough to try to take a potshot at the column from a window or rooftop. Several apparently had, so far, and she'd seen missiles destroy several buildings. She wasn't aware that any of the Qwernians had gotten a shot off at her since the landing, aside from the two tanks that had hit her just as she climbed off the beachhead.

The second shell had scuffed the smart skin "paint" in front of the driver, pissing him off, but that was the extent of their injuries.

Since then, she'd engaged every tank before they'd been able to shoot at her—not only were the drones killing off anyone stupid enough to snipe at them, they also provided advance reconnaissance of the area in front of the column. She knew where every Qwernian tank was before it ever came into sight, and over twenty pillars of smoke from burning Qwernian tanks marked Blue One's progress.

"Blue One, Eagle One sees three hostiles, directly ahead," the person tasked with reconnaissance called as they came within one intersection of the Palace.

"Blue One sees them," Pradhan replied, looking at the imagery on her corneas. "Looks like three main battle tanks in revetments in front of the Palace?" The three tanks were "hiding" behind some concrete objects that looked like the old Jersey walls that had functioned as dividers on highways back on Earth. They would *not* stop one of her rounds.

"That's affirmative, Blue One. Cleared to engage."

Pradhan snorted. As if she hadn't had that thought, all by herself.

"Roger, cleared to engage," she replied, trying to keep the sarcasm out of her voice, then switched to her company command net. "Blue Section, we're cleared to advance and engage. Blue Two, you've got the one on the left, Three, you've got the one on the right," she said, designating targets for the tanks spread to her sides and slightly behind her in a wedge formation. It wouldn't be fair for her to have *all* the fun.

Acknowledgments came back from the rest of the section.

"We've got the center one?" her own gunner asked.

"Yes," Pradhan replied.

"Cool," the gunner said.

"Blue Section, let's go," Pradhan said over the net, and the three Sanders slid smoothly forward.

"Stand by to fire!" she transmitted as her tanks flowed around the final corner, clearing the range to their targets. And then—

"Fire!"

The tank rocked a little as its main gun fired, and all three tanks in front of the Palace became burning, exploding junk heaps. Not only that . . .

"Did you just open the Palace's main doors with that shot?" Pradhan asked.

"Yeah," the gunner replied, pride in his voice. "I was trying to skip it through the tank and into the doors to make it easier for the Crunchies to get in."

"Nice shooting," Pradhan said. She looked back in front of her only to find a flood of infantry pouring out of the open doors to take positions around the revetments and destroyed tanks. She switched to the radio.

"Eagle One, Blue One. Interrogative, are you seeing the activity at the Palace?"

"Yeah, we are, Blue One. Stand by."

"Want me to light them up?" the gunner asked.

"No," Pradhan said. "We'll kill them if we have to, but nothing they have can touch us. It was fun blowing up the tanks, but massacring these guys if we don't have to would be a little too much like murder for me. Hopefully, our demonstration so far will be enough to get them to surrender."

"Blue One, Eagle One. Maintain your position there. We're going to try something else."

"Copy, Eagle One. Maintaining our position."

"What do you suppose that's all about?" the driver asked.

"I don't know," Pradhan said. "But I expect we'll find out."

· · · · ·

"**WHAT ARE THEY** doing?" Master of Lances Antryl asked as ou watched the monitor that showed the area in front of the Palace.

"Looks like they've stopped," Flythyr replied.

"For what, though? Are they afraid to approach?"

"I don't know," Flythyr admitted. "I doubt it. They could easily kill all the troopers with their main guns. They took care of our tanks easily enough," she pointed out bitterly. Then she paused as she saw specks moving in the background and muttered, "What's that . . ."

"Are you seeing this, Flock Lord Consort?" the lance in front of the Palace asked over the command center's speakers.

"I am . . . but I can't tell what's going on."

"All of their infantry just . . . launched into the air. They're *flying*!"

That, Flythyr realized, watching the monitor, wasn't exactly accurate. Not that she blamed the lance for his description . . . or that it made much difference. The armored Earthians were actually advancing in prodigious leaps, bouncing as high as a cheran and covering as much as a full tyran between touchdowns. And they could clearly alter trajectory once they'd left the ground, as well. They might as well be flying, and they came slashing forward at a preposterous speed.

"They're flying *over* us," the lance continued. "They . . . they're not even trying to attack us—they're just going past. We're trying to shoot them down, but they're moving too fast and dodging so much we—Wait . . . *they're going for the courtyard! Stop them!*"

"The courtyard?" Antryl asked. "If they get into the courtyard, they can breach the Palace and get clear down here into the War Palace."

Flythyr nodded in disagreement.

"There's no way they can do that." She motioned to the starth running the camera system. "Bring up the camera on the access portal."

The female nodded, and the main monitor changed to show the hatch that covered the access leading to the War Palace.

It was open, and Earthians could be seen landing in the courtyard on the far side of the plate glass doors near the hatch.

"I ordered that sealed!" Flythyr exclaimed. "You!" she said, motioning to a nearby starth. "Call down to the security station and tell them to shut the hatch, *now*!" She looked back to the starth at the camera system. "Bring up the view of the security station."

The starth did as she'd been ordered, and Flythyr swallowed in shock.

The monitoring station was a charnel house. At least five of her troops could be seen in the monitor; all of them were very obviously dead, most with body parts ripped off, lying in pools of their own blood. Aside from the missing limbs, none of them seemed to have been shot . . . or knifed . . . or anything. They were just obviously, violently, dead. One human sat at the main control station, and he looked over to the camera and smiled in the Earthian way. Flythyr wasn't that well versed in human emotions, but the smile the dark-skinned female gave the camera didn't appear to indicate happiness; instead, it was predatory, and she involuntarily backed away from the monitor a couple of steps.

"How did she get there?" Antryl asked.

"No idea," Flythyr replied. A glance at the other monitors showed the Earthians pouring through the access hatch into the War Palace. It was too late to seal it. "Everyone grab a rifle!" she ordered. "We have to protect the Clan Ruler!"

· · · · ·

BERKE HAD NO way of knowing how long he'd been in the cell—it seemed like at least a half-day—when a group of eight Qwernian troopers came, pulled him out, and marched him to a huge room somewhere in the War Palace. To say the room was in chaos would have been an understatement. There were at least thirty troops trying to set up fighting positions, a number of the ministers were yelling at each other, and, on the other side of the room, the clan ruler was trying to get answers to questions it seemed no one was prepared to discuss. The soldiers slammed the door after they entered and brought him forward to where Myrcal, Flythyr, and the clan ruler argued.

"This is why the Earthians are coming?" the clan ruler asked. "To get *him*?"

"I told Minister Myrcal this would never work," Flythyr said. "The Earthians value their people more than we do; I had a feeling this would drive them to action."

"Yes, he's the only Earthian we have here," Myrcal said, ignoring Flythyr. "Since they're here, I expect they're here for him. When they get here, we'll use him as a bargaining chip."

Juzhyr motioned to one of the nearby soldiers. "Give me your pistol," ou said. When the trooper did, Juzhyr leveled it between Berke's eyes. "I only want to know one thing," ou said. "What will it take to make your forces withdraw?"

Berke strained to control his bladder as he looked into the enormous maw of the pistol.

"I don't . . . I don't know," he replied, realizing they might be his final words. "I doubt they're here for just me. If they're here, they're probably—"

The door exploded. The soldiers closest to it flew through the air and the sudden, savage overpressure knocked Berke to his knees. Before he could re-cover, Juzhyr leapt forward, wrapped an arm around his throat, and shoved the cold muzzle of the pistol against his temple as troops in Heinlein armor strode into the room.

"Don't move," Juzhyr said, "or I'll kill him."

"Drop the pistol, Clan Ruler," one of the Earthians said over his armor's external speakers.

"I'll kill him!" Juzhyr snapped. The pistol against Berke's head pressed hard enough to force it to one side, and the diplomat closed his eyes.

"No, you won't," the Earthian said flatly. "And if you don't drop that pistol—now—it will be the last mistake you ever make."

"And who are you to think you can order me—the Clan Ruler of the entire Qwernian Empire—about?"

"I'm Captain Malachi Dvorak, Planetary Union Space Marines. And I'm also David Dvorak's son." The Earthian's voice was icy cold. "Personally, I'd like nothing more than for the person standing behind you to shoot you in the back of the head. Please, give him an excuse."

"If you kill me, my men will kill you and all of your troops," Juzhyr grated. "Your armor can't be that good. And don't try to bluff me! There's no one behind me but my own soldiers."

"My armor *is* that good," Malachi said, "and there *is* someone behind you." Berke's eyes popped back open, and he managed to turn his head just far enough to see Brigadier Torino suddenly materialize in the very corner of his vision and put the barrel of his own pistol against Juzhyr's head.

The entire war room froze, and the quiet hiss as the visor of Malachi Dvorak's helmet cycled upward was shockingly loud in the sudden, absolute silence. His eyes were hard as ice, his voice was even colder than they were, and the translating software projected its icy menace with perfect fidelity.

"Your choice, Clan Ruler," he said. "You may think you can kill Mister Berke before Brigadier Torino kills *you*. Personally, I don't think you have a chance in hell." He smiled. "I guess it depends on how lucky you feel. So tell me, do you feel lucky, Punk?"

· XXI ·

PUNS *VANGUARD*,
SARTH ORBIT

Dave Dvorak opened his eyes.

He didn't recognize the overhead. He was obviously back aboard *Vanguard*, but he'd never seen that particular pastel shade before, and he had no idea how he'd gotten here. In fact, he didn't seem to remember very much at all.

A corner of his brain thought that should worry him, but he felt too tranquil and too luxuriously comfortable for anything as crass as worrying. He felt . . . he felt like a man waking up from ten solid hours of good, deep sleep, he thought. Maybe even twelve hours.

He smiled faintly at the thought and raised his arms and stretched hard, luxuriating in that pure sense of good feeling. Then he froze as he realized where he was. Sick bay. What the hell was he doing in *sick bay*? He'd been healthy as a horse for the last twenty-odd years, courtesy of modern medicine, so what—?

"Hello, Papi," a soft voice said, and his head snapped over to the right as two slender hands lifted his hand to a tear-slick cheek.

"Morgana?" The hoarseness of his own voice surprised him. It sounded like something that hadn't been used in a long time, and he cleared his throat. "What . . . what the hell happened, Honey?"

"That's going to be a long story, Dad," she told him, smiling through her tears. "I'm just happy you're here to hear it!"

"But—" He broke off, his confusion evident, and she squeezed his hand again.

"You're going to need a little while to get up to speed, Dad. And right this minute, you're still pretty heavily tranked."

"I am?" He blinked at her.

"Yes. You had . . . Papi, you had a *lot* of neural damage. You were in the regen tank for *weeks*." She smiled mistily at him. "The docs weren't taking you out until the nannies fixed everything they could fix."

"And did they manage to fix everything?" Dvorak sounded far calmer than he suspected he should have, undoubtedly because of the tranquilizers.

"No," she said simply. "All your motor skills, all of your cognitive abilities—they should be fine. But you're going to have some significant memory loss."

"Oh." He considered that and managed a smile. "Do I get to pick the mistakes I forget?"

"'Fraid not." Her lips twitched and she pressed her cheek more firmly against his palm. "The good news is that most of it's going to be concentrated in fairly recent memories, and you always were a compulsive damned diarist. So even a lot of what you don't remember firsthand will still be available to you. And we've got a lot of tridee imagery and audio you can access directly through the neural educator. But you're going to have some holes, whatever we do, Dad."

"Hey," he reached up with his other hand to brush tears from her eye with his thumb, "long as I remember you, your mom, Malachi, and Maighread, I'm fine." He smiled and patted her other cheek. "Trust me, Baby. As long as I remember *you,* I'm fine."

· · · · ·

DAVE DVORAK STEPPED carefully through the hatch, only too conscious of the stiffness where the nanites were still repairing his shattered spine. It was going to be a while before—

"Attention on deck!" Admiral Francesca Swenson snapped, and he froze, eyes widening, as every man and woman in the flag briefing room rose. They snapped to attention, facing him, and he swallowed hard as he stepped fully into the compartment and crossed to the end of the enormous table.

"Please sit," he said, but they only looked back at him until he lowered himself into his own chair. Then there was a rustle and a stir as they followed suit.

"Thank you for the courtesy," he said and smiled. "I'm afraid you must've mistaken me for somebody important, but I do appreciate it."

"Not as much as we all appreciate seeing you back on your feet, Mister Secretary. We've missed you," Swenson said simply, and Dvorak felt his face heat. Fortunately—

"And some of us appreciate seeing your lazy butt up again even more than others of us do," Brigadier Robert Wilson said. "Especially those of us who were contemplating the possibility of going home to tell a certain vicious-tempered little redhead that we'd mislaid you somewhere."

"You always have such a gift for placing solemn events in context," Dvorak told him with a grateful smile.

"True, too true," Wilson acknowledged with great modesty, and a ripple of laughter ran around the briefing room.

Dvorak chuckled, as well, but then his expression sobered.

"I've been bringing myself back up to speed as quickly as my kindly physicians—" he turned to smile over his shoulder at Doctor Morgana Dvorak, who'd followed him through the hatch "—would allow. I know we lost a lot of people." His smile vanished and he shook his head. "And I know that if it's anyone's fault, it's mine."

Swenson started to protest, but Dvorak's raised hand stopped her.

"I'm not going to hammer myself with guilt, Francesca. I'm just saying that I was in charge. We all missed seeing this coming, but I had access to all the data any of you did. I didn't see it either, and all the final decisions leading up to it were mine. I still think they were sound, given what we knew when they were made, but they were *my* decisions, not yours. So nobody else in this compartment had better be blaming themselves for what happened. I know it hit all of you hard. It's probably fresher for me than for any of you, and it's going to take me time to come to terms with what happened, especially to Trish and Jane. But I'm the one who made the decisions leading up to it, so whatever else it may have been, it wasn't *your* fault. Is that clear?"

No one actively objected, although he saw disagreement in more than one set of eyes. Especially a set of stubborn blue eyes belonging to a Space Marine brigadier.

"Having said that," he continued after a moment, "I'm a little curious as to why my kindly physicians—and my no doubt loyal and supportive subordinates—have seen fit to . . . redact some of the records I've been perusing."

"Oh, give us a break!" Rob Wilson growled. "You've been out of sick bay for exactly seventeen hours. Don't you think you might give yourself—oh, I don't know; an entire *twenty-four* hours, maybe—to get fully up to speed?"

"Probably," Dvorak agreed with a faint smile. "But you know how I've always been one of those irritating people who like to read the last page of the book first?" He cocked his head, regarding his brother-in-law quizzically. "That's why I noticed that the last page of this book—" he tapped the spot on his temples where the NET fitted "—seems to be missing. So who's going to tell me what happened after my ever-eloquent son quoted Clint Eastwood to a ruling head of state?"

"With all due respect, Mister Ambassador," Admiral Swenson said with a lurking smile of her own, "it was a very appropriate quotation at the moment. And it did have the desired effect. Mostly."

"What do you mean 'mostly,' and why does your use of that particular word fill me with foreboding?" Dvorak asked. "Do we still have a problem with the Qwernians?"

He looked around the briefing room, eyebrows arched. From what he'd already learned and the expressions about him, the situation was obviously under control. But no one—aside from his brother-in-law—seemed especially eager to meet his gaze. He thought about that for a moment, then looked at the brother-in-law in question.

"Rob?"

"Oh, no," Wilson told him, shaking his head. "No problems at all with the Qwernians now."

"Oh? That sounds remarkably . . . neat and orderly, given what I do remember about Myrcal and Qwernians in general."

"Well, Myrcal's not with us anymore." Wilson's eyes turned very dark for a moment. "It seems ou wasn't very happy when ou ended up in solitary confinement in a cell under the Palace. So ou managed to hang ouself."

"Really?" Dvorak's eyes narrowed and his tone sharpened. "Did ou really kill *ouself*, Rob? Or was ou helped along by Juzhyr?"

"I'm sure Juzhyr would've been delighted to off oum, but I'm afraid Juzhyr doesn't get to make any more calls," Wilson said.

"What?" Dvorak straightened in his chair and looked around at his senior subordinates. "I realize what ou did—or allowed Myrcal to do for oum— amounts to an act of war, but we can't just go around unilaterally deposing ruling heads of state! Not if we expect anyone else to ever trust us, anyway! Maybe if the Sarthians set up a tribunal like Nuremberg or The Hague and convict oum, but until then we can't just—"

"On the contrary, we can," Abu Bakr said, speaking up for the first time. Dvorak looked at him, and Abu Bakr shrugged. "Sarthian custom's not quite like 'Earthian' custom, Dave. You know that."

"And?"

"And in this case it's the fault of—what did you call him? Your 'ever-eloquent son,' I believe?"

"Malachi? *Malachi* took it upon himself to depose a head of state?"

"Well, yes and no. It was . . . sort of an accident," Wilson said.

"An accident?" Dvorak repeated carefully. "How the hell do you depose a head of state by *accident*?! I mean, even for Malachi that's—" He broke off and shook his head. "Look, just tell me what's going on with the Qwernians!"

"Well, that's the thing," Wilson said. "You see, there aren't any more Qwernians."

"*What*?!" Dvorak stared at him in shock.

"Oh, we didn't kill them all or anything like that!" Wilson reassured him. "It's just that they aren't *Qwernians* anymore."

"Well, then what the hell *are* they?" Dvorak demanded.

"That's where Sarthian custom comes in," Abu Bakr said. "You see, Malachi defeated Juzhyr. Well, not all by himself; he did have a *little* help. But under Sarthian—and especially Qwernian, or what used to be Qwernian—custom, the individual who takes a clan ruler's surrender is considered to have personally defeated that clan ruler in combat."

"And?" Dvorak looked at his friend in considerable trepidation.

"And he took that surrender as your deputy. In fact, he specifically identified himself as your son when he did."

"Which means?"

"Which means Clan Qwern ceased to exist, and along with it the Qwernian Empire." Dvorak gaped at him, and Abu Bakr smiled. "It's now Clan Dvorak and the *Dvorakian* Empire. Good luck convincing your new subjects how it's supposed to work; Allah knows I've already tried without a lot of success! I'm sure someone as eloquent as you will manage it . . . eventually. But for right now, it means that if you want to sign any alliances in your Empire's name, Clan Ruler Dave, it'd be completely legal!"

Year 41 of the Terran Empire

W e've finished massaging the data from the first drone sweep," Stephen Buchevsky said as the dreadnought slid stealthily towards the distant star they'd come so far to reach. "The second flight is still forty-three minutes from rendezvous."

"Excellent, my Stephen," Vlad Drakulya said from the command chair at the center of the bridge, green eyes narrow as he gazed at the brilliant pinprick in the center of the main display.

At the moment, that star was approximately nineteen hundred astronomical units from *Târgoviște* as she accelerated towards it at the maximum sixty gravities her inertial compensator could sustain. She'd been in normal-space for just under two days, and her current velocity was up to 0.34c—just over 101,000 KPS. At her current acceleration it would take her another three days to attain the eighty percent of light-speed her particle screening could sustain, at which point she would be far less stealthy than she was at this moment. But by then their plan called for an open approach, showing *Târgoviște*'s original Shongair transponder. Assuming they carried all the way through to Shongaru, the Shong System's sole earthlike planet, the entire voyage—including over five and a half days of ballistic flight at 0.8c—would require another thirteen days. After their seemingly endless flight just to get here, those last thirteen days loomed before Buchevsky like thirteen centuries. If they had it to do, he wanted to get it done and be finished with it forever.

The main reason they'd made their n-space transition so far out was to allow plenty of time for their far speedier recon drones to probe the inner system before they made their presence known. They had only a single ship, and while she was thoroughly capable of sterilizing any planet, she was still only *one* ship. If they got all the way into missile range unchallenged, she could deal with any force close to the planet before it could clear for action, but all of their data was eighty Earth years out of date. It behooved them to see what might have changed in that near-century before they planned their actual attack run. And Vlad Drakulya intended for that planning to be as thorough as possible.

Buchevsky glanced at Vlad from his own chair at the tactical officer's station. The hand which actually launched those missiles would be his, and he wondered how he was going to feel about that in the unending days of a vampire's life. He didn't expect to like it very much, but at least he'd gotten Vlad to back off his plan for outright genocide. It probably wouldn't do much good for the other Shongair colonies, and Buchevsky fully understood why those other ships would unflinchingly do exactly what they'd set out to do. But there was more humanity left inside Vlad Drakulya than Vlad himself had thought before Buchevsky appealed to it. And because there was, he was prepared to settle for "only" blasting the Shongairi back into the Stone Age.

Buchevsky wished he could have convinced Vlad to accept a still less draconian outcome, but history hadn't called him Son of the Dragon for nothing. And as he'd pointed out, green eyes colder than the vacuum beyond *Târgoviște*'s hull, he intended to leave at least a third of them alive after the systematic bombardment that would destroy every trace of planetary industry.

"And that, my Stephen," he'd said in a distant, icy tone, "is far better than they intended to do to us. Indeed, in many ways, it is far more lenient than what they actually *did* do to us before we stopped them. I will leave a third of them alive, not the quarter of the human race we saved from them."

Buchevsky couldn't argue with that, and a hard and bitter part of him hadn't even wanted to. More to the point, whatever he'd wanted, that was the best he was going to get.

"No sign of any major changes from the first flight's take," he said now, bringing up a detailed schematic of the inner system. "They've got a bigger presence on Shong V than they did when Thikair left, but it's not as *much* bigger as a bunch of humans would have managed in the same time span. And their industrial base doesn't seem to have grown at all."

"No reason it should," Calvin Meyers said. Buchevsky glanced at the sandy-haired, compact ex–gunnery sergeant from the Appalachian coalfields, and Meyers shrugged. "One thing's pretty damn clear from their own records, Top. If it ain't broke, none of these Hegemony bastards waste any time fixing it. They figure what they've got's good enough, so why screw around with it?"

"True, Calvin." Vlad nodded. "They are most unlike humans in that respect, are they not?" His smile was unpleasant. "I find myself wondering what Governor Howell has accomplished during our voyage."

"Don't know," Buchevsky said. "Don't think the Hegemony's going to like it very much, though."

"I imagine not," Vlad agreed. "In fact—"

"*Madre de Dios!*" Francisco Lopez gasped. The only other survivor of Buchevsky's original group of Americans aboard *Târgoviște*, he'd shown a marked affinity for the dreadnought's sensor suite, which made him the logical choice to run it. Now Buchevsky's head snapped around as Lopez started pounding commands into his console.

"Unknown vessel at seven light-seconds!" he barked. "Closing from aft and high. Overtake velocity six thousand KPS. Acceleration—"

He stopped and swallowed hard, then looked at Vlad.

"Vlad, whatever it is, it's pulling over a *hundred* gravities," he said flatly. "And it's got a weird signature."

"What do you mean, 'weird,' Francisco?" Vlad asked in a preposterously calm tone. If Lopez' numbers were right, then whatever-the-hell-it-was was going to overtake them in less than six minutes . . . and *Târgovişte* needed twenty minutes to bring up her phase generator.

"It's got no bow wave," Lopez said, answering Vlad's question, and Buchevsky frowned. At thirty-six percent of light speed, the stranger's particle shields should have radiated at least *some* energy. At that velocity, a one-microgram particle would release 5,800 megajoules—the next best thing to the energy in 1.4 tons of TNT—when it hit its shields.

"That's . . . odd," he said out loud, changing his mind at the last moment and avoiding dirty words like "impossible."

"Indeed, my Stephen," Vlad said dryly. "Arm your weapons, please."

"Weapons hot," Buchevsky confirmed, depressing the key which released the safety interlocks. "Tracking."

"The after array has an image," Lopez said.

"Show it to us," Vlad commanded.

"Coming up now," Lopez replied, and the display which had shown the system primary suddenly displayed a very different image.

Hegemony optical systems were remarkably good. The after array had the resolution of a twelve-meter reflecting telescope, and seven light-seconds were nothing to it. Even better, there was enough vertical separation for a decent look at their pursuer, and Buchevsky swallowed hard as the display obediently superimposed a scale to give them the stranger's dimensions.

Târgovişte was over five kilometers long and her war hull was a kilometer in diameter. The stranger was almost *twenty-five* kilometers long and *four* kilometers in diameter, and there was no sign of anything remotely like a spin section. It was an enormous, silvery spindle, preposterously long for its width even with that enormous beam, with some sort of bulbous housing at what had to be its prow. There was something very peculiar about that housing, too, though he couldn't put his finger on precisely what it was. Something about the light—

"Do not fire," Vlad said, then smiled thinly as Buchevsky looked a question at him. "First," he said, "I believe discretion might be in order, given our visitors' size and the capabilities they have already shown us. And, second, I doubt that it is the Shongairi. I have no idea what it may be *instead*, but I cannot conceive of the Puppies having achieved such a radical improvement in their technology in a mere eighty years. Indeed—"

"Com laser," Ioan Draghicescu, one of Vlad's pre-invasion Romanians, announced from the communications section. "It's—"

He paused, then spoke very carefully.

"It's a communications request . . . in English."

English? Buchevsky felt his eyebrows trying to climb to the top of his skull. *English?* That was—

"'Odd,' I believe you said, my Stephen?" Vlad observed with an even thinner smile, then nodded to Draghicescu. "Put it up," he said.

"Coming up now," Draghicescu said, and Stephen Buchevsky suddenly felt as if he were still a breather who'd just been punched squarely between the eyes.

"Hello, Vlad," Dave Dvorak said from the display. "We need to talk."

PLANET SARTH

Sarth is the sole habitable planet of the 61 Cygni binary system. 61 Cygni is approximately 10.4 light-years from Earth and a distant binary whose two components orbit their common barycenter in 659 years with a mean separation of 84 AU. 61 Cygni A is a K5v star and 61 Cygni B is a K7v star. A is the more stable of the two; B has significant short-term flares on about an 11.7-year periodicity. Both exhibit flare activity, but the chromosphere of B is 25 percent more than for 61 Cygni A.

Sarth orbits 61 Cygni A at approximately 56,155,000 kilometers (0.374 AU). Its orbital period is 106.39 Earth days (approximately .29 earth years) and its rotational period is 60 hours. Mean temperature is 18° Celsius (Earth's current mean temperature is about 14.6° Celsius) and 82% of its surface is water/ice. Axial inclination is only about 8° (as opposed to Earth's almost 24°), so seasonal variations are negligible (by human standards). The planet's radius is 6,422 kilometers (44 kilometers greater than Earth's), but its gravity is only 0.85 that of Earth, indicating a less dense planet. It has two moons, each about half the size of Luna.

SARTHIAN TIMEKEEPING

Sarthians divide their planetary year into triads, each 42.5 planetary days long, and each day is divided into day-halves (roughly 30 Earth hours long) and day-quarters (roughly 15 Earth hours long). Each day-quarter is further divided as below:

Sarthian Unit	Terran Equivalent
secar	1.88 hours; 112 minutes
minaq	28.13 minutes
chequar	1.76 minutes
kysaq	52.7 seconds
seelaq	0.82 seconds

SARTHIAN DISTANCE MEASUREMENT

Sarthian unit	Kilometers	Meters	Centimeters
minran	5.325	5,324.800	532,480.000
seran	0.666	665.600	66,560.000
tyran	0.083	83.200	8,320.000
cheran	0.010	10.400	1,040.000
ran	0.001	1.300	130.000
seqran	0.000	0.163	16.250
kyran	0.000	0.020	2.031
teran	0.000	0.003	0.254

	Miles	Yards	Feet	Inches
minran	3.31	5,823.15	17,469.44	209,633.28
seran	0.41	727.89	2,183.68	26,204.16
tyran	0.05	90.99	272.96	3,275.52
cheran	0.01	11.37	34.12	409.44
ran	0.00	1.42	4.27	51.18
seqran	0.00	0.18	0.53	6.40
kyran	0.00	0.02	0.07	0.80
teran	0.00	0.00	0.01	0.10

SARTHIAN GENDERS

Sarthians have three biological genders, which are defined as male, female, and neutro. Parents are "sire," "dam," and "bearer," and "bearer" is used interchangeably with "neutro" by Sarthians. The humans' translator software uses masculine pronouns for males, feminine pronouns for females, and assigns pronouns to neutros as:

He/she = ou
His/her = ous (also the neutro plural possessive)

Him/her = oum
Them = oums
Themselves = ouselves
Sir/Ma'am = tysan

SARTHIAN NAMING CONVENTIONS

There are four main language families on Sarth: Sandian; Deltaran; Morantan; and Solahian. All of them have been influenced by most of the others—especially Diantian (and thus the Sandian language family)—but each of them also have a lot of dialects. The dialects are named after specific clans, but they are actually geographic in origin. They are simply named after the dominant clan in a given geographic location, although in a handful of cases, they are named after a clan which was defeated and absorbed into a successor.

There are two main systems of naming. One of them originated in Sanda and is used in all Sandian nations and their daughter states and has been adopted in Morant. The second originated in either Solah or Deltar (no one is entirely sure which) and continues to be used in some southern areas of Morant and—very aggressively, as a form of defiance—by the indigenous states in Deltar.

In both systems, the three adult members of any family unit are always designated numerically (first, second, and third), but the "surnames" and clan affiliation are constructed/denoted differently.

In both systems, the full family name is always the first syllable (or the complete name, in the case of monosyllabic names) of each spouse in numerical order, although the neutro spouse's first name always forms the first component of the full family name. In the Sandian system, the full family name is used by all three spouses of the triad. The complete family name is also borne by any offspring, but only until such time as they marry, at which point a new family surname is created for the new triad. In the case of a divorce (which does happen) the divorced spouse's name is removed from the family name of the remaining spouses but any offspring shared with that individual retain the full original family name. Under the Sandian system, the neutro spouse is always first spouse, while the male and female may be either second or third, the order being determined by the order in which each of them joined the triad. If the entire triad forms simultaneously (which only happens 20%–30% of the time) then the order in which the wedding vows are taken determines which comes second or third in the full family name.

In the Deltaran system, the full family name is constructed in the same manner, but each individual member of the triad uses only the first syllables of his spouses' names, not the entire family name. Moreover, the order is always neutro, male, female regardless of the order in which the spouses joined the triad.

In addition, any Sarthian's full name also includes his clan designation. In the Sandian system, only the current clan designation is retained; in the Deltaran system, clan designation includes a genealogical catalog of the no longer extant clans from which the individual is descended. In the Sandian system the clan relationship is simply designated by "nor" (Dilanto) or "nar" (Qwern), the Sandian equivalent of "of," while in the Deltaran system, the clan relationship was originally further parsed by a complex set of generational modifiers. Even the Deltarans, however, have abandoned that degree of complexity over the last three or four Sarthian generations (except on highly formal, legal occasions). They, however, use the word "shorak" (the Deltaran equivalent of "of") instead of "nor" or "nar" (for the current generation) and "bekhar" (begotten of) for the ancestral clans.

A PARTIAL SARTHIAN GLOSSARY

bearer (1)—neutro parent.

bearer (2)—priest.

Chelth—chief deity of the Myrcos Pantheon and one time chief deity of the official Diantian Pantheon. Ou is now officially merely the head of one of several legally recognized pantheons, none of which are the Republic's state religion.

Chelthian—any Sarthian who worships Chelth. All priests of Chelth renounce their "worldly" surnames and "wed" Chelth. Even the neutros among them place Chelth, the supreme and holy neutro, first in their new surname, and all of them enter Clan Chelth. This doesn't mean they are renouncing any triad they may have joined or swearing an oath of celibacy. It is simply a way of acknowledging Chelth's supremacy in their lives. The proper title of address for any priest of Chelth, regardless of gender, is "Bearer."

Chelthist—a Sarthian who doesn't merely worship Chelth but believes that Chelth should be/must be returned to Sarthian his rightful place as the true God of the Republic and, indeed, of all Sarth. The really hard-core Chelthists are perfectly prepared to embrace violence and even martyrdom in their deity's name.

Chelthite—sometimes used interchangeably with Chelthist, but properly an adjective describing Chelthists' theology and political ideology.

chyrn—the equivalent of a terrestrial owl. About the size of an owl, which would makes it much larger and rather more fearsome in comparison to the smaller Sarthians.

dau—the generic term for the Sarthian equivalent of a terrestrial dog. Like dogs on Earth, there are a huge number of different breeds and types. All of them are prefaced with "dau," however.

daurysaki—the equivalent of a terrestrial pitbull.

Deshkyr—a mythological Qwernian warrior hero revered as the founder of Clan Qwern.

Dwomo—war god and chief deity of the Pantheon of Clan Qwern. Unlike the Republic, the Empire does have a "state religion," and Dwomo is its head. Ecumenicalism is another thing the Qwernians don't understand/like about Diantians.

krat—a nuisance avian analogue of Sarth.

krylith—the equivalent of a terrestrial pig. The krylith evolved in a swamp, so whereas a terrestrial pig wallows only to stay cool, krylyths actually live in muddy/swampy enclosures.

Myrcosian—a member of the Band of Myrcos, a Chelthist organization whose avowed purpose is to restore Chelth to Ous position of primacy in the religious life of the Republic of Dianto. The Band exists as both a legal political organization, with half a dozen seats in the Sitting of Commons, but also as an extralegal terrorist organization. The terms *Myrcosian* and *Band* are used interchangeably to describe both the legal and extralegal aspects of the organization.

nata—the neutro equivalent of son/daughter.

ou/oum/ous—Sarthian neutro pronoun.

Shaymork—Chelth's mortal enemy. The agent and author of all evil in the world. I.e., the Devil of Chelthian theology.

shyrmal—the equivalent of a terrestrial eagle. This is the apex aerial predator of Sarth. Also the Qwernian Army Air Force's frontline single-engine fighter.

sorqh—the equivalent of a terrestrial cow. They tend to be placid, have an even more pronounced "herd instinct" than terrestrial cattle, and are frequently used as a metaphor for someone who is stupid and unable to or uninterested in thinking for him or herself.

starth—4-limbed, saurian-looking creatures which are the equivalent of a terrestrial horse. About the size of a quarter horse, they, too, are toe-walkers (which gives them an . . . interesting gait). They are very fast; and they are omnivorous, which means they tend to come down on the predator side of the fight-or-flight equation and makes them especially suitable as mounts for warriors, and they have long snouts, powerful jaws and teeth, and crests which are raised and unfurled in battle. Deeply revered by Clan Qwern as part of the clan's nomadic heritage.

syldak—the equivalent of a terrestrial goose. They range in weight from 12 to 20 pounds (5.5–9 kilograms).

Taysar—originally goddess of the storm and Rider of the Lightning in the Myrcos pantheon. She has changed and evolved over the centuries, especially since Chelth was dethroned as the Republic's chief deity, and is now revered by the Chelthists as Chelth's avenging angel.

terahk—the equivalent of terrestrial coffee or very, very strong hot tea.

title bearer—the (always) neutro holder of a transmittable title. The male and female members of the title bearer's triad are referred to as [title] consorts and hold only life titles (although they can become the equivalent of queen mother or queen father).

Tysan—the neutro equivalent of "sir" or "ma'am."

SARTHIAN TITLES OF NOBILITY

English	Diantian	Qwern	Deltaran
knight	swordsman	starth rider	spear
baron	sword master	charioteer	chief of spears
earl	sword lord	herdsman	master of spears
duke	arms master	flock lord	lord of spears
grand duke	lord of arms	—	grand lord of spears
prince	clan leader	clan leader	spear of the clan
king	clan master	clan master	grand spear
emperor	lord of clans	clan ruler	—

SARTHIAN MILITARY RANKS*

Planetary Union	Diantian	Qwern
Private	Dagger	Starth
Corporal	Cutlass	—
Sergeant	Pike	Leader of Eight
Staff Sergeant	Senior Pike	Leader of Twelve
Sergeant First-Class	Chief Pike	Leader of Twenty-Four
Master Sergeant	Senior Chief Pike	Leader of Thirty-Six
First Sergeant	Master Pike	Leader of Seventy-Two
Sergeant Major	Senior Master Pike	Leader of Leaders

Planetary Union	Diantian	Qwern
Second Lieutenant	Dagger Chief	Double Hand
First Lieutenant	Sword Chief	Fist
Captain	Lance Chief	Double Fist
Major	Pike Leader	Gauntlet
Lieutenant Colonel	—	Double Gauntlet
Colonel	Ship Commander	Lance
Brigadier	Commander of Eight	Double Lance
Major General	Commander of Sixty-Four	Master of Lances
Lieutenant General	Fleet Commander	Field Master
General	Navy Commander	Army Master

*Both the Republic of Dianto and the Qwernian Empire use the same ranks for both land and naval personnel.